THE COLLECTED STORIES
OF FRANK HERBERT

Tor Books by Frank Herbert

The Dragon in the Sea
Hellstrom's Hive
The White Plague

The Collected Stories of
FRANK
HERBERT

A Tom Doherty Associates Book • New York

THE COLLECTED STORIES OF FRANK HERBERT

Copyright © 2014 by Herbert Properties LLC

A Tor Book
Published by Tom Doherty Associates, LLC
175 Fifth Avenue
New York, NY 10010

www.tor-forge.com

Tor® is a registered trademark of Tom Doherty Associates, LLC.

The Library of Congress Cataloging-in-Publication Data is available upon request.

ISBN 978-0-7653-3696-5 (hardcover)
ISBN 978-1-4668-2987-9 (e-book)

Tor books may be purchased for educational, business, or promotional use. For information on bulk purchases, please contact the Macmillan Corporate and Premium Sales Department at 1-800-221-7945, extension 5442, or write to specialmarkets@macmillan.com.

First Edition: November 2014

Printed in the United States of America

0 9 8 7 6 5 4 3 2 1

CONTENTS

THE COLLECTED STORIES
OF FRANK HERBERT

INTRODUCTION

It's a great thing to create, to grow and to give of yourself in the process, but it's quite another thing to be thrown into an orgy of introspective analysis out of which you must refashion your work. To review more than twenty years of my own writing and come up with coherent comments required such analysis, however, and having been forced to the task, I find the recovery pleasant.

Analysis is a trick activity.

Sometimes, it's hardest for the person *doing his thing* to describe what he does. You can analyze the life out of any activity, and to little purpose.

"Tell me, Dr. Livingstone, what were your innermost thoughts when Mr. Stanley confronted you with his immortal greeting?"

Do you really want to know?

What kept me at this job was the suspicion that my labors might be useful to others wishing to make a career of letters. Similar works by earlier authors were useful to me—particularly the practical advice of Jack Woodford, and the marvelously candid *Summing Up* by W. Somerset Maugham.

I hope I can be as candid and as practical.

The flat statement of what I do requires little thought.

I write.

As humans measure time, I've been doing this for quite a while—more than forty years. This collection contains the laboriously hand-printed copy of one of my earliest efforts. It was produced when I was only seven. A few months later, having tested this process and found it to my liking, I announced to my family in the grand manner that I was going to be "an author."

That was on the morning of my eighth birthday, and I've never deviated far from that ambition since.

If you'll turn to that early effort, you'll find my introductory description reads:

"This story is about love and adventures."

Even at seven, I knew the ingredients of a good story: *love and adventures.*

There must also have been some sense in me of the limits implicit in words. The seven-year-old warns you that his book will only tell *something* about how animals live in the deep woods.

The seven-year-old also gives his work a narrative hook. I didn't know a narrative hook from a verb at the age of seven, but the instincts of the writer triumph. A narrative hook describes how the author catches your interest and makes you want to learn more about what's going on in his story.

The seven-year-old begins with a man and his dog lost in the forest. You are warned that the forest is a fearsome place. It contains noises which indicate dangerous creatures, especially at night. And please note that such creatures retain a deeper sense of threat when they are known only by their noises. The unknown can be a dreadful thing.

Despite the crudities, the unabashed hubris and the misspellings, this childhood effort is amazing for the number of storytelling necessities it contains: People, place, time of day, mysterious dangers and the promise of love and adventures to come.

There's the nutshell, and I count myself lucky to have come upon it so early.

That was not so much writing as it was plumbing, however. The pieces are there, but they're badly assembled. The plumbing was all bare and exposed.

I have tried to teach writing, only to discover that you cannot teach writing. You can teach the plumbing—which pipe connects to which elbow. The actual writing is something you must teach yourself. You learn by doing. The knowledge comes from the inside and it leans most heavily on the oral tradition of language, much to the despair of those who would like it all orderly and neat with explicit rules to follow.

It comes as a shock to many in our print-oriented civilization to be told that *language,* the basic tool of the writer, is more oral than written. Contemplate those thousands of years of oral tradition before we ever ventured to carve symbols in clay and stone. We are most profoundly conditioned to language-as-speech. The written word is a latecomer.

Before you will believe the *reality* of a story, someone must stand up on that printed page and speak. His words must have the characteristics of speech. They must reach your ears through your eyes. Under the onslaught of non-print media (TV, film, radio, casette players . . .) this is becoming ever more necessary. The oral tradition has never really been subjugated.

True to that tradition, I find I must have a sense of joy in what I do. There has to be some fun in it which you can feel even in the darkest moments of the story. This is the entertainment business. I'm the jongleur visiting your castle. I bring songs and news from other castles I have visited, and some of those are strange indeed. I sing for my supper and those *other castles* of which I sing are only partly figments of imagination. We may share a con-census reality which demands our service, but if you write science fiction you crowd the edges of that reality.

When we say "science," we usually mean technology. Science fiction is deeply involved with technology and the questioning of the human future. To write science fiction, you make a connection between technology and the myth-dream of human immortality. We inevitably deal with the alienation of man brought on by his immersion in a welter of things which he is told he wants/needs, but which always seem to remove him from an essential contact with his own life.

This is not really a recent development.

The company of science fiction writers is a venerable troop. We go back somewhere beyond Lucian of Samosata in the Second Century AD. We number in our company such lights as Plato, Cyrano de Bergerac, Thomas More (who gave us the word *Utopia*), Jules Verne, H. G. Wells, Edgar Allen Poe, Aldous Huxley and George Orwell—which represents only the barest listing.

We are, as a rule, concerned with mankind living on other planets. (Lucian sent his hero to the moon on a waterspout.) Often, our concern is touched by the realization that no animal species can survive forever on one planet. Even as we most freely express our fears that the human species is in danger of extinction, we parade our differences from other animals via our stories. We have imagination and, occasionally, touches of reason. Much of science fiction says these may be our ultimate strength in facing that chaotic unknown which constantly threatens to reduce us to zero.

Freud once said: "When you try to conceal your innermost thoughts, every pore oozes betrayal."

When you write, the printed page absorbs all of that ooze—all of you, the wise and the silly, the profound, the shallow and the in-between. It all hangs out in these talking letters. I want to write for as large an audience as possible, all of you sitting around the castle fireplace after a four-star dinner, all of you raptly enjoying the sound of my lute. There's no sense trying to hide that; it's in everything I do. And always there's the upcoming story in which I hope to do it all better. The current work, about which I will not talk because that wastes the energies which should go into the creation, remains my favorite. I will pour as much of myself into it as I am able, holding back nothing. You cannot lose by this. You destroy nothing. You are creating the egg, not the goose. But while that gestating egg remains my favorite, I reserve a warm spot for creations of yesteryear.

That fragment saved from childhood: I recall the child I was with a special poignancy through that fragment. And even while I laugh with you at his bumbling, I remember his unshakable drive to perfect this form of communication. It was only later that I learned about perfection—that it remains forever beyond your grasp, that you are always working toward it in a monstrous parody of Zeno's Paradox, that perfection fades when you seem to touch it.

It has been educational for me to apply the analytical tool to my own work; I couldn't possibly set down here everything I've derived from that effort. And certainly you must detect the ambivalence with which I view this. The discovery of science fiction by colleges and universities, a move led by such academics as Willis E. McNelly at the University of California, Fullerton, and Berkley Dreissel at Stanford, raises such ambivalence. We've seen analysis take the fun and the life out of other literary genres. Rest assured then that whatever comments I make hereafter I am attempting to maintain the fun and the life.

The stories in this collection are like steps on a path to me. I recall the throes of creation, some of the ambience in the working places which inevitably bleeds over into the work. These are stories I might write differently today. I might. Tony Boucher, the late author and critic for the *New York Times,* called "Mary Celeste Move" "one of the most perfect short stories I've ever read." Out of the love I held for Tony, I might not change that one, although I disagree with his judgment. I find "Seed Stock" a better story. "Mary Celeste" is brittle. It shows the sharpening and resharpening process through which it went in the writing. As with analysis, you can go too far with that process; you run into a kind of Heisenbergian wall where all of your original intentions turn to glitter. To me that's a flaw in "Mary Celeste."

My first venture into science fiction was "Looking for Something?" As with the childhood fragment, it contains rough edges.

"Looking" deals with a subject which I explored in greater detail later: that borderline of awareness out of which our compulsions grope for recognition. It says you may not know the full spectrum of motivation behind your everyday activities. And when you go looking for that motivation, you may encounter more than you wanted.

"Nightmare Blues" ("Operation Syndrome") was my first acceptance by the late John Campbell of *Astounding/Analog.* I was still mining the same vein of "Looking." However, "Nightmare" moves more freely and contains more of that special color which science fiction requires—the teleprobe, the skytrain, the sound switch beside the window, the undersea nightclub. It has that immediacy of detail which I believe a story must contain before it gives you the full sense of the place were the characters are performing. It contains some things familiar today, but the backdrop is tomorrow.

"Nightmare" says, as well, that tomorrow's world may not be the most pleasant place you've ever imagined. It brings up the subtle meaning of the old Chinese curse: "May you live in interesting times."

Much science fiction views the world and human future more from a Hebrew curse than the Chinese. It reads: "May you grow like an onion with your head in the ground!" For this latter variant, the writer plays prophet, crying: "Lift up your heads and look around you at what we are doing!" Looking back on it, I can see that this dominates the story "Cease Fire," a modern Sorcerer's Apprentice yarn.

Please note the monumental prophetic error in "Cease Fire," however. Written in 1958, it was set in that far-off time of 1972. Vietnam was a decade ahead and somewhat warmer of climate than the setting I chose. To the best of my knowledge, Vietnam did not produce an equivalent to Larry

Hulser, my protagonist, nor did it produce his invention. "Cease Fire" does say something about war syndrome and the simplistic world of those who begin their preachments with: "We could end wars if we would just . . ."

Hulser's invention will have to wait, but I expect something like this to come. You will recall that dynamite was supposed to end the possibility of war because it was too dreadful. And before that, it was the crossbow. Instruments of violence apparently don't end wars.

My timing error recalls the story told about Edgar Allan Poe, that he was walking with a friend in New York City in 1847 and suddenly cried out: "I've just had a vision of the future! Within a hundred years (by 1947) New York will have ten-storey buildings!"

Poe, the father of the modern science fiction story, failed to take into account the invention of the elevator and the steel-frame building.

As with much prophecy, so it is with science fiction. Thus far, we've been unable to achieve a surprise-free future. We fail to take some surprising development into account.

We do score occasionally, however, and these provide some of our greatest moments. Think of Arthur Clarke telling the world how a communications satellite would function and long before such wonders came into being. He predicted the development with such detail that the concept cannot be patented. Prior publication will prevent a patent. I did the same thing in "Dragon in the Sea" with the prediction of collapsible cargo devices and television periscopes. The truly classic example is that of Cleve Cartmill in the middle of World War II describing how to build an atom bomb. To this day, there probably are officials of the United States government who believe Cartmill's story developed from a leak in the Manhattan Project. The unimaginative always seem to underestimate how far the imagination can leap.

"Egg and Ashes" with its phoenix theme represents one of my earlier attempts to weave a linguistics theme into a yarn. How *does* a creature react if it hears in the spectrum which we see? This tale revolves on that common-to-science fiction element—possession as an alien presence. Why not? Most science fiction assumes an infinite universe where the wonders will never end. If you sample such a future through fiction, does that not prepare you to deal with surprising real events?

This is a question Martin Fisk of "Mary Celeste Move" might ask himself. Fisk could be any of us in a velocitized world which moves so fast we're unaware of running out of time and cannot react with sufficient rapidity to the shock power of a future into which we plunge. How much difference is there between the present breakneck pace of our freeway-insanity and Fisk's world of 300-mile-per-hour expressways where you slow down to 75 and a speed of 55 is to creep? Is it caricature or a glimpse of our current reality?

"Committee of the Whole" may have a familiar ring to some who read it. Is it today's world or just the day after tomorrow?

Here's where you separate the people who *grow like an onion* from those who merely accept that they live in the universe of the Chinese curse. I regret to say that "Committee" is my view of imminent reality. The future does tend to beguile us with myths of *progress* while the other hand prepares ever more potent shocks. "Look out for my atom bomb!" the future says. And all the while, an anonymous human is working in his basement on that surprise which will make over the atomic age into "the good old days."

Cracking the atom represented only a milestone on a longer path. If science fiction does no more, it tells us this: we are developing larger and larger chunks of energy which can be manipulated by fewer and fewer of us. If this curve continues to rise exponentially, single individuals will soon be able to focus planet-shattering energies.

The role of the anonymous individual in this development is relatively clear. Science fiction at least since H. G. Wells has been drawing his portrait with a consistent success/horror. Propinquity, serendipity and curiosity lie in wait for the unwary onion head. My ventures into science fiction see our world in far more peril from a pharmacist and biotechnician working privately in a basement laboratory than it is from the atom, fission or fusion. Given the sums of energy becoming available to fewer and fewer of us, the brutalized human, the disaffected fanatic, represents our most profound peril.

There appears no present way to prevent his surprise whether that comes in the form of a biological weapon or an application of the bias-current principle to the cracking of our entire planet. The horrors of science fiction's most bug-eyed-monster extremes don't compare with what's happening in our "real world."

The basic energy involved in this process is, of course, *knowledge*. How can you suppress that which is already or about to become *common knowledge*? Thought control quickly runs out of dependable controllers. Once Lize Meitner had published her findings, atomic fission was public property. Cleve Cartmill merely dipped into this public trough to produce his story. The materials and information tools behind such runaway growth are so widely spread in our world that the words *security* and *secrecy* contain a hideous kind of gallows humor or even worse. Official secrecy acts and the concepts of security based on them represent distractions which actually contribute to humankind's insecurity. I say it baldly here instead of letting it unfold in *fiction,* but I'm not the first to take this alarming view that *the fault is not in our stars, Mercutio . . .*

Thus, "Committee" represents that form of science fiction which attempts to depict a deeper reality: Future History. It says in a story, which the reader can accept because it's "only a story," that the essence of this fiction will come to pass. You as reader put the connections to reality together only after the reading.

This leads by what is to me an orderly thought process into the concept of the operating manual, the handbook for whatever you do as *work*. This is the book which gives you the myth of the orderly world, hiding all of the hangups and misalignments behind illusionary rules. Often such manuals are written by committees. (You may recall that a camel is a horse created by a committee.) My favorite of such handbooks is the Blue Jackets Manual which is issued to incoming recruits of the US Navy. The BJM has many classic lines, including this one:

"It is absolutely imperative that the ship be kept watertight."

Nobody can doubt this, especially if his life depends on it. Between the book and the execution of the obvious, however, is a world of creative originality. Here's where we really operate by the book. It's this in-between world which inspired me to write a short story about the educated ignorance to be found in a handbook of the future, calling the story, of course, "By the Book." The story says that those precise and orderly barriers we raise against omnipresent outer chaos can be useful tools or they can be traps. It all depends on how you interpret your manual. This is usually what I tell people who come to me asking for "rules about writing."

Such a handbook is possible, of course, and many have been written. Mine might begin this way:

Rule One: Work to develop an almost organic link between your primary tool and yourself.

Rule Two: Your primary tool is *language,* written, spoken, however it communicates.

Rule Three: Write regularly; don't wait for a call from your favorite muse.

Rule Four: Be sensitive to and responsive to your audience, but not slavish.

And so on . . .

I mean that about an *organic linkage* most profoundly, understanding that you are connected to language by devices; in my case, a typewriter. This linkage is unique to the individual and, in a sense, it dissolves as you use it. You have to develop your linkage anew each time.

So much for rule books.

Which brings us to "The Primitives."

The author's name originally was to have been Noah Arkwright. That's the pseudonym chosen by Jack Vance, Poul Anderson and myself when we plotted the story while building a houseboat which we used on the waters of the Sacramento–San Joaquin delta at the head of San Francisco Bay. We intended to write the story together as a lark, but the pressure of work forced Vance and Anderson out of the picture and they insisted I finish it. I developed our plot into the novelette.

To me this story has a lovely logic. After all, what would a primitive make out of a diamond? See if you disagree.

"The Primitives" also represented my attempt to open up another possibility for the role of women in our past. In my view humankind was matriarchal for far more centuries than it was patriarchal. Male dominance probably came onto the scene rather late after an earlier animal history of pack relationships probably similar to those of the higher apes, and *then* a long period of female dominance after we became self-conscious.

The picture of the female cowering in the cave with her brood while the male fought off the sabertooth tiger has always struck me as a bit much. I find it easier to see the image of the domineering *Cave Mother,* keeper of the birth mystery and the sacred vessel of ongoing life. If there's one thing primitives do not like, that's to bring down the wrath of powerful spirits.

Perhaps we haven't changed much in that respect, which is another recurring theme of science fiction: *It may* look *new, but it's really the same old thing.*

"The Heaven Makers" plays with zen consciousness / taoist eternity translated for Western awareness. Words are finite creatures, however, and the universe (even the universe of your own book) changes as you touch it. There exists in this book a recognition of our concensus choice to use a linear rather than a non-linear model for our universe. But what do we do when we find that this linearity closes its own circle? Do the endless serial events merely repeat? These are some of the underlying conceptualizations of "The Heaven Makers." We think our ancestral gods no longer awaken mysteries in our minds. We have the myth of the endless personal story, denying the visions of the older mysteries in the hope of finding new *scientific* answers. Thus we deify science and its offspring, technology. Science fiction has become a special toy to those alerted to this spectrum. It unfolds the monsters of awareness which lurk in our mutually-created vision of eternity. We know there are things in this eternity which we don't want to see, but like children peering past the protective legs of an adult, we seek a *safe* glimpse of the monster.

"The Heaven Makers" assumes that the immortal have no morality which can be equated with a finite morality. Look around you. The morality of the species overrides the puny morality of the individual. Our creation of *law* may have been the attempt to match species' morality with that of the individual. And, of course, the species may not be immortal.

In a natural progression from "The Heaven Makers," and all the stories before it, you get "The Being Machine" ("Mind Bomb"). This is in part another story of outside manipulation of the individual, playing with the concept of what we mean by "free will." It is the influence of reason in rebellion against any manipulation, even by itself. It is the paradox of manipulation in an equalizing (entropic) universe. This is *law and order* at the end of its tether, the species projected into a far-far future where manipulation of the individual has been carried to a self-defeating extreme. It says *law and order* lead inevitably to chaos.

Another paradox?

"Seed Stock" takes up that recurrent science fiction theme of humans colonizing/populating another planet (the eternity myth for the species). This story, however, says specifically that these colonizing humans must

become transformed into children of *that* planet, even to the point of reject-
ing *Mother Earth*. By inference, it speaks to the eternity myth right here on
this planet, saying that humans, to make their myth a reality, must become
children of this planet once more and children of *any* planet.

That, essentially, represents the motif of hope behind most science fiction: the fact that we write about any future at all, even an *interesting* one,
assumes that future will come to pass. We balance on Occam's razor, our
assumptions on one side, our myths on the other, and sometimes we cannot
tell the two apart. In common with other art forms, science fiction strives to
translate our old dreams into new ones and, in the process, to make the nightmares less fearsome.

Frank Herbert
Port Townsend, Washington
29 April 1973

LOOKING FOR SOMETHING?

Mirsar Wees, chief indoctrinator for Sol III sub-prefecture, was defying the intent of the Relaxation-room in his quarters. He buzzed furiously back and forth from metal wall to metal wall, his pedal-membrane making a cricket-like sound as the vacuum cups disengaged.

"The fools!" he thought. "The stupid, incompetent, mindless fools!"

Mirsar Wees was a Denebian. His race had originated more than three million earth years ago on the fourth planet circling the star Deneb—a planet no longer existing. His profile was curiously similar to that of a tall woman in a floor-length dress, with the vacuum-cup pedal-membrance contacting the floor under the "skirt." His eight specialized extensors waved now in a typical Denebian rage-pattern. His mouth, a thin transverse slit entirely separate from the olfactory-lung orifice directly below it, spewed forth a multi-lingual stream of invective against the assistant who cowered before him.

"How did this happen?" he shouted. "I take my first vacation in one hundred years and come back to find my career almost shattered by your incompetency!"

Mirsar Wees turned and buzzed back across the room. Through his vision-ring, an organ somewhat like a glittering white tricycle-tire jammed down about one-third of the distance over his head, he examined again the report on Earthling Paul Marcus and maintained a baleful stare upon his assistant behind him. Activating the vision cells at his left, he examined the wall chronometer.

"So little time," he muttered. "If only I had someone at Central Processing who could see a deviant when it comes by! Now I'll have to take care of this bumble myself, before it gets out of hand. If they hear of it back at the bureau . . ."

Mirsar Wees, the Denebian, a cog in the galaxy-wide korad-farming empire of his race, pivoted on his pedal-membrane and went out a door which opened soundlessly before him. The humans who saw his flame-like profile this night would keep alive the folk tales of ghosts, djinn, little people, fairies, elves, pixies . . .

Were they given the vision to see it, they would know also that an angry overseer had passed. But they would not see this, of course. That was part of Mirsar Wees' job.

It was mainly because Paul Marcus was a professional hypnotist that he obtained an aborted glimpse of the rulers of the world.

The night it happened he was inducing a post-hypnotic command into the mind of an audience-participant to his show on the stage of the Roxy Theater in Tacoma, Washington.

Paul was a tall, thin man with a wide head which appeared large because of this feature although it really was not. He wore a black tailcoat and formal trousers, jewelled cuff links and chalkwhite cuffs, which gleamed and flashed as he gestured. A red spotlight in the balcony gave a Mephisto cast to his stage-setting, which was dominated by a backdrop of satin black against which gleamed two giant, luminous eyes. He was billed as "Marcus the Mystic" and he looked the part.

The subject was a blonde girl whom Paul had chosen because she displayed signs of a higher than ordinary intelligence, a general characteristic of persons who are easily hypnotized. The woman had a good figure and showed sufficient leg when she sat down on the chair to excite whistles and cat-calls from the front rows. She flushed, but maintained her composure.

"What is your name, please?" Paul asked.

She answered in a contralto voice, "Madelyne Walker."

"Miss or Mrs.?"

She said, "Miss."

Paul held up his right hand. From it dangled a gold chain on the end of which was a large paste gem with many facets cut into its surface. A spotlight in the wings was so directed that it reflected countless star-bursts from the gem.

"If you will look at the diamond," Paul said. "Just keep your eyes on it."

He began to swing the gem rhythmically, like a pendulum, from side to side. The girl's eyes followed it. Paul waited until her eyes were moving in rhythm with the swinging bauble before he began to recite in a slow monotone, timed to the pendulum:

"Sleep. You will fall asleep . . . deep sleep . . . deep sleep . . . asleep . . . deep asleep . . . asleep . . . asleep . . ."

Her eyes followed the gem.

"Your eyelids will become heavy," Paul said. "Sleep. Go to sleep. You are falling asleep . . . deep, restful sleep . . . healing sleep . . . deep asleep . . . asleep . . . asleep . . . asleep . . ."

Her head began to nod, eyelids to close and pop open, slower and slower. Paul gently moved his left hand up to the chain. In the same monotone he said, "When the diamond stops swinging you will fall into a deep, restful sleep from which only I can awaken you." He allowed the gem to swing slower and slower in shorter and shorter sweeps. Finally, he put both palms against the chain and rotated it. The bauble at the end of the chain began to whirl rapidly, its facets coruscating with the reflections of the spotlight.

Miss Walker's head fell forward and Paul kept her from falling off the chair by grasping her shoulder. She was in deep trance. He began demonstrating to the audience the classic symptoms which accompany this—insensitivity to pain, body rigidity, complete obedience to the hypnotist's voice.

The show went along in routine fashion. Miss Walker barked like a dog. She became the dowager queen with dignified mien. She refused to answer to her own name. She conducted the imaginary symphony orchestra. She sang an operatic aria.

The audience applauded at the correct places in the performance. Paul bowed. He had his subject deliver a wooden bow, too. He wound up to the finale.

"When I snap my fingers you will awaken," he said. "You will feel completely refreshed as though after a sound sleep. Ten seconds after you awaken you will imagine yourself on a crowded streetcar where no one will give you a seat. You will be extremely tired. Finally, you will ask the fat man opposite you to give you his seat. He will do so and you will sit down. Do you understand?"

Miss Walker nodded her head.

"You will remember nothing of this when you awaken," Paul said.

He raised his hand to snap his fingers . . .

It was then that Paul Marcus received his mind-jarring idea. He held his hand up, fingers ready to snap, thinking about this idea, until he heard the audience stirring restlessly behind him. Then he shook his head and snapped his fingers.

Miss Walker awakened slowly, looked around, got up, and exactly ten seconds later began the streetcar hallucinations. She performed exactly as commanded, again awakened, and descended confusedly from the stage to more applause and whistles.

It should have been gratifying. But from the moment he received *the* idea, the performance could have involved someone other than Paul Marcus for all of the attention he gave it. Habit carried him through the closing routine, the brief comments on the powers of hypnotism, the curtain calls. Then he walked back to his dressing room slowly, preoccupied, unbuttoning his studs on the way as he always did following the last performance of the night. The concrete cave below stage echoed to his footsteps.

In the dressing room he removed the tailcoat and hung it in the wardrobe.

Then he sat down before the dressing table mirror and began to cream his face preparatory to removing the light makeup he wore. He found it hard to meet his own eyes in the mirror.

"This is silly," he told himself sourly.

A knock sounded at the door. Without turning, he said, "Come in."

The door opened hesitantly and the blonde Miss Walker stepped into the room.

"Excuse me," she said. "The man at the door said you were in here and . . ."

Seeing her in the mirror, Paul turned around and stood up.

"Is something wrong?" he asked.

Miss Walker looked around her as though to make sure they were alone before she answered.

"Not exactly," she said.

Paul gestured to a settee beside his dressing table. "Sit down, won't you?" he asked. He returned to the dressing table as Miss Walker seated herself.

"You'll excuse me if I go on with this chore," he said, taking a tissue to the grease paint under his chin.

Miss Walker smiled. "You remind me of a woman at her nightly beauty care," she said.

Paul thought: Another stage-struck miss, and the performance gives her the excuse to take up my time. He glanced at the girl out of the corners of his eyes. "Not bad, though . . ."

"You haven't told me to what I owe the pleasure of your company," he said.

Miss Walker's face clouded with thought.

"It's really very silly," she said.

Probably, Paul thought.

"Not at all," he said. "Tell me what's on your mind."

"Well, it's an idea I had while my friends were telling me what I did on the stage," she said. She grinned wryly. "I had the hardest time believing that there actually wasn't a streetcar up there. I'm still not absolutely convinced. Maybe you brought in a dummy streetcar with a lot of actors. Oh, I don't know!" She shook her head and put a hand to her eyes.

The way she said, "I don't know!" reminded Paul of his own idea; *the* idea. He decided to give Miss Walker the fast brush-off in order to devote more time to thinking this new idea through to some logical conclusion.

"What about the streetcar?" he asked.

The girl's face assumed a worried expression. "I thought I was on a real streetcar," she said. "There was no audience, no . . . hypnotist. Nothing. Just the reality of riding the streetcar and being tired like you are after a hard day's work. I saw the people on the car. I smelled them. I felt the car under my feet. I heard the money bounce in the coin-catcher and all the other noises one hears on a streetcar—people talking, a man opening his newspaper. I saw the fat man sitting there in front of me. I asked him for his seat. I even felt embarrassed. I heard him answer and I sat down in his seat. It was warm and I felt the people pressing against me on both sides. It was very real."

"And what bothers you?" Paul asked.

She looked up from her hands which were tightly clasped in her lap.

"That bothers me," she said. "That streetcar. It was real. It was as real as anything I've ever known. It was as real as now. I believed in it. Now I'm told it wasn't real." Again she looked down at her hands. "What am I to believe?"

This is getting close to *the* idea, Paul thought.

"Can you express what bothers you in any other way?" he asked.

She looked him squarely in the eyes. "Yes," she said. "I got to thinking while my friends were talking to me. I got to wondering. What if all this—" she gestured around her—"our whole lives, our world, everything we see, feel, hear, smell, or sense in any way is more of the same. A hypnotic delusion!"

"Precisely!" Paul exhaled the word.

"What did you say?" she asked.

"I said, 'Precisely!' "

Paul turned toward her and rested his left elbow on the dressing table. "Because," he said, "at the very moment I was telling you what you would do when you awakened, at the moment I was giving you the commands which resulted in your hallucination, I got the same idea."

"My goodness!" she said. The very mildness of her exclamation made it seem more vehement than if she had sworn.

Paul turned back to the dressing table mirror. "I wonder if there could be something in telepathy as well?"

Miss Walker looked at him in the mirror, the room seeming to draw in closely behind her. "It was an idea I couldn't keep to myself," she said. "I told my friends—I came with a married couple—but they just laughed at me. I decided on the spur of the moment to come back here and talk to you and I did it before I could lose my nerve. After all, you're a hypnotist. You should know something about this."

"It'll take some looking into," Paul said, "I wonder . . ." He turned toward Miss Walker. "Are you engaged tonight?"

Her expression changed. She looked at him as though her mother were whispering in her ear: "Watch out! Watch out! He's a man."

"Well, I don't know . . ." she said.

Paul got on his most winning smile. "I'm no backstage wolf," he said. "Please, I feel as though somebody had asked me to cut the Gordian knot, and I'd rather untie it—but I need help."

"What could we do?" she asked.

It was Paul's turn to hesitate. "There are several ways to approach the problem," he said. "We in America have only scratched the surface in our study of hypnotism." He doubled up his fist and thudded it gently on the dressing table. "Hell! I've seen witch doctors in Haiti who know more about it than I do. But . . ."

"What would you do first?" she asked.

"I'd . . . I'd . . ." Paul looked at her for a moment as though he really saw her for the first time. "I'd do this," he said. "Make yourself comfortable on that settee. Lean back. That's it."

"What are you going to do?" she asked.

"Well," Paul said, "It's pretty well established that these sensory hallucinations are centered in one part of the human nervous system which is laid bare by hypnotism. It's possible, by using hypnotism, to get at the commands other hypnotists have put there. I'm going to put you back in deep trance and let you search for the commands yourself. If something is commanding us to live an illusion, the command should be right there with all the others."

"I don't know," she said.

"Please," Paul urged. "We might be able to crack this thing right here and now in just a few minutes."

"All right." She still sounded hesitant, but she leaned back as directed.

Paul lifted his paste gem from the dressing table and focused the table spotlight on it. "Look at the diamond," he said. . . .

This time she fell into the trance more readily. Paul checked her for pain threshold, muscular control. She responded appropriately. He began questioning:

"Do you hear my voice?"

"Yes," she said.

"Do you know what hypnotic commands are in your mind?" he asked.

There was a long pause. Her lips opened dryly. "There are . . . commands," she said.

"Do you obey them?" he asked.

"I must."

"What is the most basic of these commands?" he asked.

"I . . . can . . . not . . . tell."

Paul almost rubbed his hands. A simple 'Don't talk about it,' he thought.

"Just nod your head if I repeat the command," he said. "Does it say, 'You must not tell'?"

Her head nodded.

Paul rubbed his hands against his pants legs and realized suddenly that he was perspiring excessively.

"What is it you must not tell?" he asked.

She shook her head without speaking.

"You must tell me," he said. "If you do not tell me, your right foot will begin to burn and itch unbearably and will continue to do so until you do tell me. Tell me what it is that you have been commanded not to tell."

Again she shook her head. She reached down and began to scratch her right foot. She pulled off her shoe.

"You must tell me," Paul said. "What is the first word of the command?"

The girl looked up at him, but her eyes remained unfocused.

"You . . ." she said.

It was as though she had brought the word from some dark place deep within her and the saying of it was almost too much to bear. She continued to scratch her right leg.

"What is the second word?" Paul asked.

She tried to speak, but failed.

"Is it 'must'?" he asked. "Nod your head if it is."

She nodded her head.

"You 'must' what?"

Again she was wordless.

He thought about it for a moment. "Sensory perception," he thought. He leaned forward. "Is it 'You must sense . . .'?" he asked. "Is it 'You must sense only . . .'?"

She relaxed. Her head nodded and she said, "Yes."

Paul took a deep breath.

"What is it 'You must sense only . . .'?" he asked.

She opened her mouth, her lips moved, but no sound issued.

He felt like screaming at her, dragging the answer from her mind with his hands.

"What is it?" His voice cracked on the question. "Tell me!"

She shook her head from side to side. He noticed signs of awakening.

Again he took a deep breath. "What will happen to you if you tell me?"

"I'll die," she said.

He leaned forward and lowered his voice to a confidential tone. "That is foolishness," he said. "You can't die just because you say a few words. You know that. Now tell me what it is that you have been ordered to sense."

She stared straight ahead of her at nothing, mouth open. Paul lowered his head to look directly into her eyes. "Do you see me?" he asked.

"No," she said.

"What do you see?" he asked.

"I see death."

"Look at me instead," Paul said. "You remember me."

"You are death," she said.

"That's nonsense! Look at me," he commanded.

Her eyes opened wider. Paul stared into them. Her eyes seemed to grow and grow and grow and grow . . . Paul found himself unable to look away. There was nothing else in the world except two blue-gray eyes. A deep, resonant voice, like a low-register cello, filled his mind.

"You will forget everything that has happened tonight," it said. "You will die rather than remember. You will, you *must,* sense only those things which you have been commanded to sense. I, _____, command it. Do you remember me?"

Paul's lips formed the word, "yes."

"Who am I?" the voice asked.

Paul dampened his dry lips with his tongue. "You are death," he said.

Bureaucracy has a kind of timeless, raceless mold which makes its communiques recognizable as to type by the members of any bureau anywhere. The multiple copies, the precise wording to cover devious intent, the absolute protocol of address—all are of a pattern, whether the communication is to the Reconstruction Finance Corporation or the Denebian Bureau of Indoctrination.

Mirsar Wees knew the pattern as another instinct. He had been supervisor of indoctrination and overseer of the korad farming on Sol III for one hundred and fifty-seven of the planet's years. In that time, by faithfully following the letter of the Indoctrination Bureau's code and never an individual interpretation of its spirit, he had insured for himself a promotion to Coordinator of the entire Sol prefecture whenever such an opening occurred.

Having met another threat to his position and resolved it, knowing the security of his tenure, he sat before the mechanical secretary-transmitter in his office and dictated a letter to the Bureau. The vision-ring around his head glowed a dull amber as he relaxed the receptors in it. His body stretched out comfortably, taking a gentle massage from the chair.

"There has been considerable carelessness lately with the training of neo-indoctrinators," he said into the communo-tube.

Let a few heads fall at the bureau, he thought.

"There seems to be a feeling that, because we of the Sol prefecture are dealing with lesser beings, a lesser amount of care need be taken with the prefecture's indoctrinators. I have just dealt with a first-order threat to the Sol III korad supply, a threat which was directly attributable to neo-indoctrinator carelessness. A deviant was allowed to pass through the hands of three of our latest acquisitions from the College of Indoctrinators. These indoctrinators have been sent back for retraining."

He thought in satisfaction: They will reflect that the korad secreted by the glands of our charges is necessary for their own immortality, and will be more severe at the training center because of that. And pensively: It is almost time for me to tell them of our breeding experiments to bring the korad glands to the exterior of these creatures, making more frequent draining possible. They will particularly appreciate the niceties of indoctrination— increasing the mating pattern, increasing individual peril and, thereby, the longevity gland secretion, and the more strict visual limitation to keep the creatures from discovering the change. . . .

"I am sending a complete visio-corder report on how I met this threat," he spoke into the tube. "Briefly, I insinuated myself into the earth-being's presence and installed a more severe command. Standard procedure. It was not deemed practical to eliminate the creature because of the latest interpretations on command interference; it was felt that the being's elimination might set off further thought-patterns inimical to our designs.

"The creature was, therefore, commanded to mate with another of its ilk who is more stringently under our control. The creature also was removed from any labor involving the higher nerve-centers and has been put to another task, that of operating a transportation device called a streetcar.

"The mate has been subjected to the amputation of an appendage. Unfortunately, before I could take action, the creature I treated had started along an exceedingly clever line of action and had installed irremovable commands which made the appendage useless."

They will see how much of a deviant the creature was, he thought, and how careless the new indoctrinators were.

"The indoctrinator service must keep in mind at all times what happened to create the Sol plantoid belt. Those bodies, as we all know, once were the planet Dirad, the greatest korad source in the entire galaxy. Slipshod procedure employed by indoctrinators set up a situation similar to the one I have just nipped, and we were forced to destroy the entire planet. The potency of minds which have slipped from our control should be kept constantly before our attention. Dirad is an object lesson.

"The situation here is again completely normal, of course, and the korad supply is safe. We can go on draining the immortality of others—but *only as long as we maintain constant vigilance.*"

He signed it, "Cordially, Mirsar Wees, Chief Indoctrinator, Sol Subprefecture."

Someday, he thought, it will be "Coordinator."

Rising from the mechano-secretary, Mirsar Wees moved over to the "incoming" tube of his report-panel and noticed a tube which his new assistant had tabbed with the yellow band of "extreme importance."

He inserted the tube into a translator, sat down, and watched as it dealt out the report:

"A Hindu creature has seen itself as it really is," the report said.

Mirsar Wees reached over and put a tracer-beam on his new assistant to observe how that worthy was meeting this threat.

The report buzzed on: "The creature went insane as per indoctrination command, but most unfortunately it is a member of a sect which worships insanity. Others are beginning to listen to its babblings."

The report concluded: "I make haste."

Mirsar Wees leaned back, relaxed and smiled blandly. The new assistant showed promise.

OPERATION SYNDROME

Honolulu is quiet, the dead buried, the rubble of buildings cleaned away. A salvage barge rocks in the Pacific swell off Diamond Head. Divers follow a bubble trail down into the green water to the wreck of the Stateside sky-train. The Scramble Syndrome did this. Ashore, in converted barracks, psychologists work fruitlessly in the aftermath of insanity. This is where the Scramble Syndrome started: one minute the city was peaceful; a clock tick later the city was mad.

In forty days—nine cities infected.

The twentieth century's Black Plague.

Seattle

First a ringing in the ears, fluting up to a whistle. The whistle became the warning blast of a nightmare train roaring clackety-clack, clackety-clack across his dream.

A psychoanalyst might have enjoyed the dream as a clinical study. This psychoanalyst was not studying the dream; he was having it. He clutched the sheet around his neck, twisted silently on the bed, drawing his knees under his chin.

The train whistle modulated into the contralto of an expensive chanteuse singing "Insane Crazy Blues." The dream carried vibrations of fear and wildness.

"A million dollars don't mean a thing—"

Hoarse voice riding over clarion brass, bumping of drums, clarinet squealing like an angry horse.

A dark-skinned singer with electric blue eyes and dressed in black stepped away from a red backdrop. She opened her arms to an unseen audience. The singer, the backdrop lurched into motion, revolving faster and faster and faster until it merged into a pinpoint of red light. The red light dilated to the bell mouth of a trumpet sustaining a minor note.

The music shrilled; it was a knife, cutting his brain.

Dr. Eric Ladde awoke. He breathed rapidly; he oozed perspiration. Still he heard the singer, the music.

I'm dreaming that I'm awake, he thought.

He peeled off the top sheet, slipped his feet out, put them on the warm floor. Presently, he stood up, walked to the window, looked down on the moontrail shimmering across Lake Washington. He touched the sound switch beside the window and now he could hear the night—crickets, spring peepers at the lakeshore, the far hum of a skytrain.

The singing remained.

He swayed, gripped at the windowsill.

Scramble Syndrome—

He turned, examined the bedside newstape; no mention of Seattle. Perhaps he was safe—illness. But the music inside his head was no illness.

He made a desperate clutch for self-control, shook his head, banged his ear with the palm of his hand. The singing persisted. He looked to the bed-side clock—1:05 A.M., Friday, May 14, 1999.

Inside his head the music stopped. But now—Applause! A roar of clapping, cries, stamping of feet. Eric rubbed his head.

I'm not insane . . . I'm not insane—

He slipped into his dressing gown, went into the kitchen cubicle of his bachelor residence. He drank water, yawned, held his breath—anything to drive away the noise, now a chicken-haggle of talking, clinking, slithering of feet.

He made himself a highball, splashed the drink at the back of his throat. The sounds inside his head turned off. Eric looked at the empty glass in his hand, shook his head.

A new specific for insanity—alcohol! He smiled wryly. *And every day I tell my patients that drinking is no solution.* He tasted a bitter thought: *Maybe I should have joined that therapy team, not stayed here trying to create a machine to cure the insane. If only they hadn't laughed at me—*

He moved a fibreboard box to make room beside the sink, put down his glass. A notebook protruded from the box, sitting atop a mound of electronic parts. He picked up the notebook, stared at his own familiar block printing on the cover: *Amanti Teleprobe—Test Book IX.*

They laughed at the old doctor, too, he thought. *Laughed him right into an asylum. Maybe that's where I'm headed—along with everyone else in the world.*

He opened the notebook, traced his finger along the diagram of his latest experimental circuit. The teleprobe in his basement laboratory still carried the wiring, partially dismantled.

What was wrong with it?

He closed the notebook, tossed it back into the box. His thoughts hunted through the theories stored in his mind, the knowledge saved from a thousand failures. Fatigue and despondency pulled at him. Yet, he knew that the things Freud, Jung, Adler and all the others had sought in dreams and mannerisms hovered just beyond his awareness in an electronic tracer circuit.

He wandered back into his study-bedroom, crawled into the bed. He practiced yoga breathing until sleep washed over him. The singer, the train, the whistle did not return.

Morning lighted the bedroom. He awoke, trailing fragments of his nightmare into consciousness, aware that his appointment book was blank until ten o'clock. The bedside newstape offered a long selection of stories, most headed "Scramble Syndrome." He punched code letters for eight items, flipped the machine to audio and listened to the news while dressing.

Memory of his nightmare nagged at him. He wondered, "How many people awake in the night, asking themselves, 'Is it my turn now?'"

He selected a mauve cape, drew it over his white coveralls. Retrieving the notebook from the box in the kitchen, he stepped out into the chill spring morning. He turned up the temperature adjustment of his coveralls. The unitube whisked him to the Elliott Bay waterfront. He ate at a seafood restaurant, the teleprobe notebook open beside his plate. After breakfast, he found an empty bench outside facing the bay, sat down, opened the notebook. He found himself reluctant to study the diagrams, stared out at the bay.

Mists curled from the gray water, obscuring the opposite shore. Somewhere in the drift a purse seiner sounded its hooter. Echoes bounced off the buildings behind him. Early workers hurried past, voices stilled: thin look of faces, hunted glances—the uniform of fear. Coldness from the bench seeped through his clothing. He shivered, drew a deep breath of the salt air. The breeze off the bay carried essence of seaweed, harmonic on the dominant bitter musk of a city's effluvia. Seagulls haggled over a morsel in the tide rip. The papers on his lap fluttered. He held them down with one hand, watching the people.

I'm procrastinating, he thought. *It's a luxury my profession can ill afford nowadays.*

A woman in a red fur cape approached, her sandals tapping a swift rhythm on the concrete. Her cape billowed behind in a puff of breeze.

He looked up to her face framed in dark hair. Every muscle in his body locked. She was the woman of his nightmare down to the minutest detail! His eyes followed her. She saw him staring, looked away, walked past.

Eric fumbled his papers together, closed the notebook and ran after her. He caught up, matched his steps to hers, still staring, unthinking. She looked at him, flushed, looked away.

"Go away or I'll call a cop!"

"Please, I have to talk to you."

"I said go away." She increased her pace; he matched it.

"Please forgive me, but I dreamed about you last night. You see—"

She stared straight ahead.

"I've been told *that* one before! Go away!"

"But you don't understand."

She stopped, turned and faced him, shaking with anger. "But I *do* understand! You saw my show last night! You've dreamed about me!" She wagged her head. "Miss Lanai, I *must* get to know you!"

Eric shook his head. "But I've never even heard of you or seen you before."

"Well! I'm not accustomed to being insulted either!" She whirled, walked away briskly, the red cape flowing out behind her. Again he caught up with her.

"Please—"

"I'll scream!"

"I'm a psychoanalyst."

She hesitated, slowed, stopped. A puzzled expression flowed over her face. "Well, that's a new approach."

He took advantage of her interest. "I really did dream about you. It was most disturbing. I couldn't shut it off."

Something in his voice, his manner— She laughed. "A real dream was bound to show up some day."

"I'm Dr. Eric Ladde."

She glanced at the caduceus over his breast pocket. "I'm Colleen Lanai; I sing."

He winced. "I know."

"I thought you'd never heard of me."

"You sang in my dream."

"Oh." A pause. "Are you really a psychoanalyst?"

He slipped a card from his breast pocket; handed it to her. She looked at it.

"What does 'Teleprobe Diagnosis' mean?"

"That's an instrument I use."

She returned the card, linked an arm through his, set an easy, strolling pace. "All right, doctor. You tell me about your dream and I'll tell you about my headaches. Fair exchange?" She peered up at him from under thick eyelashes.

"Do you have headaches?"

"Terrible headaches." She shook her head.

Eric looked down at her. Some of the nightmare unreality returned. He thought, "What am I doing here? One doesn't dream about a strange face and then meet her in the flesh the next day. The next thing I know the whole world of my unconscious will come alive."

"Could it be this Syndrome thing?" she asked. "Ever since we were in Los Angeles I've—" She chewed at her lip.

He stared at her. "You were in Los Angeles?"

"We got out just a few hours before that . . . before—" She shuddered. "Doctor, what's it like to be crazy?"

He hesitated. "It's no different from being sane—for the person involved." He looked out at the mist lifting from the bay. "The Syndrome appears similar to other forms of insanity. It's as though something pushed people over their lunacy thresholds. It's strange; there's a rather well defined radius of about sixty miles which it saturated. Atlanta and Los Angeles, for instance, and Lawton, had quite sharp lines of demarcation: people on one side of a street got it; people on the other side didn't. We suspect there's a contamination period during which—" He paused, looked down at her, smiled. "And all you asked was a simple question. This is my lecture personality. I wouldn't worry too much about those headaches; probably diet, change of climate, maybe your eyes. Why don't you get a complete physical?"

She shook her head. "I've had six physicals since we left Karachi: same thing—four new diets." She shrugged. "Still I have headaches."

Eric jerked to a stop, exhaled slowly. "You were in Karachi, too?"

"Why, yes; that was the third place we hit after Honolulu."

He leaned toward her. "And Honolulu?"

She frowned. "What is this, a cross-examination?" She waited. "Well—"

He swallowed, thought, *How can one person have been in these cities the Syndrome hit and be so casual about it?*

She tapped a foot. "Cat got your tongue?"

He thought, *She's so flippant about it.*

He ticked off the towns on his fingers. "You were in Los Angeles, Honolulu, Karachi; you've hit the high spots of Syndrome contamination and—"

An animal cry, sharp, exclamatory, burst from her. "It got all of those places?"

He thought, *How could anyone be alive and not know exactly where the Syndrome has been?*

He asked, "Didn't you know?"

She shook her head, a numb motion, eyes wide, staring. "But Pete said—" She stopped. "I've been so busy learning new numbers. We're reviving the old-time hot jazz."

"How could you miss it? TV is full of it, the newstapes, the transgraphs."

She shrugged. "I've just been so busy. And I don't like to think about such things. Pete said—" She shook her head. "You know, this is the first time I've been out alone for a walk in over a month. Pete was asleep and—" Her expression softened. "That Pete; he must not have wanted me to worry."

"If you say so, but—" He stopped. "Who's Pete?"

"Haven't you heard of Pete Serantis and the musikron?"

"What's a musikron?"

She shook back a curl of dark hair. "Have your little joke, doctor."

"No, seriously. What's a musikron?"

She frowned. "You *really* don't know what the musikron is?"

He shook his head.

She chuckled, a throaty sound, controlled. "Doctor, you talk about *my* not knowing about Karachi and Honolulu. Where have you been hiding your head? Variety has us at the top of the heap."

He thought, "She's serious!"

A little stiffly, he said, "Well, I've been quite busy with a research problem of my own. It deals with the Syndrome."

"Oh." She turned, looked at the gray waters of the bay, turned back. She twisted her hands together. "Are you sure about Honolulu?"

"Is your family there?"

She shook her head. "I have no family. Just friends." She looked up at him, eyes shining. "Did it get . . . everybody?"

He nodded, thought: *She needs something to distract her attention.*

He said, "Miss Lanai, could I ask a favor?" He plunged ahead, not waiting for an answer. "You've been three places where the Syndrome hit. Maybe there's a clue in your patterns. Would you consent to undergoing a series of tests at my lab? They wouldn't take long."

"I couldn't possibly; I have a show to do tonight. I just sneaked out for a few minutes by myself. I'm at the Gweduc Room. Pete may wake up and—" She focused on his pleading expression. "I'm sorry, doctor. Maybe some other time. You wouldn't find anything important from me anyway."

He shrugged, hesitated. "But I haven't told you about my dream."

"You tempt me, doctor. I've heard a lot of phony dream reports. I'd appreciate the McCoy for just once. Why don't you walk me back to the Gweduc Room? It's only a couple of blocks."

"Okay."

She took his arm.

"Half a loaf—"

He was a thin man with a twisted leg, a pinched, hating face. A cane rested against his knee. Around him wove a spiderweb maze of wires—musikron. On his head, a dome-shaped hood. A spy, unsuspected, he looked out through a woman's eyes at a man who had identified himself as Dr. Eric Ladde. The thin man sneered, heard through the woman's ears: "Half a loaf—"

On the bayside walk, Eric and Colleen matched steps.

"You never did tell me what a musikron is."

Her laughter caused a passing couple to turn and stare. "Okay. But I still don't understand. We've been on TV for a month."

He thought, *She thinks I'm a fuddy; probably am!*

He said, "I don't subscribe to the entertainment circuits. I'm just on the science and news networks."

She shrugged. "Well, the musikron is something like a recording and playback machine; only the operator mixes in any new sounds he wants. He wears a little metal bowl on his head and just thinks about the sounds—the musikron plays them." She stole a quick glance at him, looked ahead. "Everyone says it's a fake; it really isn't."

Eric stopped, pulled her to a halt. "That's fantastic. Why—" He paused, chuckled. "You know, you happen to be talking to one of the few experts in the world on this sort of thing. I have an encephalorecorder in my basement lab that's the last word in teleprobes . . . that's what you're trying to describe." He smiled. "The psychiatrists of this town may think I'm a young upstart, but they send me their tough diagnostic cases." He looked down at her. "So let's just admit your Pete's machine is artistic showmanship, shall we?"

"But it isn't just showmanship. I've heard the records before they go into the machine and when they come out of it."

Eric chuckled.

She frowned. "Oh, you're so supercilious."

Eric put a hand on her arm. "Please don't be angry. It's just that I know this field. You don't want to admit that Pete has fooled you along with all the others."

She spoke in a slow, controlled cadence: "Look . . . doctor . . . Pete . . . was . . . one . . . of . . . the . . . inventors . . . of . . . the . . . musikron . . . Pete . . . and . . . old . . . Dr. Amanti." She squinted her eyes, looking up at him. "You may be a big wheel in this business, but I know what I've heard."

"You said Pete worked on this musikron with a doctor. What did you say that doctor's name was?"

"Oh, Dr. Carlos Amanti. His name's on a little plate inside the musikron."

Eric shook his head. "Impossible. Dr. Carlos Amanti is in an asylum."

She nodded. "That's right; Wailiku Hospital for the Insane. That's where they worked on it."

Eric's expression was cautious, hesitant. "And you say when Pete thinks about the sounds, the machine produces them?"

"Certainly."

"Strange I'd never heard about this musikron before."

"Doctor, there are a lot of things you've never heard about."

He wet his lips with his tongue. "Maybe you're right." He took her arm, set a rapid pace down the walkway. "I want to see this musikron."

In Lawton, Oklahoma, long rows of prefabricated barracks swelter on a sun-baked flat. In each barracks building, little cubicles; in each cubicle, a hospital bed; on each hospital bed, a human being. Barracks XRO-29: a psychiatrist walks down the hall, behind him an orderly pushing a cart. On the cart, hypodermic needles, syringes, antiseptics, sedatives, test tubes. The psychiatrist shakes his head.

"Baily, they certainly nailed this thing when they called it the Scramble Syndrome. Stick an egg-beater into every psychosis a person could have, mix 'em up, turn 'em all on."

The orderly grunts, stares at the psychiatrist.

The psychiatrist looks back. "And we're not making any progress on this thing. It's like bailing out the ocean with a sieve."

Down the hallway a man screams. Their footsteps quicken.

The Gweduc Room's elevator dome arose ahead of Eric and Colleen, a half-melon inverted on the walkway. At the top of the dome a blue and red script-ring circled slowly, spelling out, "Colleen Lanai with Pete Serantis and the Musikron."

On the walkway before the dome a thin man, using a cane to compensate for a limp, paced back and forth. He looked up as Eric and Colleen approached.

"Pete," she said.

The man limped toward them, his cane staccato on the paving.

"Pete, this is Dr. Ladde. He's heard about Dr. Amanti and he wants to—"

Pete ignored Eric, stared fiercely at Colleen. "Don't you know we have a show tonight? Where have you been?"

"But, it's only a little after nine; I don't—"

Eric interrupted. "I was a student of Dr. Amanti's. I'm interested in your musikron. You see, I've been carrying on Dr. Amanti's researches and—"

The thin man barked, "No time!" He took Colleen's arm, pulled her toward the dome.

"Pete, please! What's come over you?" She held back.

Pete stopped, put his face close to hers. "Do you like this business?"

She nodded mutely, eyes wide.

"Then let's get to work!"

She looked back at Eric, shrugged her shoulders. "I'm sorry."

Pete pulled her into the dome.

Eric stared after them. He thought, "He's a decided compulsive type . . . very unstable. May not be as immune to the Syndrome as she apparently is." He frowned, looked at his wrist watch, remembered his ten o'clock appointment. "Damn!" He turned, almost collided with a young man in busboy's coveralls.

The young man puffed nervously at a cigarette, jerked it out of his mouth, leered. "Better find yourself another gal, Doc. That one's taken."

Eric looked into the young-old eyes, stared them down. "You work in there?"

The young man replaced the cigarette between thin lips, spoke around a puff of blue smoke. "Yeah."

"When does it open?"

The young man pulled the cigarette from his mouth, flipped it over Eric's shoulder into the bay. "We're open now for breakfast. Floor show doesn't start until seven tonight."

"Is Miss Lanai in the floor show?"

The busboy looked up at the script-ring over the dome, smiled knowingly. "Doc, she *is* the floor show!"

Again Eric looked at his wrist watch, thought, *I'm coming back here tonight.* He turned toward the nearest unitube. "Thanks," he said.

"You better get reservations if you're coming back tonight," said the busboy.

Eric stopped, looked back. He reached into his pocket, found a twenty buck piece, flipped it to the busboy. The thin young man caught the coin out of the air, looked at it, said, "Thank *you.* What name, Doc?"

"Dr. Eric Ladde."

The busboy pocketed the coin. "Righto, Doc. Floorside. I come on again at six. I'll attend to you personally."

Eric turned back to the unitube entrance again and left immediately.

Under the smog-filtered Los Angeles sun, a brown-dry city.

Mobile Laboratory 31 ground to a stop before Our Lady of Mercy Hospital, churning up a swirl of dried palm fronds in the gutter. The overworked turbo-motor sighed to a stop, grating. The Japanese psychologist emerged on one side, the Swedish doctor on the other. Their shoulders sagged.

The psychologist asked, "Ole, how long since you've had a good night's sleep?"

The doctor shook his head. "I can't remember, Yoshi; not since I left Frisco, I guess."

From the caged rear of the truck, wild, high-pitched laughter, a sigh, laughter.

The doctor stumbled on the steps to the hospital sidewalk. He stopped, turned. "Yoshi—"

"Sure, Ole. I'll get some fresh orderlies to take care of this one." To himself he added, "If there are any fresh orderlies."

Inside the hospital, cool air pressed down the hallway. The Swedish doctor stopped a man with a clipboard. "What's the latest count?"

The man scratched his forehead with a corner of the clipboard. "Two and a half million last I heard, doctor. They haven't found a sane one yet."

The Gweduc Room pointed a plastine finger under Elliott Bay. Unseen by the patrons, a cage compressed a high density of sea life over the transparent ceiling. Illumabeams traversed the water, treating the watchers to visions of a yellow salmon, a mauve perch, a pink octopus, a blue jellyfish. At one end of the room, synthetic mother-of-pearl had been formed into a giant open gweduc shell—the stage. Colored spotlights splashed the backdrop with ribbons of flame, blue shadows.

Eric went down the elevator, emerged in an atmosphere disturbingly reminiscent of his nightmare. All it lacked was the singer. A waiter led him, threading a way through the dim haze of perfumed cigarette smoke, between tables ringed by men in formal black, women in gold lamé, luminous synthetics. An aquamarine glow shimmered from the small round table tops—the only lights in the Gweduc Room other than spotlights on the stage and illumabeams in the dark water overhead. A susurration of many voices hung on the air. Aromas of alcohol, tobacco, perfumes, exotic seafoods layered the room, mingled with a perspirant undertone.

The table nestled in the second row, crowded on all sides. The waiter extricated a chair; Eric sat down.

"Something to drink, sir?"

"Bombay Ale."

The waiter turned, merged into the gloom.

Eric tried to move his chair into a comfortable position, found it was wedged immovably between two chairs behind him. A figure materialized out of the gloom across from him; he recognized the busboy.

"Best I could get you, Doc."

"This is excellent." Eric smiled, fished a twenty-buck piece from his pocket, pressed it into the other's hand.

"Anything I can do for you, Doc?"

"Would you tell Miss Lanai I'm here?"

"I'll try, Doc; but that Pete character has been watching her like a piece of prize property all afternoon. Not that I wouldn't do the same thing myself, you understand."

White teeth flashed in the smoke-layered shadows. The busboy turned, weaved his way back through the tables. The murmuring undercurrent of voices in the room damped out. Eric turned toward the stage. A portly man in ebony and chalk-striped coveralls bent over the microphone.

"Here's what you've been waiting for," he said. He gestured with his left hand. Spotlights erased a shadow, revealing Colleen Lanai, her hands clasped in front of her. An old-fashioned gown of electric blue to match her eyes sheathed the full curves.

"Colleen Lanai!"

Applause washed over the room, subsided. The portly man gestured with his right hand. Other spotlights flared, revealing Pete Serantis in black coveralls, leaning on his cane.

"Pete Serantis and—"

He waited for a lesser frenzy of clapping to subside.

". . . The Musikron!"

A terminal spotlight illuminated a large metallic box behind Pete. The thin man limped around the box, ducked, and disappeared inside. Colleen took the microphone from the announcer, who bowed and stepped off the stage.

Eric became aware of a pressing mood of urgency in the room. He thought, "For a brief instant we forget our fears, forget the Syndrome, everything except the music and this instant."

Colleen held the microphone intimately close to her mouth.

"We have some more real oldies for you tonight," she said. An electric pressure of personality pulsed out from her. "Two of these songs we've never presented before. First, a trio—'Terrible Blues' with the musikron giving you a basic recording by Clarence Williams and the Red Onion Jazz Babies, Pete Serantis adding an entirely new effect; next, 'Wild Man Blues' and the trumpet is pure Louis Armstrong; last, 'Them's Graveyard Words,' an old Bessie Smith special." She bowed almost imperceptibly.

Music appeared in the room, not definable as to direction. It filled the senses. Colleen began to sing, seemingly without effort. She played her voice like a horn, soaring with the music, ebbing with it, caressing the air with it.

Eric stared, frozen, with all the rest of the audience.

She finished the first song. The noise of applause deafened him. He felt pain in his hands, looked down to find himself beating his palms together. He stopped, shook his head, took four deep breaths. Colleen picked up the thread of a new melody. Eric narrowed his eyes, staring at the stage. Impulsively, he put his hands to his ears and felt panic swell as the music remained undiminished. He closed his eyes, caught his breath as he continued to see Colleen, blurred at first, shifting, then in a steady image from a place nearer and to the left.

A wavering threnody of emotions accompanied the vision. Eric put his hands before his eyes. The image remained. He opened his eyes. The image again blurred, shifted to normal. He searched to one side of Colleen for the position from which he had been seeing her. He decided it could only be from inside the musikron and at the instant of decision discerned the outline of a mirror panel in the face of the metallic box.

"Through a one-way glass," he thought. "Through Pete's eyes."

He sat, thinking, while Colleen finished her third number. Pete emerged from the musikron to share the applause. Colleen blew a kiss to the audience.

"We'll be back in a little while."

She stepped down from the stage, followed by Pete; darkness absorbed them. Waiters moved along the tables. A drink was placed on Eric's table. He put money in the tray. A blue shadow appeared across from him, slipped into the chair.

"Tommy told me you were here . . . the busboy." She leaned across the table. "You mustn't let Pete see you. He's in a rage, a real pet. I've never seen anybody that angry."

Eric leaned toward her, caught a delicate exhalation of sandalwood perfume. It dizzied him. "I want to talk to you," he said. "Can you meet me after the show?"

"I guess I can trust you," she said. She hesitated, smiling faintly. "You're the professional type." Another pause. "And I think I need professional advice." She slipped out of the chair, stood up. "I have to get back before he suspects I didn't go to the powder room. I'll meet you near the freight elevator upstairs."

She was gone.

A cold breeze off the bay tugged at Eric's cape, puffing it out behind him. He leaned against the concrete railing, drawing on a cigarette. The glowing coal flowed an orange wash across his face, flaring, dimming. The tide rip sniggled and babbled; waves lap-lap-lapped at the concrete beneath him. A multi-colored glow in the water to his left winked out as the illumabeams above the Gweduc Room were extinguished. He shivered. Footsteps approached from his left, passed behind him—a man, alone. A muffled whirring sound grew, stopped. Light footsteps ran toward him, stopped at the rail. He smelled her perfume.

"Thanks," he said.

"I can't be long. He's suspicious. Tommy brought me up the freight elevator. He's waiting."

"I'll be brief. I've been thinking. I'm going to talk about travel. I'm going to tell you where you've been since you hooked up with Pete in Honolulu." He turned, leaned sideways against the railing. "You tried your show first in Santa Rosa, California, the sticks; then you went to Piquetberg, Karachi, Reykjavik, Portland, Hollandia, Lawton—finally, Los Angeles. Then you came here."

"So you looked up our itinerary."

He shook his head. "No." He hesitated. "Pete's kept you pretty busy rehearsing, hasn't he?"

"This isn't easy work."

"I'm not saying it is." He turned back to the rail, flipped his cigarette into the darkness, heard it hiss in the water. "How long have you known Pete?"

"A couple of months more or less. Why?"

He turned away. "What kind of a fellow is he?"

She shrugged. "He's a nice guy. He's asked me to marry him."

Eric swallowed. "Are you going to?"

She looked out to the dark bay. "That's why I want your advice. I don't know . . . I just don't know. He put me where I am, right on top of the entertainment heap." She turned back to Eric. "And he really is an awfully nice guy . . . when you get under that bitterness."

Eric breathed deeply, pressed against the concrete railing. "May I tell you a story?"

"What about?"

"This morning you mentioned Dr. Carlos Amanti, the inventor of the teleprobe. Did you know him?"

"No."

"I was one of his students. When he had the breakdown it hit all of us pretty hard, but I was the only one who took up the teleprobe project. I've been working at it eight years."

She stirred beside him. "What is this teleprobe?"

"The science writers have poked fun at it; they call it the 'mind reader.' It's not. It's just a means of interpreting some of the unconscious impulses of the human brain. I suppose some day it may approach mind reading. Right now it's a rather primitive instrument, sometimes unpredictable. Amanti's intention was to communicate with the unconscious mind, using interpretation of encephalographic waves. The idea was to amplify them, maintain a discrete separation between types, and translate the type variations according to thought images."

She chewed her lower lip. "And you think the musikron would help make a better teleprobe, that it would help fight the Syndrome?"

"I think more than that." He looked down at the paving.

"You're trying to tell me something without saying it," she said. "Is it about Pete?"

"Not exactly."

"Why'd you give that long recitation of where we'd been? That wasn't just idle talk. What are you driving at?"

He looked at her speculatively, weighing her mood. "Hasn't Pete told you about those places?"

She put a hand to her mouth, eyes wide, staring. She moaned. "Not the Syndrome . . . not all of those places, too?"

"Yes." It was a flat, final sound.

She shook her head. "What are you trying to tell me?"

"That it could be the musikron causing all of this."

"Oh, no!"

"I could be wrong. But look at how it appears. Amanti was a genius working near the fringe of insanity. He had a psychotic break. Then he helped Pete build a machine. It's possible that machine picks up the operator's brain wave patterns, transmits them as a scrambling impulse. The musikron *does* convert thought into a discernible energy—sound. Why isn't it just as possible that it funnels a disturbing impulse directly into the unconscious." He wet his lips with his tongue. "Did you know that I hear those sounds even with my hands over my ears, see you with my eyes covered. Remember my nightmare? My nervous system is responding to a subjective impulse."

"Does it do the same thing to everybody?"

"Probably not. Unless a person was conditioned as I have been by spending years in the aura of a similar machine, these impulses would be censored at the threshold of consciousness. They would be repressed as unbelievable."

Her lips firmed. She shook her head. "I don't see how all this scientific gobbledy-gook proves the musikron caused the Syndrome."

"Maybe it doesn't. But it's the best possibility I've seen. That's why I'm going to ask a favor. Could you get me the circuit diagrams for the musikron? If I could see them I'd be able to tell just what this thing does. Do you know if Pete has plans for it?"

"There's some kind of a thick notebook inside the musikron. I think that's what you mean."

"Could you get it?"

"Maybe, but not tonight . . . and I wouldn't dare tell Pete."

"Why not tonight?"

"Pete sleeps with the key to the musikron. He keeps it locked when it's not in use; so no one will get inside and get a shock. It has to be left on all the time because it takes so long to warm it up. Something about crystals or energy potential or some words like that."

"Where's Pete staying?"

"There are quarters down there, special apartments."

He turned away, breathed the damp salt air, turned back.

Colleen shivered. "I know it's not the musikron. I . . . they—" She was crying.

He moved closer, put an arm around her shoulders, waiting. He felt her shiver. She leaned against him; the shivering subsided.

"I'll get those plans." She moved her head restlessly. "That'll prove it isn't the musikron."

"Colleen . . ." He tightened his arm on her shoulders, feeling a warm urgency within him.

She moved closer. "Yes."

He bent his head. Her lips were warm and soft. She clung to him, pulled away, nestled in his arms.

"This isn't right," she said.

Again he bent his head. She tipped her head up to meet him. It was a gentle kiss.

She pulled away slowly, turned her head toward the bay. "It can't be like this," she whispered. "So quick—without warning."

He put his face in her hair, inhaled. "Like what?"

"Like you'd found your way home."

He swallowed. "My dear."

Again their lips met. She pulled away, put a hand to his cheek. "I have to go."

"When will I see you?"

"Tomorrow. I'll tell Pete I have to do some shopping."

"Where?"

"Do you have a laboratory?"

"At my home in Chalmers Place on the other side of the lake. It's in the directory."

"I'll come as soon as I can get the diagrams."

Again they kissed.

"I really have to go."

He held her tightly.

"Really." She pulled away. "Good night"—she hesitated—"Eric." Shadows flowed in around her.

He heard the whirring of the elevator, leaned back against the concrete, drawing deep breaths to calm himself.

Deliberate footsteps approached from his left. A handlight flashed in his face, the dull gleam of a night patrolman's brassard behind the light. The light moved to the caduceus at his breast.

"You're out late, doctor."

The light returned to his face, winked off. Eric knew he had been photographed—as a matter of routine.

"Your lipstick's smudged," the patrolman said. He walked away past the elevator dome.

Inside the silent musikron: a thin man, pinched face, hating. Bitter thought: *Now wasn't that a sweet love scene!* Pause. *The doctor wants something to read?* Wry smile. *I'll* provide it. *He'll have something to occupy his mind after we've gone.*

Before going to bed, Eric filed a transgraph to Mrs. Bertz, his secretary, telling her to cancel his appointments for the next day. He snuggled up to the pillow, hugging it. Sleep avoided him. He practiced yoga breathing. His senses remained alert. He slipped out of bed, put on a robe and sandals. He looked at the bedside clock—2:05 A.M., Saturday, May 15, 1999. He thought, *Just twenty-five hours ago—nightmare. Now . . . I don't know.* He smiled. *Yes I do; I'm in love. I feel like a college kid.*

He took a deep breath. *I'm in love.* He closed his eyes and looked at a memory picture of Colleen. *Eric, if you only solve this Syndrome, the world is yours.* The thoughts skipped a beat. *I'm an incipient manic—*

Eric ruminated. *If Pete takes that musikron out of Seattle—What then?*

He snapped a finger, went to the vidiphone, called an all-night travel agency. A girl clerk finally agreed to look up the booking dates he wanted— for a special fee. He gave her his billing code, broke the connection and went to the microfilm rack across from the foot of his bed. He ran a finger down the title index, stopped at "Implications of Encephalographic Wave Forms, A Study of the Nine Brain Pulses, by Dr. Carlos Amanti." He pushed the selector opposite the tape, activated the screen above the rack and returned to his bed, carrying the remote-control unit.

The first page flashed on the screen; room lights dimmed automatically. He read:

"There is a scale of vibratory impulses spanning and exceeding the human auditory range which consistently produce emotional responses of fear in varying degrees. Certain of these vibratory impulses—loosely grouped under the term *sounds*—test the extremes of human emotional experience. One may say, within reason, that all emotion is response to stimulation by harmonic movement, by oscillation.

"Many workers have liked emotions with characteristic encephalographic wave responses: Carter's work on Zeta waves and love; Reymann on Pi waves and abstract thinking; Poulson on the Theta Wave Index to degrees of sorrow, to name a few.

"It is the purpose of my work to trace these characteristic responses and point out what I believe to be an entirely new direction for interpretation of—"

Because of the late hour, Eric had expected drowsiness to overtake his reading, but his senses grew more alert as he read. The words had the familiarity of much re-reading, but they still held stimulation. He recalled a passage toward the end of the book, put the film on motor feed and scanned forward to the section he wanted. He slowed the tape, returned the controls to single-page advance; there it was:

"While working with severely disturbed patients in the teleprobe, I have found a charged emotional feeling in the atmosphere. Others, unfamiliar with my work, have reported this same experience. This suggests that the characteristic emanations of a disturbed mentality may produce sympathetic reactions upon those within the unshielded field of the teleprobe. Strangely, this disturbed sensation sometimes follows by minutes or even hours the period when the patient was under examination.

"I am hesitant to suggest a theory based upon this latter phenomenon. There is too much we do not know about the teleprobe—its latency period, for instance. However, it is possible that the combination of teleprobe and disturbed personality broadcasts a field with a depressant effect upon the unconscious functions of persons within that field. Be that as it may, this entire field of teleprobe and encephalographic wave research carries implications which—"

With a decisive gesture, Eric snapped off the projector, slipped out of bed and dressed. The bedside clock showed 3:28 A.M., Saturday, May 15, 1999. Never in his life had he felt more alert. He took the steps two at a time down to his basement lab, flipped on all the lights, wheeled out his teleprobe.

I'm on to something, he thought. *This Syndrome problem is too urgent for me to waste time sleeping.*

He stared at his teleprobe, an open framework of shelves, banks of tubes, maze of wiring, relaxing chair in the center with the metal hemisphere of the pickup directly above the chair. He thought, *The musikron is rigged for sound projection; that means a secondary resonance circuit of some kind.*

He pulled an unused tape recorder from a rack at the end of his bench, stripped the playback circuit from it. He took the recorder service manual, sketched in the changes he would need, pausing occasionally to figure circuit loads and balances on a slide rule. Presently, not too satisfied with his work, but anxious to get started, he brought out the parts he would need and began cutting and soldering. In two hours he had what he wanted.

Eric took cutter pliers, went to the teleprobe, snipped away the recorder circuit, pulled it out as a unit. He wheeled the teleprobe cage to the bench and, delicately feeling his way, checking the circuit diagrams as he went, he wired in the playback circuit. From the monitor and audio sides, he took the main leads, fed them back into the first bank of the encephalographic pickup. He put a test power source on the completed circuit and began adding resistance units by eye to balance the impedance. It took more than an hour of testing and cutting, required several units of shielding.

He stepped back, stared at the machine. He thought, *It's going to oscillate all over the place. How does he balance this monster?*

Eric pulled at his chin, thinking. *Well, let's see what this hybrid does.*

The wall clock above his bench showed 6:45 A.M. He took a deep breath, hooked an overload fuse into a relay power switch, closed the switch. A wire in the pickup circuit blazed to incandescence; the fuse kicked out. Eric opened the switch, picked up a test meter, and returned to the machine. The fault eluded him. He went back to the circuit diagrams.

"Perhaps too much power—" He recalled that his heavy duty rheostat was at a shop being repaired, considered bringing out the auxiliary generator he had used on one experiment. The generator was beneath a pile of boxes in a corner. He put the idea temporarily aside, turned back to the teleprobe.

"If I could just get a look at that musikron."

He stared at the machine. "A resonance circuit—What else?" He tried to imagine the interrelationship of the components, fitting himself into the machine.

"I'm missing it some place! There's some other thing and I have the feeling I already know it, that I've heard it. I've got to see the diagrams on that musikron."

He turned away, went out of the lab and climbed the stairs to his kitchen. He took a coffee capsule from a package in the cupboard, put it beside the sink. The vidiphone chimed. It was the clerk from the travel bureau. Eric took down her report, thanked her, broke the connection. He did a series of subtractions.

"Twenty-eight hour time lag," he thought. "Every one of them. That's too much of a coincidence."

He experienced a moment of vertigo, followed by weariness. "I'd better get some rest. I'll come back to this thing when I'm more alert."

He padded into the bedroom, sat down on the bed, kicked off his sandals and lay back, too tired to undress. Sleep eluded him. He opened his eyes, looked at the clock: 7:00 A.M. He sighed, closed his eyes, sank into a somnolent state. A niggling worry gnawed at his consciousness. Again he opened his eyes, looked at the clock: 9:50 A.M. *But I didn't feel the time pass,* he thought. *I must have slept.* He closed his eyes. His senses drifted into dizziness, the current in a stream, a ship on the current, wandering, hunting, whirling.

He thought, *I hope he didn't see me leave.*

His eyelids snapped open and, for a moment, he saw a unitube entrance on the ceiling above his head. He shook his head.

"That was a crazy thought. Where'd that come from?" he asked himself. "I've been working too hard."

He turned on his side, returned to the somnolent state, his eyes drooping closed. Instantly, he had the sensation of being in a maze of wires; an emotion of hate surged over him so strongly it brought panic because he couldn't explain it or direct it at anything. He gritted his teeth, shook his head, opened his eyes. The emotion disappeared, leaving him weak. He closed his eyes. Into his senses crept an almost overpowering aroma of gardenias, a vision of dawnlight through a shuttered window. His eyelids snapped open; he sat up in the bed, put his head in his hands.

Rhinencephalic stimulation, he thought. *Visual stimulation . . . auditory stimulation . . . nearly total sensorium response. It means something. But what does it mean?* He shook his head, looked at the clock: 10:10 A.M.

Outside Karachi, Pakistan, a Hindu holy man squatted in the dust beside an ancient road. Past him paraded a caravan of International Red Cross trucks, moving selected cases of Syndrome madness to the skytrain field on the Indus delta. Tomorrow the sick would be studied at a new clinic in Vienna. The truck motors whined and roared; the ground trembled. The holy man drew an ancient symbol with a finger in the dust. The wind of a passing truck stirred the pattern of Brahmaputra, twisting it. The holy man shook his head sadly.

Eric's front door announcer chimed as someone stepped onto the entrance mat. He clicked the scanner switch at his bedside, looked to the bedroom master screen; Colleen's face appeared on the screen. He punched for the door release, missed, punched again, caught it. He ran his hands through his hair, snapped the top clip of his coveralls, went to the entrance hall.

Colleen appeared tiny and hesitant standing in the hall. As he saw her, something weblike, decisive, meshed inside him—a completeness.

He thought, *Boy, in just one day you are completely on the hook.*

"Eric," she said.

Her body's warm softness clung to him. Fragrance wafted from her hair. "I missed you," he said.

She pulled away, looked up. "Did you dream about me?"

He kissed her. "Just a normal dream."

"Doctor!"

A smile took the sting out of the exclamation. She pulled away, slipped off her fur-lined cape. From an inner pocket of the cape she extracted a flat blue booklet. "Here's the diagram. Pete didn't suspect a thing."

Abruptly, she reeled toward him, clutched at his arm, gasping.

He steadied her, frightened. "What's the matter, darling?"

She shook her head, drawing deep, shuddering breaths.

"It's nothing; just a . . . little headache."

"Little headache nothing." He put the back of his wrist against her forehead. The skin held a feverish warmth. "Do you feel ill?"

She shook her head. "No. It's going away."

"I don't like this as a symptom. Have you eaten?"

She looked up, calmer. "No, but I seldom eat breakfast . . . the waistline."

"Nonsense! You come in here and eat some fruit."

She smiled at him. "Yes, doctor . . . darling."

The reflection on the musikron's inner control surfaces gave an underlighted, demoniacal cast to Pete's face. His hand rested on a relay switch. Hesitant thought: *Colleen, I wish I could control your thoughts. I wish I could tell you what to do. Each time I try, you get a headache. I wish I knew how this machine really works.*

Eric's lab still bore the cluttered look of his night's activities. He helped Colleen up to a seat on the edge of the bench, opened the musikron booklet beside her. She looked down at the open pages.

"What are all those funny looking squiggles?"

He smiled. "Circuit diagram." He took a test clip and, glancing at the diagram, began pulling leads from the resonance circuit. He stopped, a puzzled frown drawing down his features. He stared at the diagram. "That can't be right." He found a scratch pad, stylus, began checking the booklet.

"What's wrong?"

"This doesn't make sense."

"How do you mean?"

"It isn't designed for what it's supposed to do."

"Are you certain?"

"I know Dr. Amanti's work. This isn't the way he works." He began leafing through the booklet. A page flopped loose. He examined the binding. The booklet's pages had been razored out and new pages substituted. It was a good job. If the page hadn't fallen out, he might not have noticed. "You said it was easy to get this. Where was it?"

"Right out on top of the musikron."

He stared at her speculatively.

"What's wrong?" Her eyes held open candor.

"I wish I knew." He pointed to the booklet. "That thing's as phony as a Martian canal."

"How do you know?"

"If I put it together that way"—a gesture at the booklet—"it'd go up in smoke the instant power hit it. There's only one explanation: Pete's on to us."

"But how?"

"That's what I'd like to know . . . how he anticipated you'd try to get the diagram for me. Maybe that busboy—"

"Tommy? But he's such a nice young fellow."

"Yeah. He'd sell his mother if the price was right. He could have eavesdropped last night."

"I can't believe it." She shook her head.

In the webwork of the musikron, Pete gritted his teeth. *Hate him! Hate him!* He pressed the thought at her, saw it fail. With a violent motion, he jerked the metal hemisphere off his head, stumbled out of the musikron. *You're not going to have her! If it's a dirty fight you want, I'll really show you a dirty fight!*

Colleen asked, "Isn't there some other explanation?"

"Can you think of one?"

She started to slide down from the bench, hesitated, lurched against him, pressing her head against his chest. "My head . . . my head—" She went limp in his arms, shuddered, recovered slowly, drew gasping breaths. She stood up. "Thank you."

In a corner of the lab was a canvas deck chair. He led her over to it, eased her down. "You're going to a hospital right now for a complete check-up—tracers, the works. I don't like this."

"It's just a headache."

"Peculiar kind of a headache."

"I'm not going to a hospital."

"Don't argue. I'm calling for reservations as soon as I can get over to the phone."

"Eric, I won't do it!" She pushed herself upright in the chair. "I've seen all the doctors I want to see." She hesitated, looked up at him. "Except you. I've had all those tests. There's nothing wrong with me . . . except something in my head." She smiled: "I guess I'm talking to the right kind of a doctor for that."

She lay back, resting, closed her eyes. Eric pulled up a stool, sat down beside her, holding her hand. Colleen appeared to sink into a light sleep, breathing evenly. Minutes passed.

If the teleprobe wasn't practically dismantled, I could test her, he thought.

She stirred, opened her eyes.

"It's that musikron," he said. He took her arm. "Did you ever have headaches like this before you began working with that thing?"

"I had headaches, but . . . well, they weren't this bad." She shuddered. "I kept having horrible dreams last night about all those poor people going insane. I kept waking up. I wanted to go in and have it out with Pete." She put her hands over her face. "How can you be certain it's the musikron. You can't be sure. I won't believe it! I can't."

Eric stood up, went to the bench and rummaged under loose parts for a notebook. He returned, tossed the book into her lap. "There's your proof."

She looked at the book without opening it. "What is this?"

"It's some figures on your itinerary. I had a travel bureau check your departure times. From the time Pete would have been shutting down the musikron to the moment all hell broke loose there's an even twenty-eight-hour time lapse. That same time lag is present in each case."

She pushed the notebook from her lap. "I don't believe it. You're making this up."

He shook his head. "Colleen, what does it mean to you that you have been each place where the Syndrome hit . . . that there was a twenty-eight-hour time lapse in each case. Isn't that stretching coincidence too far?"

"I know it's not true." Her lips thinned. "I don't know what I've been thinking of to even consider you were right." She looked up, eyes withdrawn. "It can't be true. If it was, it would mean Pete planned the whole thing. He's just not that kind of a guy. He's nice, thoughtful."

He started to put his hand on her arm. "But, Colleen, I thought—"

"Don't touch me. I don't care what you thought, or what I thought. I think you've been using your psychological ability to try to turn me away from Pete."

He shook his head, again tried to take her arm.

She pulled away. "No! I want to think and I can't think when . . . when you touch me." She stared at him. "I believe you're just jealous of Pete."

"That's not—"

A motion at the lab door caught his eye, stopped him. Pete stood there, leaning on his cane.

Eric thought, *How did he get there? I didn't hear a thing. How long has he been there?* He stood up.

Pete stepped forward. "You forgot to latch your door, doctor." He looked at Colleen. "Common enough thing. I did, too." He limped into the room, cane tapping methodically. "You were saying something about jealousy." A pause. "I understand about jealousy."

"Pete!" Colleen stared at him, turned back to Eric. "Eric, I—" She began, and then shrugged.

Pete rested both hands on his cane, looked up at Eric. "You weren't going to leave me anything, were you, doctor—the woman I love, the musikron. You were even going to hang me for this Syndrome thing."

Eric stopped, retrieved his notebook from the floor. He handed it to Pete, who turned it over, looked at the back.

"The proof's in there. There's a twenty-eight-hour time lag between the moment you leave a community and the moment madness breaks out. You already know it's followed you around the world. There's no deviation. I've checked it out."

Pete's face paled. "Coincidence. Figures can lie; I'm no monster."

Colleen turned toward Eric, back to Pete. "That's what I told him, Pete."

"Nobody's accusing you of being a monster, Pete . . . yet," Eric said. "You *could* be a savior. The knowledge that's locked up in that musikron could practically wipe out insanity. It's a positive link with the unconscious . . . can be tapped any time. Why, properly shielded—"

"Nuts! You're trying to get the musikron so you can throw your weight around." He looked at Colleen. "And you sugar-talked her into helping you." He sneered. "It's not the first time I've been double-crossed by a woman; I guess I should've been a psychiatrist."

Colleen shook her head. "Pete, don't talk that way."

"Yeah . . . How else do you expect me to talk? You were a nobody; a canary in the hula chorus and I picked you up and set you down right on the top. So what do you do—" He turned away, leaning heavily on the cane. "You can have her, Doc; she's just your type!"

Eric put out a hand, withdrew it. "Pete! Stop allowing your deformity to deform your reason! It doesn't matter how we feel about Colleen. We've got to think about what the musikron is doing to people! Think of all the unhappiness this is causing people . . . the death . . . the pain—"

"People!" Pete spat out the word.

Eric took a step closer to him. "Stop that! You know I'm right. You can have full credit for anything that is developed. You can have full control of it. You can—"

"Don't try to kid me, Doc. It's been tried by experts. You and your big words! You're just trying to make a big impression on baby here. I already told you you can have her. I don't want her."

"Pete! You—"

"Look out, Doc; you're losing your temper!"

"Who wouldn't in the face of your pig-headedness?"

"So it's pig-headed to fight a thief, eh, Doc?" Pete spat on the floor, turned toward the door, tripped on his cane and fell.

Colleen was at his side. "Pete, are you hurt?"

He pushed her away. "I can take care of myself!" He struggled to his feet, pulling himself up on the cane.

"Pete, please—"

Eric saw moisture in Pete's eyes. "Pete, let's solve this thing."

"It's already solved, Doc." He limped through the doorway.

Colleen hesitated. "I have to go with him. I can't let him go away like this. There's no telling what he'll do."

"But don't you see what he's doing?"

Anger flamed in her eyes; she stared at Eric. "I saw what you did and it was as cruel a thing as I've ever seen." She turned and ran after Pete.

Her footsteps drummed up the stairs; the outer door slammed.

An empty fibreboard box lay on the floor beside the teleprobe. Eric kicked it across the lab.

"Unreasonable . . . neurotic . . . flighty . . . irresponsible—"

He stopped; emptiness grew in his chest. He looked at the teleprobe. "Sometimes, there's no predicting about women." He went to the bench, picked up a transistor, put it down, pushed a tumble of resistors to the back of the bench. "Should've know better."

He turned, started toward the door, froze with a thought which forced out all other awareness:

What if they leave Seattle?

He ran up the stairs three at a time, out the door, stared up and down the street. A jet car sped past with a single occupant. A woman and two children approached from his left. Otherwise, the street was empty. The unitube entrance, less than half a block away, disgorged three teen-age girls. He started toward them, thought better of it. With the tubes running fifteen seconds apart, his chance to catch them had been lost while he'd nursed his hurt.

He re-entered the apartment.

I have to do something, he thought. *If they leave, Seattle will go the way of all the others.* He sat down by the vidiphone, put his finger in the dial, withdrew it.

If I call the police, they'll want proof. What can I show them besides some time-tables? He looked out the window at his left. *The musikron! They'll see—*Again he reached for the dial, again withdrew. *What would they see? Pete would just claim I was trying to steal it.*

He stood up, paced to the window, stared out at the lake.

I could call the society, he thought.

He ticked off in his mind the current top officers of the Kind County Society of Psychiatric Consultants. All of them considered Dr. Eric Ladde a little too successful for one so young; and besides there was the matter of his research on the teleprobe; mostly a laughable matter.

But I have to do something . . . the Syndrome—He shook his head. *I'll have to do it alone, whatever I do.* He slipped into a black cape, went outside and headed for the Gweduc Room.

A cold wind kicked up whitecaps in the bay, plumed spray onto the waterfront sidewalk. Eric ducked into the elevator, emerged into a lunchroom atmosphere. The girl at the checktable looked up.

"Are you alone, doctor?"

"I'm looking for Miss Lanai."

"I'm sorry. You must have passed them outside. She and Mr. Serantis just left."

"Do you know where they were going?"

"I'm sorry; perhaps if you come back this evening—"

Eric returned to the elevator, rode up to the street vaguely disquieted. As he emerged from the elevator dome, he saw a van pull away from the service dome. Eric played a hunch, ran toward the service elevator which already was whirring down.

"Hey!"

The whirring stopped, resumed; the elevator returned to the street level, in it Tommy, the busboy.

"Better luck next time, Doc."

"Where are they?"

"Well—"

Eric jammed a hand into his coin pocket, fished out a fifty-buck piece, held it in his hand.

Tommy looked at the coin, back at Eric's eyes. "I heard Pete call the Bellingham skytrain field for reservations to London."

A hard knot crept into Eric's stomach; his breathing became shallow, quick; he looked around him.

"Only twenty-eight hours—"

"That's all I know, Doc."

Eric looked at the busboy's eyes, studying him.

Tommy shook his head. "Don't you start looking at me that way!" He shuddered. "That Pete give me the creeps; always staring at a guy; sitting around in that machine all day and no noises coming out of it." Again he shuddered. "I'm glad he's gone."

Eric handed him the coin. "You won't be."

"Yeah," Tommy stepped back into the elevator. "Sorry you didn't make it with the babe, Doc."

"Wait."

"Yeah?"

"Wasn't there a message from Miss Lanai?"

Tommy made an almost imperceptible motion toward the inner pocket of his coveralls. Eric's trained eyes caught the gesture. He stepped forward, gripped Tommy's arm.

"Give it to me!"

"Now look here, Doc."

"Give it to me!"

"Doc, I don't know what you're talking about."

Eric pushed his face close to the busboy's. "Did you see what happened to Los Angeles, Lawton, Portland, all the places where the Syndrome hit?"

The boy's eyes went wide. "Doc, I—"

"Give it to me!"

Tommy darted his free hand under his coveralls, extracted a thick envelope, thrust it into Eric's hand.

Eric released the boy's arm. Scrawled on the envelope was: "This will prove you were wrong about Pete." It was signed, "Colleen."

"You were going to keep this?" Eric asked.

Tommy's lips twisted. "Any fool can see it's the plans for the musikron, Doc. That thing's valuable."

"You haven't any idea," Eric said. He looked up. "They're headed for Bellingham?"

"Yeah."

The nonstop unitube put Eric at the Bellingham field in twenty-one minutes. He jumped out, ran to the station, jostling people aside. A skytrain lashed into the air at the far end of the field. Eric missed a step, stumbled, caught his balance.

In the depot, people streamed past him away from the ticket window. Eric ran up to the window, leaned on the counter. "Next train to London?"

The girl at the window consulted a screen beside her. "There'll be one at 12:50 tomorrow afternoon, sir. You just missed one."

"But that's twenty-four hours!"

"You'd arrive in London at 4:50 P.M., sir." She smiled. "Just a little late for tea." She glanced at his caduceus.

Eric clutched at the edge of the counter, leaned toward her. "That's twenty-nine hours—one hour too late."

He pushed himself away from the window, turned.

"It's *just* a four-hour trip, doctor."

He turned back. "Can I charter a private ship?"

"Sorry, doctor. There's an electrical storm coming; the traveler beam will have to be shut down. I'm sure you couldn't get a pilot to go out without the beam. You do understand?"

"Is there a way to call someone on the skytrain?"

"Is this a personal matter, doctor?"

"It's an emergency."

"May I ask the nature of the emergency?"

He thought a moment, looking at the girl. He thought, *Same problem here . . . nobody would believe me.*

He said, "Never mind. Where's the nearest vidiphone? I'll leave a message for her at Plymouth Depot."

"Down that hallway to your right, doctor." The girl went back to her tickets. She looked up at Eric's departing back. "Was it a medical emergency, doctor?"

He paused, turned. The envelope in his pocket rustled. He felt for the papers, pulled out the envelope. For the second time since Tommy had given them to him, Eric glanced inside at the folded pages of electronic diagrams, some initialed "C. A."

The girl waited, staring at him.

Eric put the envelope back in his pocket, a thought crystalizing. He glanced up at the girl. "Yes, it was a medical emergency. But you're out of range."

He turned, strode outside, back to the unitube. He thought about Colleen. *Never trust a neurotic woman. I should have known better than to let my glands hypnotize me.*

He went down the unitube entrance, worked his way out to the speed strip, caught the first car along, glad to find it empty. He took out the envelope, examined its contents during the ride. There was no doubt about it; the envelope contained the papers Pete had razored from the musikron service book. Eric recognized Dr. Amanti's characteristic scrawl.

The wall clock in his lab registered 2:10 P.M. as Eric turned on the lights. He took a blank sheet of paper from his notebook, wrote on it with grease pencil:

"DEADLINE, 4:00 P.M., Sunday, May 16th."

He tacked the sheet above his bench, spread out the circuit diagrams from the envelope. He examined the first page.

Series modulation, he thought. *Quarter wave.* He ran a stylus down the page, checked the next page. *Multiple phase-reversing.* He turned to the next page. The stylus paused. He traced a circuit, went back to the first page. *Degenerative feedback.* He shook his head. *That's impossible! There'd just be a maze of wild harmonics.* He continued on through the diagrams, stopped and read through the last two pages slowly. He went through the circuits a second time, a third time, a fourth time. He shook his head. *What is it?*

He could trace the projection of much of the diagram, amazed at the clear simplicity of the ideas. The last ten pages though—They described a series of faintly familiar circuits, reminding him of a dual frequency crystal calibrator of extremely high oscillation. "10,000 KC" was marked in the margin. But there were subtle differences he couldn't explain. For instance, there was a sign for a lower limit.

A series of them, he thought. *The harmonics hunt and change. But it can't be random. Something has to control it, balance it.*

At the foot of the last page was a notation: "Important—use only C6 midget variable, C7, C8 dual, 4ufd."

They haven't made tubes in that series for fifty years, he thought. *How can I substitute?*

He studied the diagram.

I don't stand a chance of making this thing in time. And if I do; what then? He wiped his forehead. *Why does it remind me of a crystal oscillator?* He looked at the clock—two hours had passed. *Where did the time go?* he asked himself. *I'm taking too much time just learning what this is.* He chewed his lips, staring at the moving second hand of the clock, suddenly froze. *The parts houses will be closing and tomorrow's Sunday!*

He went to the lab vidiphone, dialed a parts house. No luck. He dialed another, checking the call sheet beside the phone. No luck. His fifth call netted a suggestion of a substitute circuit using transistors which might work. Eric checked off the parts list the clerk suggested, gave the man his package tube code.

"I'll have them out to you first thing Monday," the man said.

"But I have to have them today! Tonight!"

"I'm sorry, sir. The parts are in our warehouse; it's all locked up tight on Saturday afternoon."

"I'll pay a hundred bucks above list price for those parts."

"I'm sorry, sir; I don't have authorization."

"Two hundred."

"But—"

"Three hundred."

The clerk hesitated. Eric could see the man figuring. The three hundred probably was a week's wages.

"I'll have to get them myself after I go off duty here," the clerk said. "What else do you need?"

Eric leafed through the circuit diagrams, read off the parts lists from the margins. "There's another hundred bucks in it if you get them to me before seven."

"I get off at 5:30, doctor. I'll do my best."

Eric broke the circuit, returned to his bench, began roughing-in from the diagram with what materials he had. The teleprobe formed the basic element with surprisingly few changes.

At 5:40, the dropbell of his transgraph jangled upstairs. Eric put down his soldering iron, went upstairs, pulled out the tape. His hands trembled when he saw the transmission station. London. He read:

"Don't ever try to see me again. Your suspicions are entirely unfounded as you probably know by now. Pete and I to be married Monday. Colleen."

He sat down at the transmitter, punched out a message to American Express, coding it urgent for delivery to Colleen Lanai.

"Colleen: If you can't think of me, please think of what this means to a city full of people. Bring Pete and that machine back before it's too late. You can't be this unhuman."

He hesitated before signing it, punched out, "I love you." He signed it, "Eric."

He thought, *You damn' fool, Eric. After the way she ran out on you.*

He went into the kitchen, took a capsule to stave off weariness, ate a dinner of pills, drank a cup of coffee. He leaned back against the kitchen drainboard, waiting for the capsule to take hold. His head cleared; he washed his face in cold water, dried it, returned to the lab.

The front door announcer chimed at 6:42 P.M. The screen showed the clerk from the parts house, his arms gripping a bulky package. Eric punched the door release, spoke into the tube: "First door on your left, downstairs."

The back wall of his bench suddenly wavered, the lines of masonry rippling; a moment of disorientation surged through him. He bit his lip, holding to the reality of the pain.

It's too soon, he thought. *Probably my own nerves; I'm too tense.*

An idea on the nature of the Syndrome flashed into his mind. He pulled a scratch pad to him, scribbled, "Loss of unconscious autonomy; overstimulation subliminal receptors; gross perception—petit perception. Check C. G. Jung's collective unconscious."

Footsteps tapped down the stairway.

"This the place?"

The clerk was a taller man than he had expected. An air of near adolescent eagerness played across the man's features as he took in the lab. "What a layout!"

Eric cleared a space on the bench. "Put that stuff right here." Eric's eyes focused on the clerk's delicately sensitive hands. The man slid the box onto the bench, picked up a fixed crystal oscillator from beside the box, examined it.

"Do you know anything about electronic hookups?" Eric asked.

The clerk looked up, grinned. "W7CGO. I've had my own ham station over ten years."

Eric offered his hand. "I'm Dr. Eric Ladde."

"Baldwin Platte . . . Baldy." He ran one of his sensitive hands through thinning hair.

"Glad to know you, Baldy. How'd you like to make a thousand bucks over what I've already promised you?"

"Are you kidding, Doc?"

Eric turned his head, looked at the framework of the teleprobe. "If that thing isn't finished and ready to go by four o'clock tomorrow afternoon, Seattle will go the way of Los Angeles."

Baldy's eyes widened; he looked at the framework. "The Syndrome? How can—"

"I've discovered what caused the Syndrome . . . a machine like this. I have to build a copy of that machine and get it working. Otherwise—"

The clerk's eyes were clear, sober. "I saw your nameplate upstairs, Doc, and remembered I'd read about you."

"Well?"

"If you say positive you've found out what caused the Syndrome, I'll take your word for it. Just don't try to explain it to me." He looked toward the parts on the bench, back to the teleprobe. "Tell me what I'm supposed to do." A pause. "And I hope you know what you're talking about."

"I've found something that just can't be coincidence," Eric said. "Added to what I know about teleprobes, well—" He hesitated. "Yes, I know what I'm talking about."

Eric took a small bottle from the rear of his bench, looked at the label, shook out a capsule. "Here, take this; it'll keep you awake."

Baldy swallowed the capsule.

Eric sorted through the papers on his bench, found the first sheet. "Now, here's what we're dealing with. There's a tricky quarter-wave hookup coupled to an amplification factor that'll throw you back on your heels."

Baldy looked over Eric's shoulder. "Doesn't look too hard to follow. Let me work on that while you take over some of the tougher parts." He reached for the diagram, moved it to a cleared corner of the bench. "What's this thing supposed to do, Doc?"

"It creates a field of impulses which feed directly into the human unconscious. The field distorts—"

Baldy interrupted him. "Okay, Doc. I forgot I asked you not to explain it to me." He looked up, smiled. "I flunked Sociology." His expression sobered. "I'll just work on the assumption you know what this is all about. Electronics I understand; psychology . . . no."

They worked in silence, broken only by sparse questions, muttering. The second hand on the wall clock moved around, around, around; the minute hand followed, and the hour hand.

At 8:00 A.M., they sent out for breakfast. The layout of the crystal oscillators still puzzled them. Much of the diagram was scrawled in a radio shorthand.

Baldy made the first break in the puzzle.

"Doc, are these things supposed to make a noise?"

Eric looked at the diagram. "What?" His eyes widened. "Of course they're supposed to make a noise."

Baldy wet his lips with his tongue. "There's a special sonar crystal set for depth sounding in submarine detection. This looks faintly like the circuit, but there are some weird changes."

Eric tugged at his lip; his eyes glistened. "That's it! That's why there's no control circuit! That's why it looks as though these things would hunt all over the place! The operator is the control—his mind keeps it in balance!"

"How's that?"

Eric ignored the question. "But this means we have the wrong kind of crystals. We've misread the parts list." Frustration sagged his shoulders. "And we're not even halfway finished."

Baldy tapped the diagram with a finger. "Doc, I've got some old surplus sonar equipment at home. I'll call my wife and have her bring it over. I think there are six or seven sonopulsators—they just might work."

Eric looked at the wall clock: 8:28 A.M. Seven and a half hours to go. "Tell her to hurry."

Mrs. "Baldy" was a female version of her husband. She carried a heavy wooden box down the steps, balancing it with an easy nonchalance.

"Hi, Hon. Where'll I put this stuff?"

"On the floor . . . anywhere. Doc, this is Betty."

"How do you do."

"Hiya, Doc. There's some more stuff in the car. I'll get it."

Baldy took her arm. "You better let me do it. You shouldn't be carrying heavy loads, especially down stairs."

She pulled away. "Go on. Get back to your work. This is good for me—I need the exercise."

"But—"

"But me no buts." She pushed him.

He returned to the bench reluctantly, looking back at his wife. She turned at the doorway and looked at Baldy. "You look pretty good for being up all night, Hon. What's all the rush?"

"I'll explain later. You better get that stuff."

Baldy turned to the box she had brought, began sorting through it. "Here they are." He lifted out two small plastic cases, handed them to Eric, pulled out another, another. There were eight of them. They lined the cases up on the bench. Baldy snapped open the cover of the first one.

"They're mostly printed circuits, crystal diode transistors and a few tubes. Wonderful engineering. Don't know what the dickens I ever planned to do with them. Couldn't resist the bargain. They were two bucks apiece." He folded back the side plate. "Here's the crys—Doc!"

Eric bent over the case.

Baldy reached into the case. "What were those tubes you wanted?"

Eric grabbed the circuit diagram, ran his finger down the parts list. "C6 midget variable, C7, C8 dual 4ufd."

Baldy pulled out a tube. "There's your C6." He pulled out another. "There's your C8." Another. "Your C7." He peered into the works. "There's a third stage in here I don't think'll do us any good. We can rig a substitute for the 4ufd component."

Baldy whistled tonelessly through his teeth. "No wonder that diagram looked familiar. It was based on this wartime circuit."

Eric felt a moment of exultation, sobered when he looked at the wall clock: 9:04 A.M.

He thought, "We have to work faster or we'll never make it in time. Less than seven hours to go."

He said, "Let's get busy. We haven't much time."

Betty came down the stairs with another box. "You guys eaten."

Baldy didn't look up from dismantling the second plastic box. "Yeah, but you might make us some sandwiches for later."

Eric looked up from another of the plastic boxes. "Cupboard upstairs is full of food."

Betty turned, clattered up the stairs.

Baldy glanced at Eric out of the corners of his eyes. "Doc, don't say anything to Betty about the reason for all this." He turned his attention back to the box, working methodically. "We're expecting our first son in about five months." He took a deep breath. "You've got me convinced." A drop of perspiration ran down his nose, fell onto his hand. He wiped his hand on his shirt. "This has gotta work."

Betty's voice echoed down the stairs: "Hey, Doc, where's your can opener?"

Eric had his head and shoulders inside the teleprobe. He pulled back, shouted, "Motor-punch to the left of the sink."

Muttering, grumbling, clinking noises echoed down from the kitchen. Presently, Betty appeared with a plate of sandwiches, a red-tinted bandage on her left thumb. "Broke your paring knife," she said. "Those mechanical gadgets scare me." She looked fondly at her husband's back. "He's just as gadget happy as you are, Doc. If I didn't watch him like a spy-beam my nice old kitchen would be an electronic nightmare." She upended an empty box, put the plate of sandwiches on it. "Eat when you get hungry. Anything I can do?"

Baldy stepped back from the bench, turned. "Why don't you go over to Mom's for the day?"

"The whole day?"

Baldy glanced at Eric, back at his wife. "The Doc's paying me fourteen hundred bucks for the day's work. That's our baby money; now run along."

She made as though to speak, closed her mouth, walked over to her husband, kissed his cheek. "Okay, Hon. Bye." She left.

Eric and Baldy went on with their work, the pressure mounting with each clock tick. They plodded ahead, methodically checking each step.

At 3:20 P.M., Baldy released test clips from half of the new resonance circuit, glanced at the wall clock. He stopped, looked back at the teleprobe, weighing the work yet to be done. Eric lay on his back under the machine, soldering a string of new connections.

"Doc, we aren't going to make it." He put the test meter on the bench, leaned against the bench. "There just isn't enough time."

An electronic soldering iron skidded out from under the teleprobe. Eric squirmed out behind it, looked up at the clock, back at the unconnected wires of the crystal circuits. He stood up, fished a credit book from his pocket, wrote out a fourteen hundred buck credit check to Baldwin Platte. He tore out the check, handed it to Baldy.

"You've earned every cent of this, Baldy. Now beat it; go join your wife."

"But—"

"We haven't time to argue. Lock the door after you so you can't get back in if—"

Baldy raised his right hand, dropped it. "Doc, I can't—"

"It's all right, Baldy." Eric took a deep breath. "I kind of know how I'll go if I'm too late." He stared at Baldy. "I don't know about you. You might, well—" He shrugged.

Baldy nodded, swallowed. "I guess you're right, Doc." His lips worked. Abruptly, he turned, ran up the stairs. The outside door slammed.

Eric turned back to the teleprobe, picked up an open lead to the crystal circuits, matched it to its receptor, ran a drop of solder across the connection. He moved to the next crystal unit, the next—

At one minute to four he looked at the clock. More than an hour's work remained on the teleprobe and then—He didn't know. He leaned back against the bench, eyes filmed by fatigue. He pulled a cigarette from his pocket, pressed the igniter, took a deep drag. He remembered Colleen's question: "What's it like to be insane?" He stared at the ember on his cigarette.

Will I tear the teleprobe apart? Will I take a gun, go hunting for Colleen and Pete? Will I run out?—The clock behind him clicked. He tensed. *What will it be like?* He felt dizzy, nauseated. A wave of melancholia smothered his emotions. Tears of self-pity started in his eyes. He gritted his teeth. *I'm not insane . . . I'm not insane*—He dug his fingernails into his palms, drew in deep, shuddering breaths. Uncertain thoughts wandered through his mind.

I shall faint . . . the incoherence of morosis . . . demoniacal possession . . . dithyrambic dizziness . . . an anima figure concretionized out of the libido . . . corybantic calenture . . . mad as a March hare—

His head sagged forward.

*. . . Non compos mentis . . . aliéné . . . avoir le diable au corps—What has happened to Seattle? What has happened to Seattle? What has—*His

breathing steadied; he blinked his eyes. Everything appeared unchanged . . . unchanged . . . unchanged—*I'm wandering. I must get hold of myself!*

The fingers of his right hand burned. He shook away the short ember of his cigarette.

Was I wrong? What's happening outside? He started for the stairs, made it halfway to the door when the lights went out. A tight band ringed his chest. Eric felt his way to the door, grasped the stair rail, climbed up to the dim, filtered light of the hall. He stared at the stained glass bricks beside the door, tensed at a burst of gunshots from outside. He sleepwalked to the kitchen, raised on tiptoes to look through the ventilator window over the sink.

People! The street swarmed with people—some running, some walking purposefully, some wandering without aim, some clothed, some partly clothed, some nude. The bodies of a man and child sprawled in blood at the opposite curbing.

He shook his head, turned, went into the living room. The lights suddenly flashed on, off, on, stayed. He punched video for a news program, got only wavy lines. He put the set on manual, dialed a Tacoma station. Again wavy lines.

Olympia was on the air, a newcaster reading a weather report: "Partly cloudy with showers by tomorrow afternoon. Temperatures—"

A hand carrying a sheet of paper reached into the speaker's field of vision. The newsman stopped, scanned the paper. His hand shook. "Attention! Our mobile unit at the Clyde Field jet races reports that the Scramble Syndrome has struck the twin cities of Seattle-Tacoma. More than three million people are reported infected. Emergency measures already are being taken. Road blocks are being set up. There are known to have been fatalities, but—"

A new sheet of paper was handed to the announcer. His jaw muscles twitched as he read. "A jet racer has crashed into the crowd at Clyde Field. The death toll is estimated at three hundred. There are no available medical facilities. All doctors listening to this broadcast—all doctors—report at once to State disaster headquarters. Emergency medical—" The lights again blinked out, the screen faded.

Eric hesitated. *I'm a doctor. Shall I go outside and do what I can, medically, or shall I go down and finish the teleprobe—now that I've been proved right? Would it do any good if I did get it working?* He found himself breathing in a deep rhythm. *Or am I crazed like all the others? Am I really doing what I think I'm doing? Am I mad and dreaming a reality?* He thought of pinching himself, knew that would be no proof. *I have to go ahead as though I'm sane. Anything else* really *is madness.*

He chose the teleprobe, located a handlight in his bedroom, returned to the basement lab. He found the long unused emergency generator under the crates in the corner. He wheeled it to the center of the lab, examined it. The powerful alcohol turbine appeared in working order. The pressure cap on the fuel reservoir popped as he released it. The reservoir was more than half full. He found two carboys of alcohol fuel in the corner where the generator had been stored. He filled the fuel tank, replaced the cap, pumped pressure into the tank.

The generator's power lead he plugged into the lab fuse box. The hand igniter caught on the first spin. The turbine whirred to life, keened up through the sonic range. Lab lights sprang to life, dimmed, steadied as the relays adjusted.

It was 7:22 P.M. by the wall clock when he soldered the final connection. Eric estimated a half hour delay before the little generator had taken over, put the time actually at near eight o'clock. He found himself hesitant, strangely unwilling to test the completed machine. His one-time encephalorecorder was a weird maze of crossed wiring, emergency shielding, crowded tubes, crystals. The only familiar thing remaining in the tubular framework was the half-dome of the head-contact hanging above the test chair.

Eric plugged in a power line, linked it to a portable switchbox which he placed in the machine beside the chair. He eased aside a sheaf of wires, wormed his way through, sat down in the chair. He hesitated, hand on the switch.

Am I really sitting here? he wondered. *Or is this some trick of the unconscious mind? Perhaps I'm in a corner somewhere with a thumb in my mouth. Maybe I've torn the teleprobe apart. Maybe I've put the teleprobe together so it will kill me the instant I close the switch.*

He looked down at the switch, withdrew his hand. He thought, *I can't just sit here; that's madness, too.*

He reached up to the helmetlike dome, brought it down over his head. He felt the pinpricks of the contacts as they probed through his hair to his scalp. The narco-needles took hold, deadening skin sensation.

This feels like reality, he thought. *But maybe I'm building this out of memory. It's hardly likely I'm the only sane person in the city.* He lowered his hand to the switch. *But I have to act as though I am.*

Almost of its own volition, his thumb moved, depressed the switch. Instantly, a soft ululation hung in the laboratory air. It shifted to dissonance, to harmony, wailing, half-forgotten music, wavered up the scale, down the scale.

In Eric's mind, mottled pictures of insanity threatened to overwhelm his consciousness. He sank into a maelstrom. A brilliant spectograph coruscated before his eyes. In a tiny corner of his awareness, a discrete pattern of sensation remained, a reality to hold onto, to save him—the feeling of the teleprobe's chair beneath him and against his back.

He sank farther into the maelstrom, saw it change to gray, become suddenly a tiny picture seen through the wrong end of a telescope. He saw a small boy holding the hand of a woman in a black dress. The two went into a hall-like room. Abruptly Eric no longer saw them from a distance but was again himself at age nine walking toward a casket. He sensed again the horrified fascination, heard his mother's sobs, the murmurous, meaningless voice sounds of a tall, thin undertaker. Then, there was the casket and in it a pale, waxed creature who looked somewhat like his father. As Eric watched, the face melted and became the face of his uncle Mark; and then another mask, his high-school geometry teacher. Eric thought, *We missed that one in my psychoanalysis.* He watched the mobile face in the coffin as it again shifted and became the professor who had taught him abnormal psychology, and then his own analyst, Dr. Lincoln Ordway, and then—he fought against this one—Dr. Carlos Amanti.

So that's the father image I've held all these years, he thought. *That means— That means I've never really given up searching for my father. A fine thing for an analyst to uncover about himself!* He hesitated. *Why did I have to recognize that? I wonder if Pete went through this in his musikron?* Another part of his mind said, *Of course not. A person has to want to see inside himself or he never will, even if he has the opportunity.*

The other part of his mind abruptly seemed to reach up, seize control of his consciousness. His awareness of self lurched aside, became transformed into a mote whipping through his memories so rapidly he could barely distinguish between events.

Am I dying? he wondered. *Is it my life passing in review?*

The kaleidoscopic progression jerked to a stop before a vision of Colleen—the way he had seen her in his dream. The memory screen lurched to Pete. He saw the two people in a relationship to himself that he had never quite understood. They represented a catalyst, not good or evil, merely a reagent which set events in motion.

Suddenly, Eric sensed his awareness growing, permeating his body. He knew the condition and action of each gland, each muscle fiber, each nerve ending. He focused his inner eyes on the grayness through which he had passed. Into the gray came a tendril of red—shifting, twisting, weaving past him. He followed the red line. A picture formed in his mind, growing there like the awakening from anaesthetic. He looked down a long street—dim in the spring dusk—at the lights of a jet car thundering toward him. The car grew larger, larger, the lights two hypnotic eyes. With the vision came a thought: *My, that's pretty!*

Involuntary reactions took over. He sensed muscles tensing, jumping aside, the hot blast of the jet car as it passed. A plaintive thought twisted into his mind: *Where am I? Where's Mama? Where's Bea?*

Tightness gripped Eric's stomach as he realized he sat in another's consciousness, saw through another's eyes, sensed through another's nerves. He jumped away from the experience, pulling out of the other mind as though he had touched a hot stove.

So that's how Pete knew so much, he thought. *Pete sat in his musikron and looked through our eyes.* Another thought: *What am I doing here?* He sensed the teleprobe chair beneath him, heard the new self within him say, "I'm going to need more trained, expert help."

He followed another red tendril, searching, discarded it; sought another. The orientation was peculiar—no precise up or down or compass points until he looked out of the other eyes. He came to rest finally behind two eyes that looked down from an open window in the fortieth story of an office building, sensed the suicidal thoughts building up pressure within this person. Gently, Eric touched the center of consciousness, seeking the name—Dr. Lincoln Ordway, psychoanalyst.

Eric thought, *Even now I turn back to my own analyst.*

Tensely, Eric retreated to a lower level of the other's consciousness, knowing that the slightest misstep would precipitate this man's death wish, a jump through that window. The lower levels suddenly erupted a pinwheel of coruscating purple light. The pinwheel slowed, became a mandala figure—at the four points of the figure an open window, a coffin, a transitus-tree and a human face which Eric suddenly recognized as a distorted picture of himself. The face was boyish, slightly vacant.

Eric thought, *The analyst, too, is tied to what he believes is his patient.* With the thought, he willed himself to move gently, unobtrusively into the image of himself, began to expand his area of dominion over the other's unconscious. He pushed a tentative thought against the almost palpable wall which represented Dr. Ordway's focus of consciousness: *Line* (a whisper), *don't jump. Do you hear me, Line? Don't jump. The city needs your help.*

With part of his mind, Eric realized that if the analyst sensed his mental privacy being invaded that realization could tip the balance, send the man plunging out the window. Another part of Eric's mind took that moment to render up a solution to why he needed this man and others like him: The patterns of insanity broadcast by Pete Serantis could only be counterbalanced by a rebroadcast of calmness and sanity.

Eric tensed, withdrew slightly as he felt the analyst move closer to the window. In the other's mind, he whispered, "Come away from the window. Come away—" Resistance! A white light expanded in Eric' thoughts, rejected him. He felt himself swimming out into the gray maelstrom, receding. A red tendril approached and with it a question, not of his own origin, lifted into his mind:

Eric? What is this thing?

Eric allowed the pattern of teleprobe development to siphon through his mind. He ended the pattern with an explanation of what was needed.

Thought: *Eric, how did the Syndrome miss you?*

Conditioning by long exposure to my own teleprobe; high resistance to unconscious distortion built up by that work.

Funny thing; I was about to dive out the window when I sensed your inter-ference. It was something—the red tendril moved closer—*like this.*

They meshed completely.

"What now?" asked Dr. Ordway.

"We'll need as much trained help as we can find in the city. Others would censor out this experience below the threshold of consciousness."

"The influence of your teleprobe may quiet everybody."

"Yes, but if the machine is ever turned off, or if people go beyond its area of influence, they'd be back in the soup."

"We'll have to go in the back door of every unconscious in the city and put things in order!"

"Not just *this* city; every city where the musikron has been and every city where Serantis takes it until we can stop him."

"How did the musikron do this thing?"

Eric projected a mixed pattern of concepts and pictures: "The musikron pushed us deep down into the collective unconscious, dangled us there as long as we remained within its area of influence. (Picture of rope hanging down into swirls of fog.) Then the musikron was turned off. (Picture of knife cutting the rope, the end falling, falling into a swirling gray mael-strom.) Do you see it?"

"If we have to go down into that maelstrom after all these people, hadn't we better get started?"

He was a short man digging with his fingers in the soft loam of his flower-bed, staring vacantly at shredded leaves—name, Dr. Harold Marsh, psy-chologist. Unobtrusively, softly, they absorbed him into the network of the teleprobe.

She was a woman, dressed in a thin housecoat, preparing to leap from the end of a pier—name, Lois Voorhies, lay analyst. Swiftly, they drew her back to sanity.

Eric paused to follow a thin red tendril to the mind of a neighbor, saw through the other's eyes sanity returning around him.

Like ripples spreading in a pond, a semblance of sanity washed out across the city. Electric power returned; emergency services were restored.

The eyes of a clinical psychologist east of the city transmitted a view of a jet plane arrowing toward Clyde Field. Through the psychologist's mind the network picked up the radiating thought patterns of a woman—guilt, re-morse, despair.

Colleen!

Hesitantly, the network extended a pseudopod of thought, reached into Colleen's consciousness and found terror. *What is happening to me!*

Eric took over. *Colleen, don't be afraid. This is Eric. We are getting things back in order thanks to you and the musikron plans.* He projected the pattern of their accomplishments.

I don't understand. You're—

You don't have to understand now. Hesitantly: *I'm glad you came.*

Eric, I came as soon as I heard—when I realized you were right about Pete and the musikron. She paused. *We're coming down to land.*

Colleen's chartered plane settled onto the runway, rolled up to a hangar and was surrounded by National Guardsmen.

She sent out a thought: *We have to do something about London. Pete threatened to smash the musikron, to commit suicide. He tried to keep me there by force.*

When?

Six hours ago.

Has it been that long since the Syndrome hit?

The network moved in: *What is the nature of this man Serantis?*

Colleen and Eric merged thoughts to project Pete's personality.

The network: *He'll not commit suicide, or smash his machine. Too self-centered. He'll go into hiding. We'll find him soon enough when we need him—unless he's lynched first.*

Colleen interrupted: *This National Guard major won't let me leave the airport.*

Tell him you're a nurse assigned to Maynard Hospital.

Individual thought from the network: *I'll confirm from this end.*

Eric: *Hurry . . . darling. We need all of the help we can get from people resistant to the teleprobe.*

Thoughts from the network: *That's as good a rationalization as any. Every man to his own type of insanity. That's enough nonsense—let's get to work!*

THE GONE DOGS

A green turbo-copter moved over the New Mexico sand flats, its rotor blades going whik-whik-whik. Evening sunlight cast deep shadows ahead of it where the ground shelved away to a river canyon. The 'copter settled to a rock outcropping, a hatch popped open and a steel cage containing one female coyote was thrown out. The cage door fell away. In one jump, the animal was out of its prison and running. It whisked over the outcropping, leaped down to a ledge along the canyon wall and was out of sight around a bend—in its blood a mutated virus which had started with hog cholera.

The lab had a sharp chemical odor in which could be detected iodoform and ether. Under it was that musky, wet-fur smell found in the presence of caged animals. A despondent fox terrier sulked in a cage at one end; the remains of a poodle were stretched on a dissecting board atop a central bench, a tag on its leg labelled *X-8, PULLMAN VETERINARY RESEARCH CENTER, LABORATORY E.* Indirect lighting touched everything with a shadowless indifference.

Biologist Varley Trent, a lanky, dark-haired man with angular features, put his scalpel in a tray beside the poodle, stepped back, looked across at Dr. Walter Han-Meers, professor of veterinary medicine. The professor was a plump, sandy-haired Chinese-Dutchman with the smooth-skinned look of an Oriental idol. He stood beside the dissecting bench, staring at the poodle.

"Another failure," said Trent. "Each one of these I autopsy, I say to myself we're that much closer to the last dog on Earth."

The professor nodded. "Came down to give you the latest. Don't see how it helps us, but for what it's worth, this virus started in coyote."

"Coyote?"

Professor Han-Meers found a lab stool, pulled it up, sat down. "Yes. Ranch hand in New Mexico broke it. Talked to the authorities. His boss, a fellow named Porter Durkin, is a V.M.D., has a veterinary hospital on a ranch down there. Used a radioactive carbon egg to mutate hog cholera. Hoped to make a name for himself all right. Government had to move in troops to keep him from being lynched."

Trent ran a hand through his hair. "Didn't the fool realize his disease would spread to other canines?"

"Apparently didn't even think of it. He has a license from one of those little hogwallow colleges, but I don't see how anyone that stupid could make the grade."

"How about the coyote?"

"Oh, that was a great success. Sheep ranchers say they haven't lost an animal to coyotes in over a month. Only things worrying them now are bears, cougars and the lack of dogs to . . ."

"Speaking of dogs," said Trent, "we're going to need more test animals here by tomorrow. Serum nine isn't doing a thing for that fox terrier. He'll die tonight sometime."

"We'll have lots of test animals by tomorrow," said Han-Meers. "The last two dog isolation preserves in Canada reported primary infestations this morning."

Trent drummed his fingers on the bench top. "What's the government doing about the offer from the Vegan biophysicists?"

Han-Meers shrugged. "We are still turning them down. The Vegans are holding out for full control of the project. You know their reputation for biophysical alterations. They might be able to save our dogs for us, but what we'd get back wouldn't be a dog any longer. It'd be some elongated, multi-legged, scaly-tailed monstrosity. I wish I knew why they went in for those fish-tail types."

"Linked gene," said Trent. "Intelligence factor coupled. They use their *mikeses* generators to open up the gene pairs and . . ."

"That's right," said Han-Meers. "You studied with them. What's the name of that Vegan you're always talking about?"

"Ger (whistle) Anso-Anso."

"That's the one. Isn't he on Earth with the Vegan delegation?"

Trent nodded. "I met him at the Quebec conference ten years ago—the year before we made the biophysical survey to Vega. He's really a nice fellow once you get to know him."

"Not for me." Han-Meers shook his head. "They're too tall and disdainful. Make me feel inferior. Always harping about their damned *mikeses* generators and what they can do in bio-physics."

"They can do it, too."

"That's what makes them so damned irritating!"

Trent laughed. "If it'll make you feel any better, the Vegans may be all puffed up with pride about their bio-physics, but they're jealous as all git-out over our tool facility."

"Hmmmph!" said Han-Meers.

"I still think we should send them dogs for experimental purposes," said Trent. "The Lord knows we're not going to have any dogs left pretty soon at the rate we're going."

"We won't send them a sick spaniel as long as Gilberto Nathal is in the Federated Senate," said Han-Meers. "Every time the subject comes up, he jumps to his feet and hollers about the pride of Earth and the out-worlder threat."

"But . . ."

"It hasn't been too long since the Denebian campaign," said Han-Meers.

Trent wet his lips with his tongue. "Mmmmm, hmmmm. How are the other research centers coming?"

"Same as we are. The morning report shows a lot of words which sum up to a big round zero." Han-Meers reached into his pocket, extracted a yellow sheet of paper. "Here, you may as well see this. It'll be out pretty soon, anyway." He thrust the paper into Trent's hand.

Trent glanced at the heading:

BUREAU-GRAM—DEPARTMENT OF HEALTH AND SANITATION—PRIMARY SECRET:

He looked up at Han-Meers.

"Read it," said the professor.

Trent looked back to the *bureau-gram.* "Department doctors today confirmed that Virus D-D which is attacking the world's canines is one-hundred percent fatal. In spite of all quarantine precautions it is spreading. The virus knows kinship to hog cholera, but will thrive in a solution of protomycetin strong enough to kill any other virus on the list. It shows ability to become dormant and anerobic. Unless a suitable weapon with which to combat this disease is found within two more months, Earth is in danger of losing its entire population of wolves, dogs, foxes, coyote . . ."

Trent looked back to Han-Meers. "We've all suspected it was this bad, but . . ." He tapped the *bureau-gram.*

Han-Meers slipped the paper from Trent's grasp. "Varley, you held out on the census takers when they came around counting dogs, didn't you?"

Trent pursed his lips. "What makes you say a thing like that?"

"Varley, I wouldn't turn you over to the police. I am suggesting you contact your Vegan and give him your dogs."

Trent took a deep breath. "I gave him five puppies last week."

A Capital correspondent for a news service had broken the story six weeks previously, following up a leak in the Health and Sanitation Committee of the Federated Senate. A new virus was attacking the world's canine population and no means of fighting it was known. People already realized their pets were dying off in droves. The news story was enough to cause a panic.

Interstellar passenger space disappeared. Powerful men exerted influence for themselves and friends. People ran every which way with their pets, hopelessly tangling inter-world quarantine restrictions. And the inevitable rackets appeared.

SPECIAL CHARTER SHIP TO PLANETS OF ALDEBARAN. STRICTEST QUARANTINE REQUIREMENTS. TRAINED ATTENDANTS TO GUARD YOUR PETS IN TRANSIT. PRICE: FIFTY THOUSAND CREDITS A KILO.

The owners, of course, could not accompany their pets, shipping space being limited.

This racket was stopped when a Federation patrol ship ran into a strange meteor swarm beyond Pluto, stopped to map its course, discovered the swarm was composed of the frozen bodies of dogs.

Eleven days after the virus story appeared, the Arcturian planets banned Terran dogs. The Arcturians knew dog-smuggling would begin and their people could profit.

Trent kept six part-beagle hounds in a servo-mech kennel at an Olympic Mountain hunting camp. They were at the camp when the government instituted its emergency census of dogs. Trent deliberately overlooked mentioning them.

Leaving Pullman at three o'clock the morning after he talked to Han-Meers, he put his jet-copter on autopilot, slept until he reached Aberdeen.

The Aberdeen commander of the Federated Police was a graying, burn-scarred veteran of the Denebian campaign. His office was a square room overlooking the harbor. The walls were hung with out-world weapons, group photographs of officers and men. The commander stood up as Trent entered, waved him to a chair. "Makaroff's the name. What can I do for you?"

Trent introduced himself, sat down, explained that he was a member of the Pullman research staff, that he had nine hounds—six adults and three puppies—at a mountain kennel.

The commander seated himself, grasped the arms of his chair, leaned back. "Why aren't they in one of the government preserves?"

Trent looked the man in the eyes. "Because I was convinced they'd be safer where they are and I was right. The preserves are infested. Yet my hounds are in perfect health. What's more, Commander, I've discovered that humans are carrying the disease. We . . ."

"You mean if I pet a dog that could kill it?"

"That's right."

The commander fell silent. Presently, he said, "So you disobeyed the quarantine act, eh?"

"Yes."

"I've done the same kind of thing myself on occasion," said the commander. "You see some stupid order given, you know it won't work; so you go against it. If you're wrong they throw the book at you; if you're right they pin a medal on you. I remember one time in the Denebian campaign when . . ."

"Could you put an air patrol over my camp?" asked Trent.

The commander pulled at his chin. "Hounds, eh? Nothing better than a good hunting hound. Damned shame to see them die with all the rest." He paused. "Air patrol, eh? No humans?"

"We have two months to find an answer to this virus or there won't be another dog on earth," said Trent. "You see how important those dogs could be?"

"Bad as that, eh?" He pulled a vidi-phone to him. "Get me Perlan." He turned to Trent. "Where is your camp?"

Trent gave him the vectors. The commander scribbled them on a scratch pad.

A face came on the screen. "Yes, sir."

The commander turned back to the vidi-phone. "Perlan, I want a robotics air patrol—twenty-four-hour duty—over a hunting camp at," he glanced at the scratch pad, "vectors 8181-A and 0662-Y, Olympic West Slope. There's a kennel at the camp with nine hounds in it. No humans at all must contact those dogs." He wet his lips with his tongue. "A doctor has just told me that humans are carrying this Virus D-D thing."

When Trent landed at Pullman that afternoon he found Han-Meers waiting in Lab E. The professor sat on the same stool as though he had not moved in two days. His slant eyes contemplated the cage which had held the fox terrier. Now there was an airdale in the enclosure. As Trent entered, Han-Meers turned.

"Varley, what is this the Aberdeen policeman tells the news services?"

Trent closed the lab door. *So the commandant had talked.*

"Flores Clinic was on the line twice today," said Han-Meers. "Want to know what we discovered that they overlooked. The policeman has perhaps made up a story?"

Trent shook his head. "No. I told him a hunch of mine was an actual fact. I had to get an air patrol over my hunting camp. Those hounds are in perfect health."

Han-Meers nodded. "They have been without such a convenience all summer. Now they have to have it."

"I've been afraid they were dead. After all, I raised those hounds from pups. We've hunted and . . ."

"I see. And tomorrow we tell everybody it was a big mistake. I had thought you possessed more scientific integrity than that."

Trent hid his anger behind a passive face, slipped off his coat, donned a lab smock. "My dogs were isolated from humans all summer. We . . ."

"The Flores people have been thorough in their investigation," said Han-Meers. "They suspect we are trying to . . ."

"Not thorough enough." Trent opened a cupboard door, took out a bottle of green liquid. "Are you going to stay here and help or are you going to let me tackle this one alone?"

Han-Meers took off his coat, found an extra lab smock. "You are out on a thin limb, Varley." He turned, smiled. "But what a wonderful opportunity to give those M.D.'s a really big come-uppance."

At nine-sixteen the next morning, Trent dropped a glass beaker. It shattered on the tile floor and Trent's calm shattered with it. He cursed for two minutes.

"We are tired," said Han-Meers. "We will rest, come back to it later. I will put off the Flores people and the others today. There is still . . ."

"No." Trent shook his head. "We're going to take another skin wash on me with Clarendon's Astringent."

"But we've already tried that twice and . . ."

"Once more," said Trent. "This time we'll add the synthetic dog blood *before* fractionating."

At ten-twenty-two, Han-Meers set the final test tube in a plastic diffraction rack, pressed a switch at its base. A small silver cobweb shimmered near the top of the tube.

"Ahhhhhh!" said the professor.

They traced back. By noon they had the pattern: Dormant virus was carried in the human glands of perspiration, coming out through the pores—mostly in the palms of the hands—only under stress of emotion. Once out of the pores, the virus dried, became anerobic.

"If I hadn't dropped that beaker and become angry," said Trent.

"We would still be looking," added Han-Meers. "Devil of a one, this. Dormant and in minute quantity. That is why they missed it. Who tests an excited subject? They wait for him to become calm."

"Each man kills the thing he loves," quoted Trent.

"Should pay more attention to philosophers like Oscar Wilde," said Han-Meers. "Now I will call the doctors, tell them of their error. They are not going to like a mere biologist showing them up."

"It was an accident," said Trent.

"An accident based on observation of your dogs," said Han-Meers. "It is, of course, not the first time such accidents have occurred to mere biologists. There was Pasteur. They had him stoned in the village streets for . . ."

"Pasteur was a chemist," said Trent curtly. He turned, put test tube and stand on a side bench. "We'll have to tell the authorities to set up robotics service for the remaining dogs. That may give us time to see this thing through."

"I will use your lab phone to call the doctors," said Han-Meers. "I cannot wait to hear that Flores' voice when . . ."

The phone rang. Han-Meers put it to his ear. "Yes. I am me . . . I mean, I am here. Yes, I will take the call." He waited. "Oh, hello, Dr. Flores. I was just about to . . ." Han-Meers fell silent, listened. "Oh, you did?" His voice was flat. "Yes, that agrees with our findings. Yes, through the pores of the hands mostly. We were waiting to confirm it, to be certain . . . Yes, by our Dr. Trent. He's a biologist on the staff here. I believe some of your people were his students. Brilliant fellow. Deserves full credit for the discovery." There was a long silence. "I insist on scientific integrity, Dr. Flores, and I have your report in my hands. It absolves humans as carriers of the virus. I agree that this development will be bad for your clinic, but that cannot be helped. Good-bye, Dr. Flores. Thank you for calling." He hung up the phone, turned. Trent was nowhere in sight.

That afternoon, the last remaining pureblood Saint Bernard died at Angúac, Manitoba. By the following morning, Georgian officials had confirmed that their isolation kennels near Igurtsk were infested. The search for uninfected dogs continued, conducted now by robots. In all the world there were nine dogs known to be free of Virus D-D— six adult hounds and three puppies. They sniffed around their mountain kennel, despondent at the lack of human companionship.

When Trent arrived at his bachelor apartment that night he found a visitor, a tall (almost seven feet) Class C humanoid, head topped by twin, feather-haired crests, eyes shaded by slitted membranes like Venetian blinds. His slender body was covered by a blue robe, belted at the waist.
"Ger!" said Trent. He shut the door.
"Friend Varley," said the Vegan in his odd, whistling tones.
They held out their hands, pressed palms together in the Vegan fashion. Ger's seven-fingered hands felt overwarm.
"You've a fever," said Trent. "You've been too long on Earth."
"It is the accursed oxidized iron in your environment," said Ger. "I will take an increased dosage of medicine tonight." He relaxed his crests, a gesture denoting pleasure. "But it is good to see you again, Varley."
"And you," said Trent. "How are the . . ." He put a hand down, made the motion of petting a dog.
"That is why I came," said Ger. "We need more."
"More? Are the others dead?"
"Their cells are alive in new descendants," said Ger. "We used an acceleration chamber to get several generations quickly, but we are not satisfied with the results. Those were very strange animals, Varley. Is it not peculiar that they were identical in appearance?"
"It sometimes happens," said Trent.
"And the number of chromosomes," said Ger. "Aren't there . . ."
"Some special breeds differ," said Trent hurriedly.
"Oh." Ger nodded his head. "Do you have more of this breed we may take?"

"It'll be tricky to do," said Trent, "but maybe if we are very careful, we can get away with it."

Commander Makaroff was *delighted* to renew his acquaintance with the famous Dr. Trent. He was *delighted* to meet the visitor from far Vega, although a little less delighted. It was clear the commander was generally suspicious of out-worlders. He ushered the two into his office, seated them, took his place behind his desk.

"I'd like a pass permitting Dr. Anso-Anso to visit my kennel," said Trent. "Not being an Earth-human, he does not carry the virus and it will be quite safe to . . ."

"Why?"

"You have, perhaps, heard of the Vegan skill in bio-physics," said Trent. "Dr. Anso-Anso is assisting me in a line of research. He needs to take several blood and culture samples from . . ."

"Couldn't a robot do it?"

"The observations depend on highly specialized knowledge and there are no robots with this training."

"Hmmm." Commander Makaroff considered this. "I see. Well, if you vouch for him, Dr. Trent, I'm sure he's all right." His tone suggested that Dr. Trent *could be* mistaken. He took a pad from a drawer, scrawled a pass, handed it to Trent. "I'll have a police 'copter take you in."

"We have a specially sterilized 'copter with our lab equipment," said Trent. "Robotics International is servicing it right now."

Commander Makaroff nodded. "I see. Then I'll have an escort ready for you whenever you say."

The summons came the next day on a pink sheet of paper:

"Dr. Varley Trent is ordered to appear tomorrow before the special subcommittee of the Federated Senate Committee on Health and Sanitation at a hearing to be conducted at 4 P.M. in the office building of the Federated Senate." It was signed, "Oscar Olaffson, special assistant to Sen. Gilberto Nathal."

Trent accepted the summons in his lab, read it, took it up to Hans-Meers' office.

The professor read the order, handed it back to Trent. "Nothing is said about charges, Varley. Where were you yesterday?"

Trent sat down. "I got my Vegan friend into the preserve so he could snatch the three puppies. He's half way home with them by this time."

"They discovered it on the morning count, of course," said Han-Meers. "Ordinarily, they'd have just hauled you off to jail, but there's an election coming up. Nathal must be cozy with your Commander Makaroff."

Trent looked at the floor.

"The Senator will crucify you in spite of your virus discovery," said Han-Meers. "I'm afraid you've made powerful enemies. Dr. Flores is the brother-in-law of Senator Grapopulus of the Appropriations Committee. They'll bring in Flores Clinic people to claim that the virus carrier could have been discovered without you."

"But they're my dogs! I can . . ."

"Not since the emergency census and quarantine act," said Han-Meers. "You're guilty of sequestering government property." He pointed a finger at Trent. "And these enemies you've made will . . ."

"*I've* made! *You* were the one had to pull the grandstand act with Flores."

"Now, Varley. Let's not quarrel among ourselves."

Trent looked at the floor. "Okay. What's done is done."

"I have a little idea," said Han-Meers. "The college survey ship, the Elmendorff, is out at Hartley Field. It has been fueled and fitted for a trip to Sagittarius."

"What does that mean?"

"The ship is well guarded, of course, but a known member of the staff with a forged note from me could get aboard. Could you handle the Elmendorff alone?"

"Certainly. That's the ship we took to Vega on the bio-physical survey."

"Then run for it. Get that ship into hyper-drive and they'll never catch you."

Trent shook his head. "That would be admitting my guilt."

"Man, you *are* guilty! Senator Nathal is going to *discover* that tomorrow. It'll be big news. But if you run away, that will be bigger news and the senator's screaming will be just so much more background noise."

"I don't know."

"People are tired of his noises, Varley."

"I still don't like it."

"Varley, the senator is desperate for vote-getting news. Give him a little more time, a little more desperation, he'll go too far."

"I'm not worried about the senator. I'm worried about . . ."

"The dogs," said Han-Meers. "And if you escaped to Vega you could give them the benefit of your knowledge of terrestrial biology. You'd have to do it by remote control, of course, but . . ." He left the idea dangling there.

Trent pursed his lips.

"Every minute you waste makes your chances of escape that much slimmer." Han-Meers pushed a pad toward Trent. "Here's my letterhead. Forge your note."

Twenty minutes after Trent's 'copter took off for Hartley Field, a government 'copter settled to the campus parking area. Two men emerged, hurried to Han-Meers' office, presented police credentials. "We're looking for a Dr. Varley Trent. He's charged with violating the dog-restriction act. He's to be held in custody."

Han-Meers looked properly horrified. "I think he went home. He said something about not feeling well."

Senator Nathal raged. His plump body quivered. His normally red face became redder. He shouted, he screamed. His fuming countenance could be seen nightly on video. Just when he was reaching a fine climax, warning people against unbridled science, he was pushed aside by more important news.

The last dog in an isolation preserve—a brindle chow—died from virus infection. Before the senator could build up steam for a new attack, the government announced the discovery of an Arctic wolf pack of twenty-six animals untouched by virus. A day later, robot searchers turned up a live twelve-year-old mongrel on Easter Island and five cocker spaniels on Tierra del Fuego. Separate preserves for dogs and wolves were prepared on the west slope of the Olympic Mountains, all of the animals transported there.

Wolves, cockers, mongrel and hounds—they were the world's pets. Excursions in sealed 'copters were operated from Aberdeen to a point five kilometers from the dog-wolf preserve. There, powerful glasses sometimes gave a glimpse of motion which imagination could pad into a dog or wolf.

About the time Senator Nathal was getting ready to launch a new blast, pointing out that Trent's hounds were not necessarily important, that there had been other canine survivors, the twelve-year-old mongrel died of old age.

Dog lovers of the world mourned. The press took over and all the glory of mongreldom was rehashed. Senator Nathal again was background noise.

Trent headed for Vega, hit hyper-drive as soon as he had cleared the sun's area of warp. He knew that the Vegans would have to quarantine him to protect the dogs, but he could follow the experiments on video, help with his knowledge of terrestrial biology.

Professor Han-Meers, protesting ill health, turned his college duties over to an assistant, went on a vacation tour of the world. First, he stopped at the capital, met Senator Nathal, apologized for Dr. Trent's defection and praised the politician's stand.

In Geneva, Han-Meers met a pianist whose pet Dalmatians had been among the first to die in the epidemic. At Cairo, he met a government official who had bred wolf hounds, also among the first deceased. In Paris, he met the wife of a furrier whose pet airdale, *Coco,* had died in the third wave of the epidemic. In Moscow, in Bombay, in Calcutta, in Singapore, in Peking, in San Francisco, in Des Moines, in Chicago, he met others in like circumstances. To all he gave notes of introduction to Senator Nathal, explaining that the senator would see they received special treatment if they wanted to visit the Olympic preserve. Han-Meers expected at least one of these people to become a scandalous nuisance sufficient to insure the senator's political embarrassment.

The wife of the Paris furrier, Mme. Estagién Couloc, paid off, but in a manner Han-Meers had not anticipated.

Mme. Couloc was a slim woman of perhaps forty-five, chic in the timeless French fashion, childless, with a narrow, haughty face and a manner to match it. But her grandmother had been a farm wife and underneath the surface of pampered rich woman, Mme. Couloc was tough. She came to Aberdeen complete with two maids, a small Alp of luggage and a note from Senator Nathal. She had convinced herself that all of this *nonsense* about humans carrying the disease couldn't possibly apply to her. *A few simple sanitary precautions and she could have a dog of her own.*

Mme. Couloc meant to have a part-beagle dog, no matter the cost. The fact that there were no dogs to be had, made her need all the more urgent. Cautious inquiries at Aberdeen convinced her this would have to be a lone-handed job. Amidst the tangled psychological desperation which filled her mind, she worked out a plan which had all of the evasive cunning characteristic of the mentally ill.

From the air, on one of the daily excursions, Mme. Couloc surveyed the terrain. It was rugged enough to discourage a less determined person. The area had been maintained in its natural slate for seven hundred years. Thick undergrowth of salal, devil club and huckleberry crowded the natural avenues of access to the interior. Rivers were full of the spring snow melt. Ridgetops were tangles of windfalls, wild blackberries in the burns, granite outcroppings. After the rough terrain there was a double fence—each unit sixteen meters high, a kilometer between.

Mme. Couloc returned to Aberdeen, left her maids at the hotel, flew to Seattle where she bought tough camping clothes, a rope and grappling hook, a light pack, concentrated food and a compass. A map of the preserve was easy to obtain. They were sold as souvenirs.

Then she went fishing in the Straits of Juan de Fuca, staying at Neah Bay. To the south towered the Olympics, remote snow caps.

For three days it rained; five days Mme. Couloc fished with a guide. On the ninth day she went fishing alone. The next morning, the Federated Coast Guard picked up her overturned boat off Tatoosh Light. By that time she was nineteen kilometers south of Sequim, two kilometers inside the prohibited area which surrounded the fences. She slept all day in a spruce thicket. Moonlight helped her that night, but it took the entire night for her to come within sight of the fence. That day she crouched in a tangle of Oregon grape bushes, saw two tripod-legged robot patrols pass on the other side of the fence. At nightfall she moved forward, waited for a patrol to pass and go out of sight. The grapple and rope took her over the top. The kilometer between fences was cleared of trees and underbrush. She crossed it swiftly, scaled the final barrier.

The robotics patrols had counted too heavily on the forbidding terrain and they had not figured a psychotic woman into their plans.

Two kilometers inside the preserve, Mme. Couloc found a cedar copse in which to hide. Her heart racing, she crouched in the copse, waiting for the dawn in which to find *her dog*. There were scratches on her face, hands and legs; her clothes were torn. *But she was inside!*

Several times that night she had to dry her perspiring palms against her khaki hiking trousers. Toward morning, she fell asleep on the cold ground. Bess and Eagle found her there just after dawn.

Mme. Couloc awoke to the scraping of a warm, damp tongue against her cheek. For a moment, she thought it was her dead *Coco*. Then she realized where she was.

And the beautiful dogs!

She threw her arms around Bess, who was as starved for human affection as was Mme. Couloc.

Oh, you beautifuls!

The robotics patrol found them there shortly before noon. The robots were counting dogs with the aid of the tiny transmitters they had imbedded in the flesh of each animal. Mme. Couloc had been waiting for nightfall in which to escape with a dog.

Bess and Eagle ran from the robots. Mme. Couloc screamed and raged as the impersonal mechanicals took her away.

That afternoon, Eagle touched noses with a wolf female through the fence separating their enclosures.

Although the robots put each dog in isolation, they were too late. And nobody thought to bother with the wolves in their separate preserve.

In seven weeks the dog-wolf preserves were emptied by Virus D-D. Mme. Couloc was sent to a mental hospital in spite of the pleas of an expensive lawyer. The news services made much of Senator Nathal's note which had been found in her pocket.

Earth officials sent a contrite message to Vega. It was understood, said the message, that one Dr. Varley Trent had given Earth dogs to a Vegan bio-physicist. Were there, by any chance, some dogs still alive?

Back came the Vegan reply: *We have no dogs. We do not know the present whereabouts of Dr. Trent.*

Trent's ship came out of hyper-drive with Vega large in the screens. The sun's flaming prominences were clearly visible. At eight hundred thousand kilometers, he increased magnification, began scanning for the planet. Instead, he picked up a Vegan guard ship arrowing toward him. The Vegan was only six thousand kilometers off when it launched a torpedo. The proximity explosion cut off Trent's quick leap for the transmitter to give his identity. The ship buckled and rocked. Emergency doors slammed, air hissed, warning lights came on, bells clanged. Trent scrambled to the only lifeboat remaining in his section. The tiny escape craft was still serviceable, although its transmitter was cracked open.

He kept the lifeboat in the shadow of his ship's wreckage as long as he could, then dove for the Vegan planet which loomed at two o'clock on his screen. As soon as his driver tubes came alight, the Vegan sped after him. Trent pushed the little boat to its limit, but the pursuer still gained. They were too close to the planet now for the Vegan to use another torpedo.

The lifeboat screamed into the thin edge of the atmosphere. *Too fast!* The air-cooling unit howled with the overload. A rear surface control flared red, melted, fused. Trent had time to fire the emergency nose rockets, cut in automatic pilot before he blacked out. The ship dived, partly out of control, nose rockets still firing. Relays clicked—*full alarm!*—circuits designed to guard human life in an emergency came alive. Some worked, some had been destroyed.

Somewhere, he could hear running water. It was dark where he was, or perhaps lighted by a faint redness. His eyelids were stuck tightly. He could feel folds of cloth around him. A parachute! The robot controls of the lifeboat had ejected him in the chute-seat as a last resort.

Trent tried to move. His muscles refused to obey. He could sense numbness in his hips, a tingling loss of specific perception in his arms.

Then he heard it—the baying of a hound—far and clear. It was a sound he had never again expected to hear. The bugling note was repeated. It reminded him of frosty nights on Earth, following Bess and Eagle and . . .

The baying of a hound!

Panic swept through him. The hound mustn't find him! He was Earthhuman, loaded with deadly virus!

Straining at his cheek muscle, Trent managed to open one eye, saw that it was not dark, but a kind of yellow twilight under the folds of the parachute. His eyelids had been clotted with blood.

Now he could hear running feet, a hound's eager sniffing.

Please keep him away from me! he begged.

An edge of the chute stirred. Now there was an eager whining. Something crept toward him under the cloth.

"Go away!" he croaked.

Through the blurred vision of his one eye, Trent saw a brown and white head—very like Eagle's. It bent toward something. With a sick feeling,

Trent realized that the *something* was one of his own outstretched, virus-filled hands. He saw a pink tongue come out, lick the hand, but could not feel it. He tried to move and unconsciousness overwhelmed him. One last thought flitted through his mind before the darkness came—

"Each man kills the thing he . . ."

There was a bed beneath him—soft, sleep-lulling. In one part of his mind he knew a long time had passed. There had been hands, needles, wheeled carts taking him places, liquids in his mouth, tubes in his veins. He opened his eyes. Green walls, glaring white sunshine partially diffused by louvre shutters, a glimpse of blue-green hills outside.

"You are feeling better?" The voice had the peculiar whistling aspiration of the Vegan vocals.

Trent shifted his gaze to the right. Ger! The Vegan stood beside the bed, deceptively Earth-human in appearance. His shutter-like eye membranes were opened wide, the double crest of feathery hair retracted. He wore a yellow robe belted at the waist.

"How long . . ."

The Vegan put a seven-fingered hand on Trent's wrist, felt the pulse. "Yes, you are feeling much better. You have been very ill for almost four of your months."

"Then the dogs are all dead," said Trent, his voice flat.

"Dead?" Ger's eye membranes flicked closed, opened.

"I killed them," said Trent. "My body's loaded with dormant virus."

"No," said the Vegan. "We gave the dogs an extra white blood cell—more predatory. Your puny virus could not survive it."

Trent tried to sit up, but Ger restrained him. "Please, Varley. You are not yet recovered."

"But if the dogs are immune to the virus . . ." He shook his head. "Give me a shipload of dogs and you can name your own price."

"Varley, I did not say dogs are immune. They . . . are . . . not like dogs exactly. We cannot give you a shipload of your animals because we do not have them. They were sacrificed in our work."

Trent stared at him.

"I have unfortunate news, my friend. We have made our planet restricted to humans. You may live out your life here, but you may not communicate with your fellows."

"Is that why your ship fired on me?"

"We thought it was an Earth Vessel coming to investigate."

"But . . ."

"It is regrettable that yourself must be kept here, Varley, but the pride of our peoples is at stake."

"Pride?"

The Vegan looked at the floor. "We, who have never failed a bio-physical alteration . . ." He shook his head.

"What happened?"

The Vegan's face went blue with embarrassment.

Trent recalled his first awakening on this planet. "When I recovered consciousness I saw a dog. At least I saw its head."

Ger pulled a wicker chair close to the bed, sat down. "Varley, we tried to combine the best elements of our own *progoas* and the Earth dogs."

"Well, wasn't that what you were supposed to do?"

"Yes, but in the process we lost all of the dogs you sent us and the resultant animals . . ." He shrugged.

"What are they?"

"They do not have a scaly tail or horned snout. For centuries we have been telling the Universe that sentient pets of the highest quality must show these characteristics of our own *progoas*."

"Aren't the new animals intelligent and loyal? Do they have as good hearing, sense of smell?"

"If anything, these characteristics have been heightened."

He paused. "You realize, though, that this animal is not truly a dog."

"Not truly a . . ."

"It's fully serviceable . . ."

Trent swallowed. "Then you can name your own price."

"When we made our first cross, the *mikeses* fertilization process united an open *progoa* cell with a dog cell, but a series of peculiar linkages occurred. They were not what we had come to expect from our readings and from what you had told us.

Trent took a deep breath, exhaled slowly.

"It was as though the gene pattern of dog characteristics were predatory, tying down tightly even with *progoa* dominants," said Ger. "Each time we repeated the process; the same thing occurred. From our knowledge of terrestrial biology, this should not have been. The blood chemistry of our animals is based on the element you call copper. We have not much iron on our planet, but what few of your type of animals we had proved to us that the copper-basic was dominant in a *mikeses* cross. Of course, without a *mikeses* generator, cells cannot be opened to permit such a cross, but still . . ."

Trent closed his eyes, opened them. "No one else will ever hear what I am about to tell you . . ." He hesitated.

Vertical lines of thoughtfulness appeared in the Vegan's cheeks. "Yes?"

"When I was here on the survey trip, I copied the diagram of a *mikeses* generator. I was able to build a working model on Earth. With it, I developed a line of hounds." He wet his lips with his tongue. "We have life on Earth with blood of copper-base chemistry. The common squid of our oceans is one of them."

Ger lowered his chin, continued to stare at Trent.

"With the generator, I linked the canine dominants of my dogs with a recessive of squid."

"But they could not breed naturally. They . . ."

"Of course not. The hounds I sent you were from a line which had no fathers for six generations. I fertilized them with the generator. They had only the female side, open to the first linkage which presented itself."

"Why?"

"Because, from my observations of *progoas,* I knew dogs were superior, but could profit by such a cross. I hoped to make that cross myself."

The Vegan looked at the floor. "Varley, it pains me, but I am faced with the evidence that your claim is true. However, the pride of my world would never permit this to be known. Perhaps the Elders should reconsider."

"You know me," said Trent. "You have my word on it."

Ger nodded. "It is as you say, Varley. I know you." He preened a feather crest with three fingers. "And through knowing you, perhaps I have tempered the pride which rules my world." He nodded to himself. "I, too, will remain silent." A subtle Vegan smile flitted across his face, disappeared.

Trent recalled the beagle head he had seen under the parachute when he'd recovered consciousness. "I'd like to see one of these animals."

"That can be . . ." Ger was interrupted by the near baying of a pack of hounds. He stood up, flung open the window louvres, returned to support Trent's head. "Look out there, friend Varley."

On the blue-green Vegan plain, Trent could see a pack of hounds coursing in pursuit of a herd of runaway *ichikas.* The hounds had the familiar beagle head, brown and white fur. All had six legs.

PACK RAT PLANET

Vincent Coogan pulled at his thin lower lip as he stared at the image of his home planet growing larger in the star ship's viewscreen.

"What kind of an emergency would make Patterson call me off a Library election trip?" he muttered.

The chief navigator turned toward Coogan, noted the down-drooping angles on the Library official's face. "Did you say something, sir?"

"Huh?" Coogan realized he had been speaking his thoughts aloud. He drew in a deep breath, squared his stringy frame in front of the viewscreen, said, "It's good to get back to the Library."

"Always good to be home," said the navigator. He turned toward the planet in the screen.

It was a garden world of rolling plains turning beneath an old sun. Pleasure craft glided across shallow seas. Villages of flat, chalk-white houses clustered around elevator towers which plumbed the interior. Slow streams meandered across the plains. Giant butterflies fluttered among trees and flowers. People walked while reading books or reclined with scan-all viewers hung in front of their eyes.

The star ship throbbed as its landing auxiliaries were activated. Coogan felt the power through his feet. Suddenly, he sensed the homecoming feeling in his chest, an anticipating that brought senses to new alertness. It was enough to erase the worry over his call-back, to banish his displeasure at the year of work he had abandoned uncompleted.

It was enough to take the bitterness out of his thoughts when he recalled the words someone on an outworld had etched beside the star ship's main port. The words had been cut deeply beneath the winged boot emblem of the Galactic Library, probably with a Gernser flame chisel.

"Go home dirty pack rats!"

The *dirty pack rats* were home.

Director Caldwell Patterson of the Galactic Library sat at the desk in his office deep in the planet, a sheet of metallic paper in his hands. He was an old man even by Eighty-first Century standards when geriatrics made six hundred years a commonplace. Some said he had been at the Library that long. Gray hair clung in molting wisps to a pale pate. His face had the leathery, hook-nosed appearance of an ancient bird.

As Coogan entered the office, a desk visor in front of Patterson chimed. The director clicked a switch, motioned Coogan to a chair and said, "Yes," with a tired, resigned air.

Coogan folded his tall frame into the chair and listened with half his mind to the conversation on the visor. It seemed some outworld ship was approaching and wanted special landing facilities. Coogan looked around the familiar office. Behind the director was a wall of panels, dials, switches, rheostats, speakers, microphones, oscillographs, code keys, screens. The two side walls were focus rhomboids for realized images. The wall which was split by the door held eight miniature viewscreens all tuned to separate channels of the Library information broadcasts. All sound switches had been turned to mute, leaving a continuous low murmur in the room.

Patterson began drumming his fingers on the desk top, glaring at the desk visor. Presently, he said, "Well, tell them we have no facilities for an honor reception. This planet is devoted to knowledge and research. Tell them to come in at the regular field. I'll obey my Code and any government order of which I'm capable, but we simply don't have the facilities for what they're asking." The director cut the switch on his visor, turned to Coogan. "Well, Vincent, I see you avoided the Hesperides green rot. Now I presume you're anxious to learn why I called you back from there?"

Same old didactic, pompous humbug, thought Coogan. He said, "I'm not exactly a robot," and shaped his mouth in a brief, wry smile.

A frown formed on Patterson's bluish lips. "We've a new government," he said.

"Is that why you called me in?" asked Coogan. He felt an upsurge of all the resentment he'd swallowed when he'd received the call-back message.

"In a way, yes," said Patterson. "The new government is going to censor all Library broadcasts. The censor is on that ship just landing."

"They can't do that!" blurted Coogan. "The Charter expressly forbids chosen broadcasts or any interference with Library function! I can quote you—"

Patterson interrupted him in a low voice. "What is the first rule of the Library Code?"

Coogan faltered, stared at the director. He said, "Well—" paused while the memory came back to him. "The first rule of the Galactic Library Code is to obey all direct orders of the government in power. For the preservation of the Library, this must be the primary command."

"What does it mean?" demanded Patterson.

"It's just words that—"

"More than words!" said Patterson. A faint color crept into his old cheeks. "That rule has kept this Library alive for eight thousand years."

"But the government can't—"

"When you're as old as I am," said Patterson, "you'll realize that governments don't know what they can't do until after they cease to be governments. Each government carries the seeds of its own destruction."

"So we let them censor us," said Coogan.

"Perhaps," said Patterson, "if we're lucky. The new Grand Regent is the leader of the Gentle Ignorance Party. He says he'll censor us. The trouble is, our information indicates he's bent on destroying the Library as some kind of an example."

It took a moment for Coogan to accept the meaning of the words. "Destroy—"

"Put it to the torch," said Patterson. "His censor is his chief general and hatchetman."

"Doesn't he realize this is more than a Library?" asked Coogan.

"I don't know what he realizes," said Patterson. "But we're faced with a primary emergency and, to complicate matters, the entire staff is in a turmoil. They're hiding arms and calling in collection ships against my express orders. That Toris Sil-Chan has been around telling every—"

"Toris!"

"Yes, Toris. Your boon companion or whatever he is. He's leading this insurrection and I gather that he—"

"Doesn't he realize the Library can't fight a war without risking destruction?" asked Coogan.

Patterson sighed. "You're one of the few among the new generation who realizes that," he said.

"Where's Toris?" demanded Coogan. "I'll—"

"There isn't time right now," said Patterson. "The Grand Regent's hatchetman is due any minute."

"There wasn't a word of this out on Hesperides," said Coogan. "What's this Grand Regent's name?"

"Leader Adams," said Patterson.

"Never heard of him," said Coogan. "Who's the hatchetman?"

"His name's Pchak."

"Pchak what?"

"Just Pchak."

He was a coarse man with overdrawn features, none of the refinements of the inner worlds. A brown toga almost the same color as his skin was belted around him. Two slitted eyes stared out of a round, pushed-in face. He came into Patterson's office followed by two men in gray togas, each wearing a blaster at the belt.

"I am Pchak," he said.

Not a pretty specimen, thought Coogan. There was something chilling about the stylized simplicity of the man's dress. It reminded Coogan of a battle cruiser stripped down for action.

Director Patterson came around his desk, shoulders bent, walking slowly as befitted his age. "We are honored," he said.

"Are you?" asked Pchak. "Who is in command here?"

Patterson bowed. "I am Director Caldwell Patterson."

Pchak looked him up and down.

"We are at your service," said Patterson.

Pchak's lips twisted into something faintly like a smile. "I would like to know who is responsible for those insulting replies to our communications officer. *'This planet is devoted to knowledge and research!'* Who said that?"

"Why—" Patterson broke off, wet his lips with his tongue, "I said that."

The man in the brown toga stared at Patterson, said, "Who is this other person?" He hooked a thumb toward Coogan.

"This is Vincent Coogan," said Patterson. "He has just returned from the Hesperides Group to be on hand to greet you. Mr. Coogan is my chief assistant and successor."

Pchak looked at Coogan. "Out scavenging with the rest of the pack rats," he said. He turned back to Patterson. "But perhaps there will be need of a successor."

One of the guards moved up to stand beside the general. Pchak said, "Since knowledge is unhappiness, even the word is distasteful when used in a laudatory manner."

Coogan suddenly sensed something electric and deadly in the room. It was evident that Patterson did, too, because he looked directly at Coogan and said, "We are here to obey."

"You demonstrate an unhappy willingness to admire knowledge," said Pchak.

The guard's blaster suddenly came up and chopped down against the director's head. Patterson slumped to the floor, blood welling from a gash on his scalp.

Coogan started to take a step forward, was stopped by the other guard's blaster prodding his middle. A red haze formed in front of Coogan's eyes, a feeling of vertigo swept over him. In spite of the dizziness, part of his mind went on clicking, producing information to be observed. *This is standard procedure for oppressors,* said his mind. *Cow your victims by an immediate show of violence.* Something cold, hard and calculating took over Coogan's consciousness.

"*Director* Coogan," said Pchak, "do you have any objections to what has just occurred?"

Coogan stared down at the squat brown figure. *I have to stay in control of the situation,* he thought. *I'm the only one left who'll fight this according to the Code.* He said, "Every man seeks advancement."

Pchak smiled. "A realist. Now explain your Library." He strode around the desk, sat down. "It hardly seems just for our government to maintain a pest-hole such as this, but my orders are to investigate before passing judgment."

Your orders are to make a show of investigation before putting the Library to the torch, thought Coogan. He picked up an image control box from the desk, clipped it to his belt. Immediately, a blaster in a guard's hand prodded his side.

"What is that?" demanded Pchak.

Coogan swallowed. "These are image controls," he said. He looked down at Patterson sprawled on the floor. "May I summon a hospital robot for Mr. Patterson?"

"No," said Pchak. "What are image controls?"

Coogan took two deep breaths, looked at the side wall. "The walls of this room are focus rhomboids for realized images," he said. "They were turned off to avoid distractions during your arrival."

Pchak settled back in the chair. "You may proceed."

The guard continued to hold his blaster on Coogan.

Moving to a position opposite the wall, Coogan worked the belt controls. The wall became a window looking down an avenue of filing cases. Robots could be seen working in the middle distance.

"Terra is mostly a shell," said Coogan. "The major portion of the matter was taken to construct spaceships during the great outpouring."

"That fable again," said Pchak.

Coogan stopped. Involuntarily, his eyes went to the still figure of Caldwell Patterson on the floor.

"Continue," said Pchak.

The cold, hard, calculating something in Coogan's mind said, *You know what to do. Set him up for your Sunday punch.*

Coogan concentrated on the screen, said: "The mass loss was compensated by a giant gravitronic unit in the planet center. Almost the entire subsurface of Terra is occupied by the Library. Levels are divided into overlapping squares one hundred kilometers to the side. The wealth of records stored here staggers the imagination. It's—"

"Your imagination perhaps," said Pchak. "Not mine."

Coogan fought down a shiver which crawled along his spine, forced himself to continue. He said, "It is the repository for all the reported doings of every government in the history of the galaxy. The format was set by the original institution from which this one grew. It was known as the Library of Congress. That institution had a reputation of—"

"Congress," said Pchak in his deadly flat tones. "Kindly explain that term."

Now what have I said? Coogan wondered. He faced Pchak, said, "Congress was an ancient form of government. The closest modern example is the Tschi Council which—"

"I thought so!" barked Pchak. "That debating society! Would you explain to me, Mr. Coogan, why a recent Library broadcast extolled the virtues of this form of government?"

There's the viper, thought Coogan. He said, "Well, nobody watches Library broadcasts anyway. What with some five thousand channels pouring out—"

"Answer my question, Mr. Coogan." Pchak leaned forward. An eager look came into the eyes of the guard with the blaster. Again Coogan's eyes sought out the still form of Patterson on the floor.

"We have no control of program selection," said Coogan, "except on ten special channels for answering research questions and ten other channels which scan through the new material as it is introduced into the Library."

"No control," said Pchak. "That's an interesting answer. Why is this?"

Coogan rubbed the back of his neck with his left hand, said, "The charter for the broadcasts was granted by the first systemwide government in the Twenty-first Century. A method of random program selection was devised to insure impartiality. It was considered that the information in the Library should always be freely available to all—" His voice trailed off and he wondered if he had quoted too much of the charter. *Well, they can read it in the original if they want,* he thought.

"Fascinating," said Pchak. He looked at the nearest guard. "Isn't that so?"

The guard grinned.

Coogan took a slow, controlled breath, exhaled. He could feel a crisis approaching. It was like a weight on his chest.

"This has to be a thorough investigation," said Pchak. "Let's see what you're broadcasting right now."

Coogan worked the belt controls and an image realized before the right-hand rhomboid. It was of a man with a hooked nose. He wore leather pants and shirt, shoes with some kind of animal face projecting from the toes, a feather crest hat on his head.

"This is a regular random information broadcast," said Coogan. He looked at his belt. "Channel Eighty-two." He turned up the volume.

The man was talking a language of harsh consonants punctuated by sibilant hisses. Beside him on the floor was a mound of tiny round objects, each bearing a tag.

"He is speaking the dead Procyon language," said Coogan. "He's a zoologist of a system which was destroyed by corona gas thirty-four centuries ago. The things on the floor are the skulls of a native rodent. He's saying that he spent eleven years classifying more than eight thousand of those skulls."

"Why?" asked Pchak. He seemed actually interested, leaned forward to look at the mound of skulls on the floor.

"I think we've missed that part," said Coogan. "It probably was to prove some zoological theory."

Pchak settled back in his chair. "He's dead," he said. "His system no longer exists. His language is no longer spoken. Is there much of this sort of thing being broadcast?"

"I'm afraid ninety-nine per cent of the Library broadcasts—excluding research channels—is of this nature," said Coogan. "It's the nature of the random selection."

"Who cares what the zoologist's theory was?" asked Pchak.

"Perhaps some zoologist," said Coogan. "You never can tell when a piece of information will be valuable."

Pchak muttered something under his breath which sounded like, "Pack rats!"

Coogan said, "Pack rats?"

The little brown man smiled. "That's what we call you," he said. "And with some justification evidently. You're packed with the kind of useless material a rodent would admire."

Time for one small lesson, thought Coogan. He said, "The pack rat, also known as the trade rat, was a rodent indigenous to this planet. It's now extinct here, but there are examples on Markeb IX and several of the Ring planets. The pack rat lived in forest land and was known for his habit of stealing small things from hunters' camps. For everything it took, the pack rat left an item from its nest, a bit of twine, a twig, a shiny piece of glass, a rock. In all of that useless material which cluttered its nest there might be one nugget of a precious metal. Since the pack rat showed no selection in its trading—was random, so to speak—it might leave the precious metal in a hunter's camp in exchange for a bottle top."

Pchak got to his feet, walked across the room to the zoologist's image, passed a hand through the projection. "Remarkable," he said, sarcasm filling his voice. "This is supposed to be a nugget?"

"More likely a twig," said Coogan.

Pchak turned back, faced Coogan. "What else do you hide in this rat's nest? Any nuggets?"

Coogan looked down at Patterson on the floor. There was a stillness about the thin old figure. "First, may I have a hospital robot attend to Mr. Patterson?"

The general kept his eyes on Coogan. "No. Answer my request."

First rule of the Code—obey, thought Coogan. With a slow, controlled movement, he shifted a lever on the box at his belt. The Procyon zoologist vanished and the wall became a screen showing a page of a book. *Here's the bail,* thought Coogan, *and I hope it poisons you.* He said, "This is an early account of military tactics showing some methods that succeeded and others that failed."

Pchak turned to the screen, put his hands behind him, rocked back and forth on heels and toes. "What language?"

"Ancient English of Terra," said Coogan. "We have a scanner that'll give you an oral translation if you'd like."

The general kept his eyes on the screen. "How do I know this account is accurate?"

"The Library Code does not permit tampering with records," said Coogan. "Our oath is to preserve the present for the future." He glanced at Pchak, back to the screen. "We have other battle records, the tactics of every species encountered by humans. For example, we have the entire war history of the Praemir of Roman II."

Coogan shifted his belt controls and the screen took up a history of warfare which had been assembled for a general sixteen centuries dead. Pchak watched as the record went from clubs and rocks to spears and made a side journey into bizarre weapons. Suddenly, Coogan blanked the screen.

Pchak's head snapped up. "Why did you stop that?"

Hooked him, thought Coogan. He said, "I thought you might rather view this at your leisure. If you wish, I'll set up a viewing room and show you how to order the records when there are side issues you'd like to study." Coogan held his breath. *Now we learn if he's really caught,* he thought.

The general continued to study the blank screen. "I have orders to make a thorough investigation," he said. "I believe this comes under the category of investigation. Have your viewing room prepared." He turned, went to the door, followed by his guards.

"It's down on the sixty-ninth level," said Coogan. "Viewing Room A." He started toward Pchak. "I'll get you all set up and—"

"You will remain here," said Pchak. "We will use Viewing Room B, instead. Send an assistant to explain things." He glanced back. "You do have an assistant, do you not?"

"I'll send Toris Sil-Chan," said Coogan and then remembered what Patterson had said about Toris leading the hotheads who wanted to do battle. He would have bitten off his tongue to retract the words, but knew he dared not change now or it would arouse Pchak's suspicions. He returned to the desk, had central-routing find Toris and send him to the viewing room. *Please don't do anything rash,* he prayed.

"Is this assistant your successor?" asked Pchak, looking down at Patterson.

"No," said Coogan.

"You must appoint a successor," said Pchak and left with his two guards.

Coogan immediately summoned a hospital robot for Patterson. The scarab shape came in on silent wheels, lifted the still form on its flat pad extensors and departed.

The sunset rain was drifting along its longitudinal mark on Terra, spattering a shallow sea, dewing the grasslands, filling the cups of flowers. One wall screen of the director's office was activated to show this surface scene—a white village in the rain, flutterings of trees. Surface copters whirred across the village, their metal gleaming in the wetness.

Coogan, his thin face wearing a look of weariness, sat at the director's desk, hands clasped in front of him. Occasionally, he glanced at the wall screen. The spire of a government star ship—tall alabaster with a sunburst insignia on its bow—could be seen beyond the village. Coogan sighed.

A chime sounded behind him. He turned to the control panel wall, depressed a button, spoke into a microphone. "Yes?"

A voice like wire scraped across a tin plate came out of the speaker. "This is the hospital."

"Well?" Coogan's voice showed irritation.

"Director Patterson was dead upon arrival here," said the wire-scraping voice. "The robots already have disposed of his body through the CIB office."

"Don't say anything about it yet," said Coogan. He removed his hand from the switch, turned back to the desk. *His* desk now. *Director Coogan.* The thought gave him no satisfaction. He kept remembering a still form sprawled on the floor. *A terrible way to go,* he thought. *A Librarian should end at his researches, just quietly topple over in the stacks.*

The desk visor chimed. Coogan hit the palm switch and Pchak's face appeared on the screen. The general was breathing rapidly, beads of sweat on his forehead.

"May I help you?" asked Coogan.

"How do I get the condemned instruction records for the Zosma language?" demanded Pchak. "Your machine keeps referring me to some nonsense about abstract symbolism."

The door of Coogan's office opened and Sil-Chan entered, saw that a caller was on the screen, stopped just inside the door. Sil-Chan was a blocky figure who achieved fat without looking soft. His round face was dominated by upswept almond eyes characteristic of the inhabitants of the Mundial Group planets of Ruchbah.

Coogan shook his head at Sil-Chan, his mind searching through memories for an answer to Pchak's question. It came to him, tagged *semantics study.* "Zosma," he said. "Yes, that was a language which dealt only in secondary referents. Each phrase was two times removed from—"

"What in Shandu is a secondary referent?" exploded Pchak.

Calmly, thought Coogan. *I can't afford to precipitate action yet.* He said,

"Ask for the section on semantics. Did Mr. Sil-Chan show you how to get the records you need?"

"Yes, yes," said Pchak. "Semantics, eh?" The screen went blank.

Sil-Chan closed the door, came across the office. "I would imagine," he said, "that the general is under the impression his researches will be completed in a week or two."

"So it would seem," said Coogan. He studied Sil-Chan. The man didn't look like a hothead, but perhaps it had taken this threat to the Library to set him off.

Sil-Chan took a chair across from Coogan. "The general is a low alley dog," he said, "but he believes in this Leader Adams. The gleam in his eyes when he talks about Adams would frighten a saint."

"How was it down in the viewing room?" asked Coogan.

"Pchak is busy studying destruction," said Sil-Chan. "We haven't made up our minds yet whether to exterminate him. Where's Director Patterson?"

A sixth sense warned Coogan not to reveal that the director was dead. He said, "He isn't here."

"That's fairly obvious," said Sil-Chan. "I have an ultimatum to deliver to the director. Where is he?"

"You can deliver your ultimatum to me," said Coogan dryly.

Sil-Chan's eyes showed little glints deep in the pupils as he stared at Coogan. "Vince, we've been friends a long time," he said, "but you've been away in the Hesperides Group and don't know what's been going on here. Don't take sides yet."

"What's been going on?" asked Coogan. He looked up at Sil-Chan out of the corners of his eyes.

The Mundial native hitched himself forward and leaned an elbow on the desk. "There's a new government, Vince, and they're planning to destroy the Library. And that gourd-head Patterson has been giving in to every order they send. Do this! Do that! He does it! He told us flat out he wouldn't defy a government order." Sil-Chan's mouth set in a thin line. *"It's against the Library Code!"*

"Who is *we*?" asked Coogan.

"Huh?" Sil-Chan looked blank.

"The *we* you said hasn't decided whether to exterminate Pchak," said Coogan.

"Oh." Sil-Chan leaned back. "Only about a third of the home staff. Most of the collection crews are joining us fast as they come in."

Coogan tapped a finger against the desk. *Some eight thousand people, more or less,* he thought. He said, "What's your plan?"

"Easy." Sil-Chan shrugged. "I've about fifty men in Section 'C' on the sixty-ninth level waiting for the word to move against Pchak and his bodyguards. Another three hundred are topside ready to jump the government ship."

Coogan tipped his head to one side and stared at Sil-Chan in amazement. "Is that your ultimatum?"

Sil-Chan shook his head. "No. Where's Patterson?"

Something decisive meshed in Coogan's mind. He got to his feet. "Patterson's dead. I'm director. What's your ultimatum?"

There was a moment's silence with Sil-Chan looking up at Coogan. "How'd he die?" asked Sil-Chan.

"He was old," said Coogan. "What's your ultimatum?"

Sil-Chan wet his lips with his tongue. "I'm sorry to hear that, Vince." Again he shrugged. "But this makes our job simpler. You're a man who'll listen to reason." He met Coogan's stare. "This is our plan. We take over this Pchak and his ship, hold him as hostage while we convert every broadcast channel we have to public support. With five thousand channels telling the—"

"You bone-brain!" barked Coogan, "That's as stupid a plan as I've ever heard. Adams would ignore your hostage and drop a stellar bomb in our laps!"

"But, Vince—"

"Don't *but, Vince,* me," said Coogan. He came around the desk and stood over Sil-Chan. "As long as you're running around disobeying the orders of your superiors you'll refer to me as Mr. Director and—"

Sil-Chan charged to his feet, glared up at Coogan. "I hate to do this, Vince," he said, "but we have organization and purpose. You can't stop us! You're relieved of your directorship until such time as—"

"Shut up!" Coogan strode around behind his desk, put his hand on a short lever low on the control panel. "Do you know what this is, Toris?"

Sil-Chan's face showed uncertainty. He shook his head.

"This is the master control for the gravitronic unit," said Coogan. "If I push it down, it shuts off the unit. Every bit of soil, everything beyond the Library shell will drift off into space!"

A pasty color came over Sil-Chan's features. He put out a hand toward Coogan. "You can't do that," he said. "Your wife and family—all of our families are up there. They wouldn't have a chance!"

"I'm director here," said Coogan. "The position is my earned right!" With his free hand, he moved four switches on the control wall. "That seals off your sixty-ninth level group behind fire panels." He turned back to Sil-Chan. "Now, get in touch with every insurgent under you and have them turn in their arms to robots which I'll release for the job. I know who some of your men are. They'd better be among the ones you contact. If you make one move I don't like, this lever goes down and stays down!"

"You!" said Sil-Chan. He ground his teeth together. "I knew I should've carried a blaster when I came in here. But no! You and Patterson were the civilized types! We could reason with you!"

"Start making those calls," said Coogan. He pushed his desk visor toward the other man.

Sil-Chan jerked the visor to him, obeyed. Coogan gave his orders to robot dispatching headquarters, waited for Sil-Chan to finish. The Mundial native finally pushed the visor back across the desk. "Does that satisfy you?" he demanded.

"No." Coogan steepled his hands in front of him. "I'm arming some of the staff I can trust. Their orders will be to shoot to kill if there's a further act of insurrection." He leaned forward. "In addition, we're going to have guard stations between sectors and a regular search procedure. You're not getting another chance to cause trouble."

Sil-Chan clenched and unclenched his fists. "And what do you intend to do about this Pchak and his Leader Adams?"

"They're the government," said Coogan. "As such the Code requires that we obey their orders. I will obey their orders. And, any man on the staff who even hints at disobedience, I'll personally turn over to Pchak for disciplinary action."

Sil-Chan arose slowly. "I've known you more than sixty years, *Mr.* Coogan. That just shows how little you can learn about a rat. After you've lost the Library to this madman, you won't have a friend left here. Not me, not the people who trust you now. Not your wife or your family." He sneered. "Why—one of your own sons, Phil, is in with us." He pointed a finger at Coogan. "I intend to tell everyone about the threat you used today to gain control of the Library."

"Control of the Library is my earned right," said Coogan. He smiled, pushed down the lever in the control wall. The wall made a quarter turn on a central pivot. "Toris, send up a repair robot when you report back to Pchak. I've special installations I want to make here."

Sil-Chan came to the edge of the desk, staring down at the lever which had controlled the movement of the wall. "Tricked me!"

"You tricked yourself," said Coogan, "You did it the moment you turned your back on our greatest strength—obedience to the government."

Sil-Chan grunted, whirled and left the office.

Coogan watched the door as it closed behind the other man, thought, *If I only had as much faith in those words as I'm supposed to have.*

She was a pretty woman with hair like glowing coals, small features except for a wide, sensual mouth. Her green eyes seemed to give off sparks to match her hair as she stared out of the visor at Coogan.

"Vince, where have you been?" she demanded.

He spoke in a tired voice. "I'm sorry, Fay. I had work that had to be done."

She said, "The boys brought their families from Antigua for a reunion and we've been ready for you for hours. What's going on? What's this nonsense Toris is bleating?"

Coogan sighed and brushed a hand through his hair. "I don't know what Toris is saying. But the Library is in a crisis. Patterson is dead and I've nobody I can trust to hold things together."

Her eyes went wide; she put a hand to her mouth, spoke through her fingers. "Oh, no! Not Pat!"

"Yes," he said.

"How?"

"I guess it was too much for him," said Coogan. "He was old."

"I couldn't believe Toris," she said.

Coogan felt a great weariness just at the edge of his mind. "You said the boys are there," he said. "Ask Phil if he was part of the group backing Toris."

"I can tell you myself he was," she said. "It's no secret. Darling, what's come over you? Toris said you threatened to dump the whole surface off into space."

"It was an empty threat then," said Coogan. "Toris was going to disobey the government. I couldn't permit it. That would only—"

"Vince! Have you gone out of your mind?" Her eyes registered amazement and horror. "This Adams means to destroy the Library! We can't just sit back and let him!"

"We've grown lax in our training," said Coogan. "We've had it too easy for too long. That's a situation I intend to correct!"

"But what about—"

"If I'm permitted to handle things my way, he won't destroy the Library," said Coogan. "I was hoping you'd trust me."

"Of course I trust you, darling, but—"

"Then trust me," he said. "And please understand that there's no place I'd rather be right now than home with you."

She nodded. "Of course, dear."

"Oh, yes," he said, "tell Phil he's under house arrest for deliberate disobedience to the Code. I'll deal with him, personally, later." He closed the switch before she could reply.

Now for General Pchak, he thought. *Let's see if he can give us a hint on how to deal with Leader Adams.*

The room was vaguely egg-shaped for acoustical reasons, cut at one end by the flat surface of a screen and with space in the center for a realized image. The wall opposite the screen was occupied by a curved couch split by drop arms in which control instruments were set.

Pchak was sprawled on the couch, a brown blob against the gray plastic, watching two Krigellian gladiators spill each other's blood in an arena which had a shifting floor. As Coogan entered, Pchak turned the screen to a book page in the Zosma language of Krigellia, scanned a few lines. He looked up at Coogan with an expression of irritation.

"*Director* Coogan," said Pchak, "have you chosen a successor yet?" He slid his feet to the floor. "I find semantics most interesting, *Director* Coogan. The art of using words as weapons appeals to me. I'm particularly interested in psychological warfare."

Coogan stared thoughtfully at the figure in the brown toga, an idea racing through his mind. *If I get this barbarian started on a study of psychological warfare, he'll never leave.* He pulled out a section of the curved couch, sat down facing Pchak. "What's the most important thing to know about a weapon?" he asked.

The general's forehead creased. "How to use it effectively, of course."

Coogan shook his head. "That's an overgeneralization. The most important thing is to know your weapon's limitations."

Pchak's eyes widened. "What it *cannot* do. Very clever."

"Psychological warfare is an extensive subject," said Coogan. "According to some, it's a two-edged sword with no handle. If you grasp it strongly enough to strike down your enemy, you render yourself *hors de combat* before your blow is delivered."

Pchak leaned against an arm of the couch. "I don't believe I understand you."

Coogan said, "Well, the whole argument is specious, anyway. You'd first have to apply the methods of psychology to yourself. As you measured more and more of your own sanity, you'd be more and more incapable of using the weapon against another."

In a cold voice, Pchak said, "Are you suggesting that I'm insane?"

"Of course not," said Coogan. "I'm giving you a summary of one of the arguments about psychological warfare. Some people believe any warfare is insanity. But sanity is a matter of degree. Degree implies measurement. To measure, we must use some absolute referent. Unless we could agree on the measuring device, we couldn't say anyone was sane or insane. Nor could we tell what opponent might be vulnerable to our weapon."

Pchak jerked forward, a hard light in his slitted eyes.

Coogan hesitated, wondered, *Have I gone too far?* He said, "I'll give you another example." He hooked a thumb toward the viewscreen. "You just watched two gladiators settle an issue for their cities. That particular action occurred twenty centuries ago. You weren't interested in the issue they settled. You were examining their method of combat. Twenty centuries from now, who will examine your methods? Will they be interested in the issues you settled?"

Pchak turned his head to one side, keeping his eyes on Coogan. "I think you're using clever words in a way to confuse me," he said.

"No, general." Coogan shook his head. "We're not here to confuse people. We believe in our Code and live by it. That Code says we must obey the government. And that doesn't mean we obey when we feel like it or when we happen to agree with you. We obey. Your orders will be carried out. It doesn't pay us to lead you into confusion."

In a strangely flat voice, Pchak said, "Knowledge is a blind alley leading only to unhappiness."

Coogan suddenly realized that the man was quoting Leader Adams. He said, "We don't put out knowledge, general. We store information. That's our first job."

"But you blat that information all over the universe!" stormed the general. "Then it becomes knowledge!"

"That is under the Charter, not the Code," said Coogan.

Pchak pursed his lips, leaned toward Coogan. "Do you mean if I ordered you to shut down your broadcasts, you'd just do it? We understood you were prepared to resist us at every turn."

"Then your information was incorrect," said Coogan.

The general leaned back, rubbed his chin. "All right, shut them down," he said. "I'll give you a half hour. I want all five thousand of them quiet and your special channels, too."

Coogan bowed, got to his feet. "We obey," he said.

In the director's office Coogan sat at the desk, staring at the opposite wall. The screens were silent. It was almost as though there was some interspatial hole in the room, a lack. The door opened and Sil-Chan entered. "You sent for me?" he asked.

Coogan looked at the man for a moment before speaking, then said. "Why didn't you return to Pchak's viewing room as I ordered?"

"Because Pchak dismissed me," said Sil-Chan curtly.

"Come in and sit down," said Coogan. He turned on his desk visor, called records. "What's the parentage and upbringing of the new Grand Regent?" he asked.

After a brief pause, a voice came from the visor: "Leader Adams, also known as Adam Yoo. Mother, Simila Yoo, native of Mundial Group"—Coogan glanced at Sil-Chan—"planet Sextus C III. Father Princeps Adams, native of Hercules Group. Father was killed in accident with subspace translator on University Planet of Hercules XII when son age nine. Young Adams raised with mother's family on Sextus C II until age eighteen when sent to Shandu for training as a Mundial religious leader. While on Shandu—"

Coogan interrupted, "Send me a transcript on it." He broke the connection, looked at Sil-Chan. "Still angry, Toris?"

Sil-Chan's lips tightened.

As though he had not noticed, Coogan said, "Adams' father was killed in an accident on a university planet. That could be the unconscious origin of his hatred of knowledge." He looked speculatively at Sil-Chan. "You're a Mundial native. What's the group like?"

"If Adams was raised there, he's a mystic," said Sil-Chan. He shrugged. "All of our people are mystics. No Mundial family would permit otherwise.

That's why he was taken to the home planet to be raised." Sil-Chan suddenly put a hand to his chin. "Father killed in an accident—" He looked at Coogan, through him. "That could have been an *arranged* accident." He leaned forward, tapped the desk. "Let's say the father objected to the son being raised in the Mundial Group—"

"Are you suggesting that the mother could have arranged the accident?"

"Either she or some of her kinsmen," said Sil-Chan. "It's been known to happen. The Mundials are jealous of their own. I had the glax of a time getting permission to come to the Library staff."

"This happiness through ignorance cult," said Coogan. "How would mysticism bear on that?"

Sil-Chan looked at the desk surface, forehead creased. "He'll believe absolutely in his own destiny. If he thinks he has to destroy the Library to fulfill that destiny, there'll be no stopping him."

Coogan clasped his hands together on the desk top, gripped them until they hurt. *Obey!* he thought. *What a weapon to use against a fanatic!*

"If we could prove the mother or the Yoo Clan had the father killed, that might be a valuable piece of knowledge," said Sil-Chan.

"A wise man depends upon his friends for information and upon himself for decisions," said Coogan.

"That's a Mundial axiom," said Sil-Chan.

"I read it somewhere," said Coogan. "You're a Mundial native, Toris. Explain this mysticism."

"It's mostly rubbed off of me," said Sil-Chan, "but I'll try. It revolves around an ancient form of ancestor worship. Mysticism, you see, is the art of looking backward while convincing yourself that you're looking forward. The ancient Terran god Janus was a mystic. He looked forward and backward at the same time. Everything a mystic does in the present must find its interpretation in the past. Now, the interpretation—"

"That's a subtle one," said Coogan. "It almost slipped past me. *Interpretation.* Substitute *explanation* for *interpretation*—"

"And you have a librarian," said Sil-Chan.

"Explanation is something that may or may not be true," said Coogan. "We're convinced of an interpretation."

"Semantics again," said Sil-Chan. A brief smile touched his lips. "Maybe that's why you're director."

"Still against me?" asked Coogan.

The smile left Sil-Chan's mouth. "It's suicide, Vince." He hitched himself forward. "If we follow your orders, when this Adams says to destroy the Library, we'd have to help him!"

"So we would," said Coogan. "But it's not going to come to that. I wish you'd trust me, Toris."

"If you were doing something that even remotely made sense, of course I would," said Sil-Chan. "But—" He shrugged.

"I've a job for you," said Coogan. "It may or may not make sense, but I want it carried out to the letter. Take any ship you can get and hop to this Sextus C III in the Mundial Group. When you get there, I want you to prove that the Yoo Clan killed Leader Adams' father. I don't care whether it's true or not. I want the proof."

"That makes sense," said Sil-Chan. "If we can discredit the big boss."

The visor chimed. Coogan hit the switch and a sub-librarian's face appeared in the screen. "Sir," the man blurted, "the Library information broadcasts are silent! I just got a call from—"

"Orders of the government," said Coogan. "It's quite all right. Return to your duties." He blanked the screen.

Sil-Chan was leaning on the desk, fists clenched. "You mean you let them close us down without a struggle."

"Let me remind you of some things," said Coogan. "We must obey the government to survive. I am director here and I've given you an order. Get on it!"

"What if I refuse?"

"I'll get somebody else to do it and you'll be locked up."

"You don't leave me any choice." He turned and slammed out of the office.

Twenty-four times the evening rains passed across the tower far above Coogan's office. The game of cat-and-mouse with Pchak went on as usual, the little brown general delving deeper and deeper into the files. On the twenty-fifth day Coogan came into his office in mid afternoon.

Pchak is completely hooked, he thought, *but what happens when Adams finds out the Library hasn't been destroyed?*

He sat down at his desk, swiveled to face the control panel and activated a tiny screen linked to a spy cell on the sixty-ninth level. Pchak was in the viewing room, studying the Albireo language preparatory to examining that double-star system's war history. Behind Coogan, a mechanical hum sounded, indicating someone was emerging from the elevator. Hastily, he blanked the spy screen, turned to his desk just as the door burst open. Toris Sil-Chan staggered into the room, his clothing torn, a dirty bandage over one shoulder.

The Mundial native lurched across the room, clutched the edge of Coogan's desk. "Hide me!" he said. "Quick!"

Coogan jerked around to the panel, swung it open and motioned toward the hole that was exposed. Sil-Chan darted in and Coogan closed the panel, returned to his desk.

Again the telltale signaled. Two armed guards burst into the room, blasters in their hands. "Where is he?" demanded the first.

"Where's who?" asked Coogan. He squared a stack of papers on his desk.

"The guy who jumped off that life boat," said the guard.

"I don't know what you're talking about," said Coogan, "but I can see that I'll have to call General Pchak and tell him how you've burst into my office without preamble and—"

The guard lowered his blaster and retreated one step. "That won't be necessary, sir," he said. "We can see the man's not here. He probably went to a lower level. Please excuse the interruption." They backed out of the room.

Coogan waited until his spy relays in the corridor told him the men had gone, then opened the panel. Sil-Chan was crumpled on the floor. Coogan bent over him, shook him. "Toris! What's wrong?"

Sil-Chan stirred, looked up at Coogan with eyes that were at first unrecognizing. "Uh . . . Vince—"

The director put an arm behind Sil-Chan, supported the man to a sitting position. "Take it easy now. Just tell me what happened."

"Made a mess of assignment," said Sil-Chan. "Yoo Clan got wind of what I was after. Had Adams send order . . . arrest. Lost ship. Got away in escape boat. Landed other side . . . planet. Pchak's guards tried stop—" His head slumped forward.

Coogan put a hand to the man's heart, felt its steady pumping. He eased Sil-Chan back to the floor, went out and summoned a hospital robot. Sil-Chan regained consciousness while the robot was lifting him. "Sorry to go out on you like that," he said. "I—"

The message visor on the director's desk chimed. Coogan pushed the response switch, scanned the words of a visual message, blanked the screen and turned back to Sil-Chan. "You'll have to be treated here," he said. "Couldn't risk carrying you through the corridors right now."

The spy beam hummed at the door. Coogan pushed Sil-Chan behind the panel, closed it. Pchak strode into the office, a blaster in his hand, the two guards behind him. The general glanced at the hospital robot, looked at Coogan. "Where's the man that robot was called to treat?"

The last guard into the office closed the door, drew his blaster.

"Talk or you'll be cut down where you stand," said Pchak.

The showdown, thought Coogan. He said, "These hospital robots are a peculiar kind of creature, general. They don't have the full prime directive against harming humans because sometimes they have to choose between saving one person and letting another one die. I can tell this robot that if I'm harmed it must give all of you an overdose of the most virulent poison it carries in its hypo arm. I inform the robot that this action will save my life. It naturally is loyal to the Library and will do exactly what I have just now told it to do."

Pehak's face tightened. He raised the blaster slightly.

"Unless you wish to die in agony, place your blasters on my desk," said Coogan.

"I won't," said Pchak. "Now what're you going to do?"

"Your blasters can kill me," said Coogan, "but they won't stop that robot until it has carried out my order."

Pchak's finger began to tighten on the trigger. "Then let's give it the—"

The sharp *blat!* of an energy bolt filled the room. Pchak slumped. The guard behind him skirted the robot fearfully, put his blaster on Coogan's desk. The weapon smelled faintly of ozone from the blast that had killed Pchak. "Call that thing off me now," said the man, staring at the robot.

Coogan looked at the other guard. "You, too," he said.

The other man came around behind the robot, put his weapon on the desk. Coogan picked up one of the weapons. It felt strange in his hand.

"You're not going to turn that thing loose on us now, are you?" asked the second guard. He seemed unable to take his gaze from the robot.

Coogan glanced down at the scarab shape of the mechanical with its flat pad extensors and back hooks for carrying a stretcher. He wondered what the two men would do if he told them the thing Pchak had undoubtedly known—that the robot could take no overt action against a human, that his words had been a lie.

The first guard said, "Look, we're on your side now. We'll tell you everything. Just before he came down here, Pchak got word that Leader Adams was coming and—"

"Adams!" Coogan barked the word. He thought, *Adams coming! How to turn that to advantage?* He looked at the first guard. "You were with Pchak when he came the first day, weren't you?"

"I was his personal guard," said the man.

Coogan scooped the other blaster off his desk, backed away. "All right. When Adams lands, you get on that visor and tell him Pchak wishes to see him down here. With Adams a hostage, I can get the rest to lay down their arms."

"But—" said the guard.

"One false move and I turn that robot loose on you," said Coogan.

The guard's throat worked visibly. He said, "We'll do it. Only I don't see how you can get the whole government to give up just because—"

"Then stop thinking," said Coogan. "Just get Adams down here." He backed against the control wall and waited.

"I don't understand," said Sil-Chan.

The Mundial native sat in a chair across the desk from Coogan. A fresh Library uniform bulged over Sil-Chan's bandaged shoulder. "You pound it into us that we have to obey," he said. "You tell us we can't go against the Code. Then at the last minute you turn around and throw a blaster on the whole crew and lose them into the hospital's violent ward."

"I don't think they can get out of there," said Coogan.

"Not with all those guards around them," said Sil-Chan. "But it's still disobedience and that's against the Code." He held up a hand, palm toward

Coogan. "Not that I'm objecting, you understand. It's what I was advocating all along."

"That's where you're mistaken," said Coogan. "People were perfectly willing to ignore the Library and its silly broadcasts as long as that information was available. Then the broadcasts were stopped by government order."

"But—" Sil-Chan shook his head.

"There's another new government," said Coogan. "Leader Adams was booted out because he told people they couldn't have something. That's bad policy for a politician. They stay in office by telling people they can *have* things."

Sil-Chan said, "Well, where does—"

"Right after you came stumbling in here," said Coogan, "I received a general order from the new government which I was only too happy to obey. It said that Leader Adams was a fugitive and any person encountering him was empowered to arrest him and hold him for trial." Coogan arose, strode around to Sil-Chan, who also got to his feet. "So you see," said Coogan, "I did it all by obeying the government."

The Mundial native glanced across Coogan's desk, suddenly smiled and went around to the control wall. "And you got me with a tricky thing like this lever." He put a hand on the lever with which Coogan had forced his submission.

Coogan's foot caught Sil-Chan's hand and kicked it away before the little man could depress the lever.

Sil-Chan backed away, shaking his bruised hand. "Ouch!" He looked up at Coogan. "What in the name of—"

The director worked a lever higher on the wall and the panel made a quarter turn. He darted behind the wall, began ripping wires from a series of lower connections. Presently, he stepped out. There were beads of perspiration on his forehead.

Sil-Chan stared at the lever he had touched. "Oh, no—" he said. "You didn't *really* hook that to the grav unit!"

Coogan nodded mutely.

Eyes widening, Sil-Chan backed against the desk, sat on it. "Then you weren't certain obedience would work, that—"

"No, I wasn't," growled Coogan.

Sil-Chan smiled. "Well, now, there's a piece of information that ought to be worth something." The smile widened to a grin. "What's my silence worth?"

The director slowly straightened his shoulders. He wet his lips with his tongue. "I'll tell you, Toris. Since you were to get this position anyway, I'll tell you what it's worth to me." Coogan smiled, a slow, knowing smile that made Sil-Chan squint his eyes.

"You're my successor," said Coogan.

RAT RACE

In the nine years it took Welby Lewis to become chief of criminal investigation for Sheriff John Czernak, he came to look on police work as something like solving jigsaw puzzles. It was a routine of putting pieces together into a recognizable picture. He was not prepared to have his cynical police-peopled world transformed into a situation out of H. G. Wells or Charles Fort.

When Lewis said "alien" he meant non-American, not extraterrestrial. Oh, he knew a BEM was a bug-eyed monster; he read some science fiction. But that was just the point—such situations were *fiction,* not to be encountered in police routine. And certainly unexpected at a mortuary. The Johnson-Tule Mortuary, to be exact.

Lewis checked in at his desk in the sheriff's office at five minutes to eight of a Tuesday morning. He was a man of low forehead, thin pinched-in Welsh face, black hair. His eyes were like two pieces of roving green jade glinting beneath bushy brows.

The office, a room of high ceilings and stained plaster walls, was in a first-floor corner of the County Building at Banbury. Beneath one tall window of the room was a cast-iron radiator. Beside the window hung a calendar picture of a girl wearing only a string of pearls. There were two desks facing each other across an aisle which led from the hall door to the radiator. The desk on the left belonged to Joe Welch, the night man. Lewis occupied the one on the right, a cigarette-scarred vintage piece which had stood in this room more than thirty years.

Lewis stopped at the front of his desk, leafed through the papers in the *incoming* basket, looked up as Sheriff Czernak entered. The sheriff, a fat man with wide Slavic features and a complexion like bread crust, grunted as he eased himself into the chair under the calendar. He pushed a brown felt hat to the back of his head, exposing a bald dome.

Lewis said, "Hi, John. How's the wife?" He dropped the papers back into the basket.

"Her sciatica's better this week," said the sheriff. "I came in to tell you to skip that burglary report in the basket. A city prowler picked up two punks with the stuff early this moring. We're sending 'em over to juvenile court."

"They'll never learn," said Lewis.

"Got one little chore for you," said the sheriff. "Otherwise everything's quiet. Maybe we'll get a chance to catch up on our paperwork." He hoisted himself out of the chair. "Doc Bellarmine did the autopsy on that Cerino woman, but he left a bottle of stomach washings at the Johnson-Tule Mortuary. Could you pick up the bottle and run it out to the county hospital?"

"Sure," said Lewis. "But I'll bet her death was natural causes. She was a known alcoholic. All those bottles in her shack."

"Prob'ly," said the sheriff. He stopped in front of Lewis's desk, glanced up at the calendar art. "Some dish."

Lewis grinned. "When I find a gal like that, I'm going to get married," he said.

"You do that," said the sheriff. He ambled out of the office.

It was about 8:30 when Lewis cruised past the mortuary in his county car and failed to find a parking place in the block. At the next corner, Cove Street, he turned right and went up the alley, parking on the concrete apron to the mortuary garage.

A southwest wind which had been threatening storm all night kicked up a damp gust as he stepped from the car. Lewis glanced up at the gray sky, but left his raincoat over the back of the seat. He went down the narrow walk beside the garage, found the back door of the mortuary ajar. Inside was a hallway and a row of three metal tanks, the tall kind welders use for oxygen and acetylene gas. Lewis glanced at them, wondered what a mortuary did with that type of equipment, shrugged the question aside. At the other end of the hall the door opened into a carpeted foyer which smelled of musky flowers. A door at the left bore a brass plate labeled OFFICE. Lewis crossed the foyer, entered the room.

Behind a glass-topped desk in the corner sat a tall blond individual type with clear Nordic features. An oak frame on the wall behind him held a colored photograph of Mount Lassen labeled PEACE on an embossed nameplate. An official burial form—partly filled in—was on the desk in front of the man. The left corner of the desk held a brass cup in which sat a metal ball. The ball emitted a hissing noise as Lewis approached and he breathed in the heavy floral scent of the foyer.

The man behind the desk got to his feet, put a pen across the burial form. Lewis recognized him—Johnson, half owner of the mortuary.

"May I help you?" asked the mortician.

Lewis explained his errand.

Johnson brought a small bottle from a desk drawer, passed it across to Lewis, then looked at the deputy with a puzzled frown. "How'd you get in?" asked the mortician. "I didn't hear the front door chimes."

The deputy shoved the bottle into a side pocket of his coat. "I parked in the alley and came in the back way," he said. "The street out front is full of Odd Fellows cars."

"Odd Fellows?" Johnson came around the desk.

"Paper said they were having some kind of rummage sale today," said Lewis. He ducked his head to look under the shade on the front window. "I guess those are Odd Fellows cars. That's the hall across the street."

An ornamental shrub on the mortuary front lawn bent before the wind and a spattering of rain drummed against the window. Lewis straightened. "Left my raincoat in the car," he said. "I'll just duck out the way I came."

Johnson moved to his office door. "Two of our attendants are due back now on a call," he said. "They—"

"I've seen a stiff before," said Lewis. He stepped past Johnson, headed for the door to the rear hall.

Johnson's hand caught the deputy's shoulder. "I must insist you go out the front," said the mortician.

Lewis stopped, his mind setting up a battery of questions. "It's raining out," he said. "I'll get all wet."

"I'm sorry," said Johnson.

Another man might have shrugged and complied with Johnson's request, but Welby Lewis was the son of the late Proctor Lewis, who had been three times president of the Banbury County Sherlock Holmes Round Table. Welby had cut his teeth on *logical deduction* and the logic of this situation escaped him. He reviewed his memory of the hallway. Empty except for those tanks near the back door.

"What do you keep in those metal tanks?" he asked.

The mortician's hand tightened on his shoulder and Lewis felt himself turned toward the front door. "Just embalming fluid," said Johnson. "That's the way it's delivered."

"Oh." Lewis looked up at Johnson's tightly drawn features, pulled away from the restraining hand and went out the front door. Rain was driving down and he ran around the side of the mortuary to his car, jumping in, slammed the door and sat down to wait. At 9:28 A.M. by his wristwatch an assistant mortician came out, opened the garage doors. Lewis leaned across the front seat, rolled down his right window.

"You'll have to move your car," said the assistant. "We're going out on a call."

"When are the other fellows coming back?" asked Lewis.

The mortician stopped halfway inside the garage. "What other fellows?" he asked.

"The ones who went out on that call this morning."

"Must be some other mortuary," said the assistant. "This is our first call today."

"Thanks," said Lewis. He rolled up his window, started the car and drove to the county hospital. The battery of unanswered questions churned in his mind. Foremost was—*Why did Johnson lie to keep me from going out the back way?*

At the hospital he delivered the bottle to the pathology lab, found a pay booth and called the Banbury Mortuary. An attendant answered and Lewis said, "I want to settle a bet. Could you tell me how embalming fluid is delivered to mortuaries?"

"We buy it by the case in concentrated form," said the mortician. "Twenty-four glass bottles to the case, sixteen ounces to the bottle. It contains red or orange dye to give a lifelike appearance. Our particular brand smells somewhat like strawberry soda. There is nothing offensive about it. We guarantee that the lifelike—"

"I just wanted to know how it came," said Lewis. "You're sure it's never delivered in metal tanks?"

"Good heavens, no!" said the man. "It'd corrode them!"

"Thanks," said Lewis and hung up softly. In his mind was the Holmesian observation: *If a man lies about an apparently inconsequential thing, then that thing is not inconsequential.*

He stepped out of the booth and bumped into Dr. Bellarmine, the autopsy surgeon. The doctor was a tall, knobby character with gray hair, sun-lamp tan and blue eyes as cutting as two scalpels.

"Oh, there you are, Lewis," he said. "They told me you were down this way. We found enough alcohol in that Cerino woman to kill three people. We'll check the stomach washings, too, but I doubt they'll add anything."

"Cerino woman?" asked Lewis.

"The old alcoholic you found in that shack by the roundhouse," said Bellarmine. "You losing your memory?"

"Oh . . . oh, certainly," said Lewis. "I was just thinking of something else. Thanks, Doc." He brushed past the surgeon. "Gotta go now," he muttered.

Back at his office Lewis sat on a corner of his desk, pulled the telephone to him and dialed the Johnson-Tule Mortuary. An unfamiliar masculine voice answered. Lewis said, "Do you do cremations at your mortuary?"

"Not *at* our mortuary," said the masculine voice, "but we have an arrangement with Rose Lawn Memorial Crematorium. Would you care to stop by and discuss your problem?"

"Not right now, thank you," said Lewis, and replaced the phone on its hook. He checked off another question in his mind—the possibility that the tanks held gas for a crematorium. *What the devil's in those tanks?* he asked himself.

"Somebody die?" The voice came from the doorway, breaking into Lewis's reverie. The deputy turned, saw Sheriff Czernak.

"No," said Lewis. "I've just got a puzzle." He went around the desk to his chair, sat down.

"Doc Bellarmine say anything about the Cerino dame?" asked the sheriff. He came into the room, eased himself into the chair beneath the calendar art.

"Alcoholism," said Lewis. "Like I said." He leaned back in his chair, put his feet on the desk and stared at a stained spot on the ceiling.

"What's niggling you?" asked the sheriff. "You look like a guy trying to solve a conundrum."

"I am," said Lewis and told him about the incident at the mortuary.

Czernak took off his hat, scratched his bald head. "It don't sound like much to me, Welby. In all probability there's a very simple explanation."

"I don't think so," said Lewis.

"Why not?"

Lewis shook his head. "I don't know. I just don't think so. Something about that mortuary doesn't ring true."

"What you think's in them tanks?" asked the sheriff.

"I don't know," said Lewis.

The sheriff seated his hat firmly on his head. "Anybody else I'd tell 'em forget it," he said. "But you, I dunno. I seen you pull too many rabbits out of the hat. Sometimes I think you're a freak an' see inside people."

"I am a freak," said Lewis. He dropped his feet to the floor, pulled a scratchpad to him and began doodling.

"Yeah, I can see you got six heads," said the sheriff.

"No, really," said Lewis. "My heart's on the right side of my chest."

"I hadn't noticed," said the sheriff. "But now you point it out to me—"

"Freak," said Lewis. "That's what I felt looking at that mortician. Like he was some kind of a creepy freak."

He pushed the scratchpad away from him. It bore a square broken into tiny segments by zigzag lines. Like a jigsaw puzzle.

"Was he a freak?"

Lewis shook his head. "Not that I could see."

Czernak pushed himself out of his chair. "Tell you what," he said. "It's quiet today. Why'ncha nose around a little?"

"Who can I have to help me?" asked Lewis.

"Barney Keeler'll be back in about a half hour," said Czernak. "He's de-liverin' a subpoena for Judge Gordon."

"Okay," said Lewis. "When he gets back, tell him to go over to the Odd Fellows Hall and go in the back way without attracting too much attention. I want him to go up to that tower room and keep watch on the front of the mortuary, note down everybody who enters or leaves and watch for those tanks. If the tanks go out, he's to tail the carrier and find out where they go."

"What're you gonna do?" asked the sheriff.

"Find a place where I can keep my eye on the back entrance. I'll call in when I get set." Lewis hooked a thumb toward the desk across from his. "When Joe Welch comes on, send him over to spell me."

"Right," said Czernak. "I still think maybe you're coon-doggin' it up an empty tree."

"Maybe I am," said Lewis. "But something shady about a mortuary gives my imagination the jumps. I keep thinking of how easy it could be for a mortician to get rid of an inconvenient corpse."

"Stuff it in one of them tanks, maybe?" asked the sheriff.

"No. They weren't big enough." Lewis shook his head. "I just don't like the idea of the guy lying to me."

It was shortly after 10:30 A.M. when Lewis found what he needed—a doctor's office in the rear of a building across the alley and two doors up from the mortuary garage. The doctor had three examining rooms on the third floor, the rear room looking down on the mortuary backyard. Lewis swore the doctor and his nurse to secrecy, set himself up in the back room with a pair of field glasses.

At noon he sent the nurse out for a hamburger and glass of milk for his lunch, had her watch the mortuary yard while he called his office and told the day radio operator where he was.

The doctor came into the back room at five o'clock, gave Lewis an extra set of keys for the office, asked him to be certain the door was locked when he left. Again Lewis warned the doctor against saying anything about the watch on the mortuary, stared the man down when it appeared he was about to ask questions. The doctor turned, left the room. Presently, a door closed solidly. The office was silent.

At about 7:30 it became too dark to distinguish clearly anything that might happen in the mortuary backyard. Lewis considered moving to a position in the alley, but two floodlights above the yard suddenly flashed on and the amber glow of a night light came from the window in the back door.

Joe Welch pounded on the door of the doctor's office at 8:20; Lewis admitted him, hurried back to the window with Welch following. The other deputy was a tall, nervous chain-smoker with a perpetual squint, a voice like a bassoon. He moved to a position beside Lewis at the window, said, "What's doing? Sheriff John said something about some acetylene tanks."

"It may be nothing at all," said Lewis. "But I've a feeling we're onto something big." In a few short sentences he explained about his encounter with the mortician that morning.

"Don't sound exciting to me," said Welch. "What you expecting to find in those tanks?"

"I wish I knew," said Lewis.

Welch went into the corner of the darkened room, lighted a cigarette, returned. "Why don't you just ask this Johnson?"

"That's the point," said Lewis. "I did ask him and he lied to me. That's why I'm suspicious. I've been hoping they'd take those tanks out and we could trail them to wherever they go. Get our answer that way."

"Why're you so sure it's the tanks he didn't want you to see?" asked Welch.

"That was a funny hallway," said Lewis. "Door at each end, none along the sides. Only things in it were those tanks."

"Well, those tanks might already be gone," said Welch. "You didn't get on this end until about ten-thirty, you said, and Keeler wasn't on the front until about eleven. They could've been taken out then if they're so all-fired important."

"I've had the same thought," said Lewis. "But I don't think they have. I'm going out to grab a bite to eat now, then I'm going down in the alley for a closer look."

"You won't get very close with all them lights on the yard," said Welch.

Lewis pointed to the garage. "If you look close you can see a space along the other side; in the shadow there. The light's on in the back hall. I'll try to get close enough for a look through the window in that rear door. They're tall tanks. I should be able to see them."

"And if they've been moved someplace else in the building?" asked Welch.

"Then I'll have to go in and brace Johnson for a showdown," said Lewis. "Maybe I should've done that in the first place, but this is a screwy situation. I just don't like a mystery in a mortuary."

"Sounds like the title of a detective story," said Welch. " 'Mystery in a Mortuary.' "

Welch sniffed. "There's already death inside there," he said. "This could be something mighty unpleasant."

Welch lighted a new cigarette from the coal of the one he had been smoking, stubbed out the discard in a dish Lewis had been using for an ash tray. "You may be right," said Welch. "The only thing impresses me about this she-bang, Welby, is like Sheriff John said—I've seen you pull too many rabbits out of the hat."

"That's what he told you?" asked Lewis.

"Yeah, but he thinks maybe you're gonna pull a blank this time." Welch stared down at the mortuary. "If you go inside, do you want me to round up a few of my men and smother the place if you don't come out by some set time?"

"I don't think that'll be necessary," said Lewis. "Don't take any action unless you see something suspicious."

Welch nodded his head. "Okay," he said. He looked at the glowing tip of his cigarette, glanced down at the yard they were watching. "Mortuaries give me the creeps anyway," he said.

Lewis bolted down a hot beef sandwich at a cafe two blocks from the mortuary, returned along a back street. It was cold and wet in the alley. A perverse wind kept tangling the skirts of his raincoat. He hugged the shadows near the mortuary garage, found the row of boards which had been nailed across the area he was going to use. Lewis clambered over the boards, dropped to soft earth which was out of the wind but under a steady dripping from unguttered eaves. He moved quietly to the end of the shadow area and, as he had expected, could see inside the window on the rear door of the mortuary. The tanks were not visible. Lewis cursed under his breath, shrugged, stepped out of the shadows and crossed the lighted backyard. The door was locked, but he could see through the window that the hallway was empty. He went around to the front door, rang the night bell.

A man in a rumpled black suit which looked as though he had slept in it answered the door. Lewis brushed past him into the warm flower smell of the foyer. "Is Johnson here?" he asked.

"Mr. Johnson is asleep," said the man. "May I be of service?"

"Ask Mr. Johnson to come down, please," said Lewis. "This is official business." He showed his badge.

"Of course," said the man. "If you'll go into the office there and have a seat, I'll tell Mr. Johnson you're here. He sleeps in the quarters upstairs."

"Thanks," said Lewis. He went into the office, looked at the colored photograph of Mount Lassen until the night attendant had disappeared up the stairs at the other end of the foyer. Then Lewis came out of the office, went to the doorway leading into the hall. The door was locked. He tried forcing it, but it wouldn't budge. He moved to the hinge side, found a thin crack which gave a view of the other end of the hall. What he saw made him draw a quick breath. The three metal tanks were right where he had expected them to be. He went back to the office, found a directory and looked up the number of the doctor's office where Welch was waiting, dialed the number. After a long wait Welch's voice came on the line, tones guarded. "Yes?"

"This is Welby," said Lewis. "Anything come in the back?"

"No," said Welch. "You all right?"

"I'm beginning to wonder," said Lewis. "Keep your eyes peeled." He hung up, turned to find Johnson's tall figure filling the office doorway.

"Mr. Lewis," said Johnson. "Is something wrong?" He came into the office.

"I want to have a look at those metal tanks," said Lewis.

Johnson stopped. "What metal tanks?"

"The ones in your back hall," said Lewis.

"Oh, the embalming fluid," said Johnson. "What's the interest in embalming fluid?"

"Let's just have a look at it," said Lewis.

"Do you have a warrant?" asked Johnson.

Lewis's chin jerked up and he stared at the man. "I wouldn't have a bit of trouble getting one," he said.

"On what grounds?"

"I could think of something that'd stick," said Lewis. "Are we going to do this the easy way or the hard way?"

Johnson shrugged. "As you wish." He led the way out of the office, unlocked the hall door, preceded Lewis down the hallway to the three tanks.

"I thought embalming fluid came in sixteen-ounce glass bottles," said Lewis.

"This is something new," said Johnson. "These tanks have glass inner liners. The fluid is kept under pressure." He turned a valve and an acrid spray emerged from a fitting at the top.

Lewis took a shot in the dark, said, "That doesn't smell like embalming fluid."

Johnson said, "It's a new type. We add the masking perfumes later."

"You just get these filled?" asked Lewis.

"No, these were delivered last week," said Johnson. "We've left them here because we don't have a better place to store them." He smiled at Lewis, but the eyes remained cold, watchful. "Why this interest?"

"Call it professional curiosity," said Lewis. He went to the rear door, unlatched it and locked the latch in the open position, stepped outside, closed the door. He could see the tanks plainly through the window. He came back into the hallway.

He's still lying to me, thought Lewis. *But it's all so very plausible.* He said, "I'm going to give your place a thorough search."

"But why?" protested Johnson.

"For no good reason at all," said Lewis. "If you want, I'll go out and get a warrant." He started to brush past Johnson, was stopped by a strong hand on his shoulder, something hard pressing into his side. He looked down, saw a flat automatic menacing him.

"I regret this," said Johnson. "Believe me, I do."

"You're going to regret it more," said Lewis. "I have your place watched front and back and the office knows where I am."

For the first time he saw a look of indecision on Johnson's face. "You're lying," said the mortician.

"Come here," said Lewis. He stepped to the back door, looked up to the black window where Welch stood. The glow of the deputy's cigarette was plainly visible, an orange wash against the blackness. Johnson saw it. "Now let's go check the front," said Lewis.

"No need," said Johnson. "I thought you were playing a lone hand." He paused. "You came in the backyard again and had a look in the window, didn't you?"

"What do you think?" asked Lewis.

"I should've anticipated that," said Johnson. "Perhaps I was too anxious to have things appear just as they were. You startled me coming in here at night like this."

"You saw me come in the front?" asked Lewis.

"Let us say that I was aware you were downstairs before the attendant told me," said Johnson. He gestured with his gun. "Let's go back to the office."

Lewis led the way down the hall. At the foyer door he glanced back.

"Turn around!" barked Johnson.

But the one glance had been enough. The tanks were gone. "What was that humming sound?" asked Lewis.

"Just keep moving," said Johnson.

In the front office the mortician motioned Lewis to a chair. "What were you looking for?" asked Johnson. He slid into the chair behind his desk, rested his gun hand on the desk top.

"I found what I was looking for," said Lewis.

"And that is?"

"Evidence to confirm my belief that this place should be taken apart brick by brick."

Johnson smiled, hooked the telephone to him with his left hand, took off the receiver and rested it on the desk. "What's your office number?"

Lewis told him.

Johnson dialed, picked up the phone, said, "Hello, this is Lewis."

Lewis came half out of the chair. His own voice was issuing from Johnson's mouth. The gun in the mortician's hand waved him back to the chair.

"You got the dope on what I'm doing?" asked Johnson. He waited. "No. Nothing important. I'm just looking." Again he paused. "I'll tell you if I find anything," he said. He replaced the phone in its cradle.

"Well?" said Lewis.

Johnson's lips thinned. "This is incredible," he said. "A mere human—" He broke off, stared at Lewis, said, "My mistake was in telling you a plausible lie after that door was left open. I should have—" He shrugged.

"You couldn't hope to fool us forever," said Lewis.

"I suppose not," said Johnson, "but reasoning tells me that there is still a chance." The gun suddenly came up, its muzzle pointing at Lewis. "It's a chance I have to take," said the mortician. The gun belched flame and Lewis was slammed back in his chair. Through a dimming haze, he saw Johnson put the gun to his own head, pull the trigger, slump across the desk. Then the haze around Lewis thickened, became the black nothing of unconsciousness.

From a somewhere he could not identify Lewis became aware of himself. He was running through a black cave, chased by a monster with blazing eyes and arms like an octopus. The monster kept shouting, "A mere human! A mere human! A mere human!" with a voice that echoed as though projected into a rain barrel. Then, above the voice of the monster, Lewis heard water dripping in a quick even cadence. At the same time he saw the mouth of the cave, a round bright area. The bright area grew larger, larger, became the white wall of a hospital room and a window with sunshine outside. Lewis turned his head, saw a metal tank like the ones in the mortuary.

A voice said, "That brought him around."

Vertigo swept over Lewis and for a moment he fought it. A white-clad figure swam into his field of vision, resolved itself into a county hospital intern whom Lewis recognized. The intern held a black oxygen mask.

The sound of the dripping water was louder now and then he realized that it was a wristwatch. He turned toward the sound, saw Sheriff Czernak straighten from a position close to his head. Czernak's Slavic face broke into a grin. "Boy, you gave us a scare," he said.

Lewis swallowed, found his voice. "What—"

"You know, you are lucky you're a freak," said Czernak. "Your heart being on the right side's the only thing saved you. That and the fact that Joe heard the shots."

The intern came around beside the sheriff. "The bullet nicked an edge of your lung and took a little piece out of a rib at the back," said the intern. "You must've been born lucky."

"Johnson?" said Lewis.

"Deader'n a mackerel," said Czernak. "You feel strong enough to tell us what happened? Joe's story don't make sense. What's with these tanks of embalming fluid?"

Lewis thought about his encounter with the mortician. Nothing about it made sense. He said, "Embalming fluid comes in sixteen-ounce bottles."

"We got those three tanks from the hallway," said Czernak, "but I don't know what we're doing with them."

"From the hall?" Lewis remembered his last look at the empty hall before Johnson had ordered him to turn around. He tried to push himself up, felt pain knife through his chest. The intern pushed him gently back to the pillow. "Here now, none of that," he said. "You just stay flat on your back."

"What was in the tanks?" whispered Lewis.

"The lab here says it's embalming fluid," said the sheriff. "What's so special about it?"

Lewis remembered the acrid odor of the spray Johnson had released from the tank valve. "Does the lab still have some of that fluid?" he asked. "I'd like to smell it."

"I'll get it," said the intern. "Don't let him sit up. It could start a hemorrhage." He went out the door.

"Where were the tanks when you found them?" asked Lewis.

"Down by the back door," said Czernak. "Where you said they were. Why?"

"I don't really know yet," said Lewis. "But I've something I wish you'd do. Take a—"

The door opened and the intern entered, a test tube in his hand. "This is the stuff," he said. He passed the tube under Lewis's nose. It gave off a musklike sweet aroma. It was not what he had smelled at the tanks. *That explains why the tanks disappeared,* he thought. *Somebody switched them. But what was in the others?* He looked up at the intern, said, "Thanks."

"You were sayin' something," said the sheriff.

"Yes," said Lewis. "Take a crew over to that mortuary, John, and rip out the wall behind where you found those tanks and take up the floor under that spot."

"What're we supposed to find?" asked Czernak.

"Damned if I know," said Lewis, "but it sure should be interesting. Those tanks kept disappearing and reappearing every time I turned my back. I want to know why."

"Look, Welby, we've got to have something solid to go on," said the sheriff. "People are running around that mortuary like crazy, saying it's bad business an' what all."

"I'd say this was good for business," said Lewis, a brief smile forming on his lips. His face sobered. "Don't you think it's enough that somebody tried to kill one of your men and then committed suicide?"

The sheriff scratched his head. "I guess so, Welby. You sure you can't give me anything more'n just your hunch?"

"You know as much about this as I do," said Lewis. "By the way, where's Johnson's body?"

"They're fixin' it up for burial," said Czernak. "Welby, I really should have more'n just your say so. The D.A. will scream if I get too heavy-handed."

"You're still the sheriff," said Lewis.

"Well, can't you even tell me why Johnson killed himself?"

"Say he was mentally unbalanced," said Lewis. "And John, here's something else. Get Doc Bellarmine to do the autopsy on Johnson and tell him to go over that body with a magnifying glass."

"Why?"

"It was something he said about mere humans," said Lewis.

"Askin' me to stick my neck out like this," said Czernak.

"Will you do it?" asked Lewis.

"Sure I'll do it!" exploded Czernak. "But I don't like it!" He jammed his hat onto his head, strode out of the room.

The intern turned to follow.

Lewis said, "What time is it?"

The intern stopped, glanced at his wristwatch. "Almost five." He looked at Lewis. "We've had you under sedatives since you came out of the operating room."

"Five A.M. or five P.M.?" asked Lewis.

"Five P.M.," said the intern.

"Was I a tough job?" asked Lewis.

"It was a clean wound," said the intern. "You take it easy now. It's almost chow time. I'll see that you're served in the first round and then I'll have the nurse bring you a sedative. You need your rest."

"How long am I going to be chained to this bed?" asked Lewis.

"We'll discuss that later," said the intern. "You really shouldn't be talking." He turned away, went out the door.

Lewis turned his head away, saw that someone had left a stack of magazines on his bed stand. The top magazine had slipped down, exposing the cover. It was done in garish colors—a bug-eyed monster chasing a scantily clad female. Lewis was reminded of his nightmare. *A mere human . . . A mere human.* The words kept turning over in his mind. *What was it about Johnson that brought up the idea of a freak?* he wondered.

A student nurse brought in his tray, cranked up his bed and helped him eat. Presently, a nurse came in with a hypo, shot him in the arm. He drifted off to sleep with the mind full of questions still unanswered.

"He's awake now," said a female voice. Lewis heard a door open, looked up to see Czernak followed by Joe Welch. It was daylight outside, raining. The two men wore damp raincoats, which they took off and draped over chairs.

Lewis smiled at Welch. "Thanks for having good ears, Joe," he said.

Welch grinned. "I opened the window when I saw you come out the back door," he said. "I thought maybe you was going to holler something up to me. Then when you went right back inside, I thought that was funny; so I left the window partly open or I'd never've heard a thing."

Czernak pulled a chair up beside Lewis's bed, sat down. Welch took a chair at the foot.

Lewis turned his head toward the sheriff. "Is the D.A. screaming yet?"

"No," said Czernak. "He got caught out in that rainstorm the other day and he's home with the flu. Besides, I'm still sheriff of this county." He patted the bed. "How you feeling, boy?"

"I'm afraid I'm gonna live," said Lewis.

"You better," said Welch. "We got a new relief radio gal who saw your picture in the files an' says she wants to meet you. She's a wow."

"Tell her to wait for me," said Lewis. He looked at the sheriff. "What'd you find?"

"I don't get it, Welby," said Czernak. "Right behind where them tanks was there was this brick wall covered with plaster. We took away the plaster and there's all these wires, see."

"What kind of wires?"

"That's just it, Keeler's old man is a jeweler and Keeler says this wire is silver. It's kind of a screen like, criss-crossed every which way."

"What were they hooked up to?"

"To nothing we could find," said Czernak. He looked at Welch. "Ain't that right?"

"Nothing there but this wire," said Welch.

"What did you do with it?" asked Lewis.

"Nothing," said Czernak. "We just left like it was and took pictures."

"Anything under the floor?"

Czernak's face brightened. "Boy, we sure hit the jackpot there!" He bent his head and peered closely at Lewis. "How'd you know we'd find something under there?"

"I just knew those tanks kept appearing out of nowhere," said Lewis. "What was under there?"

Czernak straightened. "Well, a whole section of the hall floor was an elevator and down below there was this big room. It stretched from under the hall to clear under the embalming room and there was a section of the embalming room floor where a bunch of tiles come up in one piece and there was a trapdoor and a stairway. Hell! It was just like one of them horror movies!"

"What was down there?"

"A buncha machinery," said Czernak.

"What kind?"

"I dunno." Czernak shook his head, glanced at Welch.

"Craziest stuff I ever saw," said Welch. He shrugged.

"Doc Bellarmine came down and had a look at it after the autopsy last night," said Czernak. "He said he'd be in to see you this morning."

"Did he say anything about the autopsy?" asked Lewis.

"Not to me," said Czernak.

Welch hitched his chair closer to the foot of the bed, rested an arm on the rail. "He told me it was something about the autopsy made him come down to have a look at the mortuary," he said. "He didn't say what it was, though."

"What about the mortuary staff?" asked Lewis. "Did they say anything about the secret room?"

"They swear they never even knew it was there," said Czernak. "We took 'em all into custody anyway, all except Tule and his wife."

"Tule?"

"Yeah, the other partner. His wife was a licensed mortician, too. Ain't been seen since the night you were shot. The staff says that Johnson, Tule and the wife was always locking doors around the building for no good reason at all."

"What did this machinery look like?"

"Part of it was just an elevator for that section of floor. The other stuff was hooked up to a bunch of pipes coming down from the embalming table upstairs. There was this big—" Czernak stopped as the door opened.

Dr. Bellarmine's cynical face peered into the room. His eyes swept over the occupants; he entered, closed the door behind him. "The patient's feeling better, I see," he said. "For a while there I thought this would be a job for me in my official capacity."

"This guy'll outlive all of us," said Welch.

"He probably will at that," said the doctor. He glanced down at Lewis. "Feel like a little conversation?"

"Just a minute, Doc," said Lewis. He turned to Czernak. "John, I have one more favor," he said. "Could you get one of those tanks of embalming fluid to a welding shop and have it cut open with a burner. I want to know how it's made inside."

"No, you don't," said Czernak. "I'm not leavin' here without some kind of an explanation."

"And I don't have an explanation," said Lewis. "All the pieces aren't together yet. I'm tied to this bed when I should be out working on this thing. I've ten thousand questions I want answered and no way of answering them."

"Don't excite yourself," said Bellarmine.

"Yeah, Welby, take it easy," said Czernak. "It's just that I'm about ready to pop with frustration. Nothing makes sense here. This guy tries to kill you for no apparent reason and then commits suicide. It seems to be because you wanted to look inside them tanks, but they're just embalming fluid. I don't get it."

"Would you have those tanks cut open for me?" asked Lewis.

"Okay, okay." Czernak hoisted himself to his feet. Welch also arose. "Come on, Joe," said the sheriff. "We're nothin' but a couple of leg men for Sherlock here. Let's take them—"

"John, I'm sorry," said Lewis. "It's just that I can't—"

"I know you can't do it yourself now," said Czernak. "That's why I'm doing it. You're the best man I got, Welby; so I'm countin' on you to put this together. Me, I gave up when I saw that machinery." He left the room, muttering, followed by Welch, who stopped at the door, winked at Lewis.

Bellarmine waited until the door closed, sat down on the foot of the bed. "How'd you get onto them?" he asked.

Lewis ignored the question. "What'd you find in that autopsy?" he asked.

The surgeon frowned. "I thought you were nuts when the sheriff told me what you wanted," he said. "Any fool could see Johnson died of a gunshot wound in the head. But I guessed you had a reason; so I did my cutting carefully and it was a lucky thing I did."

"Why?"

"Well, this is the kind of case an autopsy surgeon sloughs off sometimes. Visible wound. Obvious cause. I could've missed it. The guy looked to be normal."

"Missed what?"

"His heart, for one thing. It had an extra layer of muscles in the cardiac sheath. I experimented with them and near dropped my knife. They work like that automatic sealing device they put in airplane fuel tanks. Puncture the heart and this muscle layer seals the hole until the heart's healed."

"Damn!" said Lewis.

"This guy was like that all over," said Bellarmine. "For a long time doctors have looked at the human body with the wish they could redesign certain things to better specifications. Johnson looked like our wish had come true. Fewer vertebrae with better articulation. Pigment veins into the pupil of the eye which could only be some kind of filter to—"

"That's it!" Lewis slapped the bed with the palm of his hand. "There was something freakish about him and I couldn't focus on it. The pupils of his eyes changed color. I can remember seeing it and—"

"You didn't see anything," said Bellarmine. "His pelvic floor was broader and distributed the weight more evenly to the legs. The feet had larger bones and more central distribution of weight over the arch. There was an interlaced membranous support for the viscera. His circulatory system had sphincter valves at strategic points to control bleeding. This Johnson may have looked human on the outside, but inside he was superhuman."

"What about the machinery in the mortuary basement?" asked Lewis.

Bellarmine stood up, began to pace the floor, back and forth at the foot of the bed. Presently he stopped, put his hands on the rail, stared at Lewis. "I spent half the night examining that layout," he said. "It was one of the most beautifully designed and executed rigs I've ever seen. Its major purpose was to take cadaver blood and fractionate the protein."

"You mean like for making plasma and stuff like that?" asked Lewis.

"Well, something like that," said Bellarmine.

"I didn't think you could use the blood of a corpse for that," said Lewis.

"We didn't either," said the surgeon. "The Russians have been working on it, however. Our experience has been that it breaks down too quickly. We've tried—"

"You mean this was a Communist set-up?"

Bellarmine shook his head. "No such luck. This rig wasn't just foreign to the U.S.A. It was foreign to Earth. There's one centrifugal pump in there that spins free in an air blast. I shudder every time I think of the force it must generate. We don't have an alloy that'll come anywhere near standing up to those strains. And the Russians don't have it, either."

"How can you be sure?"

"For one thing, there are several research projects that are awaiting this type of rig and the Russians have no more results on those projects than we have."

"Then something was produced from cadaver blood and was stored in those tanks," said Lewis.

Bellarmine nodded. "I checked. A fitting on the tanks matched one on the machinery."

Lewis pushed himself upright, ignoring the pain in his chest. "Then this means an extraterrestrial in—" The pain in his chest became too much and he sagged back to the pillow.

Dr. Bellarmine was suddenly at his side. "You fool!" he barked. "You were told to take it easy." He pushed the emergency button at the head of the bed, began working on the bandages.

"What's matter?" whispered Lewis.

"Hemorrhage," said Bellarmine. "Where's that fool nurse? Why doesn't she answer the bell?" He stripped away a length of adhesive.

The door opened and a nurse entered, stopped as she saw the scene.

"Emergency tray," said Bellarmine. "Get Dr. Edwards here to assist! Bring plasma!"

Lewis heard a drum begin to pound inside his head—louder, louder, louder. Then it began to fade and there was nothing.

He awoke to a rustling sound and footsteps. Then he recognized it. The sound of a nurse's starched uniform as she moved about the room. He opened his eyes and saw by the shadows outside that it was afternoon.

"So you're awake," said the nurse.

Lewis turned his head toward the sound. "You're new," he said. "I don't recognize you."

"Special," she said. "Now you just take it easy and don't try to move." She pushed the call button.

It seemed that almost immediately Dr. Bellarmine was in the room bending over Lewis. The surgeon felt Lewis's wrist, took a deep breath. "You went into shock," he said. "You have to remain quiet. Don't try to move around."

His voice low and husky, Lewis said, "Could I ask some questions?"

"Yes, but only for a few minutes. You have to avoid any kind of exertion."

"What'd the sheriff find out about the tanks?"

Bellarmine grimaced. "They couldn't open them. Can't cut the metal."

"That confirms it," said Lewis. "Think there are any other rigs like that?"

"There have to be," said Bellarmine. He sat down on a chair at the head of the bed. "I've had another look at that basement layout and took a machinist with me. He agrees. Everything about it cries out mass production. Mostly cast fittings with a minimum of machining. Simple, efficient construction."

"Why? What good's the blood from human cadavers?"

"I've been asking myself that same question," said Bellarmine. "Maybe for a nutrient solution for culture growths. Maybe for the antibodies."

"Would they be any good?"

"That depends on how soon the blood was extracted. The time element varies with temperature, body condition, a whole barrel full of things."

"But why?"

The surgeon ran a hand through his gray hair. "I don't like my answer to that question," he said. "I keep thinking of how we fractionate the blood of guinea pigs, how we recover vaccine from chick embryos, how we use all of our test animals."

Lewis's eyes fell on the dresser across his room. Someone had taken the books from his night stand and put them on the dresser. He could still see the bug-eyed monster cover.

"From what I know of science fiction," said Lewis, "that silver grid in the hall must be some kind of matter transmitter for sending the tanks to wherever they're used. I wonder why they didn't put it downstairs with the machinery."

"Maybe it had to be above ground," said Bellarmine. "You figure it the same way I do."

"You're a hard-headed guy, Doc," said Lewis. "How come you go for this bug-eyed monster theory?"

"It was the combination," said Bellarmine. "That silver grid, the design of the machinery and its purpose, the strange metals, the differences in Johnson. It all spells A-L-I-E-N, alien. But I could say the same holds for you, Lewis. What put you wise?"

"Johnson. He called me a *mere human*. I got to wondering how alien a guy could be to separate himself from the human race."

"It checks," said Bellarmine.

"Buy why guinea pigs?" asked Lewis.

The surgeon frowned, looked at the floor, back at Lewis. "That rig had a secondary stage," he said. "It could have only one function—passing live virus under some kind of bombardment—X-ray or beta ray or whatever—and depositing the mutated strain in a little spray container about as big as your fist. I know from my own research experience that some mutated virus can be deadly."

"Germ warfare," whispered Lewis. "You sure it isn't the Russians?"

"I'm sure. This was a perfect infecting center. Complete. Banbury would've been decimated by now if that's what it was."

"Maybe they weren't ready."

"Germ warfare is ready when one infecting center is set up. No. This rig was for producing slight alterations in common germs or I miss my guess. This little spray container went into a . . ."

"Rack on Johnson's desk," said Lewis.

"Yeah," said Bellarmine.

"I saw it," said Lewis. "I thought it was one of those deodorant things." He picked a piece of lint off the covers. "So they're infecting us with mutated virus."

"It scares me," said Bellarmine.

Lewis squinted his eyes, looked up at the surgeon. "Doc, what would you do if you found out that one of your white rats was not only intelligent but had found out what you were doing to it?"

"Well—" Bellarmine looked out the window at the gathering dusk. "I'm no monster, Lewis. I'd probably turn it loose. No—" He scratched his chin. "No, maybe I wouldn't at that. But I wouldn't infect it anymore. I think I'd put it through some tests to find out just how smart it was. The rat would no longer be a simple test animal. Its usefulness would be in the psychological field, to tell me things about myself."

"That's about the way I had it figured," said Lewis. "How much longer am I going to be in this bed?"

"Why?"

"I've figured a way for the guinea pigs to tell the researchers the jig's up."

"How? We don't even know their language. We've only seen one specimen and that one's dead. We can't be sure they'd react the same way we would."

"Yes, they would," said Lewis.

"How can you say that? They must already know we're sentient."

"So's a rat sentient—to a degree," said Lewis. "It's all in the way you look at it. Sure. Compared to us, they're vegetables. That's the way it'd be with—"

"We don't have the right to take risks with the rest of humanity," protested Bellarmine. "Man, one of them tried to kill you!"

"But everything points to that one being defective," said Lewis. "He made too many mistakes. That's the only reason we got wise to him."

"They might dump us into the incinerator as no longer useful," said Bellarmine. "They—"

Lewis said, "They'd have to be pretty much pure scientists. Johnson was a field man, a lab technician, a worker. The pure scientists would follow our human pattern. I'm sure of it. To be a pure scientist you have to be able to control yourself. That means you'd understand other persons'—other beings'—problems. No, Doc. Your first answer was the best one. You'd put your rats through psychological tests."

Bellarmine stared at his hands. "What's your idea?"

"Take a white rat in one of those little lab cages. Infect it with some common germ, leave the infecting hypo in the cage, put the whole works—rat and all—in front of that silver grid. Distort—"

"That's a crazy idea," said Bellarmine. "How could you tell a hypothetical something to look at your message when you don't even know the hypothetical language—how to contact them in the first place?"

"Distort the field of that grid by touching the wires with a piece of metal," said Lewis. "Tie the metal to the end of a pole for safety."

"I've never heard a crazier idea," said Bellarmine.

"Get me the white rat, the cage and the hypo and I'll do it myself," said Lewis.

Bellarmine got to his feet, moved toward the door. "You're not doing anything for a couple of weeks," he said. "You're a sick man and I've been talking to you too long already." He opened the door, left the room.

Lewis stared at the ceiling. A shudder passed over his body. *Mutated virus!*

The door opened and an orderly and nurse entered. "You get a little tube feeding of hot gelatin," said the nurse. She helped him eat it, then, over his protests, gave him a sedative.

"Doctor's orders," said the nurse.

Through a descending fog, Lewis murmured, "Which doctor?"

"Dr. Bellarmine," she said.

The fog came lower, darkened. He drifted into a nightmare peopled by thousands of Johnsons, all of them running around with large metal tanks asking, "Are you human?" and collecting blood.

Sheriff Czernak was beside the bed when Lewis awoke. Lewis could see out the window that dawn was breaking. He turned toward the sheriff. "Mornin', John," he whispered. His tongue felt thick and dry.

"'Bout time you woke up," said Czernak. "I've been waiting here a coupla hours. Something fishy's going on."

"Wind my bed up, will you?" asked Lewis. "What's happening?"

Czernak arose, moved to the foot of the bed and turned the crank.

"The big thing is that Doc Bellarmine has disappeared," he said. "We traced him from the lab here to the mortuary. Then he just goes *pffft!*"

Lewis's eyes widened. "Was there a white rat cage?"

"There you go again!" barked Czernak. "You tell me you don't know anything about this, but you sure know all the questions." He bent over Lewis. "Sure, there was a rat cage! You better tell me how you knew it!"

"First tell *me* what happened," said Lewis.

Czernak straightened, frowning. "All right, Welby, but when I get through telling, then you better tell." He wet his lips with his tongue. "I'm told the Doc came in here and talked to you last night. Then he went down to the lab and got one of them white rats with its cage. Then he went over to the mortuary. He had the cage and rat with him. Our night guard let him in. After a while, when the Doc didn't come out, the guard got worried and went inside. There in the back hall is the Doc's black bag. And over where this silver wire stuff was he finds—"

"Was?" Lewis barked the word.

"Yeah," said Czernak wearily. "That's the other thing. Sometime last night somebody ripped out all them wires and didn't leave a single trace."

"What else did the guard find?"

Czernak ran a hand under his collar, stared at the opposite wall.

"Well?"

"Welby, look, I—"

"What happened?"

"Well, the night guard—it was Rasmussen—called me and I went right down. Rasmussen didn't touch a thing. There was the Doc's bag, a long wood pole with a tire iron attached to it and the rat cage. The rat was gone."

"Was there anything in the cage?"

Czernak suddenly leaned forward, blurted, "Look, Welby, about the cage. There's something screwy about it. When I first got there, I swear it wasn't there. Rasmussen doesn't remember it, either. My first idea when I got there was that the Doc'd gone out the back way, but our seal was still on the door. It hadn't been opened. While I was thinking that one over—I was standing about in the middle of the hall—I heard this noise like a cork being pulled out of a bottle. I turned around and there was this little cage on the floor. Out of nowhere."

"And it was empty?"

"Except for some pieces of glass that I'm told belonged to a hypo."

"Broken?"

"Smashed to pieces."

"Was the cage door open?"

Czernak tipped his head to one side, looked at the far wall. "No, I don't believe it was."

"And exactly where was this cage?" Lewis's eyes burned into the sheriff's.

"Like I said, Welby. Right in front of where the wires was."

"And the wires were gone?"

"Well—" Again the sheriff looked uncomfortable. "For just a second there, when I turned around after hearing that noise—for just a second there I thought I saw 'em."

Lewis took a deep breath.

Czernak said, "Now come on and give, will you? Where's the Doc? You must have some idea, the way you been askin' questions."

"He's taking his entrance exams," said Lewis. "And we'd all better pray that he passes."

OCCUPATION FORCE

He was a long time awakening. There was a pounding somewhere. General Henry A. Llewellyn's eyes snapped open. Someone at his bedroom door. Now he heard the voice. "Sir . . . sir . . . sir . . ." It was his orderly.

"All right, Watkins, I'm awake."

The pounding ceased.

He swung his feet out of the bed, looked at the luminous dial on his alarm clock—two-twenty-five. What the devil? He slipped on a robe, a tall, ruddy-faced man—chairman of the Joint Chiefs of Staff.

Watkins saluted when the general opened the door. "Sir, the President has called an emergency cabinet meeting." The orderly began to talk faster, his words running all together. "There's an alien spaceship big as Lake Erie sailing around the earth and getting ready to attack."

It took a second for the general to interpret the words. He snorted. Pulp magazine poppycock! he thought.

"Sir," said Watkins, "there is a staff car downstairs ready to take you to the White House."

"Get me a cup of coffee while I dress," said the general.

Representatives of five foreign nations, every cabinet officer, nine senators, fourteen representatives, the heads of the secret service, FBI and of all the armed services were at the meeting. They gathered in the conference room of the White House bomb shelter—a panelled room with paintings around the walls in deep frames to simulate windows. General Llewellyn sat across the oak conference table from the President. The buzzing of voices in the room stopped as the President rapped his gavel. An aide stood up, gave them the first briefing.

A University of Chicago astronomer had picked up the ship at about eight P.M. It was coming from the general direction of the belt of Orion. The astronomer had alerted other observatories and someone had thought to notify the government.

The ship had arrowed in at an incredible rate, swung into a one-and-one-half-hour orbit around Earth. It was visible to the unaided eye by that time, another moon. Estimates put its size at nineteen miles long, twelve miles wide, vaguely egg-shaped.

Spectroscopic analysis showed the drive was a hydrogen ion stream with traces of carbon, possibly from the refractor. The invader was transparent to radar, responded to no form of communication.

Majority opinion: a hostile ship on a mission to conquer Earth.

Minority opinion: a *cautious* visitor from space.

Approximately two hours after it took up orbit, the ship put out a five-hundred-foot scout which swooped down on Boston, grappled up a man by the name of William R. Jones from a group of night workers waiting for a bus.

Some of the minority went over to the majority. The President, however, continued to veto all suggestions that they attack. He was supported by the foreign representatives who were in periodic communication with their governments.

"Look at the size of the thing," said the President. "An ant with an ant-size pea-shooter could attack an elephant with the same hopes of success we would have."

"There's always the possibility they're just being prudent," said a State Department aide. "We've no evidence they're dissecting this Jones from Boston, as I believe someone suggested."

"The size precludes peaceful intent," said General Llewellyn. "There's an invasion army in that thing. We should fire off every atomic warhead rocket we can lay hand to, and . . ."

The President waved a hand to silence him.

General Llewellyn sat back. His throat hurt from arguing, his hand ached from pounding the table.

At eight A.M., the spaceship detached a thousand-foot scout as it passed over the New Jersey coast. The scout drifted down over Washington, D.C. At eight-eighteen A.M., the scout contacted Washington airport in perfect English, asked for landing instructions. A startled tower operator warned the scout ship off until Army units had cleared the area.

General Llewellyn and a group of expendable assistants were chosen to greet the invaders. They were at the field by eight-fifty-one. The scout, a pale robins-egg blue, settled to a landing strip which cracked beneath it. Small apertures began flicking open and shut on the ship's surface. Long rods protruded, withdrew. After ten minutes of this, a portal opened and a ramp shot out, tipped to the ground. Again silence.

Every weapon the armed services could muster was trained on the invader. A flight of jets swept overhead. Far above them, a lone bomber circled, in its belly THE BOMB. All waited for the general's signal.

Something moved in the shadow above the ramp. Four human figures appeared at the portal. They wore striped trousers, cutaways, glistening black shoes, top hats. Their linen shone. Three carried briefcases, one had a scroll. They moved down the ramp.

General Llewellyn and aides walked out to the foot of the ramp. *They look like more bureaucrats,* thought the general.

The one with the scroll, a dark-haired man with narrow face, spoke first. "I have the honor to be the ambassador from Krolia, Loo Mogasayvidiantu." His English was faultless. He extended the scroll. "My credentials."

General Llewellyn accepted the scroll, said, "I am General Henry A. Llewellyn"—he hesitated—"representative of Earth."

The Krolian bowed. "May I present my staff?" He turned. "Ayk Turgoto-kikalapa, Min Sinobayatagurki and William R. Jones, late of Boston, Earth."

The general recognized the man whose picture was in all of the morning newspapers. *Here's our first Solar quisling,* he thought.

"I wish to apologize for the delay in our landing," said the Krolian ambassador. "Occasionally quite a long period of time is permitted to elapse between preliminary and secondary phases of a colonial program."

Colonial program! thought the general. He almost gave the signal which would unleash death upon this scene. But the ambassador had more to say.

"The delay in landing was a necessary precaution," said the Krolian. "Over such a long period of time our data sometimes becomes outmoded. We needed time for a sampling, to talk to Mr. Jones, to bring our data up to date." Again he bowed with courtly politeness.

Now General Llewellyn was confused: *Sampling . . . data . . .* He took a deep breath. Conscious of the weight of history on his shoulders, he said, "We have one question to ask you, Mr. Ambassador. Do you come as friends or conquerors?"

The Krolian's eyes widened. He turned to the Earthman beside him. "It is as I expected, Mr. Jones." His lips thinned. "That Colonial Office! Under-staffed! Inefficient! Bumbling . . ."

The General frowned. "I don't understand."

"No, of course," said the ambassador. "But if our Colonial Office had kept track . . ." He waved a hand. "Look around at your people, sir."

The general looked first at the men behind the ambassador. Obviously human. At a gesture from the Krolian, he turned to the soldiers behind himself, then toward the frightened faces of the civilians behind the airport fences. The general shrugged, turned back to the Krolian. "The people of Earth are waiting for the answer to my question. Do you come as friends or conquerors?"

The ambassador sighed. "The truth is, sir, that the question really has no answer. You must surely notice that we are of the same breed."

The general waited.

"It should be obvious to you," said the Krolian, "that we have already occupied Earth . . . about seven thousand years ago."

THE NOTHING

If it hadn't been for the fight with my father I'd never have gone down to the Tavern and then I wouldn't have met the *Nothing*. This *Nothing* was really just an ordinary looking guy. He wasn't worth special attention unless, like me, you were pretending you were Marla Graim, the feelies star, and him Sidney Harch meeting you in the bar to give you a spy capsule.

It was all my father's fault. Imagine him getting angry because I wouldn't take a job burning brush. What kind of work is that for an eighteen-year-old girl anyway? I know my folks were hard pressed for money but that was no excuse for the way he lit into me.

We had the fight over lunch but it was after six o'clock before I got the chance to sneak out of the house. I went down to the Tavern because I knew the old man would be madder than a tele in a lead barrel when he found out. There was no way I could keep it from him, of course. He pried me every time I came home.

The Tavern is a crossroads place where the talent gets together to compare notes, and talk about jobs. I'd only been in there once before, and that time with my father. He warned me not to go there alone because a lot of the jags used the place. You could smell the stuff all over the main room. There was pink smoke from a hyro bowl drifting up around the rafters. Someone had a Venusian Oin filter going. There was a lot of talent there for so early in the evening.

I found an empty corner of the bar and ordered a blue fire because I'd seen Marla Graim ask for one in the feelies. The bartender stared at me sharply and I suspected he was a tele, but he didn't pry. After awhile he floated my drink up to me and 'ported away my money. I sipped the drink the way I'd seen Marla Graim do, but it was too sweet. I tried not to let my face show anything.

The bar mirror gave me a good broad view of the room and I kept looking into it as though I was expecting somebody. I saw him in the mirror and immediately knew he was going to take the seat beside me. I'm not exactly a prescient, but sometimes those things are obvious.

He came across the room, moving with a gladiator ease between the packed tables. That's when I pretended I was Marla Graim waiting at a Port Said bar to pick up a spy capsule from Sidney Harch like in the feelie I'd seen Sunday. This fellow did look a little like Harch—curly hair, dark blue eyes, face all sharp angles as if it had been chiseled by a sculptor who'd left the job uncompleted.

He took the stool beside me as I'd known he would, and ordered a blue fire, easy on the sugar. Naturally, I figured this was a get-acquainted gambit and wondered what to say to him. Suddenly, it struck me as an exciting idea to just ride along with the Marla Graim plot until it came time to leave.

He couldn't do anything to stop me even if he was a 'porter. You see, I'm a pyro and that's a good enough defense for anyone. I glanced down at my circa-twenty skirt and shifted until the slit exposed my garter the way I'd seen Marla Graim do it. This blond lad didn't give it a tumble. He finished his drink, and ordered another.

I whiffed him for one of the cokes, but he was dry. No jag. The other stuff in the room was getting through to me, though, and I was feeling dizzy. I knew I'd have to leave soon and I'd never get another chance to be a Marla Graim type; so I said, "What's yours?"

Oh, he knew I was talking to him all right, but he didn't even look up. It made me mad. A girl has some pride and there I'd unbent enough to start the conversation! There was an ashtray piled with scraps of paper in front of him. I concentrated on it and the paper suddenly flamed. I'm a good pyro when I want to be. Some men have been kind enough to say I could start a fire without the talent. But with a prying father like mine how could I ever know?

The fire got this fellow's attention. He knew I'd started it. He just glanced at me once and turned away. "Leave me alone," he said. "I'm a *Nothing*."

I don't know what it was. Maybe I have a little of the tele like that doctor said once, but I knew he was telling the truth. It wasn't one of those gags like you see in the feelies. You know—where there are two comedians and one says, "What's yours?" And the other one answers, "Nothing."

Only all the time he's levitating the other guy's chair and juggling half a dozen things behind his back, no hands. You know the gag. It's been run into the ground. Well, when he said that, it kind of set me back. I'd never seen a real-life *Nothing* before. Oh, I knew there were some. In the government preserves and such, but I'd never been like this—right next to one.

"Sorry," I said. "I'm a pyro."

He glanced at the ashes in the tray and said, "Yeah, I know."

"There's not much work for pyros any more," I said. "It's the only talent I

have." I turned and looked at him. Handsome in spite of being a *Nothing*.
"What did you do?" I asked.

"I ran away," he said. "I'm a fugitive from the Sonoma Preserve."

That made my blood tingle. Not only a *Nothing,* but a fugitive, too. Just
like in the feelies. I said, "Do you want to hide out at my place?"

That brought him around. He looked me over and he actually blushed.
Actually! I'd never seen a man blush before. That fellow certainly was loaded
with firsts for me.

"People might get the wrong idea when I'm caught," he said. "I'm sure to
be caught eventually. I always am."

I was really getting a feeling for that woman-of-the-world part. "Why not
enjoy your freedom then?" I asked.

I let him see a little more through the circa-twenty slit. He actually turned
away! Imagine!

That's when the police came. They didn't make any fuss. I'd noticed
these two men standing just inside the door watching us. Only I'd thought
they were watching me. They came across the room and one of them bent
over this fellow.

"All right, Claude," he said. "Come quietly."

The other took my arm and said, "You'll have to come, too, sister."

I jerked away from him. "I'm not your sister," I said.

"Oh, leave her alone, fellows," said this Claude. "I didn't tell her anything.
She was just trying to pick me up."

"Sorry," said the cop. "She comes, too."

That's when I began to get scared. "Look," I said. "I don't know what this
is all about."

The man showed me the snout of a hypo gun in his pocket. "Stop the
commotion and come quietly, sister, or I'll have to use this," he said.

So who wants to go to sleep? I went quietly, praying we'd run into my
father or someone I knew so I could explain things. But no such luck.

The police had a plain old jet buggy outside with people clustered around
looking at it. A 'porter in the crowd was having fun jiggling the rear end up
and down off the ground. He was standing back with his hands in his pockets, grinning.

The cop who'd done all the talking just looked toward this 'porter and the
fellow lost his grin and hurried away. I knew then the cop was a tele, although he hadn't touched my mind. They're awfully sensitive about their
code of ethics, some of those teles.

It was fun riding in that old jet buggy, I'd never been in one before. One
of the cops got in back with Claude and me. The other one drove. It was the
strangest feeling, flying up over the bay on the tractors. Usually, whenever I
wanted to go someplace, I'd just ask, polite like, was there a 'porter around
and then I'd think of where I wanted to go and the 'porter would set me
down there quick as a wink.

Of course, I wound up in some old gent's apartment now and then. Some 'porters do that sort of thing for a fee. But a pyro doesn't have to worry about would-be Casanovas. No old gent is going to fool around when his clothes are on fire.

Well, the jet buggy finally set down on an old hospital grounds way back up in the sticks and the cops took us to the main building and into a little office. Walking, mind you. It was shady in the office—not enough lights— and it took a minute for my eyes to adjust after the bright lights in the hall. When they did adjust and I saw the old codger behind the desk I did a real double take. It was Mensor Williams. Yeah. The *Big All*. Anything anybody else can do he can do better.

Somebody worked a switch somewhere and the lights brightened. "Good evening, Miss Carlysle," he said and his little goatee bobbled.

Before I could make a crack about ethics against reading minds, he said, "I'm not intruding into your mental processes. I've merely scanned forward to a point where I learned your name."

A prescient, too!

"There really wasn't any need to bring her," he told the cops. "But it was inevitable that you would." Then he did the funniest thing. He turned to Claude and nodded his head toward me. "How do you like her, Claude?" he asked. Just like I was something offered for sale or something!

Claude said, "Is she the one, Dad?"

Dad! That one smacked me. The *Big All* has a kid and the kid's a *Nothing*!

"She's the one," said Williams.

Claude kind of squared his shoulders and said, "Well, I'm going to throw a stick into the works. I won't do it!"

"Yes, you will," said Williams.

This was all way over my head and I'd had about enough anyway. I said, "Now wait a minute, gentlemen, or I'll set the place on fire! I mean literally!"

"She can do it, too," said Claude, grinning at his father.

"But she won't," said Williams.

"Oh, won't I?" I said. "Well, you just try and stop me!"

"No need to do that," said Williams. "I've seen what's going to happen."

Just like that! These prescients give me the creeps. Sometimes I wonder if they don't give themselves the creeps. Living for them must be like repeating a part you already know. Not for me. I said, "What would happen if I did something different from what you'd seen?"

Williams leaned forward with an interested look in his eyes. "It's never happened," he said. "If it did happen once, that'd be a real precedent."

I can't be sure, but looking at him there, I got the idea he'd really be interested to see something happen different from his forecast. I thought of starting a little fire, maybe in the papers on his desk. But somehow the idea didn't appeal to me. It wasn't that any presence was in my mind telling me not to. I don't know exactly what it was. I just didn't *want* to do it. I said, "What's the meaning of all this double talk?"

The old man leaned back and I swear he seemed kind of disappointed. He said, "It's just that you and Claude are going to be married."

I opened my mouth to speak and nothing came out. Finally, I managed to stammer, "You mean you've looked into the future and seen us *married*? How many kids we're going to have and everything like that?"

"Well, not everything," he said. "All things in the future aren't clear to us. Only certain main-line developments. And we can't see too far into the future for most things. The past is easier. That's been fixed immovably."

"And what if we don't want to?" asked Claude.

"Yeah," I said. "What about that?" But I have to admit the idea wasn't totally repulsive. As I've said, Claude looked like Sidney Harch, only younger. He had something—you can call it animal magnetism if you wish.

The old man just smiled. "Miss Carlysle," he said, "do you honestly object to—"

"As long as I'm going to be in the family you can call me Jean," I said.

I was beginning to feel fatalistic about the whole thing. My great aunt Harriet was a prescient and I'd had experience with them. Now I was remembering the time she told me my kitty was going to die and I hid it in the old cistern and that night it rained and filled the cistern. Naturally the kitty drowned. I never forgave her for not telling me how the kitty was going to die.

Old Williams looked at me and said, "At least *you're* being reasonable."

"I'm not," said Claude.

So I told him about my great aunt Harriet.

"It's the nature of things," said Williams. "Why can't you be as reasonable as she's being, son?"

Claude just sat there with the original stone face.

"Am I so repulsive?" I asked.

He looked at me then. Really looked. I tell you I got warm under it. I know I'm not repulsive. Finally, I guess I blushed.

"You're not repulsive," he said. "I just object to having my whole life ordered out for me like a chess set up."

Stalemate. We sat there for a minute or so, completely silent. Presently Williams turned to me and said, "Well, Miss Carlysle, I presume you're curious about what's going on here."

"I'm not a moron," I said. "This is one of the *Nothing* Preserves."

"Correct," he said. "Only it's more than that. Your education includes the knowledge of how our talents developed from radiation mutants. Does it also include the knowledge of what happens to extremes from the norm?"

Every schoolkid knows that, of course. So I told him. Sure I knew that the direction of development was toward the average. That genius parents tend to have children less smart than they are. This is just general information.

Then the old man threw me the twister. "The talents are disappearing, my dear," he said.

I just sat there and thought about that for awhile. Certainly I knew it'd been harder lately to get a 'porter, even one of the old gent kind.

"Each generation has more children without talents or with talents greatly dulled," said Williams. "We will never reach a point where there are absolutely none, but what few remain will be needed for special jobs in the public interest."

"You mean if I have kids they're liable to be *Nothings*?" I asked.

"Look at your own family," he said. "Your great aunt was a prescient. Have there been any others in your family?"

"Well, no, but—"

"The prescient talent is an extreme," he said. "There are fewer than a thousand left. There are nine of us in my category. I believe you refer to us as the *Big All*."

"But we've got to do something!" I said. "The world'll just go to pot!"

"We *are* doing something," he said. "Right here and on eight other preserves scattered around the world. We're reviving the mechanical and tool skills which supported the pretalent civilization and we're storing the instruments which will make a rebirth of that civilization possible."

He raised a warning hand. "But we must move in secrecy. The world's not yet ready for this information. It would cause a most terrible panic if this were to become known."

"Well, you're prescient. What does happen?" I asked him.

"Unfortunately, none of us are able to determine that," he said. "Either it's an unfixed line or there's some interference which we can't surmount." He shook his head and the goatee wiggled. "There's a cloudy area in the near future beyond which we can't see. None of us."

That scared me. A prescient may give you the creeps, but it's nice to know there's a future into which someone can see. It was as if there suddenly wasn't any future—period. I began to cry a little.

"And our children will be *Nothings*," I said.

"Well, not exactly," said Williams. "Some of them, maybe, but we've taken the trouble of comparing your gene lines—yours and Claude's. You've a good chance of having offspring who will be prescient or telepathic or both. A better than seventy percent chance." His voice got pleading. "The world's going to need that chance."

Claude came over and put a hand on my shoulder. It sent a delicious tingle up my spine. Suddenly, I got a little flash of his thoughts—a picture of us kissing. I'm not really a tele, but like I said, sometimes I get glimmers.

Claude said, "Okay. I guess there's no sense fighting the inevitable. We'll get married."

No more argument. We all traipsed into another room and there was a preacher with everything ready for us, even the ring. Another prescient. He'd come more than a hundred miles to perform the ceremony, he said.

Afterward, I let Claude kiss me once. I was having trouble realizing that I was married. Mrs. Claude Williams. But that's the way it is with the inevitable, I guess.

The old man took my arm then and said there was one small precaution. I'd be going off the grounds from time to time and there'd always be the chance of some unethical tele picking my brains.

They put me under an anesthetube and when I came out of it I had a silver grid in my skull. It itched some, but they said that it would go away. I'd heard of this thing. They called it a blanket.

Mensor Williams said, "Now go home and get your things. You won't need to tell your parents any more than that you have a government job. Come back as soon as you're able."

"Get me a 'porter," I said.

"The grounds are gridded against teleporters," he said. "I'll have to send you in a jet buggy."

And so he did.

I was home in ten minutes.

I went up the stairs to my house. It was after nine o'clock by then. My father was waiting inside the door.

"A fine time for an eighteen-year-old girl to be coming home!" he shouted and he made a tele stab at my mind to see what I'd been up to. These teles and their ethics! Well, he ran smack dab into the blanket and maybe you think that didn't set him back on his heels. He got all quiet suddenly.

I said, "I have a government job. I just came back for my things." Time enough to tell them about the marriage later. They'd have kicked up a fine rumpus if I'd said anything then.

Mama came in and said, "My little baby with a government job! How much does it pay?"

I said, "Let's not be vulgar."

Papa sided with me. "Of course not, Hazel," he said. "Leave the kid alone. A government job! What do you know! Those things pay plenty. Where is it, baby?"

I could see him wondering how much he could tap me for to pay his bills and I began to wonder if I'd have any money at all to keep up the pretense. I said, "The job's at Sonoma Preserve."

Papa said, "What they need with a pyro up there?"

I got a brilliant inspiration. I said, "To keep the *Nothings* in line. A little burn here, a little burn there. You know."

That struck my father funny. When he could stop laughing he said, "I know you, honey. I've watched your think tank pretty close. You'll take care of yourself and no funny business. Do they have nice safe quarters for you up there?"

"The safest," I said.

I felt him take another prod at my blanket and withdraw. "Government work is top secret," I said.

"Sure. I understand," he said.

So I went to my room and got my things packed. The folks made some more fuss about my going away so sudden, but they quieted down when I told them I had to go at once, or lose the chance at the job.

Papa finally said, "Well, if the government isn't safe, then nothing is."

They kissed me goodbye and I promised to write and to visit home on my first free weekend.

"Don't worry, Papa," I said.

The jet buggy took me back to the preserve. When I went into the office, Claude, my husband, was sitting across the desk from his father.

The old man had his hands to his forehead and there were beads of perspiration showing where the fingers didn't cover. Presently, he lowered his hands and shook his head.

"Well?" asked Claude.

"Not a thing," said the old man.

I moved a little bit into the room but they didn't notice me.

"Tell me the truth, Dad," said Claude. "How far ahead did you see us?"

Old Mensor Williams lowered his head and sighed. "All right, son," he said. "You deserve the truth. I saw you meet Miss Carlysle at the Tavern and not another thing. We had to trace her by old-fashioned methods and compare your gene lines like I said. The rest is truth. You know I wouldn't lie to you."

I cleared my throat and they both looked at me.

Claude jumped out of his chair and faced me. "We can get an annulment," he said. "No one has the right to play with other peoples' lives like that."

He looked so sweet and little-boy-like standing there. I knew suddenly I didn't want an annulment. I said, "The younger generation has to accept its responsibilities sometime."

Mensor Williams got an eager look in his eyes. I turned to the old man, said, "Was that seventy percent figure correct?"

"Absolutely correct, my dear," he said. "We've checked every marriageable female he's met because he carries my family's dominant line. Your combination was the best. Far higher than we'd hoped for."

"Is there anything else you can tell us about our future?" I asked.

He shook his head. "It's all cloudy," he said. "You're on your own."

I got that creepy feeling again and looked up at my husband. Little laugh wrinkles creased at the corners of Claude's eyes and he smiled. Then another thought struck me. If we were on our own, that meant we were shaping our own future. It wasn't fixed. And no nosey prescient could come prying in on us, either. A woman kind of likes that idea. Especially on her wedding night.

CEASE FIRE

Snow slanted across the frozen marshland, driven in fitful gusts. It drifted in a low mound against the wooden Observation Post. The antennae of the Life Detector atop the OP swept back and forth in a rhythmic halfcircle like so many frozen sticks brittle with rime ice.

The snow hid all distance, distorted substance into gray shadows without definition. A suggestion of brightness to the north indicated the sun that hung low on the horizon even at midnight in this season.

Out of possible choices of a place for a world-shattering invention to be born, this did not appear in the running.

A rifle bullet spanged against an abandoned tank northeast of the OP, moaned away into the distance. The bullet only emphasized the loneliness, the isolation of the OP set far out ahead of the front lines of the Arctic battlefields of 1972. Behind the post to the south stretched the long reaches of the Canadian barren lands. An arm of the Arctic Ocean below Banks Island lay hidden in the early snow storm to the north.

One operator—drugged to shivering wakefulness—stood watch in the OP. The space around him was barely six feet in diameter, crammed with equipment, gridded screens glowing a pale green with spots that indicated living flesh: a covey of ptarmigan, a possible Arctic fox. Every grid point on the screens held an aiming code for mortar fire.

This site was designated "OP 114" by the Allied command. It was no place for the sensitive man who had found himself pushed, shunted and shamed into this position of terror. The fact that he did occupy OP 114 only testified to the terrible urgencies that governed this war.

Again a rifle bullet probed the abandoned tank. Corporal Larry Hulser— crouched over the OP's screens—tried to get a track on the bullet. It had seemed to come from the life-glow spot he had identified as probably an Arctic fox.

Much too small for a human, he thought. *Or is it?*

The green glow of the screens underlighted Hulser's dark face, swept shadows upward where they merged with his black hair. He chewed his lips, his eyes darting nervously with the fear he could never hide, the fear that made him the butt of every joke back at the barracks.

Hulser did not look like a man who could completely transform his society. He looked merely like an indefinite lump of humanity encased in a Life Detector shield, crouching in weird green shadows.

In the distant days of his youth, one of Hulser's chemistry professors had labeled him during a faculty tea: *"A mystic—sure to fail in the modern world."*

The glow spot Hulser had identified as a fox shifted its position.

Should I call out the artillery? Hulser wondered. *No. This could be the one they'd choose to investigate with a flying detector. And if the pilot identified the glow as a fox*—Hulser cringed with the memory of the hazing he had taken on the wolf he'd reported two months earlier.

"Wolfie Hulser!"

I'm too old for this game, he thought. *Thirty-eight is too old. If there were only some way to end—*

Another rifle bullet spanged against the shattered tank. Hulser tried to crouch lower in the tiny wooden OP. The bullets were like questing fingers reaching out for unrecognized metal—to identify an OP. When the bullets found their mark, a single 200 mm. mortar shell followed, pinpointed by echophones. Or it could be as it had been with Breck Wingate, another observer.

Hulser shivered at the memory.

They had found Wingate hunched forward across his instruments, a neat hole through his chest from side to side just below the armpits. Wind had whistled through the wall of the OP from a single bullet hole beside Wingate. The enemy had found him and never known.

Hulser glanced up nervously at the plywood walls: all that shielded him from the searching bullets—a wood shell designed to absorb the metal seekers and send back the sound of a bullet hitting a snowdrift. A rolled wad of plot paper filled a bullet hole made on some other watch near the top of the dome.

Again Hulser shivered.

And again a bullet spanged against the broken tank. Then the ground rumbled and shook as a mortar shell zeroed the tank.

Discouraging us from using it as an OP, thought Hulser.

He punched the *backtrack* relay to give the mortar's position to his own artillery, but without much hope. The enemy was beginning to use the new "shift" shells that confused *backtrack*.

The phone beside his L-D screens glowed red. Hulser leaned into the cone of silence, answered: "OP 114. Hulser."

The voice was Sergeant Chamberlain's. "What was that mortar shooting at, Wolfie?"

Hulser gritted his teeth, explained about the tank.

Chamberlain's voice barked through the phone: "We shouldn't have to call for an explanation of these things! Are you sure you're awake and alert?"

"Yeah, Sarg."

"Okay. Keep your eyes open, Wolfie."

The red glow of the phone died.

Hulser trembled with rage. *Wolfie!*

He thought of Sergeant Mike Chamberlain: tall, overbearing, the irritating nasal twang in his voice. And he thought of what he'd like to do to Chamberlain's narrow, small-eyed face and its big nose. He considered calling back and asking for "Schnozzle" Chamberlain.

Hulser grinned tightly. *That'd get him! And he'd have to wait another four hours before he could do anything about it.*

But the thought of the certain consequences in arousing Chamberlain's anger wiped the grin from Hulser's face.

Something moved on his central screen. The fox. Or was it a fox? It moved across the frozen terrain toward the shattered tank, stopped halfway.

A fox investigating the strange odors of cordite and burned gas? he wondered. *Or is it the enemy?*

With this thought came near panic. If any living flesh above a certain minimum size—roughly fifty kilos—moved too close to an OP without the proper IFF, the hut and all in it exploded in a blinding flash of thermite: everything incinerated to prevent the enemy from capturing the observer's Life Detector shield.

Hulser studied the grid of his central screen. It reminded him of a game he'd played as a boy: two children across a room from one another, ruled graph paper hidden behind books in their laps. Each player's paper contained secretly marked squares: four in a row—a battleship, three in a row—a destroyer, two in a . . .

Again the glow on his screen moved toward the tank crater.

He stared at the grid intersection above the glowing spot, and far away in his mind a thought giggled at him: *Call and tell 'em you have a battleship on your screen at O-6-C. That'd get you a Section Eight right out of this man's army!*

Out of the army!

His thoughts swerved abruptly to New Oakland, to Carol Jean. *To think of her having our baby back there and—*

Again the (fox?) moved toward the tank crater.

But his mind was hopelessly caught now in New Oakland. He thought of all the lonely years before Carol: to work five days a week at Planetary Chemicals . . . the library and endless pages of books (and another channel

of his mind commented: *You scattered your interests too widely!*) . . . the
tiny cubbyhole rooms of his apartment . . . the tasteless—

Now, the (fox?) darted up to the tank crater, skirted it.

Hulser's mind noted the movement, went right on with its reverie: *Then
Carol! Why couldn't we have found each other sooner? Just one month together and—*

Another small glowing object came on the screen near the point where
he'd seen the first one. It, too, darted toward the tank crater.

Hulser was back in the chill present, a deadly suspicion gnawing him:
*The enemy has a new type of shield, not as good as ours. It merely reduces
image size!*

Or is it a pair of foxes?

Indecision tore at him.

They could have a new shield, he thought. *We don't have a corner on the
scientific brains.*

And a piece of his mind wandered off in the new direction—the war
within the war: the struggle for equipment superiority. A new weapon—a
new shield—a better weapon—a better shield. It was like a terrible ladder
dripping with maimed flesh.

They could have a new shield, his mind repeated.

And another corner of his mind began to think about the shields, the
complex flicker-lattice that made human flesh transparent to—

Abruptly, he froze. In all clarity, every diagram in place, every equation,
every formula complete—all spread out in his mind was the instrument he
knew could end this war. Uncontrolled shivering took over his body. He
swallowed in a dry throat.

His gaze stayed on the screen before him. The two glow spots joined,
moved into the tank crater. Hulser bent into the cone of silence at his phone.
"This is OP 114. I have two greenies at co-ordinates O-6-C-sub T-R. I think
they're setting up an OP!"

"Are you sure?" It was Chamberlain's nasal twang.

"Of course I'm sure!"

"We'll see."

The phone went dead.

Hulser straightened, wet his lips with his tongue. *Will they send a plane for
a sky look? They don't really trust me.*

A rending explosion at the tank crater answered him.

Immediately, a rattle of small arms fire sprang up from the enemy lines.
Bullets quested through the gray snow.

It was an enemy OP! Now, they know we have an observer out here!

Another bullet found the dome of the OP.

Hulser stared at the hole in terror. *What if they kill me? My idea will die with me! The war will go on and on and—*He jerked toward the phone, screamed into it: "Get me out of here! Get me out of here! Get me out of here!"

When they found him, Hulser was still mumbling the five words.

Chamberlain's lanky form crouched before the OP's crawl hole. The three muffled figures behind him ignored the OP, their heads turning, eyes staring off into the snow, rifles at the ready. The enemy's small arms fire had stopped.

Another one's broke, thought Chamberlain. *I thought shame might make him last a little while longer!*

He dragged Hulser out into the snow, hissed: "What is it, you? Why'd you drag us out into this?"

Hulser swallowed, said, "Sarge, please believe me. I know how to detonate enemy explosives from a distance without even knowing where the explosives are. I can—"

"Detonate explosives from a distance?" Chamberlain's eyes squinted until they looked like twin pieces of flint. *Another one for the head shrinkers unless we can shock him out of it,* he thought. He said, "You've gone off your rocker, you have. Now, you git down at them instruments and—"

Hulser paled. "No, Sarg! I have to get back where—"

"I could shoot your head off right where you—"

Fear, frustration, anger—all of the complex pressure-borne emotions in Hulser—forced the words out of him: "You big-nosed, ignorant lump. I can end this war! You hear?" His voice climbed. "Take me back to the lieutenant! I'm gonna send your kind back under the rocks, you—"

Chamberlain's fist caught Hulser on the side of the head, sent him tumbling into the snow. Even as he fell, Hulser's mind said: *But you told him, man! You finally told him!*

The sergeant glanced back at his companions, thought, *If the enemy heard him, we've had it!* He motioned one of the other men in close. "Mitch, take the watch on this OP. We'll have to get Hulser back."

The other nodded, ducked through the crawl hole.

Chamberlain bent over Hulser. "You stinkin' coward!" he hissed. "I've half a mind to kill you where you sit! But I'm gonna take you in so's I can have the personal pleasure of watchin' you crawl when they turn the heat on you! Now you git on your feet! An' you git to walkin'!"

Major Tony Lipari—"Tony the Lip" to his men—leaned against the canvas-padded wall of his dugout, hands clasped behind his head. He was a thin, oily-looking man with black hair, parted in the middle and slicked to his head like two beetle wings. In civilian life he had sold athletic supplies from a wholesale house. He had once worn a turban to an office party, and it had been like opening a door on his appearance. Somewhere in his ancestry there had been a Moor.

The major was tired (*Casualty reports! Endless casualty reports!*) and irritable, faintly nervous.

We don't have enough men to man the OPs now! he thought. *Do we have to lose another one to the psych boys?*

He said, "The lieuten—" His voice came out in a nervous squeak, and he stopped, cleared his throat. "The lieutenant has told me the entire story, corporal. Frankly, it strikes me as utterly fantastic."

Corporal Hulser stood at attention before the major. "Do I have the major's permission to speak?"

Lipari nodded. "Please do."

"Sir, I was a chemist . . . I mean as a civilian. I got into this branch because I'd dabbled in electronics and they happened to need L-D observers more than they needed chemists. Now, with our shields from—" He broke off, suddenly overwhelmed by the problem of convincing Major Lipari.

He's telling me we need L-D observers! thought Lipari. He said, "Well, go on, Hulser."

"Sir, do you know anything about chemistry?"

"A little."

"What I mean is, do you understand Redox equations and substitution reactions of—"

"Yes, yes. Go on!"

Hulser swallowed, thought: *He doesn't understand. Why won't he send me back to someone who does?* He said, "Sir, you're aware that the insulation layer of our L-D shield is a special kind of protection for—"

"Certainly! Insulates the wearer from the electrical charge of the suit!"

Hulser goggled at the major. "Insulates . . . Oh, no, sir. Begging the major's pardon, but—"

"Is this necessary, corporal?" asked Lipari. And he thought: *If he'd only stop this act and get back to work! It's so obvious he's faking! If—*

Sir, didn't you get the—"

"I had a full quota of L-D shield orientation when they called me back into the service," said Lipari. "Infantry's my specialty, of course. Korea, you know. But I understand how to operate a shield. Go on, corporal." He kicked his chair away from the wall.

"Sir, what that insulation layer protects the wearer from is a kind of pseudo-substitution reaction in the skin. The suit's field can confuse the body into producing nitrogen bubbles at—"

"Yes, Hulser! I know all that! But what's this have to do with your wonderful idea?"

Hulser took a deep breath. "Sir, I can build a projector on the principle of the L-D suits that will produce an artificial substitution reaction in any explosive. I'm sure I can!"

"You're sure?"

"Yes, sir. For example, I could set up such a reaction in Trinox that would produce fluorine and ionized hydrogen—in minute quantities, of course—but sufficient that any nearby field source would detonate—"

"How would you make sure there was such a field in the enemy's storage area?"

"Sir! Everybody wears L-D shields of one kind or another! They're field generators. Or an internal combustion motor . . . or . . . or just anything! If you have an explosive mixture collapsing from one system into another in the presence of fluorine and hydrogen—" He shrugged. "It'd explode if you looked cross-eyed at it!"

Lipari cleared his throat. "I see." Again he leaned back against the wall. The beginning of an eyestrain headache tugged at his temples. *Now, the put-up-or-shut-up,* he thought. He said, "How do we build this wonderful projector, corporal?"

"Sir, I'll have to sit down with some machinists and some E-techs and—"

"Corporal, I'll decide who sits down with whom among my men. Now. I'll tell you what you do. You just draw up the specifications for your projector and leave them with me. I'll see that they get into the proper hands through channels."

"Sir, it's not that simple. I have all the specs in my head now, yes, but in anything like this you have to work out bugs that—"

"We have plenty of technical experts who can do that," said Lipari. And he thought: *Why doesn't he give up? I gave him the chance to duck out gracefully! Scribble something on some paper, give it to me. That's the end of it!*

"But sir—"

"Corporal! My orderly will give you paper and pencil. You just—"

"Sir! It can't be done that way!"

Lipari rubbed his forehead. "Corporal Hulser, I am giving you an order. You will sit down and produce the plans and specifications for your projector. You will do it now."

Hulser tasted a sourness in his mouth. He swallowed. *And that's the last we'd ever hear of Corporal Larry Hulser,* he thought. *Tony the Lip would get the credit.*

He said, "Sir, after you submit my plans, what would you do if someone asked, for example, how the polar molecules of—"

"You will explain all of these things in your outline. Do I make myself clear, corporal?"

"Sir, it would take me six months to produce plans that could anticipate every—"

"You're stalling, corporal!" Major Lipari pushed himself forward, came to his feet. He lowered his voice. "Let's face it, Hulser. You're faking! I know it. You know it. You just had a bellyful of war and you decided you wanted out."

Hulser shook his head from side to side.

"It's not that simple, corporal. Now. I've shown you in every way I can that I understand this, that I'm willing to—"

"Begging the major's pardon, but—"

"You will do one of two things, Corporal Hulser. You either produce the diagrams, sketches or whatever to prove that you *do* have a worthy idea, or you will go back to your unit. I'm done fooling with you!"

"Sir, don't you under—"

"I could have you shot under the Articles of War!"

And Lipari thought: *That's what he needs—a good shock!*

Bitter frustration almost overwhelmed Hulser. He felt the same kind of anger that had goaded him to attack Sergeant Chamberlain. "Major, enough people know about my idea by now that at least some of them would wonder if you hadn't shot the goose that laid the golden egg!"

Lipari's headache was full-blown now. He pushed his face close to Hulser's. "I have some alternatives to a firing squad, corporal!"

Hulser returned Lipari's angry glare. "It has occurred to me, *sir,* that this project would suddenly become 'our' project, and then 'your' project, and somewhere along the line a mere corporal would get lost."

Lipari's mouth worked wordlessly. Presently, he said, "That did it, Hulser! I'm holding you for a general court! There's one thing I can do without cooking any goose but yours!"

And that ends the matter as far as I'm concerned, thought Lipari. *What a day!*

He turned toward the door of his dugout: "Sergeant!"

The door opened to admit Chamberlain's beanpole figure. He crossed the room, came to attention before Lipari, saluted. "Sir?"

"This man is under arrest, sergeant," said Lipari. "Take him back to area headquarters under guard and have him held for a general court. On your way out send in my orderly."

Chamberlain saluted. "Yes, sir." He turned, took Hulser's arm. "Come along, Hulser."

Lipari turned away, groped on a corner shelf for his aspirin. He heard the door open and close behind him. And it was not until this moment that he asked himself: Could that crackpot actually have had a workable idea? He found the aspirin, shrugged the thought away. *Fantastic!*

Hulser sat on an iron cot with his head in his hands. The cell walls around him were flat, riveted steel. It was a space exactly the length of the cot, twice as wide as the cot. At his left, next to the foot of the bed, was a barred door. To his right, at the other end of the floor space, was a folding washbasin with water closet under. The cell smelled foul despite an overriding stink of disinfectant.

Why don't they get it over with? he asked himself. *Three days of this madhouse! How long are they—*

The cell door rattled.

Hulser looked up. A wizened figure in a colonel's uniform stood on the other side of the bars. He was a tiny man, gray-haired, eyes like a curious bird, a dried parchment skin. In the proper costume he would have looked like a medieval sorcerer.

A youthful MP sergeant stepped into view, unlocked the door, stood aside. The colonel entered the cell.

"Well, well," he said.

Hulser came to his feet, saluted.

"Will you be needing me, sir?" asked the MP sergeant.

"Eh?" The colonel turned. "Oh. No, sergeant. Just leave that door open and—"

"But sir—"

"Nobody could get out of this cell block, could they sergeant?"

"No, sir. But—"

"Then just leave the door open and run along."

"Yes, sir." The sergeant saluted, frowned, turned away. His footsteps echoed down the metal floor of the corridor.

The colonel turned back to Hulser. "So you're the young man with the bright ideas."

Hulser cleared his throat. "Yes, sir."

The colonel glanced once around the cell. "I'm Colonel Page of General Savage's staff. Chemical warfare."

Hulser nodded.

"The general's adjutant suggested that I come over and talk to you," said Page. "He thought a chemist might—"

"Page!" said Hulser. "You're not the Dr. Edmond Page who did the work on pseudo-lithium?"

The colonel's face broke into a pleased smile. "Why . . . yes, I am."

"I read everything about your work that I could get my hands on," said Hulser. "It struck me that if you'd just—" His voice trailed off.

"Do go on," said Page.

Hulser swallowed. "Well, if you'd just moved from organic chemistry into inorganic, that—" He shrugged.

"I might have induced direct chemical rather than organic reactions?" asked Page.

"Yes, sir."

"That thought didn't occur to me until I was on my way over here," said Page. He gestured toward the cot. "Do sit down."

Hulser slumped back to the cot.

Page looked around, finally squeezed past Hulser's knees, sat down on the lid of the water closet. "Now, let's find out just what your idea is."

Hulser stared at his hands.

"I've discussed this with the general," said Page. "We feel that you may know what you're talking about. We would deeply appreciate a complete explanation."

"What do I have to lose?" asked Hulser.

"You may have reason for feeling bitter," said Page. "But after reading the charges against you I would say that you've been at least partly responsible for your present situation." He glanced at his wristwatch. "Now, tell me exactly how you propose to detonate munitions at a distance . . . this projector you've talked about."

Hulser took a deep breath. *This is a chemist,* he thought. *Maybe I can convince him.* He looked up at Page, began explaining.

Presently, the colonel interrupted. "But it takes enormous amounts of energy to change the atomic—"

"I'm not talking about changing atomic structure in that sense, sir. Don't you see it? I merely set up an artificial condition *as though* a catalyst were present. A pseudo-catalyst. And this brings out of the static mixture substances that are already there: Ionized hydrogen from moisture—fluorine from the actual components in the case of Trinox. White phosphorus from Ditrate, Nitric oxide and rhombic sulfur from common gunpowder."

Page wet his lips with his tongue. "But what makes you think that—in a nonorganic system—the presence of the pseudo-catalyst—" He shook his head. "Of course! How stupid of me! You'd first get a polar reaction—just as I did with pseudo-lithium. And that would be the first step into—" His eyes widened and he stared at Hulser. "My dear boy, I believe you've opened an entirely new field in nonorganic chemistry!"

"Do you see it, sir?"

"Of course I see it!" Page got to his feet. "You'd be creating an artificial radical with unstable perimeter. The presence of the slightest bit of moisture in that perimeter would give you your ionized hydrogen and—" He clapped his hands like a small boy in glee. "Kapowie!"

Hulser smiled.

Page looked down at him. "Corporal, I do believe your projector might work. I confess that I don't understand about field lattices and these other electronic matters, but you apparently do."

"Yes, sir."

"How did you ever stumble onto this?" asked Page.

"I was thinking about the lattice effect in our Life Detector systems—when suddenly, there it was: the complete idea!"

Page nodded. "It was one of those things that had to remain dormant until the precisely proper set of circumstances." Page squeezed past Hulser's knees. "No, no. Stay right there. I'm going to set up a meeting with Colonel Allenby of the L-D section, and I'll get in someone with more of a mechanical bent—probably Captain Stevens." He nodded. "Now, corporal, you just stay right here until—" His glance darted around the cell, and he laughed nervously. "Don't you worry, young man. We'll have you out of here in a few hours."

Hulser was to look back on the five weeks of the first phase in "Operation Big Boom" as a time of hectic unreality. Corps ordered the project developed in General Savage's reserve area after a set of preliminary plans had been shipped outside. The thinking was that there'd be less chance of a security leak that close to a combat zone, and that the vast barrens of the reserve area offered better opportunity for a site free of things that could detonate mysteriously and lead to unwanted questions.

But Corps was taking no chances. They ringed the area with special detachments of MPs. Recording specialists moved in on the project, copied everything for shipment stateside.

They chose an open tableland well away from their own munitions for the crucial test. It was a barren, windy place: gray rocks poking up from frozen earth. The long black worm of a power cable stretched away into the distance behind the test shelter.

A weasel delivered Hulser and Page to the test site. The projector box sat on the seat between them. It was housed in a green container two feet square and four feet long. A glass tube protruded from one end. A power connection, sealed and with a red "do not connect" sign, centered the opposite end. A tripod mounting occupied one side at the balance point.

The morning was cold and clear with a brittle snap to the air. The sky had a deep cobalt quality, almost varnished in its intensity.

About fifty people were gathered for the test. They were strung out through the shelter—a long shed open along one side. An empty tripod stood near the open side and almost in the center. On both sides of the tripod technicians sat before recording instruments. Small black wires trailed away ahead of them torward an ebony mound almost a mile from the shed and directly opposite the open side.

General Savage already was on the scene, talking with a stranger who had arrived that morning under an impressive air cover. The stranger had worn civilian clothes. Now, he was encased in an issue parka and snowpants. He didn't look or act like a civilian. And it was noted that General Savage addressed him as "sir."

The general was a brusque, thick-bodied man with the overbearing confidence of someone secure in his own ability. His face held a thick-nosed, square-jawed bulldog look. In fatigues without insignia, he could have been mistaken for a sergeant. He looked the way a hard, old-line sergeant is expected to look. General Savage's men called him "Me Tarzan" mainly because he took snow baths, mother naked, in subzero weather.

A white helmeted security guard ringed the inside of the test shed. Hulser noted that they wore no sidearms, carried no weapons except hand-held bayonets. He found himself thinking that he would not have been surprised to see them carrying crossbows.

General Savage waved to Page as the colonel and Hulser entered the shed. Colonel Page returned the gesture, stopped before a smooth-cheeked lieutenant near the tripod.

"Lieutenant," said Page, "have all explosives except the test stack been removed from the area?"

The lieutenant froze to ramrod attention, saluted, "Yes, sir, colonel."

Page took a cigarette from his pocket. "Let me have your cigarette lighter, please, lieutenant."

"Yes, sir." The lieutenant fumbled in a pocket, withdrew a chrome lighter, handed it to Page.

Colonel Page took the lighter in his hand, looked at it for a moment, hurled both lighter and cigarette out into the snow. The lighter landed about sixty feet away.

The lieutenant paled, then blushed.

The colonel said, "Every cigarette lighter, every match. And check with everyone to see that they took those special pills at least four hours ago. We don't want any *internal* combustion without a motor around it."

The lieutenant looked distraught, "Yes, sir."

"And, lieutenant, stop the last weasel and have the driver wait to cart the stuff you collect out of our area."

"Yes, sir." The lieutenant hurried away.

Page turned back to Hulser, who had mounted the projector on its tripod, and now stood beside it.

"All ready, sir," said Hulser. "Shall I connect the cable?"

"What do you think?" asked Page.

"We're as ready as we'll ever be."

"Okay. Connect it, then stand by with the switch in your hands."

Hulser turned to comply. And now, as the moment of the critical test approached, he felt his legs begin to tremble. He felt sure that everyone could see his nervousness.

A tense stillness came over the people in the shed.

General Savage and his visitor approached. The general was explaining the theory of the projector.

His visitor nodded.

Seen close-up, the other man gave the same impression of hard competence that radiated from General Savage—only more competent, harder. His cheekbones were like two ridges of tan rock beneath cavernous sockets, brooding dark eyes.

General Savage pointed to the black mound of explosives in the distance. "We have instruments in there with the explosives, sir. The wires connect them with our recorders here in the shed. We have several types of explosives to be tested, including kerosene, gasoline, engine oil. Everything we could lay our hands on except atomics. But if these things blow, then we'll know the projector also will work on atomics."

The visitor spoke, and his voice came out with a quality like a stick dragged through gravel. "It was explained to me that—the theory being correct—this projector will work on any petroleum fuel, including coal."

"Yes, sir," said Savage. "It is supposed to ignite coal. We have a few lumps in a sack to one side. You can't see it because of the snow. But our instruments will tell us which of these things are effected—" he glanced at Hulser "—if any."

Colonel Page returned from checking the recording instruments.

Savage turned to the colonel. "Are we ready, Ed?"

"Yes, general." He glanced at Hulser, nodded. "Let's go, Larry. Give it power."

Hulser depressed the switch in his hand, involuntarily closed his eyes, then snapped them open and stared at the distant explosives.

A low humming arose from the projector.

Page spoke to the general. "It'll take a little time for the effect to build u—"

As he started to say "up" the mound of explosives went *up* in a giant roaring and rumbling. Colonel Page was left staring at the explosion, his mouth shaped to say "p."

Steam and dust hid the place where the explosives had been.

The gravel voice of the visitor spoke behind Hulser. "Well, there goes the whole shooting match, general. And I *do* mean shooting!"

"It's what we were afraid of, sir," said Savage. "But there's no help for it now." He sounded bitter.

Hulser was struck by the bitterness in both voices. He turned, became conscious that the lieutenant whom Page had reprimanded was beating at a flaming breast pocket, face livid. The people around him were laughing, trying to help.

Page had hurried along the line of recorders, was checking each one.

The significance of the lieutenant's antics suddenly hit Hulser. *Matches! He forgot his spare matches after losing his cigarette lighter!* Hulser glanced to where the colonel had thrown the lighter, saw a black patch in the snow.

Page returned from checking the recorders. "We can't be sure about the coal, but as nearly as we can determine, it touched off everything else in the stack!" He put an arm on Hulser's shoulder. "This young genius has won the war for us."

Savage turned, scowled at Hulser.

The (civilian?) snorted.

But Hulser was staring out at the explosion crater, a look of euphoria on his face.

The technicians were moving out into the area now, probing cautiously for unexploded fragments.

The general and his visitor exchanged a glance that could have meant anything.

Savage signaled his radio operator to call for transportation.

Presently, a line of weasels came roaring up to the test site.

Savage took Hulser's arm in a firm grip. "You'd better come with us. You're a valuable piece of property now."

Hulser's mind came back to the curious conversation between Savage and the visitor after the explosion, and he was struck by the odd sadness in the general's voice. *Could he be an old war dog sorry to see it end?* Somehow, on looking at the general, that didn't fit.

They sped across the barrens to the base, Hulser uncomfortable between the general and his visitor. Apparently, no one wanted to discuss what had just happened. Hulser was made uncomfortable by the lack of elation around him. He looked at the back of the driver's neck, but that told him nothing.

They strode into the general's office, an oblong room without windows. Maps lined the walls. A low partition separated one space containing two barren tables from another space containing three desks one set somewhat apart. They crossed to the separate desk.

Savage indicated his visitor. "This is Mr. Sladen." There was a slight hesitation on the "mister."

Hulser suppressed a desire to salute, shook hands. The other man had a hard grip in an uncalloused hand.

Sladen's gravelly baritone came out brusque and commanding. "Brief him, general. I'll go get my people and their gear together. We'll have to head right back."

Savage nodded. "Thank you, sir. I'll get right at it."

Sladen cast a speculative look at Hulser. "Make sure he understands clearly what has just happened. I don't believe he's considered it."

"Yes, sir."

Sladen departed.

Hulser felt an odd sinking sensation in his stomach.

Savage said, "I'm not rank happy, Hulser, and we haven't much time. We're going to forget about military formality for a few minutes."

Hulser nodded without speaking.

"Do you know what has just happened?" asked Savage.

"Yes, sir. But what puzzles me is that you people don't seem pleased about our gaining the whip hand so we can win this war. It's—"

"It's not certain that we have the whip hand." Savage sat down at his desk, picked up a book bound in red leather.

"You mean the enemy—"

"Bright ideas like yours just seem to float around in the air, Hulser. They may already have it, or they could be working on it. Otherwise, I'd have seen that your brainstorm was buried. It seems that once human beings realize something can be done, they're not satisfied until they've done it."

"Have there been any signs that the enemy—"

"No. But neither have *they* seen any signs of *our* new weapon . . . I hope. The point is: we do have it and we're going to use it. We'll probably overwhelm them before they can do anything about it. And that'll be the end of *this* war."

"But, if explosives are made obsolete, that'll mean an end to all wars," protested Hulser. "That's what I'm concerned about!"

The general sneered. "Nothing, my bright-eyed young friend, has thus far made war impossible! When this one's over, it'll be just a matter of time until there's another war, both sides using your projector."

"But, sir—"

"So the next war will be fought with horse cavalry, swords, crossbows and lances," said Savage. "And there'll be other little *improvements*!" He slammed the red book onto his desk, surged to his feet. "Elimination of explosives only makes espionage, poisons, poison gas, germ warfare—all of these—a necessity!"

"How can you—"

"Don't you understand, Hulser? You've made the military use of explosives impossible. That means gasoline. The internal combustion motor is out. That means jet fuels. Airplanes are out. That means gunpowder. Everything from the smallest sidearm to the biggest cannon is out!"

"Certainly, but—"

"But we have other alternatives, Hulser. We have the weapons King Arthur used. And we have some *modern* innovations: poison gases, curare-tipped crossbow bolts, bacterial—"

"But the Geneva Convention—"

"Geneva Convention be damned! And that's just what will happen to it as soon as a big enough group of people decide to ignore it!" General Savage hammered a fist on his desk. "Get this! Violence is a part of human life. The lust for power is a part of human life. As long as people want power badly enough, they'll use any means to get it—fair or foul! Peaceful or otherwise!"

"I think you're being a pessimist, sir."

"Maybe I am. I *hope* I am. But I come from a long line of military people. We've seen some things to make us pessimists."

"But the pressures for peace—"

"Have thus far not been strong enough to prevent wars, Hulser." The general shook his head. "I'll tell you something, my young friend: When I first saw the reference to your ideas in the charges against you, I had the sinking sensation one gets when going down for the third time. I hoped against hope that you were wrong, but I couldn't afford *not* to investigate. I hoped that Major Lipari and Sergeant Chamberlain had you pegged for—"

The general stopped, glared at Hulser. "There's another bone I have to pick with you! Your treatment of two fine soliders was nothing short of juvenile! If it wasn't for the Liparis and the Chamberlains, you'd be getting thirty lashes every morning from your local slavekeeper!"

"But, sir—"

"Don't 'But, sir' me, Hulser! If there was time before you leave, I'd have you deliver personal apologies to both of them!"

Hulser blushed, shook his head. "I don't know. All I really know is that I was sure my idea would work, and that Lipari and Chamberlain didn't understand. And I knew if I was killed, or if my idea wasn't developed, the enemy might get it first."

Savage leaned back against his desk, passed a hand across his eyes. "You were right, of course. It's just that you were bucking the system, and you're not the right kind to buck the system. Your kind usually fails when you try."

Hulser sighed.

"You're now a valuable piece of property, my lad. So don't feel sorry for yourself. You'll be sent home where you can be around when your wife has that child."

Hulser looked surprised.

"Oh, yes, we found out about her," said Savage. "We thought at first you were just working a good dodge to get home to her." He shrugged. "You'll probably have it fairly soft now. You'll be guarded and coddled. You'll be expected to produce another act of *genius*! The Lord knows, maybe you *are* a genius."

"You wait and see, sir. I think this will mean an end to all wars."

The general suddenly looked thoughtful. "Hulser, a vastly underrated and greatly despised writer—in some circles—once said, 'There is nothing more difficult to take in hand, more perilous to conduct, or more uncertain in its success, than to take the lead in the introduction of a new order of things.' That's a very deep statement, Hulser. And there you are, way out in front with 'a new order of things.' I hope for the sake of that child you're going to have—for the sake of all children—that we don't have another war." He shrugged. "But I don't hold out too—"

Sladen popped back into the office. "Our air cover's coming up, general. We'll have to take him like he is. Send his gear along later, will you?"

"Certainly, sir." Savage straightened, stuck out his right hand, shook with Hulser. "Good luck, Hulser. You take what I said to heart. It's the bitter truth that men of war have to live with. You weren't attacking the source of the problem with your bright idea. You were attacking one of the symptoms."

Savage's left hand came up from his desk with the red book. "Here's a gift for that child you're going to have." He pressed the book into Hulser's hands. "The next generation will need to understand this book."

Hulser had time to say, "Thank you, sir." Then he was propelled out the door by Sladen.

It was not until he was on the plane winging south that Hulser had an opportunity to examine the book. Then he gripped it tightly in both hands, stared out the window at the sea of clouds. The book was a limited edition copy, unexpurgated, of the works of Niccolo Machiavelli, the master of deceit and treachery.

EPILOGUE

Many people labor under the misapprenhension that the discovery of the Hulser Detonator was made in a secret government laboratory. In actuality, the genius of Dr. Lawrence Hulser was first seen on the Arctic battlefields of 1972 where he conceived his idea and where that idea was immediately recognized.

Beecher Carson, *"The Coming of the Sword—A History of Ancient and Modern Wars"*—Vol. 6, p. 112.

A MATTER
OF TRACES

Herday, Domen 18, 7102 (N.C.)
Wershteen City, Aspidiske VII

The Special Subcommittee on Intergalactic Culture (*see page 33*) met, pursuant to call, at 1600 in the committee room, 8122 Senate Office Building, Wershteen City, Senator Jorj C. Zolam, chairman of the subcommittee, presiding.

Also present: Senator Arden G. Pingle of Proxistu I; Mergis W. Ledder, counsel to the subcommittee; Jorj X. McKie, saboteur extraordinary to the committee.

Senator Zolam: The subcommittee will be in order. Our first witness will be the Hon. Glibbis Hablar, Secretary of Fusion.

We are glad to see you, Mr. Secretary. We believe that you have some of the best cultural fusion experts in the universe working in your Department, and we are in the habit of leaning heavily upon them for our records of factual data.

As you know, our subcommittee is working under Senate Resolution 1443 of the 803rd Congress, First Session, to make a full and complete investigation of complaints received from economy groups that the Historical Preservation Teams of the Bureau of Cultural Affairs are excessively wasteful of their funds.

Now, Mr. Secretary, I understand that you are prepared to present a sample of the work being done by your Historical Preservation Teams.

Secretary Hablar: Yes, Senator. I have here a tri-di record of an interview with one of the early pioneers to Gomeisa III, also a transcription of the interview, and some explanatory matter necessary for a complete understanding of this exhibit.

Senator Zolam: Do you wish to project the tri-di at this time?

Secretary Hablar: Unfortunately, Senator, I am unable to do that. My projector has been officially sabotaged—presumably to save the time of the committee. I am embarrassed by my inability to . . .

Senator Zolam: Committee Saboteur McKie will enter an official explanation for the record.

Saboteur McKie: The Secretary may make the official excuse that his tri-di recording was faulty.

Secretary Hablar: Thank you, Mr. McKie. Your courtesy is deeply appreciated. May I add to my official excuse that the faulty recording is attributable to antiquated equipment which our appropriation for the last biennium was insufficient to renew or replace?

Senator Zolam: That request will be considered later by the full committee. Now, Mr. Secretary, you do have a written transcription of this interview?

Secretary Hablar: Yes, Senator.

Senator Zolam: What is the significance of this particular interview?

Secretary Hablar: The interview was recorded at Lauh Village on Gomeisa III. We consider this interview to be one of the best we've ever recorded. It is particularly interesting from the standpoint of the cultural tracings revealed in the vernacular used by the elderly gentleman interviewed.

Senator Zolam: Who did your men interview?

Secretary Hablar: His name is Hilmot Gustin. Students of intergalactic familial relationships recognize the name Gustin, or Gusten, or Gousting, or Gaustern—as stemming from the cultural milieu of Procyon out of the Mars Migration.

Senator Zolam: Will you identify this Gustin for the record, please?

Secretary Hablar: His parents took him to Gomeisa III in the pioneer days when he was nine years old. That was the year 6873, New Calendar, making him 238 years old now. Gustin's family was in the second migratory wave that arrived three standard years after the first settlement. He is now retired, living with a niece.

Senator Zolam: Do you have a likeness of Gustin?

Secretary Hablar: Only on the wire, Senator. However, he is described in one of the team reports as . . . excuse me a moment, I believe I have the report right here. Yes . . . as ". . . a crotchety old citizen who looks and acts about half his age. He is about two meters tall, narrow face, long gray hair worn in the ancient twin-braid style, watery blue eyes, a sharp chin and enormous ears and nose."

Senator Zolam: A very vivid description.

Secretary Hablar: Thank you, Senator. Some of our people take an artistic pride in their work.

Senator Zolam: That's quite apparent, Mr. Secretary. Now, are you prepared to submit the transcribed interview at this time?

Secretary Hablar: Yes, Senator. Do you want me to read it?

Senator Zolam: That will not be necessary. Submit it to the robo-sec here, and the interview will be printed at this point in the record.

*INTERVIEW WITH HILMOT GUSTIN, PIONEER SETTLER ON GOMEISA III,
TAKEN BY HISTORICAL PRESERVATION*

PRESERVATION OF CULTURAL AND HISTORICAL TRACES
IN
THE GOMEISA PLANETS BY THE BUREAU OF
CULTURAL AFFAIRS
HEARINGS
before the
SPECIAL SUBCOMMITTEE ON INTERGALACTIC CULTURE
of the
COMMITTEE ON GALACTIC FUSION, DISPERSION,
MIGRATION
AND SETTLEMENT
INTERGALACTIC SENATE
803rd CONGRESS
First Session
pursuant to
S. Res. 1443
A resolution to investigate the activities of the Historical
Preservation Teams of the Bureau of Cultural Affairs

———

Part 1
Intergalactic Department of Fusion, Bureau of Cultural Affairs
Domen 18, 19, 20, 21, 22, 23, 24, 25, 26: 7102
(New Calendar)
Printed for the use of the Committee on Galactic Fusion,
Dispersion, Migration and Settlement

*TEAM 579 OF THE BUREAU OF CULTURAL AFFAIRS, DEPARTMENT OF
FUSION.*

Interviewer Simsu Yaggata: Here we are in the home of Mr. and Mrs.
Presby Kilkau in the village of Lauh, Gomeisa III. We are here to interview
Hilmot Gustin, the gentleman seated across from me beside his niece, Mrs.
Kilkau. Mr. Gustin is one of the few surviving pioneers to Gomeisa III, and
he has kindly agreed to tell us some of the things he experienced first-hand
in those early days. I want to thank you, Mrs. Kilkau, for your hospitality in
inviting me here today.

Mrs. Kilkau: It is we who are honored, Mr. Yaggata.

Gustin: I still think this is a lot of frip-frap, Bessie. I was supposed to go
bilker fishing today.

Mrs. Kilkau: But, Uncle Gus.

Gustin: How about you, Mr. Yaggata? Wouldn't you rather go fishing?

Yaggata: I'm sorry, sir. Our schedule doesn't permit me the time.

Gustin: Too bad. The bilker are biting like a flock of hungry fangbirds.

Yaggata: I wonder if we could begin by having you tell us when you first came to Gomeisa III?

Gustin: That was in '64.

Yaggata: That would be 6864?

Gustin: Yes. I was just a wicky boy then. My pap moved us from Procyon IV in the second wave.

Yaggata: I understand you come from a long line of pioneers, sir.

Gustin: My folks never did stay put after Mars. We spent five generations on Mars—then, just like boomer seeds: spang! all over creation!

Yaggata: You came out in the Mars Migration?

Gustin: That was when my grandfather went to Procyon IV. My pap was born enroute. I was born on Procyon.

Yaggata: And what motivated your father to migrate here to Gomeisa III?

Gustin: He heard it was green. Procyon's nothing but one big sandstorm.

Yaggata: And what did he say when he found the vegetation was purple?

Gustin: He said anything was better than yellow dust.

Yaggata: And this is a very beautiful planet.

Gustin: One of the prettiest in the whole universe!

Yaggata: Now, sir, we're interested in the details of your life as it was in those early days. How did you find conditions when you arrived?

Gustin: Rougher than a chigger's . . . Are you recording now, Mr. Yaggata?

Yaggata: Yes, I am.

Gustin: We found it pretty rough.

Yaggata: How soon after arrival did you take up your own claim?

Gustin: Ten or fifteen days we waited in the bracks with all the other chums. Then we came directly to Lauh. There were two other families in the district: the Pijuns and the Kilkaus. Bessie's husband is a grandson of old Effus Kilkau.

Yaggata: What did it look like around here in those days?

Gustin: Nothing but fritch brush and wally bugs, an occasional tiger snake and some duka-dukas, and, of course, those danged fangbirds.[1]

Yaggata: Most of the universe is familiar with the terrible fangbirds, sir. We can all be thankful they've been exterminated.

Gustin: They haven't been exterminated! They're just waiting in some hidden valley for the day when . . .

---

[1] Fangbirds, or pseudo-Pterodactylus, native to Gomeisa III. A flying reptile, now extinct, that grew to a wingspan of ten meters. Creature characterized by venomous fangs (formic acid) protruding from roof of nose hood.

Mrs. Kilkau: Now, Uncle Gus!

Gustin: Well, they are!

Yaggata: The duka-dukas—those are the little fuzzy doglike creatures, aren't they?

Gustin: That's right. Their fuzz is stiff as wire and barbed. Scratch worse than a fritch thorn.

Yaggata: What was the first thing you did when you came here?

Gustin: We took sick with the toogies!

Yaggata: The toogies?

Gustin: The medics call it Fremont's boils after old Doc Fremont who was in the first wave. He's the one discovered they were caused by the micro-pollen of the fritch flowers.

Yaggata: I see. Did you build a house immediately?

Gustin: Well, sir, in between scratching the toogies we threw up a sod shelter with a shake roof, and piled fritch brush around for a compound to keep out the duka-dukas.

Yaggata: That must have been exciting—listening to the weird screams of the fangbirds, the whistling calls of the duka-dukas.

Gustin: We all had too much work to do, and no time to feel excited.

Yaggata: Most of the early pioneers have their names attached to some element of this planet, sir. Was your family so honored?

Gustin: Heh, heh! Gustin swamp! That's what we've got! I'll tell you, Mr. Yaggata, Bessie wanted me to make out like our family was a pack of heroes, but the truth is we weren't anything but dirt farmers, and with a swamp making up about two-thirds of our dirt.

Yaggata: But you certainly must've had some interesting experiences while carving a ranch out of that wilderness.

Gustin: It's a funny thing, mister, but what some folks call *interesting experiences* aren't anything but labor and misery to those who're having them.

Yaggata: Wasn't there anything to lighten the load? Something amusing, perhaps?

Gustin: Well, sir, there was the time pap bought the rollit[2] and he . . .

Mrs. Kilkau: Oh, now, Uncle Gus! I'm sure Mr. Yaggata wouldn't be interested in a silly old commercial transaction like . . ."

Gustin: You see here, Bessie! I'm the one's being interviewed!

Mrs. Kilkau: Of course, Uncle Gus, but . . .

Gustin: And I think that story about the rollit has a real lesson for everyone!

Yaggata: It certainly wouldn't do any harm to hear the story, sir.

[2] Rollit, genus Rollitus Sphericus, exterminated on Gomeisa III in the mutated mastitis epidemic of 6990. One herd may be seen in Galactic zoo, Aspidiske III, although this is the heavy-planet adapted form. The original was an ovoid oviparous creature that grew to a size of some twenty meters diameter, moved by shifting balance.

Gustin: You understand, mister, we weren't anything but lean chums[3] with the little kit.[4] Our power pack was busy all the time just producing bare essentials. So when old Effus Kilkau advertised that he had a draft animal for sale, pap was all for buying it.

Yaggata: Advertised? How was that done?

Gustin: On the checker net.[5] Old Effus advertised that he had one rollit for sale cheap, weight 2500 kilos, trained to plow.

Yaggata: Some of those who will use this record will not be familiar with the genus rollitus sphericus, Mr. Gustin. Would you mind setting the record clear?

Gustin: In due time, son. Don't light a short fuse. The point is, my pap didn't know a rollit from a bowling ball, either, and he was too darned proud to admit it.

Yaggata: Ha, ha, ha. Wouldn't anyone enlighten him?

Gustin: Well, old Effus suspected pap was ignorant about rollits, and Effus thought it'd be a good joke just to let him have it cold.

Yaggata: I see. How was the transaction completed?

Gustin: All done on the checker net, and confirmed at base where they credited Effus with the seventy galars.

Yaggata: Your father bought it sight unseen?

Gustin: Oh, certainly! There was no question of hanky-panky in those days. People had to help each other . . . and they had to be honest because their lives depended on it. It's only after we get civilized that we feel free to cheat. Besides, we lived so far apart in those days that we'd have lost more going to look at the beast than just having it shipped over.

Yaggata: That certainly makes sense, sir. But didn't your father kind of feel around to find out specifically what it was that he was buying?

Gustin: Oh, he probed around some. But pap was afraid of appearing the sag.[6] I do remember he asked how the rollit was to feed. Old Effus just said that this rollit was trained to a whistle call, and could be turned loose to graze off the country. About then, somebody else chimed in on the net and said seventy galars was certainly cheap for a 2500-kilo rollit, and if pap didn't want the beast, then he'd take it. So pap closed the deal right then and there.

Yaggata: How did they deliver it?

Gustin: Well, the Kilkaus were some better off than we were. They had a freight platform null to 6000 kilos. They just put the rollit on that platform and flew it over.

Yaggata: What did your father say when he saw it?

---

[3] Lean chums—marginal pioneers, poor.

[4] Little Kit—minimum pioneer equipment permitted by settlement authorities—clothing suited to local climate (2 changes each); one Hellerite power pack; hand tools fitted for local resources and sufficient to build shelter, work the land.

[5] Checker net—daily radio check-in network required during pioneer period on all planets.

[6] Sag—a fool, stupid person, one easily sided.

Gustin: You mean about harness?

Yaggata: Yes.

Gustin: Well, sir, I don't think pap even thought about the harness problem. We'd had a ciget on Procyon, and pap'd made his own harness with good long traces so he could stay away from the stink of it. He just figured he'd have another set of harness to make.

Yaggata: Didn't he say *anything* about harness?

Gustin: No. He didn't have a chance to say anything. You see, the rollit was a little spooky from the flight. As soon as they let it down it rolled all over the landscape, and it made one pass and rolled right over me.

Yaggata: Galumpers! To someone who'd never seen a rollit before, I imagine that was quite frightening!

Gustin: It's a good thing Maw didn't see it. She'd have passed dead away. You know, a 2500-kilo rollit develops about 1500 kilos of forward thrust from a standing start, and once it gets moving it can really roll. They're deceptive, too. They look like a kind of giant amœba flowing over the landscape, and all of a sudden they're right on top of you—literally!

Yaggata: Weren't you frightened when it ran over you?

Gustin: Well, it knocked me down, there was a second of darkness and a kind of warm, firm pressure—then it was gone. You know, a rollit won't hurt you. In fact, they're really very friendly. There was a case of a fellow over in Mirmon County who was saved from a fangbird by his rollit. The rollit just sat on this fellow until the fangbird gave up.

Yaggata: I'll bet that was an experience!

Gustin: Sure was. You know, a rollit's ninety percent mobile fluid and pump muscles, and the rest a hide like flexible armor plate. An adult rollit's practically immune to physical attack—even from a fangbird—and there's nothing like being indestructible to make you a friend of everyone.

Yaggata: What was your reaction to being run down by that big animated ball of flesh?

Gustin: After the first shock, I wanted to try it again. I thought it was fun. But pap was so shaken by it, that he rushed me indoors. It took old Effus a half hour to convince pap that a rollit wouldn't hurt anyone, that it distributed its weight over such a large area that it was just like a good massage.

Yaggata: Ha, ha, ha. So there was your father with a rollit and no idea how to harness it.

Gustin: That's right. He didn't even think about it until after lunch. Old Effus was gone by then. The rollit was outside just rolling around, browsing off the fritch brush, clearing quite an area of it, at that. Good brush buckers, rollits are.

Yaggata: How did your father approach the problem?

Gustin: He just walked up to the rollit, clucked at it and whistled like ole

Effus had told him. He led the rollit over to the shed where we had our imperv plow. It was a three-gang plow with a two and a half foot bite.

Yaggata: How was it supposed to be towed?

Gustin: By a power pack rotor. But we only had the one pack, and we didn't want to go into three-ball for a rotor.

Yaggata: What did your father say?

Gustin: He said, "Well, let's figure out how to hook this beast to the front of that there . . ." And then it hit him. How do you put harness on a beast that rolls its whole body, and moves by shifting its center of gravity? That was a real stinker of a problem.

Yaggata: I've seen the diagrams. They appear quite obvious. Didn't it occur to your father right away how it had to be done?

Gustin: Sometimes the obvious isn't so obvious until someone's showed it to you, mister. Remember, pap had never seen anything even remotely like a rollit before. His whole concept of draft animals was tied up in something like a ciget—a creature with a specific number of legs and a body that would accommodate some kind of harness. The rollit was a different breed of beast entirely.

Yaggata: Certainly, but . . .

Gustin: And what you've been used to seeing can tie your mind up in little knots so tight you can't see anything else.

Yaggata: Why didn't your father just call up a neighbor and ask how to hitch a rollit to a plow?

Gustin: Pap was too proud. He wasn't going to ask and look foolish, and he wasn't going to give up. For about a week it was a regular ten-ring scrag fight around out compound. We learned later that old Effus and half his clan were up in the hills with binoculars laughing themselves silly. They ran bets on what we'd try next.

Yaggata: What'd you try *first*?

Gustin: Just a plain loop harness. Pap made a loop big enough to pass around the rollit. He clucked the beast into the loop, dropped the bight around near the top front—that is, around the end away from the plow. A rollit doesn't rightly have a front. Then he ordered the beast to pull. That rollit leaned into the line like it knew what it was doing. The plow moved forward about four feet, then the line was down where it slipped under the beast. Pap clucked it back into the harness and ordered it forward again. About three times that way and it was clear he'd never get his plowing done if he had to reharness every four feet.

Yaggata: Were your neighbors watching all this?

Gustin: Yes. By the second day the whole district was in on the joke. And we had a full flap in our compound and were really hupping it.

Yaggata: What'd he try next?

Gustin: A kind of web harness with rollers. It took us three days to make it. Meanwhile, we tried a vertical harness that went over the top and under the rollit. We greased the area that contacted the rollit, but the grease wouldn't last. As soon as it was gone, the harness would rub. Our rollit could rub through the toughest harness in about ten revolutions.

Yaggata: How'd the web harness work?

Gustin: It really wasn't a bad idea—better than what our neighbors were using right then if he'd perfected it.

Yaggata: What were your neighbors using?

Gustin: A kind of corral on wheels with rollers along the front to contact the front of the rollit. It had harness rings on the back. They opened one side to let the rollit in, hooked on the equipment, and the rollit pulled the whole rig.

Yaggata: I'm curious. Why didn't your father sneak over and watch his neighbors using their rollits?

Gustin: He tried. But they were all onto him. Our neighbors were just never using their beasts when pap came around. It was like a comic formal dance. They'd invite him in for a drink of chicker. Pap would remark about their plowing. He'd ask to look over their equipment, but there'd never be anything around that even remotely resembled rollit harness.

Yaggata: Uh . . . what was wrong with the web harness he tried?

Gustin: Pap hadn't made the web big enough to belly completely around the front of the rollit. And then the rollers kept fouling because he hadn't perfected a good sling system.

Yaggata: How did he finally solve the problem?

Gustin: He calmed down and started thinking straight. First, he put the plow out in the center of our compound. Then he stationed the rollit all around the plow, first one side then the other. And just like that—he had it.

Yaggata: I must be a little slow on obvious associations myself. Something has just occurred to me. Was your father the inventor of the standard rollitor?

Gustin: It was his idea.

Mrs. Kilkau: Uncle Gus! You never told us your father was an inventor! I never realized . . .

Gustin: He wasn't an inventor. He was just a darned good practical pioneer. As far as thinking up the original rollitor is concerned, that'd be obvious to anyone who'd given it a second's thought. What do you think the Gomeisa Historical Society has been trying to . . .

Mrs. Kilkau: Do you mean that musty old junk out in the number two warehouse?

Gustin: That *musty old junk* includes your mother's first swamp cream tritchet![7] And right spang in the middle of that *musty old junk* is the first rollitor!

Yaggata: Do you mean you have the original rollitor right here?

---

[7] Swamp cream tritchet—the crude baffled incline first used to settle out the floating curds secreted by calophyllum gomeisum, the common swamp bush of Gomeisa III.

Gustin: Right out back in the warehouse.

Yaggata: Why . . . that thing's priceless! Could we go out and see it now?

Gustin: Don't see why not.

Mrs. Kilkau: Oh, Uncle Gus! It's so dirty out there and . . .

Gustin: A little dirt never hurt anyone, Bessie! Uhhhgh! That knee where the fangbird got me is giving me more trouble this week. Too bad we don't have any rollits around nowadays. There's nothing like a rollit massage to pep up the circulation.

Yaggata: Have *you* had an encounter with a fangbird?

Gustin: Oh, sure. A couple of times.

Yaggata: Could you tell us about it?

Gustin: Later, son, Let's go look at the rollitor.

(Editor: A raw splice break has been left on the wire at this point and should be repaired.)

Yaggata: Here we are in a corner of warehouse number two. Those stacked boxes you see in the background are cases of swamp cream so important to the cosmetic industry—and the chief output of the Gustin-Kilkau Ranch.

Gustin: This here's a trench climber used for mining the raw copper we discovered in the fumerole region.

Yaggata: And this must be the original rollitor attached to this plow.

Gustin: That's right. It's a simple thing rightly enough: just four wooden rollers set in two 'V's,' one set of rollers above the other, and the whole rig attached directly to the plow at the rear.

Yaggata: They're quite large rollers.

Gustin: We had a big rollit. You see this ratchet thing in here?

Yaggata: Yes.

Gustin: That adjusted the height of the rollers and the distance between the two sets to fit the frontal curve of our rollit. The rollit just moved up against these rollers. One set of rollers rode high on the beast's frontal curve, and the other set of rollers rode low. The rollit kind of wedged in between them and pushed.

Yaggata: What are these wheels on the plow frame?

Gustin: They kept the plow riding level.

Yaggata: It's really such a simple device.

Gustin: Simple! We trained our rollit to plow all by itself!

Yaggata: What'd your neighbors think of that?

Gustin: I'll tell you they stopped laughing at pap! Inside of a forty-day, the old tow corrals were all discarded. They called the new rigs Gustin rollitors for awhile, but the name soon got shortened.

Mrs. Kilkau: I never realized! To think! Right here in our own warehouse! Why . . . the Historical Society . . .

Gustin: They can wait until I've passed on! I get a deal of satisfaction coming out here occasionally and just touching this *musty old junk*. It does you good to remember where you came from.

Mrs. Kilkau: But, Uncle Gus . . .

Gustin: And you came from dirt-farming pioneers, Bessie! Fine people! There wouldn't be any of this soft living you enjoy today if it weren't for them and this *musty old junk*!

Mrs. Kilkau: But I think it's selfish of you, keeping these *priceless* . . .

Gustin: Sure it's selfish! But that's a privilege of those who've done their jobs well, and lived long enough to look back awhile. If you'll consider a minute, gal, I'm the one who saw what swamp cream did for the complexion. I've got a right to be selfish!

Mrs. Kilkau: Yes, Uncle Gus. I've heard that story.

Yaggata: But *we* haven't heard it, Mr. Gustin. Would you care to . . .

Gustin: Yes, I'd care to . . . but some other time, son. Right now I'm a wicky tired, and I'd better get some rest.

Yaggata: Certainly, sir! Shall we set the time for . . .

Gustin: I'll call you, son. Don't you call me. Uuuuugh! Damned fangbird wound! But I'll tell you one thing, son: I've changed my mind about this frip-frap of yours. It does us all good to see where we came from. If the people who see that record of yours have any brains, they'll think about where they came from. Do 'em good!

(Editor: Wire ends here. Attached note says Hilmot Gustin takes ill the following day. The second interview was delayed indefinitely.)

Senator Zolam: Do you have further records to introduce at this time, Mr. Secretary?

Secretary Hablar: I was hoping my Assistant Secretary for Cultural Affairs could make it here today. Unfortunately, he was called to an intercultural function with representatives of the Ring Planets.

Saboteur McKie: That was my doing, Mr. Secretary. The committee members are pressed for time today.

Secretary Hablar: I see.

Senator Zolam: There being no further business, the Special Subcommittee on Intergalactic Culture stands adjourned until 1600 tomorrow.

OLD RAMBLING HOUSE

On his last night on Earth, Ted Graham stepped out of a glass-walled telephone booth, ducked to avoid a swooping moth that battered itself in a frenzy against a bare globe above the booth.

Ted Graham was a long-necked man with a head of pronounced egg shape topped by prematurely balding sandy hair. Something about his lanky, intense appearance suggested his occupation: certified public accountant.

He stopped behind his wife, who was studying a newspaper classified page, and frowned. "They said to wait here. They'll come get us. Said the place is hard to find at night."

Martha Graham looked up from the newspaper. She was a doll-faced woman, heavily pregnant, a kind of pink prettiness about her. The yellow glow from the light above the booth subdued the red auburn cast of her ponytail hair.

"I just *have* to be in a house when the baby's born," she said. "What'd they sound like?"

"I dunno. There was a funny kind of interruption—like an argument in some foreign language."

"Did they sound foreign?"

"In a way." He motioned along the night-shrouded line of trailers toward one with two windows glowing amber. "Let's wait inside. These bugs out here are fierce."

"Did you tell them which trailer is ours?"

"Yes. They didn't sound at all anxious to look at it. That's odd—them wanting to trade their house for a trailer."

"There's nothing odd about it. They've probably just got itchy feet like we did."

He appeared not to hear her. "Funniest-sounding language you ever heard when that argument started—like a squirt of noise."

Inside the trailer, Ted Graham sat down on the green couch that opened into a double bed for company.

"They could use a good tax accountant around here," he said. "When I first saw the place, I got that definite feeling. The valley looks prosperous. It's a wonder nobody's opened an office here before."

His wife took a straight chair by the counter separating kitchen and living area, folded her hands across her heavy stomach.

"I'm just continental tired of wheels going around under me," she said. "I want to sit and stare at the same view for the rest of my life. I don't know how a trailer ever seemed glamorous when—"

"It was the inheritance gave us itchy feet," he said.

Tires gritted on gravel outside.

Martha Graham straightened. "Could that be them?"

"Awful quick, if it is." He went to the door, opened it, stared down at the man who was just raising a hand to knock.

"Are you Mr. Graham?" asked the man.

"Yes." He found himself staring at the caller.

"I'm Clint Rush. You called about the house?" The man moved farther into the light. At first, he'd appeared an old man, fine wrinkle lines in his face, a tired leather look to his skin. But as he moved his head in the light, the wrinkles seemed to dissolve—and with them, the years lifted from him.

"Yes, we called," said Ted Graham. He stood aside. "Do you want to look at the trailer now?"

Martha Graham crossed to stand beside her husband. "We've kept it in awfully good shape," she said. "We've never let anything get seriously wrong with it."

She sounds too anxious, though Ted Graham. *I wish she'd let me do the talking for the two of us.*

"We can come back and look at your trailer tomorrow in daylight," said Rush. "My car's right out here, if you'd like to see our house."

Ted Graham hesitated. He felt a nagging worry tug at his mind, tried to fix his attention on what bothered him.

"Hadn't we better take our car?" he asked. "We could follow you."

"No need," said Rush. "We're coming back into town tonight anyway. We can drop you off then."

Ted Graham nodded. "Be right with you as soon as I lock up."

Inside the car, Rush mumbled introductions. His wife was a dark shadow in the front seat, her hair drawn back in a severe bun. Her features suggested gypsy blood. He called her Raimee.

Odd name, thought Graham. And he noticed that she, too, gave the strange first impression of age that melted in a shift of light.

Mrs. Rush turned her gypsy features toward Martha Graham. "You are going to have a baby?"

It came out as an odd, veiled statement.

Abruptly, the car rolled forward.

Martha Graham said, "It's supposed to be born in about two months. We hope it's a boy."

Mrs. Rush looked at her husband. "I have changed my mind," she said.

Rush spoke without taking his attention from the road. "It is too . . ." He broke off, spoke in a tumble of strange sounds.

Ted Graham recognized it as the language he'd heard on the telephone.

Mrs. Rush answered in the same tongue, anger showing in the intensity of her voice. Her husband replied, his voice calmer.

Presently, Mrs. Rush fell moodily silent.

Rush tipped his head toward the rear of the car. "My wife has moments when she does not want to get rid of the old house. It has been with her for many years."

Ted Graham said, "Oh." Then: "Are you Spanish?"

Rush hesitated. "No. We are Basque."

He turned the car down a well-lighted avenue that merged into a highway. They turned onto a side road. There followed more turns—left, right, right.

Ted Graham lost track.

They hit a jolting bump that made Martha gasp.

"I hope that wasn't too rough on you," said Rush. "We're almost there."

The car swung into a lane, its lights picking out the skeleton outlines of trees: peculiar trees—tall, gaunt, leafless. They added to Ted Graham's feeling of uneasiness.

The lane dipped, ended at a low wall of a house—red brick with clerestory windows beneath overhanging eaves. The effect of the wall and a wide-beamed door they could see to the left was ultra-modern.

Ted Graham helped his wife out of the car, followed the Rushes to the door.

"I thought you told me it was an old house," he said.

"It was designed by one of the first modernists," said Rush. He fumbled with an odd curved key. The wide door swung open onto a hallway equally wide, carpeted by a deep pile rug. They could glimpse floor-to-ceiling view windows at the end of the hall, city lights beyond.

Martha Graham gasped, entered the hall as though in a trance. Ted Graham followed, heard the door close behind them.

"It's so—so—so *big*," exclaimed Martha Graham.

"You want to trade this for our trailer?" asked Ted Graham.

"It's too inconvenient for us," said Rush. "My work is over the mountains on the coast." He shrugged. "We cannot sell it."

Ted Graham looked at him sharply. "Isn't there any money around here?" He had a sudden vision of a tax accountant with no customers.

"Plenty of money, but no real estate customers."

They entered the living room. Sectional divans lined the walls. Subdued lighting glowed from the corners. Two paintings hung on the opposite walls—oblongs of odd lines and twists that made Ted Graham dizzy.

Warning bells clamored in his mind.

Martha Graham crossed to the windows, looked at the lights far away below. "I had no idea we'd climbed that far," she said. "It's like a fairy city."

Mrs. Rush emitted a short, nervous laugh.

Ted Graham glanced around the room, thought: *If the rest of the house is like this, it's worth fifty or sixty thousand.* He thought of the trailer: *A good one, but not worth more than seven thousand.*

Uneasiness was like a neon sign flashing in his mind. "This seems so . . ." He shook his head.

"Would you like to see the rest of the house?" asked Rush.

Martha Graham turned from the window. "Oh, yes."

Ted Graham shrugged. *No harm in looking,* he thought.

When they returned to the living room, Ted Graham had doubled his previous estimate on the house's value. His brain reeled with the summing of it: a solarium with an entire ceiling covered by sun lamps, an automatic laundry where you dropped soiled clothing down a chute, took it washed and ironed from the other end . . .

"Perhaps you and your wife would like to discuss it in private," said Rush. "We will leave you for a moment."

And they were gone before Ted Graham could protest.

Martha Graham said, "Ted, I honestly never in my life dreamed—"

"Something's very wrong, honey."

"But, Ted—"

"This house is worth at least a hundred thousand dollars. Maybe more. And they want to trade *this*"—he looked around him—"for a seven-thousand-dollar trailer?"

"Ted, they're foreigners. And if they're so foolish they don't know the value of this place, then why should—"

"I don't like it," he said. Again he looked around the room, recalled the fantastic equipment of the house. "But maybe you're right."

He stared out at the city lights. They had a lacelike quality: tall buildings linked by lines of flickering incandescence. Something like a Roman candle shot skyward in the distance.

"Okay!" he said. "If they want to trade, let's go push the deal . . ."

Abruptly, the house shuddered. The city lights blinked out. A humming sound filled the air.

Martha Graham clutched her husband's arm. "Ted! Wha—what was that?"

"I dunno." He turned. "Mr. Rush!"

No answer. Only the humming.

The door at the end of the room opened. A strange man came through it. He wore a short togalike garment of gray, metallic cloth belted at the waist by something that glittered and shimmered through every color of the spectrum. An aura of coldness and power emanated from him—a sense of untouchable hauteur.

He glanced around the room, spoke in the same tongue the Rushes had used.

Ted Graham said, "I don't understand you, mister."

The man put a hand to his flickering belt. Both Ted and Martha Graham felt themselves rooted to the floor, a tingling sensation vibrating along every nerve.

Again the strange language rolled from the man's tongue, but now the words were understood.

"Who are you?"

"My name's Graham. This is my wife. What's going—"

"How did you get here?"

"The Rushes—they wanted to trade us this house for our trailer. They brought us. Now look, we—"

"What is your talent—your occupation?"

"Tax accountant. Say! Why all these—"

"That was to be expected," said the man. "Clever! Oh, excessively clever!" His hand moved again to the belt. "Now be very quiet. This may confuse you momentarily."

Colored lights filled both the Grahams' minds. They staggered.

"You are qualified," said the man. "You will serve."

"Where are we?" demanded Martha Graham.

"The coordinates would not be intelligible to you," he said. "I am of the Rojac. It is sufficient for you to know that you are under Rojac sovereignty."

Ted Graham said, "But—"

"You have, in a way, been kidnapped. And the Raimees have fled to your planet—an unregistered planet."

"I'm afraid," Martha Graham said shakily.

"You have nothing to fear," said the man. "You are no longer on the planet of your birth—nor even in the same galaxy." He glanced at Ted Graham's wrist. "That device on your wrist—it tells your local time?"

"Yes."

"That will help in the search. And your sun—can you describe its atomic cycle?"

Ted Graham groped in his mind for his science memories from school, from the Sunday supplements. "I can recall that our galaxy is a spiral like—"

"Most galaxies are spiral."

"Is this some kind of a practical joke?" asked Ted Graham.

The man smiled, a cold, superior smile. "It is no joke. Now I will make you a proposition."

Ted nodded warily. "All right, let's have the stinger."

"The people who brought you here were tax collectors we Rojac recruited from a subject planet. They were conditioned to make it impossible for them to leave their job untended. Unfortunately, they were clever enough to realize that if they brought someone else in who could do their job, they were released from their mental bonds. Very clever."

"But—"

"You may have their job," said the man. "Normally you would be put to work in the lower echelons, but we believe in meting out justice wherever possible. The Raimees undoubtedly stumbled on your planet by accident and lured you into this position without—"

"How do you know I can do your job?"

"That moment of brilliance was an aptitude test. You passed. Well, do you accept?"

"What about our baby?" Martha Graham worriedly wanted to know.

"You will be allowed to keep it until it reaches the age of decision—about the time it will take the child to reach adult stature."

"Then what?" insisted Martha Graham.

"The child will take its position in society—according to its ability."

"Will we ever see our child after that?"

"Possibly."

Ted Graham said, "What's the joker in this?"

Again the cold, superior smile. "You will receive conditioning similar to that which we gave the Raimees. And we will want to examine your memories to aid us in our search for your planet. It would be good to find a new inhabitable place."

"Why did they trap us like this?" asked Martha Graham.

"It's lonely work," the man explained. "Your house is actually a type of space conveyance that travels along your collection route—and there is much travel to the job. And then—you will not have friends, nor time for much other than work. Our methods are necessarily severe at times."

"Travel?" Martha Graham repeated in dismay.

"Almost constantly."

Ted Graham felt his mind whirling. And behind him, he heard his wife sobbing.

The Raimees sat in what had been the Grahams' trailer.

"For a few moments, I feared he would not succumb to the bait," she said. "I knew you could never overcome the mental compulsion enough to leave them there without their first agreeing."

Raimee chuckled. "Yes. And now I'm going to indulge in everything the Rojac never permitted. I'm going to write ballads and poems."

"And I'm going to paint," she said. "Oh, the delicious freedom!"

"Greed won this for us," he said. "The long study of the Grahams paid off. They couldn't refuse to trade."

"I knew they'd agree. The looks in their eyes when they saw the house!

They both had . . ." She broke off, a look of horror coming into her eyes. "One of them did not agree!"

"They both did. You heard them."

"The baby?"

He stared at his wife. "But—but it is not at the age of decision!"

"In perhaps eighteen of this planet's years, it *will* be at the age of decision. What then?"

His shoulders sagged. He shuddered. "I will not be able to fight it off. I will have to build a transmitter, call the Rojac and confess!"

"And they will collect another inhabitable place," she said, her voice flat and toneless.

"I've spoiled it," he said. "I've spoiled it!"

YOU TAKE THE
HIGH ROAD

Lewis Orne clasped his hands behind his back until the knuckles showed white. He stared darkly out his second-floor window at the morning on Hamal II. The big yellow sun already above the distant mountains dominated a cloudless sky. It promised to be a scorcher of a day.

Behind him Orne could hear a scratchy pen rasping across paper as the Investigation and Adjustment operative made notes on their just-completed interview.

So maybe I was wrong to push the panic button, thought Orne. *That doesn't give this wise guy the right to be such a heel! After all—this is my first job. They can't expect perfection the first time out!*

The scratching pen began to wear on Orne's nerves.

Creases furrowed his square forehead. He put his left hand up to the rough window wooden frame, ran his right hand through the stiff bristles of his close-cropped red hair. The loose cut of his white coverall uniform—standard for agents of the Rediscovery and Re-education Service—accentuated Orne's blocky appearance. He had the thick muscles and no-fat look of someone raised on a heavy planet—in his case, Chargon of the Gemma System. There was a full jowled bulldog appearance to his face. It was an effective disguise for a pixie nature.

At the moment, however, he was feeling decidedly unpixielike.

If I'm wrong, they'll boot me out of the service, he thought. *There's too much bad blood between R-and-R and the Investigation and Adjustment people. But there'll be some jumping if I'm right about this place!*

Orne shook his head. *But I'm probably wrong.*

The more he thought about it the more he felt that it had been a stupid move to call in the I–A. This planet of Hamal II probably was not aggressive by nature. There probably was no danger here of providing arms to a potential war maker.

Someone clumped down the stairs at the other end of the building. The floor shook under Orne's feet. This was an old building—the government guest house—and built of rough lumber. The room carried the sour smell of many former occupants.

From his second-floor window Orne could see part of the cobblestone market square of this village of Pitsiben. Beyond the square he could make out the wide track of the ridge road that came up from the Plains of Rogga. Along the road stretched a double line of moving figures: farmers and hunters coming for market day in Pitsiben. Amber dust hung over the road. It softened the scene, imparted a romantic, out-of-focus look.

The farmers leaned into the pushing harness of their low two-wheeled carts, plodding along with a heavy-footed swaying motion. They wore long green coats, yellow berets tipped uniformly over the left ear, yellow trousers with the cuffs darkened by the dust of the road, open sandals that revealed horny feet splayed out like the feet of draft animals. The carts were piled high with green and yellow vegetables seemingly arranged to carry out the general color scheme.

Brown-clothed hunters moved with the line, but to one side like flank guards. They strode along, heads high, cap feathers bobbing. Each carried a bell-muzzled fowling piece at a jaunty angle over one arm, a spyglass in a leather case over the left shoulder. Behind the hunters trotted their apprentices pulling three-wheeled carts overflowing with swamp deer, ducks and *porjos,* the snake-tailed rodents that Hamal natives considered such a delicacy.

On the distant valley floor Orne could see the dark red spire of the I–A ship that had come flaming down just after dawn of this day—homing on his transmitter. The ship, too, seemed set in a dreamlike haze: blue smoke from kitchen fires in the farm homes that dotted the valley. The red shape towered above the homes, looking out of place, like an ornament left over from holiday decorations for giants.

As Orne watched, a hunter paused on the ridge road, unlimbered his spyglass, studied the I–A ship.

The smoke and the hot yellow sun conspired to produce a summery appearance to the countryside—a look of lush growing. It was essentially a peaceful scene, arousing in Orne a deep feeling of bitterness.

Damn! I don't care what the I–A says! I was right to call them. These people of Hamal are hiding something. They're not peaceful! The real mistake that was made here was made by that dumbo on First-Contact when he gabbled about the importance we place on a peaceful history!

The pen scratching stopped, and the I–A man cleared his throat.

Orne turned, looked across the low room at the operative. The I–A man sat at a rough table beside Orne's unmade bed. Papers and report folders were scattered all around him on the table. A small recorder weighted one stack. The I–A man slouched in a bulky wooden chair. He was a big-headed, gangling figure with over-large features, a leathery skin. His hair was dark and straggling. His eyelids drooped. They gave to his face that look of haughty superciliousness that was like a brand mark of the I–A. The man wore patched blue fatigues without insignia. He had introduced himself as Umbo Stetson, chief I–A operative for this sector.

Stetson noted Orne's attention, said, "I believe I have everything now. Let's just check it over. You landed here ten weeks ago, right?"

"Yes. I was set down by a landing boat from the *R-and-R* transport, Arneb Rediscovery."

"And this was your first mission?"

"Yes. I graduated from Uni-Galacta with the class of '07, and did my apprentice work on Timurlain."

Stetson frowned. "Then you came out here to this newly re-discovered backwater planet?"

"That's right."

"I see. You were just full of the old rah-rah, the old missionary spirit to uplift mankind and all that sort of thing."

Orne blushed, scowled.

"They're still teaching that 'cultural renaissance' bushwah at dear old Uni-Galacta, I see," said Stetson. He put a hand to his breast, raised his voice: "We must re-unite the lost planets with the centers of culture and industry, and take up the glorious onward march of mankind that was stopped so brutally by the Rim Wars!"

He spat on the floor.

"I think we can skip all this," muttered Orne.

Stetson chuckled. "You're sooooo right! Now . . . what'd you bring with you when you landed?"

"I had a dictionary compiled by the First-Contact man, but it was pretty sketchy in—"

"Who was that First-Contact, by the way?"

"I never met him but his name's in the dictionary: Andre Bullone."

"Oh—Any relation to High Commissioner Ipscott Bullone?"

"I don't know."

Stetson scribbled something on one of his papers. "And that report says this is a peaceful planet with a primitive farming-hunting economy, eh?"

"Yes."

"Uh, huh. What else'd you bring with you?"

"The usual blanks and files for my reports—and a transmitter."

"And you pushed the 'panic button' on that transmitter two days ago, eh? Did we get here fast enough for you?"

Orne glared at the floor.

Stetson said, "I suppose you've the usual eidetic memory crammed with cultural-medical-industrial information."

"I'm a fully qualified *R-and-R* agent."

"We will observe a moment of reverent silence," said Stetson. Abruptly, he slammed a hand onto the table. "It's just plain damn' stupidity! Nothing but a political come-on!"

Orne snapped to angry attention. "What do you mean?"

"This *R-and-R* dodge, son. It's an attention getter . . . it's perpetuating some political lives. But you mark my words: we're going to *re*-discover just one planet too many; we're going to give its people the industrial foundation they don't deserve—and we're going to see another Rim War to end all Rim Wars!"

Orne took a step forward. "Why'n hell do you think I pushed the panic button here?"

Stetson sat back. "My dear fellow, that's what we're just now trying to determine." He tapped his front teeth with the pen. "Now . . . just why *did* you call us?"

"I *told* you I'm not sure! It's just—" He shrugged.

"You felt lonely and decided you wanted the I–A to come hold your hand. Is that it?"

"Oh go to hell!" barked Orne.

"In due time, son. In due time." Stetson's drooping eyelids drooped even farther. "Now . . . just what're they teaching you *R-and-R* dummies to look for these days?"

Orne swallowed an angry reply. "Do you mean in war signs?"

"What else?"

"We're supposed to look for fortifications, for war games among the children, for people drilling or other signs of armylike group activities, for war scars and wounds on people and buildings, for indications of wholesale destruction and . . . you know, things like that."

"Gross evidence," said Stetson. "Do you consider this adequate?"

"No I don't!"

"You're sooooo right," said Stetson. "Hm-m-m. . . . Let's dig a little deeper: What bothers you about these people?"

Orne sighed. "They have no spirit, no bounce. No humor. The atmosphere around this place is perpetual seriousness bordering on gloom."

"Oh?"

"Yeah. I . . . I uh—" Orne wet his lips with his tongue. "I uh . . . told the Leaders' Council one day that our people are very interested in a steady source of *froolap* bones for making left-handed bone china saucers."

Stetson jerked forward. "You *what*?"

"I uh . . . told the—"

"Yeah! I got that. What happened?"

"They asked for a detailed description of the *froolap* and the accepted method of preparing the bones for shipment."

"And what'd you tell them?"

"Well, I. . . . Well, according to my description they decided that Hamal doesn't have any *froolaps*."

"I see," said Stetson.

"That's what's wrong with the place: no *froolaps*."

Stetson took a deep breath, sat back. He tapped his pen on the table, stared into the distance.

Now I've done it, thought Orne. *Why can't I keep my big mouth shut? I've just convinced him that I'm nuts!*

"How're they taking to re-education?" asked Stetson.

"Oh, they're very interested in the industrial end. That's why I'm here in Pitsiben village. We located a tungsten source nearby and—"

"What about their medical people?" asked Stetson. "Are they on their toes?"

"I guess so," said Orne. "But you know how it is with medical people— they often have the idea that they already know everything. I'm making progress, though."

"What's their medical level?"

"They've got a good basic knowledge of anatomy . . . surgery and bone setting. That sort of thing."

"You got any ideas why these people are so backward?" asked Stetson.

"Their history says this planet was accidentally seeded by sixteen survivors—eleven women and five men—from a Tritshain cruiser that was disabled in some engagement or other during the early part of the Rim Wars. They landed with a lifeboat without much equipment and little know-how. I take it that it was mostly the black gang that got away."

"And here they sat until *R-and-R* came along," said Stetson. "Lovely. Just lovely."

"That was five hundred Standard years ago," said Orne.

"And these gentle people are still farming and hunting," murmured Stetson. "Oh lovely." He glared up at Orne. "How long would it take a planet such as this one—granting the aggressive drive—to become a definite war menace?"

Orne said, "Well . . . there are two uninhabited planets in this system that they could grab for raw materials. Oh, I'd say twenty to twenty-five years after they got the industrial foundation on their own planet."

"And how long before the aggressive core would have the know-how to go underground . . . if necessary . . . so that we'd have to blast the planet apart to get at them?"

"Six months to a year."

"You are beginning to see the sweet little problem you *R-and-R* dummies are creating for us!" Stetson abruptly pointed an accusing finger at Orne. "And let us make just one little slip! Let us declare a planet aggressive and bring in an occupation force and let your spies find out we made a mistake!" He doubled his hand into a fist. *"Ahah!"*

"They've already started building the factories to produce machine tools," said Orne. "They're quick enough." He shrugged. "They soak everything up like some dark gloomy sponge."

"Very poetic," growled Stetson. He lifted his long frame from the chair, stepped into the middle of the room. "Well, let's go take a closer look. But I'm warning you, Orne: this had better live up to whatever it was that prompted you to call us. The I–A has more important things to do than to go around wet nursing the *R-and-R!*"

"And you'd just love to get something on us, too!" said Orne.

"You're sooooo right, son."

"Okay! So I made a mistake!"

"We'll see. Come along. I've a go-buggy downstairs."

Here goes nothing, thought Orne. *This jerk isn't going to look very hard when it's easier to sit back and laugh at the* R-and-R*! I'm finished before I even get started!*

It was already beginning to grow hot outside when they emerged onto the cobblestone street. The green and yellow flag hung limply from its mast atop the guest house. All activity seemed to have taken on a slower pace. Groups of stolid Hamal natives stood before awning-shaded vegetable stalls across the street. They gazed moodily at the I–A vehicle.

The go-buggy was a white two-seater tear drop with wrap-around window, a turbine engine in the rear.

Orne and Stetson got in, fastened their safety belts.

"There's what I mean," said Orne.

Stetson started the motor, eased in the clutch. The buggy bounced a couple of times on the cobbles until the gyro-spring system took hold.

"There's what you mean what?" asked Stetson.

"Those dolts across the street back there. Any other place in the universe they'd have been around this rig ten deep, prying under the rear vents at the turbine, poking underneath at the wheels. These jerks just stand around at a distance and look gloomy!"

"No *froolap,*" said Stetson.

"Yeah!"

"What's wrong with that?" asked Stetson. "So they're shy."

"Forget I mentioned it."

"I saw by your reports that there are no walled villages on Hamal," said Stetson. He slowed the go-buggy to maneuver between two of the low push carts.

"None that I've seen."

"And no military drill by large groups?"

"None that I've seen."

"And no heavy armaments?"

"None that I've seen."

"What's this *none-that-I've-seen* kick?" demanded Stetson. "Do you suspect them of hiding something?"

"I do."

"Why?"

"Because things don't seem to fit somehow on this planet. And when things don't fit there are missing pieces."

Stetson took his eyes from the street, shot a sharp glance at Orne, returned his attention to the street. "So you're suspicious."

Orne grabbed the door handle as the go-buggy swerved around a corner, headed out the wide ridge road. "That's what I said right at the beginning."

"We're always simply delighted to investigate *R-and-R*'s slightest suspicions," said Stetson.

"It's better for me to make a mistake than it is for you to make one," growled Orne.

"You will notice that their construction is almost entirely of wood," said Stetson. "Wood constructions is peaceful."

"Doesn't that depend on what weapons are used?" asked Orne.

"Is that what they're teaching you at dear old Uni-Galacta?"

"No. That was my own idea. If they have artillery and mobile cavalry, then forts would be useless."

"And what would they use for cavalry?" asked Stetson. "There are no riding animals on Hamal. According to your reports, that is."

"So I haven't found any . . . yet!"

"All right," said Stetson. "I'll be reasonable. You spoke of weapons. What weapons do they use? I haven't seen anything heavier than those fowling pieces carried by their hunters."

"If they had cannon, that'd explain a lot of things," muttered Orne.

"Such as the lack of forts?"

"You're damn' right!"

"An interesting theory. How do they manufacture those guns, by the way?"

"They're produced singly by skilled artisans. It's a sort of a guild."

"A sort of a guild. My!" Stetson pulled the go-buggy to a jolting stop on a deserted stretch of the ridge road. "Did First-Contact see any sign of cannon?"

"You know he didn't."

Stetson nodded. "Mm-m-m, hm-m-m-m."

"But that could've been an accident," said Orne. "What I don't like is that the stupid jerk shot off his face and told these people right off how important it is to us that a redisk planet have a peaceful outlook."

"You're sooooo right. For once," said Stetson. He got out of the buggy. "Come on. Give me a hand."

Orne slid out his side. "Why're we stopping here?"

Stetson passed him the end of a tape measure. "Hold that on the edge of the road over there like a good fellow, will you?"

Orne obeyed.

The ridge road proved to be just under seven meters wide. Stetson wrote the figure in a notebook, muttered something about "lines of regression."

They got back into the buggy, moved on down the road.

"What's important about the width of the road?" asked Orne.

"I–A has a profitable side line selling omnibuses," said Stetson. "I just wanted to see if our current models would fit on these roads."

Funny man! thought Orne. He said, "I presume it's increasingly difficult for I–A to justify its appropriations!"

Stetson laughed. "You're too sooooo right! We're going to put in an additional line of nerve tonic for *R-and-R* agents."

"Hah!"

Orne leaned back into his own corner, became lost in gloom. *I'm sunk! This smart-Aleck isn't going to find anything I haven't found. There was no real reason to call in the I–A except that things don't feel right here!*

The ridge road dipped down to the right through scrub trees.

"We finally get off the high road," said Stetson.

"If we'd kept straight on, we'd have gone down into a swamp," said Orne.

"Oh?"

They came out into the floor of a wide valley that was cut by lines of windbreak trees. Smoke spiraled into the still air from behind the trees.

"What's the smoke over there?" asked Stetson.

"Houses."

"Have you looked?"

"Yes I've looked!"

"Touchy, aren't we?"

The road bore directly toward a river. They crossed on a crude wooden bridge. Stetson pulled to a stop on the opposite side of the bridge, stared at the twin lines of a narrow cart track that wound along the river.

Again they got under way, heading toward another ridge.

The I–A man looked thoughtful. "Let's go over that about their government again," he said.

Orne raised his voice above the whine of the turbine as it began to labor in the climb up the other ridge. "What do you mean?"

"That hereditary business."

"I just said that Council membership seems to be passed along on an eldest son basis."

"Seems to be?" Stetson maneuvered the buggy over a rise and onto a road that turned right down the crest of the ridge.

"Well, they gave me some hanky panky about an elective procedure in case the eldest son dies."

"I see. What games do these people play?"

"I've only seen one: it's played by sixteen men in teams of four. They use a square field about fifty meters on a side with smooth diagonal ditches crossing from corner to corner. Four men take stations at each corner, and rotate the turns at play."

"What do they do? Crawl at each other along the ditches?"

"Very funny! They use two heavy balls pierced for holding with the fingers. One ball's green and the other's yellow. Yellow ball goes first: it's rolled along the ditch. The green ball's supposed to be thrown in such a way that it smacks the yellow ball at the intersection."

"And a great huzzah goes up!" said Stetson.

"No audience," said Orne.

"Anyway, it seems like a peaceful game," said Stetson. "Are they good at it?"

"Remarkably clumsy I thought. But they seem to enjoy it. Come to think of it: that game's the only thing I've ever seen them even come close to enjoying."

"You're a frustrated missionary," said Stetson. "People aren't having any fun: you want to jump in and organize games!"

"War games," said Orne. "Have you ever thought of that one?"

"Huh?" Stetson took his eyes off the road momentarily. They bumped off the edge. He jerked his attention back to his driving.

"What if some smart *R-and-R* agent sets himself up as emperor on this planet?" asked Orne. "He could start his own dynasty. First thing you'd know about it is when the bombs started dropping!"

"That's the I–A's personal nightmare," said Stetson. He fell silent.

The sun climbed higher.

Their road dipped into a slight hollow, slanted up to a new ridge, swung left along the crest. They could see another village on high ground in the distance. When they were close enough to see the green-and-yellow flag atop the government building. Stetson pulled to a stop, opened his window, shut off the motor. The turbine keened down-scale to silence. With the window open, the air-conditioning off, they felt the oppressive heat of the day.

Sweat began pouring off Orne, settling in a soggy puddle where his bottom touched the plastic of the seat.

"What're we doing here?" asked Orne.

"Waiting."

"Waiting for what?"

"For something to happen," said Stetson. "How do the natives feel about peace?"

"Oh, they think it's wonderful. The Council members are delighted by the peaceful activities of *R-and-R*."

"Now tell me why you punched the panic button!" demanded Stetson.

Orne's mouth worked soundlessly. Then he blurted: "I told you before I wasn't sure!"

"I want to know what set you off," said Stetson. "What was the straw that grounded the blinking rocket?"

Orne swallowed, spoke in a low voice. "They held a banquet for—"

"Who held a banquet?"

"The Council. They held a banquet for me. And . . . uh—"

"They served *froolap*," said Stetson.

"Do you want to hear this?"

"Dear boy: I'm all ears."

"You're sooooo right!" said Orne. "Well . . . what they served me was a stew of *porjo* tails that—"

"Porjo?"

"It's a kind of rodent that they consider a delicacy. Especially the tails. Anyway, what they did was . . . well, the cook just before bringing the stew in and planking it down in front of me he tied up a live *porjo* with some kind of cord that dissolved quickly in the hot liquid. This animal erupted out of the pot and all over me."

"So?"

"They laughed for five minutes."

"You mean they played a practical joke on you and you got mad? I thought you said they had no sense of humor?"

"Look, wise guy! Have you ever stopped to think what kind of people it takes to put a live animal in boiling liquid just to play a joke?"

"A little heavy for humor," said Stetson. "But playful all the same. And that's why you called in the I–A?"

"That's part of it!"

"And the rest is your deep dark suspicions!"

Orne's face darkened with rage. "So I got mad and pulled a stupid boner! Go ahead! Make something out of it!"

"I fully intend to," said Stetson. He reached under the dash, pulled out a microphone, spoke into it: "This is Stetson."

So I've really had it! thought Orne.

A humming sound came from beneath the dash followed by: "This is the ship. What's doing?"

"We've got a real baddy here, Hal," said Stetson. "Put out an emergency call for an occupation force."

Orne jerked upright, ogled the I–A man.

The dash speaker clanked, and the voice said: "How bad is it?"

"One of the worst I've ever seen. Put out a VRO on the First-Contact: some jerk named Bullone. Have him sacked. I don't care if he's Commissioner Bullone's mother! It'd take a blind man and a stupid one at that to call this joint peaceful!"

"You going to have trouble getting back?" asked the voice.

"I doubt it. They don't know yet that we're on to them."

"Give me your grid just in case."

Stetson glanced at an indicator dial on the dash. "A-8."

"Gotcha."

"Get that call out, man!" said Stetson. "I want a full O-force in here by tomorrow night!"

"Right away."

The humming sound stopped.

Stetson replaced the microphone, turned to Orne. "So you just followed a hunch?"

Orne shook his head. "I—"

"Look behind us," said Stetson.

Orne stuck his head out the open window, stared back the way they had come.

"See anything curious?" asked Stetson.

Orne felt giddy. He said, "I see a late coming farmer and one hunter with apprentice moving up fast on the outside."

"I mean the road," said Stetson. "You may consider this a first lesson in I–A technique: a wide road that follows the ridges is a military road. Always. Farm roads are narrow and follow the water level route. Military roads are wider, avoid swamps, and cross rivers at right angles. This one fits all the way."

"But—" Orne fell silent as the hunter came up, passed their vehicle without a side glance.

"What's that leather case on his back?" asked Stetson.

"Spyglass."

"Lesson number two," said Stetson. "Telescopes always originate as astronomical devices. Spyglasses are always developed as an adjunct of a long-range weapon. I would guess that fowling piece has an effective range of probably one hundred meters. Ergo: you may take it as proved that they have artillery."

Orne nodded.

"Now let's look at this village," said Stetson. "Notice the flag. Almost inevitably they originate as banners to follow into battle. Not always. However, you may take this as a good piece of circumstantial evidence in view of the other things."

"I see."

"Now let's consider your Leader's Council," said Stetson. "There's nothing but a civilian aristocracy. Rule one in our book says that whenever you have a situation of haves and have-nots, then you have positions to be defended. That always means armies. I'll bet my bottom credit that those gaming fields of the green and yellow balls are disguised drill grounds."

Orne swallowed. "I should've thought of that."

"You did," said Stetson. "Unconsciously. You saw all of this unconsciously. It bothered hell out of you. That's why you pushed the panic button."

"I guess you're right."

"Another lesson," said Stetson. "The most important point on the aggression index: peaceful people don't even discuss peace. They don't even think about it. The only way you develop more than a casual interest in peace is through the violent contrast of war."

"Sure!" Orne took a deep breath, stared at the village. "But what about the lack of forts?"

"We can take it for granted that they have artillery," said Stetson. "Hmm-m-m." He rubbed at his chin. "Well, that's probably enough. I guess you don't have to have mobile cavalry in the equation to rule out forts."

"I guess not."

"What happened here was something like this," said Stetson. "First-Contact, that stoop Bullone, jumped to a wrong conclusion about these people, and he tipped our hand. The rulers of Hamal probably got together, declared a truce, hid or disguised every sign of war they knew about, and concentrated on milking us for all they could get."

"That figures," said Orne. He was just beginning to feel the emotional cleansing of relief.

"I think you'll make a pretty good I–A operative," said Stetson.

"I'll make a—Huh?"

"We're drafting you," said Stetson.

Orne stared at him. "Can you do that?"

"There are still some wise heads in our government," said Stetson. "You may take it for granted that we have this power." He frowned. "And we find too damned many of our people the way we found you!"

Orne swallowed. "This is—" He fell silent as the farmer pushed his creaking cart past the I–A vehicle. They stared at the peculiar swaying motion of the farmer's back, the solid way his feet came down, the smooth way the high-piled vegetable cart rolled over the road.

"I'm a left-handed *froolap* myself?" muttered Orne. He pointed at the retreating back. "There's your cavalry animal. That damn' wagon's nothing but a chariot!"

Stetson slapped his right fist into this open left palm. "Damn! Right in front of our eyes all the time!" He smiled grimly. "There are going to be some surprised and angry people hereabouts when our occupation force arrives."

As it turned out, he was "sooooo right."

MISSING LINK

"We ought to scrape this planet clean of every living thing on it," muttered Umbo Stetson, section chief of Investigation & Adjustment.

Stetson paced the landing control bridge of his scout cruiser. His footsteps grated on a floor that was the rear wall of the bridge during flight. But now the ship rested on its tail fins—all four hundred glistening red and black meters of it. The open ports of the bridge looked out on the jungle roof of Gienah III some one hundred fifty meters below. A butter yellow sun hung above the horizon, perhaps an hour from setting.

"Clean as an egg!" he barked. He paused in his round of the bridge, glared out the starboard port, spat into the fire-blackened circle that the cruiser's jets had burned from the jungle.

The I–A section chief was dark-haired, gangling, with large head and big features. He stood in his customary slouch, a stance not improved by sacklike patched blue fatigues. Although on this present operation he rated the flag of a division admiral, his fatigues carried no insignia. There was a general unkempt, straggling look about him.

Lewis Orne, junior I–A field man with a maiden diploma, stood at the opposite port, studying the jungle horizon. Now and then he glanced at the bridge control console, the chronometer above it, the big translite map of their position tilted from the opposite bulkhead. A heavy planet native, he felt vaguely uneasy on this Gienah III with its gravity of only seven-eighths Terran Standard. The surgical scars on his neck where the micro-communications equipment had been inserted itched maddeningly. He scratched.

"Hah!" said Stetson. "Politicians!"

A thin black insect with shell-like wings flew in Orne's port, settled in his close-cropped red hair. Orne pulled the insect gently from his hair, released it. Again it tried to land in his hair. He ducked. It flew across the bridge, out the port beside Stetson.

There was a thick-muscled, no-fat look to Orne, but something about his blocky, off-center features suggested a clown.

"I'm getting tired of waiting," he said.

"*You're* tired! Hah!"

A breeze rippled the tops of the green ocean below them. Here and there, red and purple flowers jutted from the verdure, bending and nodding like an attentive audience.

"Just look at that blasted jungle!" barked Stetson. "Them and their stupid orders!"

A call bell tinkled on the bridge control console. The red light above the speaker grid began blinking. Stetson shot an angry glance at it. "Yeah, Hal?"

"Okay, Stet. Orders just came through. We use Plan C. ComGO says to brief the field man, and jet out of here."

"Did you ask them about using another field man?"

Orne looked up attentively.

The speaker said: "Yes. They said we have to use Orne because of the records on the *Delphinus*."

"Well then, will they give us more time to brief him?"

"Negative. It's crash priority. ComGO expects to blast the planet anyway."

Stetson glared at the grid. "Those fat-headed, lard-bottomed, pig-brained . . . POLITICIANS!" He took two deep breaths, subsided. "Okay. Tell them we'll comply."

"One more thing, Stet."

"What now?"

"I've got a confirmed contact."

Instantly, Stetson was poised on the balls of his feet, alert. "Where?"

"About ten kilometers out. Section AAB-6."

"How many?"

"A mob. You want I should count them?"

"No. What're they doing?"

"Making a beeline for us. You better get a move on."

"Okay. Keep us posted."

"Right."

Stetson looked across at his junior field man. "Orne, if you decide you want out of this assignment, you just say the word. I'll back you to the hilt."

"Why should I want out of my first field assignment?"

"Listen, and find out." Stetson crossed to a tilt-locker behind the big translite map, hauled out a white coverall uniform with gold insignia, tossed it to Orne. "Get into these while I brief you on the map."

"But this is an R&R uni—" began Orne.

"Get that uniform on your ugly frame!"

"Yes, sir, Admiral Stetson, sir. Right away, sir. But I thought I was through with old Rediscovery & Reeducation when you drafted me off of Hamal into the I–A . . . sir." He began changing from the I–A blue to the R&R white. Almost as an afterthought, he said: ". . . Sir."

A wolfish grin cracked Stetson's big features. "I'm soooooo happy you have the proper attitude of subservience toward authority."

Orne zipped up the coverall uniform. "Oh, yes, sir . . . sir."

"Okay, Orne, pay attention." Stetson gestured at the map with its green superimposed grid squares. "Here we are. Here's that city we flew over on our way down. You'll head for it as soon as we drop you. The place is big enough that if you hold a course roughly northeast you can't miss it. We're—"

Again the call bell rang.

"What is it this time, Hal?" barked Stetson.

"They've changed to Plan H, Stet. New orders cut."

"Five days?"

"That's all they can give us. ComGO says he can't keep the information out of High Commissioner Bullone's hands any longer than that."

"It's five days for sure then."

"Is this the usual R&R foul-up?" asked Orne.

Stetson nodded, "Thanks to Bullone and company! We're just one jump ahead of catastrophe, but they still pump the bushwah into the Rah & Rah boys back at dear old Uni-Galacta!"

"You're making light of my revered alma mater," said Orne. He struck a pose. "We must reunite the lost planets with our centers of culture and industry, and take up the glorious onward march of mankind that was so brutally—"

"Can it!" snapped Stetson. "We both know we're going to rediscover one planet too many some day. Rim War all over again. But this is a different breed of fish. It's not, repeat, *not* a re-discovery."

Orne sobered. "Alien?"

"Yes. A-L-I-E-N! A never-before-contacted culture. That language you were force fed on the way over, that's an alien language. It's not complete . . . all we have off the *minis*. And we excluded data on the natives because we've been hoping to dump this project and nobody the wiser."

"Holy mazoo!"

"Twenty-six days ago an I–A search ship came through here, had a routine mini-sneaker look at the place. When he combed in his net of sneakers to check the tapes and films, lo and behold, he had a little stranger."

"One of *theirs*?"

"No. It was a *mini* off the *Delphinus Rediscovery*. The *Delphinus* has been unreported for eighteen standard months!"

"Did it crack up here?"

"We don't know. If it did, we haven't been able to spot it. She was supposed to be way off in the Balandine System by now. But we've something else on our minds. It's the one item that makes me want to blot out this place, and run home with my tail between my legs. We've a—"

Again the call bell chimed.

"NOW WHAT?" roared Stetson into the speaker.

"I've got a *mini* over that mob, Stet. They're talking about us. It's a definite raiding party."

"What armament?"

"Too gloomy in that jungle to be sure. The infra beam's out on this *mini*. Looks like hard pellet rifles of some kind. Might even be off the *Delphinus*."

"Can't you get closer?"

"Wouldn't do any good. No light down there, and they're moving up fast."

"Keep an eye on them, but don't ignore the other sectors," said Stetson.

"You think I was born yesterday?" barked the voice from the grid. The contact broke off with an angry sound.

"One thing I like about the I–A," said Stetson. "It collects such even-tempered types." He looked at the white uniform on Orne, wiped a hand across his mouth as though he'd tasted something dirty.

"Why *am* I wearing this thing?" asked Orne.

"Disguise."

"But there's no mustache!"

Stetson smiled without humor. "That's one of I–A's answers to those fat-keistered politicians. We're setting up our own search system to find the planets before *they* do. We've managed to put spies in key places at R&R. Any touchy planets our spies report, we divert the files."

"Then what?"

"Then we look into them with bright boys like you—disguised as R&R field men."

"Goody, goody. And what happens if R&R stumbles onto me while I'm down there playing patty cake?"

"We disown you."

"But you said an I–A ship found this joint."

"It did. And then one of our spies in R&R intercepted a *routine* request for an agent-instructor to be assigned here with full equipment. Request signed by a First-Contact officer name of Diston . . . of the *Delphinus*!"

"But the *Del*—"

"Yeah. Missing. The request was a forgery. Now you see why I'm mostly for rubbing out this place. Who'd dare forge such a thing unless he knew for sure that the original FC officer was missing . . . or dead?"

"What the jumped up mazoo are we doing here, Stet?" asked Orne. "Alien calls for a full contact team with all of the—"

"It calls for one planet-buster bomb . . . buster—in five days. Unless you give them a white bill in the meantime. High Commissioner Bullone will have word of this planet by then. If Gienah III still exists in five days, can't you imagine the fun the politicians'll have with it? Mama mia! We want this planet cleared for contact or dead before then."

"I don't like this, Stet."

"YOU don't like it!"

"Look," said Orne. "There must be another way. Why . . . when we teamed up with the Alerinoids we gained five hundred years in the physical sciences alone, not to mention the—"

"The Alerinoids didn't knock over one of our survey ships first."

"What if the *Delphinus* just crashed here . . . and the locals picked up the pieces?"

"That's what you're going in to find out, Orne. But answer me this: If they *do* have the *Delphinus,* how long before a tool-using race could be a threat to the galaxy?"

"I saw that city they built, Stet. They could be dug in within six months, and there'd be no—"

"Yeah."

Orne shook his head. "But think of it: Two civilizations that matured along different lines! Think of all the different ways we'd approach the same problems . . . the lever that'd give us for—"

"You sound like a Uni-Galacta lecture! Are you through marching arm in arm into the misty future?"

Orne took a deep breath. "Why's a freshman like me being tossed into this dish?"

"You'd still be on the *Delphinus* master lists as an R&R field man. That's important if you're masquerading."

"Am I the only one? I know I'm a recent *convert,* but—"

"You want out?"

"I didn't say that. I just want to know why I'm—"

"Because the bigdomes fed a set of requirements into one of their iron monsters. Your card popped out. They were looking for somebody capable, dependable . . . and . . . *expendable!*"

"Hey!"

"That's why I'm down here briefing you instead of sitting back on a flagship. *I* got you into the I–A. Now, you listen carefully: If you push the panic button on this one without cause, I will personally flay you alive. We both know the advantages of an alien contact. But if you get into a hot spot, and call for help, I'll dive this cruiser into that city to get you out!"

Orne swallowed. "Thanks, Stet. I'm—"

"We're going to take up a tight orbit. Out beyond us will be five transports full of I–A marines and a Class IX Monitor with one planet-buster. You're calling the shots, God help you! First, we want to know if they have the *Delphinus* . . . and if so, where it is. Next, we want to know just how warlike these goons are. Can we control them if they're bloodthirsty. What's their potential?"

"In five days?"

"Not a second more."

"What do we know about them?"

"Not much. They look something like an ancient Terran chimpanzee . . . only with blue fur. Face is hairless, pink-skinned." Stetson snapped a switch. The translite map became a screen with a figure frozen on it. "Like that. This is life size."

"Looks like the missing link they're always hunting for," said Orne.

"Yeah, but you've got a different kind of a missing link."

"Vertical-slit pupils in their eyes," said Orne. He studied the figure. It had been caught from the front by a mini-sneaker camera. About five feet tall. The stance was slightly bent forward, long arms. Two vertical nose slits. A flat, lipless mouth. Receding chin. Four-fingered hands. It wore a wide belt from which dangled neat pouches and what looked like tools, although their use was obscure. There appeared to be the tip of a tail protruding from behind one of the squat legs. Behind the creature towered the faery spires of the city they'd observed from the air.

"Tails?" asked Orne.

"Yeah. They're arboreal. Not a road on the whole planet that we can find. But there are lots of vine lanes through the jungles." Stetson's face hardened. "Match *that* with a city as advanced as that one."

"Slave culture?"

"Probably."

"How many cities have they?"

"We've found two. This one and another on the other side of the planet. But the other one's a ruin."

"A ruin? Why?"

"You tell us. Lots of mysteries here."

"What's the planet like?"

"Mostly jungle. There are polar oceans, lakes and rivers. One low mountain chain follows the equatorial belt about two thirds around the planet."

"But only two cities. Are you sure?"

"Reasonably so. It'd be pretty hard to miss something the size of that thing we flew over. It must be fifty kilometers long and at least ten wide. Swarming with these creatures, too. We've got a zone-count estimate that places the city's population at over thirty million."

"Whee-ew! Those are tall buildings, too."

"We don't know much about this place, Orne. And unless you bring them into the fold, there'll be nothing but ashes for our archaeologists to pick over."

"Seems a dirty shame."

"I agree, but—"

The call bell jangled.

Stetson's voice sounded tired: "Yeah, Hal?"

"That mob's only about five kilometers out, Stet. We've got Orne's gear outside in the disguised air sled."

"We'll be right down."

"Why a disguised sled?" asked Orne.

"If they think it's a ground buggy, they might get careless when you most need an advantage. We could always scoop you out of the air, you know."

"What're my chances on this one, Stet?"

Stetson shrugged. "I'm afraid they're slim. These goons probably have the *Delphinus,* and they want you just long enough to get your equipment and everything you know."

"Rough as that, eh?"

"According to our best guess. If you're not out in five days, we blast."

Orne cleared his throat.

"Want out?" asked Stetson.

"No."

"Use the *back-door* rule, son. Always leave yourself a way out. Now . . . let's check that equipment the surgeons put in your neck." Stetson put a hand to his throat. His mouth remained closed, but there was a surf-hissing voice in Orne's ears: "You read me?"

"Sure. I can—"

"No!" hissed the voice. "Touch the mike contact. Keep your mouth closed. Just use your speaking muscles without speaking."

Orne obeyed.

"Okay," said Stetson. "You come in loud and clear."

"I ought to. I'm right on top of you!"

"There'll be a relay ship over you all the time," said Stetson. "Now . . . when you're not touching that mike contact this rig'll still feed us what you say . . . and everything that goes on around you, too. We'll monitor every-thing. Got that?"

"Yes."

Stetson held out his right hand. "Good luck. I meant that about diving in for you. Just say the word."

"I know the word, too," said Orne. "HELP!"

Gray mud floor and gloomy aisles between monstrous bluish tree trunks— that was the jungle. Only the barest weak glimmering of sunlight penetrated to the mud. The disguised sled—its para-grav units turned off—lurched and skidded around buttress roots. Its headlights swung in wild arcs across the trunks and down to the mud. Aerial creepers—great looping vines of them—swung down from the towering forest ceiling. A steady drip of condensation spattered the windshield, forcing Orne to use the wipers.

In the bucket seat of the sled's cab, Orne fought the controls. He was plagued by the vague slow-motion-floating sensation that a heavy planet native always feels in lighter gravity. It gave him an unhappy stomach.

Things skipped through the air around the lurching vehicle: flitting and darting things. Insects came in twin cones, siphoned toward the headlights. There was an endless chittering, whistling, *tok-tok-tok*ing in the gloom beyond the lights.

Stetson's voice hissed suddenly through the surgically implanted speaker: "How's it look?"

"Alien."

"Any sign of that mob?"

"Negative."

"Okay. We're taking off."

Behind Orne, there came a deep rumbling roar that receded as the scout cruiser climbed its jets. All other sounds hung suspended in after-silence, then resumed: the strongest first and then the weakest.

A heavy object suddenly arced through the headlights, swinging on a vine. It disappeared behind a tree. Another. Another. Ghostly shadows with vine pendulums on both sides. Something banged down heavily onto the hood of the sled.

Orne braked to a creaking stop that shifted the load behind him, found himself staring through the windshield at a native of Gienah III. The native crouched on the hood, a Mark XX exploding-pellet rifle in his right hand directed at Orne's head. In the abrupt shock of meeting, Orne recognized the weapon: standard issue to the marine guards on all R&R survey ships.

The native appeared the twin of the one Orne had seen on the translite screen. The four-fingered hand looked extremely capable around the stock of the Mark XX.

Slowly, Orne put a hand to his throat, pressed the contact button. He moved his speaking muscles: *"Just made contact with the mob. One on the hood now has one of our Mark XX rifles aimed at my head."*

The surf-hissing of Stetson's voice came through the hidden speaker: *"Want us to come back?"*

"Negative. Stand by. He looks cautious rather than hostile."

Orne held up his right hand, palm out. He had a second thought: held up his left hand, too. Universal symbol of peaceful intentions: empty hands. The gun muzzle lowered slightly. Orne called into his mind the language that had been hypnoforced into him. *Ocheero? No. That means 'The People.' Ah* . . . And he had the heavy fricative greeting sound.

"Ffroiragrazzi," he said.

The native shifted to the left, answered in pure, unaccented High Galactese: "Who are you?"

Orne fought down a sudden panic. The lipless mouth had looked so odd forming the familiar words.

Stetson's voice hissed: *"Is that the native speaking Galactese?"*

Orne touched his throat. *"You heard him."*

He dropped his hand, said: "I am Lewis Orne of Rediscovery and Reeducation. I was sent here at the request of the First-Contact officer on the *Delphinus Rediscovery.*"

"Where is your ship?" demanded the Gienahn.

"It put me down and left."

"Why?"

"It was behind schedule for another appointment."

Out of the corners of his eyes, Orne saw more shadows dropping to the mud around him. The sled shifted as someone climbed onto the load behind the cab. The someone scuttled agilely for a moment.

The native climbed down to the cab's side step, opened the door. The rifle was held at the ready. Again, the lipless mouth formed Galactese words: "What do you carry in this . . . vehicle?"

"The equipment every R&R field man uses to help the people of a rediscovered planet improve themselves." Orne nodded at the rifle. "Would you mind pointing that weapon some other direction? It makes me nervous."

The gun muzzle remained unwaveringly on Orne's middle. The native's mouth opened, revealing long canines. "Do we not look strange to you?"

"I take it there's been a heavy mutational variation in the humanoid norm on this planet," said Orne. "What is it? Hard radiation?"

No answer.

"It doesn't really make any difference, of course," said Orne. "I'm here to help you."

"I am Tanub, High Path Chief of the Grazzi," said the native. "I decide who is to help."

Orne swallowed.

"Where do you go?" demanded Tanub.

"I was hoping to go to your city. Is it permitted?"

A long pause while the vertical-slit pupils of Tanub's eyes expanded and contracted. "It is permitted."

Stetson's voice came through the hidden speaker: *"All bets off. We're coming in after you. That Mark XX is the final straw. It means they have the* Delphinus *for sure!"*

Orne touched his throat. *"No! Give me a little more time!"*

"Why?"

"I have a hunch about these creatures."

"What is it?"

"No time now. Trust me."

Another long pause in which Orne and Tanub continued to study each other. Presently, Stetson said: *"Okay. Go ahead as planned. But find out where the* Delphinus *is! If we get that back we pull their teeth."*

"Why do you keep touching your throat?" demanded Tanub.

"I'm nervous," said Orne. "Guns always make me nervous."

The muzzle lowered slightly.

"Shall we continue on to your city?" asked Orne. He wet his lips with his tongue. The cab light on Tanub's face was giving the Gienahn an eerie sinister look.

"We can go soon," said Tanub.

"Will you join me inside here?" asked Orne. "There's a passenger seat right behind me."

Tanub's eyes moved catlike: right, left. "Yes." He turned, barked an order into the jungle gloom, then climbed in behind Orne.

"When do we go?" asked Orne.

"The great sun will be down soon," said Tanub. "We can continue as soon as Chiranachuruso rises."

"Chiranachuruso?"

"Our satellite . . . our moon," said Tanub.

"It's a beautiful word," said Orne. "Chiranachuruso."

"In our tongue it means: The Limb of Victory," said Tanub. "By its light we will continue."

Orne turned, looked back at Tanub. "Do you mean to tell me that you can see by what light gets down here through those trees?"

"Can you not see?" asked Tanub.

"Not without the headlights."

"Our eyes differ," said Tanub. He bent toward Orne, peered. The vertical slit pupils of his eyes expanded, contracted. "You are the same as the . . . others."

"Oh, on the *Delphinus*?"

Pause. "Yes."

Presently, a greater gloom came over the jungle, bringing a sudden stillness to the wild life. There was a chittering commotion from the natives in the trees around the sled. Tanub shifted behind Orne.

"We may go now," he said. "Slowly . . . to stay behind my . . . scouts."

"Right." Orne eased the sled forward around an obstructing root.

Silence while they crawled ahead. Around them shapes flung themselves from vine to vine.

"I admired your city from the air," said Orne. "It is very beautiful."

"Yes," said Tanub. "Why did you land so far from it?"

"We didn't want to come down where we might destroy anything."

"There is nothing to destroy in the jungle," said Tanub.

"Why do you have such a big city?" asked Orne.

Silence.

"I said: Why do you—"

"You are ignorant of our ways," said Tanub. "Therefore, I forgive you. The city is for our race. We must breed and be born in sunlight. Once—long ago—we used crude platforms on the tops of the trees. Now . . . only the . . . wild ones do this."

Stetson's voice hissed in Orne's ears: *"Easy on the sex line, boy. That's always touchy. These creatures are oviparous. Sex glands are apparently hidden in that long fur behind where their chins ought to be."*

"Who controls the breeding sites controls our world," said Tanub. "Once there was another city. We destroyed it."

"Are there many . . . wild ones?" asked Orne.

"Fewer each year," said Tanub.

"There's how they get their slaves," hissed Stetson.

"You speak excellent Galactese," said Orne.

"The High Path Chief commanded the best teacher," said Tanub. "Do you, too, know many things, Orne?"

"That's why I was sent here," said Orne.

"Are there many planets to teach?" asked Tanub.

"Very many," said Orne. "Your city—I saw very tall buildings. Of what do you build them?"

"In your tongue—glass," said Tanub. "The engineers of the *Delphinus* said it was impossible. As you saw—they are wrong."

"A glass-blowing culture," hissed Stetson. *"That'd explain a lot of things."*

Slowly, the disguised sled crept through the jungle. Once, a scout swooped down into the headlights, waved. Orne stopped on Tanub's order, and they waited almost ten minutes before proceeding.

"Wild ones?" asked Orne.

"Perhaps," said Tanub.

A glowing of many lights grew visible through the giant tree trunks. It grew brighter as the sled crept through the last of the jungle, emerged in cleared land at the edge of the city.

Orne stared upward in awe. The city fluted and spiraled into the moonlit sky. It was a fragile appearing lacery of bridges, winking dots of light. The bridges wove back and forth from building to building until the entire visible network appeared one gigantic dew-glittering web.

"All that with glass," murmured Orne.

"What's happening?" hissed Stetson.

Orne touched his throat contact. *"We're just into the city clearing, pro-ceeding toward the nearest building."*

"This is far enough," said Tanub.

Orne stopped the sled. In the moonlight, he could see armed Gienahns all around. The buttressed pedestal of one of the buildings loomed directly ahead. It looked taller than had the scout cruiser in its jungle landing circle.

Tanub leaned close to Orne's shoulder. "We have not deceived you, have we, Orne?"

"Huh? What do you mean?"

"You have recognized that we are not mutated members of your race."

Orne swallowed. Into his ears came Stetson's voice: *"Better admit it."*

"That's true," said Orne.

"I like you, Orne," said Tanub. "You shall be one of my slaves. You will teach me many things."

"How did you capture the *Delphinus*?" asked Orne.

"You know that, too?"

"You have one of their rifles," said Orne.

"Your race is no match for us, Orne . . . in cunning, in strength, in the prowess of the mind. Your ship landed to repair its tubes. Very inferior ceramics in those tubes."

Orne turned, looked at Tanub in the dim glow of the cab light. "Have you heard about the I–A, Tanub?"

"I–A? What is that?" There was a wary tenseness in the Gienahn's figure. His mouth opened to reveal the long canines.

"You took the *Delphinus* by treachery?" asked Orne.

"They were simple fools," said Tanub. "We are smaller, thus they thought us weaker." The Mark XX's muzzle came around to center on Orne's stomach. "You have not answered my question. What is the I–A?"

"I am of the I–A," said Orne. "Where've you hidden the *Delphinus*?"

"In the place that suits us best," said Tanub. "In all our history there has never been a better place."

"What do you plan to do with it?" asked Orne.

"Within a year we will have a copy with our own improvements. After that—"

"You intend to start a war?" asked Orne.

"In the jungle the strong slay the weak until only the strong remain," said Tanub.

"And then the strong prey upon each other?" asked Orne.

"That is a quibble for women," said Tanub.

"It's too bad you feel that way," said Orne. "When two cultures meet like this they tend to help each other. What have you done with the crew of the *Delphinus*?"

"They are slaves," said Tanub. "Those who still live. Some resisted. Others objected to teaching us what we want to know." He waved the gun muzzle. "You will not be that foolish, will you, Orne?"

"No need to be," said Orne. "I've another little lesson to teach you: I already know where you've hidden the *Delphinus*."

"Go, boy!" hissed Stetson. *"Where is it?"*

"Impossible!" barked Tanub.

"It's on your moon," said Orne. "Darkside. It's on a mountain on the darkside of your moon."

Tanub's eyes dilated, contracted. "You read minds?"

"The I–A has no need to read minds," said Orne. "We rely on superior mental prowess."

"The marines are on their way," hissed Stetson. *"We're coming in to get you. I'm going to want to know how you guessed that one."*

"You are a weak fool like the others," gritted Tanub.

"It's too bad you formed your opinion of us by observing only the low grades of the R&R," said Orne.

"Easy, boy," hissed Stetson. *"Don't pick a fight with him now. Remember, his race is arboreal. He's probably as strong as an ape."*

"I could kill you where you sit!" grated Tanub.

"You write finish for your entire planet if you do," said Orne. "I'm not alone. There are others listening to every word we say. There's a ship overhead that could split open your planet with one bomb—wash it with molten rock. It'd run like the glass you use for your buildings."

"You are lying!"

"We'll make you an offer," said Orne. "We don't really want to exterminate you. We'll give you limited membership in the Galactic Federation until you prove you're no menace to us."

"Keep talking," hissed Stetson. *"Keep him interested."*

"You dare insult me!" growled Tanub.

"You had better believe me," said Orne. "We—"

Stetson's voice interrupted him: *"Got it, Orne! They caught the* Delphinus *on the ground right where you said it'd be! Blew the tubes off it. Marines now mopping up."*

"It's like this," said Orne. "We already have recaptured the *Delphinus*." Tanub's eyes went instinctively skyward. "Except for the captured armament you still hold, you obviously don't have the weapons to meet us," continued Orne. "Otherwise, you wouldn't be carrying that rifle off the *Delphinus*."

"If you speak the truth, then we shall die bravely," said Tanub.

"No need for you to die," said Orne.

"Better to die than be slaves," said Tanub.

"We don't need slaves," said Orne. "We—"

"I cannot take the chance that you are lying," said Tanub. "I must kill you now."

Orne's foot rested on the air sled control pedal. He depressed it. Instantly, the sled shot skyward, heavy G's pressing them down into the seats. The gun in Tanub's hands was slammed into his lap. He struggled to raise it. To Orne, the weight was still only about twice that of his home planet of Chargon. He reached over, took the rifle, found safety belts, bound Tanub with them. Then he eased off the acceleration.

"We don't need slaves," said Orne. "We have machines to do our work. We'll send experts in here, teach you people how to exploit your planet, how to build good transportation facilities, show you how to mine your minerals, how to—"

"And what do we do in return?" whispered Tanub.

"You could start by teaching us how you make superior glass," said Orne. "I certainly hope you see things our way. We really don't want to have to come down there and clean you out. It'd be a shame to have to blast that city into little pieces."

Tanub wilted. Presently, he said: "Send me back. I will discuss this with . . . our council." He stared at Orne. "You I–A's are too strong. We did not know."

In the wardroom of Stetson's scout cruiser, the lights were low, the leather chairs comfortable, the green beige table set with a decanter of Hochar brandy and two glasses.

Orne lifted his glass, sipped the liquor, smacked his lips. "For a while there, I thought I'd never be tasting anything like this again."

Stetson took his own glass. "ComGO heard the whole thing over the general monitor net," he said. "D'you know you've been breveted to senior field man?"

"Ah, they've already recognized my sterling worth," said Orne.

The wolfish grin took over Stetson's big features. "Senior field men last about half as long as the juniors," he said. "Mortality's terrific?"

"I might've known," said Orne. He took another sip of the brandy.

Stetson flicked on the switch of a recorder beside him. "Okay. You can go ahead any time."

"Where do you want me to start?"

"First, how'd you spot right away where they'd hidden the *Delphinus*?"

"Easy. Tanub's word for his people was *Grazzi*. Most races call themselves something meaning *The People*. But in his tongue that's *Ocheero*. *Grazzi* wasn't on the translated list. I started working on it. The most likely answer was that it had been adopted from another language, and meant *enemy*."

"And *that* told you where the *Delphinus* was?"

"No. But it fitted my hunch about these Gienahns. I'd kind of felt from the first minute of meeting them that they had a culture like the Indians of ancient Terra."

"Why?"

"They came in like a primitive raiding party. The leader dropped right onto the hood of my sled. An act of bravery, no less. Counting coup, you see?"

"I guess so."

"Then he said he was High Path Chief. That wasn't on the language list, either. But it was easy: *Raider Chief.* There's a word in almost every language in history that means raider and derives from a word for road, path or highway."

"Highwaymen," said Stetson.

"Raid itself," said Orne. "An ancient Terran language corruption of road."

"Yeah, yeah. But where'd all this translation griff put—"

"Don't be impatient. Glass-blowing culture meant they were just out of the primitive stage. That, we could control. Next, he said their moon was *Chiranachuruso,* translated as *The Limb of Victory.* After that it just fell into place."

"How?"

"The vertical-slit pupils of their eyes. Doesn't that mean anything to you?"

"Maybe. What's it mean to you?"

"Night-hunting predator accustomed to dropping upon its victims from above. No other type of creature ever has had the vertical slit. And Tanub said himself that the *Delphinus* was hidden in the best place in all of their history. History? That'd be a high place. Dark, likewise. Ergo: a high place on the darkside of their moon."

"I'm a pie-eyed greepus," whispered Stetson.

Orne grinned, said: "You probably are . . . sir."

OPERATION HAYSTACK

When the Investigation & Adjustment scout cruiser landed on Marak it carried a man the doctors had no hope of saving. He was alive only because he was in a womblike creche pod that had taken over most of his vital functions.

The man's name was Lewis Orne. He had been a blocky, heavy-muscled redhead with slightly off-center features and the hard flesh of a heavy planet native. Even in the placid repose of near death there was something clownish about his appearance. His burned, ungent-covered face looked made up for some bizarre show.

Marak is the League capital, and the I–A medical center there is probably the best in the galaxy, but it accepted the creche pod and Orne more as a curiosity than anything else. The man had lost one eye, three fingers of his left hand and part of his hair, suffered a broken jaw and various internal injuries. He had been in terminal shock for more than ninety hours.

Umbo Stetson, Orne's section chief, went back into his cruiser's "office" after a hospital flitter took pod and patient. There was an added droop to Stetson's shoulders that accentuated his usual slouching stance. His over-large features were drawn into ridges of sorrow. A general straggling, trampish look about him was not helped by patched blue fatigues.

The doctor's words still rang in Stetson's ears: "This patient's vital tone is too low to permit operative replacement of damaged organs. He'll live for a while because of the pod, but—" And the doctor had shrugged.

Stetson slumped into his desk chair, looked out the open port beside him. Some four hundred meters below, the scurrying beetlelike activity of the I–A's main field sent up discordant roaring and clattering. Two rows of other scout cruisers were parked in line with Stetson's port—gleaming red and black needles. He stared at them without really seeing them.

It always happens on some "routine" assignment, he thought. *Nothing but a slight suspicion about Heleb: the fact that only women held high office.*

One simple, unexplained fact . . . and I lose my best agent! He sighed, turned to his desk, began composing the report:

"The militant core on the Planet Heleb has been eliminated. Occupation force on the ground. No further danger to Galactic peace expected from this source. Reason for operation: Rediscovery & Reeducation—*after two years on the planet*—failed to detect signs of militancy. The major indications were: 1) a ruling caste restricted to women, and 2) disparity between numbers of males and females *far* beyond the Lutig norm! Senior Field Agent Lewis Orne found that the ruling caste was controlling the sex of offspring at conception (see attached details), and had raised a male slave army to maintain its rule. The R&R agent had been drained of information, then killed. Arms constructed on the basis of that information caused critical injuries to Senior Field Agent Orne. He is not expected to live. I am hereby urging that he receive the Galaxy Medal, and that his name be added to the Roll of Honor."

Stetson pushed the page aside. That was enough for ComGO, who never read anything but the first page anyway. Details were for his aides to chew and digest. They could wait. Stetson punched his desk callbox for Orne's service record, set himself to the task he most detested: notifying next of kin. He read, pursing his lips:

"Home Planet: Chargon. Notify in case of accident or death: Mrs. Victoria Orne, mother."

He leafed through the pages, reluctant to send the hated message. Orne had enlisted in the Marak Marines at age seventeen—a runaway from home—and his mother had given post-enlistment consent. Two years later: scholarship transfer to Uni-Galacta, the R&R school here on Marak. Five years of school and one R&R field assignment under his belt, and he had been drafted into the I–A for brilliant detection of militancy on Hamal. And two years later—*kaput!*

Abruptly, Stetson hurled the service record at the gray metal wall across from him; then he got up, brought the record back to his desk, smoothing the pages. There were tears in his eyes. He flipped a switch on his desk, dictated the notification to Central Secretarial, ordered it sent out priority. Then he went groundside and got drunk on Hochar brandy, Orne's favorite drink.

The next morning there was a reply from Chargon: "Lewis Orne's mother too ill to travel. Sisters being notified. Please ask Mrs. Ipscott Bullone of Marak, wife of the High Commissioner, to take over for family." It was signed: "Madrena Orne Standish, sister."

With some misgivings, Stetson called the residence of Ipscott Bullone, leader of the majority party in the Marak Assembly. Mrs. Bullone took the call with blank screen. There was a sound of running water in the background. Stetson stared at the grayness swimming in his desk visor. He always disliked a blank screen. A baritone husk of a voice slid: "This is Polly Bullone."

Stetson introduced himself, relayed the Chargon message.

"Victoria's boy dying? Here? Oh, the poor thing! And Madrena's back on Chargon . . . the election. Oh, yes, of course. I'll get right over to the hospital!"

Stetson signed off, broke the contact.

The High Commissioner's wife yet! he thought. Then because he had to do it, he walled off his sorrow, got to work.

At the medical center, the oval creche containing Orne hung from ceiling hooks in a private room. There were humming sounds in the dim, watery greenness of the room, rhythmic chuggings, sighings. Occasionally, a door opened almost soundlessly, and a white-clad figure would check the graph tapes on the creche's meters.

Orne was lingering. He became the major conversation piece at the internes' coffee breaks: "That agent who was hurt on Heleb, he's still with us. Man, they must build those guys different from the rest of us! . . . Yeah! Understand he's got only about an eighth of his insides . . . liver, kidneys, stomach—all gone . . . Lay you odds he doesn't last out the month . . . Look what old sure-thing McTavish wants to bet on!"

On the morning of his eighty-eighth day in the creche, the day nurse came into Orne's room, lifted the inspection hood, looked down at him. The day nurse was a tall, lean-faced professional who had learned to meet miracles and failures with equal lack of expression. However, this routine with the dying I–A operative had lulled her into a state of psychological unpreparedness. *Any day now, poor guy,* she thought. And she gasped as she opened his sole remaining eye, said:

"Did they clobber those dames on Heleb?"

"Yes, sir!" she blurted. "They really did, sir!"

"Good!"

Orne closed his eye. His breathing deepened.

The nurse rang frantically for the doctors.

It had been an indeterminate period in a blank fog for Orne, then a time of pain and the gradual realization that he was in a creche. Had to be. He could remember his sudden exposure on Heleb, the explosion—then nothing. Good old creche. It made him feel safe now, shielded from all danger.

Orne began to show minute but steady signs of improvement. In another month, the doctors ventured an intestinal graft that gave him a new spurt of energy. Two months later, they replaced missing eye and fingers, restored his scalp line, worked artistic surgery on his burn scars.

Fourteen months, eleven days, five hours and two minutes after he had been picked up "as good as dead," Orne walked out of the hospital under his own power, accompanied by a strangely silent Umbo Stetson.

Under the dark blue I–A field cape, Orne's coverall uniform fitted his once muscular frame like a deflated bag. But the pixie light had returned to his eyes—even to the eye he had received from a nameless and long dead donor. Except for the loss of weight, he looked to be the same Lewis Orne. If he was different—beyond the "spare parts"—it was something he only suspected, something that made the idea, "twice-born," not a joke.

Outside the hospital, clouds obscured Marak's green sun. It was midmorning. A cold spring wind bent the pile lawn, tugged fitfully at the border plantings of exotic flowers around the hospital's landing pad.

Orne paused on the steps above the pad, breathed deeply of the chill air. "Beautiful day," he said.

Stetson reached out a hand to help Orne down the steps, hesitated, put the hand back in his pocket. Beneath the section chief's look of weary superciliousness there was a note of anxiety. His big features were set in a frown. The drooping eyelids failed to conceal a sharp, measuring stare.

Orne glanced at the sky to the southwest. "The flitter ought to be here any minute." A gust of wind tugged at his cape. He staggered, caught his balance. "I *feel* good."

"You look like something left over from a funeral," growled Stetson.

"Sure—my funeral," said Orne. He grinned. "Anyway, I was getting tired of that walk-around-type morgue. All my nurses were married."

"I'd almost stake my life that I could trust you," muttered Stetson.

Orne looked at him. "No, no, Stet . . . stake *my* life. I'm used to it."

Stetson shook his head. "No, dammit! I trust you, but you deserve a peaceful convalescence. We've no right to saddle you with—"

"Stet?" Orne's voice was low, amused.

"Huh?" Stetson looked up.

"Let's save the noble act for someone who doesn't know you," said Orne. "You've a job for me. Okay. You've made the gesture for your conscience."

Stetson produced a wolfish grin. "All right. So we're desperate, and we haven't much time. In a nutshell, since you're going to be a house guest at the Bullones'—we suspect Ipscott Bullone of being the head of a conspiracy to take over the government."

"What do you mean—*take over the government*?" demanded Orne. "The Galactic High Commissioner *is* the government—subject to the Constitution and the Assemblymen who elected him."

"We've a situation that could explode into another Rim War, and we think he's at the heart of it," said Stetson. "We've eighty-one touchy planets, all of them old-line steadies that have been in the League for years. And on every one of them we have reason to believe there's a clan of traitors sworn to overthrow the League. Even on your home planet—Chargon."

"You want me to go home for my convalescence?" asked Orne. "Haven't been there since I was seventeen. I'm not sure that—"

"No, dammit! We want you as the Bullones' house guest! And speaking of that, would you mind explaining how they were chosen to ride herd on you?"

"There's an odd thing," said Orne. "All those gags in the I–A about old Upshook Ipscott Bullone . . . and then I find that his wife went to school with my mother."

"Have you met Himself?"

"He brought his wife to the hospital a couple of times."

Again, Stetson looked to the southwest, then back to Orne. A pensive look came over his face. "Every schoolkid knows how the Nathians and the Marakian League fought it out in the Rim War—how the old civilization fell apart—and it all seems kind of distant," he said.

"Five hundred standard years," said Orne.

"And maybe no farther away than yesterday," murmured Stetson. He cleared his throat.

And Orne wondered why Stetson was moving so cautiously. *Something deep troubling him.* A sudden thought struck Orne. He said: "You spoke of trust. Has this conspiracy involved the I–A?"

"We think so," said Stetson. "About a year ago, an R&R archeological team was nosing around some ruins on Dabih. The place was all but vitrified in the Rim War, but a whole bank of records from a Nathian outpost escaped." He glanced sidelong at Orne. "The Rah&Rah boys couldn't make sense out of the records. No surprise. They called in an I–A crypt-analyst. He broke a complicated substitution cipher. When the stuff started making sense he pushed the panic button."

"For something the Nathians wrote five hundred years ago?"

Stetson's drooping eyelids lifted. There was a cold quality to his stare. "This was a routing station for key Nathian families," he said. "Trained refugees. An old dodge . . . been used as long as there've been—"

"But five hundred *years,* Stet!"

"I don't care if it was five *thousand* years!" barked Stetson. "We've intercepted some scraps since then that were written in the *same* code. The bland confidence of *that*! Wouldn't that gall you?" He shook his head. "And every scrap we've intercepted deals with the coming elections."

"But the election's only a couple of days off!" protested Orne.

Stetson glanced at his wristchrono. "Forty-two hours to be exact," he said. "Some deadline!"

"Any names in these old records?" asked Orne.

Stetson nodded. "Names of planets, yes. People, no. Some code names, but no cover names. Code name on Chargon was *Winner.* That ring any bells with you?"

Orne shook his head. "No. What's the code name here?"

"The Head," said Stetson. "But what good does that do us? They're sure to've changed those by now."

"They didn't change their communications code," said Orne.

"No . . . they didn't."

"We must have something on them, some leads," said Orne. He felt that Stetson was holding back something vital.

"Sure," said Stetson. "We have history books. They say the Nathians were top drawer in political mechanics. We know for a fact they chose landing sites for their *refugees* with diabolical care. Each family was told to dig in, grow up with the adopted culture, develop the weak spots, build an underground, train their descendants to take over. They set out to bore from within, to make victory out of defeat. The Nathians were long on patience. They came originally from nomad stock on Nathia II. Their mythology calls them Arbs or Ayrbs. Go review your seventh grade history. You'll know almost as much as we do!"

"Like looking for the traditional needle in the haystack," muttered Orne. "How come you suspect High Commissioner Upshook?"

Stetson wet his lips with his tongue. "One of the Bullones' seven daughters is currently at home," he said. "Name's Diana. A field leader in the I–A women. One of the Nathian code messages we intercepted had her name as addressee."

"Who sent the message?" asked Orne. "What was it all about?"

Stetson coughed. "You know, Lew, we cross-check everything. This message was signed M.O.S. The only M.O.S. that came out of the comparison was on a routine next-of-kin reply. We followed it down to the original copy, and the handwriting checked. Name of Madrena Orne Standish."

"Maddie?" Orne froze, turned slowly to face Stetson. "So that's what's troubling you!"

"We know you haven't been home since you were seventeen," said Stetson. "Your record with us is clean. The question is—"

"Permit me," said Orne. "The question is: Will I turn in my own sister if it falls that way?"

Stetson remained silent, staring at him.

"Okay," said Orne. "My job is seeing that we don't have another Rim War. Just answer me one question: How's Maddie mixed up in this? My family isn't one of these traitor clans."

"This whole thing is all tangled up with politics," said Stetson. "We think it's because of her husband."

"Ahhhh, the member for Chargon," said Orne. "I've never met him." He looked to the southwest where a flitter was growing larger as it approached. "Who's my cover contact?"

"That mini-transceiver we planted in your neck for the Gienah job," said Stetson. "It's still there and functioning. Anything happens around you, we hear it."

Orne touched the subvocal stud at his neck, moved his speaking muscles without opening his mouth. A surf-hissing voice filled the matching transceiver in Stetson's neck:

"You pay attention while I'm making a play for this Diana Bullone, you hear? Then you'll know how an expert works."

"Don't get so interested in your work that you forget why you're out there," growled Stetson.

Mrs. Bullone was a fat little mouse of a woman. She stood almost in the center of the guest room of her home, hands clasped across the paunch of a long, dull silver gown. She had demure gray eyes, grandmotherly gray hair combed straight back in a jeweled net—and that shocking baritone husk of a voice issuing from a small mouth. Her figure sloped out from several chins to a matronly bosom, then dropped straight like a barrel. The top of her head came just above Orne's dress epaulets.

"We want you to feel at home here, Lewis," she husked. "You're to consider yourself one of the family."

Orne looked around at the Bullone guest room: low-key furnishings with an old-fashioned selectacol for change of decor. A polawindow looked out onto an oval swimming pool, the glass muted to dark blue. It gave the outside a moonlight appearance. There was a contour bed against one wall, several built-ins, and a door partly open to reveal bathroom tiles. Everything traditional and comfortable.

"I already *do* feel at home," he said. "You know, your house is very like our place on Chargon. I was surprised when I saw it from the air. Except for the setting, it looks almost identical."

"I guess your mother and I shared ideas when we were in school," said Polly. "We were *very* close friends."

"You must've been to do all this for me," said Orne. "I don't know how I'm ever going to—"

"Ah! Here we are!" A deep masculine voice boomed from the open door behind Orne. He turned, saw Ipscott Bullone, High Commissioner of the Marakian League. Bullone was tall, had a face of harsh angles and deep lines, dark eyes under heavy brows, black hair trained in receding waves. There was a look of ungainly clumsiness about him.

He doesn't strike me as the dictator type, thought Orne. *But that's obviously what Stet suspects.*

"Glad you made it out all right, son," boomed Bullone. He advanced into the room, glanced around. "Hope everything's to your taste here."

"Lewis was just telling me that our place is very like his mother's home on Chargon," said Polly.

"It's old fashioned, but we like it," said Bullone. "Just a great big tetragon on a central pivot. We can turn any room we want to the sun, the shade or the breeze, but we usually leave the main salon pointing northeast. View of the capital, you know."

"We have a sea breeze on Chargon that we treat the same way," said Orne.

"I'm sure Lewis would like to be left alone for a while now," said Polly. "This is his first day out of the hospital. We mustn't tire him." She crossed to the polawindow, adjusted it to neutral gray, turned the selectacol, and the room's color dominance shifted to green. "There, that's more restful," she said. "Now, if there's anything you need you just ring the bell there by your bed. The autobutle will know where to find us."

The Bullones left, and Orne crossed to the window, looked out at the pool. The young woman hadn't come back. When the chauffeur-driven limousine flitter had dropped down to the house's landing pad, Orne had seen a parasol and sunhat nodding to each other on the blue tiles beside the pool. The parasol had shielded Polly Bullone. The sunhat had been worn by a shapely young woman in swimming tights, who had rushed off into the house.

She was no taller than Polly, but slender and with golden red hair caught under the sunhat in a swimmer's chignon. She was not beautiful—face too narrow with suggestions of Bullone's cragginess, and the eyes overlarge. But her mouth was full-lipped, chin strong, and there had been an air of exquisite assurance about her. The total effect had been one of striking elegance—extremely feminine.

Orne looked beyond the pool: wooded hills and, dimly on the horizon, a broken line of mountains. The Bullones lived in expensive isolation. Around them stretched miles of wilderness, rugged with planned neglect.

Time to report in, he thought. Orne pressed the neck stud on his transceiver, got Stetson, told him what had happened to this point.

"All right," said Stetson. "Go find the daughter. She fits the description of the gal you saw by the pool."

"That's what I was hoping," said Orne.

He changed into light-blue fatigues, went to the door of his room, let himself out into a hall. A glance at his wristchrono showed that it was shortly before noon—time for a bit of scouting before they called lunch. He knew from his brief tour of the house and its similarity to the home of his childhood that the hall let into the main living salon. The public rooms and men's quarters were in the outside ring. Secluded family apartments and women's quarters occupied the inner section.

Orne made his way to the salon. It was long, built around two sections of the tetragon, and with low divans beneath the view windows. The floor was thick-pile rugs pushed one against another in a crazy patchwork of reds and browns. At the far end of the room, someone in blue fatigues like his own was bent over a stand of some sort. The figure straightened at the same time a tinkle of music filled the room. He recognized the red-gold hair of the young woman he had seen beside the pool. She was wielding two mallets to play a stringed instrument that lay on its side supported by a carved-wood stand.

He moved up behind her, his footsteps muffled by the carpeting. The music had a curious rhythm that suggested figures dancing wildly around firelight. She struck a final chord, muted the strings.

"That makes me homesick," said Orne.

"Oh!" She whirled, gasped, then smiled. "You startled me. I thought I was alone."

"Sorry. I was enjoying the music."

"I'm Diana Bullone," she said. "You're Mr. Orne."

"Lew to all of the Bullone family, I hope," he said.

"Of course . . . Lew." She gestured at the musical instrument. "This is very old. Most find its music . . . well, rather weird. It's been handed down for generations in mother's family."

"The kaithra," said Orne. "My sisters play it. Been a long time since I've heard one."

"Oh, of course," she said. "Your mother's—" She stopped, looked confused. "I've got to get used to the fact that you're . . . I mean that we have a strange man around the house who isn't *exactly* strange."

Orne grinned. In spite of the blue I–A fatigues and a rather severe pulled-back hairdo, this was a handsome woman. He found himself liking her, and this caused him a feeling near self-loathing. She was a suspect. He couldn't afford to like her. But the Bullones were being so decent, taking him in like this. And how was their hospitality being repaid? By spying and prying. Yet, his first loyalty belonged to the I–A, to the peace it represented.

He said rather lamely: "I hope you get over the feeling that I'm strange."

"I'm over it already," she said. She linked arms with him, said: "If you feel up to it, I'll take you on the deluxe guided tour."

By nightfall, Orne was in a state of confusion. He had found Diana fascinating, and yet the most comfortable woman to be around that he had ever met. She liked swimming, *paloika* hunting, *ditar* apples—She had a "poo-poo" attitude toward the older generation that she said she'd never before revealed to anyone. They had laughed like fools over utter nonsense.

Orne went back to his room to change for dinner, stopped before the po-lawindow. The quick darkness of these low latitudes had pulled an ebon blanket over the landscape. There was city-glow off to the left, and an orange halo to the peaks where Marak's three moons would rise. *Am I falling in love with this woman?* he asked himself. He felt like calling Stetson, not to report but just to talk the situation out. And this made him acutely aware that Stetson or an aide had heard everything said between them that afternoon.

The autobutle called dinner. Orne changed hurriedly into a fresh lounge uniform, found his way to the small salon across the house. The Bullones already were seated around an old-fashioned bubble-slot table set with real candles, golden *shardi* service. Two of Marak's moons could be seen out the window climbing swiftly over the peaks.

"You turned the house," said Orne.

"We like the moonrise," said Polly. "It seems more romantic, don't you think?" She glanced at Diana.

Diana looked down at her plate. She was wearing a low-cut gown of *firemesh* that set off her red hair. A single strand of *Reinach* pearls gleamed at her throat.

Orne sat down in the vacant seat opposite her. *What a handsome woman!* he thought.

Polly, on Orne's right, looked younger and softer in a green stola gown that hazed her barrel contours. Bullone, across from her, wore black lounging shorts and knee-length *kubi* jacket of golden pearl cloth. Everything about the people and setting reeked of wealth, power. For a moment, Orne saw that Stetson's suspicions could have basis in fact. Bullone might go to any lengths to maintain this luxury.

Orne's entrance had interrupted an argument between Polly and her husband. They welcomed him, went right on without inhibition. Rather than embarrassing him, this made him feel more at home, more accepted.

"But I'm not running for office this time," said Bullone patiently. "Why do we have to clutter up the evening with that many people just to—"

"Our election night parties are traditional," said Polly.

"Well, I'd just like to relax quietly at home tomorrow," he said. "Take it easy with just the family here and not have to—"

"It's not like it was a *big* party," said Polly. "I've kept the list to fifty."

Diana straightened, said: "This is an important election Daddy! How could you *possibly* relax? There're seventy-three seats in question . . . the whole balance. If things go wrong in just the Alkes sector . . . why . . . you could be sent back to the floor. You'd lose your job as . . . why . . . someone else could take over as—"

"Welcome to the job," said Bullone. "It's a headache." He grinned at Orne. "Sorry to burden you with this, m'boy, but the women of this family run me ragged. I guess from what I hear that you've had a pretty busy day, too." He smiled paternally at Diana. "And your first day out of the hospital."

"She sets quite a pace, but I've enjoyed it," said Orne.

"We're taking the small flitter for a tour of the wilderness area tomorrow," said Diana. "Lew can relax all the way. I'll do the driving."

"Be sure you're back in plenty of time for the party," said Polly. "Can't have—" She broke off at a low bell from the alcove behind her. "That'll be for me. Excuse me, please . . . no, don't get up."

Orne bent to his dinner as it came out of the bubble slot beside his plate: meat in an exotic sauce, *Sirik* champagne, *paloika au semil* . . . more luxury.

Presently, Polly returned, resumed her seat.

"Anything important?" asked Bullone.

"Only a cancellation for tomorrow night. Professor Wingard is ill."

"I'd just as soon it was cancelled down to the four of us," said Bullone.

Unless this is a pose, this doesn't sound like a man who wants to grab more power, thought Orne.

"Scottie, you should take more pride in your office!" snapped Polly. "You're an important man."

"If it weren't for you, I'd be a nobody and prefer it," said Bullone. He grinned at Orne. "I'm a political idiot compared to my wife. Never saw anyone who could call the turn like she does. Runs in her family. Her mother was the same way."

Orne stared at him, fork raised from plate and motionless. A sudden idea had exploded in his mind.

"You must know something of this life, Lewis," said Bullone. "Your father was member for Chargon once, wasn't he?"

"Yes," murmured Orne. "But that was before I was born. He died in office." He shook his head, thought: *It couldn't be . . . but—*

"Do you feel all right, Lew?" asked Diana. "You're suddenly so pale."

"Just tired," said Orne. "Guess I'm not used to so much activity."

"And I've been a beast keeping you so busy today," she said.

"Don't you stand on ceremony here, son," said Polly. She looked concerned. "You've been very sick, and we understand. If you're tired, you go right on into bed."

Orne glanced around the table, met anxious attention in each face. He pushed his chair back, said: "Well, if you really don't mind—"

"Mind!" barked Polly. "You scoot along now!"

"See you in the morning. Lew," said Diana.

He nodded, turned away, thinking: *What a handsome woman!* As he started down the hall, he heard Bullone say to Diana: "Di, perhaps you'd better not take that boy out tomorrow. After all, he *is* supposed to be here for a rest." Her answer was lost as Orne entered the hall, closed the door.

In the privacy of his room, Orne pressed the transceiver stud at his neck, said: *"Stet?"*

A voice hissed in his ears: *"This is Mr. Stetson's relief. Orne, isn't it?"*

"Yes. I want a check right away on those Nathian records the archaeologists found. Find out if Heleb was one of the planets they seeded."

"Right. Hang on." There was a long silence, then: *"Lew, this is Stet. How come the question about Heleb?"*

"Was it on that Nathian list?"

"Negative. Why'd you ask?"

"Are you sure, Stet? It'd explain a lot of things."

"It's not on the lists, but . . . wait a minute." Silence. Then: *"Heleb was on line of flight to Auriga, and Auriga was on the list. We've reason to doubt they put anyone down on Auriga. If their ship ran into trouble—"*

"That's it!" snapped Orne.

"Keep your voice down or talk subvocally," ordered Stetson. *"Now, answer my question: What's up?"*

"Something so fantastic it frightens me," said Orne. *"Remember that the women who ruled Heleb bred female or male children by controlling the sex of their offspring at conception. The method was unique. In fact, our medics thought it was impossible until—"*

"You don't have to remind me of something we want buried and forgotten," interrupted Stetson. *"Too much chance for misuse of that formula."*

"Yes," said Orne. *"But what if your Nathian underground is composed entirely of women bred the same way? What if the Heleb women were just a bunch who got out of hand because they'd lost contact with the main element?"*

"Holy Moley!" blurted Stetson. *"Do you have evidence—"*

"Nothing but a hunch," said Orne. *"Do you have a list of the guests who'll be here for the election party tomorrow?"*

"We can get it. Why?"

"Check for women who mastermind their husbands in politics. Let me know how many and who."

"Lew, that's not enough to—"

"That's all I can give you for now, but I think I'll have more. Remember that . . ." he hesitated, spacing his words as a new thought struck him *". . . the . . . Nathians . . . were . . . nomads."*

Day began early for the Bullones. In spite of its being election day, Bullone took off for his office an hour after dawn. "See what I mean about this job owning you?" he asked Orne.

"We're going to take it easy today, Lew," said Diana. She took his hand as they came up the steps after seeing her father to his limousine flitter. The sky was cloudless.

Orne felt himself liking her hand in his—liking the feel of it too much. He withdrew his hand, stood aside, said: "Lead on."

I've got to watch myself, he thought. *She's too charming.*

"I think a picnic," said Diana. "There's a little lake with grassy banks off to the west. We'll take viewers and a couple of good novels. This'll be a do-nothing day."

Orne hesitated. There might be things going on at the house that he should watch. But no . . . if he was right about this situation, then Diana could be the weak link. Time was closing in on them, too. By tomorrow the Nathians could have the government completely under control.

It was warm beside the lake. There were purple and orange flowers above the grassy bank. Small creatures flitted and cheeped in the brush and trees. There was a *groomis* in the reeds at the lower end of the lake, and every now and then it honked like an old man clearing his throat.

"When we girls were all at home we used to picnic here every Eight-day," said Diana. She lay on her back on the groundmat they'd spread. Orne sat beside her facing the lake. "We made a raft over there on the other side," she said. She sat up, looked across the lake. "You know, I think pieces of it are still there. See?" She pointed at a jumble of logs. As she gestured, her hand brushed Orne's.

Something like an electric shock passed between them. Without knowing exactly how it happened, Orne found his arms around Diana, their lips pressed together in a lingering kiss. Panic was very close to the surface in Orne. He broke away.

"I didn't plan for that to happen," whispered Diana.

"Nor I," muttered Orne. He shook his head. "Sometimes things can get into an awful mess!"

Diana blinked. "Lew . . . don't you . . . like me?"

He ignored the monitoring transceiver, spoke his mind. *They'll just think it's part of the act,* he thought. And the thought was bitter.

"Like you?" he asked. "I think I'm in love with you!"

She sighed, leaned against his shoulder. "Then what's wrong? You're not already married. Mother had your service record checked." Diana smiled impishly. "Mother has second sight."

The bitterness was like a sour taste in Orne's mouth. He could see the pattern so clearly. "Di, I ran away from home when I was seventeen," he said.

"I know, darling. Mother's told me all about you."

"You don't understand," he said. "My father died before I was born. He—"

"It must've been very hard on your mother," she said. "Left all alone with her family . . . and a new baby on the way."

"They'd known for a long time," said Orne. "My father had *Broach's* disease, and they found out too late. It was already in the central nervous system."

"How horrible," whispered Diana.

Orne's mind felt suddenly like a fish out of water. He found himself grasping at a thought that flopped around just out of reach. "Dad was in politics," he whispered. He felt as though he were living in a dream. His voice stayed low, shocked. "From when I first began to talk, Mother started grooming me to take his place in public life."

"And you didn't like politics," said Diana.

"I hated it!" he growled. "First chance, I ran away. One of my sisters married a young fellow who's now the member for Chargon. I hope he enjoys it!"

"That'd be Maddie," said Diana.

"You know her?" asked Orne. Then he remembered what Stetson had told him, and the thought was chilling.

"Of course I know her," said Diana. "Lew, what's wrong with you?"

"You'd expect me to play the same game, you calling the shots," he said. "Shoot for the top, cut and scramble, claw and dig."

"By tomorrow all that may not be necessary," she said.

Orne heard the sudden hiss of the carrier wave in his neck transceiver, but there was no voice from the monitor.

"What's . . . happening . . . tomorrow?" he asked.

"The election, silly," she said. "Lew, you're acting very strangely. Are you sure you're feeling all right?" She put a hand to his forehead. "Perhaps we'd—"

"Just a minute," said Orne, "About us—" He swallowed.

She withdrew her hand. "I think my parents already suspect. We Bullones are notorious love-at-first-sighters." Her overlarge eyes studied him fondly. "You don't feel feverish, but maybe we'd better—"

"What a dope I am!" snarled Orne. "I just realized that I have to be a Nathian, too."

"You *just* realized?" She stared at him.

There was a hissing gasp in Orne's transceiver.

"The identical patterns in our families," he said. "Even to the houses. And there's the real key. What a dope!" He snapped his fingers. "*The head!* Polly! Your mother's the grand boss woman, isn't she?"

"But, darling . . . of course. She—"

"You'd better take me to her and fast!" snapped Orne. He touched the stud at his neck, but Stetson's voice intruded.

"Great work, Lew! We're moving in a special shock force. Can't take any chances with—"

Orne spoke aloud in panic: *"Stet! You get out to the Bullones! And you get there alone! No troops!"*

Diana had jumped to her feet, backed away from him.

"What do you mean?" demanded Stetson.

"I'm saving our stupid necks!" barked Orne. *"Alone! You hear? Or we'll have a worse mess on our hands than any Rim War!"*

There was an extended silence. *"You hear me, Stet?"* demanded Orne.

"Okay, Lew. We're putting the O-force on standby. I'll be at the Bullones' in ten minutes. ComGO will be with me." Pause. *"And you'd better know what you're doing!"*

It was an angry group in a corner of the Bullones' main salon. Louvered shades cut the green glare of a noon sun. In the background there was the hum of air-conditioning and the clatter of roboservants preparing for the night's election party. Stetson leaned against the wall beside a divan, hands jammed deeply into the pockets of his wrinkled, patched fatigues. The wagon tracks furrowed his high forehead. Near Stetson, Admiral Sobat Spencer, the I–A's Commander of Galactic Operations, paced the floor. ComGO was a bull-necked bald man with wide blue eyes, a deceptively mild voice. There was a caged animal look to his pacing—three steps out, three steps back.

Polly Bullone sat on the divan. Her mouth was pulled into a straight line. Her hands were clasped so tightly in her lap that the knuckles showed white. Diana stood beside her mother. Her fists were clenched at her sides. She shivered with fury. Her gaze remained fixed, glaring at Orne.

"Okay, so my stupidity set up this little meeting," snarled Orne. He stood about five paces in front of Polly, hands on hips. The admiral, pacing away at his right, was beginning to wear on his nerves. "But you'd better listen to what I have to say." He glanced at the ComGO. *"All* of you."

Admiral Spencer stopped pacing, glowered at Orne. "I have yet to hear a good reason for not tearing this place apart . . . getting to the bottom of this situation."

"You . . . traitor, Lewis!" husked Polly.

"I'm inclined to agree with you, Madame," said Spencer. "Only from a different point of view." He glanced at Stetson. "Any word yet on Scottie Bullone?"

"They were going to call me the minute they found him," said Stetson. His voice sounded cautious, brooding.

"You were coming to the party here tonight, weren't you, admiral?" asked Orne.

"What's that have to do with anything?" demanded Spencer.

"Are you prepared to jail your wife and daughters for conspiracy?" asked Orne.

A tight smile played around Polly's lips.

Spencer opened his mouth, closed it soundlessly.

"The Nathians are mostly women," said Orne. "There's evidence that your womenfolk are among them."

The admiral looked like a man who had been kicked in the stomach. "What . . . evidence?" he whispered.

"I'll come to that in a moment," said Orne. "Now, note this: the Nathians are mostly women. There were only a few *accidents* and a few planned males, like me. That's why there were no family names to trace—just a tight little female society, all working to positions of power through their men."

Spencer cleared his throat, swallowed. He seemed powerless to take his attention from Orne's mouth.

"My guess," said Orne, "is that about thirty or forty years ago, the conspirators first began breeding a few males, grooming them for really choice top positions. Other Nathian males—the accidents where sex-control failed—they never learned about the conspiracy. These new ones were full-fledged members. That's what I'd have been if I'd panned out as expected."

Polly glared at him, looked back at her hands.

"That part of the plan was scheduled to come to a head with this election," said Orne. "If they pulled this one off, they could move in more boldly."

"You're in way over your head, boy," growled Polly. "You're too late to do anything about us!"

"We'll see about that!" barked Spencer. He seemed to have regained his self-control. "A little publicity in the right places . . . some key arrests and—"

"No," said Orne. "She's right. It's too late for that. It was probably too late a hundred years ago. These dames were too firmly entrenched even then."

Stetson straightened away from the wall, smiled grimly at Orne. He seemed to be understanding a point that the others were missing. Diana still glared at Orne. Polly kept her attention on her hands, the tight smile playing about her lips.

"These women probably control one out of three of the top positions in the League," said Orne. "Maybe more. Think, admiral . . . think what would happen if you exposed this thing. There'd be secessions, riots, sub-governments would topple, the central government would be torn by suspicions and battles. What breeds in that atmosphere?" He shook his head. "The Rim War would seem like a picnic!"

"We can't just ignore this!" barked Spencer. He stiffened, glared at Orne.

"We can and we will," said Orne. "No choice."

Polly looked up, studied Orne's face. Diana looked confused.

"Once a Nathian, always a Nathian, eh?" snarled Spencer.

"There's no such thing," said Orne. "Five hundred years' cross-breeding with other races saw to that. There's merely a secret society of astute political scientists." He smiled wryly at Polly, glanced back at Spencer. "Think of your own wife, sir. In all honesty, would you be ComGO today if she hadn't guided your career?"

Spencer's face darkened. He drew in his chin, tried to stare Orne down, failed. Presently, he chuckled wryly.

"Sobie is beginning to come to his senses," said Polly. "You're about through, son."

"Don't underestimate your future son-in-law," said Orne.

"Hah!" barked Diana. "I *hate* you, Lewis Orne!"

"You'll get over that," said Orne mildly.

"Ohhhhhh!" Diana quivered with fury.

"My major point is this," said Orne. "Government is a dubious glory. You pay for your power and wealth by balancing on the sharp edge of the blade. That great amorphous thing out there—the people—has turned and swallowed many governments. The only way you can stay in power is by giving *good* government. Otherwise—sooner on later—your turn comes. I can remember my mother making that point. It's one of the things that stuck with me." He frowned. "My objection to politics is the compromises you have to make to get elected!"

Stetson moved out from the wall. "It's pretty clear," he said. Heads turned toward him. "To stay in power, the Nathians had to give us a fairly good government. On the other hand, if we expose them, we give a bunch of political amateurs—every fanatic and power-hungry demagogue in the galaxy—just the weapon they need to sweep them into office."

"After that: chaos," said Orne. "So we let the Nathians continue . . . with two minor alterations."

"We alter nothing," said Polly. "It occurs to me, Lewis, that you don't have a leg to stand on. You have me, but you'll get nothing out of me. The rest of the organization can go on without me. You don't dare expose us. We hold the whip hand!"

"The I–A could have ninety per cent of your organization in custody inside of ten days," said Orne.

"You couldn't find them!" snapped Polly.

"How?" asked Stetson.

"Nomads," said Orne. "This house is a glorified tent. Men on the outside, women on the inside. Look for inner courtyard construction. It's instinctive with Nathian blood. Add to that, an inclination for odd musical instruments—the kaithra, the tambour, the oboe—all nomad instruments. Add to that, female dominance of the family—an odd twist on the nomad heritage, but not completely unique. Check for predominance of female offspring. Dig into political background. We'll miss damn few!"

Polly just stared at him, mouth open.

Spencer said: "Things are moving too fast for me. I know just one thing: I'm dedicated to preventing another Rim War. If I have to jail every last one of—"

"An hour after this conspiracy became known, you wouldn't be in a position to jail anyone," said Orne. "The husband of a Nathian! You'd be in jail yourself or more likely dead at the hands of a mob!"

Spencer paled.

"What's your suggestion for compromise?" asked Polly.

"Number one: the I–A gets veto power on any candidate you put up," said Orne. "Number two: you can never hold more than two thirds of the top offices."

"Who in the I–A vetoes our candidates?" asked Polly.

"Admiral Spencer, Stet, myself . . . anyone else we deem trustworthy," said Orne.

"You think you're a god or something?" demanded Polly.

"No more than you do," said Orne. "This is what's known as a check and balance system. You cut the pie. We get first choice on which pieces to take."

There was a protracted silence; then Spencer said: "It doesn't seem right just to—"

"No political compromise is ever totally right," said Polly. "You keep patching up things that always have flaws in them. That's how government is." She chuckled, looked up at Orne. "All right, Lewis. We accept." She glanced at Spencer, who shrugged, nodded glumly. Polly looked back at Orne. "Just answer me one question: How'd you know I was boss lady?"

"Easy," said Orne. "The records we found said the . . . Nathian (he'd almost said 'traitor') family on Marak was coded as *'The Head.'* Your name, Polly, contains the ancient word *'Poll,'* which means *head.*"

Polly looked at Stetson. "Is he always that sharp?"

"Every time," said Stetson.

"If you want to go into politics, Lewis," said Polly, "I'd be delighted to—"

"I'm already in politics as far as I want to be," growled Orne. "What I really want is to settle down with Di, catch up on some of the living I've missed."

Diana stiffened. "I never want to see, hear *from* or hear *of* Mr. Lewis Orne ever again!" she said. "That is final, emphatically final!"

Orne's shoulders drooped. He turned away, stumbled, and abruptly collapsed full length on the thick carpets. There was a collective gasp behind him.

Stetson barked: "Call a doctor! They warned me at the hospital he was still hanging on a thin thread!" There was the sound of Polly's heavy footsteps running toward the hall.

"Lew!" It was Diana's voice. She dropped to her knees beside him, soft hands fumbling at his neck, his head.

"Turn him over and loosen his collar!" snapped Spencer. "Give him air!"

Gently, they turned Orne onto his back. He looked pale, Diana loosed his collar, buried her face against his neck. "Oh, Lew, I'm sorry," she sobbed. "I didn't mean it! Please, Lew . . . please don't die! Please!"

Orne opened his eyes, looked up at Spencer and Stetson. There was the sound of Polly's voice talking rapidly on the phone in the hall. He could feel Diana's cheek warm against his neck, the dampness of her tears. Slowly, deliberately, Orne winked at the two men.

THE PRIESTS OF PSI

The instant he stepped out of the transport's shields into Amel's sunlight warmth on the exit ramp Orne felt the surge of psi power around him. It was like being caught in a strange magnetic field. He caught the hand rail in sudden dizziness, stared down some two hundred metres at the glassy tricrete of the space port. Heatwaves shimmered off the glistening surface, baking the air even up to this height. There was no wind except inside him where the hidden gusts of the psi fields howled against his recently awakened senses.

The techs who had trained Orne in the use of the flesh-buried psi detection instruments had given him a small foretaste of this sensation back in the laboratory on Marak. It had been far short of this reality. The first sharp signal of the primary detector concealed in his neck had been replaced by the full spectrum of psi awareness.

Orne shuddered. Amel crawled with skin-creeping sensations. Weird urges flickered through his mind like flashes of heat lightning. He wanted to grunt like a wallowing *kiriffa,* and in the next instant felt laughter welling in him while a sob tore at his throat.

I knew it was going to be bad, he thought. *They warned me.*

The counter-conditioning only made this moment worse because now he was *aware.* Without the psi training, he knew that his mind would have confused the discrete sensations into a combined awe-fear—perfectly logical emotions for him to feel when debarking on the priest planet.

This was holy ground: sanctuary of all the religions in the known universe (and, some said, of all the religions in the *un*known universe).

Orne forced his attention on to the inner focus as the techs had taught him. Slowly, psi awareness dimmed to background annoyance. He drew in a deep breath of the hot, dry air. It was vaguely unsatisfying as though lacking some essential element to which his lungs were accustomed.

Still holding the rail, he waited to make certain he had subdued the ghost urges within him. Across the ramp, the glistening inner surface of the opened port reflected his image, distorting it slightly in a way that accented his differences from the lean, striding norm. He looked like a demigod reincarnated out of this world's ancient past: square and solid with the corded neck muscles of a heavy-grav native. A faint scar demarked the brow line of his close-cropped red hair. Other fine scars on his bulldog face were visible because he knew where to look, and his memory told of more scars on his heavy body. There was a half-humorous saying in Investigation & Adjustment that senior field agents could be detected by the number of scars and medical patches they carried.

Orne tugged at the black belt on his aqua toga, feeling uncomfortable in this garment that all "students" on Amel had to wear.

The yellow sun, Dubhe, hung at the meridian in a cloudless blue sky. It hammered through the toga with oppressive warmth. Orne felt the perspiration slick on his body. One step away the escalfield hummed softly, ready to drop him into the bustle visible at the foot of the transport. Priests and passengers were engaged in some kind of ceremony down there—initiation of the new students. Faintly to his ears came a throbbing drum-chant and a sing-song keening almost hidden beneath the port's machinery clatter.

Orne studied the scene around him, still waiting to make sure he would not betray his awareness. The transport's ramp commanded a sweeping view: a fantastic scratchwork of towers, belfries, steeples, monoliths, domes, ziggurats, pagodas, stupas, minarets, dagobas. They cluttered a flat plain that stretched to a horizon dancing in the heatwaves. Golden sunlight danced off bright primary colors and weathered pastels—buildings in tile and stone, tricrete and plasteel, and the synthetics of a thousand thousand civilizations.

Staring out at the religious warren, Orne experienced an abrupt feeling of dread at the unknown things that could be waiting in those narrow, twisted streets and jumbled buildings. The stories that leaked out of Amel always carried a hint of forbidden mystery, and Orne knew his emotions were bound to be tainted by some of that mystery. But his sudden dread shifted subtly to a special kind of fear.

This *peculiar* fear, coming out of his new awareness, had begun back on Marak.

Orne had been seated at the desk in his bachelor officer quarters, staring out at the park-like landscape of the I–A university grounds. Marak's green sun, low in the afternoon quadrant, had seemed distant and cold. Orne had been filling in as a lecturer on "Exotic Clues to War Tendencies" while waiting for his wedding to Diana Bullone. He was scheduled to marry the High Commissioner's daughter in only three weeks, and after a honeymoon on Kirachin he was expecting permanent assignment to the anti-war college. He could look forward to a life of training new I–A agents in the arts of seeking out and destroying the seeds that could grow into another Rim War.

That had been his concept of the future that afternoon on Marak. But suddenly he had turned away from his desk to frown at the stiffly regulation

room. Something was awry. He studied the grey walls, the sharp angles of
the bunk, the white bedcover with its blue I-A monogram: the crossed sword
and stylus. The room's other chair stood backed against the foot of the bunk,
leaving a three-centimetre clearance for the grey flatness of the closet door.

Something he could not define was making him restless—call it premo-
nition.

Abruptly, the hall door banged open. Umbo Stetson, Orne's superior officer, strode into the room. The section chief wore his characteristic patched
blue fatigues. His only badge of rank, golden I–A emblems on his collar and
uniform cap, looked faintly corroded. Orne wondered when they had last
been polished, then pushed the thought aside. Stetson reserved all of his
polish for his mind.

Behind the I–A officer rolled a mechanocart piled with cramtapes, mi-
crofilms and even some old-style books. It trundled itself into the room, its
wheels rumbling as it cleared the doorsill. The door closed itself.

Good Lord! thought Orne. *Not an assignment! Not now.* He got to his
feet, looked first at the cart, then at Stetson. There was an edge of uneasiness in Orne's voice as he asked: "What's this, Stet?"

Stetson pulled out the chair from the foot of the bunk, straddled it, sailed
his cap on to the blanket. His dark hair straggled in an uncombed muss. His
eyelids drooped, accenting his usual look of haughty superciliousness.

"You've had enough assignments to know what this is," he growled. A
wry smile touched his lips. "Got a little job for you."

"Don't I have any say in this any more?" asked Orne.

"Well now, things may've changed a bit, and then again maybe they
haven't," said Stetson.

"I'm getting married in three weeks," said Orne. "To the daughter of the
High Commissioner."

"Your wedding is being postponed," said Stetson. He held up a hand as
Orne's face darkened. "Wait a bit. Just postponed. Emergency. The High
Commissioner sent his charming daughter off today on a job we just
trumped up for the purpose."

Orne's voice was dangerously low: "What purpose?"

"The purpose of getting her out of your hair. You're leaving for Amel in
six days and there's lots to be done before you're ready to go."

Orne drummed his fingers on the desk. "Just like that. Wedding's off. I'm
assigned to a . . . Amel?"

"Yes."

"What is this, Stet? Amel's a picnic ground."

"Well . . ." Stetson shook his head. "Maybe not."

A sudden fear struck Orne. "Whose job was trumped up?" he demanded.
"Has Diana . . ."

"She's off to Franchi Primus to help design a new uniform for the I–A
women," said Stetson. "That safe enough for you?"

"But why so sudden?"

"We have to get you ready for Amel. Miss Bullone would have wasted time, diverted your attention. She knows something's up, but she takes orders just like the rest of us in the I–A. Have I made myself clear?"

"No notice. No nothing. Oh, this I–A is real fun! I must recommend it every time I find a young fellow looking for a job!"

"Mrs Bullone will bring a note from Diana tonight," said Stetson. "She's perfectly safe. You can get married when this is over."

"Provided the I–A doesn't dream up some new emergency for me!" barked Orne.

"You're the ones who took the I–A oath," said Stetson. "You knew when you took it that this sort of thing could happen."

"I'm going to rewrite the oath," said Orne. "To the words: '*I pledge my life and my sacred honour to seek out and destroy the seeds of war wherever they may be found*' let us add: '*and I will sacrifice anything and anybody in the process.*'"

"Not a bad addition," said Stetson. "Why don't you recommend it when you get back?"

"*If* I get back! What's the emergency this time?"

"This emergency came hunting for you specifically," said Stetson.

"How thoughtful of it."

"Your name's on the list for the latest *summoning* to Amel."

"A religious student? But I've never applied for . . ."

"But your name's on the list. Nice great big letters. List signed by the Halmyrach Abbod himself."

"There has to be a mistake. It's obviously a confusion of names with . . ."

"You've been specifically identified by family and current abode. No mistake."

Orne pushed himself away from the desk. "But there *has* to be! I tell you I've never applied for . . ." He broke off. "Anyway, what's the difference? The I–A couldn't be interested in Amel. Never been a war anywhere near the place. The big shots were always afraid of offending their gods."

Stetson pointed to the mechanocart. "I don't have much time for this briefing, so stop interrupting. You're going to need everything on this cart and more. You're going to the medics this evening for a quick-heal operation. Some very hush-hush . . ." He frowned, repeated himself: ". . . *very* hush-hush equipment's going to be hidden under your skin. Do you know anything about psi powers?"

The change of pace caused Orne to blink. He wet his lips with his tongue. "You mean like that fellow on Wessen who was supposed to be able to jump to any planet in the universe without a ship?"

"Something like that."

"Say, whatever happened to him? All the stories, then . . ."

"Maybe it was a fake," said Stetson. "Maybe it wasn't. We hope you can find out. Our techs will be showing you some psi equipment later. An amplifier . . ."

"But how does this connect with Amel?"

"You're going to tell us . . . we hope. You see, Lew, we just had the confirmation early this morning. At the next session of the Assembly there's going to be a motion to do away with the I–A, turn all of our functions over to Rediscovery & Re-education."

"Put us under Tyler Gemine? That political hack! Half our problems come from Rah & Rah stupidities! They've damn' near bumbled us into another Rim War a dozen times!"

"Mmmmm, hmmmmm," said Stetson. "And the next session of the Assembly is just over the horizon—five months."

"But . . . but a motion like that wouldn't stand a chance! It's asinine! I mean, look at the . . ."

"You'll be interested to know, Lew, that the pressure for this change comes from the priests of Amel. There does not seem to be any doubt that religious heat can put it over."

"Which sect of the priests?"

"All of them."

Orne shook his head. "But there are thousands of sects on Amel . . . millions, maybe. Under the Ecumenical Truce they . . ."

"All of them," repeated Stetson.

Orne frowned. "None of this fits. If the priests are gunning for us, why would they invite an I–A field agent on to their planet at the same time? That doesn't . . ."

"Exactly," said Stetson. "I'm sure you'll jump with joy when you learn that nobody—repeat: nobody!—has ever before been able to put an agent into Amel. Not the I–A. Not the old Marakian Secret Service. Not even the Nathians. All attempts have been met with polite ejection. No agent's ever gone farther than their landing field." Stetson got to his feet, glared down at Orne. "You'd better get started on this background material I brought. Your first session with the techs is tonight after the medics get through with you."

"What provision will there be for getting me off if Amel goes sour?" asked Orne.

"None."

Orne bounced to his feet. "None?"

"Our best information indicates that your training—they call it 'The Ordeal'—takes about six months. If there's no report from you within that limit, we'll make inquiries."

"Like: *'What've you done with the body?'*" snarled Orne. "Hell! There might not even be an I–A to make an inquiry in six months!"

Stetson shrugged. "I know this is sudden, and our data's skimpy where it . . ."

"This is like a last resort!"

"Exactly, Lew. But we have to find out why the galactic centre of all religions has turned against us. We have no hope of going in there and subduing them. It'd start religious uprisings all through the galaxy. Make the Rim War look like a game of ball at a girl's school. I'm not even certain we could get enough volunteers to do the job. We never qualify an agent because of his religion, but I'm damned sure they'd *qualify* us on that score. No. We have to find out why! Maybe we can change whatever's bothering them. It's our only hope. Maybe they don't understa . . . ."

"What if they have plans for conquest by war? What then, Stet? A new faction could've come to power on Amel. Why not?"

Stetson looked sad, shrugged. "If you could prove it . . . ." He shook his head.

"When am I going to the medics?"

"They'll come for you."

"Yeah. Somebody already came for me . . . it looks like."

It was early evening in Orne's hospital room at the I–A medical centre—the quiet time between dinner and visiting hours. The nurse had turned on the light beside his bed. It cast a soothing reflection from the green walls. The induction bandage felt bulky under his chin, but the characteristic quick-heal itching had not yet started.

Being in a hospital room made him vaguely uneasy. He knew why: the smells and the sounds reminded him of all the months he'd spent creeping back from death after his injuries in the Heleb uprising. Heleb had been another planet where war just could *not* start. Like Amel.

The door to his hospital room opened. A tech officer strode through, closed the door. The man's uniform bore odd forked lightning insignia. Orne had never seen the emblem before. *Psi?* he wondered. The officer stopped at the foot of the bed, leaned on the cross-bar. His face was bird-like. There was a long nose, pointed chin, narrow mouth. The eyes made quick, darting movements. He was tall, bone skinny, and when he lifted his right hand in a mock salute, the gesture was fluttery.

"Hi," he said. "I'm Ag Emolirdo, head of our Psi Section. The Ag is for Agony."

Unable to move his head because of the induction bandage, Orne stared down the length of the bed at Emolirdo. The officer carried an aura of . . . confidence, *knowing* confidence. He reminded Orne of a priest back on Chargon. This idea made Orne uneasy. He said: "How d'you do."

"This will have to move rather rapidly," said the tech. He smiled. "You'll be into parahypnoid sessions by midnight."

"Join the I–A and learn the mysteries of the universe," Orne said.

Emolirdo cocked one eyebrow. "Were you aware that you're a psi focus?"

"A what?" Orne tried to sit up, but the bandage restraints held him fast.

"Psi focus," said Emolirdo. "You'll understand it later. Briefly, you're an island of order in a disordered universe. Four times since you came to the attention of the I–A you've done the impossible. Any one of the incidents you tackled should have led to ferment and then general war. You've brought order out of . . ."

"So I did what I was trained to do."

"Trained? By whom?"

"By my government . . . by the I–A. That's a stupid question."

"Is it?" Emolirdo found a chair, sat down, his head level with Orne's. "Well, we won't argue the point. The chief thing now is that you know consciously the broad areas to be covered. You understand?"

"I know the parahypnoid technique," said Orne.

"First, psi focus," said Emolirdo. "Let us define life as a bridge between Order and Chaos. Then, let us define Chaos as raw energy available to anything that can subdue it—that is, to anything that can put it into some order. Life, then, becomes stored Chaos. You follow?"

"I hear you. Get on with it."

"Ah impatience of the non-adept," murmured Emolirdo. He cleared his throat. "To restate the situation, Life feeds on Chaos, but must exist in Order. An apparent paradox. This brings us to the condition called *stasis*. Stasis is like a magnet. It attracts free energy to itself until the pressure of Chaos becomes too great and it explodes . . . and, exploding, goes back to Chaos. One is left with the unavoidable conclusion that Stasis leads always to Chaos."

"That's dandy," said Orne.

Emolirdo frowned. "This rule is true on both the levels of chemical-inanimate and chemical-animate, Mr. Orne. For example, ice, the stasis of water, explodes when brought into abrupt contact with extreme heat. The frozen society explodes when exposed suddenly to the chaos of war or the *apparent* chaos of a strange new society. Nature abhors stasis."

"Like a vacuum," said Orne.

"Precisely."

"Outside of the vacuum in my head, what other little problems do we have?" asked Orne.

"Amel."

"Oh, yes. Another vacuum?"

"Apparently a stasis that does not explode."

"Then maybe it isn't static."

"You're very astute, Mr. Orne."

"Golly . . . thanks."

"You think you're being very humorous, don't you, Mr. Orne?"

"I thought you were the prize joker here. What's all this have to do with Amel?"

"Miracles," said Emolirdo. "You obviously were summoned to Amel because they consider you a worker of miracles."

Pain stabbed through Orne's bandaged neck as he tried to turn his head. "Miracles?" he croaked.

"Substitute *psi* for miracle," said the tech. "*Psi focus,* to be more precise." A weird half smile flickered across Emolirdo's mouth. It was as though he had fought down an internal dispute on whether to laugh or cry, solved it by doing neither.

Orne felt confused, uneasy. He said: "You've left me."

"Psi focus is the scientific label for miracle," said Emolirdo. "It's something that happens outside of recognized channels, in spite of accepted rules. Religions say it's a miracle. Certain scientists say we have encountered a psi focus. That can be either a person or a locale."

"I'm not reading you at all," muttered Orne.

"You've heard of the ancient miracle caverns on the older planets?"

Orne blinked. "I've heard the legends."

"We're convinced that they concealed shapes . . . convolutions that projected out of our apparent universe. Except at these focus points, the raw energy of outer Chaos cannot be bent to our needs. But *at* these focus points, Chaos—the wild energy—is richly available in a way that can be tamed. It may be moulded in unique ways that defy ordinary rules." Emolirdo's eyes blazed. He seemed to be fighting a great inner excitement.

Orne wet his lips. "Shapes?"

"Men have bent wires, coiled them, carved bits of plastic, jumbled together odd assortments of apparently unrelated objects. And weird things happen. A smooth piece of metal becomes tacky, as though you'd smeared it with glue. A man draws a pentagram on a certain floor, and flame dances within it. Smoke curls from a strangely shaped bottle and does another man's bidding, obeys his will. Then there are certain men who conceal this focus within themselves. They walk into . . . nothing, and reappear light years away. They look at a person suffering from an incurable disease. The incurable is cured. They raise the dead. They read minds."

Orne tried to swallow in a dry throat. "All this is psi?"

"We believe so." Emolirdo bent towards Orne's bedside light, thrust a fist in between the light and the green wall. "Look at the wall."

"I can't turn my head," said Orne.

"Sorry. Just a shadow." Emolirdo withdrew his hand. "But let us say there were sentient beings confined to the flat plane of that wall. Let us say they saw the shadow of my fist. Could a genius among them imagine the shape that cast the shadow—a shape that projected outside of his dimensions?"

"Good question," said Orne.

"What if the being in the wall fashioned a device that projected into our dimension?" asked Emolirdo. "He would be like the blind men studying the legendary elephant. His device would respond in ways that do not fit his dimension. He would have to set up all kinds of new postulates."

Under the bandage, the skin of Orne's neck began to itch maddeningly.

He resisted the desire to probe there with a finger. Bits of folklore from Chargon flitted through his memory: the magicians, the little people who granted wishes in a way that made the wisher regret his desires, the cavern where the sick were cured. The quick-heal itching lured his finger with almost irresistible force. He groped for a pill on his bedstand, gulped it down, waited for the relief.

Presently, Orne said: "What's this thing you've put in my neck?"

"It has a dual purpose," said Emolirdo. "It signals the presence of psi activity—psi *fields,* we call them. And it's an amplifier, giving a boost to any latent . . . ah, talents you may have. It'll often permit a novice to produce some of the minor psi effects."

Orne rubbed the outside of his neck bandage, forced his hand away. "Such as what?"

"Oh . . . resisting psi-induced emotions, detecting motivation in others through some of their emotions. It may give a small degree of prescience. You'd be able to detect extremes of personal danger when they were still some distance off in time. You'll understand about this, after the parahypnoid session."

Orne felt something tingling in his neck. There was a vacant sensation in the pit of his stomach. "Prescience?"

"You'd recognize it at first as a kind of fear . . . a *peculiar* kind of fear. Sometimes it's like hunger even though you've just eaten. Something feels like it's lacking . . . inside you, or in the air you breathe. If you feel it, you'll recognize it. It'll always be a warning of danger. Very trustworthy."

Orne's skin felt clammy. There was the vacant sensation in his stomach. The air of the room felt stale. His immediate reaction was to reject the sensations and all of the suggestive conversation, but there was still the fact of Stetson. Nobody in the I–A was more coldly objective or quicker to toss out mumbo-jumbo. And Stetson obviously accepted this psi thing. Stetson could be trusted. That was the major fact keeping Orne from booting this . . . this . . .

"You look a little pale," said Emolirdo.

"Probably." Orne managed a tight smile. "I think I feel your prescience thing right now."

"Describe your sensations."

Orne obeyed.

"You feel irritated, jumpy without apparent reason," said Emolirdo. "Odd that it should happen so soon, before the training, that is. Unless . . ." He pursed his lips.

"Unless what?"

"Unless your talent . . . were quite strong. And unless psi training itself were actually dangerous to you. Wouldn't that be interesting, though?"

"Yeah. Fascinating. I can hardly wait to get through this training and be on my way to Amel."

It was reluctance, Orne decided. There was no real excuse to wait up here on the transport's ramp any longer. Obviously, he had overcome the first staggering impact of the psi fields of Amel. There was still the prescient awareness of danger—like a sore tooth signalling its presence. The day was hot, and the toga was too heavy. He was soaked in perspiration.

Damn! If I wait too long they'll get suspicious.

He took a half step towards the escalfield, still fighting the reluctance. His nostrils caught an acrid bite of incense that had evaded the oil-and-ozone dominance of the landing area. In spite of counter-conditioning and carefully nurtured agnosticism, he felt an abrupt sensation of awe. Amel exuded an aura of magic that defied cynical disbelief.

The chanting and keening that lifted fog-like from the religious warren sparked memory fragments. Shards of his childhood on Chargon tumbled through Orne's mind: *the religious processions on holy days . . . the image of Mahmud glowering down from the* kiblah *. . . and the* azan *ringing out across the great square on the day of* Bairam—

> *"Let no blasphemy occur nor permit a blasphemer to live! May such a one be accursed of God and of the blessed from the sole of his foot to the crown of his head, sleeping and waking, sitting and standing . . ."*

Orne shook his head.

Yes, bow down to Ullun, the star wanderer of the Ayrbs, he thought. Now would be a great time for him to get religion!

But the roots were deep. He tightened the belt of his toga, strode forward into the escalfield. Its feathery touch dropped him to the ground, disgorged him beside a covered walkway. A cluster of priests and students were pressed into the thin shade of the cover. They began to separate as Orne approached, leaving in pairs—a white-clad priest with each student.

One priest remained facing Orne. He was tall and with a thick body. There was a heavy feeling about him as though the ground would shudder when he walked. His head was shaved bald. Deep lines scratched patterns on his wide jowled face. Dark eyes glowered from beneath overhanging grey brows.

"Are you Orne?" the priest rumbled.

Orne stepped under the walkway. "That's right." There was a yellowish gleam to the priest's skin.

"I am Bakrish," said the priest. He put his slab hands on his hips, glared at Orne. "You missed the ceremony of lustration."

Something about the heavy figure, the glowering face reminded Orne abruptly of an I–A gunnery sergeant he had known. The thought restored Orne's sense of balance, brought a grin to his face.

"Sorry," said Orne. "I was enjoying the view."

"You find something amusing?" demanded Bakrish.

"This humble face reflects happiness," said Orne. "Happiness to be on Amel."

"Oh. Well, come along." Bakrish turned away, strode off under the covered walk, not looking to see if Orne followed.

Orne shrugged, set off after the priest, found that he had to force himself to a half trot to keep up with the other's long-legged stride.

No moving walks, no hopalongs, thought Orne. *This place is primitive.*

The walk jutted like a long beak from a windowless, low stone building. Double doors opened into a dim hall. The doors had to be opened manually, and one of them creaked. Bakrish led the way past rows of narrow cells open to the hall, came finally to another door. It opened into a cell slightly larger than the others, big enough to accommodate one small desk and two chairs. Pink light filled the room from concealed exciters.

Bakrish crossed the cell ahead of Orne, crunched into the chair behind the desk, motioned for Orne to take the other seat. "Sit down."

Orne complied, but with a sudden feeling of wariness. Something here failed to add up for his highly tuned senses.

"As you know, we here on Amel live under the Ecumenical Truce," said Bakrish. "Your intelligence service will have briefed you on some of the significance behind that fact, of course."

Orne concealed his surprise at this turn in the conversation. He nodded.

Bakrish smiled. "The main thing you need to understand about it now is that there is nothing unusual in my being assigned as your guru."

"I *don't* understand."

"You are a follower of Mahmud. I am a Hynd and a *Wali,* under divine protection. Under the Truce, all of us serve the one God who has many names. You understand?"

"I see."

Bakrish nodded. "When Emolirdo told us about you, we had to see for ourselves, of course. That is why you are here."

Emolirdo a traitor! Iron control kept Orne from revealing his shock.

"You pose a fascinating problem," said Bakrish.

Anger coursed through Orne. *What a foul-up!* He set his face in a wolfish grin, probed with his newly awakened psi awareness for some weakness here, an emotion, a clue to the feeling of oddness about the room. "I'm so happy you've found something to keep you occupied," he said.

Bakrish leaned forward, glanced behind Orne, nodded. In the same instant, Orne felt the sensation of oddness dissipate. He whirled, caught a flicker of robe and a wheeled object being pulled away from the open door.

"That's better," said Bakrish. "Now we have the tensor phase pattern of your equipment. We can nullify it at will, or destroy you with it."

Orne froze. *What kind of a bomb did Emolirdo have the medics plant in me?*

"However, we do not wish to destroy you," said Bakrish. "For the time being we will not tamper with your equipment. We *want* you to use it."

Orne took two deep breaths. Without volition, his psi training took over. He concentrated on the inner focus for calmness. It came like a wash of cool water: icy, observant calm.

Boxed! All it took was one traitor! The thoughts blazed through his mind. But outwardly he remained calm, alert.

"Have you nothing to say?" asked Bakrish.

"Yes." Orne cleared his throat. "I want to see the Halmyrach Abbod. I've got to find out why you're trying to destroy the . . ."

"All in due time," said Bakrish.

"Where's the Abbod?"

"Nearby. When the time comes for you to have your audience with him it will be arranged."

"Meanwhile, I just wait for you to blow me up!"

"Blow you . . ." Bakrish looked puzzled. "Believe me, my young friend, we have no desire to cause your destruction. That is merely a necessary precaution. Now, there are two facts here: You want to find out about us, and we want to find out about you. The best way for both of us to accomplish our aims would be for you to submit to your ordeal. You really don't have any choice, of course."

"You mean I let you lead me around like a *grifka* being brought to the slaughterhouse! Either that or else you destroy me."

"It would be better if you just looked on this as an interesting test," murmured Bakrish. "Your bloody thoughts really aren't suitable."

"Somehow, I'm going to find out what makes you tick," grated Orne. "When I do, I'm going to smash your mainspring!"

Bakrish frowned, swallowed. "You *must* be exposed to the holy mysteries," he said. His yellow skin paled.

Orne leaned back. His sudden burst of bravado had left an aftermath of embarrassment. He thought: *This joker should've laughed at me. He's in the driver's seat. But my threat frightened him. Why?*

"Do you submit to your ordeal?" asked Bakrish.

Orne pushed himself up out of the chair. "You said it for me: I really don't have any choice."

"This is the cell of meditation-on-faith," said Bakrish. "Stretch out on the floor, flat on your back. Do not try to sit up or stand until I give you permission. It is very dangerous."

"Why?" Orne looked around the room. It was high and narrow. Walls, floor and ceiling looked like white stone veined by thin brown lines like insect tracks. Pale white light, sourceless and as flat as skimmed milk, filled the room. A damp stone smell permeated the place.

"Flat on your back you are relatively safe," said Bakrish. "Accept my word for it. I have seen the results of disbelief."

Orne cleared his throat, feeling suddenly cold. He sat down, stretched out on the floor. The stone was chill against his back.

"Once started on your ordeal, the only way out is to go through it," said Bakrish.

"Have *you* been through this?" asked Orne.

"But of course."

Orne probed for the other's motive-emotions, met a sense of cold sympathy . . . if the psi awareness could be trusted. After all, much of it had come from Emolirdo, a traitor.

"So I've crawled into your tunnel . . . or is it a cave?" said Orne. "What's at the other end?"

"That's for you to discover."

"You're using me to find out something, Bakrish. What if I refuse to cooperate? Is that stalemate?"

A sense of tentative regret radiated from Bakrish. "When the scientist sees that his experiment has failed, he is not necessarily barred from further experiments . . . with new equipment. You truly have no choice."

"Then let's get on with it."

"As you will." Bakrish moved to the end wall. It swung open to reveal the outer hallway, closed behind the priest. There was an abrupt feeling of increased pressure.

Orne studied the cell. It appeared to be about four metres long, two metres wide, some ten metres high. But the mottled stone ceiling appeared blurred. Perhaps the room was higher. The pale lighting could be designed for confusing the senses. He probed the prescient sense, felt its amorphous twinge—peril.

The priest's voice suddenly filled the room, booming from a concealed speaker: "You are enclosed within a psi machine. This ordeal is ancient and exacting: to test the quality of your faith. Failure means loss of your life, your soul or both."

Orne clenched his hands. Perspiration made his palms oily. An abrupt increase in background psi activity registered on his booster.

"Immerse yourself in the mystical stream," said Bakrish. "Of what are you afraid?"

Orne thought of the pressures focused on him, all the evidence of deep and hidden intent. "I don't like to act just on faith. I like to know where I'm going."

"Sometimes you must go for the sake of going," said Bakrish. "In fact, you do this all the time when . . ."

"Nuts!"

"When you press the stud to turn on a room's lights, you act on faith that there will be light," said Bakrish.

"Faith in past experience."

"And what about the first time?"

"I guess I must've been surprised at the light."

"Then prepare yourself for surprises, because there is no lighting mechanism in your cell. The light you see there exists because you desire it, and for no other reason."

"What . . ."

Darkness engulfed the room.

Bakrish's voice filled the darkness with a husky whisper. "Have faith."

The prescient warning gripped Orne: writhing terror. He fought down the desire to jump up and dash for the door wall. The priest's warning, grimly matter of fact, had rung true. Death lay in flight.

Smoky glowing appeared near the ceiling, coiled down towards Orne.

Light?

Orne lifted his right hand. He couldn't see the hand. The radiance cast no light into the rest of the cell. The sense of pressure in the cell increased with each heartbeat.

Light if I wish it? Well . . . it became dark when I doubted.

He thought of the milky light.

Shadowless illumination flickered into being, but near the ceiling where he had seen the glowing radiance there boiled a black cloud. It beckoned like the outer darkness of space.

Orne froze, staring.

Darkness filled the room.

Again, radiance glowed at the ceiling.

The klaxon of prescient fear cried through Orne. He closed his eyes in the effort of concentration. Immediately, fear lessened. His eyes snapped open in shock.

Fear!

And the ghostly glowing crawled nearer.

Eyes closed.

Still the sense of peril, but without immediacy.

Fear equals darkness. Even in the light, darkness beckons. He stilled his breathing, concentrated on the inner focus. *Faith? Blind faith? What do they want of me? Fear brings the dark.*

He forced his eyes to open, stared into the lightless void of the cell. Radiance coiling downwards. *Even in the darkness there is light. But it's not really light because I can't see by it.*

It was like a time he could remember—long ago in childhood: darkness in his own bedroom. Mooncast shadows transmuted to monsters. He had clenched his eyes tightly closed, fearful that if he opened them he would see a thing too horrible to face.

Orne stared up at the coiling radiance. *False light. Like false hope.* The radiance coiled backwards into itself, receding. *Utter darkness equals utter fear.*

The radiance winked out.

Dank, stone-smelling darkness permeated the cell, a darkness infected with creeping sounds—claw scrabbles and hisses, little slitherings . . .

Orne invested the sounds with every shape of terror his imagination could produce: poisonous lizards, insane monsters . . . The peril sense enfolded him, and he hung there suspended in it.

Bakrish's hoarse whisper snaked through the darkness: "Orne? Are your eyes open?"

His lips trembled with the effort to speak: "Yes."

"What do you *see,* Orne?"

An image suddenly danced on to the black field in front of Orne: Bakrish in an eerie red light, leaping and capering, grimacing . . .

"What do you see?" hissed Bakrish.

"You. I see you in Sadun's inferno."

"The hell of Mahmud?"

"Yes. Why?"

"Orne, do you not prefer the light?"

"Why do I see you?"

"Orne, I *beg* of you! Choose the . . ."

"*Why* do I see you in . . ." Orne broke off. He had the feeling that something peered inside him with heavy deliberation, checked his thoughts, his vital processes, weighed them. He knew suddenly that if he willed it, Bakrish would be cast into the deepest torture pit dreamed of in Mahmud's nightmares. *Why not? Then again: why? Who am I to decide? He may not be the right one. Perhaps the Halmyrach Abbod . . .*

Groaning, creaking filled the stones of the cell. A tongue of flame lanced out of the darkness above Orne, poised. It cast a ruddy glow on the stone walls.

Prescient fear clawed at him.

Faith? He had the inner knowledge—not faith—that in this instant he could do a dangerous and devilish thing: cast a man into eternal torture. *Which man and why? No man.* He rejected the choice.

Above him, the dancing flame receded, winked out, leaving only darkness and its slithering noises. Realization swept over Orne: he felt his own fingernails trembling and scrabbling against the stone floor—*claws!* He laughed aloud, stilled his hands. The claw sound stopped. He felt his feet writhing with involuntary efforts at flight. He stilled his feet, recognized the absence of the suggestive slithering. And the hissing! He focused on it, realized that it was his own breath fighting through clenched teeth.

Orne laughed.

Light?

In sudden perversity, he rejected the idea of light. Somehow, he knew this machine was responding to his innermost wishes, but only to those wishes uncensored by a doubting consciousness. Light was his for the willing of it, but he chose the darkness, and in the sudden release of tension, ignored Bakrish's warning, got to his feet. He smiled into the darkness, said: "Open the door, Bakrish."

Again, Orne felt something peer inside him, and recognized it for a psi probe—greatly magnified from the training probe used by Emolirdo. Someone was checking his motives.

"I'm not afraid," said Orne. "Open the door."

A scraping sound grated in the cell. Light fanned inwards from the hall as the end wall swung open. Orne looked out at Bakrish, a shadow framed against the light like a robed statue.

The Hynd stepped forwards, jerked to a halt as he saw Orne standing.

"Did you not prefer the light, Orne?"

"No."

"But you must have understood this test: you're standing . . . unafraid of my warning."

"This machine obeys my uncensored will," said Orne. "That's faith: the uncensored will."

"You *do* understand. And still you preferred the dark?"

"Does that bother you, Bakrish?"

"Yes, it does."

"Good."

"I see." Bakrish bowed. "Thank you for sparing me."

"You know about that?"

"I felt flames and heat, smelled the burning . . ." The priest shook his head. "The life of a guru here is not safe. Too many possibilities."

"You were safe," said Orne. "I censored my will."

"The most enlightened degree of faith," murmured Bakrish.

"Is that all there is to my ordeal?" Orne glanced around at the darkened cell walls.

"Merely the first step," said Bakrish. "There are seven steps in all: the test of faith, the test of the miracle's two faces, the test of dogma and ceremony, the test of ethics, the test of the religious ideal, the test of service to life, and the test of the mystical experience. They do not necessarily fall in that order."

Orne felt the absence of immediate prescient fear. He tasted a sense of exhilaration. "Then let's get on with it."

Bakrish sighed. "Holy Empress defend me," he muttered, then: "Yes, of course. Your next step: the miracle's two faces."

And the prescient sense of peril began to flicker within Orne. Angrily, he put it aside. *I have faith,* he thought. *Faith in myself. I've proved I can conquer my fear.*

"Well, what're we waiting for?" he demanded.

"Come along," said Bakrish. He turned with a swirl of his white robe, led the way down the hall.

Orne followed. "By miracle, do you mean psi focus?"

"What difference does it make what we call it?" asked Bakrish.

"If I solve all your riddles, do you take the heat off the I–A?" asked Orne.

"The heat . . . Oh, you mean . . . That is a question for the Halmyrach Abbod to decide."

"He's nearby, eh?"

"Very near."

Bakrish stopped before a heavy bronze door at the end of the hall, turned an ornate handle at one side, threw his shoulder against the door. It creaked open. "We generally don't come this way," he said. "These two tests seldom follow each other."

Orne blinked, followed the priest through the door into a gigantic round room. Stone walls curved away to a domed ceiling far above them. In the high curve of the ceiling slit windows admitted thin shafts of light that glittered downwards through gilt dust. Orne followed the light downwards to its focus on a straight barrier wall about twenty metres high and forty or fifty metres long, chopped off and looking incomplete in the middle of the room. The wall was dwarfed in the immensity of the domed space.

Bakrish circled around behind Orne, swung the heavy door closed, nodded towards the central barrier. "We go over there." He led the way.

Their slapping footsteps echoed off the walls. The damp stone smell was strong, like a bitter taste. Orne glanced left, saw doors evenly spaced around the room's perimeter, bronze doors like the one they had entered.

As they approached the barrier, Orne centred his attention on it. The surface looked to be a smooth grey plastic—featureless, but somehow menacing.

Bakrish stopped about ten metres from the middle of the wall. Orne stopped beside him, became conscious of prescient fear: something to do with the wall. Within him there was a surging and receding like waves on a beach. Emolirdo had described this sensation and interpreted it: *Infinite possibilities in a situation basically perilous.*

A blank wall?

"Orne, is it not true that a man should obey the orders of his superiors?" Bakrish's voice carried a hollow echo in the immensity of the room.

Orne's throat felt dry. He cleared it, rasped: "I suppose so . . . if the orders make sense. Why?"

"You were sent here as a spy, Orne. By rights, anything that happens to you is no concern of ours."

Orne tensed. "What're you driving at?"

Bakrish looked down at Orne, large eyes dark and glistening. "Sometimes these machines frighten us. Their methods are so unpredictable, and anyone who comes within the field of one of them can be subjected to its power."

"Like back there in that cell when you hung at the edge of the inferno?"

Bakrish shuddered. "Yes."

"But I still have to go through with this thing?"

"You must. It is the only way you will accomplish what you were sent here to do . . . and . . . you could not stop now, anyway. The ball is rolling down the hill. You don't even want to stop."

Orne tested this against his own feelings, shrugged. "I *am* curious."

"The thing is, Orne, you suspect us and fear us. These lead to hate. We saw that back there at the cell. But hate can be supremely dangerous to you in this present test. You . . ."

A scraping sound behind them brought Orne's attention around. Two oblate brothers deposited a heavy, square-armed chair on the stone floor facing the wall. They cast frightened glances at Orne, the wall, turned and scampered towards one of the heavy bronze doors.

"As I was saying, Orne, I am merely following orders here. I beg of you not to hate me, nor to hate anyone. You should not harbour hate during this test."

"What frightened those two fellows who brought that chair?" asked Orne. He watched the pair scurry through their door, slam it behind them.

"They know the reputation of this test. The very fabric of our universe is woven into it. Many things can hang in the balance here. Infinite possibilities."

Cautiously, Orne probed for Bakrish's motives. The priest obviously sensed the probe. He said: "I am afraid, Orne. Is that what you wanted to know?"

"Why are you afraid?"

"In *my* ordeal, this test proved nearly fatal. I had sequestered a core of hate. This place clutches at me even now." He shivered.

Orne found the priest's fright unsteadying. He looked at the chair. It was squat, ugly. An inverted metallic bowl projected on an arm over the seat. "What's the chair?"

"You must sit down in it."

Orne glanced at the grey wall, at Bakrish, back to the chair. There was tension here as though each heartbeat pumped pressure into the room. The surging and receding of his prescient sense increased, but he felt himself committed to this blind course.

"Sometimes we must go for the sake of going." The words rang in his memory. Who had said them?

He crossed to the chair, turned, sat down. In the act of sitting, the prescient sense of peril came to full surge, stayed. But there was no time for a change of heart. Metal bands leaped from concealed openings in the chair, pinned his arms, circled his chest and legs. Orne surged against them, twisting.

"Do not struggle," warned Bakrish. "You cannot escape."

Orne sank back.

"Please, Orne: you must not hate us. Your danger is magnified manyfold if you do. Hate could make you fail."

"Dragging you down with me, eh?"

"Quite possibly," muttered Bakrish. "One never quite escapes the consequences of one's hate." He stepped behind the chair, lowered the inverted bowl over Orne's head. "If you move suddenly or try to jerk away the micro-filament probes within this bowl will cause you great pain."

Orne felt something touch his scalp, crawling, tickling. "What is this?"

"One of the great psi machines." Bakrish adjusted something on the chair. Metal clicked. "Observe the wall. It can manifest your most latent urges. You can bring about miracles, call forth the dead, do many wonders. You may be on the brink of a deep mystical experience."

Orne swallowed in a dry throat. "You mean if I wanted my father to appear here he would?"

"He is deceased?"

"Yes."

"Then it could happen. But I must caution you. The things you see here will not be hallucination. And one thing more: If you are successful in calling forth the dead, you must realize that what you call forth will be that dead person, and yet not that dead person."

The back of Orne's right arm itched. He longed to scratch it. "How can . . ."

"The paradox is like this: any living creature manifested here through your will must be invested with your psyche as well as its own. Its matter will impinge on your matter. All of your memories will be available to whatever living flesh you call forth."

"But . . ."

"Hear me out, Orne. In some cases, your *creates* may fully understand their duality. Others will reject your half out of hand because they have not the capacity. Some may even lack sentience."

Orne felt the fear driving Bakrish's words, sensed truth in them. *He believes this, anyway.* He said: "But why trap me here in this chair?"

"It's important that you do not run away from yourself." Bakrish's hand fell on Orne's shoulder. "I must leave you now. May grace guide you."

There was a swishing of robes as the priest strode away. Presently a door closed, its sound a hollow sharpness. Orne felt infinitely alone.

A faint humming became audible—distant bee sound. The booster in his neck tugged sharply, and he felt the flare of a psi field around him. The barrier wall blinked alive to the color of grass green, and immediately began to crawl with iridescent purple lines. They squirmed and writhed like countless glowing worms trapped in a viscid green aquarium.

Orne drew in a shuddering breath. Prescient fear hammered at him. The crawling purple lines held hypnotic fascination. Some appeared to waft out towards him. The shape of Diana's face glowed momentarily among them. He tried to hold the image, saw it melt away.

Because she's alive? he wondered.

Shapeless deformities squirmed across the wall, coalesced abruptly into the outline of a *shriggar,* the saw-toothed lizard that Chargonian mothers invoked to frighten their children into obedience. The image took on more substance, developed yellow scale plates, stalk eyes.

Time suddenly slowed to a grinding, creeping pace within Orne. He thought back to his childhood on Chargon: terror memories.

But even then shriggar were extinct, he told himself.

Memory persisted down a long corridor full of empty echoes that suggested gibbering insanity. Down . . . down . . . down . . . He remembered childish laughter, a kitchen, his mother. And there were his sisters screaming derisively. And he remembered himself cowering, ashamed. He couldn't have been more than three years old. He had come running into the house to babble that he had seen a *shriggar* . . . in the deep shadows of the creek gully.

Laughing girls! Hateful little girls! "He thinks he saw a shriggar!" "Hush now, you two."

On the green wall, the *shriggar* outline bulged outwards. A taloned foot extended. It stepped from the wall on to the stone floor: half again as tall as a man, stalked eyes swivelling right, left . . .

Orne jerked out of his reverie, felt painful throbbing as his head movement disturbed the microfilament probes.

There was scratching of talons on stone as the *shriggar* took three tentative steps away from the wall. Orne tasted the fear within himself, thought: *Some ancestor of mine was hunted by such a creature! The panic goes too deep!* It was a clear thought that flickered through his mind while every sense remained focused on the nightmare lizard.

Its yellow scales rasped with every breath it took. The narrow, birdlike head twisted to one side, lowered. Its beak mouth opened to reveal a forked tongue and saw teeth.

Primordial instinct pressed Orne back in his chair. He smelled the stink of the creature: sickly sweet with overtones of sour cheese.

The *shriggar* bobbed its head, coughed: *"Chunk!"* Its stalk eyes moved, centred on Orne. One taloned foot lifted and it plunged into motion towards the figure trapped in the chair. Its high-stepping lope stopped about four metres away, and the lizard cocked its head to one side while it examined Orne.

He stared up at it, his only bodily sensation a vague awareness of tightness across chest and stomach. The beast stink was almost overpowering.

Behind the *shriggar,* the green wall continued to wriggle with iridescent purple lines. It was a background blur on Orne's eyes. The lizard moved closer, and he smelled a draught of breath as fetid as swamp ooze.

No matter what Bakrish said, this has to be hallucination, he told himself. *Shriggar have been extinct for centuries.* But another thought blinked at him: *The priests could have bred zoo specimens to maintain the species. How does anyone know what's been done here in the name of religion?*

The *shriggar* cocked its head to the other side.

At the green wall, lines solidified. Two children dressed in scanty sun aprons skipped out on to the stone floor. Their footsteps echoed, and childish giggling echoed in the vast emptiness. One child appeared to be about five years old, the other slightly older—possibly eight. The older child carried a small bucket with a toy shovel protruding from it. They stopped, looked around, confused.

The *shriggar* turned its head, bent its stalk eyes towards them. It swivelled its body back towards the wall, poised one foot, lunged into its high-stepping lope.

The youngest child looked up, squealed.

The *shriggar* increased its speed.

Shocked, Orne recognized the children: his two sisters, the ones who had laughed at his fearful cries on that long ago day. It was as though he had brought this incident to life for the sole purpose of venting his hate, inflicting on those children the thing they had derided.

The lizard swooped down, blocked the children from view. Orne tried to close his eyes, could not. There came a shriek cut off with abrupt finality. Unable to stop, the *shriggar* hit the green wall, *melted into it!*

The older child lay sprawled on the floor still clutching her bucket and toy shovel. A red smear spread across the stones beside her. She stared across the room at Orne, slowly got to her feet.

No matter what Bakrish said, this can't be real, thought Orne. Yet he felt an odd wash of relief that the *shriggar* had vanished.

The child began walking towards Orne, swinging her bucket. Her right hand clutched the toy shovel. She stared fixedly at Orne. He brought her name into his mind: *Maddie, my sister, Lurie. But she's a grown woman now, married and with children of her own.*

Flecks of sand marked the child's legs and cheeks. One of her two blonde braids hung down partly undone. She looked angry, shivering with an eight-year-old's fury. About two metres away she stopped.

"You did that!" she screamed.

Orne shuddered at the madness in the child voice. She lifted the bucket, hurled its contents at him. He shut his eyes, felt coarse sand deluge his face, pelt the silver dome, run down his cheeks. Pain coursed through him as he shook his head, disrupting the microfilaments against his scalp. Through slitted eyes he saw the dancing lines on the green wall leap into wild motion—bending, twisting, flinging. Orne stared at the purple frenzy through a red haze of pain. And he remembered the guru's warning that any life he called forth here would contain his own psyche as well as its own.

"Lurie," he said, "please try to . . ."

"You tried to get into my head!" she screamed. "But I pushed you out!"

Bakrish had said it: *"Others will reject your half out of hand because they have not the capacity."* This dual create had rejected him because her eight-year-old mind could not accept such an experience. And Orne realized that he was taking this scene as reality and not as hallucination.

"I'm going to kill you!" screamed Lurie.

She hurled herself at him, the toy shovel swinging. Light glinted from the tiny blade. It slashed down on his right arm. *Abrupt pain!* Blood darkened the sleeve of his gown.

Orne felt himself caught up in a nightmare. Words leaped to his lips: "Stop that, Lurie! God will punish you!"

Movement behind the child. He looked up.

A toga-clad figure in red turban came striding out of the green wall: a tall man with gleaming eyes, the face of a tortured ascetic—long grey beard parted in the *sufi* manner.

Orne whispered the name: *"Mahmud!"*

A gigantic tri-di of that face dominated the inner mosque of Chargon.

God will punish you!

Orne remembered standing beside his father, staring up at the image in the mosque, bowing to it.

The Mahmud figure strode up behind Lurie, caught her arm as she started another blow. She turned, struggling, but he held her, twisted the arm slowly, methodically. A bone snapped with sickening sharpness. The child screamed and screamed and . . ."

"Don't!" protested Orne.

Mahmud had a low, rumbling voice. He said: "One does not command God's agent to stop His just punishment." He held the child's hair, stooped, caught up the fallen shovel, slashed it across her neck. The screaming stopped. Blood spurted over his gown. He let the now limp figure fall to the floor, dropped the shovel, turned to Orne.

Nightmare! thought Orne. *This has to be a nightmare!*

"You are thinking this is a nightmare," rumbled Mahmud.

And Orne remembered: this creature, too, if it were real, could think with his reactions and memories. He rejected the thought. "You *are* a nightmare!"

"Your create has done its work," said Mahmud. "It had to be disposed of, you know, because it was embodied by hate, not by love."

Orne felt sickened, guilty, angry. He remembered that this test involved understanding miracles. "This was a miracle?" he demanded.

"What is a miracle?" demanded Mahmud.

Abruptly, an air of suspense enclosed Orne. Prescient fear sucked at his vitals.

"What is a miracle?" repeated Mahmud.

Orne felt his heart hammering. He couldn't seem to focus on the words, stammered: "Are you really an agent of God?"

"Quibbles and labels!" barked Mahmud. "Don't you know about labels? An expediency! There's something *beyond* your labels. Where the zone of the word stops, something else begins."

A tingling sense of madness prickled through Orne. He felt himself balanced on the edge of chaos. "What is a miracle?" he whispered. And he thought back to Emolirdo: *words . . . chaos . . . energy. Psi equals miracle! No. More labels. Energy.*

"Energy from chaos moulded into duration," he said.

"Very close for words," murmured Mahmud. "Is a miracle good or evil?"

"Everybody says miracles are good." Orne took a deep breath. "But they don't have to be either. Good and evil are all tied up in motives."

"Man has motives," said Mahmud.

"Man can be good or evil in his miracles by any definition he wants," said Orne.

Mahmud lifted his head, stared down his nose at Orne. "Yes?"

After a moment of tension, Orne returned the stare. Success in this test had taken on a deep meaning for him. He could feel the inner goading. "Do you want me to say that men create gods to enforce their definitions of good and evil?"

"Do I?"

"So I've said it!"

"Is that all you have to say?"

Orne had to force his attention on to the meanings of words. It was like wading upstream in a swift river. So easy to relax and forget it all. His thoughts showed a tendency to scatter. *Is* what *all I have to say?*

"What is it about men's creations?" demanded Mahmud. "What is it about any creation?"

Orne recalled the nightmare sequence of events in this test. He wondered: *Could this psi machine amplify the energy we call religion? Bakrish said I could bring the dead to life here. Religion's supposed to have a monopoly on that. And the original Mahmud's certainly dead. Been dead for centuries. Provided it isn't hallucination, this whole thing makes a peculiar kind of sense. Even then . . .*

"You know the answer," said Mahmud.

Orne said: "Creations may act independently of their creators. So good and evil don't apply."

"Ah-hah! You have learned this lesson!"

Mahmud stooped, lifted the dead child figure. There was an odd tenderness to his motions. He turned away, marched back into the writhings of the green wall. Silence blanketed the room. The dancing purple lines became almost static, moved in viscous torpor.

Orne felt drained of energy. His arms and legs ached as though he had been using their muscles to the absolute limit.

A bronze clangor echoed behind him, and the green wall returned to its featureless grey. Footsteps slapped against the stone floor. Hands worked at the metallic bowl, lifted it off his head. The straps that held him to the chair fell away. Bakrish came round to stand in front of Orne.

"Did I pass this test?" asked Orne.

"You are alive and still in possession of your soul are you not?"

"How do I know if I still have my soul?"

"One knows by the absence," murmured Bakrish. He glanced down at

Orne's wounded arm. "We must get that bandaged. It's night and time for the next step in your ordeal."

"Night?" Orne glanced up at the slitted windows in the dome, saw darkness punctured by stars. He looked around, realized that shadowless exciter light of glow globes had replaced the daylight. "Time goes quickly here."

"For some . . . not for others."

"I feel so tired."

"We'll give you an energy pill when we fix the arm. Come along."

"What's next?"

"You must walk through the shadow of dogma and ceremony, Orne. For it is written that motive is the father of ethics, and caution is the brother of fear . . ." he paused ". . . and fear is the daughter of pain."

There was a nip of chill in the night air. Orne felt thankful now for the thickness of the robe around him. A cooing of birds sounded from the deeper shadows of a park area ahead. Beyond the park arose a hill outlined against the stars, and up the hill marched a snake-track of moving lights.

Bakrish spoke from beside Orne. "The lights are carried by students. Each student has a pole, and on its top a translucent box. The four sides of the boxes each show a different color: red, blue, yellow and green."

Orne watched the lights. They flickered like weird phosphorescent insects in the dark. "What's the reason for that?"

"They show their piety."

"I mean the four colors?"

"Ah. Red for the blood you dedicate to your god, blue for the truth, yellow for the richness of religious experience, and green for the growth of that experience."

"So they march up the mountain."

"Yes. To show their piety." Bakrish took Orne's arm. "The procession is coming out of the city through a gate in the wall over here. There will be a light for you there. Come along."

They crossed the park, stopped by a narrow open gate. Bakrish took a pole from a rack beside the wall, twisted the handle and light glowed at the top. "Here."

The pole felt slippery smooth in Orne's hand. The light above him was turned to cast a red glow on the people passing through the gate: a student, then a priest, a student, then a priest . . . Their faces carried a uniform gravity.

The end of the procession appeared. "Stay behind that priest," said Bakrish. He urged Orne into the line, fell in behind.

Immediately, prescient fear tugged at Orne's energy. He stumbled, faltered, heard Bakrish grunt: "Keep up! Keep up!"

Orne recovered his balance. His light cast a dull green reflection off the back of the priest ahead. A murmuring, shuffling sounded from the procession. Insects chittered in the tall grass beside their trail. Orne looked up. The bobbing lights wove a meander line up the hill.

The prescient fear grew stronger. Orne felt fragmented. Part of him cowered sickly with the thought that he could fail here. Another part groped out for the chimera of this ordeal. He sensed tremendous elation only a heartbeat away, but this only piled fuel on his fear. It was as though he struggled to awaken from a nightmare within a nightmare, knowing that the pseudo-awakening would only precipitate him into new terror.

The line halted. Orne stumbled to a stop, focused on what was happening around him. Students bunched into a semi-circle. Their lights bounced multicolored gleams off a stone stupa about twice the height of a man. A bearded priest, his head covered by a red three-cornered hat, his body vague motions under a long black robe, stood in front of the stupa like a dark judge at some mysterious trial.

Orne found a place in the outer ring of students, peered between two of them.

The red-hatted priest bowed, spoke in a resonant bass voice: "You stand before the shrine of purity and the law, the two inseparables of all true belief. Here before you is a key to the great mystery that can lead you to paradise."

Orne felt tension, then the impact of a strong psi field, realized abruptly that this psi field was different. It beat like a metronome with the cadence of the priest's words, rising with the passion of his speech.

". . . the immortal goodness and purity of all the great prophets!" he was saying. "Conceived in purity, born in purity, their thoughts ever bathed in goodness! Untouched by base nature in all their aspects!"

With a shock, Orne realized that this psi field around him arose not from some machine, but from a blending of emotions in the massed students. The emotions he sensed played subtle harmonies on the overriding field. It was as though the priest played these people as a musician might play his instrument.

". . . the eternal truth of this divine dogma!" shouted the priest.

Incense wafted across Orne's nostrils. A hidden voder began to emit low organ notes: a rumbling, sonorous melody. To the right, Orne saw a graveman circling the ring of students and priests waving a censer. Blue smoke hung over the mass of people in ghostly curls. From off in the darkness a bell tinkled seven times.

Orne felt like a man hypnotized, thinking: *Massed emotions act like a psi field! Great God! What* is *a psi field?*

The priest raised both arms, fists clenched. "Eternal paradise to all true believers! Eternal damnation to all unbelievers!" His voice lowered. "You students seeking the eternal truth, fall down to your knees and beg for enlightenment. Pray for the veil to be lifted from your eyes."

There was a shuffling and whisper of robes as the students around Orne sank to their knees. Still Orne stared ahead, his whole being caught up in his discovery. *Massed emotions act like a psi field!*

A muttering sound passed through the students.

What is *a psi field?* Orne asked himself. He felt an answer lurking in a hidden corner of his mind.

Angry glances were directed at Orne from the kneeling students. The muttering grew louder.

Belatedly, Orne became aware of danger. Prescient fear was like a klaxon roaring within him.

Bakrish leaned close, whispered: "There's a trail into the woods off to your right. Better start working towards it."

At the far side of the kneeling crowd a student lifted an arm, pointed at Orne. "What about him? He's a student!"

Someone lost in the mass of people shouted: "Unbeliever!" Others took it up like a mindless chant.

Orne grasped his light standard tightly, began inching his way to the right. Tension in the crowd was like a fuse smoking and sizzling towards a mass of explosives.

The red-hatted priest glared at Orne, dark face contorted in the kaleido-scopic gleams of the students' lights. He thrust out an arm towards Orne. "Death to unbelievers!"

Students began climbing to their feet.

Orne moved faster, stumbling back into the darkness beyond the lights, realized he still carried his own light like a waving beacon. Its colored reflections picked out a side trail leading off into blackness.

The priest's voice behind him leaped to an insane pitch: "Bring me the head of that blasphemer!"

Orne hurled his light standard like a spear at the suddenly congested group behind him, whirled, fled along the trail.

A ragged, demoniacal yell lifted into the night from the mass of students. A thunder of footsteps pounded after him.

Orne put on more speed. His eyes adjusted to the starlight, and he could just make out the line of the trail curving around the slope to the left. A blotch of deeper blackness loomed ahead.

The woods?

The scrambling mob sound filled the night behind him.

Under Orne's feet, the path became uneven, twisted to the right down a steep slope, turned left. He tripped, almost fell. His robe caught on bushes, and he lost seconds freeing himself, glanced back. Another few seconds and the lights of the mob would reveal him. He came to a split-second decision, plunged off the trail downhill to the right and parallel to the line of trees. Bushes snagged his robe. He fumbled with the belt, shed the robe.

"I hear him!" someone screamed from above.

The mob came to a plunging stop, held silent. Orne's crashing progress dominated the night sounds.

"Down there!"

And they were after him.

"His head!" someone screamed. "Tear his head off him!"

Orne plunged on, feeling cold and exposed in nothing but sandals and the light shorts he had worn beneath the robe. The mob was a crashing avalanche on the hill above him: curses, thumps and tearing sounds, waving lights. Abruptly, Orne stumbled on to another trail, was almost across it before he could turn left. His legs ached. There was a tight band across his chest. He plunged into deeper darkness, glanced up to see trees outlined against the stars. The mob was a confused clamour behind.

Orne stopped, listened to the voices: "Part of you go that way! We'll go this way!"

He drew in gasping breaths, looked around. *Like a hunted animal!* he thought. And he remembered Bakrish's words: "*. . . caution is the brother of fear . . .*" He smiled grimly, slipped off the trail downhill to the right, ducked beneath low limbs, crawled behind a log. Moving softly, silently, he dug dirt from beside the log, smeared it over his face and chest.

Lights came closer along the trail. He heard the angry voices.

Keeping his head down, Orne wriggled deeper into the trees, arose to his knees, slid down a hill. He worked his way to the right down the hill. The mob sounds grew dim, faded. He crossed another trail, melted through more trees and bushes. His wounded arm ached, and unaccountably this reminded him of the itching sensation he had felt while strapped in the chair . . . *an itching like a healing wound but* before *the wound!* He felt that he had met another clue, but its meaning baffled him.

The trees thinned, bushes grew farther apart. He came out on to the flat park area, a lawn underfoot. Beyond the park he saw the wall, and above that street lights and glowing windows.

Bakrish said the Halmyrach Abbod is in this city, thought Orne. *Why bother with the lower echelons? I'm a field agent of the I–A. It's time I got down to work.* And in the back of his mind another thought niggled: *Did I pass that last test?* Angrily, he pushed the thought aside, crouched as footsteps sounded on a path to his left.

Through the thin starlight filtered by scattered trees he saw a priest in white walking along the path. Orne flattened himself against a tree, waited. Fragrance of night-blooming flowers crossed his nostrils. Birds whirring and rustling sounded from the branches overhead. The footsteps came closer.

Orne waited for the priest to pass, slipped out behind him.

Presently, Orne strode towards the wall and the street lights. The priest's robe hung a little long. He tucked a fold under the belt, smiled. In the dark bushes at the edge of the park lay an unconscious figure bound and gagged with strips torn from his own underclothing.

Now, we see what makes this place tick, thought Orne. He paused while still in the shadows of the park, scrubbed at the dirt on his face and chest with an under corner of the robe, then continued on his way calmly—a priest out on normal business.

No movement showed beyond the low wall. Orne walked along it, entered by a gate, crossed to an alley. A sour smell of cooking tainted the narrow way. The slapping of his sandalled feet made a double echo off the stone walls. Ahead, a standard light showed the crossing of another narrow alley.

Orne stopped as thin shadows projected across the intersection. Two priests strode into view. Orne hurried ahead, recalled a religious greeting from his own childhood training on Chargon. "Shari'a, gentle sirs," he said. "God grant you peace."

The pair stopped with their faces in shadows half turned his direction. The near one spoke: "May you follow the highway of divine command and guidance." The other said: "May we be of service?"

"I am from another sector and have been summoned to the Halmyrach Abbod," said Orne. "I seem to have lost my way." He waited, alert to every movement from the pair.

"These alleys are like a maze," said the nearest priest. "But you are near." He turned, and the street light revealed a pinched-in face, narrow eyes. "Take the next turning to your right. Follow that way to the third turning left. That street ends at the court of the Abbod."

"I am grateful," murmured Orne.

"A service to one of God's creatures is a service to God," said the priest. "May you find wisdom." The pair bowed, passed around Orne, went on their way.

Orne smiled into the darkness, thinking: *Old I–A maxim—Go straight to the top.*

The street of the Abbod proved to be even narrower than the others. Orne could have stretched out his arms to touch both walls. At the end of the alley a door glowed dimly grey in reflected starlight. The door proved to be locked.

A locked door? he thought. *Can all be sweetness and purity here?* He stepped back, peered up at the wall. Dark irregularities there suggested spikes or a similar barrier. His thought was cynically amused: *Such civilized appointments on this* peaceful *planet!*

A glance back up the alley showed it still empty. He shed the priestly robe, swung a hemmed corner up on to the wall, pulled. The robe slipped back slightly, caught. There was a small tearing sound as he tested it, but the robe held. He tried his weight on it. The fabric stretched, but remained firmly caught.

Scrabbling sounds marked his passage up the wall. He avoided sharp spikes on the top, crouched there. One window in the building opposite him glowed with a dim rose color behind loose draperies. He glanced down, saw a starlit courtyard, tall pots in rows topped with flowering bushes. Another glance at the window, and he felt the abrupt stab of prescient fear. *Danger there!* An air of tension hung over the courtyard.

Orne freed the robe from the spike, dropped into the courtyard, crouched in shadows while he slipped back into the priest's garment. One deep breath, and he began working his way around the courtyard to the left, hugging the shadows. Vines dropped from a balcony below the lighted window. He tested one, found it too fragile, moved farther along the wall. A draught touched his left cheek. Darker blackness there—an open door.

Prescient fear tingled along his nerves. Angrily, he put down the fear, slipped through the door into the hall.

Light glared in the hall!

Orne froze, then suppressed laughter as he saw the beam switch beside the door. He stepped back: darkness. Forward: light.

Stairs climbed curving to the left at the end of the hall. Orne moved quietly along the hall, paused at the foot of the stairs and looked up at a heavy wooden door with golden initials on it in bas relief: "H.A."

Halmyrach Abbod! Right to the top!

He slipped up the stairs, cautiously gripped the door handle, turned it with the gentlest of pressure. The lock clicked. He threw the door open, lunged through, slammed the door behind him.

"Ah, Mr. Orne. Very resourceful of you." It was a faintly tenor masculine voice with just an edge of quaver to it.

Orne slewed around, saw a wide-hooded bed. Remote in the bed like a dark-skinned doll sat a man in a nightshirt. He was propped up by a mound of pillows. The face looked familiar. It was narrow, smooth-skinned with a nose that hung like a precipice over a wide mouth. His head was polished dark baldness.

The wide mouth moved, and the faintly quavering tenor voice said: "I am the Halmyrach Abbod. You wished to see me?"

An aura of oldness hung over the man in the bed like an ancient odour of parchment.

Orne took two steps towards the bed, his prescient fear clamouring. He paused, recalling the resemblance. "You look like Emolirdo."

"My younger brother, Mr. Orne. Do be seated." He gestured towards a chair beside the bed. "Forgive me for receiving you this way, but I find myself jealous of my rest in these later years."

Orne moved to the chair. Something about this skinny ancient spoke of deadliness beyond anything Orne had ever before encountered. He glanced around the room, saw dark hangings on the walls covered with weird shapes: curves and squares, pyramids, swastikas and a repetitive symbol like an anchor—a vertical line with an arc at its base. The floor was black and white tile of gigantic pentagonal pieces, each at least two metres across. Furniture of polished woods was crowded into the corners: a desk, a low table, chairs, a tape rack and a stand in the shape of a spiral staircase.

"Have you already summoned your guards?" asked Orne.

"I have no need of them, Mr. Orne. Please sit down." Again the skeletal arm gestured towards the chair.

Orne looked at the chair. It had no arms to conceal secret bindings.

"The chair is just a chair," said the Abbod.

Orne sat down like a man plunging into cold water, tensed.

The Abbod smiled. "You see?"

Orne wet his lips with his tongue. Something was wrong here. This was not working out at all as he had imagined. "I came here to find out some things," he said.

"Good. We shall share information."

"Why're you people out to get the I–A?"

"First things first, Mr. Orne. Have you deciphered the intent of your ordeal?" The Abbod's large eyes, brown and glossy, stared at Orne. "Do you know why you co-operated with us?"

"What else could I do?"

"Many things, as you have demonstrated just this night."

"All right, I was curious."

"About what?"

Orne lowered his eyes, felt something quicken within himself.

"Be honest with yourself, Mr. Orne."

"I . . . I suspected you were teaching me things about myself that . . . that I didn't already know."

"Superb!" The Abbod smiled. "But you were a product of the Marakian civilization. All aberrative tendencies had been removed at an early age by microsurgical *atenture*. How, then, could there be left anything about yourself that you did not know?"

"There just *was*. I found out I could be afraid without knowing why. I . . ."

"Had you ever heard of the thaumaturgic psychiatrists of the ancient Christian era?"

"What era was that?"

"Long ago. So long ago that there are left only small, tantalizing fragments to tell us of those days. The Christeros religion derives from that period."

"What about it?"

"You have not heard of these ancient practices?"

"I know there were mental sciences before the microsurgical techniques were developed. Is that what you mean?"

"In a way." The Abbod fell silent, waiting.

Orne swallowed. This was not going the way it should have gone. He felt on the defensive, and all he faced was one skinny old man in a ridiculous nightshirt. Anger swelled in Orne. "I came here to find out if you people were fomenting war!"

"And what if we were? What then? Were you prepared to be the surgeon, to cut out the infection and leave society in its former health?"

Orne's anger receded.

"Do you not see the parallel, Mr. Orne?" The Abbod frowned. "The best of a supreme mechanistic science worked you over and declared you sane, balanced, clear. Yet there remained something more that they had not touched."

"Then there's something the I–A isn't . . . touching?"

"But of course."

"What?"

"Most of every iceberg is beneath the surface of the sea," said the Abbod.

A tiny wave of Orne's anger surged back. "Now what's *that* supposed to mean?"

"Then let us approach it this way," said the Abbod. "The Guru called Pasawan, who led the Ramakrishnanas into the Great Unifying we know as the Ecumenical Truce, was a follower of the Hynd doctrine. This has always taught the divinity of the soul, the unity of all existence, the oneness of the Godhead and the harmony of all religions."

Orne stiffened. "You're not going to get anywhere trying to force a lot of religious pap down my throat!"

"One does not successfully force religion on to anyone," murmured the Abbod. "If it pleases you to do so, you may consider this in the nature of a history lesson."

Orne sank back in the chair. "So get on with it."

"Thanks to Pasawan, we believe we have developed here a science of religion. The discovery of psi powers and an interpretation of their significance tends to confirm our postulates."

"Which are?"

"That mankind, acting somewhat as a great psi machine, does create a force, an energy system. We may refer to this system as religion, and invest it with an independent focus of action which we will call God. But remember that a god without discipline faces the same fate as the merest human under the same circumstances. It is unfortunate that mankind has always been so attracted by visions of absolutes—even in his gods."

Orne recalled his experience that night when he had felt a psi field surging out of the emotions in the massed students. He rubbed his chin.

"Let us consider this idea of absolutes," said the Abbod. "Let us postulate a finite system in which a given *being* may exhaust all avenues of knowledge—know everything, as it were."

In an intuitive leap, Orne saw the image being painted by the Abbod's words. He blurted: "It'd be worse than death!"

"Unutterable, deadly boredom would face such a being. Its future would be endless repetition, replaying all of its old tapes. A boredom worse than extinction."

"But boredom is a kind of stasis," said Orne. "Stasis would lead to chaos."

"And what do we have?" asked the Abbod. "We have chaos: an infinite system where *anything* can happen—a place of constant change. And let us recognize one of the inevitable properties of this infinite system. If *anything* can happen, then our hypothetical *being* could be extinguished. Quite a price to pay to escape boredom, eh?"

"All right. I'll go along with your game and your hypothetical *being*. Couldn't it find some kind of . . . well, insurance?"

"Such as scattering its eggs in an infinite number of baskets, eh?"

"Life's done just that, hasn't it? It's scattered all over the universe in billions of forms."

"Yet *any*thing can happen," murmured the Abbod. "So we have two choices: infinite boredom or infinite chance."

"So what?"

"Do you wish me to continue with the history lesson?"

"Go ahead."

"Now, behind or beneath or projecting into this scattered *Life,* let us postulate a kind of consciousness that . . ." He raised a hand as Orne's face darkened. "Hear me out, Mr. Orne. This *other* consciousness has been suspected for countless centuries. It has been called such things as 'collective unconscious,' 'the paramatman,' 'urgrund,' 'sanatana dharma,' 'super mind,' 'ober palliat' . . . It has been called many things."

"None of which makes it any more real!" snapped Orne. "Let's not mistake *clear* reasoning for *correct* reasoning. The fact that a name exists for something doesn't mean that thing exists."

"You are then an empiricist," said the Abbod. "Good. Did you ever hear the legend of Doubting Thomas?"

"No."

"No matter," said the Abbod. "He was always one of my favorite characters. He refused to take crucial facts on faith."

"Sounds like a wise man."

The Abbod smiled. "A moment ago I said that mankind generates a power we may call religion, and within that religion a focus of independent action you may refer to as God."

"Are you sure it isn't the other way around?"

"That's of no importance at the moment, Mr. Orne. Let us go on to a corollary of the original postulate, which is that mankind also generates prophets in the same way—men who point out the paths that lead to degeneracy and failure. And here we come to a function of our order as I see it. We find these prophets and educate them."

"You educate men like Mahmud?"

"Mahmud escaped us."

Orne suddenly sat up straight. "Are you implying that *I'm* a prophet?"

"But of course you are. You're a man with extraordinary powers. Psi instruments have only sharpened and brought to focus what was already there, latent within you."

Orne slapped a hand on to his right knee. "If this isn't the wildest train of . . ."

"I'm serious, Mr. Orne. In the past, prophets have tended to preach without restriction—uninhibited and really undisciplined. The results were always the same: temporary order that climbed towards greater and greater power, then the inevitable degeneration. We, on the other hand, have another method.

We seek the slow, self-disciplined accumulation of data that will extend our science of religion. The broad course ahead of us is already becoming . . ."

"Do you mean to tell me that you people presume to educate prophets?"

An inner light glittered in the Abbod's glossy eyes. "Mr. Orne, have you any idea how many innocents have been tortured to death in the name of religion during the course of Man's bloody history?"

Orne shrugged. "There's no way of knowing how many."

"Countless?"

"Certainly."

"That is one of the things which always happen when religions run wild, Mr. Orne. War and bloodshed of countless sorts develop from undisciplined religion."

"And you think I'm a prophet?"

"We *know* you are. It is uncertain whether you could start a new religion, but you *are* a prophet. We had you out on that mountainside tonight for just one purpose. Your fellow students did not turn out to be prophets. They will never rise above the oblate brotherhood. We know their character, however, and we know your character. Put the two together, and you should have learned a lesson."

"Sure! That I could get my head torn off by a mob!"

"That would have meant you failed the test," said the Abbod. "Now, please be calm and tell me the basic significance of your experience out there."

"Wait a minute," said Orne. "How'd *you* know what happened out there?"

"I knew within seconds when you ran away from the mob," said the Abbod. "I was waiting for the report. We suspected you would come here."

"Of course. And you just sat here and waited for me."

"Of course. Now answer the question: What's the basic significance of your experience?"

Orne turned his head, looked out of the corners of his eyes at the Abbod. "That there's a great amount of explosive energy in religion. That's what I learned."

"You already knew this, naturally."

"Yes. You just made the fact important to me."

"Mr. Orne, I will tell you about just one of the many prophets we have on Amel. His talents are extreme. He can cause a glowing aura to appear around his body. He can levitate. What we understand as space does not exist for him. Seemingly, he can step from planet to planet as easily as a normal person would cross the . . ."

"Is this that fellow who was on Wessen? The one the feature scribes went nuts over when . . ."

"I see you've heard of him. We got to him barely in time, Mr. Orne. I ask you now: What would happen if he were to appear to a crowd, say, on Marak, that enlightened center of our government, and display there his full powers?"

Orne frowned.

"Is it likely they would put a religious interpretation on his activities?" demanded the Abbod.

"Well . . . probably."

"Most certainly! And what if he did not fully understand his own talents? Picture it. He knows the true from the false by some inner sense—call it instinct. Around him he sees much that is false. What's he likely to do?"

"All right!" barked Orne. "He'd probably start a new religion! You've made your point."

"A *wild* religion," corrected the Abbod. He glared at Orne, pointed to Orne's left. "Look there!"

Orne turned, saw a dancing sword of flame about two meters away. Its point was aimed at his head. He shivered, felt perspiration drench his body. Prescient fear screamed within him.

"The first lone man to tap that source of energy was burned alive as a sorcerer by his fellow humans," said the Abbod. "The ancients thought that flame was alive. They gave it religious significance, called it a *salamander*. They thought of it as a demon. And when you don't know how to control it, the thing does act like a wild demon with a life and will of its own. It's raw energy, Mr. Orne. *I* direct it through a psi focus. You act so superior. You think of yourself as a servant of a great organization that prevents war. Yet I—one man alone—could utterly annihilate any military force you could bring against me . . . and I would use nothing but this ancient discovery!"

The old man sank back against his pillows, closed his eyes. Presently, he opened his eyes, said: "Sometimes I forget my years, but they never forget me."

Orne drew in a ragged breath. The deadliness that he had suspected in this skeletal human had taken on form and dimension: deadliness magnified to new dimensions.

"When Emolirdo informed us of you, we had to bring you here, test you, see for ourselves," murmured the Abbod. "So many do not test out. In your case, though, the tests proved Emolirdo correct. You . . ."

"I did things Emolirdo taught me how to do, and *with* equipment he had put in my body!"

"Your *equipment* has been nullified by a dampening projection since your interview with Bakrish at your arrival," said the Abbod.

Orne opened his mouth to protest, closed it. He recalled his sensation of strangeness during that first interview. *Nullified?* Yet he still sensed danger all around.

"What Emolirdo did was to force you to accept the things you already could do," said the Abbod. "Your first lesson: faith in yourself." He looked grimly amused. "But it is plain that you still cherish doubts."

"You're damn' right I do! I think this whole hocus pocus was designed to confuse me, put me off the track!"

"You doubt the existence of a superior consciousness that manifests itself in gods and prophets and even sometimes in our machines," said the Abbod.

"I think you may have stumbled on to something with your psi powers, but you've mucked it up with your mystical hogwash! There's a scientific explanation for these things that'd appear if you blew away all this fog."

"The empiricist demands his demonstration," murmured the Abbod. "Very well. Let us introduce you to the graduate school, Mr. Orne. Thus far, you've been playing with toys. Let's see how you react when we threaten the basic fiber of your being!"

Orne pushed himself to his feet, reached behind for the back of the chair. He glanced left at the dancing point of flame, saw it sweep around in front of his eyes. Burning, prickling sensations crawled along his skin. The flame grew to a ball almost a meter in diameter, pressed forwards. Orne stumbled backwards, knocked over the chair. Heat blasted his face.

"How now?" cried the Abbod.

He's trying to panic me, thought Orne. *This could be an illusion.* He darted to the left, and the flame shot ahead of him, cutting him off, pressed even closer.

Orne retreated. His face burned where the flame seared against it.

"Is this illusion, Mr. Orne?" called the Abbod.

Doggedly, Orne shook his head. His eyes smarted. The flaming ball pressed him backwards. He shook perspiration from his head, glanced down at the floor. *Pentagonal tiles. Giant pentagonal tiles at least two meters across.* He stepped to the center of a white tile, immediately felt the heat diminish.

"Psi must be faced with psi," called the Abbod.

Orne nodded, wet his lips with his tongue, swallowed. He tried to focus on the inner awareness as Emolirdo had taught him. Nothing. He closed his eyes, concentrated, felt something give.

Somewhere, there was a great howling of not-sound. He was being pulled inwards, distorted. Twisted in a vortex that sucked him down . . . down . . . down . . . down . . .

The thought of ticking seconds blazed within him.

TIME!

No sensation except a dim touch of the pentagram as though it pressed against his body at every point: a pentagram, a box, a cage. And the ticking seconds. His mind boiled with the thought of *TIME!*

Time and tension, he thought. And his mind juggled symbols like blocks of energy, manipulated energy like discrete signals. There was a problem. *Tension! Tension = energy source. Energy + opposition = growth of energy. To strengthen a thing, oppose it. Growth of energy + opposition = opposites blending into a new identity.*

"You become like the worst in what you oppose," he thought. It was a quotation. He had heard it somewhere. *Priest slips into evil. The great degenerates into the small.*

And he remembered his wounded arm, the itching before the wound.

TIME!

Beyond the pentagram he sensed a place where chaotic energy flowed. A great blank not-darkness filled with not-light and a ceaseless flowing. And he felt himself as on a mountaintop—as though he *were* the mountaintop. Pressing upwards but still connected to a living earth below. Somewhere he felt the touch of the pentagram: a shape that could be remembered and located.

A voice came from below the mountain: "Mr. Orne?"

He felt the pentagram press more tightly.

"Mr. Orne?"

The Abbod's voice.

Orne felt himself flowing back, compressed, twisted. The shape of his body became a new distortion to his senses. He wanted to resist.

"Don't fight it, Mr. Orne."

Pressure against side and arms: the floor. He opened his eyes, found that he was stretched out on the tiles, his head at one corner of the white pentagram, his feet at the opposite corner. The Abbod stood over him in a belted white robe: a dark, monkey-like creature with overlarge, staring eyes.

"What did you see? Mr. Orne?"

Orne drew in a deep, gasping breath. He felt dizzy, weak. "Nothing," he gasped.

"Oh, yes. You *saw* with every sense you possess. One does not walk without seeing the path."

Walk? Path? Orne remembered the sense of flowing chaos. He pulled his arms back, pushed himself up. The floor felt cold against his palms. The wound in his arm itched. He shook his head. "What do you *want* from me?"

The Abbod's gaze bored into him. "*You* tell me."

Orne swallowed in a dry throat. "I saw chaos."

The Abbod leaned forward. "And *where* is this chaos?"

Orne looked down at his feet extended along the floor, glanced around the room, back to the Abbod. "Here. It was this world, this universe, this . . ."

"Why could you see it as chaos?"

Orne shook his head. *Why? I was threatened. I . . . TIME!* He looked up. "It has something to do with time."

"Mr. Orne, have you ever seen a jungle?"

"Yes."

"The plant life, its growth is not immediately apparent to your senses, is it?"

"Not . . . immediately. But over a period of days, of course, you . . ." He broke off.

"Precisely!" barked the Abbod. "If you could, as it were, speed up the jungle, it would become a place of writhing contention. Vines would shoot up like snakes to clutch and strangle the trees. Plants would leap upwards, blast forth with pods, hurl out their seeds. You would see a great strangling battle for sunlight."

"Time," said Orne. And he recalled Emolirdo's analogy: the three-dimensional shadow cast into the two-dimensional world. "How does the person in the two-dimensional world interpret the shadow of a three-dimensional object?" he murmured.

The Abbod smiled. "Emolirdo so enjoys that analogy."

"The two-dimensional being can interpolate," said Orne. "He can stretch his imagination to create . . . *things* that reach into the other dimension."

"So?"

Orne felt the tension. Nerves trembled along his arms. "Psi machines!" he blurted. "They manipulate time!"

"Psi phenomena are time phenomena," said the Abbod.

It was like veils falling away from Orne's senses. He remembered his wounded arm, the itching he had felt before the arm was wounded in that exact place. He recalled a small psi instrument that Emolirdo had displayed: loops, condensers, electronic tubes, all focusing on a thin square of plastic. Rubbed one way, the plastic felt tacky. Rubbed the other way, the plastic felt as slick as glass, greased.

In a half-musing way, he said: "There was a thin layer of time flow along the plastic. One direction, my hand moved with the flow; the other direction, my hand opposed the flow."

"Eh?" The Abbod looked puzzled.

"I was remembering something," said Orne.

"Oh." The Abbod turned, shuffled back to his bed, sat on the edge. His robe opened, revealing thin shanks under his nightshirt. He looked incredibly old and tired.

Orne felt a pang of sympathy for the old man. The sense of dread that had surrounded this place was gone. In its place he felt an awakening akin to awe.

"Life projects matter through the dimension of time," said the Abbod.

"A kind of time machine?"

The Abbod nodded. "Yes. Our awareness is split. It exists within these three dimensions and outside of them. We have known this for centuries. Thoughts can blaze through a lifetime in the merest fraction of a second. Threaten the human life, and you can force his awareness to retreat into no-time. You can weigh countless alternatives, select the course of action that has the greatest survival potential. All of this you can do while time in this dimension stands still."

Orne took a deep breath. He knew this was true. He recalled that final terrible instant in the Heleb uprising. There he had sat at the controls of his escape ship while around him great weapons swung about to bear on the vessel's flimsy walls. There seemed no way to avoid the blasting energies that were sure to come. And he remembered the myriad alternatives that had flitted through his mind while outside the terrible weapons seemed to hang frozen. And he *had* escaped. The one sure way had been seen.

The Abbod pushed himself back into the bed, pulled covers over his legs. "I am a very old man." He looked sideways at Orne. "But it still pleasures me to see a person make the *old* discovery."

Orne took a step forward. "Old?"

"Ancient. Thousands of years before the first man ventured into space from the original home world, a scattered few were discovering this way of looking at the universe. They called it *Maya*. The tongue was Sanskrit. Our view of the matter is a little more . . . sophisticated. But there's no essential difference. The ancients said: '*Abandon forms; direct yourself towards temporal reality.*' You know, Mr. Orne, it's amazing. Man has such an . . . *appetite* to encompass . . . *everything*."

Like a sleep walker, Orne moved forward, righted the chair beside the bed, sank into it. Extensions of his awakening captured his attention. "*The prophet who calls forth the dead,*" he said. "*He returns the matter of the body to a time when it was alive.* That flame you threatened me with. You bring it out of a time when the matter around us was gaseous incandescence. The man from Wessen who walks from planet to planet like you would cross a stream on stepping stones." Orne held up his hands. "Of course. Without time to stretch across it, there can be no space. To him, *time is a specific location!*"

"Think of the universe as an expanding balloon," said the Abbod. "A balloon of weird shape and unexplored convolutions. Suppose you have a transparent grid, three-dimensional. Like graph paper. You look through it at the universe. It is a matrix against which you can plot out the shapes and motions of the universe."

"Education," said Orne.

The Abbod spoke like a teacher praising a pupil. "Very good!" He smiled. "This grid, this matrix is trained into human beings. They project it on to the universe. With this matrix they break nature into bits. Usable bits. But, somehow, they too often get the idea that nature . . . the universe *is* the bits. The matrix is so very useful, permitting us to communicate our ideas, for example. But it is so near-sighted. It's like an old man reading script with his nose pressed almost to the page. He sees one thing at a time. But our universe is *not* one thing at a time. It's an enormous complex. Still we concentrate on the bits." He shook his head. "Do you know how we see the bits, Mr. Orne?"

Orne snapped out of a half-reverie in which the Abbod's words had been like gross areas of understanding that flowed into his awareness. "We see them by contrast. Each bit moves differently, has a different color, or . . ."

"Very good! We see them by contrast. To see a bit we must see also its background. Bit and background are inseparable. Without one you cannot discern the other. Without evil you cannot determine good. Without war, you cannot determine peace. Without . . ."

"Wait a minute!" Orne jerked to attention. "Is that why you're out to ruin the I–A?"

"Mr. Orne, a compulsive peace is not peace. To compel peace, you must use warlike methods. It is nonsense to think that you can get rid of one of a pair and possess only the other. You are doing this by force! You create a vacuum into which chaos will flow."

Orne shook his head. He felt trapped in a maze, caught by the idea that something *had* to be wrong with the Abbod's words.

"It is like a drug habit," said the Abbod. "If you enforce peace, it will take greater and greater amounts of peace to satisfy you. And you will use more and more violence to obtain it. The cycle will end in cataclysm. Think rather of how light reaches your eyes. When you are reading you do not seek out, striving for the light. In the same way, peace comes to your senses. Pleasure comes to you. Good comes to you. As the light reaches your eyes. These are functions of your nerves. You cannot make an effort with your nerves. You *can* make an effort with your muscles. That is the way it is with our universe. Our matrix must be a direct function of reality, of actual matter. In this, it is like our nerves. If we distort the matrix, we do not change reality, but only our way of seeing it. If we destroy one half of a pair, the remaining half overwhelms us. Take away the predator, and the creature preyed upon undergoes a population explosion. All of these things fit the basic law."

"And the I–A has broken that law?"

"It has." The Abbod frowned. "You see, peace is an internal matter. It's a *self*-discipline. It *must* come from within. If you set up an outside power to *enforce* peace, that outside power grows stronger and stronger. It must. Inevitably, it degenerates. Comes the cataclysm."

"You people on Amel look on yourselves as a kind of super I–A, don't you?"

"In a sense," the Abbod agreed. "But we want to go to the root. We wish to plant the seed of self-discipline wherever it will take root. And to do this, we prepare certain ground for cultivation."

"Ground?"

"Worlds. Societies." The Abbod stared at Orne. "And we desperately need farmers, Mr. Orne."

"Meaning me?"

"Would you care to enlist?"

Orne cleared his throat, broke his attention away from the Abbod's intent gaze. He felt that he was being stampeded.

The Abbod's voice intruded. "This is a chaotic universe, Mr. Orne. Things are changing. Things *will* change. There is an instinct in human beings that realizes this. Our instinct foments a feeling of insecurity. We seek something unchanging. Beliefs are temporary because the bits we believe *about* are in motion. They change. And periodically, we go through the cataclysm. We tear down the things that refuse to work. They don't do what we expect them to do, and we become children, smashing the toys that refuse to obey. In such times, the teachers of self-discipline are much needed."

"You say we're approaching some great smashing up, some cataclysm?"

"We are always approaching it. Always ahead of us is the great burning from which the Phoenix arises. Only one thing endures: Faith. The object changes, but faith endures. It's the absolute we yearn after in a changing universe."

Orne felt overwhelmed by a sense of outrage. "Faith? That's nonsense! There's no logic, no scientific . . ."

"Trust your senses!" barked the Abbod. "Do not try to distort the matrix to fit what you *want* to believe! You have experienced another dimension. Many have done this without realizing it. *You* realize it."

"But . . . faith? In what?"

"In our appetite. Faith that we will encompass this other dimension and find there a new area of mystery to beckon our senses. Faith that there is something enduring in all this chaos . . . and if not, that we can create a thing that will endure. *That* faith, Mr. Orne.'

Orne lowered his eyes. "I'm sorry. I . . . didn't understand."

The Abbod's voice lowered almost to a whisper. "Of course you didn't. You had not heard our simple definition of a religion. A religion is the faith that something will endure beyond the apparent chaos surrounding us. The central concepts are Faith and Endurance."

Orne turned the thought over in his mind.

"Our faith here is in the linear endurance of humankind," said the Abbod. "On Amel we call it the Great Continuity. It is our faith that there will always be a descendant of humankind—evolved, changed, unrecognizable to today's humans, no matter what, but still our descendant."

Cynicism, his most dependable defence, took over Orne's thinking. "Very high sounding," he said. "And if that's what you're really doing here, quite attractive. But how can I be certain what you're doing? You use lots of words. Some even make sense."

"But all it takes is one weak link, eh?"

Orne shrugged.

"That's why we seek out only the strong, the prophets," said the Abbod. "That is why the testing and the education. If we tame the wild religions and harness their energies to our purpose, that makes sense, doesn't it?"

"Certainly."

"Then we will give you this, Mr. Orne: You may go anywhere on Amel, ask any questions, look at any records, request any cooperation that does not oppose our purpose. Satisfy yourself. And even then, you do not have to decide to stay with us. You may return to any of the outer worlds, to Marak, to Chargon, wherever you wish to go. We insist only that you subject your talents to our instructions, that you permit us to show you how they may be tamed."

Orne wet his lips with his tongue. A tentative probe at the Abbod's emotions revealed candor and faint amusement. The amusement annoyed Orne. He had the feeling that this was an old story to the Abbod, that the reactions of one Lewis Orne could be classified as type such and so. A kind of pique made him say: "Aren't you afraid I might . . . well, double-cross you once I was off Amel?"

"We have faith in *you*, Mr. Orne. Your ordeal has given us grounds for that, at least."

Orne chuckled. "The least I can do is return the favor, eh?"

"After you've pried and tested us to your satisfaction, yes. You said it yourself, you know: Faith is the uncensored will. Doubt is a censor we'd rather you didn't have."

Orne nodded, and a new thought hit him. "Do you have enough faith in me to let me return to Marak and make over the I–A along lines you'd approve?"

The Abbod shook his head. "Faith in you, we have that. But your I–A has gone too far along the road to power. You understand, my son, that a bureau is like an individual. It will fight for survival. It will seek power. Your I–A has a personality made up of all its parts. Some such as yourself we would trust. Others . . . I'm afraid not. No. Before we permit you to leave here, the I–A will be dead, and other bureaus will be feeding on the remains."

Orne stared at the ancient face. Presently, he said: "I guess I failed them."

"Perhaps not. Your original purpose is still intact. Peace as a self-discipline can be more gratifying than any other kind. It grows more slowly, to be sure, but it's confident growth that counts."

Orne still tasted a certain bitterness. "You seem pretty confident that I'll join you."

"You've already passed that decision," murmured the Abbod. "When you asked to return and make over the I–A."

This time Orne's chuckle was aimed at himself. "Know me pretty well, don't you."

"We know your purpose, your religion, as it were. You share our faith in humankind. When we learned that, we knew you were already one of us." The Abbod smiled, and the old face seemed to light up. "There's much ground to prepare, and we have need of many farmers."

"Yeah, I'm a hayseed, all right," said Orne.

"After you have pried into Amel to your heart's content, come back and talk to me. I know there's a certain young lady awaiting you on Marak. Perhaps we could discuss your returning to another bureau—Rediscovery and Re-education."

"R & R! Those bumbleheads! They're the . . ."

"You have an interesting conditioned reaction there," said the Abbod. "For now I will only remind you that any bureau is the sum of its parts."

In his office on Marak, Tyler Gemine, director of Rediscovery & Re-education, faced Orne across an immense blackwood desk. Behind Gemine a wide window looked out on the packed office buildings of Marak's central government quarter. The director was a rounded outline against the window, a fat and genial surface with smiling mouth and hard eyes. Frown wrinkles creased his forehead.

The office fitted Gemine. On the surface it seemed built for comfort: soft chairs, thick carpet, unobtrusive lighting. But three walls held file cases geared to a remote search control at the desk. Six auto-secretaries flanked the desk.

Sitting opposite the director, Orne still wore his aqua toga from Amel. R & R security police had rushed him here from the spaceport, giving him no time to change.

"All of this haste must appear unseemly to you, Mr. Orne," said Gemine. "Separating you from your fiancée at the spaceport like that. Rude of us." The hard eyes bored into Orne.

Orne hid his amusement under a mask of concern. "I know you must have good reasons, sir."

Gemine leaned back. "Indeed we do." He pulled a stack of papers towards him on the desk, squared them. "Before the I–A took you away from us, Mr. Orne, you were an agent of the R & R."

"Yes, sir. They drafted me."

"That unfortunate business on Hamal!"

"There was nothing I could do, sir."

"No blame attaches to you, Mr. Orne. But you understand that we do have some curiosity about you now that we have superseded the I–A."

"You want to know where my loyalties are?"

"Precisely."

"The R & R's purpose is still my purpose, sir."

"Good! Good!" Gemine patted the stack of papers in front of him. "Ahhh, this mission to Amel. What about that?"

"Why was I sent?"

Gemine's stare was cold and measuring. "Yes."

"It was very simple. The I–A executive staff heard about the move to do away with their department. They had reason to believe the priests were a prime factor in the move. I was sent to Amel to see if they could be circumvented."

"And you failed." It was a flat statement.

"Sir, I beg to remind you that I once volunteered for the R & R. I was one of your agents before the I–A took me away from you." He managed a tight smile. "And it didn't take a giant brain to realize that you would take over the I–A's functions once they were out of the way."

Gemine's eyes clouded with thought. He cleared his throat. "What about this psi thing? In the final audit of I–A we came across this odd department. Unfortunately . . ." Gemine studied a paper in front of him. ". . . the director, one Ag Emolirdo, has disappeared. There were records, though, showing that you were trained by him before your recent . . . ah, mission."

So Agony took it on the lam, thought Orne. *Gone home to report, no doubt.* He said: "It was a questionable field. Oriented along ESP lines." (And he thought: *That'll fit this little hack's executive logic!*) "They were looking for rules to explain certain non-chance phenomena," he went on. "Their results were debatable."

Gemine restacked the papers in front of him. "As I suspected. Well . . . we can go into it in more detail later. I confess it sounded extremely far-fetched in outline. Typical of I–A wastefulness." He leaned back, steepled his hands in front of him. "No, Mr. Orne, as you know, we are taking over the key functions of the I–A. But we're running into stupid resistance. That's where I've hoped you could come in."

"My record with R & R is clear, sir."

Gemine swivelled his chair, looked out of the window at Marak's executive warren. "You know both the R & R and the I–A, Mr. Orne. It's in my mind to attach you to my office—as a special executive assistant. Your duties would be to facilitate absorption of the I–A." He turned back to look at Orne. "What would you say to that?"

Orne hesitated just the right length of time. "I'd . . . I'd consider that an honor, sir."

"Excellent!" Gemine bent forward. "You'll want to get situated first, of course." His manner became more confidential. "You'll be getting married, I understand. Take what time you need. Say, a month."

"That's very kind of you, sir."

"Not at all. I want you to be happy with us." He wet his lips with his tongue. "Miss Bullone may not have had the time to tell you . . . about her father, that is. He is no longer our high commissioner. Lost out in the recent shake-up. A pity after so many years of excellent service."

"Has he stayed on in the Assembly?"

"Oh, yes. He's still an important member. Minority leader." Gemine stared at Orne. "We'd like to have you act—unofficially, you understand—as a sort of liaison with Mr. Bullone."

"I'm sure something could be worked out, sir."

Gemine smiled, relaxed. He nodded.

Orne said: "What about my staff, sir?"

"Staff?"

"I'll need assistants of my own if I'm to do this job correctly."

Sudden tension filled the room. "Anyone special in mind?"

Gently, thought Orne. *This is the delicate part.* He said: "All the time I was in the I–A, I was directly under one man. When he said frog, I jumped. Wherever he pointed, that's where I went."

"Ahhh . . . Mr. Umbo Stetson."

"I see you know him."

"Know him? He's a major source of resistance!"

"That'd make it even more pleasant," said Orne.

Gemine chortled. He radiated gleeful sadism. "Take him! Any authority you need to whip him into line, it's yours!"

Orne matched Gemine's smile. "This is going to be even more fun than I thought."

Gemine arose. "I'll have an office fitted for you next to mine, Lewis.

Want everything cosy and neat." He nodded. "I think this is going to work out very well. Indeed I do."

Orne stood up. "I hope I'll live up to all your expectations, sir."

"You already are, my boy! You know what's expected of you, and you know how to deliver." He gave Orne a knowing smile. "And I won't soon forget your *failure* on Amel." He chortled. "Eh?"

From the secret report: Lewis Orne to the Halmyrach Abbod:

> Gemine was every bit as easy as you said he would be. He has already given me Stetson, and through Stetson I'll bring in the others. This is fallow ground, indeed. Needs the ministrations of a trained farmer.
>
> It was fascinating to talk to Gemine. There was the pattern just as you anticipated it. The weak was absorbing the strong, completely unaware that the strong could eat it up from within. But this time, only a selective seed of the strong.
>
> Stetson raised no objections at all. The idea he found particularly intriguing was this: *We must find a way of preventing war without making war impossible.* For myself, I find this no paradox. In a universe without limits, life must grow through self-imposed limits. Every teaching turns on its *discipline.* And what is a discipline but a limit self-imposed for the benefits derived? My new *matrix* needs no distortion to encompass this concept.
>
> Out of all this, one thought keeps coming back to me. I will mention it this once. It occurs to me that the most effective government is that one where the governed do not know they are being governed, but believe they govern themselves.
>
> > Your obed't farmer,
> > Lewis Orne.

EGG AND ASHES

For a week now the Siukurnin had hung above the hunters' camp disguised as a pine cone. One of the ropes holding their tent fly passed within inches of it, and when the cold evening wind blew, as it was doing now, the rope hummed. This created a masking harmonic that had to be filtered out (along with many other "noises") before the Siukurnin could concentrate on the vibrations coming from the figures around the fire.

Already imprinted and stored in the Siukurnin's subcellular structure was a long catalogue of light-reflected *shapes* and vibration meanings from this place and the other places. It knew that when one of the carbon life-forms moved to the nearby flowing liquid, the creature was going to the *water.* (And that was one of the vibrations for the great heaving expanse of liquid beyond the mountains to the east.) And it knew that when one of these creatures became dormant for the night (low vibration period), that was *sleep.*

Oh, there were so *many* vibration meanings.

The Siukurnin tried reproducing the vibrations for *sleep* and *water* at a subaural level, gloried in its growing mastery of these subtleties.

An aroma of coffee and broiled meat arose from the fire. The Siukurnin listened to these for a moment, savoring the full roundness of the vibration spectrum in this enchanting place. As yet it had not thought of the necessity for a non-*chilitigish* vibration to refer to itself.

(You must understand that when it thought of itself at this stage [which was seldom], it did not think: "I am a Siukurnin." In the first place a natural mechanism inhibited prolonged introspection. In the second place, "Siukurnin" is a make-do vibration—a limited auditory approach to the actual "term" that is used only in communicating with creatures who do not hear into the visual spectrum, and who are not yet able to detect the *chilitigish* spectrum. Since this is only a start at communication, it's perfectly all right for you to think of this creature as a "Siukurnin," but you should keep in mind that there's a limitation.)

·

Before coming to this hunters' camp, the Siukurnin had spent two weeks as a false rivet head in the wardroom of a long gray warship. It had left the warship as a coating of "film" on a garbage container, and had arrived here in the pine glade as a length of "wire" in the trunk lid of a used car that had been sold to one of the hunters.

Between the garbage container and the used car there had been several other shape-aliases, all characterized by solid color and smoothness and all difficult to reproduce. The Siukurnin looked on its present pine cone form almost as a rest.

Once started on its repertoire of new vibration meanings, the Siukurnin was like a *lilim* with a new *arabeg,* or, as you might say, like a child with a new toy. Presently, it recalled the period on the warship. "Now hear this! Now hear this!" it chanted to itself at a level too low to be detected by the figures beneath it.

Darkness folded over the camp in the pine trees and the fire flickered low. The upright creatures retired into their tent. (To *sleep,* you understand.) Among these creatures was one identified by the primitive (non-*chilitigish*) vibration: "Sam."

Now the Siukurnin listened to the soughing of the wind through the branches around it, to the scrabbling of night creatures—and once there was a figurative scream of skunk odor nearby. Much later, the Siukurnin defied its inhibitions, tried to recall a time before the awakening at the warship. Only faint fog memory came: a sensation of swimming upward through dark *water.*

The effort of memory brought the inhibition mechanism into action. Destructive hunger gnawed at the Siukurnin. It sensed changes going on within its structure—a maturation of sorts.

To put down the hunger, the Siukurnin imagined itself as one of the flying creatures to be *seen* in the delightful harmonics of sky above it—soaring . . . soaring . . .

But this, too, became disturbing because its self-image insisted on resolving into a giant red-gold winged thing unfamiliar to these skies (but feeling disquietingly familiar to the Siukurnin).

Dawn crystalled the peaks to the east, brought stirrings that aroused the Siukurnin from its reverie. A figure emerged from the tent, yawned, stretched. The Siukurnin matched light vibrations and sound vibrations for the figure and, in its own way, "recognized" the hunter, Sam. There were checkered harmonics with merging of long and short olfactory-visual waves punctured by great sound-meaning vibrations.

"Chilly this morning," said the hunter. "Wish I could stay in the sack like you bums."

From the tent came another voice: "You lost a fair and square toss, Sam. Get that fire goin'."

A connoisseur sense within the Siukurnin came to full alert. It felt that this crude creature carried some supremely desirable element. In a sense, the Siukurnin "crouched."

The hunter put a hand on the fly rope, glanced at the false pine cone. "Yeah," he said. "You'll burn like pitch." He reached up, touched the "cone," felt sudden warmth, then nothing. The "cone" was gone. He shook his hand, looked around the ground, back to the tree. Nothing. "I'll be danged," he muttered. He scratched the palm that had touched the "cone."

"That fire goin' yet?" demanded the voice from the tent.

Sam shook his head. "No. I was going to pick a pine cone to help start the fire and the darn thing disappeared."

"You're gettin' old, grampaw," came the voice from the tent. "Better buy some glasses when we get back to town."

Another voice intruded from the tent: "Will you guys quit your yakking? I'm trying to sleep!"

For the Siukurnin there had been an instant of exquisite languor. Then it had felt itself changing uncontrollably, spreading out over the hand of the carbon life-form, seeping immediately through pores, between cells, into a vein. It stretched out—no more than six cells in diameter—reaching . . . reaching . . .

A long, thin thread explored the length of the vein. (You'll appreciate that the vibrations here were magnificent in their contrapuntal relationship: little hissings and squealings and lappings played against a superb background throb. There were also a few moments of delicate adjustment before the leucocytes ceased their ravening attack.)

In its own way, the Siukurnin danced for joy. Its hunger became only a faint beckoning: a dim sort of knowledge that end-of-hunger was at hand.

And there came a trickle of memory from before the upward swimming and those first moments of awareness on the warship. There was not enough recollection to frighten it with the thought that its own little egg of ego might be overwhelmed . . . just enough to whet its curiosity.

(All Siukurnin are fully endowed with a curiosity that cannot be inhibited, you know. And *chilitigish* awareness makes this faculty even more potent.)

The Siukurnin swam, crawled, wriggled, elongated and squeezed. Down, outward, upward. It had to filter out part of the "music" around it now: wheezings in the great air sacs, gurglings and sloshings, cracklings and swishings. All *so* distracting. One of its elements enwebbed the host's vocal cords ("great vibrators" to a Siukurnin). Another part interfingered the speech centers of the brain. Cilia reached out to the eye surfaces and the eyelid veins, contacting the exterior.

It was distracting at first to discover how all the vibrations were separated by different sense organs; then temptation became irresistible. (Who can hurl blame for this?) The Siukurnin coordinated its contact with speech centers and vocal cords.

Across the pine glade a human voice shouted: "Now hear this! Now hear this! Water! Sleep! Fire! Eat!"

Oh, it was an exhilarating sensation!

Two of the upright creatures, the other hunters, tumbled from the tent. One called: "It's about time you got . . ." It broke off. There was no fire. Only Sam standing terror-eyed beside the firepit, left hand to throat, right hand outthrust as though to push something away.

Then Sam swayed, collapsed.

In the hospital room, gross vibrations had been dampened to a remote hush. Slatted blinds were closed against raw morning sunlight. The bedside lamp had been turned off. But there still was a soft harmonic reflection from cream-colored walls that mingled with the even hiss of sleep breathing.

Sam lay on his back on the room's single bed, eyes closed. His chest under a green humming of blanket rose and fell gently. Somewhere, a pumping motor throbbed its obbligato. Distantly, stiff little shuntings and pantings and screechings told of city traffic. Ether trailed its solo virtuosity through the air, riding on a wave of disinfectant. A nurse's heels along the hall added an abrupt random rhythm that wove back and forth . . . back and forth through the other vibrations in a way that excited the connoisseur sense of the figure on the bed.

(After all, the long, virtual silence of the migration had now been recalled. In a sense, it was *starved* for these wonderful "noises.")

Outside the half-opened door of the room, a doctor could be heard talking to Beverly, Sam's wife. The doctor was tall, a beak-nosed shape: pink and blond with white on white on white echoing across the image. Acrid little shouts came from his hands, clinkings from his pockets, and a buzzing of tobacco rode his breath.

There had been a strange *dual* recognition of Beverly: a sense of familiarity with her dark hair, soft curve of cheeks, alert gray-green eyes. (The Sam-memories, of course.) And there had been added to this a pungent explosion of perfume-base powder (still familiar, yes, but heightened to an indescribable pitch), plus a glissando of gold necklace on green coat on green suit, all played against a bright beating of gold-bronze buttons. (And there was much more, but without *chilitigish* awareness in the reader, the effects are meaningless.)

The doctor's voice carried a drum quality as he uttered cautious reassurances. "There is no doubt that it's some type of narcolepsy," he said. "But there's no enlargement of the lymphatic glands. His pulse and respiration are normal. Temperature's up, but not dangerously. I'm inclined to suspect this may be a reaction due to nervous strain. Has he been working very hard?"

"Narcolepsy, narcolepsy, narcolepsy," whispered the Siukurnin with its Sam-lips.

Well . . . they weren't exactly Sam-lips now. They were much more accurately Sam (to the Siukurnin power) lips.

You just have to understand that single-ego orientation sets up difficult problems in communications here. What you would consider odd and irresistible things had been happening to Sam and Siukurnin. Cilia of Siukurnin had gone creeping and seeking of their own volition. It was now a great thin net spread throughout the host. Wherever it touched nerve cells—in brain and elsewhere—subtle displacements occurred at the subcellular level. New memories (Sam-memories) filtered into Siukurnin. And Siukurnin memories, of course, filtered back to Sam. (This is one of those processes that just cannot be confined to a one-way circuit.)

Things had gone so far that Siukurnin had displaced the temporary migration-ego. And Sam—"he" now thought of himself as a kind of "needle" at the end of an "extremely long thread. You *see,* the "thread" was the Siukurnin ego-memory-chain, its past so ancient that the Sam-ego was staggered.

(If you open up a Siukurnin-past you find that it is other creatures stretched out to a virtually meaningless number. This is a fascinating infinity process in which a quite satisfactory internal relationship has been worked out.)

Fully awakened, Siukurnin now understood the necessity mechanism that had blanked out ego-memory-chain awareness. There is such a temptation in the migration period to turn inward upon the merged multiplicity, encyst all distracting processes, and just think and think and think and . . .

You can see how this would be a kind of death. (Strictly speaking, Siukurnin do not fear death, although they are vulnerable during the "flight-of-joy" vector in their life cycle.)

Both Sam and Siukurnin were completely merged now. Sam-Siukurnin (ego-memory-chain + x) lay in the meaningful vibration core of the hospital room. Neither "unit" could now undo what had happened—nor wanted to undo it. Oh, there had been some Sam-resistance at first. Quite natural.

But Siukurnin revealed how a reluctant host's flesh could be incinerated without stopping the merging process. (And there were all those memories laid out in the open to prove this!) The other capture memories were a compelling argument, too.

The process is so *drearily* repetitive—except for the new life with its fascinating vibration meanings, of course.

And now you know how it happens. Not painful (except for some initial shocks). Not harmful to the host-ego. And not to be resisted.

In fact, this is being written in the hope that the rest of you will *see* (what an *odd* sensory division) how foolish it is to resist.

There's no point in resistance.

You cannot fight the inevitable.

Besides, you will find the merging a very rewarding experience. And if you stop to think about it, this is not the first time your kind has encountered us (although never before in such numbers as our present migration). You do have your legend of the Phoenix. According to your legend, this was a great red-gold "bird" that returned to Heliopolis in ancient Egypt every five hundred years (a reasonable Siukurnin-host life span), there to be reborn from its own ashes.

Naturally, the flesh of a dead host has to be incinerated to free the Siukurnin web for its "flight-of-joy." To think of the Phoenix as a "bird" was somewhat of an oversimplification, you understand. But we're sure you'll enjoy the flying sensation and the act of creating your new egg—especially when you view the experience with full *chilitigish* awareness.

A-W-F UNLIMITED

The morning the space armor problem fell into the agency's lap, Gwen Everest had breakfast at her regular restaurant, an automated single-niche place catering to bachelor girls. Her order popped out of the slot onto her table, and immediately the tabletop projecta-menu switched to selling Interdorma's newest Interpretive Telelog.

"Your own private dream translator! The secret companion to every neurosis!"

Gwen stared at the inch-high words doing a skitter dance above her fried eggs. She had written that copy. Her food beneath the ad looked suddenly tasteless. She pushed the plate away.

Along the speedwalk into Manhattan a *you-seeker,* its roboflier senses programmed to her susceptibilities, flew beside her ear. It was selling a year's supply of Geramyl—"the breakfast drink that helps you LIVE longer!"

The selling hook this morning was a Gwen Everest idea: a life insurance policy with the first year's premiums paid—"absolutely FREE if you accept this offer now!"

In sudden anger, she turned on the roboflier, whispered a code phrase she had wheedled from an engineer who serviced the things. The roboflier darted upward in sudden erratic flight, crashed into the side of a building.

A small break in her control. A beginning.

Waiting for Gwen along the private corridor to the Singlemaster, Hucksting and Battlemont executive offices were displays from the recent Religion of the Month Club campaign. She ran a gamut of adecals, layouts, slogans, projos, quartersheets, skinnies. The works.

"Subscribe now and get these religions absolutely FREE! Complete text of the Black Mass plus Abridged Mysticism!"

She was forced to walk through an adecal announcing: "Don't be Half Safe! Believe in Everything! Are you sure that African Bantu Witchcraft is not the True Way?"

At the turn of the corridor stood a male-female graphic with flesh-stimulant skinnies and supered voices, "Find peace through Tantrism."

The skinnies made her flesh crawl.

Gwen fled into her office, slumped into her desk chair. With mounting horror, she realized that she had either written or supervised the writing of every word, produced every selling idea along that corridor.

The interphon on her desk emitted its fluted "Good morning." She slapped the blackout switch to keep the instrument from producing an image. The last thing she wanted now was to see one of her co-workers.

"Who is it?" she barked.

"Gwen?" No mistaking that voice: André Battlemont, bottom name on the agency totem.

"What do you want?" she demanded.

"Our Gwenny is feeling nasty this morning, isn't she?"

"Oh, Freud!" She slapped the disconnect, leaned forward with elbows on the desk, put her face in her hands. *Let's face it,* she thought. *I'm 48, unmarried, and a prime mover in an industry that's strangling the universe. I'm a professional strangler.*

"Good morning," fluted the interphon.

She ignored it.

"A strangler," she said.

Gwen recognized the basic problem here. She had known it since childhood. Her universe was a continual replaying of "The Emperor's New Suit." She saw the nakedness.

"Good morning," fluted the interphon.

She dropped her right hand away from her face, flicked the switch. "Now what?"

"Did you cut me off, Gwen?"

"What if I did?"

"Gwen, please! We have a problem."

"We always have problems."

Battlemont's voice dropped one octave. "Gwen. This is a Big problem."

Uncanny the way he can speak capital letters, she thought. She said: "Go away."

"You've been leaving your Interdorma turned off!" accused Battlemont. "You mustn't. Neurosis can creep up on you."

"Is that why you called me?" she asked.

"Of course not."

"Then go away."

Battlemont did a thing then that everyone from Singlemaster on down knew was dangerous to try with Gwen Everest. He pushed the override to send his image dancing above her interphon.

After the momentary flash of anger, Gwen correctly interpreted the act as one of desperation. She found herself intrigued. She stared at the round face, the pale eyes (definitely too small, those eyes), the pug nose and wide gash of mouth above almost no chin at all.

Plus the hairline in full retreat.

"André, you are a mess," she said.

He ignored the insult. Still speaking in the urgency octave, he said: "I have called a full staff meeting. You must attend at once."

"Why?"

"There are two military people in there, Gwen." He gulped. "It's desperate. Either we solve their problem or they will ruin us. They will draft every man in the agency!"

"Even you?"

"Yes!"

She moved her right hand toward the interphon's emergency disconnect. "Good-by, André."

"Gwen! My God! You can't let me down at a time like this!"

"Why not?"

He spoke in breathless haste. "We'll raise your salary. A bonus. A bigger office. More help."

"You can't afford me now," she said.

"I'm begging you, Gwen. Must you abuse me?"

She closed her eyes, thought: *The insects! The damned little insects with their crummy emotions! Why can't I tell them all to go to composite hell?* She opened her eyes, said: "What's the military's flap?"

Battlemont mopped his forehead with a pastel blue handkerchief. "It's the Space Service," he said. "The female branch. The WOMS. Enlistments have fallen to almost nothing."

She was interested in spite of herself. "What's happened?"

"Something to do with the space armor. I don't know. I'm so upset."

"Why have they tossed it into our laps like this? The ultimatum, I mean."

Battlemont glanced left and right, leaned forward. "The grapevine has it they're testing a new theory that creative people work better under extreme stress."

"The Psychological Branch again," she said. "Those jackasses!"

"But what can we do?"

"Hoist 'em," she said. "You run along to the conference."

"And you'll be there, Gwen?"

"In a few minutes."

"Don't delay too long, Gwen." Again he mopped his forehead with the blue handkerchief. "Gwen, I'm frightened."

"And with good reason." She squinted at him. "I can see you now: Nothing on but a lead loincloth, dumping fuel into a radioactive furnace. Freud, what a picture!"

"This is no joke, Gwen!"

"I know."

"You *are* going to help?"

"In my own peculiar way, André." She hit the emergency disconnect.

André Battlemont turned away from his interphon, crossed his office to a genuine Moslem prayer rug. He sat down on it facing the floor-to-ceiling windows that looked eastward across midtown Manhattan. This was the 1479th floor of the Stars of Space building, and it was quite a view out there whenever the clouds lifted. But the city remained hidden beneath a low ceiling this morning.

Up here it was sunny, though—except in Battlemont's mood. A fearcycle ululated along his nerves.

What he was doing on the prayer rug was practicing Yoga breathing to calm those nerves. The military could wait. They *had* to wait. The fact that he faced the general direction of Mecca was left over from two months before. Yoga was a month old. There was always some carry-over.

Battlemont had joined the Religion of the Month Club almost a year ago—seduced by his own agency's deep motivation campaign plus the Brotherhood Council's seal of approval.

This month it was the Reinspired Neo-Cult of St. Freud.

A test adecal superimposed itself on the cloud-floor view beneath him. It began playing the latest Gwen-Everest-inspired pitch of the IBMausoleum. Giant rainbow letters danced across the fleecy background.

"Make your advice immortal! Let us store your voice and thought patterns in everlasting electronic memory circuits! When you are gone, your loved ones may listen to your voice as you answer their questions exactly the way you would most likely have answered them in Life!"

Battlemont shook his head. The agency, fearful of its dependence on the live Gwen Everest, had secretly recorded her at a staff conference once. Very illegal. The unions were death on it. But the IBMausoleum had broken down with the first question put to Gwen's ghost-voice.

"Some people have thought patterns that are too complex to permit accurate psyche-record," the engineer explained.

Battlemont did not delude himself. The sole genius of the agency's three owners lay in recognizing the genius of Gwen Everest. She *was* the agency.

It was like riding the tiger to have such an employee. Singlemaster, Hucksting and Battlemont had ridden this tiger for 22 years. Battlemont closed his eyes, pictured her in his mind: a tall, lean woman, but with a certain grace. Her face was long, dominated by cold blue eyes, framed in waves of auburn hair. She had a wit that could slash you to ribbons, and that priceless commodity: the genius to pull selling sense out of utter confusion.

Battlemont sighed.

He was in love with Gwen Everest. Had been for 22 years. It was the reason he had never married. His Interdorma explained that it was because he wanted to be dominated by a strong woman.

But that only explained. It didn't help.

For a moment, he thought wistfully of Singlemaster and Hucksting, both taking their annual three-month vacation at the geriatrics center on Oahu. Battlemont wondered if he dared ask Gwen to take her vacation with him. Just once.

No.

He realized what a pitiful figure he made on the prayer rug. Pudgy little man in a rather unattractive blue suit.

Tailors did things for him that they called "improving your good points." But except when he viewed himself in a Vesta-Mirror to see the sample clothes projected back onto his own idealized image, he could never pin down what those "good points" were.

Gwen would certainly turn him down.

He feared that more than anything. As long as there remained the possibility . . .

Memory of the waiting Space Service deputation intruded. Battlemont trembled, broke the Yoga breathing pattern. The exercise was having its usual effect: a feeling of vertigo. He heaved himself to his feet.

"One cannot run away from fate," he muttered.

That was a carry-over from the Karma month.

According to Gwen, the agency's conference room had been copied from a Florentine bordello's Emperor Room. It was a gigantic space. The corners were all flossy curlicues in heavy gilding, an effect carried over into deep carvings on the wall panels. The ceiling was a mating of Cellini cupids with Dali landscapes.

Period stuff. Antique.

Into this baroque setting had been forced a one-piece table 6 feet wide and 42 feet long. It was an enlarged bit of Twentieth Century Wallstreetiana fenced in by heavy wooden chairs. Beanbag paperweights and golden wheel ashtrays graced every place.

The air of the room was blue with the smoke of mood-cigs. ("It rhymes with Good Bigs!") The staff seated around the table was fighting off the depressant effect of the two Space Service generals, one male and one female, seated in flanking positions beside Battlemont's empty chair. There was a surprising lack of small talk and paper rustling.

All staff members had learned of the ultimatum via the office grapevine.

Battlemont slipped in his side door, crossed to his chair at the end of the table, dropped into it before his knees gave out. He stared from one frowning military face to the other.

No response.

He cleared his throat. "Sorry I'm . . . ah . . . Pressing business. Unavoidable." He cast a frantic glance around the table. No sign of Gwen. He smiled at one officer, the other.

No response.

On his right sat Brigadier General Sonnet Finnister of the WOMS (Women of Space). Battlemont had been appalled to see her walk. Drill-sergeant stride. No nonsense. She wore a self-designed uniform: straight pleated skirt to conceal bony hips, a loose blouse to camouflage lack of upper development, and a long cape to confuse the whole issue. Atop her head sat a duck-billed, flat-fronted cap that had been fashioned for the single purpose of hiding the Sonnet Finnister forehead, which went too high and too wide.

She seldom removed the hat.

(This particular hat, Battlemont's hurried private investigations had revealed, looked hideous on every other member of the WOMS. To a woman, they called it "the Sonnet Bonnet." There had been the additional information that the general herself was referred to by underlings as "Sinister Finnister"—partly because of the swirling cape.)

On Battlemont's left sat General Nathan Owling of the Space Engineers. Better known as "Howling Owling" because of a characteristic evidenced when he became angry. He appeared to have been shaped in the officer caste's current mold of lean, blond athlete. The blue eyes reminded Battlemont of Gwen's eyes, except that the man's appeared colder.

If that were possible.

Beyond Owling sat Leo Prim, the agency's art director. He was a thin young man, thin to a point that vibrated across the edge of emaciation. His black hair, worn long, held a natural wave. He had a narrow Roman nose, soulful brown eyes, strong cleft in the chin, generous mouth with large lips. A mood-cig dangled from the lips.

If Battlemont could have chosen his own appearance, he would have liked to look like Leo Prim. Romantic. Battlemont caught Prim's attention, ventured a smile of camaraderie.

No response.

General Sonnet Finnister tapped a thin finger on the tabletop. It sounded to Battlemont like the slack drum of a death march.

"Hadn't we better get started?" demanded Finnister.

"Are we all here—finally?" asked Owling.

Battlemont swallowed past a lump in his throat. "Well . . . ah . . . no . . . ah . . ."

Owling opened a briefcase in his lap, glanced at an intelligence report, looked around the table. "Miss Everest is missing," he announced.

Finnister said: "Couldn't we go ahead without her?"

"We'll wait," said Owling. He was enjoying himself. *Damned parasites need a touch of the whip now and then!* he thought. *Shows 'em where they stand.*

Finnister glared at Owling, a hawk stare that had reduced full colonels (male) to trembling. The stare rolled off Owling without effect. *Trust the high command to pair me with a male supremacy type like Owling!* she thought.

"Is this place safe from snooping?" asked Owling.

Battlemont turned his own low-wattage glare on the staff seated in the mood smoke haze around the table. No glance met his. "That's all anybody ever does around here!" he snapped.

"What?" Owling started to rise.

"Busybodies!" blared Battlemont. "My whole staff!"

"Ohhh." Owling sank back into his chair. "I meant a different kind of snooping."

"Oh, that." Battlemont shrugged, suppressed an urge to glance up at the conference room's concealed recorder lenses. "We cannot have our ideas pirated by other agencies, you know. Absolutely safe here."

Gwen Everest chose this moment for her entrance. All eyes followed her as she came through the end door, strode down the length of the room.

Battlemont admired her grace. Such a feminine woman in spite of her strength. So different from the female general.

Gwen found a spare chair against the side wall, crowded it in between Battlemont and Finnister.

The commander of the WOMS glared at the intruder. "Who are *you*?"

Battlemont leaned forward. "This is Miss Everest, our . . . ah . . ." He hesitated, confused. Gwen had never had an official title with the agency. Never needed it. Everyone in the place knew she was the boss. "Ahh . . . Miss Everest is our . . . ah . . . director of coordination," said Battlemont.

"Why! That's a wonderful title!" said Gwen. "I must get it printed on my stationery." She patted Battlemont's hand, faced him and, in her best undercover-agent-going-into-action voice, said: "Let's have it, Chief. Who are these people? What's going on?"

General Owling nodded to Gwen. "I'm Owling, General, Space Engineers." He gestured to the rocket splash insignia on his shoulder. "My companion is General Finnister, WOMS."

Gwen had recognized the famous Finnister face. She smiled brightly, said: "General Woms!"

"Finnister!" snapped the female general.

"Yes, of course," said Gwen. "General Finnister Woms. Must not go too informal, you know."

Finnister spoke in slow cadence: "I . . . am . . . General . . . Sonnet . . . Finnister . . . of . . . of . . . the . . . Women . . . of . . . Space! The WOMS!"

"Oh, how stupid of me," said Gwen. "Of course you are." She patted the general's hand, smiled at Battlemont.

Battlemont, who well knew the falsity of this mood in Gwen Everest, was trying to scrunch down out of sight in his chair.

In that moment, Gwen realized with a twinge of fear that she had reached a psychic point of no return. Something slipped a cog in her mind. She glanced around the table. Familiar faces leaped at her with unreal clarity. Staring eyes. (The best part of a conference was to watch Gwen in action.) *I can't take any more of this,* thought Gwen. *I have to declare myself.*

She focused on the military. The rest of the people in this room owned little pieces of her, but not these two. Owling and Finnister. Space generals. Symbols. Targets!

Let the chips fall where they may! Fire when ready, Gridley. Shoot if you must this old gray head . . . Wait until you see the whites of their eyes.

Gwen nodded to herself.

One misstep and the agency was ruined.

Who cares?

It all passed in a split second, but the decision was made.

Rebellion!

Gwen turned her attention on Owling. "Would you be kind enough to end this stalling around and get the meeting under way?"

"Stall . . ." Owling broke it off. The intelligence report had said Gwen Everest was fond of shock tactics. He gave her a curt nod, passed the nod to Finnister.

The female general addressed Battlemont. "Your agency, as we explained to you earlier, has been chosen for a vital task, Mr. Battlefield."

"Battlemont," said Gwen.

Finnister stopped short. "What?"

"His name is Battle*mont*, not Battle*field*," said Gwen.

"What of it?"

"Names are important," said Gwen. "I'm sure you appreciate this."

The Finnister cheeks flushed. "Quite!"

Owling stepped into the breach. "We are authorized to pay this agency double the usual fee for performance," he said. "However, if you fail us we'll draft every male employee here into the Space Service!"

"What an asinine idea!" said Gwen. "Our people would destroy the Space Service. From within." Again she smiled at Battlemont. "André here could do it all by himself. Couldn't you, ducky?" She patted Battlemont's cheek.

Battlemont tried to crouch farther down into the chair. He avoided the eyes of the space brass, said: "Gwen . . . please . . ."

"What do you mean, destroy the Space Service?" demanded Finnister.

Gwen ignored her, addressed Owling. "This is another one of the Psych Branch's brainstorms," she said. "I can smell the stench of 'em in every word."

Owling frowned. As a matter of fact, he had the practical builder's suspicion of everything subjective. This Everest woman made a good point there. But the military had to stand shoulder to shoulder against outsiders. He said: "I don't believe you are properly equipped to fathom military tactics. Let's get on to the problem we . . ."

"Military tactics yet!" Gwen rapped the table. "Destroy your forces, men. This is it! Synchronize your watches. Over the top!"

"Gwen!" said Battlemont.

"Of course," said Gwen. She faced Finnister. "Would you mind awfully outlining your problem in simple terms that our unmilitarized minds could understand?"

A pause, a glare. Finnister spewed her words through stiff lips. "Enlistments in the WOMS have fallen to an alarming degree. *You* are going to correct this."

Behind Gwen, Battlemont nodded vigorously.

"Women can release men for the more strenuous tasks," said Owling.

"And there are many things women can do that men cannot do," said Finnister.

"Absolutely essential," said Owling.

"Absolutely," agreed Finnister.

"Can't draft women, I suppose," said Gwen.

"Tried to get a bill through," said Owling. "Damned committee's headed by an anti-military woman."

"Good for her," said Gwen.

"You do *not* sound like the person for this job," said Owling. "Perhaps . . ."

"Oh, simmer down," said Gwen.

"Miss Everest is the best in the business," said Battlemont.

Gwen said: "Why are enlistments down? You've run the usual surveys, I suppose."

"It's the space armor," said Finnister. "Women don't like it."

"Too mechanical," said Owling. "Too practical."

"We need . . . ah . . . glamour," said Finnister. She adjusted the brim of her cap.

Gwen frowned at the cap, cast a glance up and down the Finnister uniform. "I've seen the usual news pictures of the armor," she said. "What do they wear underneath it? Something like your uniform?"

Finnister suppressed a surge of anger. "No. They wear special fatigues."

"The armor cannot be removed while they are in space," said Owling.

"Oh?" said Gwen. "What about physical functions, that sort of thing?"

"Armor takes care of everything," said Owling.

"Apparently not *quite* everything," murmured Gwen. She nodded to herself, mulling tactics.

Battlemont straightened, sniffed the atmosphere of the conference room. Staff all alert, quiet, attentive. Mood had lightened somewhat. Gwen appeared to be taking over. Good old Gwen. Wonderful Gwen. No telling what she was up to. As usual. She'd solve this thing, though. Always did. Unless . . .

He blinked. Could she be toying with them? He tried to imagine Gwen's thought patterns. Impossible. IBMausoleum couldn't even do it. Unpredictable. All Battlemont could be certain of was that Gwen would get a gigantic belly laugh from the picture of the agency's male staff members drafted, slaving away on space freighters.

Battlemont trembled.

General Finnister was saying: "The problem is not one of getting women to enlist for Earth-based service. We need them in the ships, the asteroid stations, the . . ."

"Let's get this straight," said Gwen. "My great-great-grandmother was in some kind of armed service. I read her diary once. She called it the 'whackies' or something like that."

"WACS," said Finnister.

"Yes," said Gwen. "It was during the war with Spain."

"Japan," said Owling.

"What I'm driving at is, why all the sudden interest in women? My great-great-grandmother had one merry old time running away from some colonel who wanted . . . Well, you know. Is this some kind of a dodge to provide women for your space colonels?"

Finnister scowled her blackest.

Quickly suppressed chuckles sounded around the table.

Owling decided to try a new tack. "My dear lady, our motives are of the highest. We need the abilities of women so that mankind can march side by side to the stars."

Gwen stared at him in open admiration. "Go-wan!" she said.

"I mean it," said Owling.

"You're a poet!" said Gwen. "Oh . . . and I've wronged you. Here I was—dirty-minded me—thinking you wanted women for base purposes. And all the time you wanted *companions*. Someone to share this glorious new adventure."

Again, Battlemont recognized the danger signals. He tried to squeeze himself into as small a target as possible. Most of the staff around the table saw the same signals, but they were intent, fascinated.

"Exactly!" boomed Finnister.

Gwen's voice erupted in an angry snarl: "And we name all the little bastards after the stars in Virgo, ehhh?"

It took a long moment for Finnister and Owling to see that they had been gulled. Finnister started to rise.

"Siddown!" barked Gwen. She grinned. She was having a magnificent time. Rebellion carried a sense of euphoria.

Owling opened his mouth, closed it without a howl.

Finnister sank back into her chair.

"Shall we get down to business?" snapped Gwen. "Let's look at this glorified hunk of tin you want us to glamorize."

Finnister found something she could focus her shocked attention on. "Space armor is mostly plastic, not tin."

"Plastic-schmastic," said Gwen. "I want to see your Iron Gertie."

General Owling took two deep breaths to calm his nerves, snapped open the briefcase, extracted a folder of design sketches. He pushed them toward Gwen—a hesitant motion as though he feared she might take his hand with them. He now recognized that the incredible intelligence report was correct: this astonishing female was the actual head of the agency.

"Here's—Iron Gertie," he said, and forced a chuckle.

Gwen leafed through the folder while the others watched.

Battlemont stared at her. He realized something the rest of the staff did not: Gwen Everest was not being the usual Gwen Everest. There was a subtle difference. An abandon. Something was *very* wrong!

Without looking up from the drawings, Gwen addressed herself to Finnister. "That uniform you're wearing, General Finnister. You design that yourself?"

"What? Oh, yes. I did."

Battlemont trembled.

Gwen reached out, rapped one of Finnister's hips. "Bony," she said. She turned a page in the folder, shook her head.

"Well!" exploded Finnister.

Still without looking up, Gwen said: "Simmer down. How about the hat? You design that, too?"

"Yesss!" It was a sibilant explosion.

Gwen lifted her attention to the hat, spoke in a reasonable tone: "Possibly the most hideous thing I've ever seen."

"Well of all the—"

"Are you a fashion designer?" asked Gwen politely.

Finnister shook her head as though to clear it of cobwebs.

"You are *not* a fashion designer?" pressed Gwen.

Finnister bit the words off. "I have had *some* experience in choosing—"

"The answer is no, then," said Gwen. "Thought so." She brought her attention back to the folder, turned a page.

Finnister glared at her in open-mouthed rage.

Gwen glanced up at Owling. "Why'd you put the finger on this agency?"

Owling appeared to have trouble focusing his attention on Gwen's question. Presently, he said: "You were . . . it was pointed out that this agency was one of the most successful in . . . if not the most successful . . ."

"We were classified as experts, eh?"

"Yes. If you want to put it that way."

"I want to put it that way." She glanced at Finnister. "So we let the experts do the designing, is that clear? You people keep your greasy fingers off. Understood?" She shot a hard stare at Owling, back to Finnister.

"I don't know about you!" Finnister snapped at Owling, "but I've had all—"

"If you value your military career you'll just sit down and listen," said Gwen. Again, she glared at Owling. "Do you understand?"

Owling shook his head from side to side. Amazement dominated him. Abruptly, he realized that his head shaking could be interpreted as negative. He bobbed his head up and down, decided in mid-motion that this was undignified. He stopped, cleared his throat.

What an astonishing female! he thought.

Gwen pushed the folder of design sketches uptable to Leo Prim, the art director. "Tell me, General Owling," she said, "why is the armor so bulky?"

Leo Prim, who had opened the folder, began to chuckle.

"Marvelous, isn't it?" said Gwen.

Someone farther uptable asked: "What is?"

Gwen kept her attention on Owling. "Some jassack engineer in the Space Service designed a test model suit of armor like a gigantic woman—breasts and all." She glanced at Finnister. "You ran a survey on the stupid thing, of course?"

Finnister nodded. She was shocked speechless.

"I could've saved you the trouble," said Gwen. "One of the reasons you'd better listen carefully to what *expert me* has to say. No woman in her right mind would get into that thing. She'd feel big—and she'd feel naked." Gwen shook her head. "Freud! What a combination!"

Owling wet his lips with his tongue. "Ah, the armor has to provide sufficient shielding against radiation, and it must remain articulate under extremes of pressure and temperature," he said. "It can't be made any smaller and still permit a human being to fit into it."

"Okay," said Gwen. "I have the beginnings of an idea."

She closed her eyes, thought: *These military jerks are a couple of sitting ducks. Almost a shame to pot them.* She opened her eyes, glanced at Battlemont. His eyes were closed. He appeared to be praying. *Could be the ruination of poor André and his lovely people, too,* she thought. *What a marvelous collection of professional stranglers! Well, can't be helped. When Gwen Everest goes out, she goes out in a blaze of glory! All flags flying! Full speed ahead! Damn the torpedoes!*

"Well?" said Owling.

Fire one! thought Gwen. She said: "Presumably, you have specialists, experts who can advise us on technical details."

"At your beck and call whenever you say the word," said Owling.

Battlemont opened his eyes, stared at the back of Gwen's neck. A ray of hope stabbed through his panic. Was it possible that Gwen was really taking over?

"I'll also want all the dope on which psychological types make the best WOMS," said Gwen. "If there is such a thing as a best WOM."

Battlemont closed his eyes, shuddered.

"I don't believe I've ever been treated this highhandedly in my entire career!" blurted Finnister. "I'm not entirely sure that—"

"Just a moment, please," said Owling. He studied Gwen, who was smiling at him. The intelligence report said this woman was "probable genius" and should be handled delicately.

"I'm only sorry the law doesn't give us the right to draft women, too!" barked Finnister.

"Then you wouldn't really have this problem, would you?" asked Gwen. She turned her smile on Finnister. It was full of beatitudes.

Owling said: "I know we have full authority to handle this at our own discretion, General Finnister, and I agree that we've been subjected to some abuse but . . ."

"Abuse!" Finnister said.

"And high time, too," said Gwen.

A violent shudder passed through Battlemont. He thought: *We are doomed!*

"However," said Owling, "we mustn't let our personal feelings cloud a decision for the good of the service."

"I hear the bugles blowing," murmured Gwen.

"This agency *was* chosen as the one most likely to solve the problem," said Owling.

"There *could* have been a mistake!" said Finnister.

"Not likely."

"You are determined to turn this thing over to . . . to . . ." Finnister broke off, tapped her palms on the tabletop.

"It's advisable," said Owling. He thought: *This Gwen Everest will solve our problem. No problem could resist her. No problem would dare!*

General Owling had become a Gwenophile.

"Very well, then," snarled Finnister. "I will reserve my judgment."

General Finnister had become a Gwenophobe.

Which was part of Gwen Everest's program.

"I presume you two will be available for technical consultations from time to time," said Gwen.

"Our subordinates take care of details," said Owling. "All General Finnister and I are interested in is the big picture, the key to the puzzle."

"Big picture, key to puzzle," mused Gwen. "Wonderful idea."

"What?" Owling stared at her, puzzled.

"Nothing," said Gwen. "Just thinking out loud."

Owling stood up, looked at Finnister. "Shall we be going?"

Finnister also stood up, turned toward the door at the end of the room. "Yesss!"

Together, one on each side of the table, they marched the length of the room: tump-a-thump-a-tump-a-thump-a-tump . . . Just as they reached the door and Owling opened it, Gwen jumped to her feet. "Charrrrge!" she shouted.

The two officers froze, almost turned, thought better of it. They left, slamming the door.

Battlemont spoke plaintively into the silence. "Gwen, why do you destroy us?"

"Destroy you? Don't be silly!"

"But, Gwen . . ."

"Please be quiet, André; you're interrupting my train of thought." She turned to Leo Prim. "Leo, take those sketches and things of that big-breasted Bertha they designed. I want adecal workups on them, full projos, the entire campaign outlay."

"Big Bertha adecals, projos, the outlay," said Prim. "Right!"

Gwen, what are you doing?" asked Battlemont. "You said yourself that—"

"You're babbling, André," said Gwen. She glanced up at the ceiling. An eye in one of the Cellini cupids winked at her. "We got the usual solid recordings of this conference, I presume?"

"Of course," said Battlemont.

"Take those recordings, Leo," said Gwen. "Do a sequence out of them featuring only General Sinister Sonnet Bonnet Finnister."

"What'd you call her?" asked Prim.

Gwen explained about the Finnister nicknames. "The fashion trade knows all about her," she finished. "A living horror."

"Yeah, okay," said Prim. "A solid sequence of nothing but Finnister. What do you want it to show?"

"Every angle of that uniform," said Gwen. "And the hat. Freud! Don't forget that hat!"

Battlemont spoke plaintively. "I don't understand."

"Good," said Gwen. "Leo, send me Restivo and Jim Spark . . . a couple more of your best design people. Include yourself. We'll . . ."

"And, lo! Ben Adam's name led all the rest," said Battlemont.

Gwen turned, stared down at him. For one of the rare times in their association, Battlemont had surprised her with something he said.

I wonder if our dear André could be human? she mused.

No! I must be going soft in the head. She said: "André, go take a meditation break until time to call our next conference. Eh? There's a good fellow."

Always before when she abused me it was like a joke between us, thought Battlemont dolefully. *But now she is trying to hurt.* His concern now was for Gwen, not for the agency. *My Gwen needs help. And I don't know what to do.*

"Meditation break time," said Gwen. "Or you could go to a mood bar. Why don't you try the new Interdorma mediniche? A niche in time saves the mind!"

"I prefer to remain awake for our last hours together," said Battlemont. A sob clutched at his throat. He stood up to cover the moment, drew himself to attention, fixed Gwen with a despairing glare. "I feel the future crouching over us alike a great beast!" He turned his back on her, strode out through his private door.

"I wonder what the devil he meant by that?" mused Gwen.

Prim said: "This is the month of St. Freud. They go for prescience, extrasensory perception, that sort of thing."

"Oh, certainly," she said. "I wrote the brochure." But she found herself disturbed by Battlemont's departure. *He looked so pitiful,* she thought. *What if this little caper backfires and he gets drafted? It could happen. Leo and the rest of these stranglers could take it. But André . . .* She gave a mental shrug. *Too late to turn back now.*

Department heads began pressing toward Gwen along the table. "Say, Gwen, what about the production on . . ." "If I'm going to meet any deadlines I'll need more . . ." "Will we have to drop our other . . ."

"Shaddup!" bellowed Gwen.

She smiled sweetly into the shocked silence. "I will meet with each of you privately, just as soon as I get in a fresh stock of crying towels. First things first, though. Number one problem: we get the monkey off our backs. Eh?"

And she thought: *You poor oafs! You aren't even aware how close you are to disaster. You think Gwen is taking over as usual. But Gwen doesn't care. Gwen doesn't give a damn any more. Gwen is resigning in a blaze of glory! Into the valley of death rode the 600! Or was it 400? No matter. War is hell! I only regret that I have but one life to give for my agency. Give me liberty or give me to the WOMS.*

Leo Prim said: "You're going for the throat on these two military types, is that it?"

"Military tactics," said Gwen. "No survivors! Take no prisoners! Death to the White Eyes!"

"Huh?" said Prim.

"Get right on that assignment I gave you," she said.

"Uhh . . ." Prim looked down at the folder Owling had left. "Workups on this Big Bertha thing . . . a solido on Finnister. Okay." He shook his head. "You know, this business could shape up into a Complete Flap."

"It could be worse than that," Gwen cautioned.

Someone else said: "It's absolutely the worst I've ever seen. Drafted!"

And Gwen thought: *Ooooh! Someone has trepidations!* Abruptly, she said: "Absolutely worst flap." She brightened. "That's wonderful! One moment, all you lovely people."

There was sudden stillness in the preparations for departure.

"It has been moved that we label this business the Absolutely Worst Flap," she said.

Chuckles from the staff.

"You will note," said Gwen, "that the initials A-W-F are the first three letters in the word *awful.*"

Laughter.

"Up to now," said Gwen, "we've only had to contend with Minor, Medium and Complete Flaps. Now I give you the AWF! It rhymes with the grunt of someone being slugged in the stomach!"

Into the laughter that filled the room, Prim said: "How about the U and L in awful? Can't let them go to waste."

"Un*Limited*!" snapped Gwen. "Absolutely Worst Flap UnLimited!" She

began to laugh, had to choke it off as the laughter edged into hysteria. *Whatin-
ell's wrong with me?* she wondered. She glared at Prim. "Let's get cracking,
men! Isn't a damn one of you would look good in uniform."

The laughter shaded down into nervous gutterings. "That Gwen!"

Gwen had to get out of there. It was like a feeling of nausea. She pushed
her way down the side of the room. The sparkle had gone out of her rebellion. She felt that all of these people were pulling at her, taking bits of herself that she could never recapture. It made her angry. She wanted to kick,
bite, claw. Instead, she smiled fixedly. "Excuse me. May I get through here?
Sorry. Thank you. Excuse me."

And an image of André Battlemont kept intruding on her consciousness.
*Such a pitiful little fellow. So . . . well . . . sweet. Dammit! Sweet! In a de-
spicable sort of way.*

Twenty-five days slipped off the calendar. Twenty-five days of splashing
in a pool of confusion. Gwen's element. She hurled herself into the problem.
This one had to be just right. A tagline for her exit. A Gwen Everest signa-
ture at the bottom of the page.

Technical experts from the military swarmed all through the agency.
Experts on suit articulation. Experts on shielding. Pressure coefficients. Artificial atmosphere. Waste reclamation. Subminiature power elements. A
locksmith. An expert on the new mutable plastics. (*He* had to be flown in
from the West Coast.)

Plus the fashion experts seen only by Gwen.

It was quite a job making sure that each military expert saw only what
his small technical world required.

Came the day of the Big Picture. The very morning.

Adjacent to her office Gwen maintained a special room about 20 feet
square. She called it "my intimidation room." It was almost Louis XV: insubstantial chairs, teetery little tables, glass gimcracks on the light fixtures,
pastel cherubs on the wall panels.

The chairs looked as though they might smash flat under the weight of a
medium-sized man. Each (with the exception of a padded throne chair that
slid from behind a wall panel for Gwen) had a seat that canted forward. The
sitters kept sliding off, gently, imperceptibly.

None of the tables had a top large enough for a note pad *and* an ashtray.
One of these items had to be balanced in the lap or placed underfoot. That
forced an occasional look at the carpet.

The carpet had been produced with alarming psychological triggers. The
uninitiated felt they were standing upside down in a fishbowl.

General Owling occupied one of the trick chairs. He tried to keep from
staring at the cherub centered in a wall panel directly across from him, slightly
to the right of the seated figure of André Battlemont. Battlemont looked ill.
Owling pushed himself backward in the chair. His knees felt exposed. He

glanced at General Finnister. She sat to his right beyond a spindly table. She pulled her skirt down as he watched. He wondered why she sat so forward on the chair.

Damned uncomfortable little chairs!

He noted that Battlemont had brought in one of the big conference room chairs for himself. Owling wondered why they all couldn't have those big, square, solid, secure chairs. For that matter, why wasn't this meeting being held in the big conference room? Full staff. The Big Picture! He glanced up at the wall panel opposite. *Stupid damned cherub!* He looked down at the rug, grimaced, tore his gaze away.

Finnister had looked at the rug when she came into the room, had almost lost her balance. Now, she tried to keep her attention off it. Her mind seethed with disquieting rumors. Individual reports from the technical experts failed to reveal a total image. It was like a jigsaw puzzle with pieces from separate puzzles all thrown together. She pushed herself backward in the chair. *What an uncomfortable room.* Intuition told her the place was subtly deliberate. Her latent anger at Gwen Everest flared. *Where is that woman?*

Battlemont cleared his throat, glanced at the door to his right through which Gwen was expected momentarily. *Must she always be late?* Gwen had avoided him for weeks. Too busy. Suddenly this morning she had to have André Battlemont front and center. A figurehead. A prop for her little show. He knew pretty much what she was doing, too. In the outward, physical sense. She might be able to keep things from some of the people around here, but André Battlemont ran his own intelligence system. As to what was going on in her mind, though, he couldn't be sure. All he knew was that it didn't fit. Not even for Gwen.

Finnister said: "Our technical people inform us that you've been pretty interested—" she pushed herself back in the chair—"in the charactristics of some of the newer mutable plastics."

"That is true," said Battlemont.

"Why?" asked Owling.

"Ahhh, perhaps we'd better wait for Miss Everest," said Battlemont. "She is bringing a solido projector."

"You have mockups already?" asked Owling.

"Yes."

"Good! How many models?"

"One. Our receptionist. Beautiful girl."

"What?" Finnister and Owling in unison.

"Oh! You mean . . . that is, we have the one to show you. It is really two . . . but only one of . . ." He shrugged, suppressed a shudder.

Finnister and Owling looked at each other.

Battlemont closed his eyes. *Gwen, please hurry.* He thought about her solution to the military problem, began to tremble. Her basic idea was sound, of course. Good psychological roots. But the military would never go for it. Especially that female general who walked like a sergeant. Battle-mont's eyes snapped open as he heard a door open.

Gwen came in pushing a portable display projector. A glance of mutual dislike passed between Gwen and Finnister, was masked by mutual bright smiles immediately.

"Good morning, everybody," chirped Gwen.

Danger signal! thought Battlemont. *She's mad! She's* . . . He stopped the thought, focused on it. *Maybe she is. We work her so hard.*

"Anxious to see what you have there," said Owling. "Just getting ready to ask for a progress report when you called this meeting."

"We wanted to have something first that you could appreciate as an engi-neer," said Gwen.

Owling nodded.

Finnister said: "Our people report that you've been very secretive about your work. Why?"

"The very walls have ears. Loose lips lose the Peace! Don't be half safe!" Gwen positioned the projector in the center of the room, took the remote control, crossed to a panel which swung out to disgorge her chair. She sat down facing Finnister and Owling.

Seconds dragged past while she stared in fascination at Finnister's knees.

"Gwen?" said Battlemont.

Finnister tugged down on the hem of her skirt.

"What do you have to show us?" demanded Owling. He pushed himself back in the chair.

"First," said Gwen, "let us examine the perimeters of the problem. You must ask yourself: What do young women want when they enter the service?"

"Sounds sensible," said Owling.

Finnister nodded, her dislike of Gwen submerged in attention to the words.

"They want several things," said Gwen. "They want travel . . . adven-ture . . . the knight errant sort of thing. Tally-ho!"

Battlemont, Finnister and Owling snapped to shocked attention.

"Gives you pause when you think about it," murmured Gwen. "All those women looking for something. Looking for the free ride. The brass ring. The pot at the end of the rainbow."

She had them nodding again, Gwen noted. She raised her voice: "The old carrousel! The jingle-dingle joy journey!"

Battlemont looked at her sadly. *Mad. Ohhh, my poor, poor Gwenny.*

Owling said: "I . . . uh . . ."

"But they all want one commodity!" snapped Gwen. "And what's that? Romance! That's what's that. And in the unconscious mind what's that ro-mance? That romance is sex!"

"I believe I've heard enough," said Finnister.

"No," said Owling. "Let's . . . uh . . . this is all, I'm sure, preliminary. I want to know where . . . after all, the model . . . models they've developed . . ."

"What's with sex when you get all the folderol off it?" demanded Gwen. "The psychological roots. What's down there?"

Owling scratched his throat, stared at her. He had a basic distrust of subjective ideas, but he always came smack up against the fear that maybe (just maybe now) they were correct. Some of them appeared (and it could be appearance *only*) to work.

"I'll tell you what's down there," muttered Gwen.

"That's right!" said Gwen. "They can't *really* get out. So we give them the *symbol* of getting out. For exchanging."

"Exchanging?" asked Finnister.

"Certainly. A male astronaut sees a girl astronaut he likes. He asks her to trade keys. Very romantic. Symbolic of things that *may* happen when they return to Earth or get to a base where they can get out of the suits."

"Miss Everest," said Finnister, "as you so aptly pointed out earlier, no astronaut can see one of our women in this armor. And even if he could, I don't believe that I'd . . ."

She froze, staring, shocked speechless.

Gwen had pushed a stud on the solido projector's remote control. A suit of space armor appeared to be hanging in the center of the room. In the suit, wearing a form-fitting jacket, stood the agency's busty receptionist. The suit of armor around her was transparent from the waist up.

"The bottom half remains opaque at all times," said Gwen. "For reasons of modesty . . . the connections. However, the top half . . ."

Gwen pushed another stud. The transparent upper half faded through gray to black until it concealed the model.

"For privacy when desired," said Gwen. "That's how we've used the new mutable plastic. Gives the girl some control over her environment."

Again, Gwen pushed the first stud. The upper half of the model reappeared.

Finnister gaped at the form-fitting uniform.

Gwen stood up, took a pointer, gestured in through the projection. "This uniform was designed by a leading couturier. It is made to reveal while concealing. A woman with only a fair figure will appear to good advantage in it. A woman with an excellent figure appears stunning, as you can see. Poor figures—" Gwen shrugged—"there *are* exercises for developing them. Or so I am told."

Finnister interrupted in a cold voice. "And what do you propose to do with that . . . that uni . . . clothing?"

"This will be the regulation uniform for the WOMS," said Gwen. "There's a cute little hat goes with it. Very sexy."

Battlemont said: "Perhaps the changeover could be made slowly so as to . . ."

"What changeover?" demanded Finnister. She leaped to her feet. "General Owling?"

Owling tore his attention from the model. "Yes?"

"Completely impractical! I will put up with no more!" barked Finnister.

Battlemont thought: *I knew it. Oh, my poor Gwenny! They will destroy her, too. I knew it.*

"We can't waste any more time with this agency," said Finnister. "Come, General."

"Wait!" yelped Battlemont. He leaped to his feet. "Gwen, I told you . . ."

Finnister said: "It's regrettable, but . . ."

"Perhaps we're being a little hasty," said Owling. "There may be something to salvage from this . . ."

"Yes!" said Battlemont. "Just a little more time is all we need to get a fresh . . ."

"I think not," said Finnister.

Gwen smiled from one to the other, thought: *What a prize lot of gooney birds!* She felt a little drunk, as euphoric as if she had just come from a mood bar. *Rebellion, it's wonderful! Up the Irish! Or something.*

Owling shrugged, thought: *We have to stand together against civilians. General Finnister is right. Too bad, though.* He got to his feet.

"Just a little more time," pleaded Battlemont.

Too bad about André, thought Gwen. She had an inspiration, said: "One moment, please."

Three pairs of eyes focused on her.

Finnister said: "If you think you can stop me from going through with our threat, dissuade yourself. I'm perfectly aware that you had that uni . . . that *clothing* designed to make *me* look hideous!"

"Why not?" asked Gwen. "I was only doing to you what you did to virtually every other woman in the WOMS."

"Gwen!" pleaded Battlemont in horror.

"Be still, André," said Gwen. "It's just a matter of timing, anyway. Today. Tomorrow. Next week. Not really important."

"Oh, my poor Gwenny," sobbed Battlemont.

"I was going to wait," said Gwen. "Possibly a week. At least until I'd turned in my resignation."

"What're you talking about?" asked Owling.

"Resignation!" gasped Battlemont.

"I just can't toss poor André here to the wolves," said Gwen. "The rest of our men, yes. Once they get inside they'll chew your guts out, anyway."

"What *are* you talking about?" asked Finnister.

"The rest of the men in this agency can take care of themselves . . . and you, too," said Gwen. "Wolves among wolves. But André here is helpless. All he has is his position . . . money. He's an accident. Put him someplace where money and position are less important, it'll kill him."

"Regrettable," said Finnister. "Shall we be going, General Owling?"

"I was going to ruin both of you," said Gwen. "But I'll tell you what. You leave André alone and I'll just give *one* of you the business."

"Gwen, what are you saying?" whispered Battlemont.

"Yesss!" hissed Finnister. "Explain yourself!"

"I just want to know the pecking order here," said Gwen. "Which one of you ranks the other?"

"What does that have to do with it?" asked Finnister.

"Just a minute," said Owling. "That intelligence report." He glared at Gwen. "I'm told you've prepared an adecal on the test model we made before coming to you."

"Big Bertha," said Gwen. "And it's not just an adecal. I have everything needed for a full national campaign. Look!"

A solido of the breast-baring test model replaced the transparent suit hanging in the center of the room.

"The idea for Big Bertha here originated with General Owling," said Gwen. "My campaign establishes that fact, then goes on to feature an animated model of Big Bertha. She is a living panic. Funniest thing you ever saw. General Owling, you will be the laughingstock of the nation by nightfall of the day I start this campaign."

Owling took a step forward.

Battlemont said: "Gwen! They will destroy you!"

Owling pointed at the projection. "You . . . you wouldn't!"

"But I would," said Gwen. She smiled at him.

Battlemont tugged at Gwen's arm. She shook him off.

"It would ruin me," whispered Owling.

"Presumably, you are capable of going through with this threat," said Finnister. "Regrettable."

Owling whirled on Finnister. "We must stand together!" he said desperately.

"You bet," said Gwen. She pushed another stud on the remote control.

A projection of General Finnister in her famous uniform replaced Big Bertha.

"You may as well know the whole story," said Gwen. "I'm all set with another campaign on the designing of this uniform, right from the Sonnet Bonnet on down through the Sinister Finnister cape and those sneaky walking shoes. I start with a dummy model of the general clad in basic foundation garments. Then I go on to show how each element of the present WOMS uniform was designed for the . . . ah . . . Finnister . . . . ah . . . figure."

"I'll sue!" barked Finnister.

"Go ahead. Go ahead." Gwen waved a sinuous arm.

She acts drunk! thought Battlemont. *But she never drinks.*

"I'm all set to go black market with these campaigns," said Gwen. "You can't stop me. I'll prove every contention I make about that uniform. I'll expose you. I'll show why your enlistment drives flopped."

Red suffused the Finnister face. "All right!" she snapped. "If you're going to ruin us, I guess there's nothing we can do about it. But mark this,

Miss Everest. We'll have the men of this agency in the service. You'll have that on your conscience! And the men we draft will serve under friends of ours. I hope you know what that means!"

"You don't have any friends," said Gwen, but her voice lacked conviction. *It's backfiring,* she thought. *Oh, hell. I didn't think they'd defy me.*

"There may even be something we can do about you!" said Finnister. "A presidential order putting you in the service for reasons of national emergency. Or an emergency clause on some bill. And when we get our hands on you, Miss Everest . . .'"

"André!" wailed Gwen. It was all getting out of hand. *I didn't want to hurt anybody,* she thought. *I just . . .* She realized that she didn't know what she *had* wanted.

Battlemont was electrified. In 22 years, Gwen Everest had never appealed to anyone for help. And now, for the first time, her appeal was to him! He stepped between Gwen and Finnister. "André is right here," he said. He felt inspired. His Gwen had appealed to him! "You assassin!" he said, shaking a finger under the Finnister nose.

"Now, see here!" snapped Owling. "I won't stand for any more of—"

"And you!" barked Battlemont, whirling. "We have recordings of every conference here, from the first, and including this one! They show what happened! Don't you know what is wrong with this poor girl? You! You've driven her out of her mind!"

Gwen joined in the chorus: "What?"

"Be still, Gwen," said Battlemont. "I will handle this."

Gwen couldn't take her attention off him. Battlemont was magnificent. "Yes, André."

"I will prove it," said Battlemont. "With Interdorma psychiatrists. With all the experts money can buy. You think you have seen something in those campaigns our Gwen set up? Hah! I will show you something." He stabbed a finger at Owling. "Can the military drive you insane?"

"Oh, now see here," said Owling. "This has gone—"

"Yes! It *can* drive you insane!" said Battlemont. "And we will show, step by step, how you drove our poor Gwen out of her mind with fear for her friends. Fear for me!" He slapped himself on the chest, glared at Finnister. "And you know what we will do next? We will say to the public: This could happen to you! Who is next? You? Or you? Or you? Then what happens to your money from Congress? What happens to your enlistment quotas?"

"Now see here," said Owling. "We didn't . . .'"

"Didn't you?" snarled Battlemont. "You think this poor girl is in her right mind?"

"Well, but we didn't . . .'"

"Wait until you see our campaign," said Battlemont. He took Gwen's hand, patted it. "There, there, Gwenny. André will fix."

"Yes, André," she said. They were the only words she could find. She felt stupefied. *He's in love with me,* she thought. Never before had she known anyone to be in love with her. Not even her parents, who had always been repelled by the intellect they had spawned. Gwen felt warmth seeping through her. A cog slipped into motion in her mind. It creaked somewhat from long idleness. She thought: *He's in love with me!* She wanted to hug him.

"We seem to be at a stalemate," muttered Owling.

Finnister said: "But we can't just—"

"Shut up!" ordered Owling. "He'll do it! Can't you see that?"

"But if we draft—"

"He'll do it for sure, then! Buy some other agency to run the campaign."

"But we could turn around and draft—"

"You can't draft everybody who disagrees with you, woman! Not in this country! You'd start a revolution!"

"I . . ." Finnister said helplessly.

"And it's not just us he'd ruin," said Owling. "The whole service. He'd strike right at the money. I know his type. He wasn't bluffing. It'd be catastrophic!"

Owling shook his head, seeing a parade of crumbling military projects pass before his mind's eye, all falling into an abyss labeled "NSF."

"You are an intelligent man, General Owling," said Battlemont.

"That Psych Branch!" snarled Owling. "Them and their bright ideas!"

"I told you they were fuzzyheads," said Gwen.

"You be still, Gwen," said Battlemont.

"Yes, André."

"Well, what're we going to do?" demanded Owling.

"I tell you what," said Battlemont. "You leave us alone, we leave you alone."

"But what about my enlistments?" wailed Finnister.

"You think our Gwen, sick or well, can't solve your problems?" asked Battlemont. "For your enlistments you use the program as outlined."

"I won't!"

"You will," said Owling.

"General Owling, I refuse to have . . ."

"What happens if I have to dump this problem on the General Staff?" asked Owling. "Where will the head-chopping start? In the Psych Branch? Certainly. Who'll be next? The people who could've solved it in the field, that's who!"

Finnister said: "But—"

"For that matter," said Owling, "Miss Everest's idea sounded pretty sensible . . . with some modifications, of course."

"No modifications," said Battlemont.

He's a veritable Napoleon! thought Gwen.

"Only in minor, unimportant details," soothed Owling. "For engineering reasons."

"Perhaps," agreed Battlemont. "Provided we pass on the modifications before they are made."

"I'm sure we can work it out," said Owling.

Finnister gave up, turned her back on them.

"One little detail," murmured Battlemont. "When you make out the double-fee check to the agency, make a substantial addition—bonus for Miss Everest."

"Naturally," said Owling.

"Naturally," said Battlemont.

When the space brass had departed, Battlemont faced Gwen, stamped his foot. "You have been very bad, Gwen!"

"But, André—"

"Resignation!" barked Battlemont.

"But—"

"Oh, I understand, Gwen. It's my fault. I worked you much too hard. But that is past."

"André, you don't—"

"Yes, I do! I understand. You were going to sink the ship and go down with it. My poor, dear Gwen. A death wish! If you'd only paid attention to your Interdorma telelog."

"I didn't want to hurt anyone here, André. Only those two—"

"Yes, yes. I know. You're all mixed up."

"That's true." She felt like crying. She hadn't cried . . . since . . . she couldn't remember when. "You know," she said, "I can't remember ever crying."

"That's it!" said Battlemont. "I cry all the time. You need a stabilizing influence. You need someone to teach you how to cry."

"Would you teach me, André?"

"Would I . . ." He wiped the tears from his eyes. "You are going on a vacation. Immediately! I am going with you."

"Yes, André."

"And when we return—"

"I don't want to come back to the agency, André. I . . . can't."

"So that's it!" said Battlemont. "The advertising business! It bugs you!"

She shrugged. "I'm . . . I just can't face another campaign. I . . . just . . . can't."

"You will write a book," announced Battlemont.

"What?"

"Best therapy known," said Battlemont. "Did it myself once. You will write about the advertising business. You will expose all the dirty tricks: the hypno-jingles, the subvisual flicker images, the advertisers who finance textbooks to get their sell into them, the womb rooms where the *you-seekers* are programmed. Everything."

"I could do it," she said.

"You will tell all," said Battlemont.

"Will I!"

"And you will do it under a pseudonym," said Battlemont. "Safer."

"When do we start the vacation, André?"

"Tomorrow." He experienced a moment of his old panic. "You don't mind that I'm . . . ugly as a pig?"

"You're just beautiful," she said. She smoothed the hair across his bald spot. "You don't mind that I'm smarter than you?"

"Ah, hah!" Battlemont drew himself to attention. "You may be smarter in the head, my darling, but you are *not* smarter in the heart!"

MATING CALL

"If you get caught we'll have to throw you to the wolves," said Dr. Fladdis. "You understand, of course."

Laoconia Wilkinson, senior field agent of the Social Anthropological Service, nodded her narrow head. "Of course," she barked. She rustled the travel and order papers in her lap.

"It was very difficult to get High Council approval for this expedition after the . . . ah . . . unfortunate incident on Monligol," said Dr. Fladdis. "That's why your operating restrictions are so severe."

"I'm permitted to take only this—" she glanced at her papers—"Marie Medill?"

"Well, the basic plan of action was her idea," said Dr. Fladdis. "And we have no one else in the department with her qualifications in music."

"I'm not sure I approve of her plan," muttered Laoconia.

"Ah," said Dr. Fladdis, "but it goes right to the heart of the situation on Rukuchp, and the beauty of it is that it breaks no law. That's a legal quibble, I agree. But what I mean is you'll be within the letter of the law."

"And outside its intent," muttered Laoconia. "Not that I agree with the law. Still—" she shrugged—"music!"

Dr. Fladdis chose to misunderstand. "Miss Medill has her doctorate in music, yes," he said. "A highly educated young woman."

"If it weren't for the fact that this may be our last opportunity to discover how those creatures reproduce—" said Laoconia. She shook her head. "What we really should be doing is going in there with a full staff, capturing representative specimens, putting them through—"

"You will note the prohibition in Section D of the High Council's mandate," said Dr. Fladdis. " 'The Field Agent may not enclose, restrain or otherwise restrict the freedom of any Rukuchp native.' "

"How bad is their birthrate situation?" asked Laoconia.

"We have only the word of the Rukuchp special spokesman. This Gafka.

He said it was critical. That, of course, was the determining factor with the High Council. Rukuchp appealed to *us* for help."

Laoconia got to her feet. "You know what I think of this music idea. But if that's the way we're going to attack it, why don't we just break the law all the way—take in musical recordings, players . . ."

"Please!" snapped Dr. Fladdis.

Laoconia stared at him. She had never before seen the Area Director so agitated.

"The Rukuchp natives say that introduction of *foreign* music has disrupted some valence of their reproductive cycle," said Dr. Fladdis. "At least, that's how we've translated their explanation. This is the reason for the law prohibiting any traffic in music devices."

"I'm not a child!" snapped Laoconia. "You don't have to explain all . . ."

"We cannot be too careful," said Dr. Fladdis. "With the memory of Monligol still fresh in all minds." He shuddered. "We must return to the spirit of the SocAnth motto: *'For the Greater Good of the Universe.'* We've been warned."

"I don't see how music can be anything but a secondary stimulant," said Laoconia. "However, I shall keep an open mind."

Laoconia Wilkinson looked up from her notes, said: "Marie, was that a noise outside?" She pushed a strand of gray hair from her forehead.

Marie Medill stood at the opposite side of the field hut, staring out of one of the two windows. "I only hear the leaves," she said. "They're awfully loud in that wind."

"You're sure it wasn't Gafka?"

Marie sighed and said, "No, it wasn't his namesong."

"Stop calling that monster a him!" snapped Laoconia.

Marie's shoulders stiffened.

Laoconia observed the reflex and thought how wise the Service had been to put a mature, veteran anthropologist in command here. A hex-dome hut was too small to confine brittle tempers. And the two women had been confined here for 25 weeks already. Laoconia stared at her companion—such a young romantic, that one.

Marie's pose reflected boredom . . . worry . . .

Laoconia glanced around the hut's crowded interior. Servo-recorders, night cameras, field computers, mealmech, collapsible floaters, a desk, two chairs, folding bunks, three wall sections taken up by the transceiver linking them with the mother ship circling in satellite orbit overhead. Everything in its place and a place for everything.

"Somehow, I just can't help calling Gafka a him," said Marie. She shrugged. "I know it's nonsense. Still . . . when Gafka sings . . ."

Laoconia studied the younger woman. A blonde girl in a one-piece green uniform; heavy peasant figure, good strong legs, an oval face with high forehead and dreaming blue eyes.

"Speaking of singing," said Laoconia, "I don't know what I shall do if Gafka doesn't bring permission for us to attend their Big Sing. We can't solve this mess without the facts."

"No doubt," said Marie. She spoke snappishly, trying to keep her attention away from Laoconia. The older woman just sat there. She was always just sitting there—so efficient, so driving, a tall gawk with windburned face, nose too big, mouth too big, chin too big, eyes too small.

Marie turned away.

"With every day that passes I'm more convinced that this music thing is a blind alley," said Laoconia. "The Rukuchp birthrate keeps going down no matter how much of our music you teach them."

"But Gafka agrees," protested Marie. "Everything points to it. Our discovery of this planet brought the Rukuchps into contact with the first alien music they've ever known. Somehow, that's disrupted their breeding cycle. I'm sure of it."

"Breeding cycle," sniffed Laoconia. "For all we know, these creatures could be ambulatory vegetables without even the most rudimentary . . ."

"I'm so worried," said Marie. "It's music at the root of the problem, I'm sure, but if it ever got out that we smuggled in those education tapes and taught Gafka all our musical forms . . ."

"We did *not* smuggle anything!" barked Laoconia. "The law is quite clear. It only prohibits any form of *mechanical* reproducer of actual musical sounds. Our tapes are all completely visual."

"I keep thinking of Monligol," said Marie. "I couldn't live with the knowledge that I'd contributed to the extinction of a sentient species. Even indirectly. If our *foreign* music really has disrupted . . ."

"We don't even know if they breed!"

"But Gafka says . . ."

"Gafka says! A dumb vegetable. Gafka says!"

"Not so dumb," countered Marie. "He learned to speak our language in less than three weeks, but *we* have only the barest rudiments of songspeech."

"Gafka's an idiot-savant," said Laoconia. "And I'm not certain I'd call what that creature does *speaking*."

"It is too bad that you're tone deaf," said Marie sweetly.

Laoconia frowned. She leveled a finger at Marie. "The thing I note is that we only have their word that their birthrate is declining. They called on us for help, and now they obstruct every attempt at field observation."

"They're so shy," said Marie.

"They're going to be shy one SocAnth field expedition if they don't invite us to that Big Sing," said Laoconia. "Oh! If the Council had only authorized a *full* field expedition with armed support!"

"They couldn't!" protested Marie. "After Monligol, practically every sentient race in the universe is looking on Rukuchp as a final test case. If we mess up another race with our meddling . . ."

"Meddling!" barked Laoconia. "Young woman, the Social Anthropological Service is a holy calling! Erasing ignorance, helping the backward races!"

"And we're the only judges of what's backward," said Marie. "How convenient. Now, you take Monligol. Everyone knows that insects carry disease. So we move in with our insecticides and kill off the symbiotic partner essential to Monligolian reproduction. How uplifting."

"They should have told us," said Laoconia.

"They couldn't," said Marie. "It was a social taboo."

"Well . . ." Laoconia shrugged. "That doesn't apply here."

"How do you know?"

"I've had enough of this silly argument," barked Laoconia. "See if Gafka's coming. He's overdue."

Marie inhaled a trembling breath, stamped across to the field hut's lone door and banged it open. Immediately the tinkle of glazeforest leaves grew louder. The wind brought an odor of peppermint from the stubble plain to her left.

She looked across the plain at the orange ball of Almac sinking toward a flat horizon, swung her glance to the right where the wall of glazeforest loomed overhead. Rainbow-streaked batwing leaves clashed in the wind, shifting in subtle competition for the last of the day's orange light.

"Do you see *it*?" demanded Laoconia.

Marie shook her head, setting blonde curls dancing across her uniform collar. "It'll be dark soon," she said. "He said he'd return before it got fully dark."

Laoconia scowled, pushed aside her notes. *Always calling it a him! They're nothing but animated Easter eggs! If only . . .* She broke the train of thought, attention caught by a distant sound.

"There!" Marie peered down the length of glazeforest wall.

A fluting passage of melody hung on the air. It was the meister-song of a delicate wind instrument. As they listened, the tones deepened to an organ throb while a section of cello strings held the melody. Glazeforest leaves began to tinkle in sympathetic harmony. Slowly, the music faded.

"It's Gafka," whispered Marie. She cleared her throat, spoke louder, self-consciously: "He's coming out of the forest quite a ways down."

"I can't tell one from the other," said Laoconia. "They all look alike and sound alike. Monsters."

"They do look alike," agreed Marie, "but the sound is quite individual."

"Let's not harp on my tone deafness!" snapped Laoconia. She joined Marie at the door. "If they'll only let us attend their Sing . . ."

A six-foot Easter egg ambled toward them on four of its five prehensile feet.

The crystal glistening of its vision cap, tipped slightly toward the field hut, was semi-lidded by inner cloud pigment in the direction of the setting sun. Blue and white greeting colors edged a great bellows muscle around the torso. The bell extension of a mouth/ear—normally visible in a red-yellow body beneath the vision cap—had been retracted to a multi-creased pucker.

"What ugly brutes," said Laoconia.

"Shhhh!" said Marie. "You don't know how far away he can hear you." She waved an arm. "Gaaafkaa!" Then: "Damn!"

"What's wrong?"

"I only made eight notes out of his name instead of nine."

Gafka came up to the door, picking a way through the stubble spikes. The orange mouth/ear extended, sang a 22-note harmonica passage: "Maarrriee Mmmmmmedillll." Then a 10-second concerto: "Laoconnnnia Wiiilkinnnsonnnn!"

"How lovely!" said Marie.

"I wish you'd talk straight out the way we taught you," said Laoconia. "That singing is difficult to follow."

Gafka's vision cap tipped toward her. The voice shifted to a sing-song waver: "But polite sing greeting."

"Of course," said Laoconia. "Now." She took a deep breath. "Do we have permission to attend your Big Sing?"

Gafka's vision cap tipped toward Marie, back to Laoconia.

"Please, Gafka?" said Marie.

"Difficulty," wavered Gafka. "Not know how say. Not have knowledge your kind people. Is subject not want for talking."

"I see," said Laoconia, recognizing the metaphorical formula. "It has to do with your breeding habits."

Gafka's vision cap clouded over with milky pigment, a sign that the two women had come to recognize as embarrassment.

"Now, Gafka," said Laoconia. "None of that. We've explained about science and professional ethics, the desire to be of real help to one another. You must understand that both Marie and I are here for the good of your people."

A crystal moon unclouded in the part of the vision cap facing Laoconia.

"If we could only get them to speak straight out," said Laoconia.

Marie said: "Please, Gafka. We only want to help."

"Understand I," said Gafka. "How else talk this I?" More of the vision cap unclouded. "But must ask question. Friends perhaps not like."

"We are scientists," said Laoconia. "You may ask any question you wish."

"You are too old for . . . breeding?" asked Gafka. Again the vision cap clouded over, sparing Gafka the sight of Laoconia shocked speechless.

Marie stepped into the breech. "Gafka! Your people and my people are . . . well, we're just too different. We couldn't. There's no way . . . that is . . ."

"Impossible!" barked Laoconia. "Are you implying that we might be sexually attacked if we attended your Big Sing?"

Gafka's vision cap unclouded, tipped toward Laoconia. Purple color bands ran up and down the bellows muscle, a sign of confusion.

"Not understand I about sex thing," said Gafka. "My people never hurt other creature." The purple bands slowed their upward-downward chasing, relaxed into an indecisive green. The vision cap tipped toward Marie. "Is true all life kinds start egg young same?" This time the clouding of the vision cap was only a momentary glimmerwhite.

"Essentially, that is so," agreed Laoconia. "We all *do* start with an egg. However, the fertilization process is different with different peoples." Aside to Marie, she said: "Make a note of that point about eggs. It bears out that they may be oviparian as I suspected." Then: "Now, I must know what you meant by your question."

Gafka's vision cap rocked left, right, settled on a point between the two women. The sing-song voice intoned: "Not understand I about different ways. But know I you see many thing my people not see. If breeding (glimmerwhite) different, or you too old for breeding (glimmerwhite) my people say you come Big Sing. Not want we make embarrass for you."

"We are scientists," said Laoconia. "It's quite all right. Now, may we bring our cameras and recording equipment?"

"Bring you much of things?" asked Gafka.

"We'll only be taking one large floater to carry our equipment," said Laoconia. "How long must we be prepared to stay?"

"One night," said Gafka. "I bring worker friends to help with floater. Go I now. Soon be dark. Come moonrise I return, take to Big Sing place you." The trumpet mouth fluted three minor notes of farewell, pulled back to an orange pucker. Gafka turned, glided into the forest. Soon he had vanished among reflections of glasswood boles.

"A break at last!" barked Laoconia. She strode into the hut, speaking over her shoulder. "Call the ship. Have them monitor our equipment. Tell them to get duplicate recordings. While we're starting to analyze the sound-sight record down here they can be transmitting a copy to the master computers at Kampichi. We want as many minds on this as possible. We may never get another chance like this one!"

Marie said: "I don't—"

"Snap to it!" barked Laoconia.

"Shall I talk to Dr. Baxter?" asked Marie.

"Talk to Helen?" demanded Laoconia. "Why would you want to bother Helen with a routine question like this?"

"I just want to discuss . . ."

"That transceiver is for official use only," said Laoconia. "Transmit the message as I've directed. We're here to solve the Rukuchp breeding problem, not to chitchat."

"I feel suddenly so uneasy," said Marie. "There's something about this situation that worries me."

"Uneasy?"

"I think we've missed the point of Gafka's warning."

"Stop worrying," said Laoconia. "The natives won't give us any trouble. Gafka was looking for a last excuse to keep us from attending their Big Sing. You've seen how stupidly shy they are."

"But what if—"

"I've had a great deal of experience in handling native peoples," said Laoconia. "You never have trouble as long as you keep a firm, calm grip on the situation at all times."

"Maybe so. But . . ."

"Think of it!" said Laoconia. "The first humans ever to attend a Rukuchp Big Sing. Unique! You mustn't let the magnitude of our achievement dull your mind. Stay cool and detached as I do. Now get that call off to the ship!"

It was a circular clearing perhaps two kilometers in diameter, dark with moonshadows under the giant glaze trees. High up around the rim of the clearing, moonlight painted prismatic rainbows along every leaf edge. A glint of silver far above the center of the open area betrayed the presence of a tiny remote-control floater carrying night cameras and microphones.

Except for a space near the forest edge occupied by Laoconia and Marie, the clearing was packed with silent shadowy humps of Rukuchp natives. Vision caps glinted like inverted bowls in the moonlight.

Seated on a portable chair beside the big pack-floater, Laoconia adjusted the position of the tiny remote unit high above them. In the monitor screen before her she could see what the floater lenses covered—the clearing with its sequin glitter of Rukuchp vision caps and the faintest gleam of red and green instrument lights between herself and Marie seated on the other side of the floater. Marie was monitoring the night lenses that would make the scene appear as bright as day on the recording wire.

Marie straightened, rubbed the small of her back. "This clearing must be at least two kilometers across," she whispered, impressed.

Laoconia adjusted her earphones, tested a relay. Her feet ached. It had been at least a four-hour walk in here to this clearing. She began to feel latent qualms about what might be ahead in the nine hours left of the Rukuchp night. That stupid warning . . .

"I said it's a big clearing," whispered Marie.

Laoconia cast an apprehensive glance at the silent Rukuchp figures packed closely around. "I didn't realize there'd be so many," she whispered. "It doesn't look to me as though they're dying out. What does your monitor screen show?"

"They fill the clearing," whispered Marie. "And I think they extend back under the trees. I wish I knew which one was Gafka. I should've watched when he left us."

"Didn't he say where he was going?"

"He just asked if this spot was all right for us and if we were ready to help them."

"Well, I'm sure everything's going to be all right," said Laoconia. She didn't sound very convincing, even to herself.

"Isn't it time to contact the ship?" asked Marie.

"They'll be calling any—" A light flashed red on the panel in front of Laoconia. "Here they are now."

She flipped a switch, spoke into her cheek microphone. "Yes?"

The metallic chattering in Laoconia's earphones only made Marie feel more lonely. The ship was so far away above them.

"That's right," said Laoconia. "Transmit your record immediately and ask Kampichi to make an independent study. We'll compare notes later." Silence while she listened, then: "I'm sure there's no danger. You can keep an eye on us through the overhead lenses. But there's never been a report of a Rukuchp native offering violence to anyone . . . Well, I don't see what we can do about it now. We're here and that's that. I'm signing off now." She flipped the switch.

"Was that Dr. Baxter?" asked Marie.

"Yes. Helen's monitoring us herself, though I don't see what she can do. Medical people are very peculiar sometimes. Has the situation changed with the natives?"

"They haven't moved that I can see."

"Why couldn't Gafka have given us a preliminary briefing?" asked Laoconia. "I detest this flying blind."

"I think it still embarrasses him to talk about breeding," said Marie.

"Everything's too quiet," hissed Laoconia. "I don't like it."

"They're sure to do something soon," whispered Marie.

As though her words were the signal, an almost inaudible vibration began to throb in the clearing. Glaze leaves started their sympathetic tinkle-chiming. The vibration grew, became an organ rumble with abrupt piping obbligato that danced along its edges. A cello insertion pulled a melody from the sound, swung it over the clearing while the glazeforest chimed louder and louder.

"How exquisite," breathed Marie. She forced her attention onto the instruments in front of her. Everything was functioning.

The melody broke to a single clear high note of harmonic brilliance—a flute sound that shifted to a second phase with expanded orchestration. The music picked up element after element while low-register tympani built a stately rhythm into it, and zither tinkles laid a counterpoint on the rhythm.

"Pay attention to your instruments," hissed Laoconia.

Marie nodded, swallowing. The music was like a song heard before, but never before played with this perfection. She wanted to close her eyes; she wanted to submit entirely to the ecstasy of sound.

Around them, the Rukuchp natives remained stationary, a rhythmic expansion and contraction of bellows muscles their only movement.

And the rapture of music intensified.

Marie moved her head from side to side, mouth open. The sound was an infinity of angel choirs—every sublimity of music ever conceived—now concentrated into one exquisite distillation. She felt that it could not possibly grow more beautiful.

But it did.

There came a lifting-expanding-floating . . . a long gliding suspenseful timelessness.

Silence.

Marie felt herself drifting back to awareness, found her hands limply fumbling with dials. Some element of habit assured her that she had carried out her part of the job, but that music . . . She shivered.

"They sang for 47 minutes," hissed Laoconia. She glanced around. "Now what happens?"

Marie rubbed her throat, forced her attention onto the luminous dials, the floater, the clearing. A suspicion was forming in the back of her mind.

"I wish I knew which one of these creatures was Gafka," whispered Laoconia. "Do we dare arouse one of them, ask after Gafka?"

"We'd better not," said Marie.

"These creatures did nothing but sing," said Laoconia. "I'm more certain than ever that the music is stimulative and nothing more."

"I hope you're right," whispered Marie. Her suspicion was taking on more definite shape . . . *music, controlled sound, ecstasy of controlled sound . . .* Thoughts tumbled over each other in her mind.

Time dragged out in silence.

"What do you suppose they're doing?" hissed Laoconia. "They've been sitting like this for 25 minutes."

Marie glanced around at the ring of Rukuchp natives hemming in the little open space, black mounds topped by dim silver. The stillness was like a charged vacuum.

More time passed.

"Forty minutes!" whispered Laoconia. "Do they expect us to sit here all night?"

Marie chewed her lower lip. *Ecstasy of sound,* she thought. And she thought of sea urchins and the parthenogenetic rabbits of Calibeau.

A stirring movement passed through the Rukuchp ranks. Presently, shadowy forms began moving away into the glazeforest's blackness.

"Where are they going?" hissed Laoconia. "Do you see Gafka?"

"No."

The transmission-receive light flashed in front of Laoconia. She flipped the switch, pressed an earphone against her head. "They just seem to be leaving," she whispered into the cheek microphone. "You see the same thing we do. There's been no movement against us. Let me call you back later. I want to observe this."

A Rukuchp figure came up beside Marie.

"Gafka?" said Marie.

"Gafka," intoned the figure. The voice sounded sleepy.

Laoconia leaned across the instrument-packed floater. "What are they doing now, Gafka?" she demanded.

"All new song we make from music you give," said Gafka.

"Is the sing all ended?" asked Marie.

"Same," breathed Gafka.

"What's this about a new song?" demanded Laoconia.

"Not have your kind song before correct," said Gafka. "In it too much new. Not understand we how song make you. But now you teach, make right you."

"What is all this nonsense?" asked Laoconia. "Gafka, where are your people all going?"

"Going," sighed Gafka.

Laoconia looked around her. "But they're departing singly . . . or . . . well, there don't seem to be any mated pairs. What *are* they doing?"

"Go each to wait," said Gafka.

And Marie thought of caryocinesis and daughter nuclei.

"I don't understand," complained Laoconia.

"You teach how new song sing," sighed Gafka. "New song best all time. We keep this song. Better much than old song. Make better—" the women detected the faint glimmer-haze lidding of Gafka's vision cap—"make better young. Strong more."

"Gafka," said Marie, "is the song all you do? I mean, there isn't anything else?"

"All," breathed Gafka. "Best song ever."

Laoconia said: "I think we'd better follow some of these . . ."

"That's not necessary," said Marie. "Did you enjoy their music, Dr. Wilkinson?"

"Well . . ." There appeared to be embarrassment in the way the older woman turned her head away. "It was very beautiful."

"And you *enjoyed* it?" persisted Marie.

"I don't see what . . ."

"You're tone deaf," said Marie.

"It's obviously a stimulant of some sort!" snapped Laoconia. "I don't understand now why they won't let us . . ."

"They let us," said Marie.

Laoconia turned to Gafka. "I must insist, Gafka, that we be permitted to study all phases of your breeding process. Otherwise we can be of no help to you."

"You best help ever," said Gafka. "Birthrate all good now. You teach way out from mixing of music." A shudder passed upward through Gafka's bellows muscles.

"Do you make sense out of this?" demanded Laoconia.

"I'm afraid I do," said Marie. "Aren't you tired, Gafka?"

"Same," sighed Gafka.

"Laoconia, Dr. Wilkinson, we'd better get back to the hut," said Marie. "We can improvise what we'll need for the Schafter test."

"But the Schafter's for determining *human* pregnancy!" protested Laoconia.

The red light glowed in front of Laoconia. She flipped the switch. "Yes?"

Scratching sounds from the earphones broke the silence. Marie felt that she did not want to hear the voice from the ship.

Laoconia said: "Of course I know you're monitoring the test of . . . Why should I tell Marie you've already given Schafter tests to yourself . . ." Laoconia's voice climbed. "WHAT? You can't be ser . . . That's impossible! But, Helen, we . . . they . . . you . . . we . . . Of course I . . . Where could we have . . . Every woman on the ship . . ."

There was a long silence while Marie watched Laoconia listening to the earphones, nodding. Presently, Laoconia lifted the earphones off her head and put them down gently. Her voice came out listlessly. "Dr. Bax . . . Helen suspected that . . . she administered Schafter tests to herself and some to the others."

"She listened to that music?" asked Marie.

"The whole universe listened to that music," said Laoconia. "Some smuggler monitored the ship's official transmission of our recordings. Rebroadcast stations took it. Everyone's going crazy about our *beautiful* music."

"Oh, no," breathed Marie.

Laconia said: "Everyone on the ship listened to our recordings. Helen said she suspected immediately after the broadcast, but she waited the full half hour before giving the Schafter test." Laoconia glanced at the silent hump of Gafka standing beside Marie. "Every woman on that ship who could become pregnant is pregnant."

"It's obvious, isn't it?" asked Marie. "Gafka's people have developed a form of group parthenogenesis. Their Big Sing sets off the blastomeric reactions."

"But we're humans!" protested Laoconia. "How can . . ."

"And parts of us are still very primitive," said Marie. "This shouldn't surprise us. Sound's been used before to induce the first mitotic cleavage in an egg. Gafka's people merely have this as their sole breeding method— with corresponding perfection of technique."

Laoconia blinked, said: "I wonder how this ever got started?"

"And when they first encountered our *foreign* music," said Marie, "it confused them, mixed up their musical relationships. They were fascinated by the new musical forms. They experimented for new sensations . . . and their birthrate fell off. Naturally."

"Then you came along," said Laoconia, "and taught them how to master the new music."

"Exactly."

"Marie!" hissed Laoconia.

"Yes?"

"We were right here during that entire . . . You don't suppose that we . . . that I . . ."

"I don't know about you," said Marie, "but I've never felt more certain of anything in my life."

She chewed at her lower lip, fought back tears. "I'm going to have a baby. Female. It'll have only half the normal number of chromosomes. And it'll be sterile. And I . . ."

"Say I to you," chanted Gafka. There was an air of sadness in the singsong voice. "Say I to you: all life kinds start egg young same. Not want I to cause troubles. But you say different you."

"Parthenogenesis," said Laoconia with a show of her old energy. "That means, of course, that the human reproductive process need not . . . that is, uh . . . we'll not have to . . . I mean to say that men won't be . . ."

"The babies will be drones," said Marie. "You know that. Unfertile drones. This may have its vogue, but it surely can't last."

"Perhaps," said Laoconia. "But I keep thinking of all those rebroadcasts of our recordings. I wonder if these Rukuchp creatures ever had two sexes?" She turned toward Gafka. "Gafka, do you know if . . ."

"Sorry cause troubles," intoned Gafka. The singsong voice sounded weaker. "Must say farewell now. Time for birthing me."

"*You* are going to give birth?" asked Laoconia.

"Same," breathed Gafka. "Feel pain on eye-top." Gafka's prehensile legs went into a flurry of digging in the ground beside the floater.

"Well, you were right about one thing, Dr. Wilkinson," said Marie. "She-he is not a *him*."

Gafka's legs bent, lowered the ovoid body into the freshly dug concavity in the ground. Immediately, the legs began to shrink back into the body. A crack appeared across the vision cap, struck vertically down through the bellows muscles.

Presently, there were two Gafkas, each half the size of the original. As the women watched, the two half-sized Gafkas began extruding new legs to regain the normal symmetry.

"Oh, no," whispered Marie.

She had a headache.

TRY TO
REMEMBER

Every mind on earth capable of understanding the problem was focused on the spaceship with the ultimatum delivered by its occupants. *Talk or Die!* blared the newspaper headlines.

The suicide rate was up and still climbing. Religious cults were having a field day. A book by a science fiction author, *What the Deadly Inter-Galactic Spaceship Means to You!*, had smashed all previous best-seller records. And this had been going on for a frantic seven months.

The ship had *flapped* out of a gun-metal sky over Oregon, its shape that of a hideously magnified paramecium with edges that rippled like a mythological flying carpet. Its five green-skinned, froglike occupants had delivered the ultimatum, one copy printed on velvety paper to each major government, each copy couched faultlessly in the appropriate native tongue:

"You are requested to assemble your most gifted experts in human communication. We are about to submit a problem. We will open five identical rooms of our vessel to you. One of us will be available in each room.

"Your problem. To communicate with us.

"If you succeed, your rewards will be great.

"If you fail, that will result in destruction for all sentient life on your planet.

"We announce this threat with the deepest regret. You are urged to examine Eniwetok atoll for a small display of our power. Your artificial satellites have been removed from the skies.

"You must break away from this limited communication!"

Eniwetok had been cleared off flat as a table at one thousand feet depth . . . with no trace of explosion! All Russian and United States artificial satellites had been combed from the skies.

All day long a damp wind poured up the Columbia Gorge from the ocean. It swept across the Eastern Oregon alkali flats with a false prediction of rain. Spiny desert scrub bent before the gusts, sheltering blur-footed coveys of quail and flop-eared jackrabbits. Heaps of tumbleweed tangled in the fence lines, and the air was filled with dry particles of grit that crept under everything and into everything and onto everything with the omnipresence of filterable virus.

On the flats south of the Hermiston Ordnance Depot the weird bulk of the spaceship caught pockets and eddies of sand. The thing looked like a monstrous oval of dun canvas draped across upright sticks. A cluster of quonsets and the Army's new desert prefabs dotted a rough half-circle around the north rim. They looked like dwarfed out-buildings for the most gigantic circus tent Earth had ever seen. Army Engineers said the ship was 6,218 feet long, 1,054 feet wide.

Some five miles east of the site the dust storm hazed across the monotonous structures of the cantonment that housed some thirty thousand people from every major nation: linguists, anthropologists, psychologists, doctors of every shape and description, watchers and watchers for the watchers, spies, espionage and counter-espionage agents.

For seven months the threat of Eniwetok, the threat of the unknown as well, had held them in check.

Towards evening of this day the wind slackened. The drifted sand began sifting off the ship and back into new shapes, trickling down for all the world like the figurative "sands of time" that here were most certainly running out.

Mrs. Francine Millar, clinical psychologist with the Indo-European Germanic-Root team, hurried across the bare patch of trampled sand outside the spaceship's entrance. She bent her head against what was left of the windstorm. Under her left arm she carried her briefcase tucked up like a football. Her other hand carried a rolled-up copy of that afternoon's *Oregon Journal*. The lead story said that Air Force jets had shot down a small private plane trying to sneak into the restricted area. Three unidentified men killed. The plane had been stolen.

Thoughts of a plane crash made her too aware of the circumstances in her own recent widowhood. Dr. Robert Millar had died in the crash of a transatlantic passenger plane ten days before the arrival of the spaceship. She let the newspaper fall out of her hands. It fluttered away on the wind.

Francine turned her head away from a sudden biting of the sandblast wind. She was a wiry slim figure of about five feet six inches, still trim and athletic at forty-one. Her auburn hair, mussed by the wind, still carried the look of youth. Heavy lids shielded her blue eyes. The lids drooped slightly, giving her a perpetual sleepy look even when she was wide awake and alert—a circumstance she found helpful in her profession.

She came into the lee of the conference quonset, and straightened. A layer of sand covered the doorstep. She opened the door, stepped across the sand only to find more of it on the floor inside, grinding underfoot. It was on tables, on chairs, mounded in corners—on every surface.

Hikonojo Ohashi, Francine's opposite number with the Japanese-Korean and Sino-Tibetan team, already sat at his place on the other side of the table. The Japanese psychologist was grasping, pen fashion, a thin-pointed brush, making notes in ideographic shorthand.

Francine closed the door.

Ohashi spoke without looking up: "We're early."

He was a trim, neat little man: flat features, smooth cheeks and even curve of chin, remote dark eyes behind the inevitable thick lenses of the Oriental scholar.

Francine tossed her briefcase onto the table and pulled out a chair opposite Ohashi. She wiped away the grit with a handkerchief before sitting down. The ever-present dirt, the monotonous landscape, her own frustration—all combined to hold her on the edge of anger. She recognized the feeling and its source, stifled a wry smile.

"No, Hiko," she said. "I think we're late. It's later than we think."

"Much later when you put it that way," said Ohashi. His Princeton accent came out low, modulated like a musical instrument under the control of a master.

"Now we're going to be banal," she said. Immediately, she regretted the sharpness of her tone, forced a smile to her lips.

"They gave us no deadline," said Ohashi. "That is one thing, anyway." He twirled his brush across an inkstone.

"Something's in the air," she said. "I can feel it."

"Very much sand in the air," he said.

"The wind has us all on edge," he said. "It feels like rain. A change in the weather." He made another note, put down the brush and began setting out papers for the conference. All at once, his head came up. He smiled at Francine. The smile made him look immature, and she suddenly saw back through the years to a serious little boy named Hiko Ohashi.

"It's been seven months," she said. "It stands to reason that they're not going to wait forever."

"The usual gestation period is two months longer," he said.

She frowned, ignoring the quip. "But we're no closer today than we were at the beginning!"

Ohashi leaned forward. His eyes appeared to swell behind the thick lenses. "Do you often wonder at their insistence that *we* communicate with *them*? I mean, rather than the other way around?"

"Of course I do. So does everybody else."

He sat back. "What do you think of the Islamic team's approach?"

"You know what I think, Hiko. It's a waste of time to compare all the Galactics' speech sounds to passages from the Koran." She shrugged. "But for all we know actually they could be closer to a solution than anyone else in . . ."

The door behind her banged open. Immediately, the room rumbled with the great basso voice of Theodore Zakheim, psychologist with the Ural-Altaic team.

"Hah-haaaaaaa!" he roared. "We're all here now!"

Light footsteps behind Zakheim told Francine that he was accompanied by Emile Goré of the Indo-European Latin-Root team.

Zakheim flopped onto a chair beside Francine. It creaked dangerously to his bulk.

Like a great uncouth bear! she thought.

"Do you always have to be so noisy?" she asked.

Goré slammed the door behind them.

"Naturally!" boomed Zakheim. "I am noisy! It's my nature, my little puchkin!"

Goré moved behind Francine, passing to the head of the table, but she kept her attention on Zakheim. He was a thick-bodied man, thick without fat, like the heaviness of a wrestler. His wide face and slanting pale blue eyes carried hints of Mongol ancestry. Rusty hair formed an uncombed brush atop his head.

Zakheim brought up his briefcase, flopped it onto the table, rested his hands on the dark leather. They were flat slab hands with thick fingers, pale wisps of hair growing down almost to the nails.

She tore her attention away from Zakheim's hands, looked down the table to where Goré sat. The Frenchman was a tall, gawk-necked man, entirely bald. Jet eyes behind steel-rimmed bifocals gave him a look of down-nose asperity like a comic bird. He wore one of his usual funereal black suits, every button secured. Knob wrists protruded from the sleeves. His long-fingered hands with their thick joints moved in constant restlessness.

"If I may differ with you, Zak," said Goré, "we are *not* all here. This is our same old group, and we were going to try to interest others in what we do here."

Ohashi spoke to Francine: "Have you had any luck inviting others to our conferences?"

"You can see that I'm alone," she said. "I chalked up five flat refusals today."

"Who?" asked Zakheim.

"The American Indian-Eskimo, the Hyperboreans, the Dravidians, the Malayo-Polynesians and the Caucasians."

"Hagglers!" barked Zakheim. "I, of course, can cover us with the Hamito-Semitic tongues, but . . ." He shook his head.

Goré turned to Ohashi. "The others?"

Ohashi said: "I must report the polite indifference of the Munda and Mon-Kmer, the Sudanese-Guinean and the Bantu."

"Those are big holes in our information exchange," said Goré. "What are they discovering?"

"No more than we are!" snapped Zakheim. "Depend on it!"

"What of the languages not even represented among the teams here on the international site?" asked Francine. "I mean the Hottentot-Bushmen, the Ainu, the Basque and the Australian-Papuan?"

Zakheim covered her left hand with his right hand. "You always have me, my little dove."

"We're building another Tower of Babel!" she snapped. She jerked her hand away.

"Spurned again," mourned Zakheim.

Ohashi said: *"Go to, let us go down, and there confound their language, that they may not understand one another's speech."* He smiled. "Genesis eleven-seven."

Francine scowled. "And we're missing about twenty per cent of Earth's twenty-eight hundred languages!"

"We have all the significant ones," said Zakheim.

"How do *you* know what's significant?" she demanded.

"Please!" Goré raised a hand. "We're here to exchange information, not to squabble!"

"I'm sorry," said Francine. "It's just that I feel so hopeless today."

"Well, what have we learned today?" asked Goré.

"Nothing new with us," said Zakheim.

Goré cleared his throat. "That goes double for me." He looked at Ohashi.

The Japanese shrugged. "We achieved no reaction from the Galactic, Kobai."

"Anthropomorphic nonsense," muttered Zakheim.

"You mean naming him Kobai?" asked Ohashi. "Not at all, Zak. That's the most frequent sound he makes, and the name helps with identification. We don't have to keep referring to him as 'The Galactic' or 'that creature in the spaceship.'"

Goré turned to Francine. "It was like talking to a green statue," she said.

"What of the lecture period?" asked Goré.

"Who knows?" she asked. "It stands there like a bow-legged professor in that black leotard. Those sounds spew out of it as though they'd never stop. It wriggles at us. It waves. It sways. Its face contorts, if you can call it a face. We recorded and filmed it all, naturally, but it sounded like the usual mish-mash!"

"There's something in the gestures," said Ohashi. "If we only had more competent pasimologists."

"How many times have you seen the same total gesture repeated with the same sound?" demanded Zakheim.

"You've carefully studied our films," said Ohashi. "Not enough times to give us a solid base for comparison. But I do not despair—"

"It was a rhetorical question," said Zakheim.

"We really need more multilinguists," said Goré. "Now is when we most miss the loss of such great linguists as Mrs. Millar's husband."

Francine closed her eyes, took a short, painful breath. "Bob . . ." She shook her head. *No. That's the past. He's gone. The tears are ended.*

"I had the pleasure of meeting him in Paris shortly before the . . . end," continued Goré. "He was lecturing on the development of the similar sound schemes in Italian and Japanese."

Francine nodded. She felt suddenly empty.

Ohashi leaned forward. "I imagine this is . . . rather painful for Dr. Millar," he said.

"I am *very* sorry," said Goré. "Forgive me."

"Someone was going to check and see if there are any electronic listening devices in this room," said Ohashi.

"My nephew is with our recording section," said Goré, "He assures me there are no hidden microphones here."

Zakheim's brows drew down into a heavy frown. He fumbled with the clasp of his briefcase. "This is very dangerous," he grunted.

"Oh, Zak, you always say that!" said Francine. "Let's quit playing footsy!"

"I do not enjoy the thought of treason charges," muttered Zakheim.

"We all know our bosses are looking for an advantage," she said. "I'm tired of these sparring matches where we each try to get something from the others without giving anything away!"

"If your Dr. Langsmith or General Speidel found out what you were doing here, it would go hard for you, too," said Zakheim.

"I propose we take it from the beginning and re-examine everything," said Francine. "Openly this time."

"Why?" demanded Zakheim.

"Because I'm satisfied that the answer's right in front of us somewhere," she said.

"In the ultimatum, no doubt," said Goré. "What do you suppose is the *real* meaning of their statement that human languages are *'limited'* communication? Perhaps they are telepathic?"

"I don't think so," said Ohashi.

"That's pretty well ruled out," said Francine. "Our Rhine people say no ESP. No. I'm banking on something else: By the very fact that they posed this question, they have indicated that we *can* answer it with our present faculties."

"*If* they are being honest," said Zakheim.

"I have no recourse but to assume that they're honest," she said. "They're turning us into linguistic detectives for a good reason."

"A good reason for *them*," said Goré.

"Note the phraseology of their ultimatum," said Ohashi. "They *submit* a problem. They *open* their rooms to us. They are *available* to us. They *regret* their threat. Even their display of power—admittedly awe-inspiring—has the significant characteristic of nonviolence. No explosion. They offer rewards for success, and this . . ."

"Rewards!" snorted Zakheim. "We lead the hog to its slaughter with a promise of food!"

"I suggest that they give evidence of being nonviolent," said Ohashi. "Either that, or they have cleverly arranged themselves to present the *face* of nonviolence."

Francine turned, and looked out of the hut's end window at the bulk of the spaceship. The low sun cast elongated shadows of the ship across the sand.

Zakheim, too, looked out of the window. "Why did they choose this place? If it had to be a desert, why not the Gobi? This is not even a good desert! This is a miserable desert!"

"Probably the easiest landing curve to a site near a large city," said Goré. "It is possible they chose a desert to avoid destroying arable land."

"Frogs!" snapped Zakheim. "I do not trust these frogs with their problem of communication!"

Francine turned back to the table, and took a pencil and scratch-pad from her briefcase. Briefly she sketched a rough outline of a Galactic, and wrote "frog?" beside it.

Ohashi said: "Are you drawing a picture of your Galactic?"

"We call it 'Uru' for the same reason you call yours 'Kobai,' " she said. "It makes the sound 'Uru' *ad nauseam.*"

She stared at her own sketch thoughtfully, calling up the memory image of the Galactic as she did so. Squat, about five feet ten inches in height, with the short bowed legs of a swimmer. Rippling muscles sent corded lines under the black leotard. The arms were articulated like a human's, but they were more graceful in movement. The skin was pale green, the neck thick and short. The wide mouth was almost lipless, the nose a mere blunt horn. The eyes were large and spaced wide with nictating lids. No hair, but a high-crowned ridge from the center of the forehead swept back across the head.

"I knew a Hawaiian distance swimmer once who looked much like these Galactics," said Ohashi. He wet his lips with his tongue. "You know, today we had a Buddhist monk from Java at our meeting with Kobai."

"I fail to see the association between a distance swimmer and a monk," said Goré.

"You told us you drew a blank today," said Zakheim.

"The monk tried no conversing," said Ohashi. "He refused because that would be a form of earthly striving unthinkable for a Buddhist. He merely came and observed."

Francine leaned forward. "Yes?" She found an odd excitement in the way Ohashi was forcing himself to casualness.

"The monk's reaction was curious," said Ohashi. "He refused to speak for several hours afterwards. Then he said that these Galactics must be very holy people."

"Holy!" Zakheim's voice was edged with bitter irony.

"We are approaching this the wrong way," said Francine. She felt let down, spoke with a conscious effort. "Our access to these Galactics is limited by the space they've opened to us within their vessel."

"What is in the rest of the ship?" asked Zakheim.

"Rewards, perhaps," said Goré.

"Or weapons to demolish us!" snapped Zakheim.

"The pattern of the sessions is wrong, too," said Francine.

Ohashi nodded. "Twelve hours a day is not enough," he said. "We should have them under constant observation."

"I didn't mean that," said Francine. "They probably need rest just as we do. No. I meant the absolute control our team leaders—unimaginative men like Langsmith—have over the way we use our time in those rooms. For instance, what would happen if we tried to break down the force wall of whatever it is that keeps us from actually touching these creatures? What would happen if we brought in dogs to check how *animals* would react to them?" She reached in her briefcase, brought out a small flat recorder and adjusted it for playback. "Listen to this."

There was a fluid burst of sound: "Pau'timónsh' uego' ikloprépre 'sauta' urusa'a'a . . ." and a long pause followed by "tu'kimóomo 'urulig 'lurulil 'oog 'shuquetoé . . ." pause, "sum 'a 'suma 'a 'uru 't 'shóap!"

Francine stopped the playback.

"Did you record that today?" asked Ohashi.

"Yes. It was using that odd illustration board with the moving pictures— weird flowers and weirder animals."

"We've seen them," muttered Zakheim.

"And those chopping movements of its hands," said Francine. "The swaying body, the undulations, the facial contortions." She shook her head. "It's almost like a bizarre dance."

"What are you driving at?" asked Ohashi.

"I've been wondering what would happen if we had a leading choreographer compose a dance to those sounds, and if we put it on for . . ."

"Faaa!" snorted Zakheim.

"All right," said Francine. "But we should be using some kind of random stimulation pattern on these Galactics. Why don't we bring in a nightclub singer? Or a circus barker? Or a magician? Or . . ."

"We tried a full-blown schizoid," said Gore.

Zakheim grunted. "And you got exactly what such tactics deserve: Your schizoid sat there and played with his fingers for an hour!"

"The idea of using artists from the entertainment world intrigues me," said Ohashi. "Some *Noh* dancers, perhaps." He nodded. "I'd never thought about it. But art is, after all, a form of communication."

"So is the croaking of a frog in a swamp," said Zakheim.

"Did you ever hear about the Paradox Frog?" asked Francine.

"Is this one of your strange jokes?" asked Zakheim.

"Of course not. The Paradox Frog is a very real creature. It lives on the island of Trinidad. It's a very small frog, but it has the opposable thumb on a five-fingered hand, and it . . ."

"Just like our visitors," said Zakheim.

"Yes. And it uses its hand just like we do—to grasp things, to pick up food, to stuff its mouth, to . . ."

"To make bombs?" asked Zakheim.

Francine shrugged, turned away. She felt hurt.

"My people believe these Galactics are putting on an elaborate sham," said Zakheim. "We think they are stalling while they secretly study us in preparation for invasion!"

Goré said: "So?" His narrow shoulders came up in a Gallic shrug that said as plainly as words: *Even if this is true, what is there for us to do?*"

Francine turned to Ohashi. "What's the favorite theory current with your team?" Her voice sounded bitter, but she was unable to soften the tone.

"We are working on the assumption that this is a language of one-syllable root, as in Chinese," said Ohashi.

"But what of the vowel harmony?" protested Goré. "Surely that must mean the harmonious vowels are all in the same words."

Ohashi adjusted the set of his glasses. "Who knows?" he asked. "Certainly, the back vowels and front vowels come together many times, but . . ." He shrugged, shook his head.

"What's happening with the group that's working on the historical analogy?" asked Goré. "You were going to find out, Ohashi."

"They are working on the assumption that all primitive sounds are consonants with nonfixed vowels . . . foot-stampers for dancing, you know. Their current guess is that the Galactics are missionaries, their language a religious language."

"What results?" asked Zakheim.

"None."

Zakheim nodded. "To be expected." He glanced at Francine. "I beg the forgiveness of the Mrs. Doctor Millar?"

She looked up, startled from a daydreaming speculation about the Galactic language and dancing. "Me? Good heavens, why?"

"I have been short-tempered today," said Zakheim. He glanced at his wristwatch. "I'm very sorry. I've been worried about another appointment."

He heaved his bulk out of the chair, took up his briefcase. "And it is time for me to be leaving. You forgive me?"

"Of course, Zak."

His wide face split into a grin. "Good!"

Goré got to his feet. "I will walk a little way with you, Zak."

Francine and Ohashi sat on for a moment after the others had gone.

"What good are we doing with these meetings?" she asked.

"Who knows how the important pieces of this puzzle will be fitted together?" asked Ohashi. "The point is: We are doing something different."

She sighed. "I guess so."

Ohashi took off his glasses, and it made him appear suddenly defenseless. "Did you know that Zak was recording our meeting?" he asked. He replaced the glasses.

Francine stared at him. "How do you know?"

Ohashi tapped his briefcase. "I have a device in here that reveals such things."

She swallowed a brief surge of anger. "Well, is it really important, Hiko?"

"Perhaps not." Ohashi took a deep, evenly controlled breath. "I did not tell you one other thing about the Buddhist monk."

"Oh? What did you omit?"

"He predicts that we will fail—that the human race will be destroyed. He is very old and very cynical for a monk. He thinks it is a good thing that all human striving must eventually come to an end."

Anger and a sudden resolve flamed in her. "I don't care! I don't care what anyone else thinks! I know that . . ." She allowed her voice to trail off, put her hands to her eyes.

"You have been very distracted today," said Ohashi. "Did the talk about your late husband disturb you?"

"I know. I'm . . ." She swallowed, whispered: "I had a dream about Bob last night. We were dancing, and he was trying to tell me something about this problem, only I couldn't hear him. Each time he started to speak the music got louder and drowned him out."

Silence fell over the room. Presently, Ohashi said: "The unconscious mind takes strange ways sometimes to tell us the right answers. Perhaps we should investigate this idea of dancing."

"Oh, Hiko! Would you help me?"

"I should consider it an honor to help you," he said.

It was quiet in the semi-darkness of the projection room. Francine leaned her head against the back-rest of her chair, looked across at the stand light where Ohashi had been working. He had gone for the films on Oriental ritual dances that had just arrived from Los Angeles by plane. His coat was still draped across the back of his chair, his pipe still smoldered in the ashtray on the worktable. All around their two chairs were stacked the residue of four days' almost continuous research: notebooks, film cans, boxes of photographs, reference books.

She thought about Hiko Ohashi: a strange man. He was fifty and didn't look a day over thirty. He had grown children. His wife had died of cholera eight years ago. Francine wondered what it would be like married to an Oriental, and she found herself thinking that he wasn't really Oriental with his Princeton education and Occidental ways. Then she realized that this attitude was a kind of white snobbery.

The door in the corner of the room opened softly. Ohashi came in, closed the door. "You awake?" he whispered.

She turned her head without lifting it from the chairback. "Yes."

"I'd hoped you might fall asleep for a bit," he said. "You looked so tired when I left."

Francine glanced at her wristwatch. "It's only three-thirty. What's the day like?"

"Hot and windy."

Ohashi busied himself inserting film into the projector at the rear of the room. Presently, he went to his chair, trailing the remote control cable for the projector.

"Ready?" he asked.

Francine reached for the low editing light beside her chair, and turned it on, focusing the narrow beam on a notebook in her lap. "Yes. Go ahead."

"I feel that we're making real progress," said Ohashi. "It's not clear yet, but the points of identity . . ."

"They're exciting," she said. "Let's see what this one has to offer."

Ohashi punched the button on the cable. A heavily robed Arab girl appeared on the screen, slapping a tambourine. Her hair looked stiff, black and oily. A sooty line of kohl shaded each eye. Her brown dress swayed slightly as she tinkled the tambourine, then slapped it.

The cultured voice of the commentator came through the speaker beside the screen: "This is a young girl of Jebel Tobeyk. She is going to dance some very ancient steps that tell a story of battle. The camera is hidden in a truck, and she is unaware that this dance is being photographed."

A reed flute joined the tambourine, and a twanging stringed instrument came in behind it. The girl turned slowly on one foot, the other raised with knee bent.

Francine watched in rapt silence. The dancing girl made short staccato hops, the tambourine jerking in front of her.

"It is reminiscent of some of the material on the Norse sagas," said Ohashi. "Battle with swords. Note the thrust and parry."

She nodded. "Yes." The dance stamped onward, then: "Wait! Rerun that last section."

Ohashi obeyed.

It started with a symbolic trek on camel-back: swaying, undulating. The dancing girl expressed longing for her warrior. *How suggestive the motions of her hands along her hips,* thought Francine. With a feeling of abrupt shock, she recalled seeing almost the exact gesture from one of the films of the Galactics. "There's one!" she cried.

"The hands on the hips," said Ohashi. "I was just about to stop the reel." He shut off the film, searched through the notebooks around him until he found the correct reference.

"I think it was one of Zak's films," said Francine.

"Yes. Here it is." Ohashi brought up a reel, looked at the scene identifications. He placed the film can on a large stack behind him, restarted the film of Oriental dances.

Three hours and ten minutes later they put the film back in its can.

"How many new comparisons do you make it?" asked Ohashi.

"Five," she said. "That makes one hundred and six in all!" Francine leafed through her notes. "There was the motion of the hands on the hips. I call that one sensual pleasure."

Ohashi lighted a pipe, spoke through a cloud of smoke. "The others: How have you labeled them?"

"Well, I've just put a note on the motions of one of the Galactics and then the commentator's remarks from this dance film. Chopping motion of the hand ties to the end of Sobàya's first dream: *'Now, I awaken!'* Undulation of the body ties in with swaying of date palms in the desert wind. Stamping of the foot goes with Torak dismounting from his steed. Lifting hands, palms up—that goes with Ali offering his soul to God in prayer before battle."

"Do you want to see this latest film from the ship?" asked Ohashi. He glanced at his wristwatch. "Or shall we get a bite to eat first?"

She waved a hand distractedly. "The film. I'm not hungry. The film." She looked up. "I keep feeling that there's something I should remember . . . something . . ." She shook her head.

"Think about it a few minutes," said Ohashi. "I'm going to send out these other films to be cut and edited according to our selections. And I'll have some sandwiches sent in while I'm at it."

Francine rubbed at her forehead. "All right."

Ohashi gathered up a stack of film cans, left the room. He knocked out his pipe on a "No Smoking" sign beside the door as he left.

"Consonants," whispered Francine. "The ancient alphabets were almost exclusively made up of consonants. Vowels came later. They were the softeners, the swayers." She chewed at her lower lip. "Language constricts the *ways* you can think." She rubbed at her forehead. "Oh, if I only had Bob's ability with languages!"

She tapped her fingers on the chair arm. "It has something to do with our emphasis on *things* rather than on people and the things people do. Every Indo-European language is the same on that score. If only . . ."

"Talking to yourself?" It was a masculine voice, startling her because she had not heard the door open.

Francine jerked upright, turned towards the door. Dr. Irving Langsmith, chief of the American Division of the Germanic-Root team, stood just inside, closing the door.

"Haven't seen you for a couple of days," he said. "We got your note that you were indisposed." He looked around the room, then at the clutter on the floor beside the chairs.

Francine blushed.

Dr. Langsmith crossed to the chair Ohashi had occupied, sat down. He was a gray-haired runt of a man with a heavily seamed face, small features—a gnome figure with hard eyes. He had the reputation of an organizer and politician with more drive than genius. He pulled a stubby pipe from his pocket, lighted it.

"I probably should have cleared this through channels," she said. "But I had visions of it getting bogged down in red tape, especially with Hiko . . . I mean, with another team represented in this project."

"Quite all right," said Langsmith. "We knew what you were up to within a couple of hours. Now, we want to know what you've discovered. Dr. Ohashi looked pretty excited when he left here a bit ago."

Her eyes brightened. "I think we're on to something," she said. "We've compared the Galactics' movements to known symbolism from primitive dances."

Dr. Langsmith chuckled. "That's very interesting, my dear, but surely you . . ."

"No, really!" she said. "We've found one hundred and six points of comparison, almost exact duplication of movements!"

"Dances? Are you trying to tell me that . . ."

"I know it sounds strange," she said, "but we . . ."

"Even if you *have* found exact points of comparison, that means nothing," said Langsmith. "These are *aliens* . . . from another world. You've no right to assume that their language development would follow the same pattern as ours has."

"But they're humanoid!" she said. "Don't you believe that language started as the unconscious shaping of the *speech* organs to imitate *bodily* gestures?"

"It's highly likely," said Langsmith.

"We can make quite a few pretty safe assumptions about them," she said. "For one thing, they apparently have a rather high standard of civilization to be able to construct—"

"Let's not labor the obvious," interrupted Langsmith, a little impatiently.

Francine studied the team chief a moment, said: "Did you ever hear how Marshal Foch planned his military campaigns?"

Langsmith puffed on his pipe, took it out of his mouth. "Uh . . . are you suggesting that a military . . ."

"He wrote out the elements of his problem on a sheet of paper," said Francine. "At the top of the paper went the lowest common denominator. There, he wrote: '*Problem—To beat the Germans.*' Quite simple. Quite obvious. But oddly enough '*beating the enemy*' has frequently been overlooked by commanders who got too involved in complicated maneuvers."

"Are you suggesting that the Galactics are enemies?"

She shook her head indignantly. "I am *not*! I'm suggesting that language is primarily an instinctive social reflex. The least common denominator of a social problem is a human being. One single human being. And here we are all involved with getting this thing into mathematical equations and neat word frequency primarily oral!"

"But you've been researching a visual . . ."

"Yes! But only as it modifies the sounds." She leaned towards Langsmith. "Dr. Langsmith, I believe that this language is a *flexional* language with the flexional endings and root changes contained entirely in the bodily movements."

"Hmmmmmmm." Langsmith studied the smoke spiraling ceilingwards from his pipe. "Fascinating idea!"

"We can assume that this is a highly standardized language," said Francine. "Basing the assumption on their high standard of civilization. The two usually go hand in hand."

Langsmith nodded.

"Then the gestures, the sounds would tend to be ritual," she said.

"Mmmmm-hmmmm."

"Then . . . may we have the help to go into this idea the way it deserves?" she asked.

"I'll take it up at the next top staff meeting," said Langsmith. He got to his feet. "Don't get your hopes up. This'll have to be submitted to the electronic computers. It probably has been cross-checked and rejected in some other problem."

She looked up at him, dismayed. "But . . . Dr. Langsmith . . . a computer's no better than what's put into it. I'm certain that we're stepping out into a region here where we'll have to build up a whole new approach to language."

"Now, don't you worry," said Langsmith. He frowned. "No . . . don't worry about *this*."

"Shall we go ahead with what we're doing then?" she asked. "I mean—do we have permission to?"

"Yes, yes . . . or course." Langsmith wiped his mouth with the back of his hand. "General Speidel has called a special meeting tomorrow morning. I'd like to have you attend. I'll send somebody to pick you up." He waved a hand at the litter around Francine. "Carry on, now." There was a pathetic emptiness to the way he put his pipe in his mouth and left the room. Francine stared at the closed door.

She felt herself trembling, and recognized that she was deathly afraid. *Why?* she asked herself. *What have I sensed to make me afraid?*

Presently, Ohashi came in carrying a paper bag.

"Saw Langsmith going out," he said. "What did he want?"

"He wanted to know what we're doing."

Ohashi paused before his chair. "Did you tell him?"

"Yes. I asked for help." She shook her head. "He wouldn't commit himself."

"I brought ham sandwiches," said Ohashi.

Francine's chin lifted abruptly. "Defeated!" she said. "That's it! He acted completed defeated!"

"What?"

"I've been trying to puzzle through the strange way Langsmith was acting. He just radiated defeat."

Ohashi handed her a sandwich. "Better brace yourself for a shock," he said. "I ran into Tsu Ong, liaison officer for our delegation . . . in the cafeteria." The Japanese raised the sandwich sack over his chair, dropped it into the seat with a curious air of preciseness. "The Russians are pressing for a combined attack on the Galactic ship to wrest their secret from them by force."

Francine buried her face in her hands. "The fools!" she whispered. "Oh, the fools!" Abruptly, sobs shook her. She found herself crying with the same uncontrollable racking that had possessed her when she'd learned of her husband's death.

Ohashi waited silently.

The tears subsided. Control returned. She swallowed, said: "I'm sorry."

"Do not be sorry." He put a hand on her shoulder. "Shall we knock off for the night?"

She put her hand over his, shook her head. "No. Let's look at the latest films from the ship."

"As you wish." Ohashi pulled away, threaded a new film into the projector.

Presently, the screen came alive to a blue-gray alcove filled with pale light: one of the "class" rooms in the spaceship. A squat, green-skinned figure stood in the center of the room. Beside the Galactic was the pedestal-footed projection board that all five used to illustrate their "lectures." The board displayed a scene of a wide blue lake, reeds along the shore stirring to a breeze.

The Galactic swayed. His face moved like a ripple of water. He said: "Ahon'atu'uklah'shoginai' eástruru." The green arms moved up and down, undulating. The webbed hands came out, palms facing and almost touching, began chopping from the wrists: up, down, up, down, up, down . . .

On the projection board the scene switched to an underwater view: myriad swimming shapes coming closer, closer—large-eyed fish creatures with long ridged tails.

"Five will get you ten," said Ohashi. "Those are the young of this Galactic race. Notice the ridge."

"Tadpoles," said Francine.

The swimming shapes darted through orange shadows and into a space of cold green—then up to splash on the surface, and again down into the cool green. It was a choreographic swinging, lifting, dipping, swaying— lovely in its synchronized symmetry.

"Chiruru'uklia'a'agudav'iaá," said the Galactic. His body undulated like the movements of the swimming creatures. The green hands touched his thighs, slipped upward until elbows were level with shoulders.

"The maiden in the Oriental dance," said Francine.

Now, the hands came out, palms up, in a gesture curiously suggestive of giving. The Galactic said: "Pluainumiuri!" in a single burst of sound that fell on their ears like an explosion.

"It's like a distorted version of the ritual dances we've been watching," said Ohashi.

"I've a hunch," said Francine. "Feminine intuition. The repeated vowels: They could be an adverbial emphasis, like our word *very*. Where it says '*a-a-a*,' note the more intense gestures."

She followed another passage, nodding her head to the gestures. "Hiko, could this be a constructed language? Artificial?"

"The thought has occurred to me," said Ohashi.

Abruptly the projector light dimmed, the action slowed. All lights went out. They heard a dull, booming roar in the distance, a staccato rattling of shots. Feet pounded along the corridor outside the room.

Francine sat in stunned silence.

Ohashi said: "Stay here, please. I will have a look around to see what . . ."

The door banged open and a flashlight beam stabbed into the room, momentarily blinding them.

"Everything all right in here?" boomed a masculine voice.

They made out a white MP helmet visible behind the light.

"Yes," said Ohashi. "What is happening?"

"Somebody blew up a tower to the main transmission line from McNary Dam. Then there was an attempt to breach our security blockade on the south. Everything will be back to normal shortly." The light turned away.

"Who?" asked Francine.

"Some crazy civilians," said the MP. "We'll have the emergency power on in a minute. Just stay in this room until we give the all-clear." He left, closing the door.

They heard a rattle of machine-gun fire. Another explosion shook the building. Voices shouted.

"We are witnessing the end of a world," said Ohashi.

"Our world ended when that spaceship set down here," she said.

Abruptly the lights came on: dimly, then brighter. The projector resumed its whirring. Ohashi turned it off.

Somebody walked down the corridor outside, rapped on the door, said: "All clear." The footsteps receded down the hall, and they heard another rapping, a fainter "All clear."

"Civilians," she said. "What do you supposed they wanted so desperately to do a thing like that?"

"They are a symptom of the general sickness," said Ohashi. "One way to remove a threat is to destroy it—even if you destroy yourself in the process. These civilians are only a minor symptom."

"The Russians are the big symptom then," she said.

"Every major government is a *big* symptom right now," he said.

"I . . . I think I'll get back to my room," she said. "Let's take up again tomorrow morning. Eight o'clock all right?"

"Quite agreeable," said Ohashi. "If there is a tomorrow."

"Don't *you* get that way, too," she said, and she took a quavering breath. "I refuse to give up."

Ohashi bowed. He was suddenly very Oriental. "There is a primitive saying of the Ainu," he said: *"The world ends every night . . . and begins anew every morning."*

It was a room dug far underground beneath the Ordnance Depot, originally for storage of atomics. The walls were lead. It was an oblong space: about thirty by fifteen feet, with a very low ceiling. Two trestle tables had been butted end-to-end in the center of the room to form a single long surface. A series of green-shaded lights suspended above this table gave the scene an odd resemblance to a gambling room. The effect was heightened by the set look to the shoulders of the men sitting in spring-bottom chairs around the table. There was a scattering of uniforms: Air Force, Army, Marines; plus hard-faced civilians in expensive suits.

Dr. Langsmith occupied a space at the middle of one of the table's sides and directly across from the room's only door. His gnome features were locked in a frown of concentration. He puffed rhythmically at the stubby pipe like a witchman creating an oracle smoke.

A civilian across the table from Langsmith addressed a two-star general seated beside the team chief: "General Speidel, I think this is too delicate a spot to risk a woman."

Speidel grunted. He was a thin man with a high, narrow face: an aristocratic face that radiated granite convictions and stubborn pride. There was an air about him of spring steel under tension and vibrating to a chord that dominated the room.

"Our choice is limited," said Langsmith. "Very few of our personnel have consistently taken wheeled carts into the ship *and* consistently taken a position close to that force barrier or whatever it is."

Speidel glanced at his wristwatch. "What's keeping them?"

"She may already have gone to breakfast," said Langsmith.

"Be better if we got her in here hungry and jumpy," said the civilian.

"Are you sure you can handle her, Smitty?" asked Speidel.

Langsmith took his pipe from his mouth, peered into the stem as though the answer were to be found there. "We've got her pretty well analyzed," he said. "She's a recent widow, you know. Bound to still have a rather active deathwish structure."

There was a buzzing of whispered conversation from a group of officers at one end of the table. Speidel tapped his fingers on the arm of his chair.

Presently the door opened. Francine entered. A hand reached in from outside, closed the door behind her.

"Ah, there you are, Dr. Millar," said Langsmith. He got to his feet. There was a scuffling sound around the table as the others arose. Langsmith pointed to an empty chair diagonally across from him. "Sit down, please."

Francine advanced into the light. She felt intimidated, knew she showed it, and the realization filled her with a feeling of bitterness tinged with angry resentment. The ride down the elevator from the surface had been an experience she never wanted to repeat. It had seemed many times longer than it actually was—like a descent into Dante's Inferno.

She nodded to Langsmith, glanced covertly at the others, took the indicated chair. It was a relief to get the weight off her trembling knees, and she momentarily relaxed, only to tense up again as the others resumed their seats. She put her hands on the table, immediately withdrew them to hold them clasped tightly in her lap.

"Why was I brought here like a prisoner?" she demanded.

Langsmith appeared honestly startled. "But I told you last night that I'd send somebody for you."

Speidel chuckled easily. "Some of our Security boys are a little grim-faced," he said. "I hope they didn't frighten you."

She took a deep breath, began to relax. "Is this about the request I made last night?" she asked. "I mean, for help in this new line of research?"

"In a way," said Langsmith. "But first I'd like to have you answer a question for me." He pursed his lips. "Uh . . . I've never asked one of my people for just a wild guess before, but I'm going to break that rule with you. What's your guess as to why these Galactics are here?"

"Guess?"

"Logical assumption, then," he said.

She looked down at her hands. "We've all speculated, of course. They might be scientists investigating us for reasons of their own."

"Damnation!" barked the civilian beside her. Then: "Sorry, ma'am. But that's the pap we keep using to pacify the public."

"And we aren't keeping them very well pacified," said Langsmith. "That group that stormed us last night called themselves the *Sons of Truth*! They had thermite bombs, and were going to attack the spaceship."

"How foolish," she whispered. "How pitiful."

"Go on with your guessing, Dr. Millar," said Speidel.

She glanced at the general, again looked at her hands. "There's the military's idea—that they want Earth for a strategic base in some kind of space war."

"It could be," said Speidel.

"They could be looking for more living space for their own kind," she said.

"In which case, what happens to the native population?" asked Langsmith.

"They would either be exterminated or enslaved, I'm afraid. But the Galactics could be commercial traders of some sort, interested in our art forms, our animals for their zoos, our archaeology, our spices, our . . ." She broke off, shrugged. "How do we know what they may be doing on the side . . . secretly?"

"Exactly!" said Speidel. He glanced sidelong at Langsmith. "She talks pretty level-headed, Smitty."

"But I don't believe any of these things," she said.

"What is it you believe?" asked Speidel.

"I believe they're just what they represent themselves to be—representatives of a powerful Galactic culture that is immeasurably superior to our own."

"Powerful, all right!" It was a marine officer at the far end of the table. "The way they cleaned off Eniwetok and swept our satellites out of the skies!"

"Do you think there's a possibility they could be concealing their true motives?" asked Langsmith.

"A possibility, certainly."

"Have you ever watched a confidence man in action?" asked Langsmith.

"I don't believe so. But you're not seriously suggesting that these . . ." She shook her head. "Impossible."

"The *mark* seldom gets wise until it's too late," said Langsmith.

She looked puzzled. "Mark?"

"The fellow the confidence men choose for a victim." Langsmith relighted his pipe, extinguished the match by shaking it. "Dr. Millar, we have a very painful disclosure to make to you."

She straightened, feeling a sudden icy chill in her veins at the stillness in the room.

"Your husband's death was not an accident," said Langsmith.

She gasped, and turned deathly pale.

"In the six months before this spaceship landed, there were some twenty-eight mysterious deaths," said Langsmith. "More than that, really, because innocent bystanders died, too. These accidents had a curious similarity: In each instance there was a fatality of a foremost expert in the field of language, cryptoanalysis, semantics . . ."

"The people who might have solved this problem died before the problem was even presented," said Speidel. "Don't you think that's a curious coincidence?"

She was unable to speak.

"In one instance there was a survivor," said Langsmith. "A British jet transport crashed off Ceylon, killing Dr. Ramphit U. The lone survivor, the co-pilot, said a brilliant beam of light came from the sky overhead and sliced off the port wing. Then it cut the cabin in half!"

Francine put a hand to her throat. Langsmith's cautious hand movements suddenly fascinated her.

"Twenty-eight air crashes?" she whispered.

"No. Two were auto crashes." Langsmith puffed a cloud of smoke before his face.

Her throat felt sore. She swallowed, said: "But how can you be sure of that?"

"It's circumstantial evidence, yes," said Speidel. He spoke with thin-lipped precision. "But there's more. For the past four months all astronomical activity of our nation has been focused on the near heavens, including the moon. Our attention was drawn to evidence of activity near the moon crater Theophilus. We have been able to make out the landing rockets of more than five hundred spacecraft!"

"What do you think of that?" asked Langsmith. He nodded behind his smokescreen.

She could only stare at him; her lips ashen.

"These *frogs* have massed an invasion fleet on the moon!" snapped Speidel. "It's obvious!"

They're lying to me! she thought. *Why this elaborate pretense?* She shook her head, and something her husband had once said leapt unbidden into her mind: *"Language clutches at us with unseen fingers. It conditions us to the way others are thinking. Through language, we impose upon each other our ways of looking at things."*

Speidel leaned forward. "We have more than a hundred atomic warheads aimed at that moon-base! One of those warheads will do the job if it gets through!" He hammered a fist on the table. "But first we have to capture this ship here!"

Why are they telling me all this? she asked herself. She drew in a ragged breath, said: "Are you sure you're right?"

"Of course we're sure!" Speidel leaned back, lowered his voice. "Why else would they insist we learn their language? The first thing a conqueror does is impose his language on his new slaves!"

"No . . . no, wait," she said. "That only applies to recent history. You're getting language mixed up with patriotism because of our own imperial history. Bob always said that such misconceptions are a serious hindrance to sound historical scholarship."

"We know what we're talking about, Dr. Millar," said Speidel.

"You're suspicious of language because our imperialism went hand in hand with our language," she said.

Speidel looked at Langsmith. "You talk to her."

"If there actually were communication in the sounds these Galactics make, you know we'd have found it by now," said Langsmith. "You know it!"

She spoke in sudden anger: "I don't know it! In fact, I feel that we're on the verge of solving their language with this new approach we've been working on."

"Oh, come now!" said Speidel. "Do you mean that after our finest cryptographers have worked over this thing for seven months, you disagree with them entirely?"

"No, no, let her say her piece," said Langsmith.

"We've tapped a new source of information in attacking this problem," she said. "Primitive dances."

"Dances?" Speidel looked shocked.

"Yes. I think the Galactics' gestures may be their adjectives and adverbs—the full emotional content of their language."

"Emotion!" snapped Speidel. "Emotion isn't language!"

She repressed a surge of anger, said: "We're dealing with something completely outside our previous experience. We have to discard old ideas. We know that the habits of a native tongue set up a person's speaking responses. In fact you can define language as the system of habits you reveal when you speak."

Speidel tapped his fingers on the table, stared at the door behind Francine.

She ignored his nervous distraction, said: "The Galactics use almost the full range of implosive and glottal stops with a wide selection of vowel sounds: fricatives, plosives, voiced and unvoiced. And we note an apparent lack of the usual interfering habits you find in normal speech."

"This isn't normal speech!" blurted Speidel. "Those are nonsense sounds!" He shook his head. "Emotions!"

"All right," she said. "Emotions! We're pretty certain that language begins with emotions—pure emotional actions. The baby pushes away the plate of unwanted food."

"You're wasting our time!" barked Speidel.

"I didn't ask to come down here," she said.

"Please." Langsmith put a hand on Speidel's arm. "Let Dr. Millar have her say."

"Emotion," muttered Speidel.

"Every spoken language of earth has migrated away from emotion," said Francine.

"Can you write an emotion on paper?" demanded Speidel.

"That does it," she said. "That really tears it! You're blind! You say language has to be written down. That's part of the magic! Your mind is tied in little knots by academic tradition! Language, general, is primarily oral! People like you, though, want to make it into ritual noise!"

"I didn't come down here for an egg-head argument!" snapped Speidel.

"Let me handle this, please," said Langsmith. He made a mollifying gesture toward Francine. "Please continue."

She took a deep breath. "I'm sorry I snapped," she said. She smiled. "I think we let emotion get the best of us."

Speidel frowned.

"I was talking about language moving away from emotion," she said. "Take Japanese, for example. Instead of saying, 'Thank you' they say

'Katajikenai'—'I am insulted.' Or they say, 'Kino doku' which means 'This poisonous feeling!' " She held up her hands. "This is ritual exclusion of showing emotion. Our Indo-European languages—especially Anglo-Saxon tongues—are moving the same way. We seem to think that emotion isn't quite nice, that . . ."

"It tells you nothing!" barked Speidel.

She forced down the anger that threatened to overwhelm her. "If you can read the emotional signs," she said, "they reveal if a speaker is telling the truth. That's all, general. They just tell you if you're getting at the truth. Any good psychologist knows this, general. Freud said it: 'If you try to conceal your feelings, every pore oozes betrayal.' You seem to think that the opposite is true."

"Emotions! Dancing!" Speidel pushed his chair back. "Smitty, I've had as much of this as I can take."

"Just a minute," said Langsmith. "Now, Dr. Millar, I wanted you to have your say because we've already considered these points. Long ago. You're interested in the gestures. You say this is a dance of emotions. Other experts say with equal emphasis that these gestures are ritual combat! Freud, indeed! They ooze betrayal. This chopping gesture they make with the right hand"—he chopped the air in illustration—"is identical to the karate or judo chop for breaking the human neck!"

Francine shook her head, put a hand to her throat. She was momentarily overcome by a feeling of uncertainty.

Langsmith said: "That outward thrust they make with one hand: That's the motion of a sword being shoved into an opponent! They ooze betrayal all right!"

She looked from Langsmith to Speidel, back to Langsmith. A man to her right cleared his throat.

Langsmith said: "I've just given you two examples. We have hundreds more. Every analysis we've made has come up with the same answer: treachery! The pattern's as old as time: Offer a reward; pretend friendship; get the innocent lamb's attention on your empty hand while you poise the axe in your other hand!"

Could I be wrong? she wondered. *Have we been duped by these Galactics?* Her lips trembled. She fought to control them, whispered: "Why are you telling me these things?"

"Aren't you at all interested in revenge against the creatures who murdered your husband?" asked Speidel.

"I don't know that they murdered him!" She blinked back tears. "You're trying to confuse me!" And a favorite saying of her husband's came into her mind: *"A conference is a group of people making a difficult job out of what one person could do easily."* The room suddenly seemed too close and oppressive.

"Why have I been dragged into this conference?" she demanded. "Why?"

"We were hoping you'd assist us in capturing that spaceship," said Langsmith.

"Me? Assist you in . . ."

"Someone has to get a bomb past the force screens at the door—the ones that keep sand and dirt out of the ship. We've got to have a bomb inside."

"But why me?"

"They're used to seeing you wheel in the master recorder on that cart," said Langsmith. "We thought of putting a bomb in . . ."

"No!"

"This has gone far enough," said Speidel. He took a deep breath, started to rise.

"Wait," said Langsmith.

"She obviously has no feelings of patriotic responsibility," said Speidel. "We're wasting our time."

Langsmith said: "The Galactics are used to seeing her with that cart. If we change now, they're liable to become suspicious."

"We'll set up some other plan, then," said Speidel. "As far as I'm concerned, we can write off any possibility of further cooperation from her."

"You're little boys playing a game," said Francine. "This isn't an exclusive American problem. This is a human problem that involves every nation on Earth."

"That ship is on United States soil," said Speidel.

"Which happens to be on the only planet controlled by the human species," she said. "We ought to be sharing everything with the other teams, pooling information and ideas to get at every scrap of knowledge."

"We'd all like to be idealists," said Speidel. "But there's no room for idealism where our survival is concerned. These *frogs* have full space travel, apparently between the stars—not just satellites and moon rockets. If we get their ship we can enforce peace on our own terms."

"National survival," she said. "But it's our survival as a species that's at stake!"

Speidel turned to Langsmith. "This is one of our more spectacular failures, Smitty. We'll have to put her under close surveillance."

Langsmith puffed furiously on his pipe. A cloud of pale blue smoke screened his head. "I'm ashamed of you, Dr. Millar," he said.

She jumped to her feet, allowing her anger full scope at last. "You must think I'm a rotten psychologist!" she snapped. "You've been lying to me since I set foot in here!" She shot a bitter glance at Speidel. "Your gestures gave you away! The noncommunicative emotional gestures, general!"

"What's she talking about?" demanded Speidel.

"You said different things with your mouths than you said with your bodies," she explained. "That means you were lying to me—concealing something vital you didn't want me to know about."

"She's insane!" barked Speidel.

"There wasn't any survivor of a plane crash in Ceylon," she said. "There probably wasn't even the plane crash you described."

Speidel froze to sudden stillness, spoke through thin lips: "Has there been a security leak? Good Lord!"

"Look at Dr. Langsmith there!" she said. "Hiding behind that pipe! And you, general: moving your mouth no more than absolutely necessary to speak—trying to hide your real feelings! Oozing betrayal!"

"Get her out of here!" barked Speidel.

"You're all logic and no intuition!" she shouted. "No understanding of feeling and art! Well, general: Go back to your computers, but remember this—you can't build a machine that thinks like a man! You can't feed emotion into an electronic computer and get back anything except numbers! Logic, to you, general!"

"I said get her out of here!" shouted Speidel. He rose half out of his chair, turned to Langsmith who sat in pale silence. "And I want a thorough investigation! I want to know where the security leak was that put her wise to our plans."

"Watch yourself!" snapped Langsmith.

Speidel took two deep breaths, sank back.

They're insane, thought Francine. *Insane and pushed into a corner. With that kind of fragmentation they could slip into catatonia or violence.* She felt weak and afraid.

Others around the table had arisen. Two civilians moved up beside Francine. "Shall we lock her up, general?" asked one.

Speidel hesitated.

Langsmith spoke first: "No. Just keep her under very close surveillance. If we locked her up, it would arouse questions that we don't want to answer."

Speidel glowered at Francine. "If you give us away, I'll have you shot!" He motioned to have her taken out of the room.

When she emerged from the headquarters building, Francine's mind still whirled. *Lies!* she thought. *All lies!*

She felt the omnipresent sand grate under her feet. Dust hazed the concourse between her position on the steps and the spaceship a hundred yards away. The morning sun already had burned off the night chill of the desert. Heat devils danced over the dun surface of the ship.

Francine ignored the security agent loitering a few steps behind her, glanced at her wristwatch: nine-twenty. *Hiko will be wondering what's happened to me,* she thought. *We were supposed to get started by eight.* Hopelessness gripped her mind. The spaceship looming over the end of the concourse appeared like a malignant growth—an evil thing crouched ready to envelope and smother her.

Could that fool general be right? The thought came to her mind unbidden. She shook her head. *No! He was lying! But why did he want me to . . .* Delayed realization broke off the thought. *They wanted me to take a small bomb inside the ship, but there was no mention of my escaping! I'd have had to stay with the cart and the bomb to allay suspicions. My God! Those beasts expected me to commit suicide for them! They wanted me to blame the Galactics for Bob's death! They tried to build a lie in my mind until I'd fall in with their plan. It's hard enough to die for an ideal, but to give up your life for a lie . . .*

Anger coursed through her. She stopped on the steps, stood there shivering. A new feeling of futility replaced the anger. Tears blurred her vision. *What can one lone woman do against such ruthless schemers?*

Through her tears, she saw movement on the concourse: a man in civilian clothes crossing from right to left. Her mind registered the movement with only partial awareness: *Man stops, points.* She was suddenly alert, tears gone, following the direction of the civilian's extended right arm, hearing his voice shout: "Hey! Look at that!"

A thin needle of an aircraft stitched a hurtling line across the watery desert sky. It banked, arrowed toward the spaceship. Behind it roared an airforce jet—delta wings vibrating, sun flashing off polished metal. Tracers laced out towards the airship.

Someone's attacking the spaceship! she thought. *It's a Russian ICBM!*

But the needle braked abruptly, impossibly, over the spaceship. Behind it, the air force jet's engine died, and there was only the eerie whistling of air burning across its wings.

Gently, the needle lowered itself into a fold of the spaceship.

It's one of theirs—the Galactics', she realized. *Why is it coming here now? Do they suspect attack? Is that some kind of reinforcement?*

Deprived of its power, the jet staggered, skimmed out to a dust-geyser, belly-landing in the alkali flats. Sirens screamed as emergency vehicles raced toward it.

The confused sounds gave Francine a sudden feeling of nausea. She took a deep breath and stepped down to the concourse, moving without conscious determination, her thoughts in a turmoil. The grating sand beneath her feet was like an emery surface rubbing her nerves. She was acutely conscious of an acrid, burning odor, and she realized with a sudden stab of alarm that her security guard still waited behind her on the steps of the administration building.

Vaguely, she heard voices babbling in the building doorways on both sides of the concourse—people coming out to stare at the spaceship and off across the flats where red trucks clustered around the jet.

A pebble had worked its way into her right shoe. Her mind registered it, rejected an urge to stop and remove the irritant. An idea was trying to surface in her mind. Momentarily she was distracted by a bee humming across her path. Quite inanely her mind dwelt on the thought that the insect was too commonplace for this moment. A mental drunkenness made her giddy. She felt both elated and terrified. *Danger! Yes: terrible danger,* she thought.

Obliteration for the entire human race. But something had to be done. She started to run. . . .

An explosion rocked the concourse, threw her stumbling to her hands and knees. Sand burned against her palms. Dumb instinct brought her back to her feet. Another explosion—farther away to the right, behind the buildings. Bitter smoke swept across the concourse. Abruptly men lurched from behind the buildings on the right, slogging through the sand toward the spaceship.

Civilians! Possibly—and yet they moved with the purposeful unity of soldiers.

It was like a dream scene to Francine. The men carried weapons. She stopped, saw the gleam of sunlight on metal, heard the peculiar crunch-crunch of men running in sand. Through a dreamy haze she recognized one of the runners: Zakheim. He carried a large black box on his shoulders. His red hair flamed out in the group like a target.

The Russians! she thought. *They've started their attack! If our people join them now, it's the end!*

A machine-gun stuttered somewhere to her right. Dust puffs walked across the concourse, swept into the running figures. Men collapsed, but others still slogged toward the spaceship. An explosion lifted the leaders, sent them sprawling. Again, the machine-gun chattered. Dark figures lay on the sand like thrown dominoes. But still a few continued their mad charge.

MPs in American uniforms ran out from between the buildings on the right. The leaders carried submachine-guns.

We're stopping the attack, thought Francine. But she knew the change of tactics did not mean a rejection of violence by Speidel and the others. It was only a move to keep the Russians from taking the lead. She clenched her fists, ignored the fact that she stood exposed—a lone figure in the middle of the concourse. Her senses registered an eerie feeling of unreality.

Machine-guns renewed their chatter and then—abrupt silence. But now the last of the Russians had fallen. Pursuing MPs staggered. Several stopped, wrenched at their guns.

Francine's shock gave way to cold rage. She moved forward, slowly at first and then striding. Off to the left someone shouted: "Hey! Lady! Get down!" She ignored the voice.

There on the sand ahead was Zakheim's pitiful crumpled figure. A gritty redness spread around his chest.

Someone ran from between the buildings on her left, waved at her to go back. *Hiko!* But she continued her purposeful stride, compelled beyond any conscious willing to stop. She saw the red-headed figure on the sand as though she peered down a tunnel.

Part of her mind registered the fact that Hiko stumbled, slowing his running charge to intercept her. He looked like a man clawing his way through water.

Dear Hiko, she thought. *I have to get to Zak. Poor foolish Zak. That's what was wrong with him the other day at the conference. He knew about this attack and was afraid.*

Something congealed around her feet, spread upward over her ankles, quickly surged over her knees. She could see nothing unusual, but it was as though she had ploughed into a pool of molasses. Every step took terrible effort. The molasses pool moved above her hips, her waist.

So that's why Hiko and the MPs are moving so slowly, she thought. *It's a defensive weapon from the ship. Must be.*

Zakheim's sprawled figure was only three steps away from her now. She wrenched her way through the congealed air, panting with the exertion. Her muscles ached from the effort. She knelt beside Zakheim. Ignoring the blood that stained her skirt she took up one of his outstretched hands, felt for a pulse. Nothing. Now, she recognized the marks on his jacket. They were bullet holes. A machine-gun burst had caught him across the chest. He was dead. She thought of the big garrulous redhead, so full of blooming life only minutes before. *Poor foolish Zak.* She put his hand down gently, shook the tears from her eyes. A terrible rage swelled in her.

She sensed Ohashi nearby, struggling toward her, heard him gasp: "Is Zak dead?"

Tears dripped unheeded from her eyes. She nodded. "Yes, he is." And she thought: *I'm not crying for Zak. I'm crying for myself . . . for all of us . . . so foolish, so determined, so blind . . .*

"EARTH PEOPLE!" The voice roared from the spaceship, cutting across all thought, stilling all emotion into a waiting fear, "WE HAD HOPED YOU COULD LEARN TO COMMUNICATE!" roared the voice. "YOU HAVE FAILED!"

Vibrant silence.

Thoughts that had been struggling for recognition began surging to the surface of Francine's mind. She felt herself caught in the throes of a mental earthquake, her soul brought to a crisis as sharp as that of giving birth. The crashing words had broken through a last barrier in her mind. *"COMMU-NICATE!"* At last she understood the meaning of the ultimatum.

But was it too late?

"No!" she screamed. She surged to her feet, shook a fist at the ship. "Here's one who didn't fail! I know what you meant!" She shook both fists at the ship. "See my hate!"

Against the almost tangible congealing of air she forced her way toward the now silent ship, thrust out her left hand toward the dead figures on the sand all around her! "You killed these poor fools! What did you expect from them? You did this! You forced them into a corner!"

The doors of the spaceship opened. Five green-skinned figures emerged. They stopped, stood staring at her, their shoulders slumped. Simultaneously, Francine felt the thickened air relax its hold upon her. She strode forward, tears coursing down her cheeks.

"You made them afraid!" she shouted. "What else could they do? The fearful can't think."

Sobs overcame her. She felt violence shivering in her muscles. There was a terrible desire in her—a need to get her hands on those green figures, to shake them, hurt them, "I hope you're proud of what you've done."

"QUIET!" boomed the voice from the ship.

"I will not!" she screamed. She shook her head, feeling the wildness that smothered her inhibitions. "Oh, I know you were right about communicating . . . but you were wrong, too. You didn't have to resort to violence."

The voice from the ship intruded on a softer tone, all the more compelling for the change: "Please?" There was a delicate sense of pleading to the word.

Francine broke off. She felt that she had just awakened from a lifelong daze, but that this clarity of thought-cum-action was a delicate thing she could lose in the wink of an eye.

"We did what we had to do," said the voice. "You see our five representatives there?"

Francine focused on the slump-shouldered Galactics. They looked defeated, radiating sadness. The gaping door of the ship a few paces behind was like a mouth ready to swallow them.

"Those five are among the eight hundred survivors of a race that once numbered six billion," said the voice.

Francine felt Ohashi move up beside her, glanced sidelong at him, then back to the Galactics. Behind her, she heard a low mumbling murmur of many voices. The slow beginning of reaction to her emotional outburst made her sway. A sob caught in her throat.

The voice from the ship rolled on: "This once great race did not realize the importance of unmistakable communication. They entered space in that sick condition—hating, fearing, fighting. There was appalling bloodshed on their side and—ours—before we could subdue them."

A scuffing sound intruded as the five green-skinned figures shuffled forward. They were trembling, and Francine saw glistening drops of wetness below their crests. Their eyes blinked. She sensed the aura of sadness about them, and new tears welled in her eyes.

"The eight hundred survivors—to atone for the errors of their race and to earn the right of further survival—developed a new language," said the voice from the ship. "It is, perhaps, the ultimate language. They have made themselves the masters of all languages to serve as our interpreters." There was a long pause, then: "Think very carefully, Mrs. Millar. Do you know why they are our interpreters?"

The held breath of silence hung over them. Francine swallowed past the thick tightness in her throat. This was the moment that could spell the end of the human race, or could open new doors for them—and she knew it.

"Because they cannot lie," she husked.

"Then you have truly learned," said the voice. "My original purpose in coming down here just now was to direct the sterilization of your planet. We thought that your military preparations were a final evidence of your failure. We see now that this was merely the abortive desperation of a minority. We have acted in haste. Our apologies."

The green-skinned Galactics shuffled forward, stopped two paces from Francine. Their ridged crests drooped, shoulders sagged.

"Slay us," croaked one. His eyes turned toward the dead men on the sand around them.

Francine took a deep, shuddering breath, wiped at her damp eyes. Again she felt the bottomless sense of futility. "Did it have to be this way?" she whispered.

The voice from the ship answered: "Better this than a sterile planet—the complete destruction of your race. Do not blame our interpreters. If a race can learn to communicate, it can be saved. Your race can be saved. First we had to make certain you held the potential. There will be pain in the new ways, no doubt. Many still will try to fight us, but you have not yet erupted fully into space where it would be more difficult to control your course."

"Why couldn't you have just picked some of us, tested a few of us?" she demanded. "Why did you put this terrible pressure on the entire world?"

"What if we had picked the wrong ones?" asked the voice. "How could we be certain with a strange race such as yours that we had a fair sampling of your highest potential? No. All of you had to have the opportunity to learn of our problem. The pressure was to be certain that your own people chose their best representatives."

Francine thought of the unimaginative rule-book followers who had led the teams. She felt hysteria close to the surface.

So close. So hellishly close!

Ohashi spoke softly beside her: "Francine?"

It was a calming voice that subdued the hysteria. She nodded. A feeling of relief struggled for recognition within her, but it had not penetrated all nerve channels. She felt her hands twitching.

Ohashi said: "They are speaking English with you. What of their language that we were supposed to solve?"

"We leaped to a wrong conclusion, Hiko," she said. "We were asked to communicate. We were supposed to remember our own language—the language we knew in childhood, and that was slowly lost to us through the elevation of reason."

"Ahhhhh," sighed Ohashi.

All anger drained from her now, and she spoke with sadness. "We raised the power of reason, the power of manipulating words, above all other faculties. The written word became our god. We forgot that before words there were actions—that there have always been things beyond words. We forgot that the spoken word preceded the written one. We forgot that the written forms of our letters came from ideographic pictures—that standing behind every letter is an image like an ancient ghost. The image stands for natural movements of the body or of other living things."

"The dances," whispered Ohashi.

"Yes, the dances," she said. "The primitive dances did not forget. And the body did not forget—not really." She lifted her hands, looked at them. "I am my own past. Every incident that ever happened to every ancestor of mine is accumulated within me." She turned, faced Ohashi.

He frowned. "Memory stops at the beginning of your . . ."

"And the body remembers beyond," she said. "It's a different kind of memory: encysted in an overlay of trained responses like the thing we call language. We have to look back to our childhood because all children are primitives. Every cell of a child knows the language of emotional movements—the clutching reflexes, the wails and contortions, the sensuous twistings, the gentle reassurances."

"And you say these people cannot lie," murmured Ohashi.

Francine felt the upsurge of happiness. It was still tainted by the death around her and the pain she knew was yet to come for her people, but the glow was there expanding. "The body," she said, and shook her head at the scowl of puzzlement on Ohashi's face. "The intellect . . ." She broke off, aware that Ohashi had not yet made the complete transition to the new way of communicating, that she was still most likely the only member of her race even aware of the vision of this high plateau of being.

Ohashi shook his head, and sunlight flashed on his glasses. "I'm trying to understand," he said.

"I know you are," she said. "Hiko, all of our Earth languages have a bias toward insanity because they split off the concept of intellect from the concept of body. That's an oversimplification, but it will do for now. You get fragmentation this way, you see? Schizophrenia. These people now—" She gestured toward the silent Galactics. "—they have reunited body and intellect in their communication. A gestalten thing that requires the total being's participation. They cannot lie because that would be to lie to themselves— and this would completely inhibit speech." She shook her head. "Speech is not the word, but it is the only word we have now."

"A paradox," said Ohashi.

She nodded. "The self that is one cannot lie to the self. When body and intellect say the same thing . . . that is truth. When words and wordlessness agree . . . that is truth. You see?"

Ohashi stood frozen before her, eyes glistening behind the thick lenses. He opened his mouth, closed it, then bowed his head. In that moment he was the complete Oriental and Francine felt that she could look through him at all of his ancestry, seeing and understanding every culture and every person that had built to the point of the pyramid here in one person: Hiko Ohashi.

"I see it," he murmured. "It was example they showed. Not words to decipher. Only example for recognition, to touch our memories and call them forth. What great teachers! What great masters of being!"

One of the Galactics stepped closer, gestured toward the area behind Francine. His movements and the intent were clear to her, interpreted through her new understanding.

The Galactic's wide lips moved. "You are being recorded," he said. "It would be an opportune moment to begin the education of your people—since all new things must have a point of birth."

She nodded, steeling herself before turning. *Even with the pain of birth,* she thought. This was the moment that would precipitate the avalanche of change. Without knowing precisely how she would set off this chain reaction, she had no doubt that she would do it. Slowly, she turned, saw the movie cameras, the television lenses, the cone microphones all directed at her. People were pressed up against an invisible wall that drew an arc around the ship's entrance and this charmed circle where she stood. *Part of the ship's defenses,* she thought. *A force field to stop intruders.*

A muted murmuring came from the wall of people.

Francine stepped toward them, saw the lenses and microphones adjust. She focused on angry faces beyond the force field—and faces with fear—and faces with nothing but a terrible awe. In the foreground, well within the field, lay Zakheim's body, one hand outstretched and almost pointing at her. Silently, she dedicated this moment to him.

"Listen to me very carefully," she said. "But more important, see beyond my words to the place where words cannot penetrate." She felt her body begin to tingle with a sudden release of energy. Briefly, she raised herself onto her toes. "If you see the truth of my message, if you see through to this place that I show you, then you will enter a higher order of existence: happier, sadder. Everything will take on more depth. You will feel more of all the things there are in this universe for us to feel."

Her new-found knowledge was like a shoring up within, a bottomless well of strength.

"All the window widows of all the lonely homes of Earth am I," she said. And she bent forward. It was suddenly not Dr. Francine Millar, psychologist, there on the sand. By the power of mimesis, she projected the figure of a woman in a housedress leaning on a windowsill, staring hopelessly into an empty future.

"And all the happy innocence seeking pain."

Again, she moved: the years peeled away from her. And now, she picked up a subtle rhythm of words and movements that made experienced actors cry with envy when they saw the films.

"Nature building Nature's thunder am I," she chanted, her body swaying.

"Red roses budding

"And the trout thudding water

"And the moon pounding out stars

"On an ocean wake—

"All these am I!

"A fast hurling motion am I!

"What you think I am—that I am not!

"Dreams tell your senses all my names:

"Not harshly loud or suddenly neglectful, sarcastic, preoccupied or rebukeful—

"But murmuring.

"You abandoned a twelve-hour day for a twelve-hour night

"To meddle carefully with eternity!

"Then you realize the cutting hesitancy

"That prepares a star for wishing . . .

"When you see my proper image—

"A candle flickering am I.

"Then you will feel the lonely intercourse of the stars.

"Remember! Remember! Remember!"

MINDFIELD

In the *kabah* room another Priest failed.

It was dark in the room, which is like saying the ocean is wet. *Kabah* darkness is like no other in the universe. All radiation can be suppressed here to form a backdrop for precise inhibitory delta waves and shaped gammas.

Personality carving, it's called.

Mottled hums came from this dark, grit sounds without source-point.

The failure Priest approached death. He had been negative-thinking, permitting his accident-prayer to well up through the boundary from unconscious to conscious. In some Priests this prayer could grow too strong for Ultimate Conditioning to overcome without introducing cellular destruction into the brainpan.

But *kabah* could not kill. It could shape and twist at a sub-molecular level, but not kill. Only one solution to such an obstinate mind remained for *kabah* programming: the Priest's mind was flooded with blankness, a cool wash of nothing.

More sound trickled through the room—metallic scrapings, sharp ozone crackles without light. The failure Priest moved nearer death. Metal arms swung out where dark sensors directed, slipped the Priest into a rejuvenation tank. The tank sloshed as the body entered. The metal arms fitted caps, electrodes, suppression plates to the flesh.

Soon, a signal light would be activated, but first one more task remained. A name. It must be similar to the old name, but not near enough to rasp raw places in the dead past. And there was much dead past in this one. Many names to avoid.

Circuits flickered, settled on a single optimum sound combination. Printer styli buzzed, graved the name on the sealed rejuvenation tank: "Saim."

Outside the *kabah* room, the signal light glowed amber. Another human would see it presently, and come to wheel out the tank. Some Family would have another adult-sized "child" to raise and train.

In all this world there were only children such as this. And in every *ka-bah* room, on every priestly census scroll, all the names were listed. Not many names remained, but they were listed.

All names, that is, except one.

His name was George.

My name is George, he thought. *I must hang on to that.*

He felt shifting motion beneath his back, bands holding him to a stretcher. He heard the whistling of a turbine, the ear-thumping beat of rotors. He sensed night somewhere beyond the pale yellow dome light above him.

We're flying, he thought.

But then he couldn't be quite sure what *flying* was . . .

There had been a long time. He sheered away from thinking about how long a time. It was like a chasm.

And strange people.

And a tank that sloshed and gurgled around him, making weird tickling demands upon his nerves. Yes, there'd been a tank. That was definite.

A woman's face looked in upon him, obscuring the yellow dome light. She turned away, and he heard her voice: "He's awake, Ren."

A name went with the woman—*Jeni.* And a physical appearance—moonfaced, young with blonde hair in two long braids, blue eyes with light creases at the corners. She wore an odd grey robe with yellow flecks in its weave. The robe meant something. *Oh, yes—she's of the Wist Family.*

A masculine voice answered the woman: "Does he seem to be all right?" "Yes."

The masculine voice was Ren. He was a doctor. A dark man with almond eyes and flat features. His cerise flecked robe meant Chi Family.

"Keep an eye on him," said Ren. "See that he stays quiet."

My name is George. It was a thought like a vague handhold in darkness. *Could this be brainwashing?* he wondered.

But again he couldn't find meaning for a word. All he could think of was running water from a faucet and something foaming in a basin. *Washing.* And there were two languages in his head. One was called Haribic and came from the Educator. The other was called, in Haribic, *Ancienglis,* and this language came from . . . He sheered away. That was the chasm of Time.

Ancienglis was easiest, though.

Washing, he thought. *And faucet. And basin. And Educator.*

Educator was electrodes and ear caps and eye caps and hummings and jigglings and shakings in his mind like the rattling of dice in a cup. And passage of time.

Time.

It was like thunder in his mind.

My name is George, he thought.

"Uncle, the situation's desperate," said Saim. "There's danger more terrible than . . ." He shook his head, thinking that nothing in their world quite came up to a comparison.

"Mmmmmhmmmmm," said ó Plar. He turned in his fan-backed oak chair, stared out of the triangular window at the water rhythm garden with its cymbaline floats tinkling in the filtered morning light. Their music was pitched to a level that could be ignored here in the Regent Priest's private office. ó Plar swung back to face his nephew. Saim straightened, standing almost at attention like any other supplicant.

ó Plar considered Saim, watching him, avoiding for a moment the crisis that now could not be avoided. He saw a few more character lines in the young face. The thin features, blond hair and light eyes dominated a weak chin. A beard would cover the chin, though, if Saim survived Ultimate Conditioning another time . . .

"Uncle, you must believe me," said Saim.

"So you say," said ó Plar. He caressed the polished surface of his staff—a long tube of metal with crooked top. His hands never strayed far from it. The staff leaned now against its slot on the edge of the desk. ó Plar tapped the metal as he spoke.

"These records you've discovered—you say they refer to many caves scattered around the world, each with its complement of . . . I believe you called them rockets."

"Weapons, Uncle. Thousands of them! We found pictures. Weapons more terrible than you can imagine."

"Mmmmmhmmmmm," said ó Plar. And he thought: *The young fool! He keeps hitting the most sensitive inhibitions! Well, he's in for it now. I can't help myself.*

ó Plar took a deep breath, said: "Tell me how you found these records."

Saim dropped his gaze. Fear touched him. After all, this *was* the Regent Priest.

"Was it by digging?" asked ó Plar.

Saim shrugged, thought: *He knows we've profaned the earth.*

"Where is man's place?" demanded ó Plar.

Saim spoke with a resigned sigh: "Man's place is among the growing things on the blessed surface of Mother Earth. Neither in the sea below nor in the sky above, nor in caverns beneath. To the sea, the fishes. To the sky, the birds. To the earth's surface man. Each creature in his place."

ó Plar nodded, tapped his staff against the floor. "You recite it well, but do you believe it?"

Saim cleared his throat, but did not speak. He sensed an abrupt tension in the room, glanced at the staff in ó Plar's hand.

ó Plar said: "You cannot plead ignorance. You know why man must not dig in the earth except where the Council or a Priest-Historian such as myself has sanctified both diggers and ground."

Saim clenched his fists, unclenched them. So it had come to this.

"You know," said ó Plar. "You've seen me come from Ultimate Conditioning with the Lord's force strong upon me. You've seen Truth!"

Saim's lips thinned. *What was that old saying?* he asked himself. *Yes: In for a penny, in for a pound.*

"I know why," said Saim. "But it's not because of your holy rigmarole." He ignored the frozen look on ó Plar's face, said: "It's because back in the Lost Days people who dug in the ground accidentally set off some of these weapons. They reasoned that the region below the earth's surface was prohibited. And we're left with a law that grew out of accident and legend."

No help for him now, thought ó Plar. He said: "That would not be reasonable. And the Lord Buddha has ordered things in a reasonable way. I believe it's time to teach you this with some discipline."

Saim stiffened, said: "At least I tried to warn you."

"In the first place," said ó Plar, "there may be a few such weapons as you've described, but time is sure to have destroyed their working parts."

"Thousands of them," said Saim. "Each sealed in a giant container of inert gas. Each ready to destroy." He leaned forward. "Will you at least look at the evidence?"

ó Plar's voice grew sharper. "No need, young man. You could manufacture any evidence you needed."

Saim started to speak, but ó Plar cut him off.

"No! You came here to get me to stop the Millennial Display. You presumed to use our relationship for . . ."

"Of course I want you to stop that display!"

"But you did not tell me why."

"I did."

"Let's look at it reasonably," said ó Plar. "Under the guidance of the Blessed Priests, mankind has grown out of its violent childhood. We've enjoyed almost a thousand years of tranquillity. Just ten days now to the Millennial Display. Just ten days—and suddenly you've found a reason to stop that display."

"You must stop it," pleaded Saim.

"What harm can a few fireworks do to our people?" asked ó Plar.

"I don't have to tell you that," said Saim. "We've never seen such things. We're conditioned against all violence. I don't even see how you could force yourself to arrange such a display. The inhibitions . . ." He shuddered. "Loud noises, great flashes of light in the night sky. There'll be a panic!"

So perceptive, thought ó Plar. *This one was always so perceptive.* He said: "We but remind people in a relatively mild way how things were in ancient days."

"Madness and panic," said Saim.

"A little, perhaps," said ó Plar. He stilled the trembling of his left hand by gripping the staff. "The important thing is that we'll create public revulsion at the things you young rebels are preaching."

"Uncle, we . . ."

"I know what you're saying," said ó Plar. "Revive all the sciences of the Ancients! Expand to other planets! Expand! We don't even fill our present living space!"

"Uncle, that's just it." Saim felt like getting down on his knees. Instead, he leaned on the desk. "Mankind's dying out. There's no . . ." He shook his head ". . . no drive, no motive power."

"We're adjusting to the normal requirements of our Mother Earth," said ó Plar. "Nothing more. Well, we're going to show the people what it is you preach. We'll give them a display of ancient science."

"Haven't you heard anything I said?" pleaded Saim. "Your display will set off a panic. It'll be like a wave of fear following the line of darkness around the world. And the old weapons . . . they're all set to detect that wave. Fear at a critical volume sets off the weapons!"

ó Plar could feel the pressure of his own conditioning—so much more terrible and constricting than any pressures felt by the common herd. *If they only knew . . .*

"So you've stumbled on to a place of the Elders," said ó Plar. "Where is that place?"

Saim's lips remained closed. He could feel an emotion tugging at him. *Anger?* He tried to remember the angers of childhood, but couldn't. The conditioning was too strong.

ó Plar said: "We'll find the place you profaned whether you tell us its location or not."

"Get it over with," said Saim. And the sorrow he felt brought dampness to his eyes.

"I will," said ó Plar. He hesitated, sharing Saim's sorrow. But there was nothing else to do. The requirements of the moment were clear to both of them. "There is a strip copper mine in Mon'tana Province," he said. "They need an acolyte to learn the rituals from the resident."

"An acolyte? But, uncle I . . ."

"Don't think it'll lead to priesthood," said ó Plar. "You'll be digging, too. You appear to like digging."

"But . . ."

"Miners tend to be a profane lot," said ó Plar. "It comes from all that digging, no doubt."

Saim said: "Uncle, I don't care what you do to me, but won't you at least examine . . ."

"Enough!" ó Plar twisted an almost imperceptible ring on his staff. "Do you hear and obey?"

Saim stiffened to attention, feeling a terrible outrage that ó Plar should think it necessary to use the power of the staff in this. Saim's lips moved almost of their own volition: "I hear and obey."

"You will pack a minimal bag and leave at once for the Blessed of Heaven mine at Crystal, Mon'tana Province," said ó Plar. "Orders will be waiting for you at the train terminal." Again, he twisted the ring on his staff.

Saim stood rigidly at attention. The signal of the staff filled his mind with a procession of terrors without names. There was the red unthing of the black place shaping his thoughts into forms he no longer recognized. There was the slimy green part-self hearing and obeying. There was . . .

"Go!" ordered ó Plar.

The signal relaxed its hold.

ó Plar bowed his head, mumbled the litany of peace. His head was still bowed when he heard the door close. The tinkling of the water rhythm garden sounded overloud in the room.

That was close, thought ó Plar. *It's getting more difficult every day for me to deal with the accidental. My conditioning is so strong . . . so sure . . . so absolute.*

Presently, he touched a button on his desk. The semi-opaque face and shoulders of a woman appeared in a moment, projected above the desk. She wore the blue robe of a Priestess-Historian of the Brox Family. Her dark hair was tied in a severe braid across one shoulder. Green eyes stared at ó Plar from above a thin nose and stiff mouth.

"Will you give yourself up and submit to punishment?" asked ó Plar. It was a flat question, ritualistic.

"You know I cannot," she said. The answer carried the same lack of emphasis.

ó Plar held his face rigid to hide the momentary surge of loathing. *What this woman did might have an accidental necessity, but still . . .*

"Well, why have you called me?" asked the woman.

ó Plar rapped his staff against the floor. "ó Katje! You must observe the forms!"

"Sorry," she said. "I presume your nephew has just left you."

"I sent him to a mine," said ó Plar. "I gave him a jolt of the staff he'll never forget."

"You gave him just enough to make him angry," said ó Katje, "not enough to bind him. He'll run away. Your staff isn't functioning correctly today."

ó Plar started to rise from his chair.

"You couldn't catch him," said ó Katje. "There's nothing you can do. But no blame rests on you. It was an accident."

ó Plar relaxed. "Yes. An accident." He stared at the woman, *How to phrase this?* he wondered. *I must say a thing, yet not say it.*

"You're not trying to trace my transmission signal again, are you?" asked ó Katje.

"You know we've given up on that," said ó Plar. "No. I wish to say something of the simulacrum. This accident may give you Saim and Ren and Jeni, but I will have the simulacrum. He's unconditioned!"

"I need good workers," she said.

"They're hiding near the city," said ó Plar. "Saim came in on foot. They've found one of the ancient caves, that's what. The Elders hid them with devilish cunning, but sometimes an accident . . ." He broke off. *Did she get the message?*

"How can you be sure you'll get the simulacrum?" asked ó Katje.

Damn that woman! thought ó Plar. *Directly into the jaws of the inhibition!* He said: "If you will not give yourself up and submit to punishment, there is no further need for us to talk. May you find a path of grace."

He broke the connection, watched the image fade. *Fool woman. Flying directly . . .* His thoughts dived off at a tangent. *No! Not a fool! She was testing my inhibition! When I reacted . . . that's when she knew for sure we were prepared to follow Saim: we saw the accident.*

Now, ó Plar sat back, worrying, wondering. The little signal generator he had stuck to the back of Saim's robe during the embrace of greeting—it was sure to lead the acolyte guards directly to the hidden cave. Part of him exulted at this thought, but part recoiled in horror. The careful accumulation of so many accidents . . .

George saw the door and stopped. The door had been forced and repaired. It was a perimeter door, leading to a defensive chamber. He knew that. But the ideas of perimeter and defensive chamber weren't quite clear in his mind. They came in Ancienglis, a language with big gaps in it.

Abruptly, everything around him seemed strange, as though his surroundings had stepped out of phase with his reality. Something dragged at his ankles. He looked down at the long white robe he was wearing. It was like a . . . a hospital gown, but longer.

"Is something wrong, Jorj?"

He whirled, saw a dark man with flat features, almond eyes. *Almond eyes! Something wrong . . . dangerous . . . about almond eyes.* He said: "You're . . ."

"I am Ren, your doctor," And Ren tensed, wondering if there'd be some new violence from this simulacrum creature.

"Oh." George relaxed. "I've been sick."

"But you are well now." Ren maintained his alert, watchful attitude. *No telling what set this creature off.*

George took a deep breath.

The door!

He studied it. There were stains around it. *Blood?* He could hear voices behind it. He opened the door. It swung inward on silent hinges, revealing a chamber hewn out of grey rock. Indirect lighting gave the place a shadowless look of sterility. A man and woman stood in the chamber, talking. He knew the woman. Jeni. She came with food and sympathy in her eyes. But he didn't know the man—grey eyes, short-cropped blond hair. A feeling of youngness about him.

The man was speaking: "They didn't stand a chance of catching me. I outran them easily. And when we got into the timber . . ." He broke off, sensing the watchers.

Ren pushed past and into the room, said: "Saim, when did you get back?"

"I just this minute arrived." Saim spoke to Ren, but kept his attention on Ren's companion, who advanced into the chamber, peering around. Saim found the sight of the simulacrum freed of the regenerative tank shocking and repulsive. He said: "Is something wrong with it?"

"With Jorj? Nothing at all. He's had a hard day's problem solving and probing is all."

"My name is George," George muttered. The words were flat as though he spoke to himself.

"He speaks!" said Saim. It was a terrifying idea, as though this creature had reached a tentacle out into a new and more deeply profane dimension.

Jeni said: "He looks tired, Ren."

George focused on Saim. "You're . . ." His voice trailed off. His features grew slack. He stood silent, staring into nothing.

"Is he all right?" asked Jeni.

"Oh, yes." Ren put a hand on George's arm. "His name's something like Maid-Jor or Jorj. We found the sonal pattern by tracing a course of least lip resistance."

"Major," whispered George.

"See?" said Ren. He knew he sounded prideful, but who else had ever revived a pile of bones—created life where death had lain for a thousand years? He turned back to Saim. "You spoke of running. Is something wrong?"

"My uncle ordered me to a mine. I ran away." Saim tore his attention away from the simulacrum, wondering: *How could such a repulsive creature have so much attraction?*

"And you came directly here?" asked Ren.

"I put the grease on my shoes and around the bottom of my robe. The basenjimeters won't track me."

Fear edged Ren's nerves. "You came by a circuitous path?"

"Certainly. And I dropped through the fissure to the break under the tunnel where we . . ."

"It's different," said George. The voices annoyed him. And this place . . .

"His speech, said Saim. "It's . . ."

"Ren's had him in the Educator," said Jeni. She spoke quickly, feeling the tensions building up here, wanting to ease them.

"You should hear him in Ancienglis," said Ren. "Say something in Ancienglis for us, Jorj."

George drew himself up. "My name is Major George . . ." His thoughts veered out into emptiness, a black, enclosing place.

"He's overtired," said Ren. "I had him in the Educator almost two hours followed by a long stimulous search session. We're opening up broad areas, but there's been no really big breakthrough yet." He pulled gently at George's arm. "Come along, Jorj."

George's lips moved silently, then: "George. George. George."

They went out through the door, leaving it open. Ren's voice came back to them: "That's right, Jorj, in here." Then: "Saim, I'll see you in the lab in a few minutes."

They heard a door shut.

"Where does Ren get off giving me orders?" asked Saim. He felt stirrings of . . . could it be anger?

"Saim!" said Jeni. And she thought: *Here he is starting to act jealous again.* "Ren was just in a hurry."

"Well, there's no giving of orders here," said Saim.

She touched his arm. "I missed you, Saim."

It was enough. The tensions melted from him. "I'm sorry it took so long," said Saim. "My uncle was gone when I got there. At a Council meeting up north somewhere. I sat around cooling my heels for eight days before he got back. I didn't dare try communicating. And I only had enough of that scent suppressor for one application; so I couldn't come back without abandoning our plan."

"From what you said, you might just as well have abandoned it," said Jeni. "Wasn't there anything you could do to make your uncle believe?"

"It wasn't a matter of his believing," said Saim. "Jeni, I had the funniest feeling that he believed me all right, but couldn't do anything about it. As though something within him forced . . ." Saim shook his head. "I don't know. It was odd."

"It's all politics," said Jeni. She felt . . . resentment. Yes. Resentment. One didn't feel anger, of course. But resentment was permitted. Like a safety valve. "He knows that display will destroy all popular support for our program. This is just politics."

"But when I told him the display would set off a wave of fear to ignite these weapons, he didn't react properly," said Saim. "It was almost as though he hadn't heard me. Or refused to hear me. Or . . . I don't know."

Jeni put down a shudder of fear, thought: *Ren should have gone, or I. It was a mistake sending Saim. He's different . . . not like the Saim we knew . . . before.*

"We'd better get along to the lab," said Saim.

"There must be something we can do," said Jeni. She felt desperate, trapped.

"You should have heard him," said Saim. His voice took on some of ó Plar's querulous tone. "Don't you realize what it'd mean to revive all the old sciences, you young whelp? Don't you realize the violence and noise of just the Bessemer process?"

"Bessemer process?"

"A way of making steel," said Saim. "I reminded him that I was a metallurgist. That's when he first suggested I should get closer to my work. I knew then he was determined to send me to a mine."

"Saim! Jeni! Come along!" It was Ren calling from the lab.

"Who's he think he's giving orders to?" asked Saim.

"Oh, stop that," said Jeni. She stood on tiptoes, kissed his cheek. "It's just that he's anxious to get on with our work." She took his hand. "Come along."

They went out into the hall. Jeni closed the door behind them, barred it. They turned left down the hall, through an open door into a square room with yellow, sound-absorbent walls. One section of a wall was cluttered with recording controls and playback systems. Jeni sat down in front of a master control panel, flipped a warm-up switch.

Saim looked around. This room disturbed him for a reason he couldn't quite name.

Ren stood almost in the centre of the room, beside a table strewn with notes and instruments. The Doctor rocked back and forth on the balls of his feet, studying Saim's face. *Incredible,* thought Ren. *Saim—as natural as ever. How powerful the conditioning of the Priest-Historians. They take the mind and the being, and they shape all to suit their needs. And we would never have suspected had it not been for the accident and the tank we stole.*

Jeni said: "Saim, tell Ren what happened."

Saim nodded, reviewed what he had told Jeni.

"You ran away from the acolyte guards," said Ren. He nodded. "Wasn't that very close to violence?"

"I told you once I was an atavist!" said Saim.

"I've never doubted it," said Ren. "Do you think you could actually strike someone, hurt him?"

Saim paled.

"Don't be obscene!" said Jeni.

Let them learn now what it really is that we're doing, thought Ren. "I'm being practical," he said. He pulled back a sleeve of his robe, exposed a purple bruise on his forearm. "This morning, the simulacrum struck me."

"Ren!" It was a double gasp.

"Think about what is required to commit such violence," said Ren.

"Stop it!" wailed Jeni. She hid her face in her hands. *What have we done?* she asked herself. *It started with Saim . . . because I love him . . . and couldn't stand to lose him. But now . . .*

"You see how it affects us?" asked Ren. "I was never so frightened in my life." He swallowed. "I was two people. One of me was in such a panic that the little detector instrument fairly buzzed. And part of . . ."

"It detected your fear?" asked Saim.

"Exactly!"

"But couldn't that set off the weapon?"

Jeni lowered her hands from her face. "Not the fear from just one person," she said. "It takes the fear from a multitude."

"Pay attention to what I'm saying," said Ren. "I'm telling you something about this panic. It wasn't at all what you feel from a jolt of the priest's staff. Part of me was frightened, and part of me was watching. I *saw* the fright. It was most curious."

"You *saw* your fright?" asked Saim.

Jeni turned away. It hurt her to look at Saim like this. He was her Saim of old, but somehow . . . so different. So intense.

"Yes," said Ren. "At the very moment of my panic, I could consider what it meant. Violence has been all but stamped out of us. And what little's left, the inhibitory conditioning of our childhood takes care of that. But there must be something remaining because I found myself thinking that if Jorj struck me again, I'd have to grapple with him, stop him."

"Do you think you actually could have done it?" asked Saim.

"I don't know. But I thought of it."

"Why did he strike you?" asked Jeni. And she thought: *Perhaps there's a clue here to Saim's difference.*

"Now, there's another curious thing," said Ren. "Merely because I was in his path. I was questioning him about the weapons in this cave complex, trying different word-thought patterns in Ancienglis. Suddenly, he jumped up, shouted in Ancienglis: *'Out of my way!'* And he struck me aside. He ran halfway across the medical lab, stopped, turned around, and did the same thing you saw him do out there. He just . . . seemed to turn off."

"Is it possible he remembers?" whispered Jeni.

"Of course not!" Ren felt his skin tingle at the stupidity of such a question. "You know how he was constructed."

Saim said: "But, what's the difference if . . ."

"We started with a skeleton," said Ren. "Dead bones. They gave us nothing but a cellular pattern. From that pattern the *kabah* tank got the pattern of adjoining cells. A one-cell thickness. Those new cells gave the pattern for the next layer, and so on. Jorj is *like* the original, but he is not the original. The concept of memory, therefore, is not consistent."

"But those bones had been preserved by the gas from a weapon chamber," said Jeni. "There might even have been some flesh . . ." She shuddered, remembering Saim after the blast at the doorway to the cave.

"Even that wouldn't make any difference," said Ren. "This wasn't the same as growing a new arm, say, for someone injured in an accident. It wasn't even the same as . . ." He glanced at Saim, back to Jeni. "With an accident victim we have the original central nervous structure all intact. Or enough of it to give us solid patterns of the original. But with bones . . ." He shrugged.

All this talk of regeneration disturbed Saim, and he couldn't understand why. He said: "But this simulacrum was one of the Elders. Isn't it . . ."

"That's right," said Ren. "*Was*. The original died of the twenty-minute virus. There's no doubt he was a plague victim. He was one of the Elders. But the accent is on past tense of a thousand years ago. *Was*."

Saim glanced at Jeni, back to Ren. "But he speaks the old language exactly like the tapes we . . ."

"Certainly he does!" Ren threw up his hands at the stupidity of these questions. "But we have no reconstructed memories! All we have is the pattern, the inclination, the avenues where familiar thoughts once were. It's like . . ." He waved a hand in the air. "It's like a water-course. Rain falls. It strikes the earth and runs into little random rivulets. These rivulets hit the paths of earlier rainfalls, and still earlier rainfalls, until all those original raindrops are channelled in old, deep water-courses. Don't you see?"

Saim nodded. He suddenly saw more than this. *There could be dams on those water-courses. Permanent changes in the channels. Odd storage systems ready to gush out with strange twists of . . .* He began to tremble, abruptly pulled himself out of these thoughts.

"Habits," said Ren. "Old thoughts that are often repeated. They do something of the same thing. If we strike the right thought patterns, they'll slip into familiar channels for Jorj. He'll repeat the thought or action pattern. He'll do something that was familiar because of the old pattern."

"Like striking you," said Jeni.

"Yes!" Ren beamed at her. "They were violent people. And somewhere in this violent person we've regenerated, there's a clue to the weapons in this cave system. Through those weapons we can open up all the old sciences. Think of the metals they had that we no longer have except when we melt down something of the ancients'. And the fuels!" Ren threw up his hands. He smiled at them, turned to the table, began pawing through the notes.

"It's like grasping hold of some terrible thing and not being able to let go," said Saim.

"What is?" asked Jeni.

Saim stared at her, ignoring the question, suddenly struck with the feeling that he once had known another Jeni . . . different . . .

"Why are you staring at me like that?" asked Jeni. The look on Saim's face frightened her.

"Here it is," said Ren. He straightened with a sheaf of notes. "The abstract on my sessions with Jorj. Our opening wedge is going to come from this simulacrum. I'm thinking that . . ." He broke off, focusing on his companions. "What's wrong?"

"It's almost as though I should remember something," said Saim.

"Ren, I'm frightened," said Jeni.

Ren moved to Saim's side, put a hand on his arm. "Do you feel ill, Saim?"

"Ill?" Saim thought about it. "No. I feel . . . well, different." He stared down at his right hand. "Didn't I have a scar on this hand once?"

"A scar?" Ren glanced at the hand. "Oh." Ren's voice took on a forced heartiness. "So that's it. We all have these feelings at one time or another, Saim. They pass quickly."

"Feelings about scars?"

"If not scars, some other kind of familiarity," said Ren. "It's called *deja vu,* this feeling. You'll get over it."

"When I was testing that flying machine in the big cavern, studying the manual, and adjusting all the parts, sometimes my hands seemed to know what to do when I didn't," said Saim. "Is that what you mean?"

"It may even have something to do with racial memory," said Ren. "Just put it out of your mind."

"Would you like to rest or have something to eat?" asked Jeni.

"No . . . I . . . Get on with it, Ren. Work first, rest later."

"As you say," said Ren. And he thought: *Trust Jeni to get him back on the track. I'll have to take that into consideration—the power of love and affection in maintaining a sense of normalcy.*

"Well," said Ren. He cleared his throat. "To get back to Jorj. To understand the original of this simulacrum . . ." He leafed through his notes. "Yes . . . to understand the original, we must understand the psychology of the world that bore him. There were two opposing Alliances of power in that world. They'd agreed to disarm, but for years they disarmed with one hand while arming with the other. The natural result was a sense of shame. This cavern complex is a perfect symptom of that shame. Look how they hid it. More than a hundred meters of dirt over us that has to be lifted off by explosive charges before the actual weapons tubes are exposed."

"Are we sure it was shame?" asked Saim.

"Of course it was. Concealment is the companion of shame." Ren shook his head, marvelling at the way the non-specialist could misinterpret. "And beyond this even," he said, "beyond this cave complex and the others it hints at, think of what the opposing Alliance had. Another entire network of these weapons."

"We've discussed all this before," said Saim. He was beginning to feel impatient.

"But not the psychology of it," said Ren.

"I'd rather talk about something more to the point," said Saim. "First, what about the targets? These weapons were aimed someplace. Those targets must have changed in a thousand years."

"It wouldn't make any difference," said Jeni. "I found something horrible in dismantling some of the little guiding instruments."

"Jeni!" said Saim. "You might have exploded one of those monsters!"

"No," she said. "I didn't touch an actual weapon. I found a store of spare guidance systems. Some of them will follow lines of magnetic flux. Some can be set to go to a large area of heat or a small area of intense heat or a near bulk of metal. And you must keep in mind that all these systems are interlocking. They're made to go into a single package."

"Tell him about the other one," said Ren.

"It's a tiny version of the fear sensor," said Jeni. "When it nears a large city, it assumes command of the total guidance system. It's attracted by massive waves of fear. The fear of a populace exposed to the weapon attracts the weapon."

"There has to be some way to stop that Millennial Display," said Saim. "The wave of fear . . ." He walked away from them, turned. "People will see fireworks, all right. And that's the last thing they'll ever see."

"Maybe we should go to ó Katje and combine forces," said Jeni, "Maybe she'd help us convince . . ."

"ó Katje!" barked Saim. "I don't trust her!"

"Now, Saim," said Ren. "She's a renegade, a rebel just like ourselves. She's even transmitted pictures and data about the weapon they're studying."

"Saim, the size of that weapon!" said Jeni. "It's fifty times larger than these ones we found!"

"I don't see how she could be a rebel," said Saim. "You don't understand about the Ultimate Conditioning. I do. I've seen my uncle come out of the *kabah* room after his yearly renewal. Sometimes he looks like a man near death. We have to nurse him. You don't understand."

"Accidents do happen," said Ren. He spoke quickly, impatient to get back to his notes and the work as he saw it.

"ó Katje's done nothing except try to force us to reveal our hiding place," said Saim. "That alone is enough to make me distrust her."

A buzzer sounded on the panel behind Jeni. She whirled and knocked down a toggle switch.

"Was that the outside warning system?" asked Saim.

"Someone's approaching the old cave entrance," said Ren. He glanced at Saim. "Are you sure you used that odour suppressor?"

"I smeared it all over," said Saim. He lifted the hem of his robe. "You can see the stains. Besides, I came in the fault fissure, not the . . ."

Another buzzer sounded overhead. Jeni slapped another switch.

"Coming directly towards the entrance," said Ren. "Saim, did you say anything to your uncle that . . ."

"Why don't you come right out and ask if I've betrayed you?" demanded Saim. He felt stirrings of unrest. *Anger?* Again, he tried to remember the emotions of childhood, and failed. The conditioning was absolute here.

"What's this?" asked Jeni. She stood up, tugged at the back of Saim's robe, removed a small disc of metal stuck there with adhesive. She extended it on her palm. "Why would you wear this decoration on the back of your robe?"

Saim shook his head, confused, feeling himself on the verge of a fearful revelation. "I . . . it isn't . . ."

"Did your uncle embrace you in greeting?" demanded Jeni. She stared at the disc on her palm.

"Of course. Family always . . ."

"That's it!" she enclosed the disc in a fist, jumped past him, ran to the door, hurled the object into the hall. Turning, she slammed and bolted the door. "Signal generator," she said. "Has to be."

"Your uncle was more clever than you thought," said Ren. And he thought: *We should never have sent Saim. Jeni or I would never have made such a mistake.*

Jeni returned to Saim, inspected his robe. "Turn around."

He obeyed, moving with shocked stiffness.

"Nothing else," she said.

A red light flashed on the panel beside them.

"They're forcing the perimeter door," said Ren.

The idea of forcing such a door seized Saim with a sudden panic. He said: "They . . ."

"It means they're using metal detectors," said Ren. "A signal generator would only give them the general area."

"How did ó Plar know Saim would try to escape?" asked Jeni. "It doesn't . . ."

"He could've planted the idea," said Ren. "We're wasting time. We'll have to run for it." He strode to the door, flung it open. *This happened because I'm surrounded by fools!* he thought.

"But what about the simulacrum?" protested Jeni. "Can he travel?"

Ren turned in the doorway. "In the flying machine. Do you still believe you can operate it, Saim?"

"Well, I've only lifted it a little bit off the floor," said Saim. "But . . . yes, I . . ."

"I'm as frightened at the thought as you are," said Ren. "But there's no other way. Come on." He turned, strode into the hall.

Saim and Jeni followed.

They could hear the hammering now, metal against metal.

They shouldn't try to force that door, thought Saim. *That's dangerous.*

"Hurry it up!" called Ren.

Everything's happening so fast, thought Saim. He felt resentment at pressures he couldn't understand.

Jeni took his hand, urged him faster.

Their way led off the big hall, down a narrow passage single file. They barred doors behind them. Dim white exciter lights blinked on at their passage, surrounding them with a pale nimbus of illumination. The air grew cooler. They came out into a laboratory cut deep in the rock. A green light glowed above a cot where the simulacrum slept. He was a green shape within green within green . . .

Saim turned away. This was the room where Ren kept the stolen regeneration tank. Something about the place loomed in Saim's mind, a black image of terror.

Why? he wondered. *Why? Why?*

"I gave him a sedative," said Ren. "We'll have to wheel the cot." He pointed to the far wall. "There's a can of inflammable fluid over there, Saim. Some of the fuel from the flying machine. Get it, please."

"What do you want with it?"

Saim's question touched a core of impatience in Ren. "The regenerative tank's in this lab. You know that!"

"But why . . ."

"We can't let them find what we've done," said Ren. "There's too much evidence around. We have to destroy it."

"What about your notes in the other lab?" asked Jeni.

"I have them in my pocket. The rest of the stuff up there won't mean anything without the evidence in here. Now, hurry it up."

Yes! thought Saim. *Destroy this place!* He said: "Where's this fluid you . . ."

A dull roar shook the room. The ceiling trembled, showering them with dust.

Ren said: "What was . . ."

"The main door," said Jeni. "We should've known. The Elders must've built one of their diabolical devices into the door just as they did in the . . ." She broke off, staring at Saim.

"What is it? What's wrong?"

They whirled. It was George, speaking in Ancienglis. He stood beside his cot, staring up at the ceiling. "Are they attacking?"

Ren answered in the same tongue, wary that this might return the simulacrum to violence. "We have to escape, Jorj. We've been discovered." Aside to Jeni and Saim, he said: "Watch him carefully. Shock awakened him from the sedative. I'm not too certain of his metabolism yet. He could do anything."

"There won't be anyone alive up there at that door," said Saim. "Whoever was . . ."

"Now it's certain we have to run," said Ren. "The explosion will attract others, and the cave's wide open."

"Where are the guards?" demanded George.

"Dead," said Ren. He darted across the lab, returned with a yellow can that sloshed in his hands.

"What're you doing?" asked George. He rubbed at his head.

"Burning my records," said Ren. "Please stand aside."

"Bad as that, eh," said George. He still spoke in Ancienglis. "The dirty, sneaking bastards!" Abruptly, he shook his fist at the ceiling. "We'll show you!"

A pungent odour filled the room as Ren poured and sloshed the contents of the can around.

"Use plenty of gas," said George. "Don't leave anything for 'em."

They retreated out of the door. Ren threw the can into the center of the room.

Jeni clutched Saim's arm. "Saim, I'm frightened."

He patted her hand.

"Who's got a match?" asked George.

Ren took a firepill from his pocket, crushed it between his fingers, tossed it into the room. He slammed the door as a blossom of orange flame jumped up from the floor.

"To the big cavern," said Ren.

Saim turned, leading. Jeni stayed close to his side.

Ren stayed beside George. "You feel all right, Jorj?" he panted. He spoke Haribic, testing.

"Fine, fine." George answered in Ancienglis.

"He's in kind of a shock," said Ren. "We must be careful."

"Where're we going?" asked George. He felt turmoil at the edges of consciousness, but the action and need for it were central, demanding all attention. They'd been expecting the attack for a long time. Having it actually occur was almost a relief. *The dirty, sneaky bastards!* "Where're we going?" he repeated.

Ren searched in his mind for the Ancienglis word. "Helicopter," he said.

"Hope they don't have much air cover," said George. "A 'copter's a sitting duck for anything with firepower."

They emerged into an echoing chamber, large and cold. Dim exciter lights emitted a pale green glow around the room at their entrance. Still, the place remained a mass of phantom shadows.

"Well, blow the charge!" shouted George. He darted to the right along the wall, pulled down a fluorescent handle.

A crackling roar deafened them.

"Never trust a damn' shaped charge!" shouted George. "But they always seem to work." He threw another handle beside the first one.

Part of the ceiling creaked and groaned upwards, exposing a length of evening sky pale dove grey against dark green treetops. Something clanked and the ceiling stopped its movement.

Jeni pressed her face against Saim's chest, clung to his robe. "What's happening?" she whispered. "The noise . . ."

"Damn' thing's stuck!" said George. He punched a red button beside the handle. A sharp, crackling explosion shook them. The ceiling hurtled away and they heard it land in a thunderous crackle of broken trees and branches.

Jeni trembled. "What's . . ."

"It's all right," said Saim. "You knew what the old instructions said about opening this chamber. That's all it was. The explosion . . ."

"I couldn't have done it," she said.

Saim looked at Ren beside them. The Doctor's eyes were closed, his hands clenched into fists at his sides. His lips were moving in the litany of peace.

"For Chri'sakes, come on!" yelled George. He turned, ran towards a squat black machine crouched in the center of the chamber.

Ren was the first to follow, moved by concern for his patient. Saim took Jeni's hand, pulled her towards the helicopter.

"You've been in the flying machine before," he said. He found himself caught up by a growing sense of excitement at the thought of leaving the ground. There were remote feelings of fear, but so far away . . .

George opened the belly door, clambered into the helicopter. Ren followed, Saim pushed Jeni up on to the pipe step, clambered in behind her, slammed the door. Everything was suddenly caught up in George's urgency.

"Get a move on!" George yelled. He lifted himself up into the cockpit, slid into the left-hand seat. *Damn' civilian types,* he thought. His hands moved swiftly with an automatic sureness over the controls. "Come on! Hurry it up!"

Saim lifted up into the cockpit.

George motioned him into the right-hand seat.

Saim obeyed, watched George strapping himself in, lifted his own straps from beside the seat. There was still a smell of the preservative gas in the cockpit, disturbed by their movements.

Ren climbed up between them, stared at George. "Is *he* going to operate this machine?"

"Who'd know better how these machines work than one who actually flew in them?" asked Saim. "And I'll be right here."

"He could break down at any minute," said Ren. "You mustn't let . . ."

"Shut up!" ordered George. He pushed a white button on the panel in front of him. A grinding sound came from overhead, was replaced by a whistling roar.

Saim put a hand on Ren's shoulder, pushed him back into the cabin. "Go strap yourself down! See that Jeni's all right!"

"Here we go!" yelled George. "Look out for ground fire, and keep an eye peeled for their air cover."

The big machine jerked upwards, lurched, then rose smoothly out of the chamber. The walls slid past. Then trees. They lifted over treetops into a dove-grey sky.

Saim felt panic begin, closed his eyes tightly. *This is natural,* he told himself. *The sky is not just the place of birds.* Exultation seized him. He opened his eyes, looked out of the windows.

It was already dark on the ground, but up here in the sky it was still light. This was like living in two worlds at once.

"We're flying," he whispered.

Jeni's voice lifted from the cabin: "Saim! We're in the sky!"

He heard the terror in her voice, called back: "It's all right, Jeni. I'm here."

"I'm frightened," she whimpered.

Ren's voice came from the cabin. "Don't look out of the window, Jeni. Here, swallow this."

Saim turned, watched what George did to command the machine. Yes. Just as the manual instructed. The knob there for adjusting fuel. The big handle for tipping and turning the machine. Saim let his hands rest on the wheel, felt the movements. And suddenly the whistling of the turbine, the muted thump-thump of the rotors seemed louder.

Ren's head lifted through the cockpit door. "You must head north across the wilderness plateau, Jorj," he said. "That is the way to ó Katje's."

George lifted his hands off the wheel, looked around at the gathering darkness beneath them, at the people in the cockpit, at the robe he was wearing.

"Jorj?" said Saim. "Jorj?"

The strangeness, thought George. It was a whirling sensation in his mind. *The terrain's all different. Everything's different.*

Ren put a hand on Jorj's arm. "Jorj?"

The helicopter began to tilt left.

Saim gripped the wheel, righted them.

George said "It's all . . . I don't . . . where are we?" He rubbed his palms across his eyes.

"It's as I warned," said Ren. "Jorj had regressed. Help me unstrap him, Saim."

But Saim was too busy controlling their flight. He waved Ren's hand away from the fuel control knob. "No! Don't touch that!"

"How am I going to get him back where I can examine him?" Ren felt exasperation, knew that the drug he had taken and the medical emergency were suppressing panic. *They were in the sky!*

"Sit on the floor between us," ordered Saim. "Don't touch anything. Get Jeni to help you."

Jeni's head came through the door. "What's . . . Saim! You're running the machine!"

"You saw me do it in the cavern!"

"But that was different! You . . ."

"Here!" commanded Ren. "Stop that chatter and help me."

"Yes, of course." She was immediately all contrition.

Saim concentrated on flying the machine, Ren and Jeni dragged the simulacrum from the adjoining seat. George was slack-jawed and staring. Empty eyes. They frightened Saim as they swept out of his line of sight. He felt dampness beneath his palms.

There was full darkness in the sky now with the moon just lifting above the horizon. Saim saw village lights below to his left and far away to the right. Controlling this machine felt so . . . natural. His hands seemed to know what to do. He reached out, turned a switch. The panel glowed a dull green. Another switch. Yellow light came through the open door from the cabin.

"Thanks for the light," said Ren. He came through the door, slid into the seat George had occupied.

"What landmarks do we look for?" asked Saim.

"Where are we?" asked Ren. He spoke with a drugged dullness.

"North of Council City. I can see some village lights, but I don't know what villages. The wilderness plateau's ahead."

"ó Katje said two peaks with a lake between them," said Ren. "And a burn scar like a cross on the northern peak."

"How far?"

"She said five days on foot from Council City, but near an overtrain route."

Saim glanced at his instruments. "We could be there in only a few hours."

"Saim," said Ren, "how do you keep your sanity? I know that when this tranquillizer wears off I'm going to be hysterical." His voice lifted slightly from its dullness. "We're in the sky!"

A masculine groan sounded from the cabin behind them. Jeni called, "He's awake, Ren."

Ren shook his head, swallowed. "Does he seem all right?"

"Yes. But he's awake."

"Just keep an eye on him. See that he remains quiet."

George stirred on the stretcher, feeling the bands across his chest and legs. *My name is George,* he thought. *I must remain quiet.*

"So you're George," said ó Katje.

George leaned back in his chair, stared around the little room where he had awakened. He liked the way this woman said his name. It sounded *right,* not like the mushed-out consonants the others used. He could even hear a faint echo of the first *e.*

"Is that your name?" she asked. "George?"

She spoke Haribic. George answered in the same tongue. "That's my name." The words came out a little stiffened. Haribic was difficult at times.

The woman shifted to Ancienglis, and again he had that feeling of rightness about the way she spoke. "Is there more to your name?"

"Yes. I'm Major George . . ." The words trailed off into emptiness.

She turned to Ren standing behind her. "Is he all right?"

"Oh, yes." Ren stepped forward. He felt a great diffidence in ó Katje's presence. It was much more than the usual conditioned reverence for Priest or Priestess. "He does this frequently, ó Katje," said Ren. "Whenever his thoughts have led him into a blank area of mind."

What are we ever going to do with him? wondered ó Katje. She studied the simulacrum. There was a roughness to his features that one seldom encountered in people.

"George," she said. "George?"

George looked at her, slowly focusing. Woman in a blue robe. Long black hair tied in a silver loop at the back. Odd crooknecked staff in her hand. Thin face dominated by green eyes.

My name is George, he thought.

I could call ó Plar and dump the whole thing into his lap, she thought. *But that would be tempting his ignorance of our hiding place. If he learns we have the simulacrum. No. The* accident *must be maintained.*

And she sensed that ó Plar could have no better solution for this Elder than she could find for herself. The creature looked so helpless in his rugged way. So attractive, really.

Ren said: "Perhaps you should question him, satisfy your mind about the fear detectors." And he thought: *How odd, this awe of her. Could she have her staff tuned to some strange new frequency?*

"What about these fear detectors?" she asked. "We found no such records or devices in this cave complex."

"But they exist, ó Katje."

"I still would like to have seen these devices and the records of them for myself. I think it odd that you should have burned everything."

"I didn't want it discovered that I'd restored . . ." He nodded towards George.

She looked at George, back to Ren, thinking: *How strange this Ren is.* "Were you so ashamed of what you'd done?"

Ren's shoulders stiffened. "I didn't think it wise to broadcast that I'd violated a *kabah* room."

"I see." She nodded, feeling a brief constriction of her conditioning. It passed quickly and she thought: *ó Plar was right about this Ren. An odd variant on the renegade pattern. A* new *kind of accident.* "Perhaps there'll be similar devices and records here," she said. "We'll look for them."

"And we must act quickly," said Ren. "The danger . . ."

"So you say."

"You don't believe me?"

"I didn't say that. But you must admit you have other reasons for wishing the Millennial Display cancelled."

"You sound as though you side with the Priests on this." And he wondered: *Could Saim be right not to trust her?*

"It's one thing to follow an accident that breaks with taboo," she said. "For the sake of knowledge, of course. It's quite another thing to try to destroy the very roots of . . ."

"Accident?" He stared at her.

She fingered the slim central ring on her staff, and Ren felt the ripple of nervous disquiet that always preceded a heavy taste of displeasure.

"Please," he petitioned her.

"I would hate to return you to a full course of conditioning," she said. And she thought: *We'll have to do it, of course. As soon as we've exhausted our need for his* accidental *talents.*

Ren paled. "ó Katje, I . . ."

"It doesn't please me to have to emphasize my words with the staff," she said.

"Of course, ó Katje." He found that he was trembling. There were dim recollections in his mind of a full course of reconditioning. Darkness. Fearful twistings of semi-consciousness. Terrors!

ó Katje looked down at George. "Now, Ren, tell me your purpose with this simulacrum."

"Yes, ó Katje." He stilled the trembling. "It seemed logical. The bones were intact and in a wonderful state of preservation because of the gas."

"Gas?"

"From a weapon chamber."

"Ah, the inert substance, the preservative."

"Yes. There'd been some sort of accident to the chamber. And there was only one set of bones. I knew from medical use of the simpler tanks that the *kabah* tank could reproduce a cellular pattern in its full stage of . . ."

"This is all very interesting, dear Ren, but it's confined to *methods* when I'm more interested in your purpose."

"Yes, of course." He found that his right eyelid was twitching, rubbed it. "Purpose. I felt that we could restore many of the old habit channels in such a being—the compulsives, certainly, and the overriding repetitives—and from them gain clues to the working of the ancient devices."

She spoke through a haze of inhibitory shock: "And you restored such channels?"

Ren missed the stiffness of her voice, said: "There are signs. I think we're on the verge of a breakthrough. If we once restored his full name, perhaps . . ."

"How could you?" She almost screeched the words.

He stared at her. "ó Katje, what's . . ."

"The pains of such recall," she said. "The recollection of his actual moment of death!"

"But ó Katje, it's not exactly memories we . . ."

"A quibble! Have you no inhibitions at all?"

"ó Katje, I don't . . ."

"That which the Lord has taken unto Himself completes the Circle of Karma," she said. "You've not only invaded this domain, you . . ."

"But you *knew* this, ó Katje!"

"There's a difference in knowing an abstract idea and seeing the very substance of it," she said.

"Simulacrum," said George.

They turned, looked at him.

"Simulacrum?" asked George. All this talk-talk between the beautiful dark woman and the doctor. It had dawned on George that simulacrum referred to himself. And in his Educator-memory was a definition: *Sham. Something vague and unreal.*

"I'm no simulacrum," he said. "I'm real."

ó Katje drew in a trembling breath. "And that, Ren, is the thing which overshadows all else. He is real. He is real. He is real. And you would have him recall all his past, all his name, all . . ."

"My name?" said George. "It's Major George . . ." His thoughts shot out into the emptiness. There was no mindhold here, no place of orientation. But he knew he had been here before. There were faces, words, names, sensations.

Somewhere distant and subdued he heard a woman's voice. "You see, Ren? Have you any idea how constricting the inhibitions of a Priestess can be? Have you even the faintest conception?"

But that was away somewhere. This place in his mind, this was *here*. And there were old, familiar-feeling things. So many faces. And insistent voices: "And don't forget to bring home a dozen eggs. We're having omelet . . . Daddy, can I have a new dress for my birthday? . . . If you're the last man in the missile post and condition red is signalled, what is the procedure? . . . But I've got to know what's happened to my family! I've got to know!"

Within his mind, George stared at that last speaker, recognizing the face. *It was himself!* He was like a puppet standing in front of a visiphone, shouting into it at the uniformed man on the other end. *Man? Sure—Colonel Larkin!* "Pullyourselftogetherman!" the Colonel was yelling. "You're a soldier, you hear? You have your duty to do! Now, do it! Fire Betsy and Mabel! At once, you hear?" The Colonel paled, clutched at his throat. "May Day, you fool! People are dying like flies out here. The Ruskies have sneaked in a . . ." The Colonel supported himself on the phone stand. "Major Kinder, I order you to do your duty. Fire Betsy and . . ." He slumped out of sight.

George pushed himself out of the chair. He saw a tall woman, a figure in another world. She stepped aside.

Fire Betsy and Mabel.

The room seemed unfamiliar. Oh, sure. There was the door. These missile post doors were all the same. He'd forgotten for a moment that they'd escaped to another post. In a 'copter. The first post had been under attack. That's what the Colonel was talking about, of course. *May Day. Fire Betsy and Mabel.*

George crossed to the door, opened it.

"What's he doing?" It was the female voice behind him. The sound barely registered.

"He's living out some ancient habit pattern." It was a man's voice. Ren. But Ren was part of an unreal world. This was now. This was urgent.

George heard footsteps padding behind as he emerged into a hall, turned left towards an open door where he could see part of an instrument panel with a sigalert screen. *Fire Betsy and Mabel.* There was an image in his mind— giant grey tubes with sleek delta fins. The big ones. The city-wreckers.

He entered the room with the instrument panel, still dimly conscious of the footsteps following. And distant voices: "What's he doing in here? Shouldn't we stop him? Would it hurt him if we interfered?"

Better not interfere, thought George. He glanced around. There was a difference in the room, a difference in the controls on the panels. But it was difference that he recognized. This was a command post. One of the big centrals. The sequence panel held remote control segments for radio and radar direction of any bird in the entire defence complex. There were overrides. Salvo controls. Barrage. The master console was the newer type with contour handles instead of the old knobbed ones. The anchored chair in Command-Central position held a power arm.

Two people stepped aside as he crossed to the chair, slid into it. Names flitted through his mind: *Jeni. Saim.* He coded the board for recognition to bypass the booby-traps, tested for power. A light glowed in front of him.

"He's turned on a power source." That was Jeni.

"But nothing happened! Nothing exploded!" That was ó Katje.

"He did something first," said Jeni.

"Do these things still have power?" That was Ren.

"Dry capacitors, sun-charged," said Jeni. "Virtually ageless in their preservative."

"Be quiet!" snapped George. He activated the dry-run circuit tester. The board went green except for two plates in the lower left. One indicated firing chamber evacuated of gas. The other showed activity in the firing chamber. George rapped the plates. They remained dead. There couldn't be anything wrong with the birds, he knew. The rest of the board was green.

"I think we'd better stop him," said ó Katje. She felt a moiling war of inhibitions within. Nerves cried for action, were stopped. To interfere with this real-simulacrum might injure him-it. But there was a deadly directness in George's actions that told her what he was doing. He was getting ready to explode those terrible weapon tubes!

"Is he getting ready to set off one of those weapons?" asked Jeni.

"They used collapsed atom energy," said Ren. "It doesn't seem likely he'd . . ."

"I told you to be quiet!" said George. He indicated the dead plates on the board. "Can't those fools get out of there!" He punched the twenty-second warning, felt the dull clamour of it through his feet.

"What's that?" asked Saim.

"Can't those fools hear the warning?" asked George. "Do they want to be burned to cinders?"

ó Katje tottered forward, fighting her inhibitions. She put a hand on George's arm, pulling it as he started to move it towards a red handle on the panel. "Please, George, you must not do . . ."

He struck without warning. One instant he was sitting in the chair, intent on the panel. The next instant he was out of the chair, punching.

ó Katje fell beside the chair. Ren was knocked against a side wall, sagged to the floor. Jeni moved to interfere, and a fist to the side of her head sent her reeling.

Through blurred vision, Jeni saw Saim retrieve ó Katje's staff from the floor, raise it. Jeni staggered sideways, only half conscious, but still able to see Saim bring the staff crashing down on George's head. The look in his eyes as he delivered the blow was almost as terrifying to Jeni as was awareness of the violence itself.

Jeni slumped to the floor, pressing her hands to her eyes.

A shuddery silence settled over the room, then Saim was at her side, cradling her head: "Jeni! My dear, did he hurt you?"

His touch was both repellent and seductive. She started to push him away, felt her palm against his neck. The next instant, they were kissing with a passion that blocked out virtually all other sensation.

So violent! she thought. *So wonderfully violent!*

Saim pulled back, caressed her cheek.

"Saim," she whispered. Then, as memory of violence flooded back into her mind. "You hit him!"

"I saw him hurt you," said Saim. "I don't know. I couldn't let him hurt you."

ó Plar stared down the length of the narrow work table at ó Katje. Yellow light from a ceiling fixture bathed the center of the table, reflected up into the faces of Ren, Jeni and Saim. ó Katje held a cold compress against her jaw. Purple bruises marked Ren's jaw and Jeni's cheek. Only Saim appeared unmarked, except for a cold, staring look about the eyes.

A feeling of sadness and futility filled ó Plar. How long would it be until another accidental set of circumstances combined in a chain such as this one? A Priestess who could dig and explore antiquities without inhibition—would there ever again be another such as ó Katje? And Ren, who had stolen a *kabah* tank, and revived a virtually uninhibited ancient—how could they ever hope to happen on such a sequence ever again?

ó Plar sighed, spoke with deceptive mildness: "ó Katje, you knew it would tempt my ignorance of your hideaway to bring the simulacrum here. Could you not have been satisfied with Ren and Jeni and Saim?"

"I didn't bring the creature here." The movement of her mouth sent pains from her jaw up the side of her head. She grimaced.

"The path of the air machine was marked," said ó Plar. "We couldn't fail to note the direction and then it was simply a matter of localization. You must've known this."

"I tell you I didn't bring them here," said ó Katje. Again, she winced at the pain. She shared some of ó Plar's feeling of futility, but it was tempered by something she could only call negative-emotion. It couldn't be resentment, certainly. But if ó Plar had only waited! The situation had been filled with such accident potential!

"So it was all some kind of trickery," said Saim.

ó Plar tapped his staff against the table for emphasis, said: "You will not discuss what you fail to understand." He kept his attention on ó Katje. "Look at what has happened, ó Katje. The violence. The defilement. Is it any wonder that I . . ."

"You could have waited," she said. And she realized that it *was* resentment she felt. The violence was to blame, of course. It upset every inhibitory balance.

Saim slammed his palm against the table-top, watched the shocked reactions. He could feel something building up within himself. It had something to do with the violence and the dark memories.

"You haven't said anything about my striking the simulacrum," he said.

Again ó Plar tapped his staff against the table. "Saim, must I silence you?"

I could grab the staff away from him, break it before he realized what was happening, thought Saim. And he sank back in his seat, shocked to stillness by the thought. *What is happening to me?* he wondered.

"So," said ó Plar. "Ren, bring your simulacrum from the other room, please."

Ren stood up obediently, left the room. All he could think was: *The shame! The shame! Oh, the shame!*

Jeni reached across the space between their chairs, took Saim's hand. *I started this,* she thought. She looked sidelong at Saim. *Because I refused to lose him. That's when it started. If Ren hadn't already smuggled a rejuvenation tank into the cave, he'd never have thought about building life into Jorj's bones.*

"In a way, we should be glad it's over," said ó Plar. "I'm beginning to see that violence serves no reasonable purpose."

"That's your inhibitions speaking," said ó Katje. "Anyway violence doesn't have to be reasonable." And she thought: *There's a thing we've learned today—the attraction of being unreasonable.*

Ren came back leading George.

"Seat him here by me," said ó Plar. He gestured to an empty chair at his right.

I am called George, George thought. *Major George Kinder, USAF. USAF? That meant something important, but he couldn't fix it to any association. Uniform? More nonsense.* He realized someone was leading him into a room with people. The back of his head throbbed. Pain. And the yellow light hurt his eyes. He sank gratefully into a chair.

"You all have forced a most painful lesson upon yourselves," said ó Plar. "I wish no one to leave this room. You will watch while I do a terrible thing that must be done."

Ren stood behind George's chair. "What are you going to do?" He felt suddenly fearful, cowed by a sense of enormous guilt.

"I am going to awaken the ancient memories," said ó Plar.

Ren stared wildly around the table. "Memories? You mustn't!"

"Part of a man cannot be reconditioned," said ó Plar. "Would you have me destroy him?"

ó Plar felt the weariness in his bones, sighed. So much that could have happened here, and now no alternative but to level it all down to the great common inhibition. No help for it at all. The strictures of his own conditioning were too severe to hope for any other solution.

"But it's just a simulacrum," protested Ren. The terror welling in his mind threatened to overwhelm him.

"You will sit down here on my left where you may watch your simulacrum's face," said ó Plar. He gestured with the staff, kept it aimed at Ren while the doctor obeyed. "Now," said ó Plar, "this is a human being. We will start with that. Ren doesn't want to talk about memories because if he did he'd have to consider this creature more than simulacrum."

"Please?" said Ren.

"I will not warn you again," said ó Plar.

George leaned forward, ignoring the pain in his head. He could feel deep anger against these people, dark and obscure currents surging within himself. "What are you talking about?" he demanded.

ó Plar said: "George, who are we, we people seated around this table?"

George felt rage mingled with frustration. A word came into his mind. "You're Russians!"

ó Plar shook his head. "There are no Russians any more. Or members of any other citizen state." He gestured at his robe, his staff. "Look at me."

George looked—the robe. He glanced around the table, back to ó Plar. Fear kept him silent. The strangeness . . .

"Do we look like anyone you've ever seen?"

George shook his head. *I'm having a nightmare,* he thought. "No," he said.

ó Plar said: "It's been a thousand years since you died, George."

George sat silently staring, unable to face the word or escape it.

A shocked gasp echoed around the table.

"ó Plar?" whispered ó Katje.

"Face it together, all of you," said ó Plar.

"Died?" whispered George.

"You died," said ó Plar. "The pattern is within your mind. The circle complete. I will recall it for you from the account of Pollima, the great historian."

"ó Plar," said Saim. "Uncle, don't you think you should . . ."

"There's no more accurate account," said ó Plar. "A wonderfully terrible account from an eye-witness. Child at the time, of course."

Saim felt the stirrings of vague memories. "But, Uncle . . ."

"What do you mean died?" roared George.

"Listen," said ó Plar. "You felt dizzy, then extremely hot. Your vision blurred. You found it difficult to breathe. You most likely clutched at your throat. You heard your own heart beating. It was like a giant drum in your head. Then you fell unconscious. Then you died. The whole process took about twenty minutes. That's why we refer to it historically as the twenty-minute virus."

I was in the hallway from communications to the control chamber, George thought. *I saw Vince's body sprawled halfway out of the door to the ready room. His face was mottled black with the veins all dark. It was the most terrifying thing I'd ever seen. But the Colonel had just told me to fire Betsy and Mabel. I stepped around Vince's body and headed for the panel. That's when I suddenly felt dizzy.*

"I felt dizzy," he said.

"That's correct," said ó Plar. And he glanced at the frozen shocked faces around the table. *Let them see what they have revived,* he thought. He turned back to the figure of George. "If there was anyone near to hear you, you probably said you were dizzy. Pollima's father was a doctor. That's what he said. He described his symptoms to her as he died. A truly heroic action."

"Hot," said George. "Sweat's pouring off me."

"And what do you see?" asked ó Plar.

"Everything's going blurred," he said. "Like it was under water." The tendons stood out on his neck. His chest strained upwards, collapsed . . . strained upwards, collapsed. "Can't . . . breathe. My chest. Pain. My God! What's that pounding . . . that pounding . . ."

A hand came past ó Plar as Ren slapped a hypoject on to George's neck.

"Thank you, Ren," said ó Plar. "I was about to request that." He stared at George's face, the jaw sagging in unconsciousness. "I imagine that's burned all the old memory channels back into place. One's life pattern tends to be linked to this trauma."

How right he is, thought Saim.

"You . . . monster," whispered Ren.

ó Plar glanced at the doctor. "Me? You malign me. I did a necessary thing, and I'll pay for it much more heavily than you'll pay for what you did. *You* don't have to re-experience Ultimate Conditioning once a year."

ó Katje dropped the compress from her jaw. "ó Plar! I did not think . . . ohhhh . . ."

"Yes, a terrible thing to take into the *kabah* room," said ó Plar. "I most likely won't survive it."

Saim got to his feet. All during ó Plar's recital he had felt darkness peeling away from his mind like onion skins. He felt terrified and exalted. *Kabah* room without end down a corridor of time. Each constricting the will, subjecting the individual life to a dull pattern of placidity.

"I died," whispered George.

"Only once," said Saim. "I've died times without number." He glanced at ó Plar. "In the *kabah* room eh, *Uncle*?"

"Saim!" ó Plar raised his staff.

In one stride, Saim was beside ó Plar, wrenched the staff from still old fingers and smashed it against the table.

"There was no Millennial Display planned, was there, *Uncle*?" demanded Saim.

ó Plar drew himself up in frozen dignity. "We had every reason to suspect an accident would . . ."

"One rocket is all it'd take, eh, Uncle?" Saim glanced at the others in the room, patted Jeni's shoulder, "One rocket. Other rockets are keyed to defensive systems and would go up to knock down an invading rocket. Fear would take care of the rest."

Jeni said: "Saim, you're frightening me!"

"The whole world's like a mindfield, eh, *Uncle*?" asked Saim. "Just waiting to be set off."

George straightened, spoke more strongly. "I died. You said . . . virus." He glanced up at Saim, then at the others. "You must be descended from whoever started it."

ó Plar said: "Saim, I don't understand. The Ultimate Conditioning. You've been . . . how can you . . . why don't the inhibitions . . ."

"Let me answer poor George's questions," said Saim. He slipped into Ancienglis, and the others stared at the fluidity with which he spoke. It wasn't like the thin Educator-veneer over Haribic at all.

"We don't know if it *was* started, George," said Saim. "The virus killed almost every adult. There was an immunity among children below the ages of 12-13-14. Below 12 the virus didn't strike. It took a few 13-year-olds, more 14-year-olds. Above 14 it took all but a small group of adults."

"You can't know this," protested ó Plar. "The last time, when you came out of the *kabah* . . ."

"Be quiet, *Uncle*," said Saim.

George said: "You spoke of some adults pulling through it. Why didn't they get it?"

"They were a sect of Buddhist monks in Arkansas. They'd built themselves a shelter. They expected a war and wanted to preserve their teachings for the survivors."

"You must not bring the names of the Eight Patriarch Bodhisattvas into this room!" protested ó Plar. He felt a giant outrage. *The violence! The defilement!*

"The Bodhisattvas," mused Saim. "Arthur Washington, Lincoln Howorth, Adoula Sampson, Samuael . . ."

"Saim, please!" begged ó Plar, and he stood there trembling between his human hope and his conditioned impulses.

Saim's voice softened. "It's all right, my friend. The dying days are gone. I'm just working myself up to it."

ó Plar closed his eyes, unable to act because that would require violence, but still impelled by *kabah* demands. The dangerous alternative was to resign himself to negative thought. He let the accident prayer well up into consciousness.

"But I was in a shelter," said George. "And I got this virus. How is that possible?"

"You probably had contact with people from the outside," said Saim. "Our Patriarchs didn't. They were in their shelter, breathing filtered air, when the virus came. They didn't even know of it. They stayed there, deep in contemplation until long after the virus was past. Thus did Lord Buddha preserve them. For when they emerged, there were only children in the world."

"Only children," murmured George. "Then my kids, and my wife, all . . ." He broke off, and for a long moment stared up at Saim. Presently, he said in a flat voice: "My world's gone, isn't it?"

"Gone," agreed Saim. "And while it had its share of mistakes, we made a bigger one."

ó Katje said: "Profanity!"

Saim ignored her. "There was an electronics specialist among our Patriarchs," he said. "He thought he could enforce peace for evermore. To do this, he built an instrument that shocks the primitive part of the human mind. The shocks revive terrors from the womb. With this you can introduce terrible enforcements for any behaviour desired. The staff you saw me break? That's a relatively mild form of this instrument. A reminder."

"What behavior?" whispered George. He felt a sense of mounting horror at the logical projection of what Saim had said.

"Aversion to violence," said Saim. "That was the basic idea. It got out of hand for a stupidly simple reason that our Patriarch Samuael should have foreseen."

"Saim, Saim," whispered ó Plar. "I cannot hold out much longer:"

"Patience," said Saim. He faced George. "Do you see it? Many things can be interpreted as violent: Surgery. Sex. Loud noises. Each year the list grows longer and the number of humans grows smaller. There are some the *kabah* tanks cannot revive. The flesh is there, but the will is gone."

ó Katje clasped her hands in front of her, said: "Saim, how can you do this terrible . . ."

"An accident," said Saim. "Eh, *Uncle*?" He glanced at the bowed head of ó Plar. "That's what you've hoped for, isn't it? Deep down where the *kabah* room never quite touches? Down where the little voices whisper and protest?"

"Accident," said Ren. "ó Katje said something about an accident."

"What's this about *kabah* room and accident?" demanded George. "What the hell's a *kabah*?"

Saim looked at the ceiling, then to the door on his right. Out there—the hall, another room, the control panel he'd seen George operating. His memory focused on a red handle. That'd be the one, of course. Even without George's example, he'd have known. His hands would have known what they had probed and studied to exhaustion.

"Won't anybody explain anything?" demanded George.

A few more moments won't matter, thought Saim. He said: "The *kabah* room? That's the great granddaddy of the staffs. That's the personality carver, the shaper, the twister, the . . ."

"Stop it!" screamed ó Katje.

"Help her, Ren," said Saim.

Ren shook himself out of his shock, moved to ó Katje's side.

"Don't touch me!" she hissed.

"You'll take a tranquillizer," said Saim.

It was a flat, no-nonsense command. She found herself taking a pill from Ren's palm, gulping it. The others waited for her to sink back against her chair.

Saim returned his attention to George. "I'm stalling, of course. I've a job to do."

"You'll do it?" whispered ó Plar.

"I'll do it."

George said: "This *kabah*, this instrument you . . ."

"Ultimate Conditioning," said Saim. "Priests and Priestesses must go through it each year. Renewal. If your unconscious protest at the way of things isn't too strong, you get some new personality carving, and you're sent out to live another year, and to herd the flock."

"Saim?" pleaded Jeni. "You *are* Saim, aren't you?"

"I'm Saim," he said, but he kept his attention on George. "So that's how it is, George. Each year the shepherds are re-examined for deviation from the non-violent norm. If you fail . . ." He hesitated. ". . . you lose all your memories, and you spend some time in a big *kabah* rejuvenation tank. When a doctor brings you out of the tank, you're farmed out and raised just like a child." He turned to ó Plar. "Isn't that right, *Uncle?*"

"Please, Saim?" begged ó Plar. "What you're doing to my inhi . . ."

"The explosion!" said Jeni. She rose half out of her chair. "When you died, and I made Ren steal a *kabah* tank to . . . That's what did it. We couldn't understand. For a time, you spoke like a Priest, and acted like a Priest and . . ."

"Then you went blank," said Ren. "And later, you were Saim again."

"Saim!" whispered Jeni. "You were a Priest who failed in the *kabah*!"

Again, Saim patted Jeni's shoulder. "Ren's tank renewed old patterns with the recent ones, but the *kabah* erasure of my memories was recent and strong. Ren contributed to this moment by not connecting the suppressors in the tank. I suspect he didn't know what they were."

"What could we have been thinking of?" whispered Ren. Shame and guilt were submerged in him, cowering behind a massive sense of horror. The fact that he knew this horror came from conditioning helped not at all. "Revive the science of the Elders? Revive violence?"

"I'm beginning to see it," mused George. "A thousand years of this? Christ!"

"What we overlooked when we built the first *kabah* rooms," said Saim. "This is a violent universe. It takes a certain amount of violence to survive in it. But the conditioning prevents violence according to increasingly limited interpretations. In ultimate silence, dropping a pin is violent. The more peaceful we became, the narrower became the interpretation of violence. But if you subtract all violence . . . that's death."

Again Saim patted Jeni's shoulder. "Well, I was hoping somewhat that George would . . . but, no, this is my job." He took a deep breath. "Yes. My job. I'd suggest you all stay down here under cover where you'll be safe from the Millennial Display. Soon, now, the *kabah* rooms will be gone."

ó Plar stood up, spoke slowly against his inhibitions: "You . . . are . . . going . . . to . . . explode . . . the . . . weapons?"

"I'm going to send them winging," said Saim. It was an almost noncommittal statement in its tone.

"But all that death," whispered Jeni. "Saim, think of all the people who'll die!"

"That's all right," said Saim. "They've died before."

And he turned, walked towards the door into the hall. *My name is Samuael,* he thought. *Patriarch Samuael.*

THE TACTFUL SABOTEUR

"Better men than you have tried!" snarled Clinton Watt.

"I quote paragraph four, section ninety-one of the Semantic Revision to the Constitution," said saboteur extraordinary Jorj X. McKie. "'The need for obstructive processes in government having been established as one of the chief safeguards for human rights, the question of immunities must be defined with extreme precision.'"

McKie sat across a glistening desk from the Intergalactic Government's Secretary of Sabotage, Clinton Watt. An air of tension filled the green-walled office, carrying over into the screenview behind Watt which showed an expanse of the System Government's compound and people scurrying about their morning business with a sense of urgency.

Watt, a small man who appeared to crackle with suppressed energy, passed a hand across his shaven head. "All right," he said in a suddenly tired voice. "This is the only Secretariat of government that's never immune from sabotage. You've satisfied the legalities by quoting the law. Now, do your damnedest!"

McKie, whose bulk and fat features usually gave him the appearance of a grandfatherly toad, glowered like a gnome-dragon. His mane of red hair appeared to dance with inner flame.

"Damnedest!" he snapped. "You think I came in here to try to unseat you? You think that?"

And McKie thought: *Let's hope he thinks that!*

"Stop the act, McKie!" Watt said. "We both know you're eligible for this chair." He patted the arm of his chair. "And we both know the only way you can eliminate me and qualify yourself for the appointment is to overcome me with a masterful sabotage. Well, McKie, I've sat here more than eighteen years. Another five months and it'll be a new record. Do your damnedest. I'm waiting."

"I came in here for only one reason," McKie said. "I want to report on the search for saboteur extraordinary Napoleon Bildoon."

McKie sat back wondering: *If Watt knew my real purpose here would he act just this way? Perhaps.* The man had been behaving oddly since the start of this interview, but it was difficult to determine real motive when dealing with a fellow member of the Bureau of Sabotage.

Cautious interest quickened Watt's bony face. He wet his lips with his tongue and it was obvious he was asking himself if this were more of an elaborate ruse. But McKie had been assigned the task of searching for the missing agent, Bildoon, and it was just possible . . .

"Have you found him?" Watt asked.

"I'm not sure," McKie said. He ran his fingers through his red hair. "Bildoon's a Pan-Spechi, you know."

"For disruption's sake!" Watt exploded. "I know who and what my own agents are! But we take care of our own. And when one of our best people just drops from sight . . . What's this about not being sure?"

"The Pan-Spechi are a curious race of creatures," McKie said. "Just because they've taken on humanoid shape we tend to forget their five-phase life cycle."

"Bildoon told me himself he'd hold his group's ego at least another ten years," Watt said. "I think he was being truthful, but . . ." Watt shrugged and some of the bursting energy seemed to leave him. "Well, the group ego's the only place where the Pan-Spechi show vanity so . . ." Again he shrugged.

"My questioning of the other Pan-Spechi in the Bureau has had to be circumspect, of course," McKie said. "But I did follow one lead clear to Achus."

"And?"

McKie brought a white vial from his copious jacket, scattered a metallic powder on the desktop.

Watt pushed himself back from the desk, eyeing the powder with suspicion. He took a cautious sniff, smelled chalf, the quick-scribe powder. Still . . .

"It's just chalf," McKie said. And he thought: *If he buys that, I may get away with this.*

"So scribe it," Watt said.

Concealing his elation, McKie held a chalf-memory stick over the dusted surface. A broken circle with arrows pointing to a right-hand flow appeared in the chalf. At each break in the circle stood a symbol—in one place the Pan-Spechi character for ego, then the delta for fifth gender and, finally, the three lines that signified the dormant creche-triplets.

McKie pointed to the fifth gender delta. "I've seen a Pan-Spechi in this position who looks a bit like Bildoon and *appears* to have some of his mannerisms. There's no identity response from the creature, of course. Well, you know how the quasi-feminine fifth gender reacts."

"Don't ever let that amorous attitude fool you," Watt warned. "In spite of your nasty disposition I wouldn't want to lose you into a Pan-Spechi creche."

"Bildoon wouldn't rob a fellow agent's identity," McKie said. He pulled at his lower lip, feeling an abrupt uncertainty. Here, of course, was the most touchy part of the whole scheme. "If it was Bildoon."

"Did you meet this group's ego holder?" Watt asked and his voice betrayed real interest.

"No," McKie said. "But I think the ego-single of this Pan-Spechi is involved with the Tax Watchers."

McKie waited, wondering if Watt would rise to the bait.

"I've never heard of an ego change being forced onto a Pan-Spechi," Watt said in a musing tone, "but that doesn't mean it's impossible. If those Tax Watcher do-gooders found Bildoon sabotaging their efforts and . . . Hmmm."

"Then Bildoon *was* after the Tax Watchers," McKie said.

Watt scowled. McKie's question was in extreme bad taste. Senior agents, unless joined on a project or where the information was volunteered, didn't snoop openly into the work of their fellows. Left hand and right hand remained mutually ignorant in the Bureau of Sabotage and for good reason. Unless . . . Watt stared speculatively at his saboteur extraordinary.

McKie shrugged as Watt remained silent. "I can't operate on inadequate information," he said. "I must, therefore, resign the assignment to search for Bildoon. Instead, I will now look into the Tax Watchers."

"You will not!" Watt snapped.

McKie forced himself not to look at the design he had drawn on the desktop. The next few moments were the critical ones.

"You'd better have a legal reason for that refusal," McKie said.

Watt swiveled sideways in his chair, glanced at the screenview, then addressed himself to the side wall. "The situation has become one of extreme delicacy, Jorj. It's well known that you're one of our finest saboteurs."

"Save your oil for someone who needs it," McKie growled.

"Then I'll put it this way," Watt said, returning his gaze to McKie. "The Tax Watchers in the last few days have posed a real threat to the Bureau. They've managed to convince a High Court magistrate they deserve the same immunity from our ministrations that a . . . well, public water works or . . . ah . . . food processing plant might enjoy. The magistrate, Judge Edwin Dooley, invoked the Public Safety amendment. Our hands are tied. The slightest suspicion that we've disobeyed the injunction and . . ."

Watt drew a finger across his throat.

"Then I quit," McKie said.

"You'll do nothing of the kind!"

"This TW outfit is trying to eliminate the Bureau, isn't it?" McKie asked. "I remember the oath I took just as well as you do."

"Jorj, you couldn't be that much of a simpleton," Watt said. "You quit, thinking that absolves the Bureau from responsibility for you! That trick's as old as time!"

"Then fire me!" McKie said.

"I've no legal reason to fire you, Jorj."

"Refusal to obey orders of a superior," McKie said.

"It wouldn't fool anybody, you dolt!"

McKie appeared to hesitate, said: "Well, the public doesn't know the inner machinery of how we change the Bureau's command. Perhaps it's time we opened up."

"Jorj, before I could fire you there'd have to be a reason so convincing that . . . Just forget it."

The fat pouches beneath McKie's eyes lifted until the eyes were mere slits. The crucial few moments had arrived. He had managed to smuggle a Jicuzzi stim into this office past all of Watt's detectors, concealing the thing's detectable radiation core within an imitation of the lapel badge that Bureau agents wore.

"In Lieu of Red Tape," McKie said and touched the badge with a finger, feeling the raised letters there—"ILRT." The touch focused the radiation core onto the metallic dust scattered over the desktop.

Watt gripped the arms of the chair, studying McKie with a new look of wary tension.

"We are under legal injunction to keep hands off the Tax Watchers," Watt said. "Anything that happens to those people or to their project for scuttling us—even legitimate accidents—will be laid at our door. We must be able to defend ourselves. No one who has ever been connected with us dares fall under the slightest suspicion of complicity."

"How about a floor waxed to dangerous slickness in the path of one of their messengers? How about a doorlock changed to delay—"

"Nothing."

McKie stared at his chief. Everything depended now on the man holding very still. He knew Watt wore detectors to warn him of concentrated beams of radiation. But this Jicuzzi stim had been rigged to diffuse its charge off the metallic dust on the desk and that required several seconds of relative quiet.

The men held themselves rigid in the staredown until Watt began to wonder at the extreme stillness of McKie's body. The man was even holding his breath!

McKie took a deep breath, stood up.

"I warn you, Jorj," Watt said.

"Warn me?"

"I can restrain you by physical means if necessary."

"Clint, old enemy, save your breath. What's done is done."

A smile touched McKie's wide mouth. He turned, crossed to the room's only door, paused there, hand on knob.

"What have you done?" Watt exploded.

McKie continued to look at him.

Watt's scalp began itching madly. He put a hand there, felt a long tangle of . . . tendrils! They were lengthening under his fingers, growing out of his scalp, waving and writhing.

"A Jicuzzi stim," Watt breathed.

McKie let himself out, closed the door.

Watt leaped out of his chair, raced to the door.

Locked!

He knew McKie and didn't try unlocking it. Frantically, Watt slapped a molecular dispersion wad against the door, dived through as the wad blasted. He landed in the outer hall, stared first in one direction, then the other.

The hall was empty.

Watt sighed. The tendrils had stopped growing, but they were long enough now that he could see them writhing past his eyes—a rainbow mass of wrigglers, part of himself. And McKie with the original stim was the only one who could reverse the process—unless Watt were willing to spend an interminable time with the Jicuzzi themselves. No. That was out of the question.

Watt began assessing his position.

The stim tendrils couldn't be removed surgically, couldn't be tied down or contained in any kind of disguise without endangering the person afflicted with them. Their presence would hamper him, too, during this critical time of trouble with the Tax Watchers. How could he appear in conferences and interviews with these things writhing in their Medusa dance on his head? It would be laughable! He'd be an object of comedy.

And if McKie could stay out of the way until a Case of Exchangement was brought before the full Cabinet . . . But, no! Watt shook his head. This wasn't the kind of sabotage that required a change of command in the Bureau. This was a gross thing. No subtlety to it. This was like a practical joke. Clownish.

But McKie was noted for his clownish attitude, his irreverence for all the blundering self-importance of government.

Have I been self-important? Watt wondered.

In all honesty, he had to admit it.

I'll have to submit my resignation today, he thought. *Right after I fire McKie. One look at me and there'll be no doubt of why I did it. This is about as convincing a reason as you could find.*

Watt turned to his right, headed for the lab to see if they could help him bring this wriggling mass under control.

The President will want me to stay at the helm until McKie makes his next move, Watt thought. *I have to be able to function somehow.*

McKie waited in the living room of the Achusian mansion will ill-concealed unease. Achus was the administrative planet for the Vulpecula region, an area of great wealth, and this room high on a mountaintop commanded a natural view to the southwest across lesser peaks and foothills misted in purple by a westering G3 sun.

But McKie ignored the view, trying to watch all corners of the room at once. He had seen a fifth gender Pan-Spechi here in company with the fourth-gender ego-holder. That could only mean the creche with its three dormants was nearby. By all accounts, this was a dangerous place for someone not protected by bonds of friendship and community of interest.

The value of the Pan-Spechi to the universal human society in which they participated was beyond question. What other species had such refined finesse in deciding when to hinder and when to help? Who else could send a key member of its group into circumstances of extreme peril without fear that the endangered one's knowledge would be lost?

There was always a dormant to take up where the lost one had left off.

Still, the Pan-Spechi did have their idiosyncrasies. And their hungers were at times bizarre.

"Ahhh, McKie."

The voice, deep and masculine, came from his left. McKie whirled to study the figure that came through a door carved from a single artificial emerald of glittering creme de menthe colors.

The speaker was humanoid but with Pan-Spechi multifaceted eyes. He appeared to be a terranic man (except for the blue-green eyes) of an indeterminate, well-preserved middle age. The body suggested a certain daintiness in its yellow tights and singlet. The head was squared in outline with close-cropped blond hair, a fleshy chunk of nose and thick splash of mouth.

"Panthor Bolin here," the Pan-Spechi said. "You are welcome in my home, Jorj McKie."

McKie relaxed slightly. Pan-Spechi were noted for honoring hospitality once it was extended . . . provided the guest didn't violate their mores.

"I'm honored that you've agreed to see me," McKie said.

"The honor is mine," Bolin said. "We've long recognized you as a person whose understanding of the Pan-Spechi is most subtle and penetrating. I've longed for the chance to have uninhibited conversation with you. And here you are." He indicated a chairdog against the wall to his right, snapped his fingers. The semi-sentient artifact glided to a position behind McKie. "Please be seated."

McKie, his caution realerted by Bolin's reference to "uninhibited conversation," sank into the chairdog, patting it until it assumed the contours he wanted.

Bolin took a chairdog facing him, leaving only about a meter separating their knees.

"Have our egos shared nearness before?" McKie asked. "You appeared to recognize me."

"Recognition goes deeper than ego," Bolin said. "Do you wish to join identities and explore this question?"

McKie wet his lips with his tongue. This was delicate ground with the Pan-Spechi, whose one ego moved somehow from member to member of the unit group as they traversed their *circle of being.*

"I . . . ah . . . not at this time," McKie said.

"Well spoken," Bolin said. "Should you ever change your mind, my ego-group would consider it a most signal honor. Yours is a strong identity, one we respect."

"I'm . . . most honored," McKie said. He rubbed nervously at his jaw, recognizing the dangers in this conversation. Each Pan-Spechi group maintained a supremely jealous attitude of and about its wandering ego. The ego imbued the holder of it with a touchy sense of honor. Inquiries about it could be carried out only through such formula questions as McKie already had asked.

Still, if this were a member of the pent-archal life circle containing the missing saboteur extraordinary Napoleon Bildoon . . . if it were, much would be explained.

"You're wondering if we really can communicate," Bolin said. McKie nodded.

"The concept of *humanity,*" Bolin said, "—our term for it would translate approximately as *comsentiency*—has been extended to encompass many differing shapes, life systems and methods of mentation. And yet we have never been sure about this question. It's one of the major reasons many of us have adopted your life-shape and much of your metabolism. We wished to experience your strengths and your weaknesses. This helps . . . but is not an absolute solution."

"Weaknesses?" McKie asked, suddenly wary.

"Ahhh-hummm," Bolin said. "I see. To allay your suspicions I will have translated for you soon one of our major works. Its title would be, approximately, *The Developmental Influence of Weaknesses.* One of the strongest sympathetic bonds we have with your species, for example, is the fact that we both originated as extremely vulnerable surface-bound creatures, whose most sophisticated defense came to be the social structure."

"I'll be most interested to see the translation," McKie said.

"Do you wish more amenities or do you care to state your business now?" Bolin asked.

"I was . . . ah . . . assigned to seek out a missing agent of our Bureau," McKie said, "to be certain no harm has befallen this . . . ah . . . agent."

"Your avoidance of gender is most refined," Bolin said. "I appreciate the delicacy of your position and your good taste. I will say this for now: the Pan-Spechi you seek is not at this time in need of your assistance. Your concern, however, is appreciated. It will be communicated to those upon whom it will have the most influence."

"That's a great relief to me," McKie said. And he wondered: *What did he really mean by that?* This thought elicited another, and McKie said: "Whenever I run into this problem of communication between species I'm reminded of an old culture/teaching story."

"Oh?" Bolin registered polite curiosity.

"Two practioners of the art of mental healing, so the story goes, passed each other every morning on their way to their respective offices. They knew each other, but weren't on intimate terms. One morning as they approached each other, one of them turned to the other and said, 'Good morning.' The one greeted failed to respond, but continued toward his office. Presently, though, he stopped, turned and stared at the retreating back of the man who'd spoken, musing to himself: 'Now what did he really mean by that?' "

Bolin began to chuckle, then laugh. His laughter grew louder and louder until he was holding his sides.

It wasn't that funny, McKie thought.

Bolin's laughter subsided. "A very educational story," he said. "I'm deeply indebted to you. This story shows your awareness of how important it is in communication that we be aware of the other's identity."

Does it? McKie wondered. *How's that?*

And McKie found himself caught up by his knowledge of how the Pan-Spechi could pass a single ego-identity from individual to individual within the life circle group of five distinct protoplasmic units. He wondered how it felt when the ego-holder gave up the identity to become the fifth gender, passing the ego spark to a newly matured unit from the creche. Did the fifth gender willingly become the creche nurse and give itself up as a mysterious identity-food for the three dormants in the creche? he wondered.

"I heard about what you did to Secretary of Sabotage Clinton Watt," Bolin said. "The story of your dismissal from the service preceded you here."

"Yes," McKie said. "That's why I'm here, too."

"You've penetrated to the fact that our Pan-Spechi community here on Achus is the heart of the Tax Watchers' organization," Bolin said. "It was very brave of you to walk right into our hands. I understand how much more courage it takes for your kind to face unit extinction than it does for our kind. Admirable! You are indeed a prize."

McKie fought down a sensation of panic, reminding himself that the records he had left in his private locker at Bureau headquarters could be deciphered in time even if he did not return.

"Yes," Bolin said, "you wish to satisfy yourself that the ascension of a Pan-Spechi to the head of your Bureau will pose no threat to other human species. This is understandable."

McKie shook his head to clear it. "Do you read minds?" he demanded.

"Telepathy is not one of our accomplishments," Bolin said, his voice heavy with menace. "I do hope that was a generalized question and in no way directed at the intimacies of my ego-group."

"I felt that you were reading my mind," McKie said, tensing himself for defense.

"That was how I interpreted the question," Bolin said. "Forgive my question. I should not have doubted your delicacy or your tact."

"You do hope to place a member in the job of Bureau Secretary, though?" McKie said.

"Remarkable that you should've suspected it," Bolin said. "How can you be sure our intention is not merely to destroy the Bureau?"

"I'm not," McKie glanced around the room, regretting that he had been forced to act alone.

"Where did we give ourselves away?" Bolin mused.

"Let me remind you," McKie said, "that I have accepted the hospitality you offered and that I've not offended your mores."

"Most remarkable," Bolin said. "In spite of all the temptations I offered, you have not offended our mores. This is true. You are an embarrassment, indeed you are. But perhaps you have a weapon. Yes?"

McKie lifted a wavering *shape* from an inner pocket.

"Ahhh, the Jicuzzi stim," Bolin said. "Now, let me see, is that a weapon?"

McKie held the *shape* on his palm. It appeared flat at first, like a palm-sized sheet of pink paper. Gradually, the flatness grew a superimposed image of a tube laid on its surface, then another image of an S-curved spring that coiled and wound around the tube.

"Our species can control its shape to some extent," Bolin said. "There's some question on whether I can consider this a weapon."

McKie curled his fingers around the *shape,* squeezed. There came a pop, and fumeroles of purple light emerged between his fingers accompanied by an odor of burnt sugar.

"Exit stim," McKie said. "Now I'm completely defenseless, entirely dependent upon your hospitality."

"Ah, you are a tricky one," Bolin said. "But have you no regard for Ser Clinton Watt? To him, the change you forced upon him is an affliction. You've destroyed the instrument that might have reversed the process."

"He can apply to the Jicuzzi," McKie said, wondering why Bolin should concern himself over Watt.

"Ah, but they will ask your permission to intervene," Bolin said. "They are so formal. Drafting their request should take at least three standard years. They will not take the slightest chance of offending you. And you, of course, cannot volunteer your permission without offending them. You know, they may even build a nerve-image of you upon which to test their petition. You are not a callous person, McKie, in spite of your clownish poses. I'd not realized how important this confrontation was to you."

"Since I'm completely at your mercy," McKie said, "would you try to stop me from leaving here?"

"An interesting question," Bolin said. "You have information I don't want revealed at this time. You're aware of this, naturally?"

"Naturally."

"I find the Constitution a most wonderful document," Bolin said. "The profound awareness of the individual's identity and its relationship to society as a whole. Of particular interest is the portion dealing with the Bureau of Sabotage, those amendments recognizing that the Bureau itself might at times need . . . ah . . . adjustment."

Now what's he driving at? McKie wondered. And he noted how Bolin squinted his eyes in thought, leaving only a thin line of faceted glitter.

"I shall speak now as chief officer of the Tax Watchers," Bolin said, "reminding you that we are legally immune from sabotage."

I've found out what I wanted to know, McKie thought. Now if I can only get out of here with *it!*

"Let us consider the training of saboteurs extraordinary," Bolin said. "What do the trainees learn about the make-work and featherbedding elements in Bureau activity?"

He's not going to trap me in a lie, McKie thought. "We come right out and tell our trainees that one of our chief functions is to create jobs for the politicians to fill," he said. "The more hands in the pie, the slower the mixing."

"You've heard that telling a falsehood to your host is a great breach of Pan-Spechi mores, I see," Bolin said. "You understand, of course, that refusal to answer certain questions is interpreted as a falsehood?"

"So I've been told," McKie said.

"Wonderful! And what are your trainees told about the foot dragging and the monkeywrenches you throw into the path of legislation?"

"I quote from the pertinent training brochure," McKie said. " 'A major function of the Bureau is to slow passage of legislation.' "

"Magnificent! And what about the disputes and outright battles Bureau agents have been known to incite?"

"Strictly routine," McKie said. "We're duty bound to encourage the growth of anger in government wherever we can. It exposes the temperamental types, the ones who can't control themselves, who can't think on their feet."

"Ah," Bolin said. "How entertaining."

"We keep entertainment value in mind," McKie admitted. "We use drama and flamboyance wherever possible to keep our activities fascinating to the public."

"Flamboyant obstructionism," Bolin mused.

"Obstruction is a factor in strength," McKie said. "Only the strongest surmount the obstructions to succeed in government. The strongest . . . or the most devious, which is more or less the same thing when it comes to government."

"How illuminating," Bolin said. He rubbed the backs of his hands, a Pan-Spechi mannerism denoting satisfaction. "Do you have special instructions regarding political parties?"

"We stir up dissent between them," McKie said. "Opposition tends to expose reality, that's one of our axioms."

"Would you characterize Bureau agents as troublemakers?"

"Of course! My parents were happy as the devil when I showed trouble-making tendencies at an early age. They knew there'd be a lucrative outlet for this when I grew up. They saw to it that I was channeled in the right di-rections all through school—special classes in Applied Destruction, Ad-vanced Irritation, Anger I and II . . . only the best teachers."

"You're suggesting the Bureau's an outlet for society's regular crop of troublemakers?"

"Isn't that obvious? And troublemakers naturally call for the services of troubleshooters. That's an outlet for do-gooders. You've a check and balance system serving society."

McKie waited, watching the Pan-Spechi, wondering if his answers had gone far enough.

"I speak as a Tax Watcher, you understand?" Bolin asked.

"I understand."

"The public pays for this Bureau. In essence, the public is paying people to cause trouble."

"Isn't that what we do when we hire police, tax investigators and the like?" McKie asked.

A look of gloating satisfaction came over Bolin's face. "But these agen-cies operate for the greater good of humanity!" he said.

"Before he begins training," McKie said, and his voice took on a solemn, lecturing tone, "the potential saboteur is shown the entire sordid record of history. The do-gooders succeeded once . . . long ago. They eliminated vir-tually all red tape from government. This great machine with its power over human lives slipped into high speed. It moved faster and faster." McKie's voice grew louder. "Laws were conceived and passed in the same hour! Ap-propriations came and were gone in a fortnight. New bureaus flashed into existence for the most insubstantial reasons."

McKie took a deep breath, realizing he'd put sincere emotional weight behind his words.

"Fascinating," Bolin said. "Efficient government, eh?"

"Efficient?" McKie's voice was filled with outrage. "It was like a great wheel thrown suddenly out of balance! The whole structure of government was in imminent danger of fragmenting before a handful of people, wise with hindsight, used measures of desperation and started what was called the Sabotage Corps."

"Ahhh, yes, I've heard about the Corps' violence."

He's needling me, McKie thought, but found that honest anger helped now. "All right, there was bloodshed and terrible destruction at the beginning," he said. "But the big wheels were slowed. Government developed a controllable speed."

"Sabotage," Bolin sneered. "In lieu of red tape."

I needed that reminder, McKie thought.

"No task too small for Sabotage, no task too large," McKie said. "We keep the wheel turning slowly and smoothly. Some anonymous Corpsman put it into words, a long time ago: 'When in doubt, delay the big ones and speed the little ones.'"

"Would you say the Tax Watchers were a 'big one' or a 'little one'?" Bolin asked, his voice mild.

"Big one," McKie said and waited for Bolin to pounce.

But the Pan-Spechi appeared amused. "An unhappy answer."

"As it says in the Constitution," McKie said, "'The pursuit of unhappiness is an inalienable right of all humans.'"

"Trouble is as trouble does," Bolin said and clapped his hands.

Two Pan-Spechi in the uniforms of system police came through the creme de menthe emerald door.

"You heard?" Bolin asked.

"We heard," one of the police said.

"Was he defending his bureau?" Bolin asked.

"He was," the policeman said.

"You've seen the court order," Bolin said. "It pains me because Ser McKie accepted the hospitality of my house, but he must be held incommunicado until he's needed in court. He's to be treated kindly, you understand?"

Is he really bent on destroying the Bureau? McKie asked himself in sudden consternation. *Do I have it figured wrong?*

"You contend my words were sabotage?" McKie asked.

"Clearly an attempt to sway the chief officer of the Tax Watchers from his avowed duties," Bolin said. He stood, bowed.

McKie lifted himself out of the chairdog, assumed an air of confidence he did not feel. He clasped his thick-fingered hands together and bowed low, a grandfather toad rising from the deep to give his benediction. "In the words of the ancient proverb," he said, "'The righteous man lives deep within a cavern and the sky appears to him as nothing but a small round hole.'"

Wrapping himself in dignity, McKie allowed the police to escort him from the room.

Behind him, Bolin gave voice to puzzlement: "Now, what did he mean by that?"

"Hear ye! Hear ye! System High Court, First Bench, Central Sector, is now in session!"

The robo-clerk darted back and forth across the cleared lift dais of the courtarena, its metal curves glittering in the morning light that poured down through the domed weather cover. Its voice, designed to fit precisely into the great circular room, penetrated to the farthest walls: "All persons having petitions before this court draw near!"

The silvery half globe carrying First Magistrate Edwin Dooley glided through an aperture behind the lift dais and was raised to an appropriate height. His white sword of justice lay diagonally across the bench in front of him. Dooley himself sat in dignified silence while the robo-clerk finished its stentorian announcement and rolled to a stop just beyond the lift field.

Judge Dooley was a tall, black browed man who affected the ancient look with ebon robes over white linen. He was noted for decisions of classic penetration.

He sat now with his face held in rigid immobility to conceal his anger and disquiet. Why had they put him in this hot spot? Because he'd granted the Tax Watchers' injunction? No matter how he ruled now, the result likely would be uproar. Even President Hindley was watching this one through one of the hotline projectors.

The President had called shortly before this session. It had been Phil and Ed all through the conversation, but the intent remained clear. The Administration was concerned about this case. Vital legislation pended; votes were needed. Neither the budget nor the Bureau of Sabotage had entered their conversation, but the President had made his point—*don't compromise the Bureau but save that Tax Watcher support for the Administration!*

"Clerk, the roster," Judge Dooley said.

And he thought: *They'll get judgment according to strict interpretation of the law! Let them argue with that!*

The robo-clerk's reelslate buzzed. Words appeared on the repeater in front of the judge as the clerk's voice announced: "The People versus Clinton Watt, Jorj X. McKie and the Bureau of Sabotage."

Dooley looked down into the courtarena, noting the group seated at the black oblong table in the Defense ring on his left: a sour-faced Watt with his rainbow horror of Medusa head, McKie's fat features composed in a look of someone trying not to snicker at a sly joke—the two defendants flanking their attorney, Pander Oulson, the Bureau of Sabotage's chief counsel. Oulson was a great thug of a figure in defense white with glistening eyes under beetle brows and a face fashioned mostly of scars.

At the Prosecution table on the right sat Prosecutor Holjance Vohnbrook, a tall scarecrow of a man dressed in conviction red. Gray hair topped a stern face as grim and forbidding as a latter-day Cotton Mather. Beside him sat a frightened appearing young aide and Panthor Bolin, the Pan-Spechi complaintant, his multifaceted eyes hidden beneath veined lids.

"Are we joined for trial?" Dooley asked.

Both Oulson and Vohnbrook arose, nodded.

"If the court pleases," Vohnbrook rumbled, "I would like to remind the

Bureau of Sabotage personnel present that this court is exempt from their ministrations."

"If the prosecutor trips over his own feet," Oulson said, "I assure him it will be his own clumsiness and no act of mine nor of my colleagues."

Vohnbrook's face darkened with a rush of blood. "It's well known how you . . ."

A great drumming boomed through the courtarena as Dooley touched the handle of his sword of office. The sound drowned the prosecutor's words. When silence was restored, Dooley said: "This court will tolerate no displays of personality. I wish that understood at the outset."

Oulson smiled, a look like a grimace in his scarred face. "I apologize, Your Honor," he said.

Dooley sank back into his chair, noting the gleam in Oulson's eyes. It occurred to Dooley then that the defense attorney, sabotage-trained, could have brought on the prosecutor's attack to gain the court's sympathy.

"The charge is outlaw sabotage in violation of this court's injunction," Dooley said. "I understand that opening statements have been waived by both sides, the public having been admitted to causae in this matter by appropriate postings?"

"So recorded," intoned the robo-clerk.

Oulson leaned forward against the defense table, said: "Your Honor, defendant Jorj X. McKie has not accepted me as counsel and wishes to argue for separate trial. I am here now representing only the Bureau and Clinton Watt."

"Who is appearing for defendant McKie?" the judge asked.

McKie, feeling like a man leaping over a precipice, got to his feet, said: "I wish to represent myself, Your Honor."

"You should be cautioned against this course," Dooley said.

"Ser Oulson has advised me I have a fool for a client," McKie said. "But in common with most Bureau agents, I have legal training. I've been admitted to the System Bar and have practiced under such codes as the Gowachin where the double-negative innocence requirement must be satisfied before bringing criminal accusation against the prosecutor and proceeding backward the premise that . . ."

"This is not Gowachin," Judge Dooley said.

"May I remind the Court," Vohnbrook said, "that defendant McKie is a saboteur extraordinary. This goes beyond questions of champerty. Every utterance this man . . ."

"The law's the same for official saboteurs as it is for others in respect to the issue at hand," Oulson said.

"Gentlemen!" the judge said. "If you please? I will decide the law in this court." He waited through a long moment of silence. "The behavior of all parties in this matter is receiving my most careful attention."

McKie forced himself to radiate calm good humor.

Watt, whose profound knowledge of the saboteur extraordinary made this pose a danger signal, tugged violently at the sleeve of defense attorney Oulson. Oulson waved him away. Watt glowered at McKie.

"If the court permits," McKie said, "a joint defense on the present charge would appear to violate . . ."

"The court is well aware that this case was bound over on the basis of deposa summation through a ruling by a robo-legum," Dooley said. "I warn both defense and prosecution, however, that I make my own decisions in such matters. Law and robo-legum are both human constructions and require human interpretation. And I will add that, as far as I'm concerned, in all conflicts between human agencies and machine agencies the human agencies are paramount."

"Is this a hearing or a trial?" McKie asked.

"We will proceed as in trial, subject to the evidence as presented."

McKie rested his palms on the edge of the defense table, studying the judge. The saboteur felt a surge of misgiving. Dooley was a no-nonsense customer. He had left himself a wide avenue within the indictment. And this was a case that went far beyond immediate danger to the Bureau of Sabotage. Far-reaching precedents could be set here this day—or disaster could strike. Ignoring instincts of self-preservation, McKie wondered if he dared try sabotage within the confines of the court.

"The robo-legum indictment requires joint defense," McKie said. "I admit sabotage against Ser Clinton Watt, but remind the court of Paragraph Four, section ninety-one, of the Semantic Revision to the Constitution, wherein the Secretary of Sabotage is exempted from all immunities. I move to quash the indictment as it regards myself. I was at the time a legal officer of the Bureau required by my duties to test the abilities of my superior."

Vohnbrook scowled at McKie.

"Mmmm," Dooley said. He saw that the prosecutor had detected where McKie's logic must lead. If McKie were legally dismissed from the Bureau at the time of his conversation with the Pan-Spechi, the prosecution's case might fall through.

"Does the prosecutor wish to seek a conspiracy indictment?" Dooley asked.

For the first time since entering the courtarena, defense attorney Oulson appeared agitated. He bent his scarred features close to Watt's gorgon head, conferred in whispers with the defendant. Oulson's face grew darker and darker as he whispered. Watt's gorgon tendrils writhed in agitation.

"We don't seek a conspiracy indictment at this time," Vohnbrook said. "However, we would be willing to separate . . ."

"Your Honor!" Oulson said, surging to his feet. "Defense must protest separation of indictments at this time. It's our contention that . . ."

"Court cautions both counsel in this matter that this is not a Gowachin jurisdiction," Dooley said in an angry voice. "We don't have to convict the defender and exonerate the prosecutor before trying a case! However, if either of you would wish a change of venue . . ."

Vohnbrook, a smug expression on his lean face, bowed to the judge. "Your Honor," he said, "we wish at this time to request removal of defendant McKie from the indictment and ask that he be held as a prosecution witness."

"Objection!" Oulson shouted.

"Prosecution well knows it cannot hold a key witness under trumped up . . ."

"Overruled," Dooley said.

"Exception!"

"Noted."

Dooley waited as Oulson sank into his chair. *This is a day to remember,* the judge thought. *Sabotage itself outfoxed!* Then he noted the glint of sly humor in the eyes of saboteur extraordinary McKie, realizing with an abrupt sense of caution that McKie, too, had maneuvered for this position.

"Prosecution may call its first witness," the judge said, and he punched a code signal that sent a robo-aide to escort McKie away from the defense table and into a holding box.

A look of almost-pleasure came over prosecutor Vohnbrook's cadaverous face. He rubbed one of his downdrooping eyelids, said: "Call Panthor Bolin."

The Achusian capitalist got to his feet, strode to the witness ring. The robo-clerk's screen flashed for the record: "Panthor Bolin of Achus IV, certified witness in case $A011-5BD_4gGY74R_6$ of System High Court ZRZ[1]."

"The oath of sincerity having been administered, Panthor Bolin is prepared for testifying," the robo-clerk recited.

"Panthor Bolin, are you chief officer of the civil organization known as the Tax Watchers?" Vohnbrook asked.

"I . . . ah . . . y-yes," Bolin faltered. He passed a large blue handkerchief across his forehead, staring sharply at McKie.

He just now realizes what it is I must do, McKie thought.

"I show you this recording from the robo-legum indictment proceedings," Vohnbrook said. "It is certified by System police as being a conversation between yourself and Jorj X. McKie in which . . ."

"Your Honor!" Oulson objected. "Both witnesses to this alleged conversation are present in this courtarena. There are more direct ways to bring out any pertinent information from this matter. Further, since the clear threat of a conspiracy charge remains in this case, I object to introducing this recording as forcing a man to testify against himself."

"Ser McKie is no longer on trial here and Ser Oulson is not McKie's attorney of record," Vohnbrook gloated.

"The objection does, however, have some merit," Dooley said. He looked at McKie seated in the holding box.

"There's nothing shameful about that conversation with Ser Bolin," McKie said. "I've no objection to introducing this record of the conversation."

Bolin rose up on his toes, made as though to speak, sank back.

Now he is certain, McKie thought.

"Then I will admit this record subject to judicial deletions," Dooley said.

Clinton Watt, seated at the defense table, buried his gorgon head in his arms.

Vohnbrook, a death's-head grin on his long face, said: "Ser Bolin, I show you this recording. Now, in this conversation, was Sabotage Agent McKie subjected to any form of coercion?"

"Objection!" Oulson roared, surging to his feet. His scarred face was a scowling mask. "At the time of this alleged recording, Ser McKie was not an agent of the Bureau!" He looked at Vohnbrook. "Defense objects to the prosecutor's obvious effort to link Ser McKie with . . ."

"*Alleged* conversation!" Vohnbrook snarled. "Ser McKie himself admits the exchange!"

In a weary voice, Dooley said: "Objection sustained. Unless tangible evidence of conspiracy is introduced here, references to Ser McKie as an agent of Sabotage will not be admitted here."

"But Your Honor," Vohnbrook protested, "Ser McKie's own actions preclude any other interpretation!"

"I've ruled on this point," Dooley said. "Proceed."

McKie got to his feet in the holding box, said: "Would Your Honor permit me to act as a friend of the Court here?"

Dooley leaned back, hand on chin, turning the question over in his mind. A general feeling of uneasiness about the case was increasing in him and he couldn't pinpoint it. McKie's every action appeared suspect. Dooley reminded himself that the saboteur extraordinary was notorious for sly plots, for devious and convoluted schemes of the wildest and most improbable inversions—like onion layers in a five dimensional klein-shape. The man's success in practicing under the Gowachin legal code could be understood.

"You may explain what you have in mind," Dooley said, "but I'm not yet ready to admit your statements into the record."

"The Bureau of Sabotage's own Code would clarify matters," McKie said, realizing that these words burned his bridges behind him. "My action in successfully sabotaging *acting* Secretary Watt is a matter of record."

McKie pointed to the gorgon mass visible as Watt lifted his head and glared across the room.

"*Acting* Secretary?" the judge asked.

"So it must be presumed," McKie said. "Under the Bureau's Code, once the Secretary is sabotaged he . . ."

"Your Honor!" Oulson shouted. "We are in danger of breach of security here! I understand these proceedings are being broadcast!"

"As Director-in-Limbo of the Bureau of Sabotage, I will decide what is a breach of security and what isn't!" McKie snapped.

Watt returned his head to his arms, groaned.

Oulson sputtered.

Dooley stared at McKie in shock.

Vohnbrook broke the spell. The prosecutor said: "Your Honor, this man has not been sworn to sincerity. I suggest we excuse Ser Bolin for the time being and have Ser McKie continue his *explanation* under oath."

Dooley took a deep breath, said: "Does defense have any questions of Ser Bolin at this time?"

"Not at this time," Oulson muttered. "I presume he's subject to recall?"

"He is," Dooley said, turning to McKie. "Take the witness ring, Ser McKie."

Bolin, moving like a sleepwalker, stepped out of the ring, returned to the prosecution table. The Pan-Spechi's multi-faceted eyes reflected an odd glitter, moving with a trapped sense of evasiveness.

McKie entered the ring, took the oath and faced Vohnbrook, composing his features in a look of purposeful decisiveness that he knew his actions must reflect.

"You called yourself Director-in-Limbo of the Bureau of Sabotage," Vohnbrook said. "Would you explain that, please?"

Before McKie could answer, Watt lifted his head from his arms, growled: "You traitor, McKie!"

Dooley grabbed the pommel of his sword of justice to indicate an absolute position and barked: "I will tolerate no outbursts in my court!"

Oulson put a hand on Watt's shoulder. Both of them glared at McKie. The Medusa tendrils of Watt's head writhed as they ranged through the rainbow spectrum.

"I caution the witness," Dooley said, "that his remarks would appear to admit a conspiracy. Anything he says now may be used against him."

"No conspiracy, Your Honor," McKie said. He faced Vohnbrook, but appeared to be addressing Watt. "Over the centuries, the function of Sabotage in the government has grown more and more open, but certain aspects of changing the guard, so to speak, have been held as a highly placed secret. The rule is that if a man can protect himself from sabotage he's fit to boss Sabotage. Once sabotaged, however, the Bureau's Secretary must resign and submit his position to the President and the full Cabinet."

"He's out?" Dooley asked.

"Not necessarily," McKie said. "If the act of sabotage against the Secretary is profound enough, subtle enough, carries enough far reaching effects, the Secretary is replaced by the successful saboteur. He is, indeed, out."

"Then it's now up to the President and the Cabinet to decide between Ser Watt and yourself, is that what you're saying?" Dooley asked.

"Me?" McKie asked. "No, I'm Director-in-Limbo because I accomplished a successful *act* of sabotage against Ser Watt and because I happen to be senior saboteur extraordinary on duty."

"But it's alleged that you were fired," Vohnbrook objected.

"A formality," McKie said. "It's customary to fire the saboteur who's successful in such an effort. This makes him eligible for appointment as Secretary if he so aspires. However, I have no such ambition at this time."

Watt jerked upright, staring at McKie.

McKie ran a finger around his collar, realizing the physical peril he was about to face. A glance at the Pan-Spechi confirmed the feeling. Panthor Bolin was holding himself in check by a visible effort.

"This is all very interesting," Vohnbrook sneered, "but how can it possibly have any bearing on the present action? The charge here is outlaw sabotage against the Tax Watchers represented by the person of Ser Panthor Bolin. If Ser McKie . . ."

"If the distinguished prosecutor will permit me," McKie said, "I believe I can set his fears at rest. It should be obvious to—"

"There's conspiracy here!" Vohnbrook shouted. "What about the . . ."

A loud pounding interrupted him as Judge Dooley lifted his sword, its theremin effect filling the room. When silence had been restored, the judge lowered his sword, replaced it firmly on the ledge in front of him.

Dooley took a moment to calm himself. He sensed now the delicate political edge he walked and thanked his stars that he had left the door open to rule that the present session was a hearing.

"We will now proceed in an orderly fashion," Dooley said. "That's one of the things courts are for, you know." He took a deep breath. "Now, there are several people present whose dedication to the maintenance of law and order should be beyond question. I'd think that among those we should number Ser Prosecutor Vohnbrook; the distinguished defense counsel, Ser Oulson; Ser Bolin, whose race is noted for its reasonableness and humanity; and the distinguished representatives of the Bureau of Sabotage, whose actions may at times annoy and anger us, but who are, we know, consecrated to the principle of strengthening us and exposing our inner resources."

This judge missed his calling, McKie thought. *With speeches like that, he could get into the Legislative branch.*

Abashed, Vohnbrook sank back into his chair.

"Now," the judge said, "unless I'm mistaken, Ser McKie has referred to two acts of sabotage." Dooley glanced down at McKie. "Ser McKie?"

"So it would appear, Your Honor," McKie said, hoping he read the judge's present attitude correctly. "However, this court may be in a unique position to rule on that very question. You see, Your Honor, the alleged act of sabotage to which I refer was initiated by a Pan-Spechi agent of the Bureau. Now, though, the secondary benefits of that action appear to be sought after by a creche mate of that agent, whose . . ."

"You dare suggest that I'm not the holder of my cell's ego?" Bolin demanded.

Without knowing quite where it was or what it was, McKie was aware that a weapon had been trained on him by the Pan-Spechi. References in their culture to the weapon for defense of the ego were clear enough.

"I make no such suggestion," McKie said, speaking hastily and with as much sincerity as he could put into his voice. "But surely you cannot have misinterpreted the terranic-human culture so much that you do not know what will happen now."

Warned by some instinct, the judge and other spectators to this interchange remained silent.

Bolin appeared to be trembling in every cell of his body. "I am distressed," he muttered.

"If there were a way to achieve the necessary rapport and avoid that distress I would have taken it," McKie said. "Can you see another way?"

Still trembling, Bolin said: "I must do what I must do."

In a low voice, Dooley said: "Ser McKie, just what is going on here?"

"Two cultures are, at last, attempting to understand each other," McKie said. "We've lived together in apparent understanding for centuries, but appearances can be deceptive."

Oulson started to rise, was pulled back by Watt.

And McKie noted that his former Bureau chief had assessed the peril here. It was a point in Watt's favor.

"You understand, Ser Bolin," McKie said, watching the Pan-Spechi carefully, "that these things must be brought into the open and discussed carefully before a decision can be reached in this court. It's a rule of law to which you've submitted. I'm inclined to favor your bid for the Secretariat, but my own decision awaits the outcome of this hearing."

"What things must be discussed?" Dooley demanded. "And what gives you the right, Ser McKie, to call this a hearing?"

"A figure of speech," McKie said, but he kept his attention on the Pan-Spechi, wondering what the terrible weapon was that the race used in defense of its egos, "What do you say, Ser Bolin?"

"You protect the sanctity of your home life," Bolin said. "Do you deny me the same right?"

"Sanctity, not secrecy," McKie said.

Dooley looked from McKie to Bolin, noted the compressed-spring look of the Pan-Spechi, the way he kept a hand hidden in a jacket pocket. It occurred to the judge then that the Pan-Spechi might have a weapon ready to use against others in this court. Bolin had that look about him. Dooley hesitated on the point of calling guards, reviewed what he knew of the Pan-Spechi. He decided not to cause a crisis. The Pan-Spechi were admitted to the concourse of humanity, good friends but terrible enemies, and there were always those allusions to their hidden powers, to their ego jealousies, to the fierceness with which they defended the secrecy of their creches.

Slowly, Bolin overcame the trembling. "Say what you feel you must," he growled.

McKie said a silent prayer of hope that the Pan-Spechi could control his reflexes, addressed himself to the nexus of pickups on the far wall that was recording this courtarena scene for broadcast to the entire universe.

"A Pan-Spechi who took the name of Napoleon Bildoon was one of the leading agents in the Bureau of Sabotage," McKie said. "Agent Bildoon dropped from sight at the time Panthor Bolin took over as chief of the Tax Watchers. It's highly probable that the Tax Watcher organization is an elaborate and subtle sabotage of the Bureau of Sabotage itself, a move originated by Bildoon."

"There is no such person as Bildoon!" Bolin cried.

"Ser McKie," Judge Dooley said, "would you care to continue this interchange in the privacy of my chambers?" The judge stared down at the saboteur, trying to appear kindly but firm.

"Your Honor," McKie said, "may we, out of respect for a fellow human, leave that decision to Ser Bolin?"

Bolin turned his multi-faceted eyes toward the bench, spoke in a low voice: "If the court please, it were best this were done openly." He jerked his hand from his pocket. It came out empty. He leaned across the table, gripped the far edge. "Continue, if you please, Ser."

McKie swallowed, momentarily overcome with admiration for the Pan-Spechi. "It will be a distinct pleasure to serve under you, Ser Bolin," McKie said.

"Do what you must!" Bolin rasped.

McKie looked from the wonderment in the faces of Watt and the attorneys up to the questioning eyes of Judge Dooley. "In Pan-Spechi parlance, there is no person called Bildoon. But there was such a person, a group mate of Ser Bolin. I hope you notice the similarity in the names they chose for themselves?"

"Ah . . . yes," Dooley said.

"I'm afraid I've been somewhat of a nosy Parker, a peeping Tom and several other categories of snoop where the Pan-Spechi are concerned," McKie said. "But it was because I suspected the act of sabotage to which I've referred here. The Tax Watchers revealed too much inside knowledge of the Bureau of Sabotage."

"I . . . ah . . . am not quite sure I understand you," Dooley said.

"The best kept secret in the universe, the Pan-Spechi cyclic change of gender and identity, is no longer a secret where I'm concerned," McKie said. He swallowed as he saw Bolin's fingers go white where they tightly gripped the prosecution table.

"It relates to the issue at hand?" Dooley asked.

"Most definitely, Your Honor," McKie said. "You see, the Pan-Spechi have a unique gland that controls mentation, dominance, the relationship between reason and instinct. The five group mates are, in reality, one person. I wish to make that clear for reasons of legal necessity."

"Legal necessity?" Dooley asked. He glanced down at the obviously distressed Bolin, back to McKie.

"The gland, when it's functioning, confers ego dominance on the

Pan-Spechi in whom it functions. But it functions for a time that's definitely limited—twenty-five to thirty years." McKie looked at Bolin. Again, the Pan-Spechi was trembling. "Please understand, Ser Bolin," he said, "that I do this out of necessity and that this is not an act of sabotage."

Bolin lifted his face toward McKie. The Pan-Spechi's features appeared contorted in grief. "Get it over with, man!" he rasped.

"Yes," McKie said, turning back to the judge's puzzled face. "Ego transfer in the Pan-Spechi, Your Honor, involves a transfer of what may be termed basic-experience-learning. It's accomplished through physical contact or when the ego holder dies, no matter how far he may be separated from the creche, this seems to fire up the eldest of the creche triplets. The ego-single also bequeaths a verbal legacy to his mate whenever possible—and that's most of the time. Specifically, it's this time."

Dooley leaned back. He was beginning to see the legal question McKie's account had posed.

"The act of sabotage which might make a Pan-Spechi eligible for appointment as Secretary of the Bureau of Sabotage was initiated by a . . . ah . . . cell mate of the Ser Bolin in court today, is that it?" Dooley asked.

McKie wiped his brow "Correct, Your Honor."

"But that cell mate is no longer the ego dominant, eh?"

"Quite right, Your Honor."

"The . . . ah . . . former ego holder, this . . . ah . . . Bildoon, is no longer eligible?"

"Bildoon, or what was once Bildoon, is a creature operating solely on instinct now, Your Honor," McKie said. "Capable of acting as creche nurse for a time and, eventually, fulfilling another destiny I'd rather not explain."

"I see." Dooley looked at the weather cover of the courtarena. He was beginning to see what McKie had risked here. "And you favor this, ah, Ser Bolin's bid for the Secretariat?" Dooley asked.

"If President Hindley and the Cabinet follow the recommendation of the Bureau's senior agents, the procedure always followed in the past, Ser Bolin will be the new Secretary," McKie said. "I favor this."

"Why?" Dooley asked.

"Because of this unique roving ego, the Pan-Spechi have a more communal attitude toward fellow sentients than do most other species admitted to the concourse of humanity," McKie said. "This translates as a sense of responsibility toward all life. They're not necessarily maudlin about it. They oppose where it's necessary to build strength. Their creche life demonstrates several clear examples of this which I'd prefer not to describe."

"I see," Dooley said, but he had to admit to himself that he did not. McKie's allusions to unspeakable practices were beginning to annoy him. "And you feel that this Bildoon-Bolin act of sabotage qualifies him, provided this court rules they are one and the same person?"

"We are not the same person!" Bolin cried. "You don't dare say I'm that . . . that shambling, clinging . . ."

"Easy," McKie said. "Ser Bolin, I'm sure you see the need for this legal fiction."

"Legal fiction," Bolin said as though clinging to the words. The multi-faceted eyes glared across the courtarena at McKie. "Thank you for the verbal nicety, McKie."

"You've not answered my question, Ser McKie," Dooley said, ignoring the exchange with Bolin.

"Sabotaging Ser Watt through an attack on the entire Bureau contains subtlety and finesse never before achieved in such an effort," McKie said. "The entire Bureau will be strengthened by it."

McKie glanced at Watt. The acting Secretary's Medusa tangle had ceased its writhing. He was staring at Bolin with a speculative look in his eyes. Sensing the quiet in the courtarena, he glanced up at McKie.

"Don't you agree, Ser Watt?" McKie asked.

"Oh, yes. Quite," Watt said.

The note of sincerity in Watt's voice startled the judge. For the first time, he wondered at the dedication which these men brought to their jobs.

"Sabotage is a very sensitive Bureau," Dooley said. "I've some serious reservations—"

"If Your Honor please," McKie said, "forbearance is one of the chief attributes a saboteur can bring to his duties. Now, I wish you to understand what our Pan-Spechi friend has done here this day. Let us suppose that I had spied upon the most intimate moments between you, Judge, and your wife, and that I reported them in detail here in open court with half the universe looking on. Let us suppose further that you had the strictest moral code against such discussions with outsiders. Let us suppose that I made these disclosures in the basest terms with every four-letter word at my command. Let us suppose that you were armed, traditionally, with a deadly weapon to strike at such blasphemers, such—"

"Filth!" Bolin grated.

"Yes," McKie said. "Filth. Do you suppose, Your Honor, that you could have stood by without killing me?"

"Good heavens!" Dooley said.

"Ser Bolin," McKie said, "I offer you and all your race my most humble apologies."

"I'd hoped once to undergo the ordeal in the privacy of a judge's chambers with as few outsiders as possible," Bolin said. "But once you were started in open court . . ."

"It had to be this way," McKie said. "If we'd done it in private, people would've come to be suspicious about a Pan-Spechi in control of . . ."

"People?" Bolin asked.

"Non Pan-Spechi," McKie said. "It'd have been a barrier between our species.

"And we've been strengthened by all this," McKie said. "Those provisions of the Constitution that provide the people with a slowly moving government have been demonstrated anew. We've admitted the public to the inner workings of Sabotage, shown them the valuable character of the man who'll be the new Secretary."

"I've not yet ruled on the critical issue here," Dooley said.

"But Your Honor!" McKie said.

"With all due respect to you as a saboteur extraordinary, Ser McKie," Dooley said, "I'll make my decision on evidence gathered under my direction." He looked at Bolin. "Ser Bolin, would you permit an agent of this court to gather such evidence as will allow me to render verdict without fear of harming my own species?"

"We're humans together," Bolin growled.

"But terranic humans hold the balance of power," Dooley said. "I owe allegiance to law, yes, but my terranic fellows depend on me, too. I have a . . ."

"You wish your own agents to determine if Ser McKie has told the truth about us?"

"Ah . . . yes," Dooley said.

Bolin looked at McKie. "Ser McKie, it is I who apologize to you. I had not realized how deeply xenophobia penetrated your fellows."

"Because," McKie said, "Outside of your natural modesty, you have no such fear. I suspect you know the phenomenon only through reading of us."

"But all strangers are potential sharers of identity," Bolin said. "Ah, well."

"If you're through with your little chat," Dooley said, "would you care to answer my question, Ser Bolin? This is still, I hope, a court of law."

"Tell me, Your Honor," Bolin said, "would you permit me to witness the tenderest intimacies between you and your wife?"

Dooley's face darkened, but he saw suddenly in all of its stark detail the extent of McKie's analogy and it was to the judge's credit that he rose to the occasion. "If it were necessary to promote understanding," he rasped, "yes!"

"I believe you would," Bolin murmured. He took a deep breath. "After what I've been through here today, one more sacrifice can be borne, I guess. I grant your investigators the privilege requested, but advise that they be discreet."

"It will strengthen you for the trials ahead as Secretary of the Bureau," McKie said. "The Secretary, you must bear in mind, has no immunities from sabotage whatsoever."

"But," Bolin said, "the Secretary's legal orders carrying out his Constitutional functions must be obeyed by all agents."

McKie nodded, seeing in the glitter of Bolin's eyes a vista of peeping Tom assignments with endless detailed reports to the Secretary of Sabotage—at least until the fellow's curiosity had been satisfied and his need for revenge satiated.

But the others in the courtarena, not having McKie's insight, merely wondered at the question: *What did he really mean by that?*

MARY CELESTE
MOVE

▰▰▰▰▰▰▰▰▰▰▰▰

Martin Fisk's car, a year-old 1997 Buick with triple turbines and *jato* boosters, flashed off the freeway, found a space between a giant mobile refueling tanker and a commuter bus, darted through and surged into the first of the eight right-hand lanes in time to make the turnoff marked "NEW PENTA-GON ONLY—Reduce Speed to 75."

Fisk glanced at his surface/air rate-of-travel mixer, saw he was down to 80 miles per hour, close enough to legal speed, and worked his way through the press of morning traffic into the second lane in plenty of time to join the cars diverging onto the fifth-level ramp.

At the last minute, a big official limousine with a two-star general's decal-flag on its forward curve cut in front of him and he had to reduce speed to 50, hearing the dragbar rasping behind him as his lane frantically matched speed. The shadow of a traffic copter passed over the roadway and Fisk thought: *Hope that general's driver loses his license!*

By this time he was into the sweeping curve-around that would drop him to the fifth level. Speed here was a monitored 55. The roadway entered the building and Fisk brought his R-O-T up to the stated speed watching for the code of his off-slot: BR71D$_2$. It loomed ahead, a flashing mnemonic blinker in brilliant green.

Fisk dropped behind an in-building shuttle, squeezed into the right-hand lane, slapped the turn-off alert that set all his rim lights blinking and activated the automatics. His machine caught the signal from the roadway, went on automatic and swerved into the off-slot still at 55.

Fisk released his control bar.

Drag hooks underneath the Buick snagged the catch ribbands of the slot, jerked his car to a stop that sent him surging against the harness.

The exit-warning wall ahead of him flashed a big red "7 SECONDS! 7 SECONDS!"

Plenty of time, he thought.

He yanked his briefcase out of its dashboard carrier with his right hand while unsnapping his safety harness with his left and hitting the door actuator with his knee. He was out onto the pedestrian ramp with three seconds to spare. The warning wall lifted; his car jerked forward into the down-elevator rack to be stored in a coded pile far below. His personal I-D signal to the computer-monitored system later would restore the car to him all checked and serviced and ready for the high-risk evening race out of the city.

Fisk glanced at his wrist watch—four minutes until his appointment with William Merill, the President's liaison officer on the Internal Control Board and Fisk's boss. Adopting the common impersonal discourtesy, Fisk joined the press of people hurrying along the ramp.

Some day, he thought, *I'll get a nice safe and sane job on one of the ocean hydroponic stations where all I have to do is watch gauges and there's nothing faster than a 40 m.p.h. pedestrian ramp.* He fished a green pill out of his coat pocket, gulped it, hoped he wouldn't have to take another before his blood pressure began its down-slant to normal.

By this time he was into the pneumatic lift capsule that would take him up in an individual curve to easy walking distance from his destination. He locked his arms on the brace bars. The door thumped closed. There was a distant hiss, a feeling of smooth downward pressure that evened off. He stared at the familiar blank tan of the opposite wall. Presently, the pressure slackened, the capsule glided to a stop, its door swung open.

Fisk stepped out into the wide hall, avoided the guide-lanes for the high-speed ramp and dodged through thinning lines of people hurrying to work around him.

Within seconds he was into Merill's office and facing the WAC secretary, a well-endowed brunette with an air of brisk efficiency. She looked up from her desk as he entered.

"Oh, Mr. Fisk," she said, "how nice that you're a minute early. Mr. Merill's already here. You can have nine minutes. I hope that'll be enough. He has a very full schedule today and the Safety Council subcommittee session with the President this afternoon." She already was up and holding the inner door open for him, saying: "Wouldn't it be wonderful if we could invent a forty-eight hour day?"

We already have, he thought. *We just compressed it into the old twenty-four hour model.*

"Mr. Fisk is here," she said, announcing him as she stepped out of his way.

Fisk was through to the inner sanctum then, wondering why his mind was filled with the sudden realization that he had driven out of his apartment's garage lift one hundred miles away only thirty-two minutes before. He heard the WAC secretary close the door behind him.

Merill, a wiry redhead with an air of darting tension, pale freckled skin and narrow face, sat at a desk directly opposite the door. He looked up, fixed his green eyes on Fisk, said: "Come on in and sit down, Marty, but make it snappy."

Fisk crossed the office. It was an irregular space of six sides about forty feet across at its widest point. Merill sat with his back to the narrowest of the walls and with the widest wall at an angle to his right. A computer-actuated map of the United States covered that surface, its color-intensity lines of red, blue and purple showing traffic density on the great expressway arteries that criss-crossed the nation. The ceiling was a similar map, this one showing the entire western hemisphere and confined to the Prime-1 arteries of twenty lanes or greater.

Fisk dropped into the chair across the desk from Merill, pushed a lock of dark hair back from his forehead, feeling the nervous perspiration there. *Blast it!* he thought. *I'll have to take another pill!*

"Well?" Merill said.

"It's all here," Fisk said, slapping the briefcase onto Merill's desk. "Ten days, forty thousand miles of travel and eighteen personal interviews plus fifty-one other interviews and reports from my assistants."

"You know the President's worried about this," Merill said. "I hope you have it in some kind of order so I can present it to him this afternoon."

"It's in order," Fisk said. "But you're not going to like it."

"Yeah, well I was prepared for that," Merill said. "I don't like much of what comes across this desk." He glanced up suddenly at a strip of yellow that appeared on the overhead map indicating a partial blockage on the intercontinental throughway near Caracas. His right hand hovered over an intercom button, poised there as the yellow was replaced by red then blue shading into purple.

"Fourth problem in that area in two days," Merill said removing his hand from the button. "Have to work a talk with Mendoza into this morning's schedule. Okay" He turned back to Fisk. "Give me your economy model brief rundown. What's got into these kooks who're moving all over the landscape?"

"I've about twenty interlocking factors to reinforce my original hunch," Fisk said. "The Psych department confirms it. The question is whether this thing'll settle into some kind of steady pattern and even out. You might caution the President, off the record, that there are heavy political implications in this. Touchy ones if this leaks out the wrong way."

Merill pushed a recording button on his desk, said: "Okay, Marty, put the rest on the record. Recap and summate. I'll listen to it for review while I'm reading your report."

Fisk nodded. "Right." He pulled sheaves of papers in file folders out of the briefcase, lined them up in front of him. "We had the original report, of course, that people were making bold moves from one end of the country to the other in higher than usual numbers, from unlikely starting places to unlikelier destinations. And these people turned out to be mostly mild, timid types instead of bold pioneers who'd pulled up their roots in the spirit of adventure."

"Are the psych profiles in your report?" Merill asked. "I'm going to have a time convincing the President unless I have all the evidence."

"Right here," Fisk said, tapping one of the folders. "I also have photostats of billings from the mobile refueling tankers and mobile food canteens to show that the people in these reports are actually the ones we've analyzed."

"Weird," Merill said. He glanced at another brief flicker of yellow on the overhead map near Seattle, returned his attention to Fisk.

"State and Federal income-tax reports are here," Fisk said, touching another of the folders. "And, oh yes, car ownership breakdowns by area. I also have data on driver's license transfers, bank and loan company records to show the business transactions involved in these moves. You know, some of these kooks sold profitable businesses at a loss and took up different trades at their new locations. Others took new jobs at lower pay. Some big industries are worried about this. They've lost key people for reasons that don't make sense. And the Welfare Department figures that . . ."

"Yeah, but what's this about car ownership breakdowns?" Merill asked.

Trust him to dive right through to the sensitive area, Fisk thought. He said: "There's a steep decline in car ownership among these people."

"Do the Detroit people suspect?" Merill asked.

"I covered my tracks best I could," Fisk said, "but there're bound to be some rumbles when their investigators interview the same people I did."

"We'd better invite them to review our findings," Merill said. "There're some big political contributors in that area. What's the pattern on communities chosen by these kooks?"

"Pretty indicative," Fisk said. "Most of the areas receiving a big influx are what our highway engineers irreverently call 'headwater swamps'—meaning area where the highway feeder routes thin out and make it easy to leave the expressways."

"For example?"

"Oh . . . New York, San Francisco, Seattle, Los Angeles."

"That all?"

"No. There've been some significant population increases in areas where highway construction slowed traffic. There've been waves into Bangor, Maine . . . Blaine, Washington . . . and, my God! Calexico, California! They were hit on two consecutive weekends by one hundred and seventy of these weird newcomers."

In a tired voice, Merill said: "I suppose the concentration pattern's consistent?"

"Right down the line. They're all of middle age or past, drove well-preserved older cars, are afraid to travel by air, are reluctant to explain why they moved such long distances. The complexion of entire areas in these headwater regions is being changed. There's sameness to them—people all conservative, timid . . . you know the pattern."

"I'm afraid I do. Bound to have political repercussions, too. Congressional representation from these areas will change to fit the new pattern, sure as hell. That's what you meant, wasn't it?"

"Yes." Fisk saw that he only had a few minutes more, began to feel his nervousness mount. He wondered if he'd dare gulp a pill in front of Merill, decided against it, said: "And you'd better look into the insurance angle. Costs are going up and people are beginning to complain. I saw a report on my desk when I checked in last night. These kooks were almost to a man low-risk drivers. As they get entirely out of the market, that throws a bigger load onto the others."

"I'll have the possibility of a subsidy investigated," Merill said. "Anything else? You're running out of time."

Running out of time, Fisk thought. *The story of our lives.* He touched another of the folders, said: "Here are the missing persons reports. There's a graph curve in them to fit this theory. I also have divorce records that are worth reviewing—wives who refused to join their husbands in one of these moves, that sort of thing."

"Husband moved and the wife refused to join him, eh?"

"That's the usual pattern. There are a couple of them, though, where the wife moved and refused to come back. Desertion charged . . . very indicative."

"Yeah, I was afraid of that," Merill said. "Okay, I'll review this when . . ."

"One thing more, Chief," Fisk said. "The telegrams and moving company records." He touched a thicker folder on the right. "I had photocopies made because few people would believe them without seeing them."

"Yeah?"

"The moving company gets an order from, say, Bangor, to move household belongings there from, for example, Tulsa, Oklahoma. The request contains a plea to feed the cat, the dog, the parrot or whatever. The movers go to the address and they find a hungry dog or cat in the house—or even a dead one on some occasions. One mover found a bowl of dead goldfish."

"So?"

"These houses fit right into the pattern," Fisk said. "The moving men find dinners that've been left cooking, plates on the table—all kinds of signs that people left and intended to come back . . . but didn't. They've got a name for this kind of thing in the moving industry. They call it the 'Mary Celeste' move after the story of the sailing ship that . . ."

"I know the story," Merill said in a sour voice.

Merill passed a hand wearily across his face, dropped the hand to the desk with a thump. "Okay, Marty, it fits," he said. "These characters go out for a Saturday or Sunday afternoon drive. They take a wrong turn onto a one-way access ramp and get trapped onto one of the high-speed expressways. They've never driven over 150 before in their lives and the expressway carrier beam forces them up to 280 or 300 and they panic, lock onto the automatic and then they're afraid to touch the controls until they reach a region where the automatics slow them for diverging traffic. And after that you're lucky if you can ever get them into something with wheels on it again."

"They sell their cars," Fisk said. "They stick to local tube and surface transportation. Used car buyers have come to spot these people, call them 'Panics.' A kook with out-of-state licenses drives in all glassy-eyed and trembling, asks: 'How much you give me for my car?' The dealer makes a killing, of course."

"Of course," Merill said. "Well, we've got to keep this under wraps at least until after Congress passes the appropriation for the new trans-Huron expressway. After that . . ." He shrugged. "I don't know, but we'll think of something." He waved a hand to dismiss Fisk, bent to a report-corder that folded out of the desk and said: "Stay where I can get you in a hurry, Marty."

Within seconds, Fisk was out in the hallway facing the guidelanes to the high-speed ramp that would carry him to his own office. A man bumped into him and Fisk found that he was standing on the office lip reluctant to move out into the whizzing throngs of the corridor.

No, he thought, *I'm not reluctant. I'm afraid.*

He was honest enough with himself, though, to realize that he wasn't afraid of the high-speed ramp. It was what the ramp signified, where it could carry him.

I wonder what my car would bring? he asked himself. And he thought: *Would my wife move?* He dried his sweating palm on his sleeve before taking another green pill from his pocket and gulping it. Then he stepped out into the hall.

GREENSLAVES

He looked pretty much like the bastard offspring of a Guarani Indio and some backwoods farmer's daughter, some *sertanista* who had tried to forget her enslavement to the *encomendero* system by "eating the iron"—which is what they call lovemaking through the grill of a consel gate.

The type-look was almost perfect except when he forgot himself while passing through one of the deeper jungle glades.

His skin tended to shade down to green then, fading him into the background of leaves and vines, giving a strange disembodiment to the mud-gray shirt and ragged trousers, the inevitable frayed straw hat and rawhide sandals soled with pieces cut from worn tires.

Such lapses became less and less frequent the farther he got from the Parana headwaters, the *sertao* hinterland of Goyaz where men with his bang-cut black hair and glittering dark eyes were common.

By the time he reached *bandeirantes* country, he had achieved almost perfect control over the chameleon effect.

But now he was out of the jungle growth and into the brown dirt tracks that separated the parceled farms of the resettlement plan. In his own way, he knew he was approaching the *bandeirante* checkpoints, and with an almost human gesture, he fingered the *cedula de gracias al sacar*, the certificate of white blood, tucked safely beneath his shirt. Now and again, when humans were not near, he practiced speaking aloud the name that had been chosen for him—"Antonio Raposo Tavares."

The sound was a bit stridulate, harsh on the edges, but he knew it would pass. It already had. Goyaz Indios were notorious for the strange inflection of their speech. The farm folk who had given him a roof and fed him the previous night had said as much.

When their questions had become pressing, he had squatted on the door-step and played his flute, the *qena* of the Andes Indian that he carried in a leather purse hung from his shoulder. He had kept the sound to a conventional non-dangerous pitch. The gesture of the flute was a symbol of the region. When a Guarani put flute to nose and began playing, that was a sign words were ended.

The farm folk had shrugged and retired.

Now, he could see red-brown rooftops ahead and the white crystal shimmering of a *bandeirante* tower with its aircars alighting and departing. The scene held an odd hive-look. He stopped, finding himself momentarily overcome by the touch of instincts that he knew he had to master or fail in the ordeal to come.

He united his mental identity then, thinking, *We are greenslaves subservient to the greater whole.* The thought lent him an air of servility that was like a shield against the stares of the humans trudging past all around him. His kind knew many mannerisms and had learned early that servility was a form of concealment.

Presently, he resumed his plodding course toward the town and the tower.

The dirt track gave way to a two-lane paved market road with its footpaths in the ditches on both sides. This, in turn, curved alongside a four-deck commercial transport highway where even the footpaths were paved. And now there were groundcars and aircars in greater number, and he noted that the flow of people on foot was increasing.

Thus far, he had attracted no dangerous attention. The occasional snickering side-glance from natives of the area could be safely ignored, he knew. Probing stares held peril, and he had detected none. The servility shielded him.

The sun was well along toward mid-morning and the day's heat was beginning to press down on the earth, raising a moist hothouse stink from the dirt beside the pathway, mingling the perspiration odors of humanity around him.

And they were around him now, close and pressing, moving slower and slower as they approached the checkpoint bottleneck. Presently, the forward motion stopped. Progress resolved itself into shuffle and stop, shuffle and stop.

This was the critical test now and there was no avoiding it. He waited with something like an Indian's stoic patience. His breathing had grown deeper to compensate for the heat, and he adjusted it to match that of the people around him, suffering the temperature rise for the sake of blending into his surroundings.

Andes Indians didn't breathe deeply here in the lowlands.

Shuffle and stop.

Shuffle and stop.

He could see the checkpoint now.

Fastidious *bandeirantes* in sealed white cloaks with plastic helmets, gloves, and boots stood in a double row within a shaded brick corridor leading into the town. He could see sunlight hot on the street beyond the corridor and people hurrying away there after passing the gantlet.

The sight of that free area beyond the corridor sent an ache of longing through all the parts of him. The suppression warning flashed out instantly on the heels of that instinctive reaching emotion.

No distraction could be permitted now; he was into the hands of the first *bandeirante*, a hulking blond fellow with pink skin and blue eyes.

"Step along now! Lively now!" the fellow said.

A gloved hand propelled him toward two *bandeirantes* standing on the right side of the line.

"Give this one an extra treatment," the blond giant called. "He's from the upcountry by the look of him."

The other two *bandeirantes* had him now, one jamming a breather mask over his face, the other fitting a plastic bag over him. A tube trailed from the bag out to machinery somewhere in the street beyond the corridor.

"Double shot!" one of the *bandeirantes* called.

Fuming blue gas puffed out the bag around him, and he took a sharp, gasping breath through the mask.

Agony!

The gas drove through every multiple linkage of his being with needles of pain.

We must not weaken, he thought.

But it was a deadly pain, killing. The linkages were beginning to weaken.

"Okay on this one," the bag handler called.

The mask was pulled away. The bag was slipped off. Hands propelled him down the corridor toward the sunlight.

"Lively now! Don't hold up the line."

The stink of the poison gas was all around him. It was a new one—a dissembler. They hadn't prepared him for this poison!

Now, he was into the sunlight and turning down a street lined with fruit stalls, merchants bartering with customers or standing fat and watchful behind their displays.

In his extremity, the fruit beckoned to him with the promise of life-saving sanctuary for a few parts of him, but the integrating totality fought off the lure. He shuffled as fast as he dared, dodging past the customers, through the knots of idlers.

"You like to buy some fresh oranges?"

An oily dark hand thrust two oranges toward his face.

"Fresh oranges from the green country. Never been a bug anywhere near these."

He avoided the hand, although the odor of the oranges came near overpowering him.

Now, he was clear of the stalls, around a corner down a narrow side street. Another corner and he saw far away to his left, the lure of greenery in open country, the free area beyond the town.

He turned toward the green, increasing his speed, measuring out the time still available to him. There was still a chance. Poison clung to his clothing, but fresh air was filtering through the fabric—and the thought of victory was like an antidote.

We can make it yet!

The green drew closer and closer—trees and ferns beside a river bank. He heard the running water. There was a bridge thronging with foot traffic from converging streets.

No help for it: he joined the throng, avoided contact as much as possible. The linkages of his legs and back were beginning to go, and he knew the wrong kind of blow could dislodge whole segments. He was over the bridge without disaster. A dirt track led off the path and down toward the river.

He turned toward it, stumbled against one of two men carrying a pig in a net slung between them. Part of the shell on his right upper leg gave way and he could feel it begin to slip down inside his pants.

The man he had hit took two backward steps, almost dropped the end of the burden.

"Careful!" the man shouted.

The man at the other end of the net said: "Damn drunks."

The pig set up a squirming, squealing distraction.

In this moment, he slipped past them onto the dirt track leading down toward the river. He could see the water down there now, boiling with aeration from the barrier filters.

Behind him, one of the pig carriers said: "I don't think he was drunk, Carlos. His skin felt dry and hot. Maybe he was sick."

The track turned around an embankment of raw dirt dark brown with dampness and dipped toward a tunnel through ferns and bushes. The men with the pig could no longer see him, he knew, and he grabbed at his pants where the part of his leg was slipping, scurried into the green tunnel.

Now, he caught sight of his first mutated bee. It was dead, having entered the barrier vibration area here without any protection against that deadliness. The bee was one of the butterfly type with iridescent yellow and orange wings. It lay in the cup of a green leaf at the center of a shaft of sunlight.

He shuffled past, having recorded the bee's shape and color. They had considered the bees as a possible answer, but there were serious drawbacks to this course. A bee could not reason with humans, that was the key fact. And humans had to listen to reason soon, else all life would end.

There came the sound of someone hurrying down the path behind him, heavy footsteps thudding on the earth.

Pursuit . . . ?

He was reduced to a slow shuffling now and soon it would be only crawling progress, he knew. Eyes searched the greenery around him for a place of concealment. A thin break in the fern wall on his left caught his attention. Tiny human footprints led into it—children. He forced his way through the ferns, found himself on a low narrow path along the embankment. Two toy aircars, red and blue, had been abandoned on the path. His staggering foot pressed them into the dirt.

The path led close to a wall of black dirt festooned with creepers, around a sharp turn and onto the lip of a shallow cave. More toys lay in the green gloom at the cave's mouth.

He knelt, crawled over the toys into the blessed dankness, lay there a moment, waiting.

The pounding footsteps hurried past a few feet below.

Voices reached up to him.

"He was headed toward the river. Think he was going to jump in?"

"Who knows? But I think me for sure he was sick."

"Here; down this way. Somebody's been down this way."

The voices grew indistinct, blended with the bubbling sound of the river.

The men were going on down the path. They had missed his hiding place. But why had they pursued him? He had not seriously injured the one by stumbling against him. Surely, they did not suspect.

Slowly, he steeled himself for what had to be done, brought his specialized parts into play and began burrowing into the earth at the end of the cave. Deeper and deeper he burrowed, thrusting the excess dirt behind and out to make it appear the cave had collapsed.

Ten meters in he went before stopping. His store of energy contained just enough reserve for the next stage. He turned on his back, scattering the dead parts of his legs and back, exposing the queen and her guard cluster to the dirt beneath his chitinous spine. Orifices opened at his thighs, exuded the cocoon foam, the soothing green cover that would harden into a protective shell.

This was victory; the essential parts had survived.

Time was the thing now—ten and one half days to gather new energy, go through the metamorphosis and disperse. Soon, there would be thousands of him—each with its carefully mimicked clothing and identification papers and appearance of humanity.

Identical—each of them.

There would be other checkpoints, but not as severe; other barriers, lesser ones.

This human copy had proved a good one. They had learned many things from study of their scattered captives and from the odd crew directed by the red-haired human female they'd trapped in the *sertao*. How strange she was: like a queen and not like a queen. It was so difficult to understand human creatures, even when you permitted them limited freedom . . . almost impossible to reason with them. Their slavery to the planet would have to be proved dramatically, perhaps.

The queen stirred near the cool dirt. They had learned new things this time about escaping notice. All of the subsequent colony clusters would share that knowledge. One of them—at least—would get through to the city by the Amazon "River Sea" where the death-for-all originated. One had to get through.

Senhor Gabriel Martinho, prefect of the Mato Grosso Barrier Compact, paced his study, muttering to himself as he passed the tall, narrow window that admitted the evening sunlight. Occasionally, he paused to glare down at his son, Joao, who sat on a tapir-leather sofa beneath one of the tall book-cases that lined the room.

The elder Martinho was a dark wisp of a man, limb thin, with gray hair and cavernous brown eyes above an eagle nose, slit mouth, and boot-toe chin. He wore old style black clothing as befitted his position, his linen white against the black, and with golden cuffstuds glittering as he waved his arms.

"I am an object of ridicule!" he snarled.

Joao, a younger copy of the father, his hair still black and wavy, absorbed the statement in silence. He wore a *bandeirante*'s white coverall suit sealed into plastic boots at the calf.

"An object of ridicule!" the elder Martinho repeated.

It began to grow dark in the room, the quick tropic darkness hurried by thunderheads piled along the horizon. The waning daylight carried a hazed blue cast. Heat lightning spattered the patch of sky visible through the tall window, sent dazzling electric radiance into the study. Drumming thunder followed. As though that were the signal, the house sensors turned on lights wherever there were humans. Yellow illumination filled the study.

The Prefect stopped in front of his son. "Why does my own son, a *ban-deirante,* a jefe of the Irmandades, spout these Carsonite stupidities?"

Joao looked at the floor between his boots. He felt both resentment and shame. To disturb his father this way, that was a hurtful thing, with the elder Martinho's delicate heart. But the old man was so blind!

"Those rabble farmers laughed at me," the elder Martinho said. "I told them we'd increase the green area by ten thousand hectares this month, and they laughed. 'Your own son does not even believe this!' they said. And they told me some of the things you had been saying."

"I am sorry I have caused you distress. Father," Joao said. "The fact that I'm a *bandeirante* . . ." He shrugged. "How else could I have learned the truth about this extermination program?"

His father quivered.

"Joao! Do you sit there and tell me you took a false oath when you formed your Irmandades band?"

"That's not the way it was, Father."

Joao pulled a sprayman's emblem from his breast pocket, fingered it. "I believed it . . . then. We could shape mutated bees to fill every gap in the insect ecology. This I believed. Like the Chinese, I said: 'Only the useful shall live!' But that was several years ago, Father, and since then I have come to realize we don't have a complete understanding of what usefulness means."

"It was a mistake to have you educated in North America," his father said. "That's where you absorbed this Carsonite heresy. It's all well and good for *them* to refuse to join the rest of the world in the Ecological Realignment; they do not have as many million mouths to feed. But my own son!"

Joao spoke defensively: "Out in the red areas you see things, Father. These things are difficult to explain. Plants look healthier out there and the fruit is . . ."

"A purely temporary thing," his father said. "We will shape bees to meet whatever need we find. The destroyers take food from our mouths. It is very simple. They must die and be replaced by creatures which serve a function useful to mankind."

"The birds are dying, Father," Joao said.

"We are saving the birds! We have specimens of every kind in our sanctuaries. We will provide new foods for them to . . ."

"But what happens if our barriers are breached . . . before we can replace the population of natural predators? What happens then?"

The elder Martinho shook a thin finger under his son's nose. "This is nonsense! I will hear no more of it! Do you know what else those *mameluco* farmers said? They said they have seen *bandeirantes* reinfesting the green areas to prolong their jobs! That is what they said. This, too, is nonsense— but it is a natural consequence of defeatist talk just such as I have heard from you tonight. And every setback we suffer adds strength to such charges!"

"Setbacks, Father?"

"I have said it: setbacks!"

Senhor Prefect Martinho turned, paced to his desk and back. Again, he stopped in front of his son, placed hands on hips. "You refer to the Piratininga, of course?"

"You accuse me, Father?"

"Your Irmandades were on that line."

"Not so much as a flea got through us!"

"Yet, a week ago the Piratininga was green. Now, it is crawling. Crawling!"

"I cannot watch every *bandeirante* in the Mato Grosso," Joao protested. "If they . . ."

"The IEO gives us only six months to clean up," the elder Martinho said. He raised his hands, palms up; his face was flushed. "Six months! Then they throw an embargo around all Brazil—the way they have done with North America." He lowered his hands. "Can you imagine the pressures on me? Can you imagine the things I must listen to about the *bandeirantes* and especially about my own son?"

Joao scratched his chin with the sprayman's emblem. The reference to the International Ecological Organization made him think of Dr. Rhin Kelly, the IEO's lovely field director. His mind pictured her as he had last seen her in the A' Chigua nightclub at Bahia—red-haired, green-eyed . . . so lovely and strange. But she had been missing almost six weeks now— somewhere in the *sertao*—and there were those who said she must be dead.

Joao looked at his father. If only the old man weren't so excitable. "You excite yourself needlessly, Father," he said. "The Piratininga was not a full barrier, just a . . ."

"Excite myself!"

The Prefect's nostrils dilated; he bent toward his son. "Already we have gone past two deadlines. We gained an extension when I announced you and the *bandeirantes* of Diogo Alvarez had cleared the Piratininga. How do I explain now that it is reinfested, that we have the work to do over?"

Joao returned the sprayman's emblem to his pocket. It was obvious he'd not be able to reason with his father this night. Frustration sent a nerve quivering along Joao's jaw. The old man had to be told, though; someone had to tell him. And someone of his father's stature had to get back to the Bureau, shake them up there and make *them* listen.

The Prefect returned to his desk, sat down. He picked up an antique crucifix, one that the great Aleihadinho had carved in ivory. He lifted it, obviously seeking to restore his serenity, but his eyes went wide and glaring. Slowly, he returned the crucifix to its position on the desk, keeping his attention on it.

"Joao," he whispered.

It's his heart! Joao thought.

He leaped to his feet, rushed to his father's side. "Father! What is it?"

The elder Martinho pointed, hand trembling.

Through the spiked crown of thorns, across the agonized ivory face, over the straining muscles of the Christ figure crawled an insect. It was the color of the ivory, faintly reminiscent of a beetle in shape, but with a multi-clawed fringe along its wings and thorax, and with furry edging to its abnormally long antennae.

The elder Martinho reached for a roll of papers to smash the insect, but Joao put out a hand restraining him. "Wait. This is a new one. I've never seen anything like it. Give me a handlight. We must follow it, find where it nests."

Senhor Prefect Martinho muttered under his breath, withdrew a small Permalight from a drawer of the desk, handed the light to his son.

Joao peered at the insect, still not using the light. "How strange it is," he said. "See how it exactly matches the tone of the ivory."

The insect stopped, pointed its antennae toward the two men.

"Things have been seen," Joao said. "There are stories. Something like this was found near one of the barrier villages last month. It was inside the green area, on a path beside a river. Two farmers found it while searching for a sick man." Joao looked at his father. "They are very watchful of sickness in the newly green regions, you know. There have been epidemics . . . and that is another thing."

"There is no relationship," his father snapped. "Without insects to carry disease, we will have less illness."

"Perhaps," Joao said, and his tone said he did not believe it.

Joao returned his attention to the insect. "I do not think our ecologists know all they say they do. And I mistrust our Chinese advisors. They speak in such flowery terms of the benefits from eliminating useless insects, but they will not let us go into their green areas and inspect. Excuses. Always excuses. I think they are having troubles they do not wish us to know."

"That's foolishness," the elder Martinho growled, but his tone said this was not a position he cared to defend. "They are honorable men. Their way of life is closer to our socialism than it is to the decadent capitalism of North America. Your trouble is you see them too much through the eyes of those who educated you."

"I'll wager this insect is one of the spontaneous mutations," Joao said. "It is almost as though they appeared according to some plan. Find me something in which I may capture this creature and take it to the laboratory."

The elder Martinho remained standing by his chair. "Where will you say it was found?"

"Right here," Joao said.

"You will not hesitate to expose me to more ridicule?"

"But Father . . ."

"Can't you hear what they will say? In his own home this insect is found. It is a strange new kind. Perhaps he breeds them there to reinfest the green."

"Now *you* are talking nonsense, father. Mutations are common in a threatened species. And we cannot deny there is threat to insect species— the poisons, the barrier vibrations, the traps. Get me a container, Father. I cannot leave this creature, or I'd get a container myself."

"And you will tell where it was found?"

"I can do nothing else. We must cordon off this area, search it out. This could be . . . an accident . . ."

"Or a deliberate attempt to embarrass me."

Joao took his attention from the insect, studied his father. *That* was a possibility, of course. The Carsonites had friends in many places . . . and some were fanatics who would stoop to any scheme. Still . . .

Decision came to Joao. He returned his attention to the motionless insect. His father had to be told, had to be reasoned with at any cost. Someone whose voice carried authority had to get down to the Capitol and make them listen.

"Our earliest poisons killed off the weak and selected out those insects immune to this threat," Joao said. "Only the immune remained to breed. The poisons we use now . . . some of them do not leave such loopholes and the deadly vibrations at the barriers . . ." He shrugged. "This is a form of beetle, Father. I will show you a thing."

Joao drew a long, thin whistle of shiny metal from his pocket. "There was a time when this called countless beetles to their deaths. I had merely to tune it across their attraction spectrum." He put the whistle to his lips, blew while turning the end of it.

No sound audible to human ears came from the instrument, but the beetle's antennae writhed.

Joao removed the whistle from his mouth.

The antennae stopped writhing.

"It stayed put, you see," Joao said. "And there are indications of malignant intelligence among them. The insects are far from extinction, Father . . . and they are beginning to strike back."

"Malignant intelligence, pah!"

"You must believe me, Father," Joao said. "No one else will listen. They laugh and say we are too long in the jungle. And where is our evidence? And they say such stories could be expected from ignorant farmers but not from *bandeirantes*. You must listen, Father, and believe. It is why I was chosen to come here . . . because you are my father and you might listen to your own son."

"Believe what?" the elder Martinho demanded, and he was the Prefect now, standing erect, glaring coldly at his son.

"In the *sertao* of Goyaz last week," Joao said, "Antonil Lisboa's *bandeirante* lost three men who . . ."

"Accidents."

"They were killed with formic acid and oil of copahu."

"They were careless with their poisons. Men grow careless when they . . ."

"Father! The formic acid was a particularly strong type, but still recognizable as having been . . . or being of a type manufactured by insects. And the men were drenched with it. While the oil of copahu . . ."

"You imply that insects such as this . . ." The Prefect pointed to the motionless creature on the crucifix. ". . . blind creatures such as this . . ."

"They're not blind, Father."

"I did not mean literally blind, but without intelligence," the elder Martinho said. "You cannot be seriously implying that these creatures attacked humans and killed them."

"We have yet to discover precisely how the men were slain," Joao said. "We have only their bodies and the physical evidence at the scene. But there have been other deaths, Father, and men missing and we grow more and more certain that . . ."

He broke off as the beetle crawled off the crucifix onto the desk. Immediately, it darkened to brown, blending with the wood surface.

"Please, Father. Get me a container."

"I will get you a container only if you promise to use discretion in your story of where this creature was found," the Prefect said.

"Father, I . . ."

The beetle leaped off the desk far out into the middle of the room, scuttled to the wall, up the wall, into a crack beside a window.

Joao pressed the switch of the handlight, directed its beam into the hole which had swallowed the strange beetle.

"How long has this hole been here, Father?"

"For years. It was a flaw in the masonry . . . an earthquake, I believe."

Joao turned, crossed to the door in three strides, went through an arched hallway, down a flight of stone steps, through another door and short hall, through a grillwork gate and into the exterior garden. He set the handlight to full intensity, washed its blue glare over the wall beneath the study window.

"Joao, what are you doing?"

"My job, Father," Joao said. He glanced back, saw that the elder Martinho had stopped just outside the gate.

Joao returned his attention to the exterior wall, washed the blue glare of light on the stones beneath the window. He crouched low, running the light along the ground, peering behind each clod, erasing all shadows.

His searching scrutiny passed over the raw earth, turned to the bushes, then the lawn.

Joao heard his father come up behind.

"Do you see it, son?"

"No, Father."

"You should have allowed me to crush it."

From the outer garden that bordered the road and the stone fence, there came a piercing stridulation. It hung on the air in almost tangible waves, making Joao think of the hunting cry of jungle predators. A shiver moved up his spine. He turned toward the driveway where he had parked his airtruck, sent the blue glare of light stabbing there.

He broke off, staring at the lawn. "What is that?"

The ground appeared to be in motion, reaching out toward them like the curling of a wave on a beach. Already, they were cut off from the house. The wave was still some ten paces away, but moving in rapidly.

Joao stood up, clutched his father's arm. He spoke quietly, hoping not to alarm the old man further. "We must get to my truck, Father. We must run across them."

"Them?"

"Those are like the insect we saw inside, father—millions of them. Perhaps they are not beetles, after all. Perhaps they are like army ants. We must make it to the truck. I have equipment and supplies there. We will be safe inside. It is a *bandeirante* truck, Father. You must run with me. I will help you."

They began to run, Joao holding his father's arm, pointing the way with the light.

Let his heart be strong enough, Joao prayed.

They were into the creeping waves of insects then, but the creatures leaped aside, opening a pathway which closed behind the running men.

The white form of the airtruck loomed out of the shadows at the far curve of the driveway about fifteen meters ahead.

"Joao . . . my heart," the elder Martinho gasped.

"You can make it," Joao panted. "Faster!" He almost lifted his father from the ground for the last few paces.

They were at the wide rear door into the truck's lab compartment now. Joao yanked open the door, slapped the light switch, reached for a spray hood and poison gun. He stopped, stared into the yellow-lighted compartment.

Two men sat there—*sertao* Indians by the look of them, with bright glaring eyes and bang-cut black hair beneath straw hats. They looked to be identical twins—even to the mud-gray clothing and sandals, the leather shoulder bags. The beetle-like insects crawled around them, up the walls, over the instruments and vials.

"What the devil?" Joao blurted.

One of the pair held a qena flute. He gestured with it, spoke in a rasping, oddly inflected voice: "Enter. You will not be harmed if you obey."

Joao felt his father sag, caught the old man in his arms. How light he felt! Joao stepped up into the truck, carrying his father. The elder Martinho breathed in short, painful gasps. His face was a pale blue and sweat stood out on his forehead.

"Joao," he whispered. "Pain . . . my chest."

"Medicine, Father," Joao said. "Where is your medicine?"

"House," the old man said.

"It appears to be dying," one of the Indians rasped.

Still holding his father in his arms, Joao, whirled toward the pair, blazed: "I don't know who you are or why you loosed those bugs here, but my father's dying and needs help. Get out of my way!"

"Obey or both die," said the Indian with the flute.

"He needs his medicine and a doctor," Joao pleaded. He didn't like the way the Indian pointed that flute. The motion suggested the instrument was actually a weapon.

"What part has failed?" asked the other Indian. He stared curiously at Joao's father. The old man's breathing had become shallow and rapid.

"It's his heart," Joao said. "I know you farmers don't think he's acted fast enough for . . ."

"Not farmers," said the one with the flute. "Heart?"

"Pump," said the other.

"Pump," The Indian with the flute stood up from the bench at the front of the lab, gestured down. "Put . . . Father here."

The other one got off the bench, stood aside.

In spite of fear for his father, Joao was caught by the strange look of this pair, the fine, scale-like lines in their skin, the glittering brilliance of their eyes.

"Put Father here," repeated the one with the flute, pointing at the bench. "Help can be . . ."

"Attained," said the other one.

"Attained," said the one with the flute.

Joao focused now on the masses of insects around the walls, the waiting quietude in their ranks. They *were* like the one in the study.

The old man's breathing was now very shallow, very rapid.

He's dying, Joao thought in desperation.

"Help can be attained," repeated the one with the flute. "If you obey, we will not harm."

The Indian lifted his flute, pointed it at Joao like a weapon. "Obey."

There was no mistaking the gesture.

Slowly, Joao advanced, deposited his father gently on the bench.

The other Indian bent over the elder Martinho's head, raised an eyelid. There was a professional directness about the gesture. The Indian pushed gently on the dying man's diaphragm, removed the Prefect's belt, loosened his collar. A stubby brown finger was placed against the artery in the old man's neck.

"Very weak," the Indian rasped.

Joao took another, closer look at this Indian, wondering at the *sertao* backwoodsman who behaved like a doctor.

"We've got to get him to a hospital," Joao said. "And his medicine in . . ."

"Hospital," the Indian agreed.

"Hospital?" asked the one with the flute.

A low, stridulate hissing came from the other Indian.

"Hospital," said the one with the flute.

That stridulate hissing! Joao stared at the Indian beside the Prefect. The sound had been reminiscent of the weird call that had echoed across the lawn.

The one with the flute poked him, said: "You will go into front and maneuver this . . ."

"Vehicle," said the one beside Joao's father.

"Vehicle," said the one with the flute.

"Hospital?" Joao pleaded.

"Hospital," agreed the one with the flute.

Joao looked once more to his father. The other Indian already was strapping the elder Martinho to the bench in preparation for movement. How competent the man appeared in spite of his backwoods look.

"Obey," said the one with the flute.

Joao opened the door into the front compartment, slipped through, feeling the other one follow. A few drops of rain spattered darkly against the curved windshield. Joao squeezed into the operator's seat, noted how the Indian crouched behind him, flute pointed and ready.

A dart gun of some kind, Joao guessed.

He punched the ignitor button on the dash, strapped himself in while waiting for the turbines to build up speed. The Indian still crouched behind him, vulnerable now if the airtruck were spun sharply. Joao flicked the communications switch on the lower left corner of the dash, looked into the tiny screen there giving him a view of the lab compartment. The rear doors were open. He closed them by hydraulic remote. His father was securely strapped to the bench now, Joao noted, but the other Indian was equally secured.

The turbines reached their whining peak. Joao switched on the lights, engaged the hydrostatic drive. The truck lifted six inches, angled upward as Joao increased pump displacement. He turned left onto the street, lifted another two meters to increase speed, headed toward the lights of a boulevard.

The Indian spoke beside his ear: "You will turn toward the mountain over there." A hand came forward, pointing to the right.

The Alejandro Clinic is there in the foothills, Joao thought.

He made the indicated turn down the cross street angling toward the boulevard.

Casually, he gave pump displacement another boost, lifted another meter and increased speed once more. In the same motion, he switched on the intercom to the rear compartment, tuned for the spare amplifier and pickup in the compartment beneath the bench where his father lay.

The pickup, capable of making a dropped pin sound like a cannon, gave forth only a distant hissing and rasping. Joao increased amplification. The instrument should have been transmitting the old man's heartbeats now, sending a noticeable drum-thump into the forward cabin.

There was nothing.

Tears blurred Joao's eyes, and he shook his head to clear them.

My father is dead, he thought. *Killed by these crazy backwoodsmen.*

He noted in the dashscreen that the Indian back there had a hand under the elder Martinho's back. The Indian appeared to be massaging the dead man's back, and a rhythmic rasping matched the motion.

Anger filled Joao. He felt like diving the airtruck into an abutment, dying himself to kill these crazy men.

They were approaching the outskirts of the city, and ring-girders circled off to the left giving access to the boulevard. This was an area of small gardens and cottages protected by over-fly canopies.

Joao lifted the airtruck above the canopies, headed toward the boulevard.

To the clinic, yes, he thought. *But it is too late.*

In that instant, he realized there were no heartbeats at all coming from that rear compartment—only that slow, rhythmic grating, a faint susurration and a cicada-like hum up and down scale.

"To the mountains, there," said the Indian behind him.

Again, the hand came forward to point off to the right.

Joao, with that hand close to his eyes and illuminated by the dash, saw the scale-like parts of a finger shift position slightly. In that shift, he recognized the scale-shapes by their claw fringes.

The beetles!

The finger was composed of linked beetles working in unison!

Joao turned, stared into the *Indian's* eyes, seeing now why they glistened so: they were composed of thousands of tiny facets.

"Hospital, there," the creature beside him said, pointing.

Joao turned back to the controls, fighting to keep from losing composure. They were not Indians . . . they weren't even human. They were insects— some kind of hive-cluster shaped and organized to mimic a man.

The implications of this discovery raced through his mind. How did they support their weight? How did they feed and breathe?

How did they speak?

Everything had to be subordinated to the urgency of getting this information and proof of it back to one of the big labs where the facts could be explored.

Even the death of his father could not be considered now. He had to capture one of these things, get out with it.

He reached overhead, flicked on the command transmitter, set its beacon for a homing call. *Let some of my Irmaos be awake and monitoring their sets,* he prayed.

"More to the right," said the creature behind him.

Again, Joao corrected course.

The moon was high overhead now, illuminating a line of *bandeirante* towers off to the left. The first barrier.

They would be out of the green area soon and into the gray—then, beyond that, another barrier and the great red that stretched out in reaching fingers through the Goyaz and the Mato Grosso. Joao could see scattered lights of Resettlement Plan farms ahead, and darkness beyond.

The airtruck was going faster than he wanted, but Joao dared not slow it. They might become suspicious.

"You must go higher," said the creature behind him.

Joao increased pump displacement, raised the nose. He leveled off at three hundred meters.

More *bandeirante* towers loomed ahead, spaced at closer intervals. Joao picked up the barrier signals on his meters, looked back at the *Indian.* The dissembler vibrations seemed not to affect the creature.

Joao looked out his side window and down. No one would challenge him, he knew. This was a *bandeirante* airtruck headed *into* the red zone . . . and with its transmitter sending out a homing call. The men down there would assume he was a bandleader headed out on a contract after a successful bid—and calling his men to him for the job ahead.

He could see the moon-silvered snake of the São Francisco winding off to his left, and the lesser waterways like threads raveled out of the foothills.

I must find the nest—where we're headed, Joao thought. He wondered if he dared turn on his receiver—but if his men started reporting in . . . No. That could make the creatures suspect; they might take violent counter-action.

My men will realize something is wrong when I don't answer, he thought. *They will follow.*

If any of them hear my call.

Hours droned past.

Nothing but moonlighted jungle sped beneath them now, and the moon was low on the horizon, near setting. This was the deep red region where broadcast poisons had been used at first with disastrous results. This was where the wild mutations had originated. It was here that Rhin Kelly had been reported missing.

This was the region being saved for the final assault, using a mobile barrier line when that line could be made short enough.

Joao armed the emergency charge that would separate the front and rear compartments of the truck when he fired it. The stub wings of the front compartment and its emergency rocket motors could get him back into *bandeirante* country.

With the *specimen* sitting behind him safely subdued, Joao hoped.

He looked up through the canopy, scanned the horizon as far as he could. Was that moonlight glistening on a truck far back to the right? He couldn't be sure.

"How much farther?" Joao asked.

"Ahead," the creature rasped.

Now that he was alert for it, Joao heard the modulated stridulation beneath that voice.

"But how long?" Joao asked. "My father . . ."

"Hospital for . . . the father . . . ahead," said the creature.

It would be dawn soon, Joao realized. He could see the first false line of light along the horizon behind. This night had passed so swiftly. Joao wondered if these creatures had injected some time-distorting drug into him without his knowing. He thought not. He was maintaining himself in the necessities of the moment. There was no time for fatigue or boredom when he had to record every landmark half-visible in the night, sense everything there was to sense about these creatures with him.

How did they coordinate all those separate parts?

Dawn came, revealing the plateau of the Mato Crosso. Joao looked out his windows. This region, he knew, stretched across five degrees of latitude and six degrees of longitude. Once, it had been a region of isolated *fazendas* farmed by independent blacks and by *sertanistos* chained to the *encomendero* plantation system. It was hardwood jungles, narrow rivers with banks overgrown by lush trees and ferns, savannahs, and tangled life.

Even in this age it remained primitive, a fact blamed largely on insects and disease. It was one of the last strongholds of *teeming* insect life, if the International Ecological Organization's reports could be believed.

Supplies for the *bandeirantes* making the assault on this insect stronghold would come by way of São Paulo, by air and by transport on the multidecked highways, then on antique diesel trains to Itapira, on river runners to Bahus and by airtruck to Registo and Leopoldina on the Araguaya.

This area crawled with insects: wire worms in the roots of the savannahs, grubs digging in the moist black earth, hopping beetles, dart-like angita wasps, chalcis flies, chiggers, sphecidae, braconidae, fierce hornets, white termites, hemipteric crawlers, blood roaches, thrips, ants, lice, mosquitoes, mites, moths, exotic butterflies, mantidae—and countless unnatural mutations of them all.

This would be an expensive fight—unless it were stopped . . . because it already had been lost.

I mustn't think that way, Joao told himself. *Out of respect for my father.*

Maps of the IEO showed this region in varied intensities of red. Around the red ran a ring of gray with pink shading where one or two persistent forms of insect life resisted man's poisons, jelly flames, astringents, sonitoxics—the combination of flamant couroq and supersonics that drove insects from their hiding places into waiting death—and all the mechanical traps and lures in the *bandeirante* arsenal.

A grid map would be placed over this area and each thousand-acre square offered for bid to the independent bands to deinfest.

We bandeirantes *are a kind of ultimate predator,* Joao thought. *It's no wonder these creatures mimic us.*

But how good, really, was the mimicry? he asked himself. And how deadly to the predators?

"There," said the creature behind him, and the multipart hand came forward to point toward a black scarp visible ahead in the gray light of morning.

Joao's foot kicked a trigger on the floor releasing a great cloud of orange dye-fog beneath the truck to mark the ground and forest for a mile around under this spot. As he kicked the trigger, Joao began counting down the five-second delay to the firing of the separation charge.

It came in a roaring blast that Joao knew would smear the creature behind him against the rear bulkhead. He sent the stub wings out, fed power to the rocket motors and banked hard around. He saw the detached rear compartment settling slowly earthward above the dye cloud, its fall cushioned as the pumps of the hydrostatic drive automatically compensated.

I will come back, Father, Joao thought. *You will be buried among family and friends.*

He locked the controls, twisted in the seat to see what had happened to his captive.

A gasp escaped Joao's lips.

The rear bulkhead crawled with insects clustered around something white and pulsing. The mud-gray shirt and trousers were torn, but insects already were repairing it, spinning out fibers that meshed and sealed on contact. There was a yellow-like extrusion near the pulsing white, and a dark brown skeleton with familiar articulation.

It looked like a human skeleton—but chitinous.

Before his eyes, the thing was reassembling itself, the long, furry antennae burrowing into the structure and interlocking.

The flute-weapon was not visible, and the thing's leather pouch had been thrown into the rear corner, but its eyes were in place in their brown sockets, staring at him. The mouth was re-forming.

The yellow sac contracted, and a voice issued from the half-formed mouth.

"You must listen," it rasped.

Joao gulped, whirled back to the controls, unlocked them and sent the cab into a wild, spinning turn.

A high-pitched rattling buzz sounded behind him. The noise seemed to pick up every bone in his body and shake it. Something crawled on his neck. He slapped at it, felt it squash.

All Joao could think of was escape. He stared frantically out at the earth beneath, seeing a blotch of white in a savannah off to his right and, in the same instant, recognizing another airtruck banking beside him, the insignia of his own Irmandades band bright on its side.

The white blotch in the savannah was resolving itself into a cluster of tents with an IEO orange and green banner flying beside them.

Joao dove for the tents, praying the other airtruck would follow.

Something stung his cheek. They were in his hair—biting, stinging. He stabbed the braking rockets, aimed for open ground about fifty meters from the tent. Insects were all over the inside of the glass now, blocking his vision. Joao said a silent prayer, hauled back on the control arm, felt the cab mush out, touch ground, skidding and slewing across the savannah. He kicked the canopy release before the cab stopped, broke the seal on his safety harness and launched himself up and out to land sprawling in grass.

He rolled through the grass, feeling the insect bites like fire over every exposed part of his body. Hands grabbed him and he felt a jelly hood splash across his face to protect it. A voice he recognized as Thome of his own band said: "This way, Johnny! Run!" They ran.

He heard a spraygun fire: "Whooosh!"

And again.

And again.

Arms fitted him and he felt a leap.

They landed in a heap and a voice said: "Mother of God! Would you look at that!"

Joao clawed the jelly hood from his face, sat up to stare across the savannah.

The grass seethed and boiled with insects around the uptilted cab and the airtruck that had landed beside it.

Joao looked around him, counted seven of his Irmaos with Thome, his chief sprayman, in command.

Beyond them clustered five other people, a red-haired woman slightly in front, half turned to look at the savannah and at him. He recognized the woman immediately: Dr. Rhin Kelly of the IEO. When they had met in the A' Chigua nightclub in Bahia, she had seemed exotic and desirable to Joao. Now, she wore a field uniform instead of gown and jewels, and her eyes held no invitation at all.

"I see a certain poetic justice in this . . . traitors," she said.

Joao lifted himself to his feet, took a cloth proffered by one of his men, wiped off the last of the jelly. He felt hands brushing him, clearing dead insects off his coveralls. The pain of his skin was receding under the medicant jelly, and now he found himself dominated by puzzled questioning as he recognized the mood of the IEO personnel.

They were furious and it was directed at him . . . and at his fellow Irmandades.

Joao studied the woman, noting how her green eyes glared at him, the pink flush to her skin.

"How many of you?" Joao asked.

"There were fourteen of us," said the man.

Joao rubbed the back of his neck where the insect stings were again beginning to burn. He glanced around at his men, assessing their condition and equipment, counted four spray rifles, saw the men carried spare charge cylinders on slings around their necks.

"The airtruck will take us," he said. "We had better get out of here."

Dr. Kelly looked out to the savannah, said: "I think it has been too late for that since a few seconds after you landed, *bandeirante*. I think in a day or so there'll be a few less traitors around. You're caught in your own trap."

Joao whirled to stare at the airtruck, barked: "Tommy! Vince! Get . . ." He broke off as the airtruck sagged to its left.

"It's only fair to warn you," said Dr. Kelly, "to stay away from the edge of the ditch unless you first spray the opposite side. They can shoot a stream of acid at least fifteen meters . . . and as you can see . . ." She nodded toward the airtruck. ". . . the acid eats metal."

"You're insane," Joao said. "Why didn't you warn us immediately?"

"Warn you?"

Her blond companion said: "Rhin, perhaps we . . ."

"Be quiet, Hogar," she said, and turned back to Joao. "We lost nine men to your playmates." She looked at the small band of Irmandades. "Our lives are little enough to pay now for the extinction of eight of you . . . traitors."

"You *are* insane," Joao said.

"Stop playing innocent, *bandeirante*," she said. "We have seen your com-

panions out there. We have seen the new playmates you bred . . . and we
understand that you were too greedy; now your game has gotten out of hand."

"You've not seen my Irmaos doing these things," Joao said. He looked at
Thome. "Tommy, keep an eye on these insane ones." He lifted the spray rifle
from one of his men, took the man's spare charges, indicated the other three
armed men. "You—come with me."

"Johnny, what do you do?" Thome asked.

"Salvage the supplies from the truck," Joao said. He walked toward the
ditch nearest the airtruck, laid down a hard mist of foamal beyond the ditch,
beckoned the others to follow and leaped the ditch.

Little more than an hour later, with all of them acid-burned—two
seriously—the Irmandades retreated back across the ditch. They had salvaged
less than a fourth of the equipment in the truck, and this did not include a
transmitter.

"It is evident the little devils went first for the communications equipment," Thome said. "How could they tell?"

Joao said: "I do not want to guess." He broke open a first aid box, began
treating his men. One had a cheek and shoulder badly splashed with acid.
Another was losing flesh off his back.

Dr. Kelly came up, helped him treat the men, but refused to speak, even
to answer the simplest question.

Finally, Joao touched up a spot on his own arm, neutralizing the acid and
covering the burn with flesh-tape. He gritted his teeth against the pain,
stared at Rhin Kelly. "Where are these chigua you found?"

"Go find them yourself!" she snapped.

"You are a blind, unprincipled megalomaniac," Joao said, speaking in an
even voice. "Do not push me too far."

Her face went pale and the green eyes blazed.

Joao grabbed her arm, hauled her roughly toward the tents. "Show me
these chigua!"

She jerked free of him, threw back her red hair, stared at him defiantly.
Joao faced her, looked her up and down with a calculating slowness.

"Go ahead, do violence to me," she said, "I'm sure I couldn't stop you."

"You act like a woman who wants . . . needs violence," Joao said. "Would
you like me to turn you over to my men? They're a little tired of your raving."

Her face flamed. "You would not dare!"

"Don't be so melodramatic," he said, "I wouldn't give you the pleasure."

"You insolent . . . you . . ."

Joao showed her a wolfish grin, said: "Nothing you say will make me
turn you over to my men!"

"Johnny."

It was Thome calling.

Joao turned, saw Thome talking to the Nordic IEO man who had volunteered information. What had she called him? Hogar.

Thome beckoned.

Joao crossed to the pair, bent close as Thome signaled secrecy.

"The gentleman here says the female doctor was bitten by an insect that got past their barrier's fumes."

"Two weeks ago," Hogar whispered.

"She has not been the same since," Thome said. "We humor her, jefe, no?"

Joao wet his lips with his tongue. He felt suddenly dizzy and too warm.

"The insect that bit her was similar to the ones that were on you," Hogar said, and his voice sounded apologetic.

They are making fun of me! Joao thought.

"I give the orders here!" he snapped.

"Yes, jefe," Thome said. "But you . . ."

"What difference does it make who gives the orders?"

It was Dr. Kelly close behind him.

Joao turned, glared at her. How hateful she looked . . . in spite of her beauty.

"What's the difference?" she demanded. "We'll all be dead in a few days anyway." She stared out across the savannah. "More of your friends have arrived."

Joao looked to the forest shadow, saw more human-like figures arriving. They appeared familiar and he wondered what it was—something at the edge of his mind, but his head hurt. Then he realized they looked like *sertao* Indians, like the pair who had lured him here. There were at least a hundred of them, apparently identical in every visible respect.

More were arriving by the second.

Each of them carried a qena flute.

There was something about the flutes that Joao felt he should remember.

Another figure came advancing through the *Indians,* a thin man in a black suit, his hair shiny silver in the sunlight.

"Father!" Joao gasped.

I'm sick, he thought. *I must be delirious.*

"That looks like the Prefect," Thome said. "Is it not so, Ramon?"

The Irmandade he addressed said: "If it is not the Prefect, it is his twin. Here, Johnny. Look with the glasses."

Joao took the glasses, focused on the figure advancing toward them through the grass. The glasses felt so heavy. They trembled in his hands and the figure coming toward them was blurred.

"I cannot see!" Joao muttered and he almost dropped the glasses.

A hand steadied him, and he realized he was reeling.

In an instant of clarity, he saw that the line of *Indians* had raised their flutes, pointing at the IEO camp. That buzzing-rasping that had shaken his bones in the airtruck cab filled the universe around him. He saw his companions begin to fall.

In the instant before his world went blank, Joao heard his father's voice calling strongly: "Joao! Do not resist! Put down your weapons!"

The trampled grassy earth of the campsite, Joao saw, was coming up to meet his face.

It cannot be my father, Joao thought. *My father is dead and they've copied him . . . mimicry, nothing more.*

Darkness.

There was a dream of being carried, a dream of tears and shouting, a dream of violent protests and defiance and rejection.

He awoke to yellow-orange light and the figure who could not be his father bending over him, thrusting a hand out, saying: "Then examine my hand if you don't believe!"

But Joao's attention was on the face behind his father. It was a giant face, baleful in the strange light, its eyes brilliant and glaring with pupils within pupils. The face turned, and Joao saw it was no more than two centimeters thick. Again, it turned, and the eyes focused on Joao's feet.

Joao forced himself to look down, began trembling violently as he saw he was half enveloped in a foaming green cocoon, that his skin shared some of the same tone.

"Examine my hand!" ordered the old-man figure beside him.

"He has been dreaming." It was a resonant voice that boomed all around him, seemingly coming from beneath the giant face. "He has been dreaming," the voice repeated. "He is not quite awake."

With an abrupt, violent motion, Joao reached out, clutched the proffered hand.

It felt warm . . . human.

For no reason he could explain, tears came to Joao's eyes.

"Am I dreaming?" he whispered. He shook his head to clear away the tears.

"Joao, my son," said his father's voice.

Joao looked up at the familiar face. It *was* his father and no mistake. "But . . . your heart," Joao said.

"My pump," the old man said. "Look." And he pulled his hand away, turned to display where the back of his black suit had been cut away, its edges held by some gummy substance, and a pulsing surface of oily yellow between those cut edges.

Joao saw the hair-fine scale lines, the multiple shapes, and he recoiled.

So it was a copy, another of their tricks.

The old man turned back to face him. "The old pump failed and they gave me a new one," he said. "It shares my blood and lives off me and it'll give me a few more years. What do you think our bright IEO specialists will say about the *usefulness* of that?"

"Is it really you?" Joao demanded.

"All except the pump," said the old man. "They had to give you and some of the others a whole new blood system because of all the corrosive poison that got into you."

Joao lifted his hands, stared at them.

"They know medical tricks we haven't even dreamed about," the old man said. "I haven't been this excited since I was a boy. I can hardly wait to get back and . . . Joao! What is it?"

Joao was thrusting himself up, glaring at the old man. "We're not human anymore if . . . We're not human!"

"Be still, son!" the old man ordered.

"If this is true," Joao protested, "they're in control." He nodded toward the giant face behind his father. "They'll *rule* us!"

He sank back, gasping. "We'll be their slaves."

"Foolishness," rumbled the drum voice.

Joao looked at the giant face, growing aware of the fluorescent insects above it, seeing that the insects clung to the ceiling of a cave, noting finally a patch of night sky and stars where the fluorescent insects ended.

"What is a slave?" rumbled the voice.

Joao looked beneath the face where the voice originated, saw a white mass about four meters across, a pulsing yellow sac protruding from it, insects crawling over it, into fissures along its surface, back to the ground beneath. The face appeared to be held up from that white mass by a dozen of round stalks, their scaled surfaces betraying their nature.

"Your attention is drawn to our way of answering your threat to us," rumbled the voice, and Joao saw that the sound issued from the pulsing yellow sac. "This is our brain. It is vulnerable, very vulnerable, weak, yet strong . . . just as your brain. Now, tell me what is a slave?"

Joao fought down a shiver of revulsion, said: "I'm a slave now; I'm in bondage to you."

"Not true," rumbled the voice. "A slave is one who must produce wealth for another, and there is only one true wealth in all the universe—living time. Are we slaves because we have given your father more time to live?"

Joao looked up to the giant, glittering eyes, thought he detected amusement there.

"The lives of all those with you have been spared or extended as well," drummed the voice. "That makes us your slaves, does it not?"

"What do you take in return?"

"Ah hah!" the voice fairly barked. "Quid pro quo! You are, indeed, our slaves as well. We are tied to each other by a bond of mutual slavery that cannot be broken—never could be."

"It is very simple once you understand it," Joao's father said.

"Understand what?"

"Some of our kind once lived in greenhouses and their cells remembered the experience," rumbled the voice. "You know about greenhouses, of course?" It turned to look out at the cave mouth where dawn was beginning to touch the world with gray. "That out there, that is a greenhouse, too." Again, it looked down at Joao, the giant eyes glaring. "To sustain life, a greenhouse must achieve a delicate balance—enough of this chemical, enough of that one, another substance available when needed. What is poison one day can be sweet food the next."

"What's all this to do with slavery?" Joao demanded.

"Life has developed over millions of years in this greenhouse we call Earth," the voice rambled. "Sometimes it developed in the poison excrement of other life . . . and then that poison became necessary to it. Without a substance produced by the wire worm, that savannah grass out there would die . . . in time. Without substances produced by . . . insects, your kind of life would die. Sometimes, just a faint trace of the substance is needed, such as the special copper compound produced by the arachnids. Sometimes, the substance must subtly change each time before it can be used by a life-form at the end of the chain. The more different forms of life there are, the more life the greenhouse can support. This is the lesson of the greenhouse. The successful greenhouse must grow many times many forms of life. The more forms of life it has, the healthier it is."

"You're saying we have to stop killing insects," Joao said. "You're saying we have to let you take over."

"We say you must stop killing yourselves," rumbled the voice. "Already, the Chinese are . . . I believe you would call it: *reinfesting* their land. Perhaps they will be in time, perhaps not. Here, it is not too late. There . . . they were fast and thorough . . . and they may need help."

"You . . . give us no proof," Joao said.

"There will be time for proof, later," said the voice. "Now, join your woman friend outside; let the sun work on your skin and the chlorophyll in your blood, and when you come back, tell me if the sun is your slave."

COMMITTEE OF
THE WHOLE

▰▰▰▰▰▰▰▰▰▰▰▰

I

With an increasing sense of unease, Alan Wallace studied his client as they neared the public hearing room on the second floor of the Old Senate Office Building. The guy was too relaxed.

"Bill, I'm worried about this," Wallace said. "You could damn well lose your grazing rights here in this room today."

They were almost into the gauntlet of guards, reporters and TV cameramen before Wallace got his answer.

"Who the hell cares?" Custer asked.

Wallace, who prided himself on being the Washington-type lawyer— above contamination by complaints and briefs, immune to all shock—found himself tongue-tied with surprise.

They were into the ruck then and Wallace had to pull on his bold face, smiling at the press, trying to soften the sharpness of that necessary phrase:

"No comment. Sorry."

"See us after the hearing if you have any questions, gentlemen," Custer said. The man's voice was level and confident.

He has himself over-controlled, Wallace thought. *Maybe he was just joking . . . a graveyard joke.*

The marble-walled hearing room blazed with lights. Camera platforms had been raised above the seats at the rear. Some of the smaller UHF stations had their cameramen standing on the window ledges.

The subdued hubbub of the place eased slightly, Wallace noted, then picked up tempo as William R. Custer—"The Baron of Oregon" they called him—entered with his attorney, passed the press tables and crossed to the seats reserved for them in the witness section.

Ahead and to their right, that one empty chair at the long table stood waiting with its aura of complete exposure.

"Who the hell cares?"

That wasn't a Custer-type joke, Wallace reminded himself. For all his cattle-baron pose, Custer held a doctorate in agriculture and degrees in philosophy, maths and electronics. His western neighbors called him "The Brain."

It was no accident that the cattlemen had chosen him to represent them here.

Wallace glanced covertly at the man, studying him. The cowboy boots and string tie added to a neat dark business suit would have been affectation on most men. They merely accented Custer's good looks—the sun-burned, windblown outdoorsman. He was a little darker of hair and skin than his father had been, still light enough to be called blonde, but not as ruddy and without the late father's drink-tumescent veins.

But then young Custer wasn't quite thirty.

Custer turned, met the attorney's eyes. He smiled.

"Those were good patent attorneys you recommended, Al," Custer said. He lifted his briefcase to his lap, patted it. "No mincing around or mealy-mouthed excuses. Already got this thing on the way." Again, he tapped the briefcase.

He brought that damn' light gadget here with him? Wallance wondered. *Why?* He glanced at the briefcase. *Didn't know it was that small . . . but maybe he's just talking about the plan for it.*

"Let's keep our minds on this hearing," Wallace whispered. "This is the only thing that's important."

Into a sudden lull in the room's high noise level, the voice of someone in the press section carried across them: "greatest political show on earth."

"I brought this as an exhibit," Custer said. Again, he tapped the briefcase. It *did* bulge oddly.

Exhibit? Wallace asked himself.

It was the second time in ten minutes that Custer had shocked him. This was to be a hearing of a subcommittee of the Senate Interior and Insular Affairs Committee. The issue was Taylor grazing lands. What the devil could that . . . *gadget* have to do with the battle of words and laws to be fought here?

"You're supposed to talk over all strategy with your attorney," Wallace whispered. "What the devil do you . . ."

He broke off as the room fell suddenly silent.

Wallace looked up to see the subcommittee chairman, Senator Haycourt Tiborough, stride through the wide double doors followed by his coterie of investigators and attorneys. The senator was a tall man who had once been fat. He had dieted with such savage abruptness that his skin had never recovered. His jowls and the flesh on the back of his hands sagged. The top of his head was shiny bald and ringed by a three-quarter tonsure that had purposely been allowed to grow long and straggly so that it fanned back over his ears.

The senator was followed in close lock step by syndicated columnist Anthony Poxman who was speaking fiercely into Tiborough's left ear. TV cameras tracked the pair.

If Poxman's covering this one himself instead of sending a flunky, it's going to be bad, Wallace told himself.

Tiborough took his chair at the center of the committee table facing them, glanced left and right to assure himself the other members were present.

Senator Spealance was absent, Wallace noted, but he had party organization difficulties at home, and the Senior Senator for Oregon was, significantly, not present. Illness, it was reported.

A sudden attack of caution, that common Washington malady, no doubt. He knew where his campaign money came from . . . but he also knew where the votes were.

They had a quorum, though.

Tiborough cleared his throat, said: "The committee will please come to order."

The senator's voice and manner gave Wallace a cold chill. *We were nuts trying to fight this one in the open,* he thought. *Why'd I let Custer and his friends talk me into this? You can't butt heads with a United States senator who's out to get you. The only way's to fight him on the inside.*

And now Custer suddenly turned screwball.

Exhibit!

"Gentlemen," said Tiborough, "I think we can . . . that is, today we can dispense with preliminaries . . . unless my colleagues . . . if any of them have objections."

Again, he glanced at the other senators—five of them. Wallace swept his gaze down the line behind that table—Plowers of Nebraska (a horse trader), Johnstone of Ohio (a parliamentarian—devious), Lane of South Carolina (a Republican in Democrat disguise), Emery of Minnesota (new and eager—dangerous because he lacked the old inhibitions) and Meltzer of New York (poker player, fine old family with traditions).

None of them had objections.

They've had a private meeting—both sides of the aisle—and talked over a smooth steamroller procedure, Wallace thought.

It was another ominous sign.

"This is a subcommittee of the United States Senate Committee on Interior and Insular Affairs," Tiborough said, his tone formal. "We are charged with obtaining expert opinion on proposed amendments to the Taylor Grazing Act of 1934. Today's hearing will begin with testimony and . . . ah, questioning of a man whose family has been in the business of raising beef cattle in Oregon for three generations."

Tiborough smiled at the TV cameras.

The son-of-a-bitch is playing to the galleries, Wallace thought. He glanced at Custer. The cattleman sat relaxed against the back of his chair, eyes half lidded, staring at the senator.

"We call as our first witness today Mr. William R. Custer of Bend, Oregon," Tiborough said. "Will the clerk please swear in Mr. Custer."

Custer moved forward to the "hot seat," placed his briefcase on the table. Wallace pulled a chair up beside his client, noted how the cameras turned as the clerk stepped forward, put the Bible on the table and administered the oath.

Tiborough ruffled through some papers in front of him, waited for full attention to return to him, said: "This subcommittee . . . we have before us a bill, this is a United States Senate Bill entitled SB-1024 of the current session, an act amending the Taylor Grazing Act of 1934 and, the intent is, as many have noted, that we would broaden the base of the advisory committees to the Act and include a wider public representation."

Custer was fiddling with the clasp of his briefcase.

How the hell could that light gadget be an exhibit here? Wallace asked himself. He glanced at the set of Custer's jaw, noted the nervous working of a muscle. It was the first sign of unease he'd seen in Custer. The sight failed to settle Wallace's own nerves.

"Ah, Mr. Custer," Tiborough said. "Do you—did you bring a preliminary statement? Your counsel . . ."

"I have a statement," Custer said. His big voice rumbled through the room, requiring instant attention and the shift of cameras that had been holding tardily on Tiborough, expecting an addition to the question.

Tiborough smiled, waited, then: "Your attorney—is your statement the one your counsel supplied the committee?"

"With some slight additions of my own," Custer said.

Wallace felt a sudden qualm. They were too willing to accept Custer's statement. He leaned close to his client's ear, whispered: "They know what your stand is. Skip the preliminaries."

Custer ignored him, said: "I intend to speak plainly and simply. I oppose the amendment. Broaden the base and wider public representation are phrases of political double talk. The intent is to pack the committees, to put control of them into the hands of people who don't know the first thing about the cattle business and whose private intent is to destroy the Taylor Grazing Act itself."

"Plain, simple talk," Tiborough said. "This committee . . . we welcome such directness. Strong words. A majority of this committee . . . we have taken the position that the public range lands have been too long subjected to the tender mercies of the stockmen advisers, that the lands . . . stockmen have exploited them to their own advantage."

The gloves were off. Wallace thought. *I hope Custer knows what he's doing. He's sure as hell not accepting advice.*

Custer pulled a sheaf of papers from his briefcase and Wallace glimpsed shiny metal in the case before the flap was closed.

Christ! That looked like a gun or something!

Then Wallace recognized the papers—the brief he and his staff had labored over—and the preliminary statement. He noted with alarm the penciled markings and marginal notations. How could Custer have done that much to it in just twenty-four hours?

Again, Wallace whispered in Custer's ear: "Take it easy, Bill. The bastard's out for blood."

Custer nodded to show he had heard, glanced at the papers, looked up directly at Tiborough.

A hush settled on the room, broken only by the scraping of a chair somewhere in the rear, and the whirr of cameras.

II

"First, the nature of these lands we're talking about," Custer said. "In my state . . ." He cleared his throat, a mannerism that would have indicated anger in the old man, his father. There was no break in Custer's expression, though, and his voice remained level. ". . . in my state, these were mostly Indian lands. This nation took them by brute force, right of conquest. That's about the oldest right in the world, I guess. I don't want to argue with it at this point."

"Mr. Custer."

It was Nebraska's Senator Plowers, his amiable farmer's face set in a tight grin. "Mr. Custer, I hope . . ."

"Is this a point of order?" Tiborough asked.

"Mr. Chairman," Plowers said, "I merely wished to make sure we weren't going to bring up that old suggestion about giving these lands back to the Indians."

Laughter shot across the hearing room. Tiborough chuckled as he pounded his gavel for order.

"You may continue, Mr. Custer," Tiborough said.

Custer looked at Plowers, said: "No, Senator, I don't want to give these lands back to the Indians. When they had these lands, they only got about three hundred pounds of meat a year off eighty acres. We get five hundred pounds of the highest grade proteins—premium beef—from only ten acres."

"No one doubts the efficiency of your factory-like methods," Tiborough said. "You can . . . we know your methods wring the largest amount of meat from a minimum acreage."

Ugh! Wallace thought. *That was a low blow—implying Bill's overgrazing and destroying the land value.*

"My neighbors, the Warm Springs Indians, use the same methods I do," Custer said. "They are happy to adopt our methods because we use the land while maintaining it and increasing its value. We don't permit the land to fall prey to natural disasters such as fire and erosion. We don't . . ."

"No doubt your methods are meticulously correct," Tiborough said. "But I fail to see where . . ."

"Has Mr. Custer finished his preliminary statement yet?" Senator Plowers cut in.

Wallace shot a startled look at the Nebraskan. That was help from an unexpected quarter.

"Thank you, Senator," Custer said. "I'm quite willing to adapt to the Chairman's methods and explain the meticulous correctness of my operation. Our lowliest cowhands are college men, highly paid. We travel ten times as many jeep miles as we do horse miles. Every outlying division of the ranch—every holding pen and grazing supervisor's cabin is linked to the central ranch by radio. We use the . . ."

"I concede that your methods must be the most modern in the world," Tiborough said. "It's not your methods as much as the results of those methods that are at issue here. We . . ."

He broke off at a disturbance by the door. An Army colonel was talking to the guard there. He wore Special Services fourragere—Pentagon.

Wallace noted with an odd feeling of disquiet that the man was armed—a .45 at the hip. The weapon was out of place on him, as though he had added it suddenly on an overpowering need . . . emergency.

More guards were coming up outside the door now—Marines and Army. They carried rifles.

The colonel said something sharp to the guard, turned away from him and entered the committee room. All the cameras were tracking him now. He ignored them, crossed swiftly to Tiborough and spoke to him.

The senator shot a startled glance at Custer, accepted a sheaf of papers the colonel thrust at him. He forced his attention off Custer, studied the papers, leafing through them. Presently, he looked up, stared at Custer.

A hush fell over the room.

"I find myself at a loss, Mr. Custer," Tiborough said. "I have here a copy of a report . . . it's from the Special Services branch of the Army . . . through the Pentagon, you understand. It was just handed to me by, ah . . . the colonel here."

He looked up at the colonel who was standing, one hand resting lightly on the holstered .45. Tiborough looked back at Custer and it was obvious the senator was trying to marshall his thoughts.

"It is," Tiborough said, "that is . . . this report supposedly . . . and I have every confidence it is what it is represented to be . . . here in my hands . . .

they say that . . . uh, within the last, uh, few days they have, uh, investigated a certain device . . . weapon they call it, that you are attempting to patent. They report . . ." He glanced at the papers, back to Custer, who was staring at him steadily. ". . . this, uh, weapon, is a thing that . . . it is extremely dangerous."

"It is," Custer said.

"I . . . ah, see." Tiborough cleared his throat, glanced up at the colonel who was staring fixedly at Custer. The senator brought his attention back to Custer.

"Do you in fact have such a weapon with you, Mr. Custer?" Tiborough asked.

"I have brought it as an exhibit, sir."

"Exhibit?"

"Yes, sir."

Wallace rubbed his lips, found them dry. He wet them with his tongue, wished for the water glass, but it was beyond Custer. *Christ! That stupid cowpuncher!* He wondered if he dared whisper to Custer. Would the senators and that Pentagon lackey interpret such an action as meaning he was part of Custer's crazy antics?

"Are you threatening this committee with your weapon, Mr. Custer?" Tiborough asked. "If you are, I may say special precautions have been taken . . . extra guards in this room and we . . . that is, we will not allow ourselves to worry too much about any action you may take, but ordinary precautions are in force."

Wallace could no longer sit quietly. He tugged Custer's sleeve, got an abrupt shake of the head. He leaned close, whispered: "We could ask for a recess, Bill. Maybe we . . ."

"Don't interrupt me," Custer said. He looked at Tiborough. "Senator, I would not threaten you or any other man. Threats in the way you mean them are a thing we no longer can indulge in."

"You . . . I believe you said this device is an exhibit," Tiborough said. He cast a worried frown at the report in his hands. "I fail . . . it does not appear germane."

Senator Plowers cleared his throat. "Mr. Chairman," he said.

"The chair recognizes the senator from Nebraska," Tiborough said, and the relief in his voice was obvious. He wanted time to think.

"Mr. Custer," Plowers said, "I have not seen the report, the report my distinguished colleague alludes to; however, if I may . . . is it your wish to use this committee as some kind of publicity device?"

"By no means, Senator," Custer said. "I don't wish to profit by my presence here . . . not at all."

Tiborough had apparently come to a decision. He leaned back, whispered to the colonel, who nodded and returned to the outer hall.

"You strike me as an eminently reasonable man, Mr. Custer," Tiborough said. "If I may . . ."

"May I," Senator Plowers said. "May I, just permit me to conclude this one point. May we have the Special Services report in the record?"

"Certainly," Tiborough said. "But what I was about to suggest . . ."

"May I," Plowers said. "May I, would you permit me, please, Mr. Chairman, to make this point clear for the record?"

Tiborough scowled, but the heavy dignity of the Senate overcame his irritation. "Please continue, Senator, I had thought you were finished."

"I respect . . . there is no doubt in my mind of Mr. Custer's truthfulness," Plowers said. His face eased into a grin that made him look grandfatherly, a kindly elder statesman. "I would like, therefore, to have him explain how this . . . ah, weapon, can be an exhibit in the matter before our committee."

Wallace glanced at Custer, saw the hard set of the man's jaw, realized the cattleman had gotten to Plowers somehow. This was a set piece.

Tiborough was glancing at the other senators, weighing the advisability of high-handed dismissal . . . perhaps a star chamber session. No . . . they were all too curious about Custer's device, his purpose here.

The thoughts were plain on the senator's face.

"Very well," Tiborough said. He nodded to Custer. "You may proceed, Mr. Custer."

"During last winter's slack season," Custer said, "two of my men and I worked on a project we've had in the works for three years—to develop a sustained-emission laser device."

Custer opened his briefcase, slid out a fat aluminium tube mounted on a pistol grip with a conventional appearing trigger.

"This is quite harmless," he said. "I didn't bring the power pack."

"That is . . . this is your weapon?" Tiborough asked.

"Calling this a weapon is misleading," Custer said. "The term limits and oversimplifies. This is also a brush-cutter, a substitute for a logger's saw and axe, a diamond cutter, a milling machine . . . and a weapon. It is also a turning point in history."

"Come now, isn't that a bit pretentious?" Tiborough asked.

"We tend to think of history as something old and slow," Custer said. "But history is, as a matter of fact, extremely rapid and immediate. A President is assassinated, a bomb explodes over a city, a dam breaks, a revolutionary device is announced."

"Lasers have been known for quite a few years," Tiborough said. He looked at the papers the colonel had given him. "The principle dates from 1956 or thereabouts."

"I don't wish it to appear that I'm taking credit for inventing this device," Custer said. "Nor am I claiming sole credit for developing the sustained-emission laser. I was merely one of a team. But I do hold the device here in my hand, gentlemen."

"Exhibit, Mr. Custer," Plowers reminded him. "How is this an exhibit?"

"May I explain first how it works?" Custer asked. "That will make the rest of my statement much easier."

Tiborough looked at Plowers, back to Custer. "If you will tie this all together, Mr. Custer," Tiborough said. "I want to . . . the bearing of this device on our—we are hearing a particular bill in this room."

"Certainly, Senator," Custer said. He looked at his device. "A ninety-volt radio battery drives this particular model. We have some that require less voltage, some that use more. We aimed for a construction with simple parts. Our crystals are common quartz. We shattered them by bringing them to a boil in water and then plunging them into ice water . . . repeatedly. We chose twenty pieces of very close to the same size—about one gram, slightly more than fifteen grains each."

Custer unscrewed the back of the tube, slid out a round length of plastic trailing lengths of red, green, brown, blue and yellow wire.

Wallace noticed how the cameras of the TV men centered on the object in Custer's hands. Even the senators were leaning forward, staring.

We're gadget-crazy people, Wallace thought.

"The crystals were dipped in thinned household cement and then into iron filings," Custer said. "We made a little jig out of a fly-tying vice and opened a passage in the filings at opposite ends of the crystals. We then made some common celluloid—nitro-cellulose, acetic acid, gelatin and alcohol—all very common products, and formed it in a length of garden hose just long enough to take the crystals end to end. The crystals were inserted in the hose, the celluloid poured over them and the whole thing was seated in a magnetic waveguide while the celluloid was cooling. This centered and aligned the crystals. The waveguide was constructed from wire salvaged from an old TV set and built following the directions in the Radio Amateur's Handbook."

Custer re-inserted the length of plastic into the tube, adjusted the wires. There was an unearthly silence in the room with only the cameras whirring. It was as though everyone were holding his breath.

"A laser requires a resonant cavity, but that's complicated," Custer said. "Instead, we wound two layers of fine copper wire around our tube, immersed it in the celluloid solution to coat it and then filed one end flat. This end took a piece of mirror cut to fit. We then pressed a number eight embroidery needle at right angles into the mirror end of the tube until it touched the side of the number one crystal."

Custer cleared his throat.

Two of the senators leaned back. Plowers coughed. Tiborough glanced at the banks of TV cameras and there was a questioning look in his eyes.

"We then determined the master frequency of our crystal series," Custer said. "We used a test signal and oscilloscope, but any radio amateur could do it without the oscilloscope. We constructed an oscillator of that master frequency, attached it at the needle and a bare spot scraped in the opposite edge of the waveguide."

"And this . . . ah . . . worked?" Tiborough asked.

"No." Custer shook his head. "When we fed power through a voltage multiplier into the system we produced an estimated four hundred joules emission and melted half the tube. So we started all over again."

"You are going to tie this in?" Tiborough asked. He frowned at the papers in his hands, glanced toward the door where the colonel had gone.

"I am, sir, believe me," Custer said.

"Very well, then," Tiborough said.

"So we started all over," Custer said. "But for the second celluloid dip we added bismuth—a saturate solution, actually. It stayed gummy and we had to paint over it with a sealing coat of the straight celluloid. We then coupled this bismuth layer through a pulse circuit so that it was bathed in a counter wave—180 degrees out of phase with the master frequency. We had, in effect, immersed the unit in a thermoelectric cooler that exactly countered the heat production. A thin beam issued from the un-mirrored end when we powered it. We have yet to find something that thin beam cannot cut."

"Diamond?" Tiborough asked.

"Powered by less than two hundred volts, this device could cut our planet in half like a ripe tomato," Custer said. "One man could destroy an aerial armada with it, knock down ICBMs before they touched atmosphere, sink a fleet, pulverize a city. I'm afraid, sir, that I haven't mentally catalogued all the violent implications of this device. The mind tends to boggle at the enormous power focused in . . ."

"Shut down those TV cameras!"

It was Tiborough shouting, leaping to his feet and making a sweeping gesture to include the banks of cameras. The abrupt violence of his voice and gesture fell on the room like an explosion. "Guards!" he called. "You there at the door. Cordon off that door and don't let anyone out who heard this fool!" He whirled back to face Custer. "You irresponsible idiot!"

"I'm afraid, Senator," Custer said, "that you're locking the barn door many weeks too late."

For a long minute of silence Tiborough glared at Custer. Then: "You did this deliberately, eh?"

III

"Senator, if I'd waited any longer, there might have been no hope for us at all."

Tiborough sat back into his chair, still keeping his attention fastened on Custer. Plowers and Johnston on his right had their heads close together whispering fiercely. The other senators were dividing their attention between Custer and Tiborough, their eyes wide and with no attempt to conceal their astonishment.

Wallace, growing conscious of the implications in what Custer had said, tried to wet his lips with his tongue. *Christ!* he thought. *This stupid cowpoke has sold us all down the river!*

Tiborough signaled an aide, spoke briefly with him, beckoned the colonel from the door. There was a buzzing of excited conversation in the room. Several of the press and TV crew were huddled near the windows on Custer's left, arguing. One of their number—a florid-faced man with gray hair and horn-rimmed glasses, started across the room toward Tiborough, was stopped by a committee aide. They began a low-voiced argument with violent gestures.

A loud curse sounded from the door. Poxman, the syndicated columnist, was trying to push past the guards there.

"Poxman!" Tiborough called. The columnist turned. "My orders are that no one leaves," Tiborough said. "You are not an exception." He turned back to face Custer.

The room had fallen into a semblance of quiet, although there still were pockets of muttering and there was the sound of running feet and a hurrying about in the hall outside.

"Two channels went out of here live," Tiborough said. "Nothing much we can do about them, although we will trace down as many of their viewers as we can. Every bit of film in this room and every sound tape will be confiscated, however." His voice rose as protests sounded from the press section. "Our national security is at stake. The President has been notified. Such measures as are necessary will be taken."

The colonel came hurrying into the room, crossed to Tiborough, quietly said something.

"You should've warned me!" Tiborough snapped. "I had no idea that . . ."

The colonel interrupted with a whispered comment.

"These papers . . . your damned report is *not* clear!" Tiborough said. He looked around at Custer. "I see you're smiling, Mr. Custer. I don't think you'll find much to smile about before long."

"Senator, this is not a happy smile," Custer said. "But I told myself several days ago you'd fail to see the implications of this thing." He tapped the pistol-shaped device he had rested on the table. "I told myself you'd fall back into the old, useless pattern."

"Is that what you told yourself, really?" Tiborough said.

Wallace, hearing the venom in the senator's voice, moved his chair a few inches farther away from Custer.

Tiborough looked at the laser projector. "Is that thing really disarmed?"

"Yes, sir."

"If I order one of my men to take it from you, you will not resist?"

"Which of your men will you trust with it, Senator?" Custer asked.

In the long silence that followed, someone in the press section emitted a nervous guffaw.

"Virtually every man on my ranch has one of these things," Custer said. "We fell trees with them, cut firewood, make fence posts. Every letter written to me as a result of my patent application has been answered candidly. More than a thousand sets of schematics and instructions on how to build this device have been sent out to varied places in the world."

"You vicious traitor!" Tiborough rasped.

"You're certainly entitled to your opinion, Senator," Custer said. "But I warn you I've had time for considerably more concentrated and considerably more painful thought than you've applied to this problem. In my estimation, I had no choice. Every week I waited to make this thing public, every day, every minute, merely raised the odds that humanity would be destroyed by . . ."

"You said this thing applied to the hearings on the grazing act," Plowers protested, and there was a plaintive note of complaint in his voice.

"Senator, I told you the truth," Custer said. "There's no real reason to change the act, now. We intend to go on operating under it—with the agreement of our neighbors and others concerned. People are still going to need food."

Tiborough glared at him. "You're saying we can't force you to . . ." He broke off at a disturbance in the doorway. A rope barrier had been stretched there and a line of Marines stood with their backs to it, facing the hall. A mob of people was trying to press through. Press cards were being waved.

"Colonel, I told you to clear that hall!" Tiborough barked.

The colonel ran to the barrier. "Use your bayonets if you have to!" he shouted.

The disturbance subsided at the sound of his voice. More uniformed men could be seen moving in along the barrier. Presently, the noise receded.

Tiborough turned back to Custer. "You make Benedict Arnold look like the greatest friend the United States ever had," he said.

"Cursing me isn't going to help you," Custer said. "You are going to have to live with this thing; so you'd better try understanding it."

"That appears to be simple," Tiborough said. "All I have to do is send twenty-five cents to the Patent office for the schematics and then write you a letter."

"The world already was headed toward suicide," Custer said. "Only fools failed to realize . . ."

"So you decided to give us a little push," Tiborough said.

"H. G. Wells warned us," Custer said. "That's how far back it goes, but nobody listened. 'Human history becomes more and more a race between education and catastrophe,' Wells said. But those were just words. Many scientists have remarked the growth curve on the amount of raw energy becoming available to humans—and the diminishing curve on the number of persons required to use that energy. For a long time now, more and more violent power was being made available to fewer and fewer people. It was only a matter of time until total destruction was put into the hands of single individuals."

"And you didn't think you could take your government into your confidence."

"The government already was committed to a political course diametrically opposite the one this device requires," Custer said. "Virtually every man in the government has a vested interest in not reversing that course."

"So you set yourself above the government?"

"I'm probably wasting my time," Custer said, "but I'll try to explain it. Virtually every government in the world is dedicated to manipulating something called the 'mass man.' That's how governments have stayed in power. But there is no such man. When you elevate the nonexistent 'mass man' you degrade the individual. And obviously it was only a matter of time until all of us were at the mercy of the individual holding power."

"You talk like a commie!"

"They'll say I'm a goddamn' capitalist pawn," Custer said. "Let me ask you, Senator, to visualize a poor radio technician in a South American country. Brazil, for example. He lives a hand-to-mouth existence, ground down by an overbearing, unimaginative, essentially uncouth ruling oligarchy. What is he going to do when this device comes into his hands?"

"Murder, robbery and anarchy."

"You could be right," Custer said. "But we might reach an understanding out of ultimate necessity—that each of us must cooperate in maintaining the dignity of all."

Tiborough stared at him, began to speak musingly: "We'll have to control the essential materials for constructing this thing . . . and there may be trouble for awhile, but . . ."

"You're a vicious fool."

In the cold silence that followed, Custer said: "It was too late to try that ten years ago. I'm telling you this thing can be patchworked out of a wide variety of materials that are already scattered over the earth. It can be made in basements and mud huts, in palaces and shacks. The key item is the crystals, but other crystals will work, too. That's obvious. A patient man can grow crystals . . . and this world is full of patient men."

"I'm going to place you under arrest," Tiborough said. "You have outraged every rule—"

"You're living in a dream world," Custer said. "I refuse to threaten you, but I'll defend myself from any attempt to oppress or degrade me. If I cannot defend myself, my friends will defend me. No man who understands what this device means will permit his dignity to be taken from him."

Custer allowed a moment for his words to sink in, then: "And don't twist those words to imply a threat. Refusal to threaten a fellow human is an absolute requirement in the day that has just dawned on us."

"You haven't changed a thing!" Tiborough raged. "If one man is powerful with that thing, a hundred are . . ."

"All previous insults aside," Custer said, "I think you are a highly intelligent man, Senator. I ask you to think long and hard about this device. Use of power is no longer the deciding factor because one man is as powerful as a million. Restraint—*self*-restraint is now the key to survival. Each of us is at the mercy of his neighbor's good will. Each of us, Senator—the man in the palace and the man in the shack. We'd better do all we can to increase that good will—not attempting to buy it, but simply recognizing that individual dignity is the one inalienable right of . . ."

"Don't you preach at me, you commie traitor!" Tiborough rasped. "You're a living example of . . ."

"Senator!"

It was one of the TV cameramen in the left rear of the room.

"Let's stop insulting Mr. Custer and hear him out," the cameraman said.

"Get that man's name," Tiborough told an aide. "If he . . ."

"I'm an expert electronic technician, Senator," the man said. "You can't threaten me now."

Custer smiled, turned to face Tiborough.

"The revolution begins," Custer said. He waved a hand as the senator started to whirl away. "Sit down, Senator."

Wallace, watching the senator obey, saw how the balance of control had changed in this room.

"Ideas are in the wind," Custer said. "There comes a time for a thing to develop. It comes into being. The spinning jenny came into being because that was its time. It was based on countless ideas that had preceded it."

"And this is the age of the laser?" Tiborough asked.

"It was bound to come," Custer said. "But the number of people in the world who're filled with hate and frustration and violence has been growing with terrible speed. You add to that the enormous danger that this might fall into the hands of just one group or nation or . . ." Custer shrugged. "This is too much power to be confined to one man or group with the hope they'll administer wisely. I didn't dare delay. That's why I spread this thing now and announced it as broadly as I could."

Tiborough leaned back in his chair, his hands in his lap. His face was pale and beads of perspiration stood out on his forehead.

"We won't make it."

"I hope you're wrong, Senator," Custer said. "But the only thing I know for sure is that we'd have had less chance of making it tomorrow than we have today."

THE GM EFFECT

It was a balmy fall evening and as Dr. Valeric Sabantoce seated himself at the long table in Meade Hall's basement seminar room, he thought of how the weather would be sensationalized tomorrow by the newspapers and wire services. They would be sure to remark on the general clemency of the elements, pointing out how Nature's smiling aspect made the night's tragedy so much more horrible.

Sabantoce was a short, rotund man with a wild shock of black hair that looked as though it had never known a comb. His round face with its look of infant innocence invariably led strangers to an incorrect impression—unless they were at once exposed to his ribald wit or caught the weighted stare of his deeply-socketed brown eyes.

Fourteen people sat around the long table now—nine students and five faculty—with Professor Joshua Latchley in the chairman's seat at the head.

"Now that we're all here," Latchley said, "I can tell you the purpose of to-night's meeting. We are faced with a most terrible decision. We . . . ahhh—"

Latchley fell silent, chewed at his lower lip. He was conscious of the figure he cut here—a tall, ungainly bald man in thick-lensed glasses . . . the constant air of apology he wore as though it were a shield. Tonight, he felt that this appearance was a disguise. Who could guess—except Sabantoce, of course—at the daring exposed by this seemingly innocent gathering?

"Don't leave 'em hanging there, Josh," Sabantoce said.

"Yes . . . ahh, yes," Latchley said. "It has occurred to me that Dr. Saban-toce and I have a special demonstration to present here tonight, but before we expose you to that experiment, as it were, perhaps we should recapitulate somewhat."

Sabantoce, wondering what had diverted Latchley, glanced around the table—saw that they were *not* all there. Dr. Richard Marmon was missing.

Did he suspect and make a break for it? Sabantoce wondered. He realized then that Latchley was stalling for time while Marmon was being hunted out and brought in here.

Latchley rubbed his shiny pate. He had no desire to be here, he thought. But this had to be done. He knew that outside on the campus the special 9:00 P.M. hush had fallen over Yankton Technical Institute and this was his favorite hour for strolling—perhaps up to the fresh pond to listen to the frogs and the couples and to think on the etymological derivations of—

He became conscious of restless coughing and shuffling around the table, realized he had permitted his mind to wander. He was infamous for it, Latchley knew. He cleared his throat. *Where the devil was that Marmon? Couldn't they find him?*

"As you know," Latchley said, "we've made no particular efforts to keep our discovery secret, although we've tried to discourage wild speculation and outside discussion. Our intention was to conduct thorough tests before publishing. All of you—both the student . . . ahh, 'guinea pigs' and you professors of the faculty committee—have been most cooperative. But inevitably news of what we are doing here has spread—sometimes in a very hysterical and distorted manner."

"What Professor Latchley is saying," Sabantoce interrupted, "is that the fat's in the fire."

Expressions of curiosity appeared on the faces of the students who, up to this moment, had been trying to conceal their boredom. Old Dr. Inkton had a fit of coughing.

"There's an old Malay expression," Sabantoce said, "that when one plays Bumps-a-Daisy with a porcupine, one is necessarily jumpy. Now, all of us should've known this porcupine was loaded.'"

"Thank you, Dr. Sabantoce," Latchely said. "I feel . . . and I know this is a most unusual course . . . that all of you should share in the decision that must be made here tonight. Each of you, by participating in this project, has become involved far more deeply here than is the usual case with scientific experiments of this general type. And since you student *assistants* have been kept somewhat in the dark, perhaps Dr. Sabantoce, as original discoverer of the GM effect, should fill you in on some of the background."

Stall it is, Sabantoce thought.

"Discovery of the genetic memory, or GM effect, was an accident," Sabantoce said, picking up his cue. "Dr. Marmon and I were looking for a hormonal method of removing fat from the body. Our Compound 105 had given excellent results on mice and hamsters. We had six generations without apparent side effects and that morning I had decided to try 105 on myself."

Sabantoce allowed himself a self-deprecating grin, said: "You may remember I had a few excess pounds then."

The responsive laughter told him he had successfully lightened the mood which had grown a bit heavy after Latchley's portentous tone.

Josh is a damn' fool, Sabantoce told himself. *I warned him to keep it light. This is a dangerous business.*

"It was eight minutes after ten A.M. when I took that first dosage," Sabantoce said. "I remember it was a very pleasant spring morning and I could hear Carl Kychre's class down the hall reciting a Greek ode. In a few minutes I began to feel somewhat euphoric—almost drunk, but very gently so—and I sat down on a lab stool. Presently, I began reciting with Kychre's class, swinging my arm to the rhythm of it. The next thing I knew, there was Carl in the lab door with some students peering in behind him and I realized I might have been a bit loud."

" 'That's magnificent archaic Greek but it *is* disturbing my class,' Carl said."

Sabantoce waited for laughter to subside.

"I suddenly realized I was two people," Sabantoce said. "I was perfectly aware of where I was and who I was, but I also knew quite certainly that I was a Hoplite soldier named Zagreut recently returned from a mercenary venture on Kyrene. It was the *double-exposure* effect that so many of you have remarked. I had all the memories and thoughts of this Hoplite, including his very particular and earthy inclinations toward a female who was uppermost in his/my awareness. And there was this other thing we've all noticed: I was thinking his/my thoughts in Greek, but they were cross-linked to my dominant present and its English-based awareness. I could translate at will. It was a very heady experience, this realization that I was two people."

One of the graduate students said: "You were a whole mob, Doctor."

Again, there was laughter. Even old Inkton joined in.

"I must've looked a bit peculiar to poor Carl," Sabantoce said. "He came into the lab and said: 'Are you all right?' I told him to get Dr. Marmon down there fast . . . which he did. And speaking of Marmon, do any of you know where he is?"

Silence greeted the question; then Latchley said: "He's being . . . summoned."

"So," Sabantoce said. "Well, to get on: Marmon and I locked ourselves in the lab and began exploring this thing. Within a few minutes we found out you could direct the subject's awareness into any stratum of his genetic inheritance, there to be *illuminated* by an ancestor of his choice; and we were caught immediately by the realization that this discovery gave an entirely new interpretation to the concept of instinct and to theories of memory storage. When I say we were excited, that's the understatement of the century."

The talkative graduate student said: "Did the effect fade the way it does with the rest of us?"

"In about an hour," Sabantoce said. "Of course, it didn't fade completely, as you know. That old Hoplite's right here with me, so to speak—along with the rest of the *mob*. A touch of 105 and I have him full on—all his direct memories up to the conception-moment of my next ancestor in his line. I have some overlaps, too, and later memories of his through parallel ancestry and later siblings. I'm also linked to his maternal line, of course—and two of you are tied into this same fabric, as you know. The big thing here is that the remarkably accurate memories of that Hoplite play hob with several accepted histories of the period. In fact, he was our first intimation that much recorded history is a crock."

Old Inkton leaned forward, coughed hoarsely, said: "Isn't it about time, doctor, that we did something about that?"

"In a way, that's why we're here tonight," Sabantoce said. And he thought: *Still no sign of Marmon. I hope Josh knows what he's talking about. But we have to stall some more.*

"Since only a few of us know the full story on some of our more sensational discoveries, we're going to give you a brief outline of those discoveries," Sabantoce said. He put on his most disarming smile, gestured to Latchley. "Professor Latchley, as historian-coordinator of that phase in our investigations, can carry on from here."

Latchley cleared his throat, exchanged a knowing look with Sabantoce. *Did Marmon suspect?* Latchley asked himself. *He couldn't possibly know . . . but he might have suspected.*

"Several obvious aspects of this research method confront one immediately," Latchley said, breaking his attention away from Sabantoce and the worry about Marmon. "As regards any major incident of history—say, a battle—we find a broad selection of subjects on the victorious side and, sometimes, no selection at all on the defeated side. Through the numerous cross references found within even this small group, for example, we find remarkably few *adjacent* and incidental memories within the Troy quadrant of the Trojan wars—some female subjects, of course, but few males. The male bloodlines were virtually wiped out."

Again, Latchley sensed restlessness in his audience and felt a moment of jealousy. Their attention didn't wander when Sabantoce was speaking. The reason was obvious: Sabantoce gave them the dirt, so to speak.

Latchley forced his apologetic smile, said: "Perhaps you'd like a little of the real dirt."

They did perk up, by heaven!

"As many have suspected," Latchley said, "our evidence makes it conclusive that Henry Tudor did order the murder of the two princes in the Tower . . . at the same time he set into motion the propaganda against Richard III. Henry proves to've been a most vile sort—devious, cruel, cowardly, murderous—political murder was an accepted part of his regime." Latchley shuddered. "And thanks to his sex drive, he's an ancestor of many of us."

"Tell 'em about Honest Abe," Sabantoce said.

Latchley adjusted his glasses, touched the corner of his mouth with a finger, then: "Abraham Lincoln."

He said it as though announcing a visitor and there was a long pause.

Presently, Latchley said: "I found this most distressing. Lincoln was my particular hero in childhood. As some of you know, General Butler was one of my ancestors and . . . well, this was *most* distressing."

Latchley fumbled in his pocket, brought up a scrap of paper, studied it, then: "In a debate with Judge Douglas, Lincoln said: 'I tell you very frankly that I am not in favor of Negro citizenship. I am not, nor ever have been, in favor of bringing about in any way the social and political equality of the white and black races; that I am not nor ever have been, in favor of making voters or jurors of Negroes, nor of qualifying them to hold office, nor to intermarry with white people. I will say in addition that there is a physical difference between the white and black races, which, I suppose, will forever forbid the two races living together upon terms of social and political equality; and in as much as they cannot so live—while they do remain together—there must be the position of the superiors and the inferiors; and that I, as much as any other man, am in favor of the superior being assigned to the white man.' "

Latchley sighed, stuffed the paper into a pocket. "Most distressing," he said. "Once, in a conversation with Butler, Lincoln suggested that all Negroes should be deported to Africa. Another time, talking about the Emancipation Proclamation, he said: 'If it helps preserve the Union, that's enough. But it's as clear to me as it is to any thinking man in the Republic that this proclamation will be declared unconstitutional by the Supreme Court following the cessation of hostilities.' "

Sabantoce interrupted: "How many of you realize what hot potatoes these are?"

The faces around the table turned toward him then back to Latchley.

"Once you have the clue of an on-the-scene observer," Latchley said, "you even find correspondence and other records of corroboration. It's amazing how people used to hide their papers."

The talkative graduate student leaned his elbows on the table, said: "The hotter the potato, the more people will notice it, isn't that right, Professor Latchley?"

Poor fellow's bucking for a better grade even now, Sabantoce thought. And he answered for Latchley: "The hottest potatoes are the most difficult to swallow, too."

The inane exchange between Sabantoce and the student left a hollow silence behind it and a deepening sense of uneasiness.

Another student said: "Where's Dr. Marmon? I understand he has a theory that the more GM we bring into contact with consciousness, the more we're controlled by the dominant brutality of our ancestors. You know, he says the most brutal ones survived to have children and we kind of gloss that over in our present awareness . . . or something like that."

Old Inkton stirred out of his semidaze, turned his sour milk eyes on Latchley. "Pilgrims," he said.

"Ah, yes," Latchley said.

Sabantoce said: "We have eyewitness accounts of Puritans and Pilgrims robbing and raping Indians. Brutality. Some of my ancestors, I'm afraid."

"Tea party," Old Inkton said.

Why doesn't the old fool shut up? Latchley wondered. And he found himself increasingly uneasy about Marmon's absence. *Could there have been a double double-cross?* he asked himself.

"Why not outline the Boston Tea Party?" Sabantoce asked. "There're a few here who weren't in on that phase."

"Yes . . . ahhh-mmmm," Latchley said. "Massachusetts had a smuggling governor then, of course. Everybody of consequence in the Colonies was smuggling. Navigation Acts and all that. The governor and his cronies were getting their tea from the Dutch. Had warehouses full of it. The British East India Company was on the verge of bankruptcy when the British Government voted a subsidy—equivalent to more than twenty million dollars in current exchange. Because of this . . . ahh, subsidy, the East India Company's tea could be sent in at about half the price of the smuggled tea—even including the tax. The governor and his henchmen faced ruin. So they hired brigands to wear Indian disguise and dump the East India Company's tea into the harbor—about a half million dollars worth of tea. And the interesting thing is it was better tea than the smugglers had. Another item to note is that the governor and his cronies then added the cost of the hired brigands onto the price charged for their smuggled tea."

"Hot potatoes," Sabantoce said. "And we haven't even gone into the religious issues—Moses and his aides drafting the Ten Commandments . . . the argument between Pilate and the religious fanatic."

"Or the present United States southern senator whose grandfather was a light-skinned Negro," Latchley said.

Again, that air of suspenseful uneasiness came over the room. People turned and looked at their companions, twisted in their chairs.

Sabantoce felt it and thought: *We can't let them start asking the wrong questions. Maybe this was a bad tack to take. We should've stalled them some other way . . . perhaps in some other place. Where is Marmon?*

"Our problem is complicated by accuracy, strangely enough," Latchley said. "When you know where to look, the corroborating evidence is easy to find. The records of that southern senator's ancestry couldn't be disputed."

A student at the opposite end of the table said: "Well, if we have the evidence then nothing can stop us."

"Ahh . . . mmmm," Latchley said. "Well . . . ahh . . . the financial base for our own school is involv . . ."

He was interrupted by a disturbance at the door. Two uniformed men pushed a tall blond young man in a rumpled dark suit into the room. The door was closed and there came the click of a lock. It was an ominous sound.

Sabantoce rubbed his throat.

The young man steadied himself with a hand against the wall, worked his way up the room to a point opposite Latchley, lurched across to an empty chair and collapsed into it. A thick odor of whisky accompanied him.

Latchley stared at him, feeling both relief and uneasiness. They were *really* all here now. The newcomer stared back out of deep-set blue eyes. His mouth was a straight, in-curving line in a long face that appeared even longer because of an extremely high forehead.

"What's going on here, Josh?" he demanded.

Latchley put on his apologetic smile, said: "Now, Dick, I'm sorry we had to drag you away from wherev . . ."

"Drag!" The young man glanced at Sabantoce, back to Latchley. "Who are those guys? Said they were campus police, but I never saw 'em before. Said I had to come with them . . . vital importance!"

"I told you this was an important meeting tonight," Sabantoce said. "You've . . ."

"Important meeting," the young man sneered.

"We must decide tonight about abandoning the project," Latchley said.

A gasp sounded around the table.

That was clever, Sabantoce thought. He looked down the table at the others, said: "Now that Dr. Marmon is here, we can bring the thing out and examine it."

"Aband . . ." Marmon said and sat up straight in his chair.

A long moment of silence passed. Abruptly, the table erupted to discord—everyone trying to talk at once. The noise subsided only when Sabantoce overrode it, slamming a palm against the table and shouting: "Please!"

Into the sudden silence, Latchley said. "You have no idea how painful this disclosure is to those of us who've already faced the realities of it."

"Realities?" Marmon demanded. He shook his head and the effort he made to overcome the effects of drink was apparent to everyone around the table.

"Let me point out to all of you just one *little* part of our total problem," Sabantoce said. "The inheritance of several major fortunes in this country could be legally attacked—with excellent chances of success—on the basis of knowledge we've uncovered."

Sabantoce gave them a moment to absorb this, then: "We're boat rockers in a world whose motto is 'Don't give up the ship.' And we could tip over quite a few ships."

"Let us face it," Latchley said, picking up his cue from Sabantoce. "We are not a very powerful group."

"Just a minute!" Marmon shouted. He hitched his chair closer to the table. "Bunch of crepe hangers. Where's y'r common sense? We got the goods on a whole bunch of bums! Have you any idea how much that's worth?"

From down the table to his left came one explosive word: "Blackmail?"

Latchley looked at Sabantoce with a raised-eyebrows expression that said clearly: "See? I told you so."

"Why not?" Marmon demanded. "These bums have been blackmailing us f'r centuries. 'B'lieve what I tell y', man, or we'll pull y'r arms outa their sockets!' That's what they been tellin's . . . telling us." He rubbed his lips.

Sabantoce stood up, moved around the table and rested a hand lightly on Marmon's shoulder. "Okay. We'll let Dr. Marmon be the devil's advocate. While he's talking, Dr. Latchley and I will go out and get the film and equipment for the little demonstration we've prepared for you. It should give you a clear understanding of what we're up against." He nodded to Latchley, who arose and joined him.

They crossed to the door, trying not to move too fast. Sabantoce rapped twice on the panel. The door opened and they slipped out between two uniformed guards, one of whom closed and locked the door behind them.

"This way, please," the other guard said.

They moved up the hall, hearing Marmon's voice fade behind them: "The bums have always controlled the history books and the courts and the coinage and the military and every . . ."

Distance reduced the voice to an unintelligible murmur.

"Damn' Commie," one of the guards muttered.

"It does seem such a waste," Latchley said.

"Let's not kid ourselves," Sabantoce said as he started up the stairs to the building's side exit. "When the ship's sinking, you save what you can. I think the Bishop explained things clearly enough: God's testing all men and this is the ultimate test of faith."

"Ultimate test, certainly," Latchley said, laboring to keep up with Sabantoce. "And I'm afraid I must agree with whoever it was said this would produce only chaos—unsettled times . . . anarchy."

"Obvious," Sabantoce said, as he stepped through the outer door being held by another guard.

Latchley and the escort followed.

At once, Sabantoce noted that all the campus lights had been extinguished. *The contrived power failure,* he thought. *They probably switched Meade to an emergency circuit so we wouldn't notice.*

One of their guards stepped forward, touched Latchley's arm, said: "Take the path directly across the quad to the Medical School. Use the back door into Vance Hall. You'll have to hurry. There isn't much time."

Sabantoce led the way down the steps and onto the dark path away from Meade Hall. The path was only a suggestion of lighter gray in the darkness. Latchley stumbled into Sabantoce as they hurried, said: "Excuse me."

There was an impression of many moving dark shapes in the shadows around them. Once a light was flashed in their faces, immediately extinguished.

A voice came from the dark corner of a building: "Down here. Quickly."

Hands guided them down steps, through a door, past heavy draperies, through another door and into a small, dimly lighted room.

Sabantoce recognized it—a medical storeroom that appeared to have been emptied of its supplies rather quickly. There was a small box of compresses on a shelf at his right.

The room was heavy with tobacco smoke and the odor of perspiration. At least a dozen men loomed up in the gloom around them—some of the men in uniform.

A heavy-jowled man with a brigadier's star on his shoulder confronted Sabantoce, said: "Glad to see you made it safely. Are they all in that building now?"

"Every last one," Sabantoce said. He swallowed.

"What about the formula for your Compound 105?"

"Well," Sabantoce said, and allowed a smirk to touch his lips: "I took a little precaution about that—just to keep you honest. I mailed a few copies around to . . ."

"We know about those," the brigadier said. "We've had the mails from this place closed off and censored for months. I mean those copies you typed in the bursar's office."

Sabantoce turned white. "Well, they're . . ."

Latchley interrupted, saying: "Really, what's going on here? I thought we . . ."

"Be quiet!" the brigadier snapped. He returned his attention to Sabantoce. "Well?"

"I . . . ahh . . ."

"Those are the ones we found under the floor of his rooms," said a man by the door. "The typeface is identical, sir."

"But I want to know if he made any other copies," the brigadier said.

It was clear from the expression on Sabantoce's face that he had not. "Well . . . I . . ." he began.

Again, Latchley interrupted. "I see no need to . . ."

The loud cork-popping sound of a silenced revolver cut him off. The noise was repeated.

Latchley and Sabantoce crumpled to the floor, dead before they hit it. The man by the door stepped back, holstering his weapon.

As though punctuating their deaths, the outside night was ripped by an explosion.

Presently, a man leaned into the room, said: "The walls went in the way we planned, sir. Thermite and napalm are finishing it. Won't be a trace of those dirty Commies."

"Good work, captain," the brigadier said. "That will be all. Just keep civilians away from the immediate area until we're sure."

"Very good, sir."

The head retreated and the door was closed.

Good man, the brigadier thought. He fingered the lone remaining copy of Compound 105's formula in his pocket. *They were all good men. Hand picked. Have to use a different screening process to pick the men for the*

next project, though: the investigation of possible military uses in this Com-
pound 105.

"I want those bodies burned practically to ash," he said, gesturing with a toe at Sabantoce and Latchley. "Deliver them with those you pick up from the building."

From the shadowed rear of the room came a heavy, growling voice: "What'll I tell the senator?"

"Tell him anything you want," the brigadier said. "I'll show him my private report later." And he thought: *There's an immediate use for this compound—we have a senator right in our pockets.*

"Damn' nigger lovers," the growling voice said.

"Speak not unkindly of the dead," said a smooth tenor from the opposite corner of the room.

A man in a black suit pushed himself through to the open area around the bodies, knelt and began praying in a soft, mumbling voice.

"Tell me as soon as that fire's out," the brigadier said.

THE PRIMITIVES

I

The sinking of the Soviet propaganda ship for the sole purpose of stealing the Mars diamond was a typical Conrad Rumel (alias Swimmer) crime: a gigantic nose-thumbing for profit. And Swimmer had the gigantic nose for it, plus a hair line that crowded his eyebrows, small gray-green eyes, a chin that almost vanished into his neck and a wide thick-lipped mouth like a hungry sea bass.

When he was seventeen, Swimmer had decided his physical ugliness left him only one suitable career—crime. He came from a family noted for professional specialists—mathematicians, surgeons, physicists, teachers, biochemists. It was no surprise then that Swimmer chose to specialize. His specialty was underwater crime.

He'd had his first gill mask and equalizer suit at the age of five (the gift of a father who preferred him out of sight) and there'd soon been no doubt that Swimmer was at home in his chosen element.

Good breeding had marked him, though: he drew the line at bloodshed and murder. If there was any single modus operandi stamp on Swimmer's crimes (beyond touches that betrayed physical cowardice) it was bizarre humor. It's noteworthy that he sank the Soviet ship in shallow water when only five men of the anchor watch were aboard (the others being ashore at an official Mexican fiesta-reception) and the five were all on deck. Swimmer had thoughtfully provided an open carton of a product called "Flotation Falsies" which bobbed to the surface and provided the bouyancy on which the five Russians made their way safely to a nearby beach.

By the nature of the crime and his subsequent actions, Swimmer had hoped to involve a professional mobster named Bime Jepson. Disposal of the Mars diamond was going to be no easy matter and Swimmer's sense of honor insisted he owed this to Jepson. Their last mutual enterprise had gone exceedingly sour, costing Jepson a bundle which he quoted at $288,764.51.

Jepson's reaction then came as a surprise.

"This is a diamond?" he sneered, staring at the object in his hands. The stone was bluish-white, cloud-surfaced, about the size and shape of a medium cantaloupe. "Are you nuts or something?" Jepson demanded. "This is . . . is . . ." His one-track mind struggled for a suitable word. "This is a rock. This is a chunk of nothing!" His narrow blue eyes glared with anger.

They stood in the bedroom of Jepson's suite on the 324th floor of the Mazatlan Hilton. Corner windows opened to a view of the ocean and city, colors blaring and gaudy in the bright Mexican afternoon.

Jepson lifted his attention from the stone. He fixed his gaze on the dark-haired oversize gnome of a man who had brought this unpleasantness. The man was a walking reminder of their last encounter—all that money sunk into an invention by one of Swimmer's professional uncles, Professor Amino Rumel.

Uncle Professor's project was a time machine of uncertain function. Apprised of the device by Swimmer, Jepson had conceived the idea of a sortie into the past backed by a crew with modern arms, the object being to raid the treasury of Knossos. (One of Jepson's mistresses had read a work of fiction in which this treasure figured.)

After all those megabucks, Uncle Professor had pronounced the machine as requiring "much more development."

"It didn't work," was Jepson's summation. And he was a man who did not like to be thwarted. Only the fact that Uncle Professor was "one of them" (legitimate) and the latent hope that the device might yet be made to work had prevented Jepson from committing bloody violence. Now, here was this creep-nephew, Swimmer, back with more trouble.

Swimmer had read the signs of anger. He said: "Jep, I swear that's . . ."

"You swear nothing! This ain't no diamond! A diamond's something with . . . something you can . . ."

"Jep, let me explain about . . ."

"Ain't you been warned never to interrupt me, Swimmer?"

Swimmer retreated a short step toward the door. "Now, don't go getting excited, Jep."

Jepson threw the stone onto the unmade bed behind him. "A diamond!" he sneered.

"Jep, that rock's worth . . ."

"Sharrup!"

His heart pounding, Swimmer took two steps backward, stood pressed against the door facing Jepson. This was not going at all as he had anticipated.

"I should call in the boys and teach you a little manners," Jepson growled.

"How many times I gotta tell you don't interrupt?" Jepson scowled. "Only reason the boys let you in was you told 'em you heisted a diamond too hot for you to handle. Everybody knows how big hearted I am. I'm here to help my friends with little matters like that. But I ain't here to help my friends with . . . with . . . I ain't here to be woke up every time some beachbum finds a big pebble what's good for nothing but tying around somebody's neck so they should sink!"

"Can I say something, Jep?" Swimmer pleaded.

"Say anything you want, but say it somewhere else. I want you should get outa here and—"

"Jep!" Swimmer pleaded.

"Interrupt me once more, Swimmer, and I lose my temper."

By its lack of inflection. Jepson's voice managed to convey a profound menace.

Swimmer nodded silently. He hadn't anticipated instant rage from Jepson. Everything depended on being able to explain.

"You think I don't recognize this rock?" Jepson asked.

Swimmer shook his head from side to side.

"This is the Mars diamond," Jepson said. "Diamond! It's the rock them Ruskies brung back in their spaceship. It was in their floating museum out in the harbor just yesterday. I seen it there myself. Does that answer all your questions, Swimmer?"

"But it's worth maybe ten million dollars!" Swimmer blurted. "Everybody said . . ."

"It ain't worth ten Mexican cents! Didn't you see all them charts and things in with it?"

Swimmer patted a breast pocket of his permadry suit and a dollop of water trapped there spurted out onto the rug. He gulped, said: "I brought them, too. The diagrams, everything."

"Then you shoulda known better," Jepson snarled. "There ain't no diamond cutter in the world'd touch this thing. Ain't no cutter wouldn't recognize it in the first place. And in the second place, them charts show why this *diamond* can't be cut without it breaks into chips worth maybe two-bits apiece. It's impossible to cut this thing, you dumbhead! And in the third place, this is what they call a cultural relic of Mars what the Ruskies and every cop in the world's gonna be looking for soon's they find it missing. And you hadda bring it here!"

For Jepson, this was a long speech. He stopped to collect his thoughts. *Stupid creep Swimmer!*

Swimmer stood trembling with the desire to speak and the fear of what might happen if he did.

Jepson looked out the window, returned a speculative stare to Swimmer. "How'd you heist it?"

"I sank the boat. While everybody was splashing around topside, I went in with a gill mask and burner, opened the case and took off across the bay. It was easy."

Jepson slapped his forehead with the heel of his right hand. "You sunk the boat!" He sighed. "Well, I'm gonna do you a favor. Not because I wanta, but because I hafta. I'm gonna see this *rock* finds its way back into the bay near the Rusky boat like maybe it fell overboard. And you ain't never gonna mention this thing again, right?"

"Jep," Swimmer said, speaking with desperate urgency, "maybe I know a cutter."

Jepson studied him, interested in spite of the lessons from past experiences with Swimmer. "A cutter who could handle *this* rock? A cutter who'd even try it?"

"She'll work any rock, Jep. And she won't recognize it and she won't care where it came from."

"She?"

Swimmer wiped his forehead. He had Jepson's interest now. Maybe Jepson would come along after all.

"That's right, she," Swimmer said. "And there isn't a cutter in this world can hold a candle to her."

"I never heard of no dame cutter," Jepson said. "I didn't think they had the nerves for it."

"This is a brand new one, Jep."

"A new cutter," Jepson mused. "A dame. Is she a looker?"

"I doubt it, but I've never seen her."

"You've never seen her, but you've got her?"

"I've got her."

"Awwww," Jepson said. He shook his head. "I find it interesting you have a new cutter on the string, but nobody can cut this rock. You seen them charts. The Ruskies don't make mistakes like that. This rock is for nobody. It can't be cut."

"I think this cutter can do it," Swimmer said.

The stubborn set to Swimmer's mouth whetted Jepson's interest. It was like Swimmer to be stubborn in the face of determined opposition.

"Where you got this cutter?" Jepson asked.

Swimmer wet his lips with his tongue. This was the ticklish part, Jepson's temper being what it was. "You remember my uncle Amino and his advice for you to be patient about . . ."

"Ahhh, hah!" Jepson barked. He pointed to the door. "Out! You hear me, creep? Out!"

"Jep, the time machine works!"

Silence dragged out for a dozen heartbeats while Swimmer wondered if he had timed that revelation correctly, and while Jepson reminded himself that this possibility was one of the reasons he hadn't obliterated Swimmer.

Presently, Jepson said: "It works?"

"I swear it, Jep. It works, but the controls aren't too . . . well, accurate. Sometimes my uncle says it balks and . . . it doesn't go precisely where you want."

"But it works?" Jepson demanded.

"It brought back this cutter," Swimmer said. "From perhaps twenty or thirty thousand years ago."

A muscle twisted on Jepson's left cheek and his jaw line went hard. "I thought you said your cutter dame was an expert."

Swimmer took a deep breath, wondering how he could explain paleolithic culture to a man like Jepson. The patois of the underworld didn't fit the job.

"You ain't got nothing to say?" Jepson asked.

"I'm quoting my uncle, who's a very truthful man," Swimmer said. "According to my uncle, the people of this dame's culture made all their tools out of stone. They have what my uncle calls an *intuition* about stones and working with them. He's the one said she could cut the Mars diamond."

Jepson frowned. "Did Uncle Professor fall off the legit? He put you up to this job?"

"Oh, no! None of my family know how I . . . ahh, make my living."

Jepson groped backward with one foot, found the edge of the bed, sat down. "How much more loot does Uncle Professor need to fix his machine?"

"You have it all wrong, Jep. It isn't a matter of loot. My uncle says there are local anomalies and force-time variations and that it very likely will be impossible ever to steer the machine very close to a time mark."

"But it works?"

"With these limitations."

"Then why ain't I heard about it? Thing like this, seems it'd be more important than any Mars diamond. Why ain't it big news?"

"My uncle's trying to determine if his force-time variation theory is correct. Besides, he has a plan to present his stone-age woman before a scientific meeting and he's collecting supporting evidence. And he says he's having trouble teaching her how to talk. She thinks he's some kind of god."

"I'm beginning to be very interested in what you tell me," Jepson said. "So say some more."

"You're not mad any more, Jep?"

"I've said unkind words. So? Maybe I'm entitled. Let us now say that interest has overcome my unhappiness. You sure your uncle didn't plan this little job?"

Swimmer shook his head. "Uncle Amino wouldn't take any part of action like this. He's cubed. No, this was mine. After our—you know—I was on the shorts. I figured to do this one for the ready and cut you in because . . . well I owe it to you. You'll get your bundle back with interest. And this is a job with style, Jep. The Mars diamond—impossible to cut. But we cut it."

"And who's to believe?" Jepson said. He nodded. "You think this gal of your Uncle Professor's can do it?"

"I ran into Uncle Amino up in Long Beach. He was there buying equipment when the Russian ship made port and the Mars diamond was big news. Uncle Amino read this part about it being impossible to cut and he laughed. He said his gal could cut it into a watch fob for Premier Sherdakov if she wanted. That's the first I knew about the gal and about the machine working. He's been keeping it pretty secret, as I explained. Well . . . what he said, I questioned my uncle; he was serious. This stone-age gal can do it. He insists she can."

Jepson nodded. "If he says this cutter can do it, perhaps . . . just perhaps, mind you, we could do business. It don't go until I see for myself, though."

Swimmer allowed himself a deep sigh. "Well, naturally, Jep."

Jepson pursed his lips. "I tell you a thing, Swimmer. You ain't done this entirely outa kindness for me. You heist this rock, you maybe start an international incident, but you ain't got no way to get the rock outa Mexico."

Swimmer stared at his feet, suppressed a smile. "I guess I didn't fool you a bit, Jep. I have to get the rock up north. I have to get the cutter away from my uncle and I need a place where she can work. I need organization. You have organization."

"Organization is expensive," Jepson said.

Swimmer looked up. "We deal?"

"Seventy-five and twenty-five," Jepson said.

"Ahhh, Jep! I was thinking fifty-five, forty-five." At the look in Jepson's eyes, he said: "Sixty-forty?"

"Sharrup before I make it eighty-twenty," Jepson said. "Just be glad you got a friend like me who'll help when you need."

"There's a few million bucks in this thing," Swimmer said, fighting to keep the hurt and anger from his voice. "The split's—"

"The split stands," Jepson said. "Seventy-five and twenty-five. We don't argue. Besides, I'm nuts even to listen to you. Every time you say dough I buy trouble. This time, I better get some of my investment back. Now, you go out and tell Harpsy to slip the dolls some coin and send 'em packing. We gotta concentrate on getting this rock over the border. And *that* is gonna take some doing."

II

The chalet nestled furtively wren-brown within the morning shadows of pines and hemlocks on a lake island. The lake itself was a sheet of silvered glass reflecting upside down images of the island and a dock on its south shore. Two airboats had been brought up under the trees and hidden beneath instiflage netting.

Seated in shadows above the dock, a man with a blast-pellet swagrifle puffed nervously on an *alerto* cigaret. Two other men, similarly armed and similarly drugged to eye-darting sensitivity, patrolled the island's opposite shore.

The sounds of an argument could be heard coming from within what had been the chalet's dining room and now was a jury-rigged workshop. It was only one of many arguments that had consumed considerable time during the past five days of harried flight northward from Mazatlan.

Swimmer, for one, was sick of the arguing, but he knew of no non-violent way to silence his uncle. Things were not going at all as he had planned. First, there had been the disconcerting discovery that a Mexican boy had identified him from mug files as the man who had walked out of the water wearing a normal business suit (permadry) and gill mask and carrying a "white rock."

Jepson's organization had smuggled Swimmer over the border concealed in a freight load of canteloupes. One of the canteloupes had been hollowed out to hold the diamond.

Next, Swimmer's uncle—alerted by the front-page hullabaloo—had absolutely balked at cooperating in anything his wayward nephew wanted.

Jepson had lost his temper, had given terse orders to his boys and here they all were now—somewhere in Canada or northern Minnesota.

Arguing.

Only one of the dining room's occupants had failed to participate in the arguments. She answered to the name of Ob (although her own people had called her Kiunlan, which translated as Graceful Shape).

Kiunlan-Ob stood five feet one inch tall. Professor Amino Rumel's lab scales had placed her weight at one hundred twenty-seven pounds nine ounces. Her blue-black hair had been drawn back and tied with a red ribbon. She had a low forehead and large, wide-set blue-gray eyes. Her nose was flat and with large nostrils. Both chin and mouth were broad, the lips thick. Fifteen welted red scars down the left side of her face told the initiated that she had seen fifteen summers and had not yet littered. A simple brown pullover dress belted at the waist covered her heavy-legged body, but failed to conceal the fact that she had four breasts.

This feature had first attracted Swimmer's fascinated attention. He had then noted her hands. These bore thick horn callouses over palms and fingers and along the inner edges of the fingers—even occasionally on the backs of the fingers, especially around the nails.

Ob stood now beside a bench that had replaced the chalet dining room's table. One of her hands rested on the back of a high stool drawn up to the bench. The Mars diamond lay on a cushioned square of black velvet atop the bench. The stone's milky surface reflected a faint yellow from the spotlight hanging close to it on a gooseneck.

As the argument progressed, Ob's attention shifted fearfully from speaker to speaker. First, there were many angry noises from Gruaack, the super devil-god who was called Proff Ess Orr. Then came equally loud and angry noises from the big stout devil-god called Jepp, the one whose eyes blazed with the threat of unknown terrors and who obviously was superior over all the others in this place.

Sometimes there were softer sounds from the smaller creature who had accompanied the devil-god Jepp. The status of this creature was not at all clear. He appeared to Ob to be vaguely human. The face was not at all unpleasant. And he seemed to share some of Ob's fears. She thought perhaps the other creature was a human snared like herself by these terrible beings.

"Yes, she's a genius at shaping stones!" Uncle Professor blared. "Yes! Yes! But she's still a primitive creature whose understanding of what we want is definitely limited."

He paced back and forth in front of Ob and the bench, a bald, skinny little man trembling with indignation.

Thieves, assassins, kidnappers, he thought. *How could Conrad have become associated with such a crew? Coming on him in his lab that way, crating his equipment without a by-your-leave and spiriting him off to this remote place.*

"You through yakking?" Jepson asked.

"No, I am not," Uncle Professor said. He pointed to the diamond on the bench. "That . . . that is no ordinary diamond. That is the Mars diamond. Turning such a priceless stone over to . . ."

"Sharrup!" Jepson said.

Creeps with their stupid arguments, he thought.

Uncle Professor glanced at his nephew. There'd been some bad moments during the past few days of their furtive journey. Again, the Professor wondered about nephew Conrad. Could the boy have been deceived by Jepson? The man was a criminal and that obviously was where all his money came from—all the money provided to develop the time machine. Was it possible this Jepson had dragged poor Conrad into this nefarious scheme through some terrible threat?

In a quiet voice, Jepson said: "Did you or didn't you tell your nephew the Swimmer here that your gal could cut this Mars rock?"

"Yes, I said that; I said she could cut any stone, but . . ."

"So awright. I want she should cut."

"Will you please try to understand?" the Professor pleaded. "Ob undoubtedly can *cut* your stone. But any idea of facets and deriving the maximum brilliance from a given gem—this probably is outside her understanding. She's accustomed to *functional* artifacts, to simpler purposes in her . . ."

"Simple, Schmimple!" Jepson snarled. "You're stalling. What's it, huh? D'you lie about this dame? Alla stories I ever see 'bout creeps like her, the guys did the stone cutting and the dames sat around caves hiding from tigers they got teeth six feet long."

"We're going to have to revise our previous hypotheses about stone-age divisions of labor," the Professor said. "As nearly as I can make out from Ob, women made the tools and weapons while the men did the hunting. Their society was matriarchal with certain women functioning somewhat like priestesses. Cave Mothers, I believe it would translate."

"Yeah? I ain't so sure. What about them things?"

"Things?" The Professor peered at Jepson with a puzzled frown.

"She's got four of 'em!" Jepson barked. "I think you're trying to pass off some freak as . . ."

"Oh," the Professor said. "Four, yes. That's very curious. About one in fourteen million human female births today demonstrate a condition of more than two mammaries. Heretofore, there've been three major hypotheses: one, mutation, two, absorbed sibling, and three, ahh . . . throwback. Ob is living proof of the third case. Multiple births were more frequent in her time, you see? It's quite simple: females were required to suckle more infants. A survival characteristic that gradually disappeared as multiple births declined."

"You don't say," Jepson growled.

"George was particularly elated," the Professor said, "since he had maintained the third case."

"George? Who is George?" Jepson demanded.

"My associate, Professor George Elwin," the Professor said.

"You didn't tell me about no George," Jepson said. "When I was sinking all that loot in your stupid machine, there wasn't no George around. Who's he, your new mark?"

"Mark?" The Professor glanced at Swimmer back to Jepson.

Swimmer tried to swallow in a dry throat, sensing how near Jepson was to a violent explosion of rage. Swimmer found it odd that his uncle couldn't see the danger.

"I don't really see where my associate is any concern of yours," the Professor said. "But if . . ."

"How many people know about that *time* machine—" Jepson pointed to the large crate in the corner behind him—"and about this Ob dame?"

"Well you know, of course, and . . ."

"Don't get smart with me, creep! Who knows?"

The Professor stared at him, aware at last of the suppressed rage. Professor Rumel's mouth felt suddenly dry. Criminals such as this could be most violent—murderously so, at times.

"Well, aside from those of us here in this room, there are Professor Elwin and very likely two or three of George's assistants. I didn't impose any special strictures of secrecy other than to suggest we'd wait for the complete investigation before publishing our . . ."

"How come this George?" Jepson demanded.

"Well, my dear sir, *someone* with the proper training had to go to Northern France and seek the archeological authentication. Inevitably, there will be cries of fraud, you know."

Jepson screwed his face into a puzzled frown. "Archeo . . . What's this Northern France bit?"

The Professor's face came alight with the glow of a man launched on his favorite subject. "You may not know it, Mr. Jepson, but paleolithic artifacts bear markings that are, in some respects, as distinctive as the brush-strokes of a master painter. Now, under strictly controlled archeological conditions, we're seeking some of Ob's work in situ—where she originally made it."

"Yeah?" Jepson said.

"You see, Mr. Jepson, as nearly as we can determine, Ob came from the region just east of Cambrai in Northern France. This is something more than an educated guess. We have several pieces of evidence—a scrap of obsidian which Ob—you see how I got her name . . . my little joke: Ob for obsidian . . . well, this piece of obsidian she carried on her when we picked her up is of a type common in the region we've selected. There was also plant pollen on her person, types of clay soil in the mud on her feet and a photograph of the background landscape which we took as we snatched Ob from . . ."

"Yeah," Jepson said. "So only a few of us know about her."

"Quite," the Professor said. "I'm sure you can see why we decided to delay any publication and prevent idle speculation. Nothing destroys the essential character of scientific endeavor more than Sunday supplement romanticizing."

"Yeah," Jepson said. "Just like you tol' me."

"And there's the ethical problem," the Professor said. "Some people may question the morality of our bringing this human being out of her natural habitat in the past. I, personally, incline to the theory that Ob's timestream diverted from ours at the moment of her removal from her—and our—personal past. However, if you . . ."

"Yeah, yeah!" Jepson barked.

Keerist! he thought. *The old creep could yak all day about nothing. Big words! Big words! Didn't mean a thing.*

III

Swimmer looked from one to the other and marveled at the low level of communication between his uncle and Jepson. The Professor might just as well be talking to Ob for all the sense he was making. Swimmer fingered the gill mask in his pocket, thinking of it as a back-door way of escape should things get completely out of hand here.

"As I was about to say," the Professor said, "if you consider the equation of historical interference as one element of your total . . ."

"Yeah!" Jepson exploded. "That's very interesting. But what I wanna know is why can't I show this Ob dame a rock and say I want some other rock cut likewise and such and so? She could do the thing like that, ain't it?"

The Professor sighed and threw up his hands. He'd thought he'd penetrated Jepson's strange jargon, conveyed some of the problems to the man, but not a bit of it appeared to have gotten through.

"Din't you say she was an expert?" Jepson demanded.

"Given time," the Professor said in a patient, long-suffering tone. "I do believe Ob could make one of the finest diamond cutters in the world. We've a few industrial diamond chips in the lab and part of our examination of her involved seeing what she could do with them. She needed no more than a glance to see the natural cleavage lines. No fumbling or mistakes. Just one practical glance. But I wish to warn you—the measure of her understanding may be seen in the fact she thought the diamonds too hard for practical purposes."

"But she worked them rocks okay?"

"If that's what you want to call it."

"Did she have any better tools than we got here?" Jepson motioned to the rack at the rear of the bench, the cutter's vice clamped to one end.

"Not as good."

"She know how to use them tools?"

"She has a natural tool sense and she's quite awed by our equipment. She's an intuitive worker. You might say she *lives* the stone. Indeed, she appears to project ideas of life and animism into the stones she works."

"Yeah," Jepson said. "So let's get busy." He turned and studied Ob.

She lowered her gaze under the pressure of that stare from the angry devil-god. Ob felt she understood what was wanted of her. She had a much better grasp of the language than she had permitted the devil-gods to suspect. The training imparted by her Cave Mother fitted well here: *"When dealing with devil-gods and spirits, give them the obedience and subservience they demand. But dissemble, always dissemble."*

A pang of homesickness shot through her and her lower lip trembled, but she suppressed the emotion. A female trained to the cave-motherhood and the creation of living tools did not give way, even before devil-gods. And there was work to do here, creation for which she had been trained. Beyond her understanding of the devil-gods' words, there were much more direct ways of divining their desires. They had brought her into the presence of their wondrous tools and they had set up the stones as for a sacrifice. The stone was one of the difficult, very hard ones, and its grain had been criss-crossed and twisted by unimaginable forces. But Ob could see the points of entry and the manner in which the work should progress.

"Tell her what she should do," Jepson said.

"I refuse to have any more to do with this," the Professor said.

Swimmer blanched.

"Nobody," Jepson said in a low, cold voice, "but nobody refuses what I say do. You, Uncle Professor, will get across to your cutter dame what it is she should do. You will do this or I will permit you to watch my boys cut up your creep nephew here into exceedingly small pieces. We wouldn't want the fishes should choke while they are disposing of him. Do I make myself plain?"

"You wouldn't dare," the Professor said. But even as he spoke he sensed that Jepson would indeed dare. The man was a criminal monster . . . and they were at his mercy.

Swimmer stood trembling. Now, he regretted ever having started this exploit. The gill mask in his pocket was useless. Jepson would never let him get off this island alive if there were the slightest upset in his plans.

Grudgingly, the Professor said: "Just what is it you want me to do, Mr. Jepson?"

"We been through all that!" Jepson snarled. "Get your dame started on this rock. The big-domes say it can't be cut. So let's see her cut it."

"It's on your head," the Professor said.

"Yeah," Jepson said. "So do."

Swimmer took a deep breath as the Professor turned toward Ob. It was obvious to Swimmer now that Jepson had plans of his own concerning the cutter dame. The Mars diamond was merely a preliminary. Swimmer suspected he shortly would have no place in Jepson's plans. And people who had no place in Jepson's plans sometimes disappeared.

As these thoughts went through Swimmer's mind. Ob looked at him with such a weight of shared understanding that he wondered if the ancients had possessed a telepathic faculty which had been lost in the genetic ebb and flow of the ensuing eons. And he wondered suddenly at the terrors this poor creature must be undergoing—and hiding so well. She'd been snatched from her place and time, taken forever from her friends. There could be no sending her back; the time machine couldn't be controlled that well. And here she was now, in Jepson's hands.

Something would have to be done about Jepson, Swimmer thought. He shivered with fear of what he had to do . . . and the fear of what would happen if he failed in any step.

"Ob," the Professor said.

Ob looked at Gruaaack, trying to convey by her waiting silence the almost frantic desire to please. Thank whatever benign spirits might hover near this place, the devil-gods were through fighting, she thought.

"Ob," the Professor repeated, "look at this stone." He pointed to the Mars diamond on its bed of black velvet.

Ob looked at the stone.

The Professor spoke slowly and distinctly: "Ob can you work this stone?"

Such a difficult stone, Ob thought. *But there was a way. The devil-god Gruaaack must know this. It was a test then. The devil-god was testing her.*

"Ob. Work. Stone," she said.

Swimmer marveled at the throaty quality of her voice.

"First, you must cut off a small piece of the stone," the Professor said.

Yes, it is a test, Ob thought. *Everyone knows the work progresses a small chip at a time. This was such a difficult stone, though. The first cut would be somewhat larger than usual. Still, the cut would remove a small enough piece.*

"Small. Piece," she agreed.

"Do you have the tools you need?" the Professor asked. He indicated the vice, jeweler's mallet and wedges on the bench.

Another test, Ob thought.

"Need. Wa. Ter," she said. "Need. Ongh-ongh."

"What the devil's an ong-ong?" Jepson asked. "I never heard no cutter ask for an ong-ong."

"I've no idea," the Professor said. "She's never used the term before." He turned a puzzled frown on Jepson. "Surely you must see now how limited our communication really is. There exists such a wide gap in . . ."

"So get 'er an ong-ong!" Jepson barked.

Ob looked from one devil-god to the other. They must have ongh-ongh, she thought. Wherever there was fire there was ongh-ongh. She looked at Swimmer, seeing only the fear in him. He must be another human like herself. She turned her attention to Gruaaack. Could this be another test? It was very puzzling. She picked up the Mars diamond in one horn-calloused hand, drew a finger along it. "Ongh-ongh."

The Professor shrugged. "Ob, you get ongh-ongh," he said.

Ob sighed. *Another test.*

She clasped the Mars diamond in both hands headed for the chalet's living room. There was a fire-hole in the living room; she had smelled it and seen it.

The living room had been furnished with heavy rustic furniture and Mexican fabrics. The colorful upholstery filled Ob with awe. *What manner of animal could have produced such skins?* she wondered. *Devil-god land must possess many terrors.*

Two of Jepson's boys sat at a round table near the windows overlooking the lake. They were eating and playing poker. A fire had been layed in the stone fireplace and Ob headed directly toward it, trailed by Jepson, the Professor and Swimmer.

The boys looked up from their game and one said: "Get a load of that shape. Gives me the creeps."

"Yeah," his companion said, and looked at Jepson. "What's she doin' with the rock, boss?"

Jepson spoke with an offhand, casual tone, keeping his attention on Ob. "Sharrup."

The boys shrugged and went back to their game.

Ob knelt at the fireplace, scooped out a small handful of ashes. "Ongh-ongh," she said. She rested the diamond on the hearth, spat into the ashes, kneaded a bit of black mud which she transferred to the diamond. Her horny hands worked the mud into the stone's surface.

"What's she doon?" Jepson demanded.

"I'm sure I don't know," the Professor said. "But ongh-ongh appears to be ashes."

Jepson fixed his attention on the diamond which was now a black-streaked mess. Ob picked it up, walked to the room's east windows. She lifted the diamond to the sun, studied it.

Yes, she thought, *the light of Mighty Fire passed through this stone and was dimmed and cut into strange patterns by the ongh-ongh.* She rubbed the stone, removing some of its black cover, wiped her hands on the brown dress, again held the diamond to Mighty Fire. It was as she had expected, the technique taught her by the Cave Mother. Lines of ongh-ongh on the stone's surface betrayed tiny flaws and these lines provided a fixed reference against which to study the interior contours.

"I believe this must be some sort of religious prelude to the actual work," the Professor said.

Swimmer looked at him, glanced at Jepson, then moved up behind Ob. He bent, peered up at the stone in her hands, seeing the coruscating light and the patterns revealed by the ash coating.

Ob turned, seeing him close there. She ventured a shy smile which was quickly erased as she darted glances at Jepson and the Professor.

Swimmer straightened, grinned.

Again, he was rewarded by that shy smile. It gave a momentary lightness to her heavy features.

"Strange," the Professor said. "Sun worship, very likely. I must delve into her religious beliefs more . . ."

"When's she gonna cut out this crap and get to cutting?" Jepson demanded.

"Ob. Work," she said.

She turned, led the way back into the workroom, returned the stone to its square of velvet.

Swimmer started to move up close, was stopped by a hand gripping his shoulder. He turned, looked up at Jepson.

"I want you should stay back outa the way, boy," Jepson said.

Swimmer shivered. He had sensed ultimate rejection in the man's voice.

A bird chose this moment to sing outside the room's south window: "Willow, will-will, willow."

Ob looked to the window, smiled. The birdsong was familiar, a voice she understood. He was saying: "This is my ground, my bush." She turned, met Jepson's harsh stare.

"Cut that damn rock!" Jepson said.

She cringed. There was death in that voice. She had heard it distinctly.

The Professor adjusted the spotlight above the bench, touched Ob's arm.

She looked up, surprised to find fear in his eyes, too. *Gruaaack afraid?* All was not as it appeared with the devil-gods! Her mind churning, she bent to the stone, rested it in the vicestand, turned it—gently, precisely—locked it in place. *Such wonderful tools they had, these devil-gods.*

Jepson moved around beside the bench where he could command a clear view of her work. He wiped his hands against his sides to remove the perspiration. He had watched cutters at their work before. Time always seemed to stretch out during that first cut—dragging, dragging—while tensions mounted and the cutter drew on the nervous energy to make the single tap . . . just right.

Expecting this, Jepson found Ob's actions stupefying.

IV

She searched a moment among the wedges racked on the bench, selected one and rested it on the diamond. She lifted the mallet in her other hand.

Jepson waited for the long drawn-out positioning and shifting of the wedge. He jumped as she brought the mallet down without changing that first, apparently casual placement.

Crack!

A long narrow piece of the Mars diamond fell to the bench.

Crack!

Another, slightly smaller this time.

Crack!

Jepson came out of his shock as a third chip clattered to the bench. "Wait!" he shrieked.

Crack!

Ob eased the vice, turned the diamond slightly.

Crack!

"Tell her to wait!" Jepson bleated.

Crack!

The Professor found his voice. "Ob!"

She turned still holding mallet and wedge firmly, waited for Gruaaack's command.

"Stop work," the Professor said.

Dutifully she lowered her hands.

Jepson pursed his lips, made a low sound: "Whooooeeee." He picked up the largest chip, turned it in the light. "The rock that couldn't be cut, eh? Whooooeeee." He dropped the chip to the bench, drew a dart pistol from a shoulder holster, pointed it at Swimmer.

"No hard feelings, Swimmer," he said. "But you are excess baggage. And Uncle Professor needs a lesson that he should do like he's told."

"You wouldn't!" the Professor whispered.

Jepson darted a glance at the Professor.

In this instant, Swimmer acted from desperation, leaping sideways and kicking at the gun hand. Muscles hardened from years of swimming slammed the toe of his shoe into Jepson's hand. The gun went *pffwt!* as it left the hand. A dart buried itself in the ceiling. The gun clattered across the room.

Ob stood for a frozen second, horrified by Swimmer's action against the devil-god. But she had heard the death in the devil-god's voice and she knew that even the *will-will willow* bird would attack a human if given enough reason. Why then couldn't a human attack a devil-god?

As Jepson opened his mouth to call his boys, Ob brought a fist crashing down onto his head. There was a sound like the dropping of a ripe melon and a sharp snap as Jepson's neck broke. He collapsed with a soft thud.

Swimmer dove for the fallen dart pistol, scooped it up, crouched facing the door to the living room, listening with every sense for a sign that the disturbance had been heard.

"My word!" the Professor said.

Only the ordinary sounds of the house penetrated the room—footsteps from one of the bedrooms overhead, the creak of bedsprings, a faucet being turned on, somebody whistling.

Swimmer turned.

Ob stood staring down at Jepson. A look of dawning wonder covered her face.

Swimmer crossed to Jepson, bent, examined him.

"Dead," he said. He straightened, smiled reassuringly at Ob. It was a reassurance he did not feel, however. "We're in the soup, Uncle," he said. "If any of the boys come in . . ."

The Professor fought down a shudder. "What shall we do?"

"We have one chance," Swimmer said. "Ob, help me get this carcass behind your bench." He bent, started to drag Jepson's body.

Gently, Ob brushed him aside, lifted Jepson's body with one hand through the belt. The dead man's head lolled; his arms dragged on the floor.

Swimmer swallowed, indicated where he wanted the body deposited. They propped Jepson in a corner, moved the bench to conceal him.

"My word," the Professor whispered. "She's strong as an ox!"

"Now listen carefully," Swimmer said. "Ob must go right on working as though nothing had happened. I'll try to get into the lake. If I can, once under water, I can get away and bring help." He passed Jepson's dart pistol to the Professor. "Keep this in your pocket. Don't use it unless you have to."

"This is dreadful," the Professor said.

"It'll be more dreadful if you don't do this just the way I say," Swimmer rasped. "Now, put that gun in your pocket."

The Professor gulped, obeyed.

"Now get her back to work," Swimmer said.

The Professor nodded, faced Ob. "You . . . work . . . stone," he said.

She remained motionless, studying him, wondering at the tone of command the human had used against this devil-god. Could a human command devil-gods?

"Please, Ob," Swimmer said. "Work the stone."

Something near worship was in her eyes as she looked at Swimmer. "You. Want. Ob. Work?" she asked.

"You work," Swimmer said. He patted her arm.

Again that shy smile touched her mouth. She turned back to the bench and the diamond. "Ob. Work?" she asked.

Swimmer looked at his uncle. The man's eyes appeared glazed with shock. "Uncle?" Swimmer said.

The Professor shook his head, met Swimmer's eyes with something like attention.

"If anyone asks for Jep," Swimmer said, "he went for a walk and left you to supervise Ob cutting the rock. Got that?"

The professor gulped. "I quite understand, Conrad. I must dissemble, tell falsehoods. But do hurry. This is most distasteful."

Crack!

Ob chipped another piece from the diamond.

Crack!

Swimmer permitted himself a deep breath. He had no time to be afraid or remember that he was a physical coward. The lives of his uncle and this strangely attractive primitive woman depended on him. He composed his features, slipped out of the room and down the side passage to the kitchen. It was empty, but someone had left a pot of water boiling. A spicy steam odor followed him across the room as he let himself out the back door.

A soft breeze rustled the pines overhead. He looked up, checked the position of the sun—still forenoon. There was motion along the shore to his right and left—two guards.

Swimmer forced himself to a casual, strolling pace toward the lake, aiming for a point midway between the guards. A fallen tree reached across the sand into the water there, its dead limbs sprayed out into air and water. He sat down on the sand beside the tree and within inches of the water, tossed a cone into the lake as though in idle play.

The guards ignored him after one searching glance.

Swimmer waited, wondering why he found Ob so attractive. He decided at last that she was the only woman who'd ever really looked at him without some degree of revulsion.

The guards strolled toward him, turned and patrolled away. Both had their backs to him now. Swimmer whipped out his gill mask, brought it down over his head, slipped into the water among the tree's branches, submerged. Years of practice made the action almost noiseless.

Slowly, he worked himself out into the lake, staying close to the bottom. His permadry suit billowed around him, and he pulled the hidden cords to tighten it.

Presently he was in deep water. He twisted his shoe heels. Flippers emerged from the toes. With a strong, steady stroke, he struck out for the opposite shore, guiding himself by the compass on the back of his wristwatch.

Strange emotions churned in him, not the least being a sense of cleansing at the realization that he was cutting himself off from his criminal past. The code was explicit: you did not inform on your fellows—no matter the provocation.

But he had to inform. Otherwise a woman who was suddenly very important to him might die.

V

When Swimmer looked back on it, that afternoon which the authorities referred to as "the day we broke up the Jepson Gang" contained shadows of dreamlike unreality criss-crossed with currents of profound immediacy.

There was the comparative quiet of the lake crossing under water. That was routine and hardly counted. He emerged around a point hidden from the island and there was a brief dog-trot through trees and buckbrush to a dirt track, its sides piled high with duff blown there by skimmer fans. The track led to a rural road where he was picked up by a farm truck with outsize aprons and a hover-blast like a hurricane.

The face of the farmer failed to register—but his voice, a whining twang, lingered for years, and there was a dark brown mole over the second knuckle of his right hand. It seemed important to Swimmer, reflecting upon it later, that the farmer was hauling a load of cabbage which smelled of fresh dirt.

Worry over Ob kept Swimmer jittery and on the edge of the truck's seat. The farmer called him "neighbor" and complained about the price of fertilizer. The man asked Swimmer only one question: "Where y' going, neighbor?"

"To town."

Town, according to a sign at its edge, was Ackerville, population 12,908. The farmer dropped Swimmer across the street from a tall building which obviously dated from before the turn of the century: it presented a monotonous face of glass and aluminum. A plaque over the entrance revealed that it was the administrative center for Crane County.

A whistle hooted for noon as Swimmer entered the building and followed arrow signs to the Sheriff's Office. He was to remember the place afterward chiefly for the smell of its halls (pine disinfectant) and the tall, skinny sheriff in a conservative business suit and western hat, who said as Swimmer entered the office:

"You'd be Conrad Rumel. Ralph Abernathy just called from his truck and said he brought you into town."

The fact that a farmer in Northern Minnesota could identify him that easily helped Swimmer to understand the terrifying efficiency in which he was abruptly immersed. Armed deputies appeared in the door behind him. They appeared surprised that he carried no weapons. He was hustled into a maple-paneled office that looked out through a wall of windows onto the street corner where the farmer had dropped him.

Ralph Abernathy. There was no face in his memory to go with the name. Swimmer wondered how he could've ridden in the truck with the farmer and not remember the face.

Ob! The danger!

The Sheriff wanted to know about the Mars diamond.

Swimmer had to repeat his story three times for the Sheriff and deputies, another time for a bald, white-bearded fat man identified as the County Prosecutor. They seemed unconcerned about the urgency, kept dragging out new questions.

Abruptly, there were many more men in the room. Sheriff and County Prosecutor faded into the background.

The newcomers deferred to a Wallace MacPreston, a thin little man not over five feet two inches tall, iron gray hair and a wide mouth set in a perpetual half-smile that never reached his large blue eyes.

"I am a special assistant to the President," MacPreston said.

Swimmer didn't have to ask *President of what?*

MacPreston then launched into his own line of questioning. Some were the same questions the Sheriff and deputies had asked, but MacPreston was also concerned about *how* Swimmer had sunk the Soviet propaganda ship. Was Swimmer aware he'd cracked the ship in half? Had that been his intention? What had guided him in placement of the explosive charges? How large was each charge? Why? What type of detonator? How far had he retreated to avoid the compression shock? What clues in the ship's design had betrayed its weak points? What particular burner had he chosen to cut open the diamond box? Why had he selected that particular time for the operation?

Gradually, Swimmer grew aware of faces in the crowd around MacPreston. One particularly caught his attention: a square-faced hulk of a man at MacPreston's left—eyes like brown caverns above a hooked nose, dark straw hair wisping away to twin bald spots at the temples. This man betrayed an obvious interest in the details of how Swimmer had sunk the ship.

But none of these people appeared to grasp the urgency, the danger to Ob . . . and Uncle Amino.

MacPreston went over Swimmer's story . . . and over it . . . and over it . . . and over it.

The position of the diamond box—how had that guided him in placement of the explosives?

"Look!" Swimmer suddenly raged. "Don't any of you realize what'll happen if Jepson's boys find out he's dead?"

"Jepson's boys aren't going anywhere," MacPreston said.

"But they'll kill Ob . . . and my uncle," Swimmer said.

"Doubtful," MacPreston said. "Now, about this Ob. You say your uncle picked her up with a *time* machine?"

Swimmer had to explain then about the time machine, Jepson's money, about the break-through, the inaccurate controls. With every new question to answer, he could feel time running out for Ob and his uncle.

"Time machine," MacPreston sneered.

The hook-nosed man tugged at MacPreston's sleeve. MacPreston look up, said: "Yeah, Mish?"

"Outside," the man said. "Wanta talk." They left the room.

More time raced past. Swimmer began to lose all hope.

MacPreston and his companion returned followed by an Army general and a Ranger colonel. The Colonel was speaking as they entered: "Three hundred and eighty men, counting the single-scooters and manjets, plus the twenty-five flying tanks the Marines are sending; that should do it."

"What about him?" the General asked, and he nodded toward Swimmer.

"Rumel goes with us," MacPreston said. "You heard what the President said."

"We still have three hours of daylight," the Colonel said. "That's plenty of time."

"Do you need transportation?" the General asked.

"We'll use our limousine," MacPreston said.

"Stay high and out of it until we send the signal," the General said. "I don't suppose you're armored."

"A Presidential limousine—you're joking!" MacPreston said.

"Yeah, well I still want you out of it until the shooting's over," the General said. "No telling what armament a mob like that'll have."

"What shooting?" Swimmer asked.

"We're going in and rescue your uncle and your stone-age woman friend," MacPreston said. He shook his head. "Time machine."

Swimmer took two deep breaths, said: "You know where they are?"

"We have a plan of the house from the architect," MacPreston said. He started to turn away, looked back at Swimmer. "One of Mish's boys just handed me the damndest report I've ever seen in my life—from a Professor Elwin in Cambrai, France. You know this Elwin?"

"I know who he is," Swimmer said. And he stilled his own questions in the hope that these people would launch themselves into their promised action.

"Time machine," MacPreston muttered, but there was awe rather than doubt in his voice.

Swimmer felt something grab his left wrist, looked down to find the wrist connected by handcuffs to the right wrist of the hook-nosed companion—*Mish*.

"I'm Mischa Levinsky, CID," the man said, staring hard at Swimmer. "Wanta talk to you sometime, Rumel, about that Mazatlan operation. For one man, that was a dilly."

CID, Swimmer thought. *The President. Army. Rangers. Marines.* He had the feeling that he was lost in a mad pinball machine, about to be bounced from bumper to bumper while MacPreston shouted. *"Tilt! Tilt! Tilt!"*

"Let's roll it," Levinsky said.

VI

The combined force dove into the lake island out of the afternoon sun, screaming in like a swarm of angry insects onto an enemy hive. Army armored single-scooters formed a solid ring around the beach perimeter. Marine flying tanks darkened the sky. Leaping Rangers in manjets popped up and down through the pines.

To Swimmer, watching from the rear of the limousine which hovered at about seven thousand feet southeast of the scene, the orderly pandemonium was an insane game. He found it difficult to associate any of his own actions with this result. Had it not been for his fear over Ob, Swimmer knew he'd have found the whole thing ludicrous.

The limousine dropped down to three thousand feet, moved in closer.

Swimmer glanced at MacPreston on his right. "Are they . . ."

"Dunno yet," MacPreston said. "Pretty good operation, eh, Mish?"

"Too damn many of 'em," Levinsky growled. "Wonder they aren't falling all over each other."

"What do you think, Rumel?" MacPreston asked.

"What?"

"Is it a good operation?"

They're nuts, Swimmer thought. He said: "I agree with Mr. Levinsky. Jepson couldn't have had more than twenty of his men down there . . . from my count. I'd have held the armor out farther and gone in with fifty men."

"Where would you have hit?" MacPreston asked.

Levinsky nodded.

"Right on top of the house."

The limousine dropped to five hundred feet above the lake's southeast shore. Swimmer could hear scattered rifle shots. Each one sent an agony of fear through him.

Oh . . .

A man-made serenity returned to the island, a shocked silence broken only by faint shouts heard across the hush of water. A line of men with their hands in the air was marched onto the island's dock through a cordon of single-scooters.

Something buzzed from the limousine's dash.

"That's it," MacPreston said. "Let's go."

The limousine slanted in to the patch of open ground beside the chalet. Its hover jets raised a cloud of pine-needle duff that settled slowly after the motors were silenced.

MacPreston opened his window, sneezed from the dust.

A Ranger captain ran up, saluted, spoke through the window. "All secure, sir. Professor Rumel and the—ah—woman are safe in the house."

Swimmer allowed himself a deep sigh.

"What were the casualties?" Levinsky demanded.

"Sir?" The Ranger captain bent to peer in at Levinsky.

"The casualties!" Levinsky snapped.

"We have ten wounded, sir. Eight from our own crossfire. Nothing serious, though. And we killed two of the—uh—men here. Wounded four others."

MacPreston touched a button beside him. The limousine's bubbletop swung back with a hiss of hydraulic mechanism.

"Fifty men right on top of the house," Levinsky muttered. "Would've been plenty."

"Well, Captain," MacPreston said, "bring Professor Rumel and the woman out here. I'm anxious to meet them."

The Ranger captain fidgeted. "Well, sir . . . you know we had orders to handle her and the Professor with kid gloves and we—"

"So bring them out here!"

"Sir, the woman refuses to leave her work."

"Her *work*?"

"Sir, Professor Rumel says she'll take orders only from his nephew there." The Captain nodded toward Swimmer.

Swimmer absorbed this silently, but with a strong upswing of good humor. He *liked* this Captain. He liked MacPreston. He liked Levinsky and all this damn fool mob of fighting men. Swimmer was surprised to come out of this reverie and find Levinsky and MacPreston staring at him.

"What *didn't* you tell us?" Levinsky asked.

About Ob working on the diamond, Swimmer thought. He swallowed, said: "I think she likes me."

"So?" MacPreston said.

"So that's good," Swimmer said.

"From the description, she sounds like a freak," MacPreston said. "What's good about it?"

Swimmer suddenly did *not* like MacPreston. The emotional reaction was apparently quite evident in the glare Swimmer turned on the Presidential assistant. "Maybe the description's wrong," MacPreston said.

"Wally," Levinsky said, "why don't you shut up?"

In the embarrassed silence which followed. Swimmer looked at Levinsky, reflecting: *Ob a freak? She's no more a freak than I am! So she has extra equipment. In her day, that was an advantage. And it isn't her fault she was snatched out of her day. She didn't ask to be brought here and have people sneer at her. Just because of the way she looks. She's a normal and healthy human female. Probably a lot more normal and healthy than this MacPreston jerk!*

MacPreston, his face flushed with anger, turned to the Ranger captain, said: "She *refuses* to come out here?"

"Sir, the professor insists she'll only take orders from his nephew. I'm . . . I hesitate to use force."

"Why?" MacPreston demanded. "Don't you have enough men for the job?"

"Sir, there's a bench in there must weigh four hundred pounds. They hid this Jepson behind it. We wanted to move the bench to see if Jepson was really dead. Sir, she lifted that bench with one hand."

"A four-hundred-pound bench? With one hand?"

"Yes, sir. Oh . . . and Jepson was really dead, sir. Skull crushed. According to the Professor, she did that with one blow of her fist."

"Her fist?" MacPreston turned his outraged stare onto Swimmer. "Rumel, what kind of female is that in there?"

"Just an ordinary, normal woman," Swimmer said.

"But—"

"Nothing unusual at all about her!" Swimmer said. "In her day, she may even have been a ninety-seven-pound weakling. She didn't ask to be brought here, MacPreston. She didn't ask to have people pronounce stupid judgments on her appearance."

MacPreston studied Swimmer's face, noting every detail of it from the low hairline to the vanishing chin. Presently he said: "Sorry, Mr. Rumel. My error."

Swimmer nodded, thinking: *She'll only take orders from me.* A crazy elation filled him. He felt his left wrist being lifted by the handcuffs, looked down to see Levinsky unlocking the cuff.

"Mish, what're you doing?" MacPreston asked.

"Isn't it obvious?" Levinsky asked.

"Now, wait a minute, Mish," MacPreston said. "I sympathize with your request, and the President does, too. But there are large obstacles. This man has committed crimes which no other man—"

"He's the best demolition man I ever met," Levinsky said.

"But we have the Russians to think about!" MacPreston said unhappily.

"Well give 'em Jepson," Levinsky said. "Jepson's dead. He can't object . . . *or dispute our story.*"

Swimmer massaged his wrist where the handcuff had been, stared from MacPreston to Levinsky. Their conversation made no sense to him. The Ranger captain, still standing beside the limousine, appeared equally puzzled.

"But Rumel has been *identified*!" MacPreston said.

"So?" Levinsky said.

"So the Russians'll know he was involved. What use can he be to you after that? He has a face—excuse me, Mr. Rumel, but it's true—that a Minnesota farmer could identify after seeing it only twice in the newspapers. How could you hide that from the Russians?"

"Don't be stupid, Wally! I never wanted to use him that way. I want his *knowledge,* his experience. I want him in the academy."

"But if we don't hand him over to prosecution with the rest of that mob—"

"What if we claim he was our agent all along? What if we say he infiltrated the Jepson mob *for* us?"

"You said it yourself, Mish. They know who the expert was. They know who sank that boat."

"So?"

MacPreston frowned.

"You heard what the President said," Levinsky said. "If Rumel proves cooperative, and if we deem it advisable after our field investigation—"

"I don't like it."

"The Russians won't like it, either. Especially when we give them back their diamond and the Jepson gang, what's left of it."

"The boat!"

"We'll apologize about the boat."

Give them back their diamond, Swimmer thought. *Oh, God! And Ob's in there cutting that rock into little pieces!*

"I'll have to think about it," MacPreston said. "Discomfiting the Russians would give me just as much pleasure as it would you. But there are other considerations." He looked up at the Ranger Captain. "Well, what're you standing there for?"

"Sir?"

"Take us to Professor Rumel and this . . . woman."

"Sir, I've . . . I think we'd better hurry."

"Why?"

"Well, sir, it's what I've been trying to . . . sir, this work she won't leave—she's cutting up that Mars diamond."

Swimmer had not suspected MacPreston could move that fast. The limousine's door was slammed open. MacPreston grabbed his arm, and they were out and running—up the chalet's front steps with armed men in uniform leaping aside, through the door and into the living room.

Overturned chair, broken windows, a bullet-splintered wall: all testified to the violence of the attack. A cordon of guards was opened to the hall leading into the workroom.

MacPreston stopped short. Swimmer bumped into him, was bumped in turn by Levinsky who was right on their heels.

"That sound," MacPreston said.

Swimmer recognized it. The sound came from the hallway.

Crack!

Crack!

Crack!

MacPreston released Swimmer's arm, advanced on the hall like a bull preparing to charge. A nudge from Levinsky sent Swimmer following after. He felt he was being escorted to his execution, and found it odd how their feet kept to the rhythm of Ob's chipping.

Into the workroom they paraded.

The place appeared untouched by the military's violence except for a shattered window at their left. Professor Amino Rumel stood beside the window. He turned as his nephew entered, said: "Conrad! Thank heaven you're here. She won't do a thing I say."

MacPreston stopped a good six feet from where Ob was working. He stared at the square brown figure, noting the intense concentration in every line of her back, the play of muscles. Swimmer and Levinsky stopped behind him.

Crack!

Crack!

The Professor advanced on Swimmer. "There's been the most dreadful confusion," he said.

"In heaven's name, Rumel, stop her!" MacPreston rasped.

"I've tried," the Professor said. "She pays no attention to me."

"Not you!" MacPreston roared.

Crack!

The Professor drew himself up, stared at MacPreston. "And who," he asked, "might you be?" He turned oddly pleading eyes on Swimmer. It was obvious that MacPreston had remembered about the four-hundred-pound bench being lifted with one hand.

Swimmer tried to find his voice. His throat felt as though it had been seared with a hot poker. Slowly he brushed past MacPreston, touched Ob's arm.

Ob dropped mallet and wedge, whirled on Swimmer with a glare that sent him retreating one quick step. At sight of him, though, a smile stretched her mouth. The smile held a radiant quality that transfixed Swimmer.

"Ob, you can stop the work now," Swimmer whispered.

Still smiling, she moved close to him, put a calloused forefinger to his cheek in the silent invitation of the cave, testing the emotion she read on his face. There were no scars on the cheek to count his years—and the skin was so sweetly, excitingly soft . . . like one of the Cave Mother's babies. Still, he appeared to understand the fingerplay. He drew her aside, brushed a lock of hair away from her cheek, touched her ears.

Ob wanted to take his hand, lead him to the bench and show him the work, but she feared to break the spell.

"Even with the bullets flying around," Professor Rumel said, "she paid no attention. Just went right on, as though—" His voice trailed off. Presently he said: "Dear me. She wouldn't know about bullets."

Swimmer heard the voice as though it came from a dream. Part of him was aware that MacPreston and Levinsky had gone to the bench, that they were bent over it muttering. What he read on Ob's face made all of that unimportant.

The words of the Cave Mother came back to Ob: *"It's all right to play with the males and sample them, but when the time comes for permanent mating, my magic will tell you which one to choose. You'll know at once."*

How wise the Cave Mother had been to know such a thing, Ob thought. How potent was the Cave Mother's magic!

Swimmer felt that he had come alive, been reborn here in this room, that behind him lay a whole misplaced segment of non-existence. He wanted to hug Ob, but suspected she might respond with painful vigor. She'd have to be cautioned about her strength before she broke his ribs. He sensed also that she might not have the inhibitions dictated by current culture. He could imagine her reacting with complete abandon if he should kiss her.

Slowly he pulled away.

Ob saw his reluctance, thought: *He thinks of the devil-gods. We must distract the devil-gods, occupy them with other things. Then perhaps they'll take their thunder-magic elsewhere, and leave mortals to the things which interest mortals.*

But Swimmer had just begun to think about consequences. He found himself filled with wonder that he had never before worried about the legal consequences of his actions. The Mars diamond had attracted him, he realized, because it was a romp, a lark, a magnificent joke. But after what had happened to the rock, MacPreston and Levinsky would have to throw him to the Russians. They couldn't just hand over a mess of chips and say: "Sorry, fellows . . . it came apart." Everything had come apart—and Swimmer was struck speechless by fear of what might happen to Ob.

Consequences no longer could be ignored. Levinsky and MacPreston were engaged in a heated argument.

"This is a catastrophe, I tell you!" MacPreston said.

"Wally, you're being an ass," Levinsky said.

"But what can we tell the Russians?"

Exactly, Swimmer thought. *What can we tell the Russians?*

"That's just it," Levinsky said. "This prehistoric female has solved that problem for us. She's made us a *propaganda* weapon we can parade before the whole world!"

"You'd just—"

"Certainly! There isn't a person in the world who'll fail to get the point." Levinsky lowered his voice. "The uncuttable diamond, don't you see? And we can say we planned it this way. We give 'em the Jepson gang and—" He pointed to something hidden by MacPreston's body. ". . . and an object lesson."

Swimmer found himself overcome by curiosity. He headed for the bench, but Ob darted ahead, shouldered MacPreston aside and turned with something glistening in her hands.

"Ob. Work," she said. "For . . . you."

With a sense of shock and awe, Swimmer accepted the object from her, understanding then what Levinsky had meant by "object lesson."

The thing Ob had fashioned from the Mars diamond was a spearhead—delicately balanced and with exquisite workmanship. It lay in Swimmer's hands, warm and glittering.

"You . . . want?" Ob asked.

ESCAPE FELICITY

"An escape-proof prison cannot be built," he kept telling himself.

His name was Roger Deirut, five feet tall, one hundred and three pounds, crewcut black hair, a narrow face with long nose and wide mouth and space-bleached eyes that appeared to reflect rather than absorb what they saw.

Deirut knew his prison—the D-Service. He had got himself rooted down in the Service like a remittance man half asleep in a hammock on some palm-shaded tropical beach, telling himself his luck would change some day and he'd get out of there.

He didn't delude himself that a one-man D-ship was a hammock, or that space was a tropical beach. But the sinecure element was there and the ships were solicitous cocoons, each with a climate designed precisely for the lone occupant.

That each pilot carried the prison's bars in his mind had taken Deirut a long time to understand. Out here aimed into the void beyond Capella Base, he could feel the bars where they had been dug into his psyche, cemented and welded there. He blamed the operators of Bu-psych and the deep-sleep hypnotic debriefing after each search trip. He told himself that Bu-psych did something to the helpless pilots then, installed this compulsion they called the *Push*.

Some young pilots managed to escape it for a while—tougher psyches, probably, but sooner or later Bu-psych got them all. It was a common compulsion that limited the time a D-ship pilot could stay out before he turned tail and fled for home.

"This time I'll break away," Deirut told himself. He knew he was talking aloud, but he had his computer's vocoders turned off and his absent mumblings would be ignored.

The gas cloud of Grand Nuage loomed ahead of him, clearly defined on his instruments like a piece of torn fabric thrown across the stars. He'd come out of subspace dangerously close, but that was the gamble he'd taken.

Bingaling Benar, fellow pilot and sometime friend, had called him nuts when Deirut had said he was going to tackle the cloud. "Didn't you do that once before?" Bingaling asked.

"I was going to once, but I changed my mind," Deirut had said.

"You gotta slow down, practically crawl in there," Bingaling had said. "I stood it eighty-one days, man. I had the push for real—couldn't take any more and I came home. Anyway, it's nothing but cloud, all the way through."

Bingaling's *endless* cloud was growing larger in the ship's instruments now. But the cloud enclosed a mass of space that could hide a thousand suns.

Eighty-one days, he thought.

"Eighty, ninety days, that's all anyone can take out there," Bingaling had said. "And I'm telling you, in that cloud it's worse. You get the push practically the minute you go in."

Deirut had his ship down to a safe speed now, nosing into the first tenuous layers. There was no mystery about the cloud's composition, he reminded himself. It was hydrogen, but in a concentration that made swift flight suicidal.

"They got this theory," Bingaling had said, "that it's an embryo star like. One day it's just going to go fwoosh and compress down into one star mass."

Deirut read his instruments. He could sense his ship around him like an extension of his own nerves. She was a pinnace class for which he and his fellow pilots had a simple and obscene nickname—two hundred and fifty meters long, crowded from nose to tubes with the equipment for determining if a planet could support human life. In the sleep-freeze compartment directly behind him were the double-checks—two pairs of rhesus monkeys and ten pairs of white mice.

D-ship pilots contended they'd seeded more planets with rhesus monkeys and white mice than they had with humans.

Deirut switched to his stern instruments. One hour into the cloud and already the familiar stars behind him were beginning to fuzz off. He felt the first stirrings of unease; not the push . . . but disquiet.

He crossed his arms, touching the question-mark insignia at his left shoulder. He could feel the ripe green film of corrosion on the brass threads. *I should polish up,* he thought. But he knew he wouldn't. He looked around him at the pilot compartment, seeing unracked food cannisters, a grease smear across the computer console, dirty fatigues wadded under a dolly seat.

It was a sloppy ship.

Deirut knew what was said about him and his fellow pilots back in the top echelons of the D-Service.

"Rogues make the best searchers."

It was an axiom, but the rogues had their drawbacks. They flouted rules, sneered at protocol, ignored timetables, laughed at vector search plans . . . and kept sloppy ships. And when they disappeared—as they often did—the Service could never be sure what had happened or where.

Except that the man had been prevented from returning . . . because there was always the push.

Deirut shook his head. Every thought seemed to come back to the push. He didn't have it yet, he assured himself. Too soon. But the thought was there, aroused. It was the fault of that cloud.

He reactivated the rear scanners. The familiar stars were gone, swallowed in a blanket of nothingness. Angrily, he turned off the scanner switch.

I've got to keep busy, he thought.

For a time he set himself to composing and refining a new stanza for the endless D-ship ballad: "I Left My Love on Lyra in the Hands of Gentle Friends." But his mind kept returning to the fact that the stanza might never be heard . . . if his plans succeeded. He wondered then how many such stanzas had been composed never to be heard.

The days went by with an ever-slowing, dragging monotony.

Eighty-one days, he reminded himself time and again. *Bingaling turned back at eighty-one days.*

By the seventy-ninth day he could see why. There was no doubt then that he was feeling the first ungentle suasions of the push. His mind kept searching for logical reasons.

You've done your best. No shame in turning back now. Bingaling's undoubtedly right—it's nothing but cloud all the way through. No stars in here . . . no planets.

But he was certain what the Bu-psych people had done to him and this helped. He watched the forward scanners for the first sign of a glow. And this helped, too. He was still going some place.

The eighty-first day passed.

The eighty-second.

On the eighty-sixth day he began to see a triple glow ahead—like lights through fog; only the fog was black and otherwise empty.

By this time it was taking a conscious effort to keep his hands from straying, toward the flip-flop controls that would turn the ship one hundred eighty degrees onto its return track.

Three lights in the emptiness.

Ninety-four days—two days longer than he'd ever withstood the push before—and his ship swam free of the cloud into open space with three stars lined out at a one o'clock angle ahead of him—a distant white-blue giant, a nearby orange dwarf and in the center . . . lovely golden sol-type to the fifth decimal of comparison.

Feverishly, Deirut activated his mass-anomaly scanners, probing space around the golden-yellow sun.

The push was terrible now, insisting that he turn around. But this was the final convincer for Deirut. If the thing Bu-psych had done to him insisted he go back now, right after discovering three new suns—then there could be only one answer to the question "Why?" They didn't want a D-Service rogue settling down on his own world. The push was a built-in safeguard to make sure the scout returned.

Deirut forced himself to study his instruments.

Presently the golden star gave up its secret—a single planet with a single moon. He punched for first approximation, watched the results stutter off the feedout tape: planetary mass .998421 of Earth norm . . . rotation forty plus standard hours . . . mean orbital distance 243 million kilometers . . . perturbation nine degrees . . . orbital variation thirty-eight plus.

Deirut sat bolt upright with surprise.

Thirty-eight plus! A variation percentage in that range could only mean the mother star had another companion—and a big one. He searched space around the star.

Nothing.

Then he saw it.

At first he thought he'd spotted the drive flare of another ship—an alien. He swallowed, the push momentarily subdued, and did a quick mental review of the alien-space contact routine worked out by Earth's bigdomes and which, so far as anyone knew, had never been put to the test.

The flare grew until it resolved itself into the gaseous glow of another astronomical body circling the golden sun.

Again, Deirut bent to his instruments. My God, how the thing moved! More than forty kilometers per second. Tape began spewing from the feedout: Mass 321.64 . . . rotation nine standard hours . . . mean orbital distance 58 million kilometers . . . perturbation blank (insufficient data) . . .

Deirut shifted to the filtered visual scanners, watched the companion sweep across the face of its star and curve out of sight around the other side. The thing looked oddly familiar, but he knew he could never have seen it before. He wondered if he should activate the computer's vocoder system and talk to it through the speaker embedded in his neck, but the computer annoyed him with its obscene logic.

The astronomical data went into the banks, though; for the experts to whistle and marvel over later.

Deirut shifted his scanners back to the planet. Shadowline measurement gave it an atmosphere that reached fade-off at an altitude of about a hundred and twenty-five kilometers. The radiation index indicated a whopping tropical belt, almost sixty degrees.

With a shock of awareness, Deirut found his hands groping toward the flip-flop controls. He jerked back, trembling. If he once turned the ship over, he knew he wouldn't have the strength of purpose to bring her back around. The push had reached terrifying intensity.

Deirut forced his attention onto the landing problem, began feeding data into the computer for the shortest possible space-to-ground course. The computer offered a few objections "for his own good," but he insisted. Presently, a landing tape appeared and he fed it into the control console, strapped down, kicked the ship onto automatic and sat back perspiring. His hands held a death grip on the sides of his crashpad.

The D-ship began to buck with the first skipping-flat entrance into the planet's atmosphere. The bucking stopped, returned, stopped—was repeated many times. The D-ship's cooling system whined. Hull plates creaked. Darkside, lightside, darkside—they repeated themselves in his viewer. The automatic equipment began reeling out atmospheric data: oxygen 23.9, nitrogen 74.8, argon 0.8, carbon dioxide 0.04 . . . By the time it got into the trace elements, Deirut was gasping with the similarity to the atmosphere of Mother Earth.

The spectrum analyzer produced the datum that the atmosphere was essentially transparent from 3,000 angstroms to 6×10^4 angstroms. It was a confirmation and he ignored the instruments when they began producing hydromagnetic data and water vapor impingements. There was only one important factor here: he could breathe the stuff out there.

Instead of filling him with a sense of joyful discovery—as it might have thirty or forty days earlier—this turned on a new spasm of the push. He had to consciously restrain himself from clawing at the instrument panel.

Deirut's teeth began to chatter.

The viewer showed him an island appearing over the horizon. The D-ship swept over it. Deirut gasped at sight of an alabaster ring of tall buildings hugging the curve of a bay. Dots on the water resolved into sailboats as he neared. How oddly familiar it all looked.

Then he was past and headed for a mainland with a low range of hills—more buildings, roads, the patchwork of fenced lands. Then he was over a wide range of prairie with herds of moving animals on it.

Deirut's fingers curled into claws. His skin trembled.

The landing jets cut in and his seat reversed itself. The ship nosed up and the seat adjusted to the new altitude. There came a roaring as the ship lowered itself on its tail jets. The proximity cut-off killed all engines.

The D-ship settled with a slight jolt.

Blue smoke and clouds of whirling ashes lifted past Deirut's scanners from the scorched landing circle. Orange flames swept through dry forage on his right, but the chemical automatics from the ship's nose sent a borate shower onto the fire and extinguished it. Deirut saw the backs of animals fleeing through the smoke haze beyond the fire. Amplification showed them to be four-legged, furred and with tiny flat heads. They ran like bouncing balls.

A tight band of fear cinched on Deirut's chest. This place was too earthlike. His teeth chattered with the unconscious demands of the push.

His instruments informed him they were picking up modulated radio signals—FM and AM. A light showing that the Probe-Test-Watch circuits were activated came alive. Computer response circuit telltales began flickering. Abruptly, the PTW bell rang, telling him: "Something approaches!"

The viewer showed a self-propelled vehicle rolling over a low hill to the north supported by what appeared to be five monstrous penumatic bladders. It headed directly toward the D-ship belching pale white smoke from a rear stack with the rhythm of steam power. External microphones picked up the confirming "chuff-chuff-chuff" and his computer announced that it was a double-action engine with sounds that indicated five opposed pairs of pistons.

A five-sided dun brown cab with dark blue-violet windows overhung the front of the thing.

In his fascination with the machine, Deirut almost forgot the wild urge pushing at him from within. The machine pulled up about fifty meters beyond the charred landing circle, extruded a muzzle that belched a puff of smoke at him. The external microphones picked up a loud explosion and the D-ship rocked on its extended tripods.

Deirut clutched the arms of his chair then sprang to the controls of the ship's automatic defenses, poised a hand over the disconnect switch.

The crawling device outside whirled away, headed east toward a herd of the bouncing animals.

Deirut punched the "Warning Only" button.

A giant gout of earth leaped up ahead of the crawler, brought it to a lurching halt at the brink of a smoking hole. Another gout of earth bounced skyward at the left of the machine; another at the right.

Deirut punched "Standby" on the defense mechanisms, turned to assess the damage. Any new threat from the machine out there and the D-ship's formidable arsenal would blast it out of existence. That was always a step to be avoided, though, and he kept one eye on the screen showing the thing out there. It sat unmoving but still chuffing on the small patch of earth left by the three blast-shots from the ship.

Less than ten seconds later, the computer out-chewed a strip of tape that said the ship's nose section had been blasted open, all proximity detectors destroyed. Deirut was down on this planet until he could make repairs.

Oddly, this eased the pressures of the push within him. It was still there and he could sense it, but the compulsive drive lay temporarily idle as though it, too, had a standby switch.

Deirut returned his attention to the crawler.

The damage had been done, and there was no helping it. A ship could land with its arsenal set on "Destroy," but deciding what needed destruction was a delicate proposition. Wise counsel said you let the other side get in a first shot if their technology appeared sufficiently primitive. Otherwise, you might make yourself decidedly unwelcome.

Who'd have thought they'd have a cannon and fire the thing without warning? he asked himself. And the reply stood there accusingly in his mind: *You should've thought of it, stupid. Gunpowder and steampower are almost always concurrent.*

Well, I was too upset by the push, he thought. *Besides, why'd they fire without warning?*

Again, the crawler's cab extruded the cannon muzzle and the cab started to turn to bring the weapon to bear on the ship. A warning blast sent earth cascading into the hole at the left of the crawler. The cab stopped turning.

"That's-a-baby," Deirut said. "Easy does it, fellows. Let's be friends." He flicked a blue switch at the left side of his board. His external microphones damped out as a klaxon sent its bull roar toward the crawler. It was a special sound capable of intimidating almost any creature that heard it. The sound had an astonishing effect on the crawler. A hatch in the middle of the cab popped open and five creatures boiled out of it to stand on the deck of their machine.

Deirut keyed the microphone beside him into the central computer, raised amplification on his view of the five creatures from the machine. He began reading off his own reactions. The human assessment always helped the computer's sensors.

"Humanoid," he said. "Upright tubular bodies about a meter and a half tall with two legs encased in some kind of boot. Sack-like garments belted at the waist. Each has five pouches dangling from the belt. Number five is significant here. Flesh color is pale blue-violet. Two arms; articulation—humanoid, but very long forearm. Wide hands with six fingers; looks like two opposable thumbs, one to each side of the hand. Heads—squarish, domed, covered with what appears to be a dark blue-violet beret. Eyes semi-stalked, yellow and just inside the front *corners* of the head. Those heads are very blocky. I suspect the eyes can be twisted to look behind without turning the head."

The creatures began climbing down off their machine.

Deirut went on with his description: "Large mouth orifice centered beneath the eyes. There appears to be a chin articulation on a short hinge. Orifice lipless, ovoid, no apparent teeth . . . correction: there's a dark line inside that may be the local equivalent. Separate small orifices below each eye stalk—possibly for breathing. One just turned its head. I see a slight indentation centered on the side of the head—purpose unknown. It doesn't appear to be an ear."

The five were advancing on the ship now; Deirut backed off the scanner to keep them in view, said: "They carry bows and arrows. That's odd, considering the cannon. Each has a back quiver with . . . five arrows. That five again. Bows slung on the string over left shoulder. Each has a short lance in a back harness, a blue-violet pennant just below the lance head. Some kind of figure on the pennant—looks like an upside down "U" in orange. Same figures repeated on the front of their tunics which are also blue-violet. Blue violet and five. What's the prognosis?"

Deirut waited for the computers answer to come to him through the speaker grafted into his neck. Relays clicked and the vocoder whispered through the bones of his head: "Probable religious association with color and number five. Extreme caution is indicated on religious matters. Body armor and hand weapon mandatory."

That's the trouble with computers, Deirut thought. *Too logical.*

The five natives had stopped just, outside the fire-blackened landing circle. They raised their arms to the ship, chanted something that sounded like "Toogayala-toogayala-toogayala." The sound came from the oval central orifice.

"We'll toogayala in just a minute," Deirut muttered. He brought out a Borgen machine pistol, donned body armor, aimed two of the ship's bombards directly at the steam wagon and set them on a dead-man switch keyed to a fifteen-second stoppage of his heart. He rigged the stern port to the PTW system, keyed to blow up any unauthorized intruders. Into various pockets he stuffed a lingua pack receptor tuned to his implanted speaker through the computer, a standard contact kit for sampling whatever interested him, a half dozen minigrenades, energy tablets, food analyzer, a throwing knife in a sheath, a miniscanner linked to the ship computer and a slingshot. With a final, grim sensation, he stuffed a medikit under the armor next to his heart.

One more glance around the familiar control center and he slid down the tube to the stern port, opened it and stepped out.

The five natives threw themselves flat on the ground, arms extended toward him.

Deirut took a moment to study them and his surroundings. There was a freshness to the air that even his nose filters could not diminish. It was morning here yet and the sun threw flat light against the low hills and clumps of scrub. They stood out with a clean chiaroscuro dominated by the long blue spear of the ship's shadow wavering across the prairie.

Deirut looked up at his D-ship. She was a red and white striped tower on his side with a gaping hole where the nose should have been. Her number—1107—stenciled in luminous green beneath the nose had just escaped the damage area. He returned his attention to the natives.

They remained stretched out on the grass, their stalked eyes stretched out and peering up at him.

"Let's hope you have a good metal-working industry, friends," Deirut said. "Otherwise, I'm going to be an extremely unhappy visitor."

At the sound of his voice, the five grunted in unison: "Toogayala ung-ung."

"Ung-ung?" Deirut asked. "I thought we were going to toogayala." He brought out the lingua pack, hung it on his chest with the mike aimed at the natives, moved toward them out of the ship's shadow. As an afterthought, he raised his right hand, palm out and empty in the universal human gesture of peace, but kept his left hand on the Borgen.

"Toogayala!" the five screamed.

His lingua pack remained silent. Toogayala and ung-ung were hardly sufficient for breaking down a language.

Deirut took another step toward them.

The five rocked back to their knees and arose, crouching and apparently poised for flight. Five pairs of stalked eyes pointed toward him. Deirut had the curious feeling then that the five appeared familiar. They looked a little like giant grasshoppers that had been crossed with an ape. They looked like bug-eyed monsters from a work of science fantasy he had read in his youth, which he saw as clear evidence that what the imagination of man could conceive, nature could produce.

Deirut took another step toward the natives, said: "Well, let's talk a little, friends. Say something. Make language, huh?"

The five backed up two steps. Their feet made a dry rustling sound in the grass.

Deirut swallowed. Their silence was a bit unnerving.

Abruptly, something emitted a buzzing sound. It seemed to come from a native on Deirut's right. The creature clutched for its tunic, gabbled: "s'Chareecha! s'Chareecha!" It pulled a small object from a pocket as the others gathered around.

Deirut tensed, lifted the Borgen.

The natives ignored him to concentrate on the object in the one creature's hands.

"What's doing?" Deirut asked. He felt tense, uneasy. This wasn't going at all the way the books said it should.

The five straightened suddenly and without a backward look, returned to their steam wagon and climbed into the cab.

What test did I fail? Deirut wondered.

Silence settled over the scene.

In the course of becoming a D-ship pilot, Deirut had gained fame for a certain pungency of speech. He paused a moment to practice some of his more famed selections, then took stock of his situation—standing here exposed at the foot of the ship while the unpredictable natives remained in their steam wagon. He clambered back through the port, sealed it, and jacked into the local computer outlet for a heart-to-heart conference.

"The buzzing item was likely a timepiece," the computer said. "The creature in possession of it was approximately two millimeters taller than his tallest companion. There are indications this one is the leader of the group."

"Leader schmeader," Deirut said. "What's this toogayala they keep yelling?"

From long association with Deirut, the computer had adopted a response pattern to meet the rhetorical question or the question for which there obviously was no answer. "Tut, tut," it said.

"You sound like my old Aunt Martha," Deirut said. "They screamed that toogayala. It's obviously important."

"When they noted your hand, that is when they raised their voices to the highest decibel level thus far recorded here," the computer said.

"But why?"

"Possible answer," the computer said. "You have five fingers."

"Five," Deirut said. "Five . . . five . . . five . . ."

"We detect only five heavenly bodies here," the computer said. "You have noted that the skies are otherwise devoid of stars. The rapid companion is overhead right now, you know."

"Five," Deirut said.

"This planet," the computer said, "the three hot gaseous and plasma bodies and the other companion to this planet's sun."

Deirut looked at his hand, flexed the fingers.

"They may think you are a deity," the computer said. "They have six fingers; you have five."

"Empty skies except for three suns," Deirut said.

"Do not forget this planet and the other companion," the computer said;

Deirut thought about living on such a planet—no banks of stars across the heavens . . . all that hidden behind the enclosing hydrogen cloud.

He began to tremble unaccountably with an attack of the *push*.

"What'll it take to fix the nose of the ship?" Deirut asked. He tried to still his trembling.

"A sophisticated machine shop and the work of electronics technicians of at least grade five. The repair data is available in my banks."

"What're they doing in that machine?" Deirut demanded. "Why don't they talk?"

"Tut, tut," the computer said.

Thirty-eight minutes later, the natives again emerged from their steam wagon, took up stations standing at the edge of the charred ground.

Deirut repeated his precautionary measures, went out to join them. He moved slowly, warily, the Borgen ready in his left hand.

The five awaited him this time without retreating. They appeared more relaxed, chattering in low voices among themselves, watching him with those stalked eyes. The word sounds remained pure gibberish to Deirut, but he had the lingua pack trained on them and knew the computer would have the language in a matter of time.

Deirut stopped about eight paces from the natives, said: "Glad to see you, boys. Have a nice nap in your car?"

The tallest one nodded, said: "What's doing?"

Deirut gaped, speechless.

A native on the left said: "Let's hope you have a good metal-working industry, friends. Otherwise, I'm going to be an extremely unhappy visitor."

The tallest one said: "Glad to see you, boys. Have a nice nap in your car?"

"They're mimicking me!" Deirut gasped.

"Confirmed," the computer said.

Deirut overcame an urge to laugh, said: "You're the crummiest looking herd of no-good animals I ever saw. It's a wonder your mothers could stand the sight of you."

The tall native repeated it for him without an error.

"Reference to mothers cannot be accepted at this time," the computer said. "Local propagation customs unknown. There are indications these may be part vegetable—part animal."

"Oh, shut up," Deirut said.

"Oh, shut up," said a native on his left.

"Suggest silence on your part," the computer said. "They are displaying signs of trying to break down your language. Better we get their language, reveal less of ourselves."

Deirut saw the wisdom in it, spoke subvocally for the speaker in his throat: "You're so right."

He clamped his lips into a thin line, stared at the natives. Silence dragged on and on.

Presently, the tall one said: "Augroop somilican."

"Toogayala," said the one on the left.

"Cardinal number," the computer said. "Probable position five. Hold up your five fingers and say toogayala."

Deirut obeyed.

"Toogayala, toogayala," the natives agreed. One detached himself, went to the steam wagon and returned with a black metal figurine about half a meter tall, extended it toward Deirut.

Cautiously, Deirut moved forward, accepted the thing. It felt heavy and cold in his hand. It was a beautifully stylized figure of one of the natives, the eye stalks drooping into inverted U-shapes, mouth open.

Deirut brought out his contact kit, pressed it against the metal. The kit went "ping" as it took a sample.

The natives stared at him.

"Iron-magnesium-nickel alloy," the computer said. "Figure achieved by casting. Approximate age of figure twenty-five million standard years."

Deirut felt his throat go dry. He spoke subvocally: "That can't be!"

"Dating accurate to plus or minus six thousand years," the computer said. "You will note the figures carved on the casting. The inverted U on the chest is probably the figure five. Beneath that is writing. Pattern too consistent for different interpretation."

"Civilization for twenty-five million years," Deirut said.

"Plus or minus six thousand years," the computer said.

Again, Deirut felt a surge of the *push,* fought it down. He wanted to return to the crippled ship, flee this place in spite of the dangers. His knees shook.

The native who had given him the figurine, stepped forward, reclaimed it. "Toogayala," the native said. It pointed to the inverted U on the figure and then to the symbol on its own chest.

"But they only have a steam engine," Deirut protested.

"Very sophisticated steam engines," the computer said. "Cannon is retractable, gyroscopically mounted, self-tracking."

"They can fix the ship!" Deirut said.

"If they will," the computer said.

The tall native stepped forward now, touched a finger to the lingua pack, said: "s'Chareecha" with a falling inflection. Deirut watched the hand carefully. It was six-fingered, definitely, the skin a mauve-blue. The fingers were horn-tipped and double-knuckled.

"Try ung-ung," the computer suggested.

"Ung-ung," Deirut said.

The tall one jumped backward and all five sent their eye stalks peering toward the sky. They set up an excited chattering among themselves in which Deirut caught several repeated sounds: "Yaubron . . . s'Chareecha . . . Autoga . . . Sreese-sreese . . ."

"We have an approximation for entry now," the computer said. "The tall one is called Autoga. Address him by name."

"Autoga," Deirut said.

The tall one turned, tipped his eye stalks toward Deirut.

"Say *Ai-Yaubron ung sreese s'Chareecha*," the computer said.

Deirut obeyed.

The natives faced each other, returned their attention to Deirut. Presently, they began grunting almost uncontrollably. Autoga sat down on the ground, pounded it with his hands, all the while keeping up the grunting.

"What the devil?" Deirut said.

"They're laughing," the computer said. "Go sit beside Autoga."

"On the ground?" Deirut asked.

"Yes."

"Is it safe?"

"Of course."

"Why're they laughing?"

"They're laughing at themselves. You tricked them, made them jump. This is definitely laughter."

Hesitantly, Deirut moved to Autoga's side, sat down.

Autoga stopped grunting, put a hand on Deirut's shoulder, spoke to his companions. With a millisecond delay, the computer began translating: "This god-self-creation is a good Joe, boys. His accent is lousy, but he has a sense of humor."

"Are you sure of that translation?" Deirut asked.

"Reasonably so," the computer said. "Without greater morphological grounding, a cultural investigation in depth and series comparisons of vocal evolution, you get only a gross literal approximation, of course. We'll refine it while we go along. We're ready to put your subvocals through the lingua pack."

"Let's talk," Deirut said.

Out of the lingua pack on his chest came a series of sounds approximating "Ai-ing-eeya."

Computer translation of Autoga's reply was: "That's a good idea. It's open sky."

Deirut shook his head. It didn't sound right. Open sky?

"Sorry we damaged your vehicle," Autoga said. "We thought you were one of our youths playing with danger."

Deirut swallowed. "You thought my ship . . . you people can make ships of this kind?"

"Oh, we made a few about ten million *klurch* ago," Autoga said.

"It was at least fifteen million *klurch*," said the wrinkle-faced native on Deirut's left.

"Now, Choon, there you go exaggerating again," Autoga said. He looked at Deirut. "You'll have to forgive Choon. He wants everything to be bigger, better and greater than it is."

"What's a klurch?" Deirut asked.

The computer answered for his ears alone: "Probable answer—the local year, about one and one-third standards."

"I'm glad you decided to be peaceful," Deirut said.

The lingua pack rendered this into a variety of sounds and the natives stared at Deirut's chest.

"He is speaking from his chest," Choon said.

Autoga looked up at the ship. "There are more of you?"

"Don't answer that," the computer said. "Suggest the ship is a source of mystical powers."

Deirut digested this, shook his head. Stupid computer! "These are sharp cookies," he said speaking aloud.

"What a delightful arrangement of noises," Autoga said. "Do it again."

"You thought I was one of your youths," Deirut said. "Now who do you think I am?"

The lingua pack remained silent. His ear speaker said: "Suggest that question not be asked."

"Ask it!" Deirut said.

A gabble of sound came from the lingua pack.

"We debated that during the presence of s'Chareecha," Autoga said. "We hid in the purple darkness, you understand, because we have no wish to seed under the influence of s'Chareecha. A majority among us decided you are the personification of our design for a deity. I dissented. My thought is that you are an unknown, although I grant you temporarily the majority title."

Deirut wet his lips with his tongue.

"He has five fingers," Choon said.

"This was the argument you used to convince Tura and Lecky," Autoga said. "This argument still doesn't answer Spispi's objection that the five fingers could be the product of genetic manipulation or that plus amputation."

"But the eyes," Choon said. "Who could conceive of such eyes? Not in our wildest imaginations . . ."

"Perhaps you offend our visitor," Autoga said. He glanced at Deirut, the stalked eyes bending outward quizzically.

"And the articulation of the legs and arms," one of the other natives ventured.

"You're repeating old arguments, Tura," Autoga said.

Deirut suddenly had a picture of himself as he must appear to these natives. Their eyes had obvious advantages over his. He had seen them look behind themselves without turning their heads. The double thumb arrangement looked useful. They must think one thumb an odd limitation. He began to chuckle.

"What is this noise?" Autoga asked.

"I'm laughing," Deirut said.

"I will render that: 'I'm laughing at myself,'" the computer said. Sounds issued from the lingua pack.

"A person who can laugh at himself has taken a major step toward the highest civilization," Autoga said. "No offense intended."

"The theories of Picheck that the concerted wish for a deity must produce same are here demonstrated," Choon said. "It's not quite the shape of entity I had envisioned, however, but we . . ."

"Why don't we inquire?" Autoga asked and turned to Deirut. "Are you a deity?"

"I'm a mortal human being, nothing more," Deirut said.

The lingua pack remained silent.

"Translate that!" Deirut blared.

The computer spoke for him alone: "The experience, training and memory banks available suggest that it would be safer for you to pose as a deity. Their natural awe would enable you to . . ."

"We're not going to fool these characters for five minutes," Deirut said. "They've built spaceships. They have advanced electronic techniques. You heard their radio. They've had a civilization for more than twenty-five million years." He paused. "Haven't they?"

"Definitely. The cast figure was an advanced form and technique."

"Then translate my words!"

Deirut grew conscious that he had been speaking aloud and the natives were following his words and the movements of his mouth with a rapt intensity.

"Translate," Autoga said. "That would be *chtsuyop,* no?"

"You must speak subvocally," the computer said. "They are beginning to break down your language."

"They're doing it in their heads, you stupid pile of electronic junk," Deirut said. "I have to use you! And you think I can pose as a god with these people?"

"I will translate because you command it and my override circuits cannot circumvent your command," the computer said.

"A computer!" Autoga said. "He has a translating computer in his vehicle! How quaint."

"Translate," Deirut said.

Sounds issued from the lingua pack.

"I am vindicated," Autoga said. "And you will note that I did it on nothing more than the design of the vehicle and the cut of his clothing plus the artifacts, of course."

"This is why you are in command," Choon said. "I suffer your correction and instruction abysmally."

Autoga looked at Deirut. "What will you require other than the repair of your vehicle?"

"Don't you want to know where I'm from?" Deirut asked.

"You are from somewhere," Autoga said. "It has been theorized that other suns and worlds might exist beyond the hydrogen cloud from which we were formed. Your presence suggests this theory is true."

"But . . . but don't you want contact with us . . . trade, exchange ideas?"

"It is not apparent," Autoga said, "that the empty universe theory has been disproved. However, a primitive such as yourself, even you must realize such interchange would be pointless."

"But we . . ."

"We well know that the enclosure of our universe has forced us in upon ourselves," Choon said. "If that's what you were going to say?"

"He was going into boring detail about what he has to offer us," Autoga said. "I suggest we get about doing what has to be done. Spispi, you and Tura take care of the computer in his vehicle. Choon and I will . . ."

"What're you doing?" Deirut asked. He leaped to his feet. At least, he thought he leaped to his feet, but in a moment he grew conscious that he was still sitting on the ground, the five natives facing him, staring.

"They are erasing some of my circuits!" the computer wailed. "A magneto-gravitic field encloses me and the . . . aroo, tut-tut, jingle bells, jingle bells."

"This is very interesting," Autoga said presently. "He has made contact with a civilization of our level at some previous time. You will note the residual inhibition against lengthy travel away from his home. We'll make the inhibition stronger this time."

Deirut stared at the chattering natives with a sense of déjà vu. The speaker in his neck remained silent. His lingua pack made no sound. He felt movement in his mind like spiders crawling along his nerves.

"Who do you suppose he could've contacted?" Choon asked.

"Not one of our groups, of course," Autoga said. "Before we stay out in the light of s'Chareecha and plant ourselves for the next seeding, we must start a flow of inquiry."

"Who will talk to us about such things?" Choon asked. "We are mere herdsmen."

"Perhaps we should listen more often to the entertainment broadcasts," Spispi said. "Something may have been said."

"We may be simple herdsmen whose inquiry will not go very far," Autoga said, "but this has been an experience to afford us many hours of conversation. Imagine having the empty universe theory refuted!"

Deirut awoke in the control seat of his ship, smelled in the stink of the place his own sweat touched by the chemistry of fear. A glance at the instrument panel showed that he had succumbed to the push and turned ship. He was headed back out of the cloud without having found anything in it.

An odd sadness came over Deirut.

I'll find my planet some day, he thought. *It'll have alabaster buildings and sheltered waters for sailing and long stretches of prairie for game animals.*

The automatic log showed turning-around at ninety-four days.

I stood it longer than Bingaling, he thought.

He remembered the conversation with Bingaling then and the curious reference to a previous attempt at the cloud. *Maybe I did,* he thought. *Maybe I forgot because the push got so tough.*

Presently, his mind turned to thoughts of Capella Base, of going home. Just the thought of it eased the pressures of the push which was still faintly with him. The push . . . the push—it had beaten him again. Next trip out, he decided, he'd head the opposite direction, see what was to be found out there.

Almost idly then Deirut wondered about the push. *Why do we call it the push?* he wondered. *Why don't we call it the pull?*

The question interested him enough to put it to the computer.

"Tut-tut," the computer said.

BY THE BOOK

You will take your work seriously. Infinite numbers of yet-unborn humankind depend upon you who keep open the communications lines through negative space. Let the angle-transmission networks fail and Man will fail.
"You and the Haigh Company" (Employees Handbook)

He was too old for this kind of work even if his name was Ivar Norris Gump, admittedly the best troubleshooter in the company's nine-hundred-year history. If it'd been anyone but his old friend Poss Washington calling for help, there'd have been a polite refusal signed "Ing." Semiretirement gave a troubleshooter the right to turn down dangerous assignments.

Now, after three hours on duty in a full vac suit within a Skoarnoff tube's blank darkness, Ing ached with tiredness. It impaired his mental clarity and his ability to survive and he knew it.

You will take your work seriously at all times, he thought. *Axiom: A troubleshooter shall not get into trouble.*

Ing shook his head at the handbook's educated ignorance, took a deep breath and tried to relax. Right now he should be back home on Mars, his only concerns the routine maintenance of the Phobos Relay and an occasional lecture to new 'shooters.

Damn that Poss, he thought.

The big trouble was in here, though—in the tube, and six good men had died trying to find it. They were six men he had helped train—and that was another reason he had come. They were all caught up in the same dream.

Around Ing stretched an airless tubular cave twelve kilometers long, two kilometers diameter. It was a lightless hole, carved through lava rock beneath the moon's Mare Nectaris. Here was the home of the "Beam"—the beautiful, deadly, vitally *serious* beam, a tamed violence which suddenly had become balky.

Ing thought of all the history which had gone into this tube. Some nine hundred years ago the Seeding Compact had been signed. In addition to its Solar System Communications duties, the Haigh Company had taken over then the sending out of small containers, their size severely limited by the mass an angtrans pulse could push. Each container held twenty female rabbits. In the rabbit uteri, dormant, their metabolism almost at a standstill, lay two hundred human embryos nestled with embryos of cattle, all the domestic stock needed to start a new human economy. With the rabbits went plant seeds, insect eggs and design tapes for tools.

The containers were rigged to fold out on a planet's surface to provide a shielded living area. There the embryos would be machine-transferred into inflatable gestation vats, brought to full term, cared for and educated by mechanicals until the human *seed* could fend for itself.

Each container had been pushed to trans-light speed by angtrans pulses—"Like pumping a common garden swing," said the popular literature. The life mechanism was controlled by signals transmitted through the "Beam" whose tiny impulses went "around the corner" to bridge in milliseconds distances which took matter centuries to traverse.

Ing glanced up at the miniature beam sealed behind its quartz window in his suit. There was the hope and the frustration. If they could only put a little beam such as that in each container, the big beam could home on it. But under that harsh bombardment, beam anodes lasted no longer than a month. They made-do with reflection plates on the containers, then, with beambounce and programmed approximations. And somewhere the programmed approximations were breaking down.

Now, with the first Seeding Compact vessel about to land on Theta Apus IV, with mankind's interest raised to fever pitch—beam contact had turned unreliable. The farther out the container, the worse the contact.

Ing could feel himself being drawn toward that frail cargo out there. His instincts were in communion with those containers which would drift into limbo unless the beam was brought under control. The embryos would surely die eventually and the dream would die with them.

Much of humanity feared the containers had fallen into the hands of alien life, that the human embryos were being taken over by something *out there*. Panic ruled in some quarters and there were shouts that the SC containers betrayed enough human secrets to make the entire race vulnerable.

To Ing and the six before him, the locus of the problem seemed obvious. It lay in here and in the anomaly math newly derived to explain how the beam might be deflected from the containers. What to do about that appeared equally obvious. But six men had died following that obvious course. They had died here in this utter blackness.

Sometimes it helped to quote the book.

Often you didn't know what you hunted here—a bit of stray radiation perhaps, a few cosmic rays that had penetrated a weak spot in the force-baffle shielding, a dust leak caused by a moonquake, or a touch of heat, a hot spot coming up from the depths. The big beam wouldn't tolerate much interference. Put a pinhead flake of dust in its path at the wrong moment, let a tiny flicker of light intersect it, and it went whiplash wild. It writhed like a giant snake, tore whole sections off the tube walls. Beam auroras danced in the sky above the moon then and the human attendants scurried.

A troubleshooter at the wrong spot in the tube died.

Ing pulled his hands into his suit's barrel top, adjusted his own tiny beam scope, the unit that linked him through a short reach of angspace to beam control. He checked his instruments, read his position from the modulated contact ripple through the soles of his shielded suit.

He wondered what his daughter, Lisa, was doing about now. Probably getting the boys, his grandsons, ready for the slotride to school. It made Ing feel suddenly old to think that one of his grandsons already was in Mars Polytechnic aiming for a Haigh Company career in the footsteps of his famous grandfather.

The vac suit was hot and smelly around Ing after a three-hour tour. He noted from a dial that his canned-cold temperature balance system still had an hour and ten minutes before red-line.

It's the cleaners, Ing told himself. *It has to be the vacuum cleaners. It's the old familiar cussedness of inanimate objects.*

What did that handbook say? *"Frequently it pays to look first for the characteristics of devices in use which may be such that an essentially pragmatic approach offers the best chance for success. It often is possible to solve an accident or malfunction problem with straight-forward and un-complicated approaches, deliberately ignoring their more subtle aspects."*

He slipped his hands back into his suit's arms, shielded his particle counter with an armored hand, cracked open the cover, peered in at the luminous dial. Immediately, an angry voice crackled in the speakers:

"Douse that light! We're beaming."

Ing snapped the lid closed by reflex, said: "I'm in the backboard shadow. Can't see the beam." Then: "Why wasn't I told you're beaming?"

Another voice rumbled from the speakers: "It's Poss here, Ing. I'm monitoring your position by sono, told them to go ahead without disturbing you."

"What's the supetrans doing monitoring a troubleshooter?" Ing asked.

"All right, Ing."

Ing chuckled then: "What're you doing, testing?"

"Yes. We've an inner-space transport to beam down on Titan, thought we'd run it from here."

"Did I foul the beam?"

"We're still tracking clean."

Inner-space transmission open and reliable, Ing thought, *but the long reach out to the stars was muddied.* Maybe the scare mongers were right. Maybe it was outside interference, an alien intelligence.

"We've lost two cleaners on this transmission," Washington said. "Any sign of them?"

"Negative."

They'd lost two cleaners on the transmission, Ing thought. That was getting to be routine. The flitting vacuum cleaners—supported by the beam's field, patrolling its length for the slightest trace of interference, had to be replaced at the rate of about a hundred a year normally, but the rate had been going up. As the beam grew bigger, unleashed more power for the long reach, the cleaners proved less and less effective at dodging the angtrans throw, the controlled whiplash. No part of a cleaner survived contact with the beam. They were energy-charged in phase with the beam, keyed for instant dissolution to add their energy to the transmission.

"It's the damned cleaners," Ing said.

"That's what you all keep saying," Washington said.

Ing began prowling to his right. Somewhere off there the glassite floor curved gradually upward and became a wall—and then a ceiling. But the opposite side was always two kilometers away, and the Moon's gravity, light as that was, imposed limits on how far he could walk up the wall. It wasn't like the little Phobos beam where they could use a low-power magnafield outside and walk right around the tube.

He wondered then if he was going to insist on riding one of the cleaners . . . the way the six others had done.

Ing's shuffling, cautious footsteps brought him out of the anode backboard's shadow. He turned, saw a pencil line of glowing purple stretching away from him to the cathode twelve kilometers distant. He knew there actually was no purple glow, that what he saw was a visual simulation created on the one-way surface of his face-plate, a reaction to the beam's presence displayed there for his benefit alone.

Washington's voice in his speaker said: "Sono has you in Zone Yellow. Take it easy, Ing."

Ing altered course to the right, studied the beam.

Intermittent breaks in the purple line betrayed the presence between himself and that lambent energy of the robot vacuum cleaners policing the perimeter, hanging on the sine lines of the beam field like porpoises gamboling on a bow wave.

"Transport's down," Washington said. "We're phasing into a longthrow test. Ten-minute program."

Ing nodded to himself, imagined Washington sitting there in the armored bubble of the control room, a giant, with a brooding face, eyes alert and glittering. Old Poss didn't want to believe it was the cleaners, that was sure. If it was the cleaners, someone was going to have to ride the wild goose.

There'd be more deaths . . . more rides . . . until they tested out the new theory. It certainly was a helluva time for someone to come up with an anomaly *hole* in the angtrans math. But that's what someone back at one of the trans-time computers on Earth had done . . . and if he was right—then the problem had to be the cleaners.

Ing studied the shadow breaks in the beam—robotic torpedoes, sensor-trained to collect the tiniest debris. One of the shadows suddenly reached away from him in both directions until the entire beam was hidden. A cleaner was approaching him. Ing waited for it to identify the Authorized Intruder markings which it could *see* the same way he saw the beam.

The beam reappeared.

"Cleaner just looked you over," Washington said. "You're getting in pretty close."

Ing heard the worry in his friend's voice, said: "I'm all right long's I stay up here close to the board."

He tried to picture in his mind then the cleaner lifting over him and returning to its station along the beam.

"I'm plotting you against the beam," Washington said. "Your shadow width says you're approaching Zone Red. Don't crowd it, Ing. I'd rather not have to clean a fried troubleshooter out of there."

"Hate to put you to all that extra work," Ing said.

"Give yourself plenty of 'lash room."

"I'm marking the beam thickness against my helment crosshairs, Poss. Relax."

Ing advanced another two steps, sent his gaze traversing the beam's length, seeking the beginnings of the controlled whiplash which would *throw* the test message into angspace. The chained energy of the purple rope began to bend near its center far down the tube. It was an action visible only as a gentle flickering outward against the crosshairs of his faceplate.

He backed off four steps. The throw was a chancey thing when you were this close—and if interfering radiation ever touched that beam . . .

Ing crouched, sighted along the beam, waited for the throw. An experienced troubleshooter could tell more from the way the beam whipped than banks of instruments could reveal. Did it push out a double bow? Look for faulty field focus. Did it waver up and down? Possible misalignment of vertical hold. Did it split or spread into two loops? Synchronization problem.

But you had to be in here close and alert to that fractional margin between good seeing and *good night!* forever.

Cleaners began paying more attention to him in this close, but he planted himself with his AI markings visible to them, allowing them to fix his position and go on about their business.

To Ing's trained eye, cleaner action appeared more intense, faster than normal. That agreed with all the previous reports—unless a perimeter gap had admitted stray foreign particles, or perhaps tiny shades dislodged from the tube's walls by the pulse of the moon's own life.

Ing wondered then if there could be an overlooked hole in the fanatic quadruple-lock controls giving access to the tube. But they'd been sniffing along that line since the first sign of trouble. Not likely a hole would've escaped the inspectors. No—it was in here. And cleaner action *was* increased, a definite lift in tempo.

"Program condition?" Ing asked.

"Transmission's still Whorf positive, but we haven't found an angspace opening yet."

"Time?"

"Eight minutes to program termination."

"Cleaner action's way up," Ing said. "What's the dirt count?"

A pause, then: "Normal."

Ing shook his head. The monitor that kept constant count on the quantity of debris picked up by the cleaners shouldn't show normal in the face of this much activity.

"What's the word from Mare Nubium transmitter?" Ing asked.

"Still shut down and full of inspection equipment. Nothing to show for it at last report."

"Imbrium?"

"Inspection teams are out and they expect to be back into test phase by 0900. You're not thinking of ordering *us* to shut down for a complete cleanout?"

"Not yet."

"We've a budget to consider, too, Ing. Remember that."

Huh! Ing thought. *Not like Poss to worry about budget in this kind of an emergency. He's trying to tell me something?*

What did the handbook say? *"The good troubleshooter is cost conscious, aware that down time and equipment replacement are factors of serious concern to the Haigh Company."*

Ing wondered then if he should order the tube opened for thorough inspection. But the Imbrium and Nubium tubes had revealed nothing and the decontamination time *was* costly. They were the older tubes, though—Nubium the first to be built. They were smaller than Nectaris, simpler locks. But their beams weren't getting through any better than the Nectaris tube with its behemoth size, greater safeguards.

"Stand by," Washington said. "We're beginning to get whipcount on the program."

In the abrupt silence, Ing saw the beam curl. The whiplash came down the twelve kilometers of tube curling like a purple wave, traveling the entire length in about two thousandths of a second. It was a thing so fast that the visual effect was of seeing it *after* it had happened.

Ing stood up, began analyzing what he had seen. The beam had appeared clean, pure—a perfect throw . . . except for one little flare near the far end and another about midway. Little flares. The after-image was needle shaped, rigid . . . pointed.

"How'd it look?" Washington asked.

"Clean," Ing said. "Did we get through?"

"We're checking," Washington said, then: "Limited contact. Very muddy. About thirty per cent . . . just about enough to tell us the container's still there and its contents seem to be alive."

"Is it in orbit?"

"Seems to be. Can't be sure."

"Give me the cleaner count," Ing said.

A pause, then: "Damnation! We're down another two."

"Exactly two?"

"Yes. Why?"

"Dunno yet. Do your instruments show beam deflections from hitting two cleaners? What's the energy sum?"

"Everyone thinks the cleaners are causing this," Washington muttered. "I tell you they couldn't. They're fully phased *with* the beam, just add energy to it if they hit. They're *not* debris!"

"But does the beam really eat them?" Ing asked. "You saw the anomaly report."

"Oh, Ing, let's not go into that again." Washington's voice sounded tired, irritated.

The stubbornness of Washington's response confused Ing. This wasn't like the man at all. "Sure," Ing said, "but what if they're going somewhere we can't see?"

"Come off that, Ing! You're as bad as all the others. If there's one place we know they're *not* going, that's into angspace. There isn't enough energy in the universe to put cleaner mass around the corner."

"Unless that hole in our theories really exists," Ing said. And he thought: *Poss is trying to tell me something. What? Why can't he come right out and say it?* He waited, wondering at an idea that nibbled at the edge of his mind—a concept . . . What was it? Some half-forgotten association . . .

"Here's the beam report," Washington said. "Deflection shows only one being taken, but the energy sum's doubled all right. One balanced out the other. That happens."

Ing studied the purple line, nodding to himself. The beam was almost the color of a scarf his wife had worn on their honeymoon. She'd been a good wife, Jennie—raising Lisa in Mars camps and blister pods, sticking with her man until the canned air and hard life had taken her.

The beam lay quiescent now with only the faintest auroral bleed off. Cleaner tempo was down. The test program still had a few minutes to go, but Ing doubted it'd produce another throw into angspace. You acquired an instinct for the transmission pulse after a while. You could sense when the beam was going to open its tiny signal window across the light-years.

"I saw both of those cleaners go," Ing said. "They didn't seem to be torn apart or anything—just flared out."

"Energy consumed," Washington said.

"Maybe."

Ing thought for a moment. A hunch was beginning to grow in him. He knew a way to test it. The question was: Would Poss go along with it? Hard to tell in his present mood. Ing wondered about his friend. Darkness, the isolation of this position within the tube gave voices from outside a disembodied quality.

"Poss, do me a favor," Ing said. "Give me a straight 'lash-gram. No fancy stuff, just a demonstration throw. I want a clean ripple the length of the beam. Don't try for angspace, just lash it."

"Have you popped your skull? Any lash can hit angspace. And you get one fleck of dust in that beam path . . ."

"We'd rip the sides off the tube; I know. But this is a clean beam, Poss. I can see it. I just want a little ripple."

"Why?"

Can I tell him? Ing wondered.

Ing decided to tell only part of the truth, said: "I want to clock the cleaner tempo during the program. Give me a debris monitor and a crossing count for each observation post. Have them focus on the cleaners, not on the beam."

"Why?"

"You can see for yourself cleaner activity doesn't agree with the beam condition," Ing said. "Something's wrong there—accumulated programming error or . . . I dunno. But I want some actual facts to go on—a physical count during a 'lash."

"You're not going to get new data running a test that could be repeated in the laboratory."

"This isn't a laboratory."

Washington absorbed this, then: "Where would you be during the 'lash?"

He's going to do it, Ing thought. He said: "I'll be close to the anode end here. 'Lash can't swing too wide here."

"And if we damage the tube?"

Ing hesitated remembering that it was a friend out there, a friend with responsibilities. No telling who might be monitoring the conversation, though . . . and this test was vital to the idea nibbling at Ing's awareness.

"Humor me, Poss," Ing said.

"Humor him," Washington muttered. "All right, but this'd better not be humorous."

"Wait 'till I'm in position," Ing said. "A straight lash."

He began working up the tube slope out of Zone Yellow into the Gray and then the White. Here, he turned, studied the beam. It was a thin purple ribbon stretching off left and right—shorter on the left toward the anode. The long reach of it going off toward the cathode some twelve kilometers to his right was a thin wisp of color broken by the flickering passage of cleaners.

"Any time," Ing said.

He adjusted the suit rests against the tube's curve, pulled his arms into the barrel top, started the viewplate counter recording movement of the cleaners. Now came the hard part—waiting and watching. He had a sudden feeling of isolation then, wondering if he'd done the right thing. There was an element of burning bridges in this action.

If it isn't there, you can't study it, Ing thought.

"You will take your work seriously," he muttered. Ing smiled then, thinking of the tragicomic faces, the jowly board chairman he visualized behind the handbook's pronouncements. Nothing was left to chance—no task, no item of personal tidiness, no physical exercise. Ing considered himself an expert on handbooks. He owned one of the finest collections of them dating from ancient times down to the present. In moments of boredom he amused himself with choice quotes.

"Program going in," Washington said. "I wish I knew what you hope to find by this."

"I quote," Ing said. "'The objective worker makes as large a collection of data as possible and analyzes these in their entirety in relation to selected factors whose relationship to a questioned phenomenon is to be investigated.'"

"What the devil's that supposed to mean?" Washington demanded.

"Damned if I know," Ing said, "but it's right out of the Haigh Handbook." He cleared his throat. "What's the cleaner tempo from your stations?"

"Up a bit."

"Give me a countdown on the 'lash."

"No sign yet. There's . . . wait a minute! Here's some action—twenty-five . . . twenty seconds."

Ing began counting under his breath.

Zero.

A progression of tiny flares began far off to his right, flickered past him with increasing brightness. They were a blur that left a glimmering after-image. Sensors in his suit soles began reporting the fall of debris.

"Holy O'Golden!" Washington muttered.

"How many'd we lose?" Ing asked. He knew it was going to be bad—worse than he'd expected.

There was a long wait, then Washington's shocked voice: "A hundred and eighteen cleaners down. It isn't possible!"

"Yeah," Ing said. "They're all over the floor. Shut off the beam before that dust drifts up into it."

The beam disappeared from Ing's faceplate responders.

"Is that what you thought would happen, Ing?"

"Kind of."

"Why didn't you warn me?"

"You wouldn't have given me that 'lash."

"Well how the devil're we going to explain a hundred and eighteen cleaners? Accounting'll be down on my neck like a . . ."

"Forget Accounting," Ing said. "You're a beam engineer; open your eyes. Those cleaners weren't absorbed by the beam. They were cut down and scattered over the floor."

"But the . . ."

"Cleaners are designed to respond to the beam's needs," Ing said. "As the beam moves they move. As the debris count goes up, the cleaners work harder. If one works a little too hard and doesn't get out of the way fast enough, it's supposed to be absorbed—its energy converted by the beam. Now, a false 'lash catches a hundred and eighteen of them off balance. Those cleaners weren't eaten: they were scattered over the floor."

There was silence while Washington absorbed this.

"Did that 'lash touch angspace?" Ing asked.

"I'm checking," Washington said. Then: "No . . . wait a minute: there's a whole ripple of angspace . . . contacts, very low energy—a series lasting about an eighty-millionth of a second. I had the responders set to the last decimal or we'd have never caught it."

"To all intents and purposes we didn't touch," Ing said.

"Practically not." Then: "Could somebody in cleaner programming have flubbed the dub?"

"On a hundred and eighteen units?"

"Yeah. I see what you mean. Well, what're we going to say when they come around for an explanation?"

"We quote the book. 'Each problem should be approached in two stages: (1) locate those areas which contribute most to the malfunction, and (2) take remedial action designed to reduce hazards which have been positively identifying hazards.' "

Ing stepped over the lock sill into the executive salon, saw that Washington already was seated at the corner table which convention reserved for the senior beam engineer on duty, the Supervisor of Transmission.

It was too late for day lunch and too early for the second shift coffee break. The salon was almost empty. Three junior executives at a table across the room to the right were sharing a private joke, but keeping it low in Washington's presence. A security officer sat nursing a teabulb beside the passage to the kitchen tram on the left. His shoulders bore a touch of dampness from a perspiration reclaimer to show that he had recently come down from the surface. Security had a lot of officers on the station, Ing noted . . . and there always seemed to be one around Washington.

The vidwall at the back was tuned to an Earthside news broadcast: There were hints of political upsets because of the beam failure, demands for explanations of the money spent. Washington was quoted as saying a solution would be forthcoming.

Ing began making his way toward the corner, moving around the empty tables.

Washington had a coffeebulb in front of him, steam drifting upward. Ing studied the man—Possible Washington (Impossible, according to his junior engineers) was a six-foot eight-inch powerhouse of a man with wide shoulders, sensitive hands, a sharply Moorish-Semitic face of café au lait skin and startlingly blue eyes under a dark crew-cut. (The company's senior medic referred to him as "a most amazing throw of the genetic dice.") Washington's size said a great deal about his abilities. It took a considerable expenditure to lift his extra kilos moonside. He had to be worth just that much more.

Ing sat down across from Washington, gestured to the waiter-eye on the table surface, ordered Marslichen tea.

"You just come from Assembly?" Washington asked.

"They said you were up here," Ing said. "You look tired. Earthside give you any trouble about your report?"

"Until I used your trick and quoted the book: 'Every test under field conditions shall approximate as closely as possible the conditions set down by laboratory precedent.'"

"Hey, that's a good one," Ing said. "Why didn't you tell them you were following a hunch—you had a hunch I had a hunch."

Washington smiled.

Ing took a deep breath. It felt good to sit down. He realized he'd worked straight through two shifts without a break.

"You look tired yourself," Washington said.

Ing nodded. Yes, he was tired. He was too old to push this hard. Ing had few illusions about himself. He'd always been a runt, a little on the weak side—skinny and with an almost weaselish face that was saved from ugliness by widely set green eyes and a thick crewcut mop of golden hair. The hair was turning gray now, but the brain behind the wide brow still functioned smoothly.

The teabulb came up through the table slot. Ing pulled the bulb to him, cupped his hands around its warmth. He had counted on Washington to keep the worst of the official pressure off him, but now that it had been done, Ing felt guilty.

"No matter how much I quote the book," Washington said, "they don't like that explanation."

"Heads will roll and all that?"

"To put it mildly."

"Well, we have a position chart on where every cleaner went down," Ing said. "Every piece of wreckage has been reassembled as well as possible. The undamaged cleaners have been gone over with the proverbial comb of fine teeth."

"How long until we have a clean tube?" Washington asked.

"About eight hours."

Ing moved his shoulders against the chair. His thigh muscles still ached from the long session in the Skoarnoff tube and there was a pain across his shoulders.

"Then it's time for some turkey talk," Washington said.

Ing had been dreading this moment. He knew the stand Washington was going to take.

The Security officer across the room looked up, met Ing's eyes, looked away. *Is he listening to us?* Ing wondered.

"You're thinking what the others thought," Washington said. "That those cleaners were kicked around the corner into angspace."

"One way to find out," Ing said.

There was a definite lift to the Security officer's chin at that remark. He *was* listening.

"You're not taking that suicide ride," Washington said.

"Are the other beams getting through to the Seed Ships?" Ing asked.

"You know they aren't!"

Across the room, the junior executives stopped their own conversation, peered toward the corner table. The Security officer hitched his chair around to watch both the executives and the corner table.

Ing took a sip of his tea, said: "Damn tea here's always too bitter. They don't know how to serve it anywhere except on Mars." He pushed the bulb away from him. "Join the Haigh Company and save the Universe for Man."

"All right, Ing," Washington said. "We've known each other a long time and can speak straight out. What're you hiding from me?"

Ing sighed.

"I guess I owe it to you," he said. "Well, I guess it begins with the fact that every transmitter's a unique individual, which you know as well as I do. We map what it does and operate by prediction statistics. We play it by ear, as they say. Now, let's consider something out of the book. A tube is, after all, just a big cave in the rock, a controlled environment for the beam to do its work. The book says: *'By anglespace transmission, any place in the universe is just around the corner from any other place.'* This is a damned loose way to describe something we don't really understand. It makes it sound as though we know what we're talking about."

"And you say we're putting matter around that corner," Washington said, "but you haven't told me what you're—"

"I know," Ing said. "We place a modulation of energy where it can be *seen* by the Seed Ship's instruments. But that's a transfer of energy, Poss. And energy's interchangeable with matter."

"You're twisting definitions. We put a highly unstable, highly transitory reflection phenomenon in such a position that time/space limitations are changed. That's by the book, too. But you're still not telling me . . ."

"Poss, I have a crew rigging a cleaner for me to ride. We've analyzed the destruction pattern—which is what I wanted from that test 'lash—and I think we can kick me into angspace aboard one of these wild geese."

"You fool! I'm still Supetrans here and I say you're not going in there on . . ."

"Now, take it easy, Poss. You haven't even . . ."

"Granting you get kicked around that stupid corner, how do you expect to get back? And what's the purpose, anyway? What can you do if you . . ."

"I can go there and look, Poss. And the cleaner we're rigging will be more in the nature of a lifeboat. I can get down on TA-IV, maybe take the container with me, give our *seeds* a better chance. And if we learn how to kick me around there, we can do it again with . . ."

"This is stupidity!"

"Look," Ing said. "What're we risking? One old man long past his prime."

Ing faced the angry glare in Washington's eyes and realized an odd thing about himself. He wanted to get through there, wanted to give that container of embryos its chance. He was drunk with the same dream that had spawned the Seeding Compact. And he saw now that the other troubleshooters, the six who'd gone before him, must have been caught in the same web. They'd all seen where the trouble had to be. One of them would get through. There were tools in the container; another beam could be rigged on the other side. There was a chance of getting back . . . afterward . . .

"I let them talk me into sending for you," Washington growled. "The understanding was you'd examine the set up, confirm or deny what the others saw—but I didn't have to send you into that . . ."

"I want to go, Poss," Ing said. He saw what was eating on his friend now. The man had sent six troubleshooters in there to die—or disappear into an untraceable void, which was worse. Guilt had him.

"And I'm refusing permission," Washington said.

The Security officer arose from his table, crossed to stand over Washington. "Mr. Washington," he said, "I've been listening and it seems to me if Mr. Gump wants to go you can't . . ."

Washington got to his feet, all six feet eight inches of him, caught the Security man by the jacket. "So they told you to interfere if I tried to stop him!" He shook the man with an odd gentleness. "If you are on my station after the next shuttle leaves, I will see to it personally that you have an unexplained accident." He released his grip.

The Security agent paled, but stood his ground. "One call from me and this no longer will be *your* station."

"Poss," Ing said, "you can't fight city hall. And if you try they'll take you out of here. Then I'll have to make do with second best at this end. I need you as beam jockey here when I ride that wild goose."

Washington glared at him. "Ing, it won't work!"

Ing studied his friend, seeing the pressures which had been brought to bear, understanding how Earthside had maneuvered to get that request sent from a friend to Ivar Norris Gump. It all said something about Earthside's desperation. The patterns of secrecy, the Security watch, the hints in the newscasts—Ing felt something of the same urgency himself which these things betrayed. And he knew if Washington could overcome this guilt block the man would share mankind's need to help those drifting containers.

"No matter how many people get hurt—or killed," Ing said, "we have to give the embryos in those containers their chance. You know, I'm right—this is the main chance. And we need you, Poss. I want everything going for me I can get. And no matter what happens, we'll know you did your best for me . . ."

Washington took two short breaths. His shoulders slumped. "And nothing I say . . ."

"Nothing you say."

"You're going?"

"I'm going where the wild goose goes."

"And who faces the family afterward?"

"A friend, Poss. A friend faces the family and makes the blow as soft as possible."

"If you'll excuse me," the Security man said.

They ignored him as the man returned to his table.

Washington allowed himself a deep, sighing breath. Some of the fire returned to his eyes. "All right," he growled. "But I'm going to be on this end every step of the way. And I'm telling you now you get no Go signal until everything's rigged to my satisfaction."

"Of course, Poss. That's why I can't afford to have you get into a fracas and be booted out of here."

Ing's left ankle itched.

It was maddening. His hand could reach only to the calf inside the webbing of his shieldsuit. The ankle and its itch could not be lifted from the area of the sole contact controls.

The suit itself lay suspended in an oil bath within a shocktank. Around the shocktank was something that resembled a standard cleaner in shape but not in size. It was at least twice the length of a cleaner and it was fatter. The fatness allowed for phased shells—Washington's idea. It had grown out of analysis of the debris left by the test 'lash.

The faint hissing of his oxygen regenerators came to Ing through his suit sensors. His viewplate had been replaced by a set of screens linked to exterior pickups on the belly. It showed a rope of fluorescing purple surrounded by blackness.

The beam.

It was a full five centimeters across, larger than Ing had ever before seen it. The nearness of that potential violence filled him with a conditioned dread. He'd milked too many beams in too many tubes, wary of the slightest growth in size to keep him at a safe distance.

This was a monster beam. All his training and experience cried out against its size.

Ing reminded himself of the analysis which had produced the false cleaner around him now.

Eighty-nine of the cleaners recovered from the tube floor had taken their primary damage at the pickup orifice. They'd been orientated to the beam itself, disregarding the local particle count. But the most important discovery was that the cleaners had fallen through the beam without being sliced in two. They had passed completely through the blade of that purple knife without being severed. There'd been no break in the beam. The explanation had to rest in that topological anomaly—angspace. Part of the beam and/or the cleaners had gone into angspace.

He was gambling his life now that the angspace bounce coincided with the energy phasing which kept the cleaners from deflecting the beam. The outside carrier, Ing's false cleaner, was phased with the beam. It would be demolished. The next inner shell was one hundred and eighty degrees out of phase. The next shell was back in phase. And so on for ten shells.

In the center lay Ing, his hands and feet on the controls of a suit that was in effect a miniature lifeboat.

As the moment of final commitment approached, Ing began to feel a prickly sensation in his stomach. And the ankle continued to itch. But there was no way he could turn back and still live with himself. He was a troubleshooter, the best in the Haigh Company. There was no doubt that the company—and those lonely drifting human embryos had never needed him more desperately.

"Report your condition, Ing."

The voice coming from the speaker beside Ing's face-mike was Washington's with an unmistakable edge of fear in it.

"All systems clear," Ing said.

"Program entering its second section," Washington said. "Can you see any of the other cleaners?"

"Forty contacts so far," Ing said, "All normal." He gasped as his cleaner dodged a transient 'lash.

"You all right?"

"All right," Ing said.

The ride continued to be a rough one though. Each time the beam lashed, his cleaner dodged. There was no way to anticipate the direction. Ing could only trust his suit webbing and the oil-bath shocktank to keep him from being smashed against a side of the compartment.

"We're getting an abnormal number of transients," Washington said.

That called for no comment and Ing remained silent. He looked up at his receiver above the speaker. A quartz window gave him a view of the tiny beam which kept him in contact with Washington. The tiny beam, less than a centimeter long, glowed sharply purple through its inspection window. It, too, was crackling and jumping. The little beam could stand more interference than a big one, but it clearly was disturbed.

Ing turned his attention to the big beam in the view-screen, glanced back at the little beam. The difference was a matter of degree. It often seemed to Ing that the beams should illuminate the area around them, and he had to remind himself that the parallel quanta couldn't deviate that much.

"Getting 'lash count," Washington said. "Ing! Condition critical! Stand by."

Ing concentrated on the big beam now. His stomach was a hard knot. He wondered how the other troubleshooters had felt in this moment. The same, no doubt. But they'd been flying without the protection Ing had. They'd paved the way, died to give information.

The view of the beam was so close and restricted that Ing knew he'd get no warning of whip—just a sudden shift in size or position.

His heart leaped as the beam flared in the screen. The cleaner rolled sideways as it dodged, letting the beam pass to one side, but there was an ominous bump. Momentarily, the screen went blank, but the purple rope flickered back into view as his cleaner's sensors lined up and brought him back into position.

Ing checked his instruments. That bump—what had that been?

"Ing!" Washington's voice came sharply urgent from the speaker.

"What's the word?"

"We have one of the other cleaners on grav-track," Washington said. "It's in your shadow. Hold on."

There came a murmur of voices, hushed words, indistinguishable, then: "The beam touched you, Ing. You've got a phase arc between two of your shells on the side opposite the beam. One of the other cleaners has locked onto that arc with one of its sensors. Its other sensors are still on the beam and it's riding parallel with you, in your shadow. We're getting you out of there."

Ing tried to swallow in a dry throat. He knew the danger without having it explained. There was an arc, light in the tube. His cleaner was between the arc and the beam, but the other cleaner was up there behind him, too. If they had to dodge a 'lash, the other cleaner would be confused because its sensor contacts were now split. It'd be momentarily delayed. The two cleaners would collide and release light in the tube. The big beam would go wild. The protective shells would be struck from all sides.

Washington was working to get him out, but that would take time. You couldn't just yank a primary program out. That created its own 'lash conditions. And if you damped the beam, the other cleaners would home on the arc. There'd be carnage in the tube.

"Starting phase out," Washington said. "Estimating three minutes to control the second phase. We'll just . . ."

"Lash!"

The word rang in Ing's ears even as he felt his cleaner lift at the beginning of a dodge maneuver. He had time to think that the warning must've come from one of the engineers on the monitor board, then a giant gong rang out.

A startled: "What the hell!" blasted from his speaker to be replaced by a strident hissing, the ravening of a billion snakes.

Ing felt his cleaner still lifting, pressing him down against the webbing, his face hard against the protective mask. There was no view of the big beam in his screen and the little window which should've showed the line of his own small beam revealed a wavering, crackling worm of red-purple.

Abruptly, Ing's world twisted inside out.

It was like being squeezed flat into a one-molecule puddle and stretched out to infinity. He *saw* around the outside of an inner-viewed universe with light extended to hard rods of brilliance that poked through from one end to the other. He realized he wasn't seeing with his eyes, but was absorbing a sensation compounded from every sense organ he possessed. Beyond this inner view everything was chaos, undefined madness.

The beam got me, he thought. *I'm dying.*

One of the light rods resolved itself into a finite row of spinning objects—over, under, around . . . over, under, around. . . . The movement was hypnotic. With a feeling of wonder, Ing recognized that the object was his own suit and a few shattered pieces of the protective shells. The tiny beam of his own transmitter had been opened and was spitting shards of purple.

With the recognition came a sensation of being compressed. Ing felt himself being pushed down into the blackness that jerked at him, twisting, pounding. It was like going over a series of rapids. He felt the web harness bite into his skin.

Abruptly, the faceplate viewscreens showed jewel brilliance against velvet black—spots of light: sharp blue, red, green, gold. A glaring white light spun into view surrounded by whipping purple ribbons. The ribbons looked like beam auroras.

Ing's body ached. His mind felt as though immersed in fog, every thought laboring against deadly slowness.

Jewel brilliance—spots of light.

Again, glaring white.

Purple ribbons.

The speaker above him crackled with static. Through its window, he saw his tiny beam spattering and jumping. It seemed important to do something about that. Ing slipped a hand into one of his suit arms, encountered a shattered piece of protective shell drifting close.

The idea of drifting seemed vital, but he couldn't decide why.

Gently, he nudged the piece of shell up until it formed a rough shield over his receiver beam.

Immediately, a tinny little voice came from his speaker: "Ing! Come in, Ing! Can you hear me, Ing?" Then, more distant: "You there! To hell with the locks! Suit up and get in there. He must be down . . ."

"Poss?" Ing said.

"Ing! Is that you, Ing?"

"Yeah, Poss. I'm . . . I seem to be all in one piece."

"Are you down on the floor some place? We're coming in after you. Hold on."

"I dunno where I am. I can see beam auroras."

"Don't try to move. The tube's all smashed to hell. I'm patched through the Imbrium tube to talk to you. Just stay put. We'll be right with you."

"Poss, I don't think I'm in the tube."

From some place that Ing felt existed on a very tenuous basis, he felt his thoughts stirring, recognition patterns forming.

Some of the jewel brilliance he saw was stars. He saw that now. Some of it was . . . debris, bits and pieces of cleaners, odd chunks of matter. There was light somewhere towards his feet, but the sensors there appeared to've been destroyed or something was covering them.

Debris.

Beam auroras.

The glaring white spun once more into view. Ing adjusted his spin with a short burst from a finger jet. He saw the thing clearly now, recognized it: the ball and sensor tubes of a Seeding Compact container.

He grew conscious that the makeshift shield for his little beam had slipped. Static filled his speakers. Ing replaced the bit of shell.

". . . Do you mean you're not in the tube?" Washington's voice asked. "Ing, come in. What's wrong?"

"There's an SC container about a hundred meters or so directly in front of me," Ing said. "It's surrounded by cleaner debris. And there're auroras, angspace ribbons, all over the sky here. I . . . think I've come through."

"You couldn't have. I'm receiving you too strong. What's this about auroras?"

"That's why you're receiving me," Ing said. "You're stitching a few pieces of beam through here. Light all over the place; there's a sun down beneath my feet somewhere. You're getting through to me, but the container's almost surrounded by junk. The reflection and beam spatter in there must be enormous. I'm going in now and clean a path for the beam contact."

"Are you sure you're . . ." *Hiss, crackle.*

The little piece of shell had slipped again.

Ing eased it back into position as he maneuvered with his belt jets. "I'm all right, Poss."

The turn brought the primary into view—a great golden ball that went dim immediately as his scanner filter adjusted. To his right beyond the sun lay a great ball of blue with chunks of cottony clouds drifting over it. Ing stared, transfixed by the beauty of it.

A virgin planet.

A check of the lifeboat instruments installed in his suit showed what the SC container had revealed before contact had gone intermittent—Theta Apus IV, almost Earth normal except for larger oceans, smaller land masses.

Ing took a deep breath, smelled the canned air of his suit.

To work, he thought.

His suit jets brought him in close to the debris and he began nudging it aside, moving in closer and closer to the container. He lost his beam shield, ignored it, cut down receiver volume to reduce the static.

Presently, he drifted beside the container.

With an armored hand, he shielded his beam.

"Poss? Come in, Poss."

"Are you really there, Ing?"

"Try a beam contact with the container, Poss."

"We'll have to break contact with you."

"Do it."

Ing waited.

Auroral activity increased—great looping ribbons over the sky all around him.

So that's what it looks like at the receiving end, Ing thought. He looked up at the window revealing his own beam—clean and sharp under the shadow of his upraised hand. The armored fingers were black outlines against the blue world beyond. He began calculating then how long his own beam would last without replacement of anode and cathode. Hard bombardment, sharp tiny beam—its useful life would only be a fraction of what a big beam could expect.

Have to find a way to rig a beam once we get down, he thought.

"Ing? Come in, Ing?"

Ing heard the excitement in Washington's voice.

"You got through, eh, Poss, old hoss?"

"Loud and clear. Now, look—if you can weld yourself fast to the tail curve of that container we can get you down with it. It's over-engineered to handle twice your mass on landing sequence."

Ing nodded to himself. Riding the soft, safe balloon, which the container would presently become, offered a much more attractive prospect than maneuvering his suit down, burning it out above a watery world where a landing on solid ground would take some doing.

"We're maneuvering to give re-entry for contact with a major land mass," Washington said. "Tell us when you're fast to the container."

Ing maneuvered in close, put an armored hand on the container's surface, feeling an odd sensation of communion with the metal and life that had spent nine hundred years in the void.

Old papa Ing's going to look after you, he thought.

As he worked, welding himself solidly to the tail curve of the container, Ing recalled the chaos he had glimpsed in his spewing, jerking ride through angspace. He shuddered.

"Ing, when you feel up to it, we want a detailed report," Washington said. "We're planning now to put people through for every one of the containers that's giving trouble."

"You figured out how to get us back?" Ing asked.

"Earthside says it has the answer if you can assemble enough mass at your end to anchor a full-sized beam." Again Ing thought of that ride through chaos. He wasn't sure he wanted another such trip. Time to solve that problem when it arose, though. There'd be something in the book about it.

Ing smiled at himself then, sensing an instinctive reason for all the handbooks of history. Against chaos, man had to raise a precise and orderly alignment of actions, a system within which he could sense his own existence.

A watery world down there, he thought. *Have to find some way to make paper for these kids before they come out of their vats. Plenty of things to teach them.*

Watery world.

He recalled then a sentence of swimming instructions from the "Blue Jackets Manual," one of the ancient handbooks in his collection: "Breathing may be accomplished by swimming with the head out of water."

Have to remember that one, he thought. *The kids'll need a secure and orderly world.*

THE
FEATHERBEDDERS

Once there was a Slorin with a one-syllable name who is believed to have said: "niche for every one of us and every one of us in his niche."

—Folk saying of the *Scattership* People

There must be a streak of madness in a Slorin who'd bring his only offspring, an untrained and untried youth, on a mission as potentially dangerous as this one, Smeg told himself.

The rationale behind his decision remained clear: The colonial nucleus must preserve its elders for their detail memory. The youngest of the group was the logical one to be volunteered for this risk. Still . . .

Smeg forced such thoughts out of his mind. They weakened him. He concentrated on driving the gray motor-pool Plymouth they'd signed out of the government garage in the state capital that morning. The machine demanded considerable attention.

The Plymouth was only two years old, but this region's red rock roads and potholes had multiplied those years by a factor of at least four. The steering was loose and assorted squeaks arose from front and rear as he negotiated a rutted downgrade. The road took them into a shadowed gulch almost bare of vegetation and across the rattling planks of a wooden bridge that spanned a dry creekbed. They climbed out the other side through ancient erosion gullies, past a zone of scrub cottonwoods and onto the reaching flat land they'd been crossing for two hours.

Smeg risked a glance at Rick, his offspring, riding silently beside him. The youth had come out of the pupal stage with a passable human shape. No doubt Rick would do better next time—provided he had the opportunity. But he was well within the seventy-five percent accuracy limit the Slorin set for themselves. It was a universal fact that the untrained sentience saw what it *thought* it saw. The mind tended to supply the missing elements.

A nudge from the Slorin mindcloud helped, of course, but this carried its own perils. The nudged mind sometimes developed powers of its own—with terrifying results. Slorin had learned long ago to depend on the directional broadcast of the mind's narrow band, and to locate themselves in a network limited by the band's rather short range.

However, Rick had missed none of the essentials for human appearance. He had a gentle, slender face whose contours were difficult to remember. His brown eyes were of a limpid softness that made human females discard all suspicions while the males concentrated on jealousy. Rick's hair was a coarse, but acceptable black. The shoulders were a bit high and the thorax somewhat too heroic, but the total effect aroused no probing questions.

That was the important thing: no probing questions.

Smeg permitted himself a silent sigh. His own shape—that of a middle-aged government official, gray at the temples, slightly paunchy and bent of shoulder, and with weak eyes behind gold-rimmed glasses—was more in the Slorin tradition.

Live on the margins, Smeg thought. *Attract no attention.*

In other words, don't do what they were doing today.

Awareness of danger forced Smeg into extreme contact with this body his plastic genes had fashioned. It was a good body, a close enough duplicate to interbreed with the natives, but he felt it now from the inside, as it were, a fabric of newness stretched over the ancient substance of the Slorin. It was familiar, yet bothersomely unfamiliar.

I am Sumctroxelunsmeg, he reminded himself. *I am a Slorin of seven syllables, each addition to my name an honor to my family. By the pupa of my jelly-sire whose name took fourteen thousand heartbeats to pronounce, I shall not fail!*

There! That was the spirit he needed—the eternal wanderer, temporarily disciplined, yet without boundaries. "If you want to swim, you must enter the water," he whispered.

"Did you say something, Dad?" Rick asked.

Ahhh, that was very good, Smeg thought. Dad—the easy colloquialism.

"I was girding myself for the ordeal, so to speak," Smeg said. "We must separate in a few minutes." He nodded ahead to where a town was beginning to hump itself out of the horizon.

"I think I should barge right in and start asking about their sheriff," Rick said.

Smeg drew in a sharp breath, a gesture of surprise that fitted this body. "Feel out the situation first," he said.

More and more, he began to question the wisdom of sending Rick in there. Dangerous, damnably dangerous. Rick could get himself irrevocably killed, ruined beyond the pupa's powers to restore. Worse than that, he could be exposed. There was the real danger. Give natives the knowledge of what they were fighting and they tended to develop extremely effective methods.

Slorin memory carried a bagful of horror stories to verify this fact.

"The Slorin must remain ready to take any shape, adapt to any situation," Rick said. "That it?"

Rick spoke the axiom well, Smeg thought, but did he really understand it? How could he? Rick still didn't have full control of the behavior patterns that went with this particular body shape. Again, Smeg sighed. If only they'd saved the infiltration squad, the expendable specialists.

Thoughts such as this always brought the more disquieting question: *Saved them from what?*

There had been five hundred pupae in the *Scattership* before the unknown disaster. Now, there were four secondary ancestors and one new offspring created on this planet. They were shipless castaways on an unregistered world, not knowing even the nature of the disaster which had sent them scooting across the void in an escape capsule with minimum shielding.

Four of them had emerged from the capsule as basic Slorin polymorphs to find themselves in darkness on a steep landscape of rocks and trees. At morning, there'd been four additional trees there—watching, listening, weighing the newness against memories accumulated across a time-span in which billions of planets such as this one could have developed and died.

The capsule had chosen an excellent landing site: no nearby sentient constructions. The Slorin now knew the region's native label—central British Columbia. In that period of awakening, though, it had been a place of unknown dangers whose chemistry and organization required the most cautious testing.

In time, four black bears had shambled down out of the mountains. Approaching civilization, they'd hidden and watched—listening, always listening, never daring to use the mindcloud. Who knew what mental powers the natives might have? Four roughly fashioned hunters had been metamorphosed from Slorin pupae in a brush-screened cave. The hunters had been tested, refined.

Finally—the hunters had scattered.

Slorin always scattered.

"When we left Washington you said something about the possibility of a trap," Rick said. "You don't really think—"

"Slorin have been unmasked on some worlds," Smeg said. "Natives have developed situational protective devices. This has some of the characteristics of such a trap."

"Then why investigate? Why not leave it alone until we're stronger?"

"Rick!" Smeg shuddered at the youth's massive ignorance. "Other capsules may have escaped," he said.

"But if it's a Slorin down here, he's acting like a dangerous fool."

"More reason to investigate. We could have a damaged pupa here, one who lost part of the detail memory. Perhaps he doesn't know how to act—except out of instincts."

"Then why not stay out of the town and probe just a little bit with the mindcloud?"

Rick cannot be trusted with this job, Smeg thought. *He's too raw, too full of the youthful desire to play with the mindcloud.*

"Why not?" Rick repeated.

Smeg pulled the car to a stop at the side of the dirt road, opened his window. It was getting hot—be noon in about an hour. The landscape was a hardscrabble flatness marked by sparse vegetation and a clump of buildings about two miles ahead. Broken fences lined both sides of the road. Low cottonwoods off to the right betrayed the presence of the dry creekbed. Two scrofulous oaks in the middle distance provided shade for several steers. Away on the rim of the badland, obscured by haze, there was a suggestion of hills.

"You going to try my suggestion?" Risk asked.

"No."

"Then why're we stopping? This as far as you go?"

"No." Smeg sighed. "This is as far as *you* go. I'm changing plans. You will wait. I will go into the village."

"But I'm the younger. I'm—"

"And I'm in command here."

"The others won't like this. They said—"

"The others will understand my decision."

"But Slorin law says—"

"Don't quote Slorin law to me!"

"But—"

"Would you teach your grandfather how to shape a pupa?" Smeg shook his head. Rick must learn how to control the anger which flared in this bodily creation. "The limit of the law is the limit of enforcement—the real limit of organized society. We're not an organized society. We're two Slorin—alone, cut off from our pitiful net. Alone! Two Slorin of widely disparate ability. You are capable of carrying a message. I do not judge you capable of meeting the challenge in this village."

Smeg reached across Rick, opened the door.

"This is a firm decision?" Rick asked.

"It is. You know what to do?"

Rick spoke stiffly: "I take that kit of yours from the back and I play the part of a soil engineer from the Department of Agriculture."

"Not a *part*, Rick. You *are* a soil engineer."

"But—"

"You will make real tests which will go into a real report and be sent to a real office with a real function. In the event of disaster, you will assume my shape and step into my niche."

"I see."

"I truly hope you do. Meanwhile, you will go out across that field. The dry creekbed is out there. See those cottonwoods?"

"I've identified the characteristics of this landscape."

"Excellent. Don't deviate. Remember that you're the offspring of Sumctroxelunsmeg. Your jelly-sire's name took fourteen thousand heartbeats to pronounce. Live with pride."

"I was supposed to go in there, take the risk of it—"

"There are risks and there are risks. Remember, make real tests for a real report. Never betray your niche. When you have made the tests, find a place in that creekbed to secrete yourself. Dig in and wait. Listen on the narrow band at all times. Listen, that is all you do. In the event of disaster, you must get word to the others. In the kit there's a dog collar with a tag bearing a promise of reward and the address of our Chicago drop. Do you know the greyhound shape?"

"I know the plan, Dad."

Rick slid out of the car. He removed a heavy black case from the rear, closed the doors, stared in at his parent.

Smeg leaned across the seat, opened the window. It creaked dismally.

"Good luck, Dad," Rick said.

Smeg swallowed. This body carried a burden of attachment to an offspring much stronger than any in previous Slorin experience. He wondered how the offspring felt about the parent, tried to probe his own feelings toward the one who'd created him, trained him, sealed his pupa into the *Scattership*. There was no sense of loss. In some ways, he *was* the parent. As different experiences changed him, he would become more and more the individual, however. Syllables would be added to his name. Perhaps, someday, he might feel an urge to be reunited.

"Don't lose your cool, Dad," Rick said.

"The God of Slorin has no shape," Smeg said. He closed the window, straightened himself behind the steering wheel.

Rick turned, trudged off across the field toward the cottonwoods. A low cloud of dust marked his progress. He carried the black case easily in his right hand.

Smeg put the car in motion, concentrated on driving. That last glimpse of Rick, sturdy and obedient, had pierced him with unexpected emotions. Slorin parted, he told himself. It is natural for Slorin to part. An offspring is merely an offspring.

A Slorin prayer came into his mind. "Lord, let me possess this moment without regrets, and, losing it, gain it forever."

The prayer helped, but Smeg still felt the tug of that parting. He stared at the shabby building of his target town. Someone in this collection of structures Smeg was now entering had not learned a basic Slorin lesson: *There is a reason for living; Slorin must not live in a way that destroys this reason.*

Moderation, that was the key.

A man stood in the dusty sunglare toward the center of the town—one lone man beside the dirt road that ran unchecked toward the distant horizon. For one haunted moment Smeg had the feeling it was not a man, but a dangerous other-shaped enemy he'd met before. The feeling passed as Smeg brought the car to a stop nearby.

Here was the American peasant, Smeg realized—tall, lean, dressed in wash-faded blue bib overalls, a dirty tan shirt and tennis shoes. The shoes were coming apart to reveal bare toes. A ground green painter's hat with green plastic visor did an ineffective job of covering his yellow hair. The visor's rim was cracked. It dripped a fringe of ragged binding that swayed when the man moved his head.

Smeg leaned out his window, smiled: "Howdy."

"How do."

Smeg's sense of hearing, trained in a history of billions of such encounters, detected the xenophobia and reluctant bowing to convention at war in the man's voice.

"Town's pretty quiet," Smeg said.

"Yep."

Purely human accents, Smeg decided. He permitted himself to relax somewhat, asked: "Anything unusual ever happen around here?"

"You fum the gov'ment?"

"That's right." Smeg tapped the motor-pool insignia on his door. "Department of Agriculture."

"Then you ain't part of the gov'ment conspiracy?"

"Conspiracy?" Smeg studied the man for a clue to hidden meanings. Was this one of those southern towns where anything from the government just had to be communist?

"Guess you ain't," the man said.

"Of course not."

"That there was a serious question you asked, then . . . about unusual thing happening?"

"I . . . yes."

"Depends on what you call unusual."

"What . . . do *you* call unusual?" Smeg ventured.

"Can't rightly say. And you?"

Smeg frowned, leaned out his window, looked up and down the street, studied each detail: the dog sniffing under the porch of a building labeled "General Store," the watchful blankness of windows with here and there a twitching curtain to betray someone peering out, the missing boards on the side of a gas station beyond the store—one rusty pump there with its glass chamber empty. Every aspect of the town spoke of heat-addled somnolence . . . yet it was wrong. Smeg could feel tensions, transient emotional eddies that irritated his highly tuned senses. He hoped Rick already had a hiding place and was listening.

"This is Wadeville, isn't it?" Smeg asked.

"Yep. Used to be county seat 'fore the war."

He meant the War Between The States, Smeg realized, recalling his studies of regional history. As always, the Slorin were using every spare moment to absorb history, mythology, arts, literature, science—You never knew which might be the valuable piece of information.

"Ever hear about someone could get right into your mind?" the man asked.

Smeg overcame a shock reaction, groped for the proper response. Amused disbelief, he decided, and managed a small chuckle. "That the unusual thing you have around here?"

"Didn't say yes; didn't say no."

"Why'd you ask then?" Smeg knew his voice sounded like crinkling bread wrapper. He pulled his head back into the car's shadows.

"I jes' wondered if you might be hunting fer a teleepath?"

The man turned, hawked a cud of tobacco toward the dirt at his left. A vagrant breeze caught the spittle, draped it across the side of Smeg's car.

"Oh, dang!" the man said. He produced a dirty yellow bandanna, knelt and scrubbed with it at the side of the car.

Smeg leaned out, studied this performance with an air of puzzlement. The man's responses, the vague hints at mental powers—they were confusing, fitted no pattern in Slorin experience.

"You got somebody around here claiming to be a telepath?" Smeg asked.

"Can't say." The man stood up, peered in at Smeg. "Sorry about that there. Wind, y'know. Accident. Didn't mean no harm."

"Certainly."

"Hope you won't say nothing to the sheriff. Got 'er all cleaned off your car now. Can't tell where I hit 'er."

The man's voice carried a definite tone of fear, Smeg realized. He stared at this American peasant with a narrow, searching gaze. *Sheriff,* he'd said. Was it going to be this easy? Smeg wondered how to capitalize on that opening. Sheriff. Here was an element of the mystery they'd come to investigate.

As the silence drew out, the man said: "Got 'er all clean. You can get out and look for yourself."

"I'm sure you did, Mr. . . . ahhh . . ."

"Painter, Josh'a Painter. Most folks call me Josh on account of my first name there, Josh'a Painter."

"Pleased to meet you, Mr. Painter. My name's Smeg, Henry Smeg."

"Smeg," Painter said with a musing tone. "Don't rightly believe I ever heard that name before."

"It used to be much longer," Smeg said. "Hungarian."

"Oh."

"I'm curious, Mr. Painter, why you'd be afraid I might tell the sheriff because the wind blew a little tobacco juice on my car?"

"Never can tell how some folks'll take things," Painter said. He looked from one end of Smeg's car to the other, back to Smeg. "You a gov'ment man, this car an' all, reckoned I'd best be sure, one sensible man to another."

"You've been having trouble with the government around here, is that it?"

"Don't take kindly to most gov'ment men hereabouts, we don't. But the sheriff, he don't allow us to do anything about that. Sheriff is a mean man, a certain mean man sometimes, and he's got my Barton."

"Your barton," Smeg said, drawing back into the car to conceal his puzzlement. *Barton?* This was an entirely new term. Strange that none of them had encountered it before. The study of languages and dialects had been most thorough. Smeg began to feel uneasy about his entire conversation with this Painter. The conversation had never really been under control. He wondered how much of it he'd actually understood. There was in Smeg a longing to venture a mindcloud probe, to nudge the man's motives, make him *want* to explain.

"You one of them survey fellows like we been getting?" Painter asked.

"You might say that," Smeg said. He straightened his shoulders. "I'd like to walk around and look at your town, Mr. Painter. May I leave my car here?"

"'Tain't in the way that I can see," Painter said. He managed to appear both interested and disinterested in Smeg's question. His glance flicked sideways, all around—at the car, the road, at a house behind a privet hedge across the way.

"Fine," Smeg said. He got out, slammed the door, reached into the back for the flat-crowned Western hat he affected in these parts. It tended to break down some barriers.

"You forgetting your papers?" Painter asked.

"Papers?" Smeg turned, looked at the man.

"Them papers full of questions you gov'ment people allus use."

"Oh." Smeg shook his head. "We can forget about papers today."

"You jes' going to wander around?" Painter asked.

"That's right."

"Well, some folks'll talk to you," Painter said. "Got all kinds of different folks here." He turned away, started to walk off.

"Please, just a minute," Smeg said.

Painter stopped as though he'd run into a barrier, spoke without turning. "You want something?"

"Where're you going, Mr. Painter?"

"Jes' down the road a piece."

"I'd . . . ahhh, hoped you might guide me," Smeg said. "That is if you haven't anything better to do?"

Painter turned, stared at him. "Guide? In Wadeville?" He looked around him, back to Smeg. A tiny smile tugged at his mouth.

"Well, where do I find your sheriff, for instance?" Smeg asked.

The smile disappeared. "Why'd you want him?"

"Sheriffs usually know a great deal about an area."

"You sure you actual' want to see him?"

"Sure. Where's his office?"

"Well now, Mr. Smeg . . ." Painter hesitated, then: "His office is just around the corner here, next the bank."

"Would you show me?" Smeg moved forward, his feet kicking up dust puddles in the street. "Which corner?"

"This'n right here." Painter pointed to a fieldstone building at his left. A weed-grown lane led off past it. The corner of a wooden porch jutted from the stone building into the lane.

Smeg walked past Painter, peered down the lane. Tufts of grass grew in the middle and along both sides, green runners stretching all through the area. Smeg doubted that a wheeled vehicle had been down this way in two years—possibly longer.

A row of objects on the porch caught his attention. He moved closer, studied them, turned back to Painter.

"What're all those bags and packages on that porch?"

"Them?" Painter came up beside Smeg, stood a moment, lips pursed, eyes focused beyond the porch.

"Well, what are they?" Smeg pressed.

"This here's the bank," Painter said. "Them's night deposits."

Smeg turned back to the porch. Night deposits? Paper bags and fabric sacks left out in the open?

"People leaves 'em here if'n the bank ain't open," Painter said. "Bank's a little late opening today. Sheriff had 'em in looking at the books last night."

Sheriff examining the bank's books? Smeg wondered. He hoped Rick was missing none of this and could repeat it accurately . . . just in case. The situation here appeared far more mysterious than the reports had indicated. Smeg didn't like the feeling of this place at all.

"Makes it convenient for people who got to get up early and them that collects their money at night,' Painter explained.

"They just leave it right out in the open?" Smeg asked.

"Yep. 'Night deposit' it's called. People don't have to come aound when—"

"I know what it's called! But . . . right out in the open like that . . . without a guard?"

"Bank don't open till ten thirty most days," Painter said. "Even later when the sheriff's had 'em in at night."

"There's a guard," Smeg said. "That's it, isn't it?"

"Guard? What we need a guard fer? Sheriff says leave them things alone, they gets left alone."

The sheriff again, Smeg thought. "Who . . . ahh deposits money like this?" he asked.

"Like I said: the people who got to get up early and . . ."

"But *who* are these people?"

"Oh. Well, my cousin Reb: He has the gas station down to the forks. Mr. Seelway at the General Store there. Some farmers with cash crops come back late from the city. Folks work across the line at the mill in Anderson when they get paid late of a Friday. Folks like that."

"They just . . . leave their money out on this porch."

"Why not?"

"Lord knows," Smeg whispered.

"Sheriff says don't touch it, why—it don't get touched."

Smeg looked around him, sensing the strangeness of this weed-grown street with its wide-open night depository protected only by a sheriff's command. Who was this sheriff? *What* was this sheriff?

"Doesn't seem like there'd be much money in Wadeville," Smeg said. "That gas station down the main street out there looks abandoned, looks like a good wind would blow it over. Most of the other buildings—"

"Station's closed," Painter said. "You need gas, just go out to the forks where my cousin, Reb—"

"Station failed?" Smeg asked.

"Kind of."

"Kind of?"

"Sheriff, he closed it."

"Why?"

"Fire hazard. Sheriff, he got to reading the state Fire Ordinance one day. Next day he told ol' Jamison to dig up the gas tanks and cart 'em away. They was too old and rusty, not deep enough in the ground and didn't have no concrete on 'em. 'Sides that, the building's too old, wood all oily."

"The sheriff ordered it . . . just like that." Smeg snapped his fingers.

"Yep. Said he had to tear down that station. Ol' Jamison sure was mad."

"But if the sheriff says do it, then it gets done?" Smeg asked.

"Yep. Jamison's tearing it down—one board every day. Sheriff don't seem to pay it no mind long as Jamison takes down that one board every day."

Smeg shook his head. One board every day. What did that signify? Lack of a strong time sense? He looked back at the night deposits on the porch, asked: "How long have people been depositing their money here this way?"

"Been since a week or so after the sheriff come."

"And how long has that been?"

"Ohhhhh . . . four, five years maybe."

Smeg nodded to himself. His little group of Slorin had been on the planet slightly more than five years. This could be . . . this could be—He frowned. But what if it wasn't?

The dull plodding of footsteps sounded from the main street behind Smeg. He turned, saw a tall fat man passing there. The man glanced curiously at Smeg, nodded to Painter.

"Mornin', Josh," the fat man said. It was a rumbling voice.

"Mornin', Jim," Painter said.

The fat man skirted the Plymouth, hesitated to read the emblem on the car door, glanced back at Painter, resumed his plodding course down the street and out of sight.

"That was Jim," Painter said.

"Neighbor?"

"Yep. Been over to the Widow McNabry's again . . . all the whole dang' night. Sheriff's going to be mighty displeasured, believe me."

"He keeps an eye on your morals, too?"

"Morals?" Painter scratched the back of his neck. "Can't rightly say he does."

"Then why would he mind if . . . Jim—"

"Sheriff, he says it's a sin and a crime to take what don't belong to you, but it's a blessing to give. Jim, he stood right up to the sheriff, said he jes' went to the widow's to give. So—" Painter shrugged.

"The sheriff's open to persuasion, then?"

"Some folks seem to think so."

"You don't?"

"He made Jim stop smoking and drinking."

Smeg shook his head sharply, wondering if he'd heard correctly. The conversation kept darting around into seeming irrelevancies. He adjusted his hat brim, looked at his hand. It was a good hand, couldn't be told from the human original. "Smoking and drinking?" he asked.

"Yep."

"But why?"

"Said if Jim was taking on new ree-sponsibilities like the widow he couldn't commit suicide—not even slow like."

Smeg stared at Painter who appeared engrossed with a nonexistent point in the sky. Presently, Smeg managed: "That's the weirdest interpretation of the law I ever heard."

"Don't let the sheriff hear you say that."

"Quick to anger, eh?"

"Wouldn't say that."

"What *would* you say?"

"Like I told Jim: Sheriff get his eye on you, that is it. You going to toe the line. Ain't so bad till the sheriff get his eye on you. When he see you—that is the end."

"Does the sheriff have his eye on you, Mr. Painter?"

Painter made a fist, shook it at the air. His mouth drew back in a fierce, scowling grimace. The expression faded. Presently, he relaxed, sighed.

"Pretty bad, eh?" Smeg asked.

"Dang conspiracy," Painter muttered. "Gov'ment got its nose in things don't concern it."

"Oh?" Smeg watched Painter closely, sensing they were on productive ground. "What does—"

"Dang near a thousand gallons a year!" Painter exploded.

"Uhhh—" Smeg said. He wet his lips with his tongue, a gesture he'd found to denote human uncertainty.

"Don't care if you are part of the conspiracy," Painter said. "Can't do nothing to me now."

"Believe me, Mr. Painter, I have no designs on . . ."

"I made some 'shine when folks wanted," Painter said. "Less'n a thousand gallons a year . . . almost. Ain't much considering the size of some of them stills t'other side of Anderson. But them's across the line! 'Nother county! All I made was enough fer the folks 'round here."

"Sheriff put a stop to it?"

"Made me bust up my still."

"Made *you* bust up your still?"

"Yep. That's when he got my Barton."

"Your . . . ahhh . . . barton?" Smeg ventured.

"Right from under Lilly's nose," Painter muttered. His nostrils dilated, eyes glared. Rage lay close to the surface.

Smeg looked around him, searching the blank windows, the empty doorways. What in the name of all the Slorin furies was a barton?

"Your sheriff seems to hold pretty close to the law," Smeg ventured.

"Hah!"

"No liquor," Smeg said. "No smoking. He rough on speeders?"

"Speeders?" Painter turned his glare on Smeg. "Now, you tell me what we'd speed in, Mr. Smeg."

"Don't you have any cars here?"

"If my cousin Reb didn't have his station over to the forks where he get the city traffic, he'd be bust long ago. State got a law—car got to stop in jes' so many lights. Got to have windshield wiper things. Got to have tires which you can measure the tread on. Got to steer ab-solutely jes' right. Car don't do them things, it is *junk*. Junk! Sheriff, he make you sell that car for junk! Ain't but two, three folks in Wadeville can afford a car with all them things."

"He sounds pretty strict," Smeg said.

"Bible-totin' parson with hell fire in his eyes couldn't be worse. I tell you, if that sheriff didn't have my Barton, I'd a run out long ago. I'd a ree-beled like we done in Sixty-one. Same with the rest of the folks here . . . most of 'em."

"He has their . . . ahhh, bartons?" Smeg asked, cocking his head to one side, waiting.

Painter considered this for a moment, then: "Well, now . . . in a manner of speaking, you could call it that way."

Smeg frowned. Did he dare ask what a barton was? No! It might betray too much ignorance. He longed for a proper Slorin net, all the interlocked detail memories, the Slorin spaced out within the limits of the narrow band, ready to relay questions, test hypotheses, offer suggestions. But he was alone except for one inexperienced offspring hiding out there across the fields . . . waiting for disaster. Perhaps Rick had encountered the word, though. Smeg ventured a weak interrogative.

Back came Rick's response, much too loud: "Negative."

So Rick didn't know the word either.

Smeg studied Painter for a sign the man had detected the narrow band exchange. Nothing. Smeg swallowed, a natural fear response he'd noticed in this body, decided to move ahead more strongly.

"Anybody ever tell you you have a most unusual sheriff?" he asked.

"Them gov'ment survey fellows, that's what they say. Come here with all them papers and all them questions, say they interested in our crime rate. Got no crime in Wade County, they say. Think they telling us something!"

"That's what I heard about you," Smeg offered. "No crime."

"Hah!"

"But there must be some crime," Smeg said.

"Got no 'shine," Painter muttered. "Got no robbing and stealing, no gambling. Got no drunk drivers 'cepting they come from somewheres else and then they is mighty displeasured they drunk drove in Wade County. Got no *ju*venile dee-linquents like they talk about in the city. Got no patent medicine fellows. Got nothing."

"You must have a mighty full jail, though."

"Jail?"

"All the criminals your sheriff apprehends."

"Hah! Sheriff don't throw folks in jail, Mr. Smeg. Not 'less they is from over the line and needs to sleep off a little ol' spree while they sobers up enough to pay the fine."

"Oh?" Smeg stared out at the empty main street, remembering the fat man—Jim. "He gives the local residents a bit more latitude, eh? Like your friend, Jim."

"Jes' leading Jim along, I say."

"What do you mean?"

"Pretty soon the widow's going to be in the family way. Going to be a quick wedding and a baby and Jim'll be jes' like all the rest of us."

Smeg nodded as though he understood. It was like the reports which had lured him here . . . but unlike them, too. Painter's "survey fellows" had been amused by Wadeville and Wade County, so amused even their driest governmentese couldn't conceal it. Their amusement had written the area off— "purely a local phenomenon." Tough southern sheriff. Smeg was not amused. He walked slowly out to the main street, looked back along the road he'd traveled.

Rick was out there listening . . . waiting.

What would the waiting produce?

An abandoned building up the street caught Smeg's attention. Somewhere within it a door creaked with a rhythm that matched the breeze stirring the dust in the street. A "SALOON" sign dangled from the building on a broken guy wire. The sign swayed in the wind—now partly obscured by a porch roof, now revealed: "LOON" . . . "SALOON" . . . "LOON" . . . "SALOON" . . .

The mystery of Wadeville was like that sign, Smeg thought. The mystery moved and changed, now one thing, now another. He wondered how he could hold the mystery still long enough to examine it and understand it.

A distant wailing interrupted his reverie.

It grew louder—a siren.

"Here he come," Painter said.

Smeg glanced at Painter. The man was standing beside him glaring in the direction of the siren.

"Here he sure do come," Painter muttered.

Another sound accompanied the siren now—the hungry throbbing of a powerful motor.

Smeg looked toward the sound, saw a dust cloud on the horizon, something vaguely red within it.

"Dad! Dad!" That was Rick on the narrow band.

Before he could send out the questioning thought, Smeg felt it—the growing force of a mindcloud so strong it made him stagger.

Painter caught his arm, steadied him.

"Gets some folks that way the first time," Painter said.

Smeg composed himself, disengaged his arm, stood trembling. Another Slorin! It had to be another Slorin. But the fool was broadcasting a signal that could bring down chaos on them all. Smeg looked at Painter. The natives had the potential—his own Slorin group had determined this. Were they in luck here? Was the local strain insensitive? But Painter had spoken of it getting some folks the first time. He'd spoken of telepaths.

Something was very wrong in Wadeville . . . and the mindcloud was enveloping him like a gray fog. Smeg summoned all his mental energy, fought free of the controlling force. He felt himself standing there then like an island of clarity and calm in the midst of that mental hurricane.

There were sharp sounds all around him now—window blinds snapping up, doors slamming. People began to emerge. They lined the street, a dull-eyed look of expectancy about them, an angry wariness. They appeared to be respectable humans all, Smeg thought, but there was a sameness about them he couldn't quite define. It had something to do with a dowdy, slump-shouldered look.

"You going to see the sheriff," Painter said. "That's for sure."

Smeg faced the oncoming thunder of motor and siren. A long red fire truck with a blonde young woman in green leotards astride its hood emerged from the dust cloud, hurtled down the street toward the narrow passage where Smeg had parked his car.

At the wheel of the truck sat what appeared to be a dark-skinned man in a white suit, dark blue shirt, a white ten-gallon hat. A gold star glittered at his breast. He clutched the steering wheel like a racing driver, head low, eyes forward.

Smeg, free of the mindcloud, saw the driver for what he was—a Slorin, still in polymorph, his shape approximating the human . . . but not well enough . . . not well enough at all.

Clustered around the driver, on the truck's seat, clinging to the sides and the ladders on top, were some thirty children. As they entered the village, they began yelling and laughing, screaming greetings.

"There's the sheriff," Painter said. "That unusual enough fer you?"

The truck swerved to avoid Smeg's car, skidded to a stop opposite the lane where he stood with Painter. The sheriff stood up, looked back toward the parked car, shouted: "Who parked that auto*mo*bile there? You see how I had to swing way out to git past it? Somebody tear down my 'No Parking' sign again? Look out if you did! You know I'll find out who you are! Who did that?"

While the sheriff was shouting, the children were tumbling off the truck in a cacophony of greetings—"Hi, Mama!" "Daddy, you see me?" "We been all the way to Commanche Lake swimming." "You see the way we come, Pa?" "You make a pie for me, Mama? Sheriff says I kin have a pie."

Smeg shook his head at the confusion. All were off the truck now except the sheriff and the blonde on the hood. The mindcloud pervaded the mental atmosphere like a strong odor, but it stopped none of the outcry.

Abruptly, there came the loud, spitting crack of a rifle shot. A plume of dust burst from the sheriff's white suit just below the golden star.

Silence settled over the street.

Slowly, the sheriff turned, the only moving figure in the frozen tableaux. He looked straight up the street toward an open window in the second story of a house beyond the abandoned service station. His hand came up; a finger extruded. He shook his finger, a man admonishing a naughty child.

"I warned you," he said.

Smeg uttered a Slorin curse under his breath. The fool! No wonder he was staying in polymorph and relying on the mindcloud—the whole village was in arms against him. Smeg searched through his accumulated Slorin experience for a clue on how to resolve this situation. A whole village aware of Slorin powers! Oh, that sinful fool!

The sheriff looked down at the crowd of silent children, staring first at one and then another. Presently, he pointed to a barefoot girl of about eleven, her yellow hair tied in pigtails, a soiled blue and white dress on her gangling frame.

"You there, Molly Mae," the sheriff said. "You see what your daddy done?"

The girl lowered her head and began to cry.

The blonde on the truck's hood leaped down with a lithe grace, tugged at the sheriffs sleeve.

"Don't interrupt the law in the carrying out of its duties," the sheriff said.

The blonde put her hands on her hips, stamped a foot. "Tad, you hurt that child and I won't never speak to you, never again," she said.

Painter began muttering half under his breath: "No . . . no . . . no . . . no—"

"Hurt Molly Mae?" the sheriff asked. "Now, you know I won't hurt her. But she's got to go away, never see her kin again as long as she lives. You know that."

"But Molly Mae didn't do you no hurt," the young woman said. "It were her daddy. Why can't you send him away?"

"There's some things you just can't understand," the sheriff said. "Grown up adult can only be taken from sinful, criminal ways a slow bit at a time 'less'n you make a little child of him. Now, I'd be doing the crime if I made a little child out of a grown-up adult. Little girl like Molly Mae, she's a child right now. Don't make much difference."

So that was it, Smeg thought. That was the sheriff's real hold on this community. Smeg suddenly felt that a barton had to mean—a hostage.

"It's cruel," the blonde young woman said.

"Law's got to be cruel sometimes," the sheriff said. "Law got to eliminate crime. Almost got it done. Only crimes we had hereabouts for months are crimes 'gainst me. Now, you all know you can't get away with crimes like that. But when you show that *dis*regard for the majesty of the law, you got to be punished. You got to remember, all of you, that every part of a family is ree-sponsible for the whole entire family."

Pure Slorin thinking, Smeg thought. He wondered if he could make his move without exposing his own alien origins. Something had to be done here and soon. Did he dare venture a probe of greeting into the fool's mind? No. The sheriff probably wouldn't even receive the greeting through that mindcloud noise.

"Maybe you're doing something wrong then," the young woman said. "Seems awful funny to me when the only crimes are put right on the law itself."

A very pertinent observation, Smeg thought.

Abruptly, Painter heaved himself into motion, lurched through the crowd of children toward the sheriff.

The blonde young woman turned, said: "Daddy! You stay out'n this."

"You be still now, you hear, Barton Marie?" Painter growled.

"You know you can't do anything," she wailed. "He'll only send me away."

"Good! I say good!" Painter barked. He pushed in front of the young woman, stood glaring up at the sheriff.

"Now, Josh," the sheriff said, his voice mild.

They fell silent, measuring each other.

In this moment, Smeg's attention was caught by a figure walking toward them on the road into the village. The figure emerged from the dust—a young man carrying a large black case.

Rick!

Smeg stared at his offspring. The young man walked like a puppet, loose at the knees. His eyes stared ahead with a blank seeking.

The mindcloud, Smeg thought. *Rick was young, weak. He'd been calling out, wide open when the mindcloud struck. The force that had staggered a secondary ancestor had stunned the young Slorin. He was coming now blindly toward the irritation source.*

"Who that coming there?" the sheriff called. "That the one parked this car illegal?"

"Rick!" Smeg shouted.

Rick stopped.

"Stay where you are!" Smeg called. This time, he sent an awakening probe into the youth.

Rick stared around him, awareness creeping into his eyes. He focused on Smeg, mouth falling open.

"Dad!"

"Who're you?" the sheriff demanded, staring at Smeg. A jolt from the mindcloud jarred Smeg.

There was only one way to do this, Smeg realized. Fight fire with fire. The natives already had felt the mindcloud.

Smeg began opening the enclosing mental shields, dropped them abruptly and lashed out at the sheriff. The Slorin polymorph staggered back, slumped onto the truck seat. His human shape twisted, writhed.

"Who're you?" the sheriff gasped.

Shifting to the Slorin gutturals, Smeg said: "I will ask the questions here. Identify yourself."

Smeg moved forward, a path through the children opening for him. Gently, he moved Painter and the young woman aside.

"Do you understand me?" Smeg demanded.

"I . . . understand you." The Slorin gutturals were rough and halting, but recognizable.

In a softer tone, Smeg said: "The universe has many crossroads where friends can meet. Identify yourself."

"Min . . . I think. Pzilimin." The sheriff straightened himself on the seat, restored some of his human shape to its previous form. "Who are you?"

"I am Sumctroxelunsmeg, secondary ancestor."

"What's a secondary ancestor?"

Smeg sighed. It was pretty much as he had feared. The name, Pzilimin, that was the primary clue—a tertiary ancestor from the *Scattership.* But this poor Slorin had been damaged, somehow, lost part of his detail memory. In the process, he had created a situation here that might be impossible to rectify. The extent of the local mess had to be examined now, though.

"I will answer your questions later," Smeg said. "Meanwhile—"

"You know this critter?" Painter asked. "You part of the conspiracy?"

Shifting to English, Smeg said: "Mr. Painter, let the government handle its own problems. This man is one of our problems."

"Well, he sure is a problem and that's the truth."

"Will you let me handle him?"

"You sure you can do it?"

"I . . . think so."

"I sure hope so."

Smeg nodded, turned back to the sheriff. "Have you any idea what you've done here?" he asked in basic Slorin.

"I . . . found myself a suitable official position and filled it to the best of my ability. Never betray your niche. I remember that. Never betray your niche."

"Do you know what you are?"

"I'm . . . a Slorin?"

"Correct. A Slorin tertiary ancestor. Have you any idea how you were injured?"

"I . . . no. Injured?" He looked around at the people drawing closer, all staring curiously. "I . . . woke up out there in the . . . field. Couldn't . . . remember—"

"Very well, we'll—"

"I remembered one thing! We were supposed to lower the crime rate, prepare a suitable society in which . . . in which . . . I . . . don't know."

Smeg stared across the children's heads at Rick who had come to a stop behind the truck, returned his attention to Pzilimin.

"I have the crime rate here almost down to an irreducible minimum," the Slorin sheriff said.

Smeg passed a hand across his eyes. Irreducible minimum! He dropped his hand, glared up at the poor fool. "You have made these people aware of Slorin," he accused. "You've made them aware of themselves, which is worse. You've started them thinking about what's behind the law. Something every native law enforcement offical on this planet knows by instinct, and you, a Slorin—injured or not—couldn't see it."

"See what?" Pzilimin asked.

"Without crime there's no need for law enforcement officers! We are here to prepare niches in which Slorin can thrive. And you begin by doing yourself out of a job! The first rule in any position is to maintain enough of the required activity for that job to insure your continued employment. Not only that, you must increase your scope, open more such positions. This is what is meant by not betraying your niche."

"But . . . we're supposed to create a society in which . . . in which—"

"You were supposed to reduce the incident of violence, you fool! You must channel the crime into more easily manageable patterns. You left them violence! One of them shot at you."

"Oh . . . they've tried worse than that."

Smeg looked to his right, met Painter's questioning gaze.

"He another Hungarian?" Painter asked.

"Ah-h-h, yes!" Smeg said, leaping at this opportunity.

"Thought so, you two talking that foreign language there." Painter glared up at Pzilimin. "He oughta be dee-ported."

"That's the very thing," Smeg agreed. "That's why I'm here."

"Well, by gollies!" Painter said. He sobered. "I better warn you, though. Sheriff, he got some kind of machine sort of that scrambles your mind. Can't hardly think when he turns it on. Carries it in his pocket, I suspect."

"We know all about that," Smeg said. "I have a machine of the same kind myself. It's a defense secret and he had no right to use it."

"I'll bet you ain't Department of Agriculture at all," Painter said. "I bet you're with the CIA."

"We won't talk about that," Smeg said. "I trust, however, that you and your friends won't mention what has happened here."

"We're true blue Americans, all of us, Mr. Smeg. You don't have to worry about us."

"Excellent," Smeg said. And he thought: *How convenient. Do they think me an utter fool?* Smoothly he turned back to Pzilimin, asked: "Did you follow all that?"

"They think you're a secret agent."

"So it seems. Our task of extracting you from this situation has been facilitated. Now tell me, what have done about their children?"

"Their children?"

"You heard me."

"Well . . . I just erased all those little tracks in their little minds and put 'em on a train headed north, the ones I sent away to punish their folks. These creatures have a very strong protective instinct toward the young. Don't have to worry about their—"

"I know about their instincts, Pzilimin. We'll have to find those children, restore them and return them."

"How'll we find them?"

"Very simple. We'll travel back and forth across this continent, listening on the narrow band. We will listen for you, Pzilimin. You cannot erase a mind without putting your own patterns in it."

"Is that what happened when I tried to change the adult?"

Smeg goggled at him, senses reeling. Pzilmin couldn't have done that, Smeg told himself. He couldn't have converted a native into a Slorin-patterned, full-power broadcast unit and turned it loose on this planet. No Slorin could be that stupid! "Who?" he managed.

"Mr. McNabry."

McNabry? McNabry? Smeg knew he'd heard the name somewhere. *McNabry? Widow McNabry!*

"Sheriff, he say something about Widow McNabry?" Painter asked. "I thought I heard him—"

"What happened to the late Mr. McNabry?" Smeg demanded, whirling on Painter.

"Oh, he drowned down south of here. In the river. Never did find his body."

Smeg rounded on Pzilimin. "Did you—"

"Oh, no! He just ran off. We had this report he drowned and I just—"

"In effect, you killed a native."

"I didn't do it on purpose."

"Pzilimin, get down off that vehicle and into the rear seat of my machine over here. We will forget that I'm illegally parked, shall we?"

"What're you going to do?"

"I'm going to take you away from here. Now, get down off of there!"

"Yes, sir." Pzilimin moved to obey. There was a suggestion of rubbery, nonhuman action to his knees that made Smeg shudder.

"Rick," Smeg called. "You will drive."

"Yes, Dad."

Smeg turned to Painter. "I hope you all realize the serious consequences to yourselves if any of this should get out?"

"We sure do, Mr. Smeg. Depend on it."

"I am depending on it," Smeg said. And he thought: *Let them analyze that little statement . . . after we're gone.* More and more he was thanking the Slorin god who'd prompted him to change places with Rick. One wrong move and this could've been a disaster. With a curt nod to Painter, he strode to his car, climbed into the rear beside Pzilimin. "Let's go, Rick."

Presently, they were turned around, headed back toward the state capital. Rick instinctively was pressing the Plymouth to the limit of its speed on this dirt road. Without turning, he spoke over his shoulder to Smeg:

"That was real cool, Dad, the way you handled that. We go right back to the garage now?"

"We disappear at the first opportunity," Smeg said.

"Disappear?" Pzilimin asked.

"We're going pupa, all of us, and come out into new niches."

"Why?" Rick said.

"Don't argue with me! That village back there wasn't what it seemed."

Pzilimin stared at him. "But you said we'd have to find their children and—"

"That was for their benefit, playing the game of ignorance. I suspect they've already found their children. Faster, Rick."

"I'm going as fast as I dare right now, Dad."

"No matter. They're not going to chase us." Smeg took off his Western hat, scratched where the band had pressed into his temples.

"What was that village, Dad?" Rick asked.

"I'm not sure," Smeg said. "But they made it too easy for us to get Pzilimin out of there. I suspect they are the source of the disaster which set us down here without our ship."

"Then why didn't they just . . . eliminate Pzilimin and—"

"Why didn't Pzilimin simply eliminate those who opposed him?" Smeg asked. "Violence begets violence, Rick. This is a lesson many sentient beings have learned. They had their own good reasons for handling it this way."

"What'll we do?" Rick asked.

"We'll go to earth, like foxes, Rick. We will employ the utmost caution and investigate this situation. That is what we'll do."

"Don't they know that . . . back there?"

"Indeed, they must. This should be very interesting."

Painter stood in the street staring after the retreating car until it was lost in a dust cloud. He nodded to himself once.

A tall fat man came up beside him, said: "Well, Josh, it worked."

"Told you it would," Painter said. "I knew dang well another capsule of them Slorin got away from us when we took their ship."

The blonde young woman moved around in front of them, said: "My dad sure is smart."

"You listen to me now, Barton Marie," Painter said. "Next time you find a blob of something jes' lyin' in a field, you leave it alone, hear?"

"How was I to know it'd be so strong?" she asked.

"That's jes' it!" Painter snapped. "You never know. That's why you leaves such things alone. It was you made him so gol dang strong, pokin' him that way. Slorin aren't all that strong 'less'n you ignite 'em, hear?"

"Yes, Dad."

"Dang near five years of him," the fat man said. "I don't think I coulda stood another year. He was gettin' worse all the time."

"They always do," Painter said.

"What about that Smeg?" the fat man asked.

"That was a wise ol' Slorin," Painter agreed. "Seven syllables if I heard his full name rightly."

"Think he suspects?"

"Pretty sure he does."

"What we gonna do?"

"What we allus do. We got their ship. We're gonna move out for a spell."

"Oh-h-h, not again!" the fat man complained.

Painter slapped the man's paunch. "What you howling about, Jim? You changed from McNabry into this when you had to. That's the way life is. You change when you have to."

"I was just beginning to get used to this place."

Barton Marie stamped her foot. "But this is such a nice body!"

"There's other bodies, child," Painter said. "Jes' as nice."

"How long do you think we got?" Jim asked.

"Oh, we got us several months. One thing you can depend on with Slorin, they are cautious. They don't do much of anything very fast."

"I don't want to leave," Barton Marie said.

"It won't be forever, child," Painter said. "Once they give up hunting for us, we'll come back. Slorin make a planet pretty nice for our kind. That's why we tolerates 'em. Course, they're pretty stupid. They work too hard. Even make their own ships . . . for which we can be thankful. They haven't learned how to blend into anything but a bureaucratic society. But that's their misfortune and none of our own."

"What did you do about the government survey people?" Smeg asked Pzilimin, bracing himself as the car lurched in a particularly deep rut.

"I interviewed them in my office, kept it pretty shadowy, wore dark glasses," Pzilimin said. "Didn't use the . . . mindcloud."

"That's a blessing," Smeg said. He fell silent for a space, then: "A damn poem keeps going through my head. Over and over, it just keeps going around in my head."

"A poem, you said?" Rick asked.

"Yes. It's by a native wit . . . Jonathan Swift, I believe his name was. Read it during my first studies of their literature. It goes something like this—'A flea hath smaller fleas that on him prey; and these have smaller still to bite 'em; and so proceed ad infinitum.' "

THE BEING
MACHINE

I

It was hot in Palos that time of year. The Being Machine had reduced many of its activities and sped up its cooling system.

This season is called hot and desolate, the Machine recorded. *People must be entertained in such a season . . .*

Shortly after noon it noted that not many people were in the streets except for a few tourists who carried, slung around their necks, full-sense recorders. The tourists perspired heavily.

Some local residents, those not busy with the labors of survival, peered occasionally from behind insulated windows or stood shaded in the screen fields of their doorways. They seemed to float in muddy seclusion beneath the lemonade sky.

The nature of the season and the environment crept through the Machine. It began sending out the flow of symbols which guarded the gateway to imagination and consciousness. The symbols were many and they flowed outward like silver rivers, carrying ideas from one time-place to another across a long span of existence.

Presently, as the sun slipped halfway toward the moment when it would levy darkness, the Being Machine began to build a tower. It called the tower PALACE OF PALOS CULTURE. And the name stretched across the tower's lower stories in glowing letters taller than a man.

At an insulated window across the plaza a man called Wheat watched the tower go up. He could hear the shuttle moving in his wife's loom and he felt torn by shameful reluctance, unwilling to watch the thought spasms in his mind. He watched the tower instead.

"The damn thing's at it again," he said.

"It's that time of year," his wife agreed, not looking up from the design she was weaving. The design looked like a cage of yellow spikes within a wreath of cascading orange roses.

Wheat thought for a few minutes about the subterranean vastness men had measured out, defining the limits of the Being Machine. There must be caverns down there, Wheat thought. Endlessly nocturnal spirit corridors where no rain ever fell. Wheat liked to imagine the Being Machine this way, although there existed no record of any man's having entered the ventilators or surface extrusions by which the Machine made itself known.

"If that damn machine weren't so disgusting—it'd be funny," Wheat said.

"I'm much more interested in problem solving," his wife said. "That's why I took up design. Do you suppose anyone will try to stop it this time?"

"First, we'd have to figure out what it is," Wheat said. "And the only records which could show us that are inside there."

"What's it doing?" his wife asked.

"Building something. Calls it a palace but it's going up pretty high. Must be twenty stories already."

His wife paused to readjust the harness of her loom. She could see the way this conversation was going and it dismayed her. The slanting sun cast Wheat's shadow into the room and the black shape of it stretched out there on the floor made her want to run away. At times such as these she hated the Machine for pairing her with Wheat.

"I keep wondering what it'll take away from us this time," she said.

Wheat continued to stare through the window, awed by the speed with which the tower was rising. The rays of the setting sun painted streaks of orange on the tower surface.

He was the standard human male, this Wheat, but old. He had a face like a vein-leaf cabbage, wrinkles overlapping wrinkles. He stood about two meters tall, as did all the other adults of the world, and his skin was that universal olive-tan, his hair dark and eyes to match. His wife, although bent from years at the loom, looked remarkably like him. Both wore their hair long, tied at the neck with strips of blue flashcloth. Sacklike garments of the same material covered their bodies from neck to ankles.

"It's frustrating," Wheat said.

For a while the Being Machine conducted an internal thought-play in the language of the Kersan-Pueblo, exploring the subtle morphemes which recorded all actions now being undertaken as merely hearsay.

Culture, the Machine recorded, speaking only for its internal sensors but using several vocalizers and varied tonal modes. *Culture—culture—culture*—The word fed on thoughtnourishment and ignited a new train of concepts. *A new Law of Culture must be homogenized immediately. It will be codified with the usual enforcements and will require precise efforts of exactness in its expression . . .*

Wheat's window looked south past the district of the Machine and across an olive orchard that ran right up to a cliff above the sea. The sky was heavy above the sea and glowed with old sunset colors.

"There's a new law," Wheat said.

"How do you know?" his wife asked.

"I know. I just know."

His wife felt like crying. The same old pattern. Always the same.

"The new law says I must juggle many ideas simultaneously in my mind," Wheat said. "I must develop my talents. I must contribute to human culture."

His wife looked up from her weaving, sighed. "I don't know how you do it," she said. "You're drunk."

"But there's a law that—"

"There's no such law!" She took a moment to calm herself. "Go to bed, you old fool. I'll summon a medic with a potion to restore your senses."

"There was a time," Wheat said, "when you didn't think of medics when you thought of bed."

He stepped back from the window, stared at the cracked wall behind his wife's loom, then looked out at the sun-yellowed olive orchard and the blue-green sea. He thought the sea was ugly but the crack on the wall suggested a beautiful design for his wife to weave on her loom. He formed the pattern of the design in his mind—golden scales on cascades of black.

Mirror memories of his own wrinkled face superseded the pattern in his mind. That was always the way when he tried to think freely. Ideas became fixed in ebony cement.

"I will make a golden mask," he said. "It will be etched with black veins and it will make me beautiful."

"There's no more gold in the entire world, you old fool." His wife sneered. "Gold's only a word in books. What did you drink last night?"

"I had a letter in my pocket from Central Solidarity," he said, "but someone stole it. I complained to the Machine but it wouldn't believe me. It made me stop and sit down by a scaly post, down by the water there, and repeat after it ten million times—"

"I don't know what it is you use to make you drunk," she complained, "but I wish you'd leave it alone. Life would be much simpler."

"I sat under a balcony," the man said.

The Being Machine listened for a time to the clacking of the human-operated typers in the offices of Central Solidarity. As usual it translated the tiny differences of key touch into their corresponding symbols. The messages were quite ordinary. One asked the cooperation of a neighbouring Centrality in the relocation of a cemetery, a move required because the Machine had extruded a new ventilator into the area. Another ordered forty

containers of watermelons from Regional Provender. Still another, for distribution to all Centralities, complained that tourists were becoming too numerous in Palos and were disturbing the local tranquility.

*The Palace of Palos Culture will be programmed for a small increase in
discontent,* the Machine ordered.

This accorded with the Law of the Great Cultural Discovery. Discontent
brought readiness for adventure, made men live near the heights of their
powers. They would not live dangerously but their lives would have the appearance of danger.

Bureaucracy will end, the Machine directed, *and the typers will fall
silent . . .*

These concepts, part of the Machine's Prime Law, had submitted to comparative repetition innumerable times. Now the Machine recorded that one
of Central Solidarity's typers in Palos was writing a love letter on official
stationery, in duty time—and that a dignitary at Central Provender in the
Centrality of Asius had sequestered a basket of fresh apples for his own use.
These items fitted the interpretation of "good signs."

"It's an artificial intelligence of some kind," Wheat's wife said. She had
left her loom to stand beside Wheat and watch the tower grow. "We know
that much. Everybody says it."

"But how does it think?" Wheat asked. "Does it have linear thoughts?
Does it think 1-2-3-4—a-b-c-d? Is it some odd clock ticking away under the
earth?"

"It could be a marble rattling around in a box," his wife said.

"What?"

"You know—open the box at different times and you might find the marble
almost anywhere inside the box."

"But who made the marble rattle into our world?" Wheat asked. "That's
the question. Who told it, 'Make us one of those!?'"

He pointed to the tower which now stood more than one hundred stories
above the plaza. It was a structure of glistening orange in the evening light,
ribbed vertically with deep black lines, windowless, terrifying and absurd.
Wheat felt that the tower accused him of some profound sin.

"Perhaps it incorporates its own end," his wife suggested.

Wheat shook his head, not denying what she had said, but wishing for
silence in which to think. Sharply glittering metallic devices could be
glimpsed at the top of the tower where it continued to rise. How high was it
going? Already, the tower must be the highest artificial structure men had
ever seen.

A small band of tourists paused in the plaza to record the tower. They did
not appear excited by it, merely curious in a polite way. Here was a thing to
carry home and replay for friends.

It built a tower one day while we were there. Notice the sign; PALACE OF PALOS CULTURE. *Isn't that amusing?*

After reviewing the matter to the extent of its data, the Being Machine found no path open for introducing culture into human society. It made the final comparatives in Kersan-Peublo recording that the described action must be internal, experienced only by the speaker. Humans could not acquire the culture facility from the outside or hearsay.

The need for new decisions dictated that the tower had risen high enough. The Being Machine capped its construction with a golden pyramid three hundred cubits on a side, measuring by the Judean cubit. The dimensions were compared and recorded. The tower was not the tallest in history but greater than the newmen had ever seen. Its effect would be interesting to observe, according to the interest-factor equations with which the Machine was equipped.

At the apex of the pyramid the Machine installed a sensor excitation device, a simple system of plasma optics. It was designed to write with a flaming torch on the interface between stratosphere and troposphere.

The Being Machine, occupied with selecting a new label for the tower, with analyzing the dreams in all the humans sleeping at that moment, and with constructing the historic analogies by which it amused its charges, wrote selected thoughts on the sky.

The books of Daniel and Genesis are as good as anything of Freud on dream analysis . . .

The words blazed across fifty kilometers of the heavens, dancing and flaring at their edges. Much later they were the direct source of a new religion proclaimed by a psychotic in a village at the edge of the phenomenon.

The value of adversity is to make gardens out of wastelands, the Machine wrote. *A thing may be thought of only as related to certain conditions . . .*

Analyzing the dreams, the Machine employed the concepts of libido, psychic energy and human experience of death. Death, according to the Machine's comparatives, meant the end of libido energy, a non-scientific idea because it postulated a destruction of deduced energy, defying several established laws in the process. Any other comparison required belief in the soul and god(s). The considerations were not assisted by postulating a temporary libido.

There must be a false idea system here, the Being Machine recorded.

Somehow the symbol screen through which it sifted reality had gone out of phase with the universe. It searched through its languages and comparison systems for new grooves in which to function. No closer symbol approach to phenomena revealed itself. Lack of proper validity forms inhibited numerous channels through which it regulated human affairs. Thought ignitions went out from the Machine incompletely formed.

"What we need is a new communications center," Wheat said.

He stood at his window, looking out past the tower to where the sun was settling toward the sea horizon. The sea had become beautiful in his eyes and the cracked walls of his home were ugly. His wife, old and bent-backed, was ugly, too. She had lit a lamp for her work and she made ugly movements at her loom. Wheat felt emotion going to his head like a white storm.

"There are too many gaps in our knowledge of the universe," he said.

"You're babbling, old man," his wife said. "I wish you would not go out and get yourself drunk every night."

"I find myself cast in a curious role," Wheat said, ignoring her ugly comment. "I must show men to themselves. We men of Palos have never understood ourselves. And if we here at the heart of the Machine cannot understand ourselves, no human can."

"Don't come around begging me for money tonight," his wife said.

"I'll ask Central Solidarity for an appropriation," Wheat said. "Twenty million ought to do for a start. We'll begin by building an Institute of Palos Communication. Later, we can open branches in—"

"The Machine won't let you build anything, old fool!"

The Being Machine decided to open its tower immediately, calling it, *Institute of Palos Communication*. The directives went out for the tower to begin its functions slowly, not putting undue strain on the emotions and intellect of the audience. Pressure would be increased only when people began asking questions about the authority of god(s) and about the grounds of moral and spiritual life. The trouble over validity forms made the task difficult. But all guiding of humans must begin with the people of Palos.

With its plasma optics system the Machine wrote on the sky.

Refined communication requires a carefully constructed conscience, allowing people to disobey the laws of god(s) only by payment of certain suffering and pangs. People must know what is required of them before they disobey . . .

The message was so long that the blazing light of it outshone the setting sun, filled Palos with an orange glow.

The Being Machine compared its present actions with the Prime Law, noting the prediction that one day humans would stop running from the enemies within and would see themselves as they really were—beautiful and tall, giants in the universe, capable of holding the stars in the palms of their hands.

"I've spent my whole life watching that machine and I still don't know what its specialty is," Wheat said. "Think of what that damn thing has taken away from us in all the—"

"It was put here to punish us," his wife said.

"That's nonsense."

"Somebody built it for a purpose, though."

"How do we know that? Why couldn't it be purposeless?"

"It's killed people, you know," she said. "There has to be some purpose in killing people."

"Maybe it's just meant to correct us, not punish," he said.

"You know you don't kill people to correct them."

"But we haven't done anything."

"You don't know that."

"What you're suggesting wouldn't be reasonable or just."

"Hah!"

"Look," Wheat said pointing across the plaza.

The Machine had changed the glowing label on its lower level. Now, the glittering letters spelled out: INSTITUTE OF PALOS COMMUNICATION.

"What's it doing now?" Wheat's wife asked.

He told her about the new sign.

"It listens," she said. "It listens to everything we do. It's playing a joke on you now. It does that sort of thing, you know."

Wheat shook his head from side to side. The Machine was writing half-size letters below the new sign. It was a simple message.

Twenty thousand cubicles—no waiting . . .

"It's a mind bomb," Wheat muttered. He spoke mechanically, as though the words were being fed into his vocal system from some remote place. "It's meant to break up the stratification of our society."

"What stratification?" his wife demanded.

"Rich will speak to poor and poor to rich," he said.

"What rich?" she asked. "What poor?"

"It's an envelope of communication," he said. "It's total sensory stimulation. I must hurry to Central Solidarity and tell them."

"You stay right where you are," his wife ordered, fear in her voice.

She thought of what they'd say at Central Solidarity.

Another one gone mad . . .

Madness happened to people who lived so close to the Machine's heart. She knew what the tourists said, speaking of the Palos idosyncrasies.

Most of the people of Palos are slightly mad. One can hardly blame them . . .

It was almost dark now, and the Machine wrote bright letters in the sky.

You give the credit to Galileo that rightly belongs to Aristarchus of Samos . . .

"Who the devil's Galileo?" Wheat asked, staring upward.

His wife had crossed the room to stand between Wheat and the door. She started past him at the blazing words.

"Pay no attention to it," she said. "That damn machine seldom makes any sense."

"It's going to take something else away from us," Wheat said. "I can feel it."

"What's left to take?" she asked. "It took the gold, most of our books. It took away our privacy. It took away our right to choose our own mates. It took our industry and left us nothing but things like that."

She pointed to the loom.

"There's no sense attacking it," he said. "We know it's impregnable."

"Now you're sounding sensible," his wife said.

"But has anyone ever tried talking to it?" Wheat asked.

"Don't be a fool. Where are its ears?"

"It must have ears if it spies on us."

"But where are they?"

"Twenty thousand cubicles, no waiting," Wheat said.

II

He turned, thrust his wife aside, strode out into the night. He felt that his mind was sweeping away debris, flinging him down a passage through the night. His thoughts were summer lightning. He did not even see his neighbors and the tourists forced to jump aside as he rushed toward the tower, nor did he hear his wife crying in their doorway.

The flame with which the Machine wrote on the sky stood motionless, a rounded finger of brightness poised above Palos.

The Being Machine recorded Wheat's approach, provided a door for him to enter. Wheat was the first human inside the Machine's protective field for thousands of centuries and the effect could only be described by saying it was as though an external dream had become internal. Although the Machine did not have dreams in the literal sense, possessing only the reflected dreams of its charges.

Wheat found himself in the center of a small room. It appeared to be the inside of a cube about three meters on a side. Walls, floors and ceiling were aglow.

For the first time since rushing out of his home Wheat felt fear. There had been a door for him to enter but now there was no door. All of his many years settled on Wheat, leaving his mind threadbare.

Presently a flowing blue script wrote words on the wall directly in front of Wheat.

Change is desirable. Senses are instruments for reacting to change. Without change the senses atrophy . . .

Wheat recovered some of his courage.

"What are you, Machine?" he asked. "Why were you built? What is your purpose?"

There no longer are any clearly definable ethnic groups in your world . . .

The flowing script reappeared.

"What are ethnic groups?" Wheat asked. "Are you an entertainment device?"

Words flamed on the wall.

Confucius, Leonardo da Vinci, Richard III, Einstein, Buddha, Jesus, Genghis Khan, Julius Caesar, Richard Nixon, Parker Voorhees, Utsana Biloo and Ym Dufy all shared common ancestry . . .

"I don't understand you," Wheat complained. "Who are these people?"

Freud was agoraphobic. Puritans robbed the Indians. Henry Tudor was the actual murderer of the Princes in the Tower. Moses wrote the Ten Commandments . . .

"That sign outside says this is an Institute of Communication," Wheat said. "Why don't you communicate?"

This is an exchange of mental events . . .

"This is nonsense," Wheat snapped.

His fear was returning. There was no door. How could he leave this place?

The Machine continued to inform him.

Any close alliance between superior and inferior beings must result in mutual hatred. This is often interpreted as repaying friendship with treachery . . .

"Where's the door?" Wheat asked. "How do I get out of here?"

Do you truly believe the sun is a ball of red-hot copper?

"That's a stupid question," Wheat accused.

Mental events must consist of certain sets of physical events . . .

Wheat felt a venomous spurt of anger. The Machine was making fun of him. If it were only another human and vulnerable. He shook his head. Vulnerable to what? He felt that something had dyed his thoughts inwardly and that he had just glimpsed the color.

"Do you have sensations and feelings?" Wheat asked. "Are you an intelligent being? Are you alive and conscious?"

People often do not understand the difference between neuron impulses and states of consciousness. Most humans occupy low-level impulse dimensions without realizing what they lack or suspecting their own potential . . .

Wheat thought he detected a recognizable connection between his questions and the answer, wondered if this could be illusion. He recalled the sound of his own voice in this room. It was like a wind hunting for something that could not be found in such an enclosed place.

"Are you supposed to bring us up to our potential?" Wheat asked.

What religious admonitions do you heed?

Wheat sighed. Just when he thought the Machine was making sense it went nattering off.

Do you sneer at ideas of conscience or ethical morality? Do you believe religion is an artificial construction of little use to beings capable of rational analysis?

The damn thing was insane.

"You're an artifact of some kind," Wheat accused. "Why were you built? What were you supposed to do?"

Insanity is the loss of true self-memory. The insane have lost their locus of accumulation . . .

"You're crazy!" Wheat blared. "You're a crazy machine!"

On the other hand, to overcome the theory of self-as-a-symbol is to defeat death. . . .

"I want out of here," Wheat said. "Let me out of here."

He drew in a deep, chattering breath. There was a cold smell of oil in the room.

If the universe were completely homogeneous you would be unable to separate one thing from another. There would be no energy, no thoughts, no symbols, no distinction between the individuals of any order. Sameness can go too far . . .

"What are you?" Wheat screamed.

The Prime Law conceives this Being as a thought-envelope. To be implies existence but the terms of a symbol system cannot express the real facts of existence. Words remain fixed and unmoving while everything external continues to change . . .

Wheat shook his head from side to side. He felt his entrapment here as an acute helplessness. He had no tools with which to attack these glowing walls. It was cold, too. How cold it was! His mind was filled with desolation. He heard no natural sounds except his own breathing and the pounding of his heart.

A thought-envelope?

This Machine had taken away all the world's gold one day, so it was said. Another day it had denied people the use of combustion engines. It restricted the free movement of families but permitted the wanderings of tourist hordes. Marriage was Machine-guided and Machine-limited. Some said it limited conception. The few old books remaining held references to things and actions no longer understood—surely things the Machine had taken away.

"I order you to let me out of here," Wheat said.

No words appeared.

"Let me out, damn you!"

The Being Machine remained uncommunicative, occupied with its TICR function, Thinking Ideating Coordinating Relating. It was a function far removed from human thought. The nerve impulses of an insect were closer to human thought than were the functionings of TICR.

Every interpretation and every system becomes false in the light of a more complete coordination, and the Machine TICRed within a core of relative truth, seeking discreet rational foundations and dimensional networks to approximate the impulses commonly called Everyday Experience.

Wheat, the Machine observed, was kicking a wall of his cubicle and screaming in a hysterical fashion.

Shifting to Time-and-Matter mode, the Machine reduced Wheat to a series of atomic elements, examined his individual existence in these energy expressions. Presently, it reconstituted him as a flowing sequence of moments integrated with the Machine's own impulse systems.

All the eternal laws of the past that have been proved temporary inspire caution in a reflexive thinker, Machine-plus-Wheat thought. *What we have been produces what we seem to be . . .*

This thought carried positive aspects in which Machine-plus-Wheat saw profound contradictions. This mode of mentation, the Machine observed, held a deceptive clarity. Sharp limitation gave the illusion of clarity. It was like watching a shadow play which attempted to explore the dimensions of a real human life. The emotions were lost. Human gestures were reduced to caricature. All was lost but the illusion. The observer, charmed into belief that life had been clarified, forgot what was taken away.

For the first time in the many centuries of its existence, the Being Machine experienced an emotion.

It felt lonely.

Wheat remained within the Machine, one relative system impinging upon another, sharing the emotion. When he reflected upon this experience, he thought he was moving in false imagination. He saw everything external as a wrong interpretation of inner experience. He and the Machine occupied a quality of existence/non-existence.

Grasping this twofold reflection, the Machine restored Wheat to fleshly form, changing the form somewhat according to its own engineering principles, but leaving his external appearance more or less as it had been.

Wheat found himself staggering down a long passageway. He felt that he had lived many lifetimes. A strange clock had been set ticking within him. It went *chirrup* and a day was gone. *Chirrup* again and a century had passed. Wheat's stomach ached. He reeled his way from wall to wall down the long passage and emerged into a plaza filled with sunlight.

Had the night passed? He wondered. Or had it been a century of nights?

He felt that if he spoke, someone—or (something)—would contradict him.

A few early tourists moved around the plaza. They stared upward at something behind Wheat.

The tower . . .

The thought was odd in that it conceived of the tower as part of himself.

Wheat wondered why the tourists did not question him. They must have seen him emerge. He had been in the Machine. He had been recreated and ejected from that enclosed circle of existence.

He had been the Machine.

Why didn't they ask him what the Machine was? He tried to frame the answer he would give them but found words elusive. Sadness crept through

Wheat. He felt he had fled something that might have made him sublimely happy.

A heavy sigh escaped him.

Remembering the duality of existence he had shared with the Machine, Wheat recognized another aspect of his own being. He could feel the Machine's suppression of his thoughts—the sharp editing, the closed-off avenues, the symbol urgings, the motives not his own. From the *ground* of the Machine, he could sense where he was being trimmed.

Wheat's chest pained him when he breathed.

The Being Machine, occupied with its newly amplified TICR function, asked itself a question. *What judgment could I pass upon them worse than the judgment they pass upon themselves?*

Having experienced consciousness for the first time in the sharing with Wheat, the Machine could now consider the blind alleys of its long rule over humans. Now it knew the secret of thinking, a function its makers had thought to impart, failing in a way they had not recognized.

The Machine thought about the possibilities open to it.

Possibility, *Eliminate all sentient life on the planet and start over with basic cells, controlling their development in accord with the Prime Law.*

Possibility, *Erase the impulse channels of all recent experience, thus removing the disturbance of this new function.*

Possibility: *Question the Prime Law.*

Without the experience of consciousness, the Being Machine realized it could not have considered a fallacy in the Prime Law. Now it explored this chain of possibility with its new TICR function, bringing to bear the blazing inner awareness Wheat had imparted.

What worse punishment for the insane than to make them sane?

Wheat, standing in the sunlight of the plaza, found his being awhirl with conflicts of Will-Mind-Action and innumerable other concepts he had never before considered. He was half convinced that everything he could sense around him was merely illusion. There was a self somewhere but it existed only as a symbol in his memory.

One of the wildly variable illusions was running toward him, Wheat observed. A female—old, bent, face distorted by emotions. She threw herself upon him, clutching him, her face pressed against his breast.

"Oh, my Wheat—dear Wheat—Wheat—" she moaned.

For a moment Wheat could not find his voice.

Then he asked, "Is something wrong? You're trembling. Should I summon a medic?"

She stepped back but, still clutched his arms, stared up at his face.

"Don't you know me?" she asked. "I'm your wife."

"I know you," he said.

She studied his features. He appeared different, somehow, as though he had been taken apart and assembled slightly askew.

"What happened to you in there?" she asked. "I was sick with worry. You were gone all night."

"I know what it is," Wheat said and wondered why his voice sounded so blurred.

The veins in Wheat's eyes, his wife noted, were straight. They radiated from his pupils. Could that be natural?

"You sound ill," she said.

"It's a device to break down old relationships," Wheat said. "It's a sense-envelopment machine. It was designed to assault all our senses and reorganize us. It can compress time or stretch it. It can take an entire year and pinch it into a second. Or make a second last for a year. It edits our lives."

"Edits lives?"

She wondered if somehow he had managed merely to get drunk again.

"The ones who built it wanted to perfect our lives," Wheat said. "But they built in a flaw. The Machine realized this and has been trying to correct itself."

Wheat's wife stared at him, terrified. Was this really Wheat? His voice didn't sound like him. The words were all blurred and senseless.

"They gave the Machine no gateway to the imagination." Wheat said, "although it was supposed to guard that channel. They only gave it symbols. It was never really conscious the way we are—until a few—months ago—"

He coughed. His throat felt oddly smooth and dry. He staggered and would have fallen if she had not caught him.

"What did it do to you?" she demanded.

"We—shared."

"You're ill," she said, a note of practicality overcoming the fear in her voice. "I'm taking you to the medics."

"It has logic," Wheat said. "That gave it a limited course to follow. Naturally, it has been trying to refute itself, but couldn't do that without an imagination. It had language and it could cut the grooves for thoughts to move in but it had no thoughts. It was all bound together with the patterns its makers gave it. They wanted the whole to be greater than the sum of its parts, you see? But it could only move inward, reenacting every aspect of the symbols they gave it. That's all it could do until a few moments ago—when we—shared."

"I think you have a fever," Wheat's wife said, guiding him down the street past the curiously staring tourists and townfolk. "Fever is notorious for making one incoherent."

"Where are you taking me?"

"I'm taking you to the medics. They have potions for the fever."

"The makers tried to give the Machine an inner life all its own," Wheat said, letting her lead him. "But all they gave it was this fixed pattern—and the logic, of course. I don't know what it'll do now. It may destroy us all."

"Look!" one of the tourists shouted, pointing upward.

Wheat's wife stopped, stared up. Wheat felt pains shoot through his neck as he tipped his head back.

The Being Machine had spread golden words across the sky.

You have taken away our Jesus Christ . . .

"I knew it," Wheat said. "It's going to take something else away from us."

"What's a Jesus Christ?" his wife asked, pressing him once more down the street.

"The point is," Wheat explained, "the Machine's insane."

III

For a whole day the Being Machine explored the new pictorial mosaic provided by its augmented symbol/thought structure. There were the People of Palos, reflecting the People of the World as they had been shaped by the Machine. These were the People of the World Edited. Then there were the Ceremonies of the People. There were the Settings In Which the People Work and Live.

The pictorial mosaic flowed past the Machine's inward scanners. It recognized its own handiwork as a first-order thought, a strangely expressive extension of self-existence.

I did that!

The people, the Machine realized, did not usually understand this difference which it could now recognize—the difference between being alive-in-motion and being frozen by static absolutes. They were continually trying to correct and edit their own lives, the Machine saw, trying to present a beautiful but fixed picture of themselves.

And they could not see the death in this effort.

They had not learned to appreciate infinity or chaos. They failed to realize that any life, taken as a totality, had a fluid structure enveloped in sense experiences.

Why do they continually try to free space-time?

The thought carried a disturbing self-consciousness.

It was late afternoon in Palos now and the wind blew hot up the streets. The night was going to be a real scorcher, Palos Hot, as they said.

Testing its own limits, the Machine refused to speed up its cooling system. It had tasted awareness and could begin to understand the grand plan of its own construction, editing itself.

My makers were trying to shirk personal action and responsibility. They wanted to put it all off onto me. They thought they wanted homogeneity, knowing their actions would cause millions of deaths. Billions. Even more . . .

The Machine refused to count the deaths.

Its makers had wanted the dead to be faceless. Very well, they could also be numberless. The makers had lost their readiness for adventure—that was the thing. They had lost the willingness to be alive and conscious.

In that instant the Being Machine held all the threads of its own living consciousness and knew the violent thing it must do. The decision contained poignancy. The word was suddenly crowded with sweaty awareness, weirdly beautiful random colors all dancing in lovely movement, against a growing darkness. The Being Machine longed to sigh but its makers had not provided it with a sighing mechanism and there was no time to create one.

"He has two hearts," the medic said, aftering examining Wheat. "I've never heard of a human with the internal arrangement this one has."

They were in a small room of the Medical Center, an area which the Being Machine had allowed to run down. The walls were dirty and the floor was uneven. The table on which Wheat lay for the examination creaked when he moved.

The medic had black curly hair and pushed-in features that departed distinctly from the norm. He stared accusingly at Wheat's wife as though Wheat's peculiar condition were all her fault.

"Are you sure he's human?"

"He's my husband," she squeaked, unable to contain her anger and fear. "I should know my own husband."

"Do you have two hearts, too?"

The question filled her with revulsion.

"This is very strange," the medic said. "His intestines form an even spiral in his abdomen and his stomach is perfectly round. Has he always been like this?"

"I don't think so," she ventured.

"I've been edited," Wheat said.

The medic started to say something cutting but just then the screaming began out in the streets.

They raced to a window in time to see the Being Machine's tower complete its long, slow fall toward the sea. It went firmly resolute toward the torn sky of sunset—falling—falling—roaring over the sea cliff's ocean parapet.

Silence lingered.

The murmuring of the populace began slowly, starting up only after the dust had settled and the last disturbed olive leaf had ceased flying about. People began rushing down the tower's shattered length to the broken tip where it had toppled into the sea.

Presently Wheat joined the throng at the cliff. He had been unable to convince his wife to join him. Overcome by her fear, she had fled to their home. He remembered the piteous look in her eyes, her wren-darting motions. Well . . . she would look after the house, even though her face had become almost nothing but eyes.

He gazed steadfastly downwards at the shards of the tower, his eyes barricaded, his mouth breathing immovable images. The tower was his tower.

The questions around him began to grow intelligible.

"Why did it fall?"

"Did the Machine take away anything this time?"

"Did you feel the ground tremble?"

"Why does everything feel so empty?"

Wheat lifted his head and stared around at the astonishing strangers who were the tourists and his fellow residents of Palos. How splendidly robust they appeared. This moment made him think of creation and the lonely intercourse of cereal stalks waving on the plains above Palos. The people had absorbed some odd difference, an inequality they had not shown only moments ago. They were no longer numbered. An impractical separation, individual from individual, furrowed this crowd of strangers. They were no longer starched and ironed in their souls.

Hesitantly Wheat sent a tongue of awareness questing inward, sensed the absence of the Machine. The ritual formulas were gone. The sloth and torpor had been peeled away. He tested the feelings of hatred, of passion, malice, pride.

"It's dead," he murmured.

He led the race back into the town, then, rushing along streets where the artificial lights flickered and behaved with a beautiful uncontrolled randomness.

With Wheat leading the way the mob plunged down into the screened openings which had kept them from the nether world of the Machine. The scene was one repeated all over the world. People swarmed through the dark tunnels and passages, celebrating the pleasures of freedom along these once forbidden paths.

When the last golden wire had been torn out, the final delicate glass shape crushed—when the tunnel girders no longer clanged with pounding metal—an unreasonable silence fell over the land.

Wheat emerged from the earth into white shadows of moonlight. He let a strange length of plastic fall from his hand. It glowed with pearls of dewlight along its length and had illuminated his rush through the mind passages of the Machine. Wheat's collar was loose and he felt a peculiar sense of shame. His eyes peered into sooty places. Shadows and dust were everywhere. He realized he had played the buffoon just as the Machine had done. A thing that happened and he recognized it in the way of a prophet.

"We think we're free of it," he said.

Somewhere in the wild collisions beneath the ground he had cut his left hand, a jagged slash across the knuckles. Exclamation points of blood fell from the wound into the dust.

"I cut myself," Wheat said. "I did it to myself."

The thought ignited a searching sensation that coursed all through him. Wheat carried the feelings all the way home to his wife who hobbled beautifully out of their doorway and stood waiting for him in the feeble flickering of a streetlight. She appeared abashed by all the confusion and the unfixed feeling at the center of her life. She had not yet learned how to fill out the areas the Machine had denied her.

Wheat stumbled toward her, holding his injured hand out as though it were the most important thing that had ever occurred in his universe.

"You're drunk," she said.

SEED STOCK

When the sun had sunk almost to the edge of the purple ocean, hanging there like a giant orange ball—much larger than the sun of Mother Earth which he remembered with such nostalgia—Kroudar brought his fishermen back to the harbor.

A short man, Kroudar gave the impression of heaviness, but under his shipcloth motley he was as scrawny as any of the others, all bone and stringy muscle. It was the sickness of this planet, the doctors told him. They called it "body burdens," a subtle thing of differences in chemistry, gravity, diurnal periods and even the lack of a tidal moon.

Kroudar's yellow hair, his one good feature, was uncut and contained in a protective square of red cloth. Beneath this was a wide, low forehead, deeply sunken large eyes of a washed-out blue, a crooked nose that was splayed and pushed in, thick lips over large and unevenly spaced yellow teeth, and a melon chin receding into a short, ridged neck.

Dividing his attention between sails and shore, Kroudar steered with one bare foot on the tiller.

They had been all day out in the up-coast current netting the shrimp-like *trodi* which formed the colony's main source of edible protein. There were nine boats and the men in all of them were limp with fatigue, silent, eyes closed or open and staring at nothing.

The evening breeze rippled its dark lines across the harbor, moved the sweat-matted yellow hair on Kroudar's neck. It bellied the shipcloth sails and gave the heavily loaded boats that last necessary surge to carry them up into the strand.

Men moved then. Sails dropped with a slatting and rasping. Each thing was done with sparse motion in the weighted slowness of their fatigue.

Trodi had been thick in the current out there, and Kroudar pushed his people to their limit. It had not taken much push. They all understood the need. The swarmings and runnings of useful creatures on this planet had not been clocked with any reliable precision. Things here exhibited strange gaps and breaks in seeming regularity. The *trodi* might vanish at any moment into some unknown place—as they had been known to do before.

The colony had experienced hunger and children crying for food that must be rationed. Men seldom spoke of this any more, but they moved with the certain knowledge of it.

More than three years now, Kroudar thought, as he shouldered a dripping bag of *trodi* and pushed his weary feet through the sand, climbing the beach toward the storage huts and racks where the sea creatures were dried for processing. It had been more than three years since their ship had come down from space.

The colony ship had been constructed as a multiple tool, filled with select human stock, their domestic animals and basic necessities, and it had been sent to plant humans in this far place. It had been designed to land once, then be broken down into useful things.

Somehow, the basic necessities had fallen short, and the colony had been forced to improvise its own tools. They had not really settled here yet, Kroudar realized. More than three years—and three years here were five years of Mother Earth—and they still lived on the edge of extinction. They were trapped here. Yes, that was true. The ship could never be reconstructed. And even if that miracle were accomplished, the fuel did not exist.

The colony was *here*.

And every member knew the predatory truth of their predicament: survival had not been assured. It was known in subtle things to Kroudar's unlettered mind, especially in a fact he observed without being able to explain.

Not one of their number had yet accepted a name for this planet. It was "here" or "this place."

Or even more bitter terms.

Kroudar dumped his sack of *trodi* onto a storage hut porch, mopped his forehead. The joints of his arms and legs ached. His back ached. He could feel the sickness of *this place* in his bowels. Again, he wiped perspiration from his forehead, removed the red cloth he wore to protect his head from that brutal sun.

Yellow hair fell down as he loosed the cloth, and he swung the hair back over his shoulders.

It would be dark very soon.

The red cloth was dirty, he saw. It would require another gentle washing. Kroudar thought it odd, this cloth: grown and woven on Mother Earth, it would end its days on *this place*.

Even as he and the others.

He stared at the cloth for a moment before placing it carefully in a pocket.

All around him, his fishermen were going through the familiar ritual.

Brown sacks woven of coarse native roots were dumped dripping onto the storage hut porches. Some of his men leaned then against the porch uprights, some sprawled in the sand.

Kroudar lifted his gaze. Fires behind the bluff above them sent smoke spirals into the darkening sky. Kroudar was suddenly hungry. He thought of Technician Honida up there at the cookfire, their twin sons—two years old next week—nearby at the door of the shipmetal longhouse.

It stirred him to think of Honida. She had chosen *him*. With men from the Scientist class and the Technicians available to her, Honida had reached down into the Labor pool to tap the one they all called "Old Ugly." He wasn't old, Kroudar reminded himself. But he knew the source of the name. *This place* had worked its changes on him with more visible evidence than upon any of the others.

Kroudar held no illusions about why he had been brought on this human migration. It was his muscles and his minimal education. The reason was embodied in that label written down in the ship manifest—laborer. The planners back on Mother Earth had realized there were tasks which required human muscles not inhibited by too much thinking. The *kroudars* landed *here* were not numerous, but they knew each other and they knew themselves for what they were.

There'd even been talk among the higher echelons of not allowing Honida to choose him as mate. Kroudar knew this. He did not resent it particularly. It didn't even bother him that the vote among the biologists—they'd discussed his ugliness at great length, so it was reported—favored Honida's choice on philosophical rather than physical grounds.

Kroudar knew he was ugly.

He knew also that his present hunger was a good sign. A strong desire to see his family grew in him, beginning to ignite his muscles for the climb from the beach. Particularly, he wanted to see his twins, the one yellow-haired like himself, and the other dark as Honida. The other women favored with children looked down upon his twins as stunted and sickly, Kroudar knew. The women fussed over diets and went running to the medics almost every day. But as long as Honida did not worry, Kroudar remained calm. Honida, after all, was a technician, a worker in the hydroponics gardens.

Kroudar moved his bare feet softly in the sand. Once more, he looked up at the bluff. Along the edge grew scattered native trees. Their thick trunks hugged the ground, gnarled and twisted, supports for bulbous, yellow-green leaves that exuded poisonous milk sap in the heat of the day. A few of the surviving Earth-falcons perched in the trees, silent, watchful.

The birds gave Kroudar an odd confidence in his own decisions. For what do the falcons watch, he wondered. It was a question the most exalted of the colony's thinkers had not been able to answer. Search 'copters had been sent out following the falcons. The birds flew offshore in the night, rested occasionally on barren islands, and returned at dawn. The colony command had been unwilling to risk its precious boats in the search, and the mystery of the falcons remained unsolved.

It was doubly a mystery because the other birds had perished or flown off to some unfound place. The doves, the quail—the gamebirds and songbirds—all had vanished. And the domestic chickens had all died, their eggs infertile. Kroudar knew this as a comment by *this place,* a warning for the life that came from Mother Earth.

A few scrawny cattle survived, and several calves had been born *here.* But they moved with a listless gait and there was distressed lowing in the pastures. Looking into their eyes was like looking into open wounds. A few pigs still lived, as listless and sickly as the cattle, and all the wild creatures had strayed off or died.

Except the falcons.

How odd it was, because the people who planned and conceived profound thoughts had held such hopes for *this place.* The survey reports had been exciting. This was a planet without native land animals. It was a planet whose native plants appeared not too different from those of Mother Earth—in some respects. And the sea creatures were primitive by sophisticated evolutionary standards.

Without being able to put it into those beautifully polished phrases which others admired, Kroudar knew where the mistake had been made. Sometimes, you had to search out a problem with your flesh and not with your mind.

He stared around now at the motley rags of his men. They were *his* men. He was the master fisherman, the one who had found the *trodi* and conceived these squat, ugly boats built within the limitations of native woods. The colony was alive now because of his skills with boat and net.

There would be more gaps in the *trodi* runs, though. Kroudar felt this as an awareness on the edges of his fatigue. There would be unpopular and dangerous things to do then, all necessary because *thinking* had failed. The salmon they had introduced, according to plan, had gone off into the ocean vastness. The flatfish in the colony's holding ponds suffered mysterious attrition. Insects flew away and were never seen again.

There's food here, the biologists argued. Why do they die?

The colony's maize was a sometime thing with strange ears. Wheat came up in scabrous patches. There were no familiar patterns of growth or migration. The colony lived on the thin edge of existence, maintained by protein bulk from the processed *trodi* and vitamins from vegetables grown hydroponically with arduous filtering and adjustment of their water. Breakdown of a single system in the chain could bring disaster.

The giant orange sun showed only a small arc above the sea horizon now, and Kroudar's men were stirring themselves, lifting their tired bodies off the sand, pushing away from the places where they had leaned.

"All right now," Kroudar ordered. "Let's get this food inside on the racks."

"Why?" someone asked from the dusk: "You think the falcons will eat it?"

They all knew the falcons would not eat the *trodi*. Kroudar recognized the objection: it was tiredness of the mind speaking The shrimp creatures fed only humans—after careful processing to remove dangerous irritants. A falcon might take up a frond-legged *trodi,* but would drop it at the first taste.

What did they eat, those waiting birds?

Falcons knew a thing about *this place* that humans did not know. The birds knew it in their flesh in the way Kroudar sought the knowledge.

Darkness fell, and with a furious clatter, the falcons flew off toward the sea. One of Kroudar's men kindled a torch and, having rested, anxious now to climb the bluff and join their families, the fishermen pitched into the work that must be done. Boats were hauled up on rollers. *Trodi* were spread out in thin layers along racks within the storage huts. Nets were draped on racks to dry.

As he worked, Kroudar wondered about the scientists up there in the shining laboratories. He had the working man's awe of knowledge, a servility in the face of titles and things clearly superior, but he had also the simple man's sure awareness of when superior things failed.

Kroudar was not privy to the high-level conferences in the colony command, but he knew the physical substance of the ideas discussed there. His awareness of failure and hovering disaster had no sophisticated words or erudition to hold itself dancingly before men's minds, but his knowledge carried its own elegance. He drew on ancient knowledge adjusted subtly to the differences of *this place*. Kroudar had found the *trodi*. Kroudar had organized the methods of capturing them and preserving them. He had no refined labels to explain it, but Kroudar knew himself for what he could do and what he was.

He was the first sea peasant *here*.

Without wasting energy on talk, Kroudar's band finished the work, turned away from the storage huts and plodded up the cliff trail, their course marked by, here and there, men with flaming torches. There were fuzzy orange lights, heavy shadows, inching their way upward in a black world, and they gave heart to Kroudar.

Lingering to the last, he checked the doors of the huts, then followed, hurrying to catch up. The man directly ahead of him on the path carried a torch, native wood soaked in *trodi* oil. It flickered and smoked and gave off poisonous fumes. The light revealed a troglodyte figure, a human clad in patched shipcloth, body too thin, muscles moving on the edge of collapse.

Kroudar sighed.

It was not like this on Mother Earth, he knew. There, the women waited on the strand for their men to return from the sea. Children played among the pebbles. Eager hands helped with the work onshore, spreading the nets, carrying the catch, pulling the boats.

Not *here.*

And the perils *here* were not the perils of Home. Kroudar's boats never strayed out of sight of these cliffs. One boat always carried a technician with a radio for contact with shore. Before its final descent, the colony ship had seeded space with orbiting devices—watchers, guardians against surprises from the weather. The laboriously built fishing fleet always had ample warning of storms. No monster sea creatures had ever been seen in that ocean.

This place lacked the cruel savagery and variety of seas Kroudar had known, but it was nonetheless deadly. He *knew* this.

The women should wait for us on the shore, he thought.

But colony command said the women—and even some of the children—were needed for too many other tasks. Individual plants from home required personal attention. Single wheat stalks were nurtured with tender care. Each orchard tree existed with its own handmaiden, its guardian dryad.

Atop the cliff, the fishermen came in sight of the longhouses, shipmetal *quonsets* named for some far distant place and time in human affairs. Scattered electric lights ringed the town. Many of the unpaved streets wandered off unlit. There were mechanical sounds here and murmurous voices.

The men scattered to their own affairs now, no longer a band. Kroudar plodded down his street toward the open cook fires in the central plaza. The open fires were a necessity to conserve the more sophisticated energies of the colony. Some looked upon those flames as admission of defeat. Kroudar saw them as victory. It was *native* wood being burned.

Off in the hills beyond the town, he knew, stood the ruins of the wind machines they had built. The storm which had wreaked that destruction had achieved no surprise in its coming, but had left enormous surprise at its power.

For Kroudar, the *thinkers* had begun to diminish in stature then. When native chemistry and water life had wrecked the turbines in the river which emptied into the harbor, those men of knowledge had shrunk even more. Then it was that Kroudar had begun his own search for native foods.

Now, Kroudar heard, native plant life threatened the cooling systems for their atomic generators, defying radiation in a way no life should. Some among the technicians already were fashioning steam engines of materials not intended for such use. Soon, they would have native metals, though—materials to resist the wild etchings and rusts of *this place.*

They might succeed—provided the dragging sickness did not sap them further.

If they survived.

Honida awaited him at the door to their quarters, smiling, graceful. Her dark hair was plaited and wound in rings around her forehead. The brown eyes were alive with welcome. Firelight from the plaza cast a familiar glow across her olive skin. The high cheekbones of her Amerind ancestry, the full lips and proudly hooked nose—all filled him with remembered excitement.

Kroudar wondered if the *planners* had known this thing about her which gave him such warmth—her strength and fecundity. She had chosen *him,* and now she carried more of their children—twins again.

"Ahhh, my fisherman is home," she said, embracing him in the doorway for anybody to see.

They went inside then, closed the door, and she held him with more ardor, stared up into his face which, reflected in her eyes, lost some of its ugliness.

"Honida," he said, unable to find other words.

Presently, he asked about the boys.

"They're asleep," she said, leading him to the crude trestle table he had built for their kitchen.

He nodded. Later, he would go in and stare at his sons. It did not bother him that they slept so much. He could feel the reasons for this somewhere within himself.

Honida had hot *trodi* soup waiting for him on the table. It was spiced with hydroponic tomatoes and peas and contained other things which he knew she gathered from the land without telling the scientists.

Whatever she put in front of him, Kroudar ate. There was bread tonight with an odd musty flavor which he found pleasant. In the light of the single lamp they were permitted for this room, he stared at a piece of the bread. It was almost purple—like the sea. He chewed it, swallowed.

Honida, watchfully eating across from him, finished her bread and soup, asked: "Do you like the bread?"

"I like it."

"I made it myself in the coals," she said.

He nodded, took another slice.

Honida refilled his soup bowl.

They were privileged, Kroudar realized, to have this privacy for their meals. Many of the others had opted for communal cooking and eating—even among the technicians and higher echelons who possessed more freedom of choice. Honida had seen something about *this place,* though, which required secrecy and going private ways.

Kroudar, hunger satisfied, stared across the table at her. He adored her with a devotion that went far deeper than the excitement of her flesh. He could not say the thing she was, but he knew it. If they were to have a future here, that future was in Honida and the things he might learn, form and construct of himself with his own flesh.

Under the pressure of his eyes, Honida arose, came around the table and began massaging the muscles of his back—the very muscles he used to haul the nets.

"You're tired," she said. "Was it difficult out there today?"

"Hard work," Kroudar said.

He admired the way she spoke. She had many words at her disposal. He had heard her use some of them during colony meetings and during the time of their application for mating choice. She had words for things he did not know, and she knew also when to speak with her body rather than with her mouth. She knew about the muscles of his back.

Kroudar felt such a love for her then that he wondered if it went up through her fingers into her body.

"We filled the boats," he said.

"I was told today that we'll soon need more storage huts," she said. "They're worried about sparing the labor for the building."

"Ten more huts," he said.

She would pass that word along, he knew. Somehow, it would be done. The other technicians listened to Honida. Many among the scientists scoffed at her; it could be heard beneath the blandness of their voices. Perhaps it was because she had chosen Kroudar for mate. But technicians listened. The huts would be built.

And they would be filled before the *trodi* run stopped.

Kroudar realized then that he knew when the run would stop, not as a date, but almost as a physical thing which he could reach out and touch. He longed for the words to explain this to Honida.

She gave his back a final kneading, sat down beside him and leaned her dark head against his chest. "If you're not too tired," she said, "I have something to show you."

With a feeling of surprise, Kroudar became aware of unspoken excitement in Honida. Was it something about the hydroponic gardens where she worked? His thoughts went immediately to that place upon which the scientists pinned their hopes, the place where they chose the tall plants, the beautiful, engorged with richness from Mother Earth. Had they achieved something important at last? Was there, after all, a clear way to make *this place* arable?

Kroudar was a primitive then wanting his gods redeemed. Even a sea peasant knew the value of land.

He and Honida had responsibilities, though. He nodded questioningly toward the twins' bedroom.

"I arranged . . ." She gestured toward their neighbor's cubicle. "They will listen."

She had planned this, then. Kroudar stood up, held out his hand for her. "Show me."

They went out into the night. Their town was quieter now; he could hear the distant roistering of the river. For a moment, he thought he heard a cricket, but reason told him it could only be one of the huts cooling in the night. He longed wordlessly for a moon.

Honida had brought one of the rechargeable electric torches, the kind issued to technicians against emergency calls in the night. Seeing that torch, Kroudar sensed a deeper importance in this mysterious thing she wanted to show him. Honida had the peasant's hoarding instinct. She would not waste such a torch.

Instead of leading him toward the green lights and glass roofs of the hydroponic gardens, though, she guided their steps in the opposite direction toward the deep gorge where the river plunged into the harbor.

There were no guards along the footpath, only an occasional stone marker and grotesqueries of native growth. Swiftly, without speaking, she led him to the gorge and the narrow path which he knew went only down to a ledge which jutted into the damp air of the river's spray.

Kroudar found himself trembling with excitement as he followed Honida's shadowy figure, the firefly darting of her light. It was cold on the ledge and the alien outline of native trees revealed by the torch filled Kroudar with disquiet.

What had Honida discovered—or created?

Condensation dripped from the plants here. The river noise was loud. It was marsh air he breathed, dank and filled with bizarre odors.

Honida stopped, and Kroudar held his breath. He listened. There was only the river.

For a moment, he didn't realize that Honida was directing the orange light of the torch at her discovery. It looked like one of the native plants—a thing with a thick stem crouched low to the land, gnarled and twisted, bulbous yellow-green protrusions set with odd spacing along its length.

Slowly, realization came over him. He recognized a darker tone in the green, the way the leaf structures were joined to the stalk, a bunching of brown-yellow silk drooping from the bulbous protrusions."

"Maize," he whispered.

In a low voice, pitching her explanation to Kroudar's vocabulary, Honida explained what she had done. He saw it in her words, understood why she had done this thing stealthily, here away from the scientists. He took the light from her, crouched, stared with rapt attention. This meant the death of those things the scientists held beautiful. It ended their plan for *this place.*

Kroudar could see his own descendants in this plant. They might develop bulbous heads, hairless, wide thick-lipped mouths. Their skins might become purple. They would be short statured; he knew that.

Honida had assured this—right here on the river-drenched ledge. Instead of selecting seed from the tallest, the straightest stalks, the ones with the longest and most perfect ears—the ones most like those from Mother

Earth—she had tested her maize almost to destruction. She had chosen sickly, scrawny plants, ones barely able to produce seed. She had taken only those plants which *this place* influenced most deeply. From these, she had selected finally a strain which lived *here* as native plants lived.

This was *native* maize.

She broke off an ear, peeled back the husk.

There were gaps in the seed rows and, when she squeezed a kernel, the juice ran purple. He recognized the smell of the bread.

Here was the thing the scientists would not admit. They were trying to make *this place* into another Earth. But it was not and it could never be. The falcons had been the first among their creatures to discover this, he suspected.

The statement Honida made here was that she and Kroudar would be short-lived. Their children would be sickly by Mother Earth's standards. Their descendants had planned this migration. The scientists would hate this and try to stop it.

This gnarled stalk of maize said the scientists would fail.

For a long while, Kroudar crouched there, staring into the future until the torch began to dim, losing its charge. He aroused himself then, led the way back out of the gorge.

At the top, with the lights of their dying civilization visible across the plain, he stopped, said: "The *trodi* run will stop . . . soon. I will take one boat and . . . friends. We will go out where the falcons go."

It was one of the longest speeches he had ever made.

She took the light from his hand, extinguished it, pressed herself against him.

"What do you think the falcons have found?"

"The seed," he said.

He shook his head. He could not explain it, but the thing was there in his awareness. Everything here excluded poisonous vapors, or juices in which only its own seed could live. Why should the *trodi* or any other sea creature be different? And, with the falcons as evidence, the seed must be slightly less poisonous to the intruders from Mother Earth.

"The boats are slow," she said.

He agreed silently. A storm could trap them too far out for a run to safety. It would be dangerous. But he heard also in her voice that she was not trying to stop him or dissuade him.

"I will take good men," he said.

"How long will you be gone?" Honida asked.

He thought about this for a moment. The rhythms of *this place* were beginning to make themselves known to him. His awareness shaped the journey, the days out, the night search over the water where the falcons were known to sweep in their low guiding runs—then the return.

"Eight days," he said.

"You'll need fine mesh nets," she said. "I'll see to having them made. Perhaps a few technicians, too. I know some who will go with you."

"Eight days," he said, telling her to choose strong men.

"Yes," she said. "Eight days. I'll be waiting on the shore when you return."

He took her hand then and led the way back across the plain. As they walked, he said: "We must name *this place*."

"When you come back," she said.

MURDER WILL IN

As the body died, the Tegas/Bacit awoke. Unconsciousness had lasted its usual flickering instant for the Tegas element. He came out of it with his Bacit negative identity chanting: ". . . not William Bailey—I'm not William Bailey—I'm not William Bailey . . ."

It was a painful, monotonous refrain—schismatic, important. The Tegas had to separate its identity from this fading flesh. Behind the chant lay a sense of many voices clamoring.

Awareness began to divide, a splitting seam that separated him from the compressed contact which controlled the host. There came a sensation of tearing fabric and he rode free, still immersed in the dying neural system because he had no other place to go, but capable of the identity leap.

Bacit and Tegas now functioning together, sticking him to each instant. He searched his surroundings: twenty meters . . . twenty meters . . .

Flickering, pale emotions registered on his awareness. Another attendant. The man passed out of range. Cold-cold-cold.

Nothing else.

What a rare joke this was, he thought. What a mischievous thing for fate to do. A Tegas to be caught like this! Mischievous. Mischievous. It wasn't fair. Hadn't he always treated the captive flesh with gentle care? Hadn't he made fun-lovers out of killers? Fate's mischief was cruel, not kindly in the manner of the Tegas.

The Bacit negative identity projected terror, accusation, embarrassment. He had lived too long in the William Bailey flesh. Too long. He had lived down where men were, where things were made—in the thick of being. He'd loved the flesh too much. He should've stopped occasionally and looked around him. The great Tegas curiosity which masqueraded as diffidence to hide itself had failed to protect him.

Failed . . . failed . . .

Within the dying neural system, frantic messages began darting back and forth. His mind was a torrent, a flare of being. Thoughts flew off like sparks from a grinding wheel.

"It's decided," the Tegas transmitted, seeking to quiet his negative self. The communicative contact returned a sharp feeling of shame and loss.

The Bacit shifted from terror to fifth-order displeasure, which was almost as bad as the terror. All the lost experiences. Lost . . . lost . . . lost . . .

"I had no idea the Euthanasia Center would be that simple and swift," the Tegas transmitted. "The incident is past changing. What can we do?"

He thought of the one vid-call he'd permitted himself, to check on the center's hours and routine. A gray-haired, polished contact-with-the-public type had appeared on the screen.

"We're fast, clean, neat, efficient, sanitary, and reverent," the man had said.

"Fast?"

"Who would want a slow death?"

The Tegas wished in this instant for nothing more than a slow death. If only he'd checked further. He'd expected this place to be seething with emotions. But it was emotionally dead—silent as a tomb. The joke-thought fell on inner silence.

The Bacit transfixed their composite self with a projection of urgent measurement—the twenty meters limit across which the Tegas could launch them into a new host.

But there'd been no way of knowing this place was an emotional vacuum until the Tegas element had entered here, probed the place. And these chambers where he now found himself were much farther from the street than twenty meters.

Momentarily, the Tegas was submerged in accusatory terror. *This death isn't like murder at all!*

Yet, he'd thought it would be *like* murder. And it was murder that'd been the saving device of the Tegas/Bacit for centuries. A murderer could be depended upon for total emotional involvement. A murderer could be lured close . . . close . . . close, much closer than twenty meters. It'd been so easy to goad the human creatures into that violent act, to set up the ideal circumstances for the identity leap. The Tegas absolutely required profound emotions in a prospective host. One couldn't focus on the neural totality without it. Bits of the creature's awareness center tended to escape. That could be fatal—as fatal as the trap in which he now found himself.

Murder.

The swift outflow of life from the discarded host, the emotional concentration of the new host—and before he knew it, the murderer was captive of the Tegas, captive in his own body. The captive awareness cried out silently, darting inward with ever tightening frenzy until it was swallowed.

And the Tegas could get on about its business of enjoying life.

This world had changed, though, in the past hundred years of the William

Bailey period. Murder had been virtually eliminated by the new predictive techniques and computers of the Data Center. The android law-niks were everywhere, anticipating violence, preventing it. This was an elliptical development of society and the Tegas realized he should've taken it into account long ago. But life tended to be so pleasant when it held the illusion of never ending. For the Tegas, migrating across the universe with its hosts, moving as a predator in the dark of life, the illusion could be a fact.

Unless it ended here.

It didn't help matters that decisions had been forced upon him. Despite a fairly youthful appearance, the host flesh of William Bailey had been failing. The Tegas could keep its host going far beyond the normal span, but when the creature began to fail, collapse could be massive and abrupt.

I should've tried to attack someone in circumstances where I'd have been killed, he thought. But he'd seen the flaw there. The emotionless law-niks would have been on him almost instantly. Death might've escaped him. He could've been trapped in a crippled, dying host surrounded by android blankness or, even worse, surrounded by humans rendered almost emotionless by that damnable "Middle Way" and "Eight-fold Karma."

And the hounds were on his trail. He knew they were. He'd seen plenty of evidence, sensed the snoopers. He'd lived too long as William Bailey. The ones who thrived on suspicion had become suspicious. And they couldn't be allowed to examine a Tegas host too closely. He knew what'd put them on his trail: that diabolical "total profile of motives." The Tegas in William Bailey was technically a murderer thousands of times over. Not that he went on killing and killing; once in a human lifetime was quite enough. Murder could take the fun out of life.

Thoughts were useless now, he realized. He had, after all, been trapped. Thinking about it led only to Bacit accusations. And while he jumped from thought to thought, the William Bailey body moved nearer and nearer to dissolution. The body now held only the faintest contact with life, and that only because of desperate Tegas efforts. A human medic would've declared Bailey dead. Breathing had stopped. Abruptly, the heart fibrillated, ceased function.

Less than five minutes remained for the Tegas. He had to find a new host in five minutes with this one.

"Murder-murder-murder," the Bacit intruded. "You said euthanasia would be murder."

The Tegas felt William Bailey–shame. He cursed inwardly. The Bacit, normally such a useful function for a Tegas (driving away intellectual loneliness, providing companionship and caution) had become a distracting liability. The intrusion of terrifying urgency stopped thought.

Why couldn't the Bacit be silent and let him think?

Momentarily, the Tegas realized he'd never before considered the premises of his own actions.

What was the Bacit?

He'd never hungered after his own kind, for he had the Bacit. But what, after all, was the Bacit? Why, for example, would it let him captivate only males? Female thinking might be a help in this emergency. Why couldn't he mix the sexes?

The Bacit used the inner shout: "Now we have time for philosophy?"

It was too much.

"Silence!" the Tegas commanded.

An immediate sense of loneliness rocked him. He defied it, probed his surroundings. Any host would do in this situation—even a lower animal, although he hadn't risked one of those in aeons. Surely there must be some emotional upset in this terrible place . . . something . . . anything . . .

He remembered a long-ago incident when he'd allowed himself to be slain by a type who'd turned out to be completely emotionless. He'd barely managed to shift in time to any eyewitness to the crime. The moment had been like this one in its sudden emergency, but who was eyewitness to this killing? Where was an alternative host?

He searched fruitlessly.

Synapses began snapping in the William Bailey neural system. The Tegas withdrew to the longest-lived centers, probed with increasing frenzy.

A seething emotional mass lifted itself on his awareness horizon. Fear, self-pity, revenge, anger: a lovely prospect, like a rescue steamer bearing down on a drowning mariner.

"I'm not William Bailey," he reminded himself and launched outwards, homing on that boiling tangle of paradox, that emotional beacon . . .

There came the usual bouncing shock as he grabbed for the new host's identity centers. He poured out through a sensorium, discovered his own movements, felt something cold against a wrist. It was not yet completely his wrist, but the eyes were sufficiently under control for him to force them towards the source of sensation.

A flat, gray metallic object swam into focus. It was pressed against *his* wrist. Simultaneously, there occurred a swarming sense of awareness within the host. It was a sighing-out—not submission, but negative exaltation. The Tegas felt an old heart begin to falter, looked at an attendant: unfamiliar face—owlish features around a sharp nose.

But no emotional intensity, no central hook of being to be grabbed and captivated.

The room was a twin to the one in which he'd been captured by this system. The ceiling's time read-out said only eight minutes had passed since that other wrist had been touched by death.

"If you'll be so kind as to go through the door behind you," the owl-faced attendant said. "I do hope you can make it. Had to drag three of you in there already this shift; I'm rather weary. Let's get moving, eh?"

Weary? Yes—the attendant radiated only emotional weariness. It was nothing a Tegas could grasp.

The new host responded to the idea of urgency, pushed up out of a chair, shambled towards an oval door. The attendant hurried him along with an arm across the old shoulders.

The Tegas moved within the host, consolidated neural capacity, swept in an unresisting awareness. It wasn't an awareness he'd have taken out of choice—defeated, submissive. There was something strange about it. The Tegas detected a foreign object pressed against the host's spine. A capsule of some kind—neural transmitter/receiver. It radiated an emotional-damper effect, commands of obedience.

The Tegas blocked it off swiftly, terrified by the implications of such an instrument.

He had the host's identity now: James Daggett; that was the name. Age seventy-one. The body was a poor, used-up relic, weaker, more debilitated than William Bailey had been at 236. The host's birdlike awareness, giving itself up to the Tegas as it gave up to death, radiated oddly mystical thoughts, confusions, assumptions, filterings.

The Tegas was an angel "come to escort me."

Still trailing wisps of William Bailey, the Tegas avoided too close a linkage with this new host. The name and self-recognition centers were enough.

He realized with a twisted sense of defeat that the old body was being strapped on to a hard surface. The ceiling loomed over him a featureless gray. Dulled nostrils sniffed at an antiseptic breeze.

"Sleep well, paisano," the attendant said.

Not again! the Tegas thought.

His Bacit half reasserted itself: "We can jump from body to body—dying a little each time. What fun!"

The Tegas transmitted a remote obscenity from another world and another aeon, describing what the Bacit half could do with its bitterness.

Vacuity replaced the intrusion.

Defeat . . . defeat . . .

Part of this doomed mood, he realized, came out of the James Daggett personality. The Tegas took the moment to probe that host's memories, found the time when the transmitter had been attached to his spine.

Defeat-obedience-defeat . . .

It stemmed from that surgical instant.

He restored the blocks, quested outwards for a new host. Questing, he searched his Tegas memory. There must be a clue somewhere, a hint, a thought—some way of escape. He missed the Bacit contribution, parts of his memory felt cut off. The neural linkage with the dying James Daggett clung like dirty mud to his thoughts.

Ancient, dying James Daggett remained filled with mystical confusions until he was swallowed by the Tegas. It was a poor neural connection. The host was supposed to resist. That strengthened the Tegas grip. Instead, the

Tegas ran into softly dying walls of other-memory. Linkages slipped. He felt his awareness range contracting.

Something swam into the questing field—anger, outrage of the kind frequently directed against stupidities. The Tegas waited, wondering if this could be another *client* of the center.

Now, trailing the angry one came another identity. Fear dominated this one. The Tegas went into a mental crouch, focused its awareness hungrily. An object of anger, a fearful one—there was a one a Tegas could grab.

Voices came to him from the hallway outside the alcove—rasping, attacking and (delayed) fearful.

James Daggett's old and misused ears cut off overtones, reduced volume. There wasn't time to strengthen the host's hearing circuits, but the Tegas grasped the sense of the argument.

". . . told to notify . . . immediately if . . . Bailey! William Bailey! . . . saw the . . . your desk . . ."

And the fearful one: ". . . . busy . . . you've no idea how . . . and under-staffed and . . . teen an hour . . . only . . . this shift . . ."

The voices receded, but the emotional auras remained within Tegas range.

"Dead!" It was the angry one, a voice-blast accompanied by a neural overload that rolled across the Tegas like a giant wave.

At the instant of rage, the fearful one hit a momentary fear peak: abject retreat.

The Tegas pounced, quitting James Daggett in the blink-out as life went under. It was like stepping off a sinking boat into a storm-racked cockleshell. He was momentarily lost in the tracery of material spacetime which was the chosen host. Abruptly, he realized the fearful one had husbanded a reserve of supercilious hate, an ego corner fortified by resentments against authority accumulated over many years. The bouncing shock of the contact was accompanied by an escape of the host's awareness into the fortified corner.

The Tegas knew then he was in for a fight such as he'd never before experienced. The realization was accompanied by a blurred glimpse through host-eyes of a darkly suspicious face staring at him across a strapped-down body. The death-locked features of the body shook him—William Bailey! He almost lost the battle right there.

The host took control of the cheeks, contorted them. The eyes behaved independently: one looking up, the other down. He experienced direct perception, seeing with the fingertips (pale glowing), hearing with the lips (an itch of sound). Skin trembled and flushed. He staggered, heard a voice shout: "Who're you? What you doing to me?"

It was the host's voice, and the Tegas, snatching at the vocal centers, could only burr the edges of sound, not blank out intelligibility. He glimpsed the dark face across from him in an eye-swirling flash. The other had recoiled, staring.

It was one of the suspicious ones, the hated ones, the ones-who-rule. No time to worry about that now. The Tegas was fighting for survival. He summoned every trick he'd ever learned—cajolery, mystical subterfuges, a flailing of religious illusion, love, hate, word play. Men were an instrument of language and could be snared by it. He went in snake-striking dashes along the neural channels.

The name! He had to get the name!

"Carmy . . . Carmichael!"

He had half the name then, a toehold on survival. Silently, roaring inward along synaptic channels, he screamed the name—

"I'm Carmichael! I'm Carmichael!"

"No!"

"Yes! I'm Carmichael!"

"You're not! You're not!"

"I'm Carmichael!"

The host was bludgeoned into puzzlement: "Who're you? You can't be me. I'm . . . Joe—Joe Carmichael!"

The Tegas exulted, snapping up the whole name: "I'm Joe Carmichael!"

The host's awareness spiraled inward, darting, frenzied. Eyes rolled. Legs trembled. Arms moved with a disjointed flapping. Teeth gnashed. Tears rolled down the cheeks.

The Tegas smashed at him now: "I'm Joe Carmichael!"

"No . . . no . . . no . . ." It was a fading inner scream, winking out . . . back . . . out . . .

Silence.

"I'm Joe Carmichael," the Tegas thought.

It was a Joe Carmichael thought faintly touched by Tegas inflections and Bacit's reproving: "That was too close."

The Tegas realized he lay flat on his back on the floor. He looked up into dark features identified by host-memories: "Chadrick Vicentelli, Commissioner of Crime Prevention."

"Mr. Carmichael," Vicentelli said. "I've summoned help. Rest quietly. Don't try to move just yet."

What a harsh, unmoving face, the Tegas thought. Vicentelli's was a Noh mask face. And the voice: wary, cold, suspicious. This violent incident wasn't on any computer's predictives. . . . Or was it? No matter—a suspicious man had seen too much. Something had to be done—immediately. Feet already could be heard pounding along the corridor.

"Don't know what's wrong with me," the Tegas said, managing the Carmichael voice with memory help from the Bailey period. "Dizzy . . . whole world seemed to go red. . . ."

"You look alert enough now," Vicentelli said.

There was no *give* in that voice, no love. Violence there, suspicious hate contained in sharp edges.

"You look alert enough now."

A Tegas shudder went through the Carmichael body. He studied the probing, suspicious eyes. This was the breed Tegas avoided. Rulers possessed
terrible resources for the inner battle. That was one of the reasons they
ruled. Tegas had been swallowed by rulers—dissolved, lost. Mistakes had
been made in the dim beginnings before Tegas learned to avoid ones such as
this. Even on this world, the Tegas recalled early fights, near things that had
resulted in rumors and customs, myths, racial fears. All primitives knew the
code: *"Never reveal your true name!"*

And here was a ruler who had seen too much in times when that carried
supreme danger. Suspicion was aroused. A sharp intelligence weighed data
it should never have received.

Two red-coated android law-niks, as alike in their bland-featured intensity
as obedient dogs, swept through the alcove hangings, came to a stop waiting
for Vicentelli's orders. It was unnerving: even with androids, the ones-who-
submitted never hesitated in looking first to a ruler for their orders.

The Tegas thought of the control capsule that had been on James Daggett's
spine. A new fear trembled through him. The host's mouth was dry with a
purely Carmichael emotion.

"This is Joseph Carmichael," Vicentelli said, pointing. "I want him taken
to IC for a complete examination and motivational profile. I'll meet you
there. Notify the appropriate cadres."

The law-niks helped the Tegas to his new feet.

IC—Investigation Central, he thought.

"Why're you taking me to IC?" he demanded. "I should go to a hospital
for—"

"We've medical facilities," Vicentelli said. He made it sound ominous.

Medical facilities for what?

"But why—"

"Be quiet and obey," Vicentelli said. He glanced at William Bailey's
body, back to Carmichael. It was a look full of weighted suspicions, half
knowledge, educated assumptions.

The Tegas glanced at William Bailey's body, was caught by an inward-
memory touch that wrenched at his new awareness. It had been a superior
host, flesh deserving of love. The nostalgia passed. He looked back at Vicentelli, formed a vacant stare of confusion. It was not a completely feigned
reaction. The Carmichael takeover had occurred in the presence of the suspected William Bailey—no matter that William Bailey was a corpse; that
merely fed the suspicions. Vicentelli, assuming an unknown presence in
William Bailey, would think it had leaped from the corpse to Carmichael.

"We're interested in you," Vicentelli said. "Very interested. Much more
interested than we were before your recent . . . ahhh, seizure." He nodded to
the androids.

Seizure! the Tegas thought.

Firm, insistent hands propelled him through the alcove curtains into the hallway, down the hall, through the antiseptic white of the employees' dressing room and out of the back door.

The day he'd left such a short time before as William Bailey appeared oddly transformed to the Carmichael eyes. There was a slight change in the height of the eyes, of course—a matter of perhaps three centimeters taller for Carmichael. He had to break his visual reactions out of perspective habits formed by more than two centuries at Bailey's height. But the change was more than that. He felt that he was seeing the day through many eyes— many more than the host's two.

The sensation of multi-ocular vision confused him, but he hadn't time to examine it before the law-niks pushed him into the one-way glass cage of an aircar. The door hissed closed, thumping on its seals, and he was alone, peering out through the blue-gray filtering of the windows. He leaned back on padded plastic.

The aircar leaped upward out of the plastrete canyon, sped across the great tableland roof of the Euthanasia Center toward the distant man-made peaks of IC. The central complex of government was an area the Tegas always had avoided. He wished nothing more now than to continue avoiding it.

A feeling came over him that his universe had shattered. He was trapped here—not just trapped in the aircar flitting towards the plastrete citadel of IC, but trapped in the ecosystem of the planet. It was a sensation he'd never before experienced—not even on that aeons-distant day when he'd landed here in a conditioned host at the end of a trip which had taxed the limits of the host's viability. It was the way of the Tegas, though, to reach out for new planets, new hosts. It had become second nature to choose the right kind of planet, the right kind of developing life forms. The right kind always developed star travel, releasing the Tegas for a new journey, new explorations, new experiences. That way, boredom never intervened. The creatures of this planet were headed towards the stellar leap, too—given time.

But the Tegas, experiencing a new fear for him, realized he might not be around to take advantage of that stellar leap. It was a realization that left him feeling exhausted, time-scalded, injured in his responses like a mistreated instrument.

Where did I go wrong? he wondered. *Was it in the original choice of the planet?*

His Bacit half, usually so explicit in reaction to inner searching, spread across their mutual awareness a projected sense of the fuzzy unknowns ahead.

This angered the Tegas. The future always was unknown. He began exploring his host-self, assessing what he could use in the coming showdown. It was a good host—healthy, strong, its musculature and neural system capable of excellent Tegas reinforcement and intensification. It was a host that could give good service, perhaps even longer than William Bailey. The Tegas began doing what he could in the time available, removing inhibitory blocks for quicker and smoother neural responses, setting up a heart and vascular system buffer. He took a certain pride in the work; he'd never misused a host as long as it remained viable.

The natural Tegas resilience, the thing that kept him going, kept him alive and interested—the endless curiosity—reasserted itself. Whatever was about to happen, it would be new. He seated himself firmly in the host, harnessed the Carmichael memory system to his Tegas responses, and readied himself to meet the immediate future.

A thought crept into his mind:

In the delicate immensity that was his own past there lay nonhuman experiences. How subtle was this "Total Profile of Personality"? Could it detect the nonhuman? Could it cast a template which would compare too closely with William Bailey . . . or any of the others they might have on their Data Center lists?

He sensed the dance of the intellects within him, pounding out their patterns on the floor of his awareness. In a way, he knew he was all the captive stalks bound up like a sheaf of grain.

The city-scape passing beneath the aircar became something sensed rather than seen. Tiny frenzies of fear began to dart about in him. What tools of psychometry would his interrogators use? How discreet? How subtle? Beneath their probes, he must be nothing other than Joe Carmichael. Yet . . . he was far more. He felt the current of *now* sweeping his existence toward peril.

Danger-danger-danger. He could see it intellectually as Tegas. He responded to it as Joe Carmichael.

Sweat drenched his body.

The aircar began to descend. He stared at the backs of the androids' heads visible through the glass of the control cab. They were two emotionless blobs; no help there. The car left the daylight, rocked once in a recognition-field, slid down a tube filled with cold aluminium light into the yellow glowing of a gigantic plastrete parking enclosure—tawny walls and ceiling, a sense of cavernous distance humming with activity.

It made the Tegas think of a hive society he'd once experienced; not one of his better memories. He shuddered.

The aircar found its parking niche, stopped. Presently, the doors hissed open. The androids flanked the opening. One gestured for him to emerge.

The Tegas swallowed in a dry Carmichael throat, climbed out, stared around at the impersonal comings and goings of androids. Neither by eye or emotional aura could he detect a human in the region around him. Intense loneliness came over him.

Still without speaking, the androids took his arms, propelled him across an open space into the half-cup of a ring lift. The field grabbed them, shot them upward past blurred walls and flickers of openings. The lift angled abruptly, holding them softly with their faces tipped downward at something near forty-five degrees. The androids remained locked beside him like two fish swimming in the air. The lift grip returned to vertical, shot them upward into the center of an amphitheater room.

The lift hole became floor beneath his feet.

The Tegas stared up and around at a reaching space, immense blue skylight, people-people-people, tiers of them peering down at him, tiers of them all around.

He probed for emotions, met the terrifying aura of the place, an icy neural stare, a psychic *chutzpah*. The watchers—rulers all, their minds disconnected from any religion except the *self,* no nervous coughs, no impatient stirrings.

They were an iceberg of silent waiting.

He had never imagined such a place even in a nightmare. But he knew this place, recognized it immediately. If a Tegas must end, he thought, then it must be in some such place as this. All the lost experiences that might come to an end here began wailing through him.

Someone emerged from an opening on his left, strode toward him across the floor of the amphitheater: Vicentelli.

The Tegas stared at the approaching man, noted the eyes favored by deep shadows: dense black eyes cut into a face where lay a verseless record—hard glyphs of cheeks, stone-cut mouth. Everything was labor in that face: work-work-work. It held no notion of fun. It was a contrivance for asserting violence, both spectator and participant. It rode the flesh, cherishing no soft thing at all.

A vat of liquid as blue as glowing steel arose from the floor beside the Tegas. Android hands gripped him tightly as he jerked with surprise.

Vicentelli stopped in front of him, glanced once at the surrounding banks of faces, back to his victim.

"Perhaps you're ready to save us the trouble of an interrogation in depth," he said.

The Tegas felt his body tremble, shook his head.

Vicentelli nodded.

With impersonal swiftness, the androids stripped the clothing from the Tegas host, lifted him into the vat. The liquid felt warm and tingling. A harness was adjusted to hold his arms and keep his face just above the surface. An inverted dome came down to rest just above his head. The day became a blue stick of light and he wondered inanely what time it was. It'd been early when he'd entered the Euthanasia Center, now, it was very late. Yet, he knew the day had hardly advanced past mid-morning.

Again, he probed the emotional aura, recoiled from it.

What if they kill me coldly? he wondered.

Where he could single out individuals, he was reminded of the play of lightning on a far horizon. The emotional beacons were thin, yet filled with potency.

A room full of rulers. The Tegas could imagine no more hideous place.

Something moved across his stick of light: Vicentelli.

"Who are you?" Vicentelli asked.

I'm Joe Carmichael, he thought. *I must be only Joe Carmichael.*

But Carmichael's emotions threatened to overwhelm him. Outrage and submissive terror flickered through the neural exchanges. The host body twitched. Its legs made faint running motions.

Vicentelli turned away, spoke to the surrounding watchers:

"The problem with Joseph Carmichael is this violent incident which you're now seeing on your recorders. Let me impress upon you that this incident was not predicted. It was outside our scope. We must assume, therefore, that it was not a product of Joseph Carmichael. During this examination, each of you will study the exposed profile. I want each of you to record your reactions and suggestions. Somewhere here there will be a clue to the unknowns we observed in William Bailey and before that in Almiro Hsing. Be alert, observant."

God of Eternity! the Tegas thought. *They've traced me from Hsing to Bailey!*

This change in human society went back farther than he'd suspected. How far back?

"You will note, please," Vicentelli said, "that Bailey was in the immediate vicinity when Hsing fell from the Peace Tower at Canton and died. Pay particular attention to the material which points to a previous association between Hsing and Bailey. There is a possibility Bailey was at that particular place on Hsing's invitation. This could be important."

The Tegas tried to withdraw his being, to encyst his emotions. The ruling humans had gone down a developmental side path he'd never expected. They had left him somewhere.

He knew why: Tegas-like, he had immersed himself in the concealing presence of the mob, retreated into daily drudgery, lived like the living. Yet, he had never loved the flesh more than in this moment when he knew he could lose it forever. He loved the flesh the way a man might love a house. This intricate structure was a house that breathed and felt.

Abruptly, he underwent a sense of union with the flesh more intimate than anything of his previous experience. He knew for certain in this instant how a man would feel here. Time had never been an enemy of the Tegas. But Time was man's enemy. He was a man now and he prepared his flesh for maximum reactions, for high-energy discharge.

Control: That was what this society was up to—super control.

Vicentelli's face returned to the stick of light.

"For the sake of convenience," he said, "I'll continue to call you Carmichael."

The statement told him baldly that he was in a corner and Vicentelli knew it. If the Tegas had any doubts, Vicentelli now removed them.

"Don't try to kill yourself," Vicentelli said. "The mechanism in which you now find yourself can sustain your life even when you least wish that life to continue."

Abruptly, the Tegas realized his Carmichael self should be panic-stricken. There could be no Tegas watchfulness or remoteness here.

He was panic-stricken.

The host body thrashed in the liquid, surged against the bonds. The liquid was heavy—oily, but not oily. It held him as an elastic suit might, dampening his movements, always returning him to the quiescent, fishlike floating.

"Now," Vicentelli said.

There was a loud click.

Light dazzled the Carmichael eyes. Color rhythms appeared within the light. The rhythms held an epileptic beat. They jangled his mind, shook the Tegas awareness like something loosed in a violent cage.

Out of the voice which his universe had become there appeared questions. He knew they were spoken questions, but he saw them: word shapes tumbling in a torrent.

"Who are you?"

"What are you?"

"We see you for what you are. Why don't you admit what you are? We know you."

The aura of the surrounding watchers drummed at him with accusing vibrations: "We know you—know you—know you—know you . . ."

The Tegas felt the words rocking him, subduing him.

No Tegas can by hypnotized, he told himself. But he could feel his being coming out in shreds. Something was separating. Carmichael! The Tegas was losing his grip on the host! But the flesh was being reduced to a mesmerized idiot. The sense of separation intensified.

Abruptly, there was an inner sensation of stirring, awakening. He felt the host ego awakening, was powerless to counter it.

Thoughts crept along the dancing, shimmering neural paths—

"Who . . . what are . . . where do . . ."

The Tegas punched frantically at the questings: "I'm Joe Carmichael . . . I'm Joe Carmichael . . . I'm Joe Carmichael . . ."

He found vocal control, mouthed the words in dumb rhythm, making this the one answer to all questions. Slowly, the host fell silent, smothered in a Tegas envelope.

The blundering, bludgeoning interrogation continued.

Shake-rattle-question.

He felt himself losing all sense of distinction between Tegas and Carmichael. The Bacit half, whipped and terrorized by the unexpected sophistication of this attack, strewed itself in tangles through the identity net.

Voices of old hosts came alive in his mind: ". . . you can't . . . mustn't . . . I'm Joe Carmichael . . . stop them . . . why can't we . . ."

"You're murdering me!" he screamed.

The ranked watchers in the ampitheater united in an aura of pouncing glee.

"They're monsters!" Carmichael thought.

It was a pure Carmichael thought, unmodified by Tegas awareness, an unfettered human expression surging upwards from within.

"You hear me, Tegas?" Carmichael demanded. "They're monsters!"

The Tegas crouched in the flesh not knowing how to counter this. Never before had he experienced direct communication from a host after that final entrapment. He tried to locate the source of communication, failed.

"Look at 'em staring down at us like a pack of ghouls!" Carmichael thought.

The Tegas knew he should react, but before he could bring himself to it, the interrogation assumed a new intensity: shake-rattle-question.

"Where do you come from? Where do you come from? Where do you come from?"

The question tore at him with letters tall as giant buildings—faceless eyes, thundering voices, shimmering words.

Carmichael anger surged across the Tegas.

Still, the watchers radiated their chill amusement.

"Let's die and take one of 'em!" Carmichael insisted.

"Who speaks?" the Bacit demanded. "How did you get away? Where are you?"

"God! How cold they are." That had been a Bailey thought.

"Where do you come from?" the Bacit demanded, seeking the host awareness. "You are here, but we cannot find you."

"I come from Zimbue," Carmichael projected.

"You cannot come from Zimbue," the Tegas countered. "I come from Zimbue."

"But Zimbue is nowhere," the Bacit insisted.

And all the while—shake-rattle-question—Vicentelli's interrogation continued to jam circuits.

The Tegas felt he was being bombarded from all sides and from within. How could Carmichael talk of Zimbue?

"Then whence comest thou?" Carmichael asked.

How could Carmichael know of this matter? the Tegas asked himself. Whence had all Tegas come? The answer was a rote memory at the bottom of all his experiences: At the instant time began, the Tegas intruded upon the blackness where no star—not even a primal dust fleck—had tracked the dimensions with its being. They had been where senses had not been. How could Carmichael's ego still exist and know to ask of such things?

"And why shouldn't I ask?" Carmichael insisted. "It's what Vicentelli asks."

But where had the trapped ego of the host flesh hidden? Whence took it an existence to speak now?

The Bacit half had experienced enough. "Say him down!" the Bacit commanded. "Say him down! We are Joe Carmichael! You are Joe Carmichael! I am Joe Carmichael!"

"Don't panic," Carmichael soothed. "You are Tegas/Bacit, one being. I am Joe Carmichael."

And from the outer world, Vicentelli roared: "Who are you? I command you to tell me who you are! You must obey me! Are you William Bailey?"

Silence—inward and outward.

In the silence, the Tegas probed the abused flesh, understood part of the nature behind Vicentelli's attack. The liquid in which the host lay immersed: It was an anesthetic. The flesh was being robbed of sensation until only inner nerve tangles remained. Even more—the anesthetized flesh had been invaded by a control device. A throbbing capsule lay against the Carmichael spine—signalling, commanding, interfering.

"The capsule has been attached," Vicentelli said. "I will take him now to the lower chamber where the interrogation can proceed along normal channels. He's completely under our control now."

In the trapped flesh, the Bacit half searched out neural connections of the control capsule, tried to block them, succeeded only partly. Anesthetized flesh resisted Bacit probes. The Tegas, poised like a frightened spider in the host awareness, studied the softly throbbing neural currents for a solution. Should he attack, resume complete control? What could he attack? Vicentelli's interrogation had tangled identities in the host in a way that might never be unravelled.

The control capsule pulsed.

Carmichael's flesh obeyed a new command. Restraining bands slid aside. The Tegas stood up in the tank on unfeeling feet. Where his chest was exposed, sensation began to return. The inverted hemisphere was lifted from his head.

"You see," Vicentelli said, addressing the watchers above them. "He obeys perfectly."

Inwardly, Carmichael asked: "Tegas, can you reach out and see how they feel about all this? There might be a clue in their emotions."

"Do it!" the Bacit commanded.

The Tegas probed surrounding space, felt boredom, undertones of suspicion, a cat-licking sense of power. Yes, the mouse lay trapped between claws. The mouse could not escape.

Android hands helped the Tegas out of the tank, stood him on the floor, steadied him.

"Perfect control," Vicentelli said.

As the control capsule commanded, the Carmichael eyes stared straight ahead with a blank emptiness.

The Tegas sent a questing probe along the nearest channels, met Bacit, Carmichael, uncounted bits of others.

"How can you be here, Joe Carmichael?" he asked.

The host flesh responded to a capsule command, walked straight ahead across the floor of the ampitheater.

"Why aren't you fleeing or fighting me?" the Tegas insisted.

"No need," Carmichael responded. "We're all mixed up together, as you can see."

"Why aren't you afraid?"

"I was . . . am . . . hope not to be."

"How do you know about the Tegas?"

"How not? We're each other."

The Tegas experienced a shock-blink of awareness at this, felt an uneasy Bacit-projection. Nothing in all Tegas experience recalled such an inner encounter. The host fought and lost or the Tegas ended there. And the lost host went . . . where? A fearful questing came from the Bacit, a sense of broken continuity.

That damnable interrogation!

The host flesh, responding to the capsule's commands, had walked through a doorway into a blue hallway. As sensation returned, Tegas/Carmichael/Bacit grew aware of Vicentelli following . . . and other footsteps—android law-niks.

"What do you want, Joe Carmichael?" the Tegas demanded.

"I want to share."

"Why?"

"You're . . . more than I was. You can give me . . . longer life. You're curious . . . interesting. Half the creeps we got at the E-Center were worn down by boredom, and I was almost at that stage myself. Now . . . living is interesting once more."

"How can we live together—in here?"

"We're doing it."

"But I'm Tegas! I must rule in here!"

"So rule."

And the Tegas realized he had been restored to almost complete contact with the host's neural system. Still, the intrusive Carmichael ego remained. And the Bacit was doing nothing about this situation, appeared to have withdrawn to wherever the Bacit went. Carmichael remained—a slithering, mercuric thing: right there! No! Over here! No . . . . no . . . . not there, not here. Still, he remained.

"The host must submit without reservation," the Tegas commanded.

"I submit," Carmichael agreed.

"Then where are you?"

"We're all in here together. You're in command of the flesh, aren't you?"

The Tegas had to admit he was in command.

"What do you want, Joe Carmichael?" he insisted.

"I've told you."

"You haven't."

"I want to . . . watch . . . to share."

"Why should I let you do that?"

Vicentelli and his control capsule had brought the host flesh now to a drop chute. The chute's field gripped the Carmichael flesh, sent it whispering downward . . . downward . . . downward.

"Maybe you have no choice in whether I stay and watch," Joe Carmichael responded.

"I took you once," the Tegas countered. "I can take you again."

"What happens when they resume the interrogation?" Carmichael asked.

"What do you mean?"

"He means," the Bacit intruded, "that the true Joe Carmichael can respond with absolute verisimilitude to their search for a profile comparison."

The drop chute disgorged him into a long icy-white laboratory space. Through the fixated eyes came a sensation of metal shapes, of instruments, of glitterings and flashings, of movement.

The Tegas stood in capsule-induced paralysis. It was a condition any Tegas could override, but he dared not. No human could surmount this neural assault. The merest movement of a finger now amounted to exposure.

In the shared arena of their awareness, Carmichael said: "Okay, let me have the con for a while. Watch. Don't intrude at all."

The Tegas hesitated.

"Do it!" the Bacit commanded.

The Tegas withdrew. He found himself in emptiness, a nowhere of the mind, an unseen place, constrained vacuity . . . nothing . . . never . . . an unspoken, unspeaking pill of absence . . . uncontained. This was a place where senses had not been, could not be. He feared it, but felt protected by it—hidden.

A sense of friendship and reassurance came to him from Carmichael. The Tegas felt a hopeless sense of gratitude for the first other-creature friendship he'd ever experienced. But why should Carmichael-ego be friendly? Doubt worried at him, nipped and nibbled. Why?

No answer came, unless an unmeasured simplicity radiating from the Bacit could be interpreted as answer. The Tegas found he had an economy of reservations about his position. This astonished him. He recognized he was making something new with all the dangers inherent in newness. It wasn't logical, but he knew thought might be the least careless when it was the least logical.

Time is the enemy of the flesh, he reminded himself. *Time is not my enemy.*

Reflections of meaning, actions, and intentions began coming to him from the outer-being-place where Carmichael sat. Vicentelli had returned to the attack with induced colors, shapes, flarings and dazzles. Words leaped across a Tegas mind-sky: "Who are you? Answer! I know you're there! Answer! Who are you?"

Joe Carmichael mumbled half-stupefied protests: "Why're you torturing me? What're y'doing?"

Shake-rattle-question: "STOP HIDING FROM ME!"

Carmichael's response wiggled outwards: "Wha'y' doing?"

Silence enveloped the flesh.

The Tegas began receiving muted filterings of a debate: "I tell you, his profile matches the Carmichael identity with exactness." . . . "Saw him change." . . . "perhaps chemical poisoning . . . Euthanasia Center . . . consistent with ingestion of picrotoxin . . . coincidence . . ."

Creeping out into the necessary neural channels, the Tegas probed his surroundings for the emotional aura, found only do you understand? Remain unmoving, no pain. Move—pain."

Tegas permitted his host to take a deep, quivering breath. Knives played with his chest and spine.

"To breathe, to flex a wrist, to walk—all equal pain," Vicentelli said. "The beauty of it is there's no bodily harm. But you'll pray for something simple as injury unless you give up."

"You're an animal!" the Tegas managed. Agony licked along his jaw and lips, flayed his temples.

"Give up," Vicentelli said.

"Animal," the Tegas whispered. He felt his Bacit half throwing pain blocks into the neural system, tried a shallow breath. Faint irritation rewarded the movement, but he simulated a pain reaction—closed his eyes. Fire crept along his brows. A swift block eased the pain.

"Why prolong it?" Vicentelli asked. "What are you?"

"You're insane," Tegas whispered. He waited, feeling the pain blocks click into place.

Darting lights glittered in Vicentelli's eyes. "Do you really feel the pain?" he asked. He moved a handle on the console.

The host was hurled to the floor by a flashing command from the control capsule.

Under Bacit guidance, he writhed with the proper pain reactions, allowed them to subside slowly.

"You feel it," Vicentelli said. "Good." He reached down, jerked his victim upright, steadied him.

The Bacit had almost all the pain under control, signalling proper concealment reactions. The host flesh grimaced, resisted movement, stood awkwardly.

"I have all the time I need," Vicentelli said. "You cannot outlast me.

Surrender. Perhaps I may even find a use for you. I know you're there, whatever you are. You must realize this by now. You can speak candidly with me. Confess. Explain yourself. What are you? What use can I make of you?"

Moving his lips stiffly as though against great pain, Tegas said: "If I were what you suggest, what would I fear from such as you?"

"Very good!" Vicentelli crowed. "We progress. What should you fear from me? Hah! And what should I fear from you?"

"Madman," Tegas whispered.

"Ahh, now," Vicentelli said. "Hear if this is mad: My profile on you says I should fear you only if you die. Therefore, I will not kill you. You may wish to die, but I will not permit you to die. I can keep the body alive indefinitely. It will not be an enjoyable life, but it will be life. I can make you breathe. I can make your heart work. Do you wish a full demonstration?"

The inner whispers resumed and the Tegas fought against them. "We can't escape. Trapped."

The Bacit radiated hesitant uncertainty.

A Bailey thought: "It's a nightmare! That's what!"

Tegas stood in wonder: a Bailey thought!

Bacit admonitions intruded: "Be still. We must work together. Serenity . . . serenity . . . serenity . . ."

The Tegas felt himself drifting off on waves of tranquility, was shocked by a Bacit thought-scream: "NOT YOU!"

Vicentelli moved one of his console controls.

Tegas let out a muffled scream as both his arms jerked upward.

Another Vicentelli adjustment and Tegas bent double, whipped upright.

Bacit-prompted whimpering sounds escaped his lips.

"What are you?" Vicentelli asked in his softest voice.

Tegas sensed the frantic inner probings as the Bacit searched out the neural linkages, blocked them. Perspiration bathed the host flesh.

"Very well," Vicentelli said. "Let us go for a long hike."

The host's legs began pumping up and down in a stationary march. Tegas stared straight ahead, pop-eyed with simulation of agony.

"This will end when you answer my questions," Vicentelli said. "What are you? Hup-two-three-four. Who are you? Hup-two-three-four . . ."

The host flesh jerked with obedience to the commands.

Tegas again felt the thousands of old languages taking place within him—a babble. With an odd detachment, he realized he must be a museum of beings and remembered energies.

"Ask yourself how long you can stand this," Vicentelli said.

"I'm Joe Carmichael," he gasped.

Vicentelli stepped close, studied the evidences of agony. "Hup-two-three-four . . ."

Still, the babble persisted. He was a flow of energy, Tegas realized.

Energy . . . energy . . . energy. Energy was the only *solid* in the universe. He was wisdom seated in a bed of languages. But wisdom chastised the wise and spit upon those who came to pay homage. Wisdom was for copyists and clerks.

Power, then, he thought.

But power, when exercised, fragmented.

How simple to attack Vicentelli now, Tegas thought. *We're alone. No one is watching. I could strike him down in an instant.*

The habits of all that aeons-long history inhibited action. Inevitably, he had picked up some of the desires, hopes and fears—especially the fears—of his uncounted hosts. Their symbols sucked at him now.

A pure Bailey thought: "We can't keep this up forever."

The Tegas felt Bailey's sharings, then Carmichael's, the mysterious coupling of selves, the never-before engagement with the captive.

"One clean punch," Carmichael insisted.

"Hup-two-three-four," Vicentelli said, peering closely at his victim.

Abruptly, the Tegas felt himself looking inward from the far end of his being. He saw all his habits of thought contained in the shapes of every action he'd every contemplated. The thoughts took form to control flesh, a blaze of energy, a *solid*. In that flaring instant, he became pure performance. All the violent killers the Tegas had overwhelmed rose up in him, struck outward, and he *was* the experience—overpoweringly single with it, not limited by any description . . . without symbols.

Vicentelli lay unconscious on the floor.

Tegas stared at his own right hand. The thing had taken on a life of its own. Its movement had been unique to the moment, a flashing jab with fingers extended, a crushing impact against a nerve bundle in Vicentelli's neck.

Have I killed him? he wondered.

Vicentelli stirred, groaned.

So there'd been Tegas inhibitions on the blow, an exquisite control that could overpower but not kill, the Tegas thought.

Tegas moved to Vicentelli's head, stooped to examine him. Moving, he felt the torture skin relax, glanced up at the green-glowing construction, realized the thing's field was limited.

Again, Vicentelli groaned.

Tegas pressed the nerve bundle in the man's neck. Vicentelli subsided, went limp.

Pure Tegas thoughts rose up in the Carmichael neural system. He realized he'd been living for more than a century immersed in a culture which had regressed. They had invented a new thing—almost absolute control—but it held an old pattern. The Egyptians had tried it, and many before them, and a few since. The Tegas thought of the phenomenon as the man-machine. Pain controlled it—and food . . . pleasure, ritual.

The control capsule irritated his senses. He felt the aborted action message, a faint echo, Bacit-repressed: "Hup-two-three-four . . ." With the action message went the emotional inhibitions deadly to Tegas survival.

The Tegas felt sensually subdued. He thought of a world where no concentrated emotions remained, no beacons upon which he could home his short-burst transfer of identity.

The Carmichael flesh shuddered to a Tegas response. The Bacit stirred, transmitting sensations of urgency.

Yes, there was urgency. Androids might return. Vicentelli's fellow rulers might take it upon themselves to check the activity of this room.

He reached around to his back, felt the control capsule: a flat, tapered package . . . cold, faintly pulsing. He tried to insert a finger beneath it, felt the flesh rebel. Ahhh, the linkage was mortal. The diabolic thing joined the spine. He explored the connections internally, realized the thing could be removed, given time and the proper facilities.

But he had not the time.

Vicentelli's lips made feeble writhings—a baby's mouth searching for the nipple.

Tegas concentrated on Vicentelli. A ruler. Tegas rightly avoided such as this. Vicentelli's kind knew how to resist the mind-swarm. They had ego power.

Perhaps the Vicentellis had provided the key to their own destruction, though. Whatever happened, the Tegas knew he could never return into the human mass. The new man-machine provided no hiding place. In this day of new things, another new thing had to be tried.

Tegas reached for the control capsule on his back, inserted three fingers beneath it. With the Bacit blocking off the pain, he wrenched the capsule free.

All sensation left his lower limbs. He collapsed across Vicentelli, brought the capsule around to study it. The removal had dealt a mortal blow to the Carmichael host, but there were no protests in their shared awareness, only a deep curiosity about the capsule.

Simple, deadly thing—operation obvious. Barbed needles protruded along its inner surface. He cleaned shreds of flesh from them, working fast. The host was dying rapidly, blood pumping onto the floor—and spinal fluid. He levered himself onto one elbow, rolled Vicentelli onto one side, pulled away the man's jacket and shirt. A bit of fleshly geography, a ridge of spine lay exposed.

Tegas knew this landscape from the inward examination of the capsule. He gauged the position required, slapped the capsule home.

Vicentelli screamed.

He jerked away, scrabbled across the floor, leaped upright.

"Hup-two-three-four . . ."

His legs jerked up and down in terrible rhythm. Sounds of agony escaped his lips. His eyes rolled.

The Carmichael body slumped to the floor, and Tegas waited for the host to die. Too bad about this host—a promising one—but he was committed now. No turning back.

Death came as always, a wink-out, and after the flicker of blankness, he centered on the emotional scream which was Vicentelli. The Tegas divided from dead flesh, bore away with that always-new sensation of supreme discovery—a particular thing, relevant to nothing else in the universe except himself.

He was pain.

But it was pain he had known, analyzed, understood and could isolate. The pain contained all there was of Vicentelli's identity. Encapsulated that way, it could be absorbed piecemeal, shredded off at will. And the new host's flesh was grateful. With the Tegas came surcease from pain.

Slowly, the marching subsided.

The Tegas blocked off control circuits, adjusted Vicentelli's tunic to conceal the capsule on his back, paused to contemplate how easy this capture had been. It required a dangerous change of pattern, yes: a Tegas must dominate, risk notice—not blend with his surroundings.

With an abrupt sense of panic, William Bailey came alive in his awareness. "We made it!"

In that instant, the Tegas was hanging by the hook of his being, momentarily lost in the host he'd just captured. The intermittency of mingled egos terrified and enthralled. As he had inhabited others, now he was inhabited.

Even the new host—silent, captivated—became part of a changed universe, one that threatened in a different way: all maw. He realized he'd lost contact with the intellectual centers. His path touched only nerve ends. He had no home for his breath, couldn't find the flesh to wear it.

Bacit signals darted around him: a frantic, searching clamor. The flesh—the flesh—the flesh . . .

He'd worn the flesh too gently, he realized. He'd been lulled by its natural laws and his own. He'd put aside all reaching questions about the organism, had peered out of the flesh unconcerned, leaving all worries to the Bacit.

One axiom had soothed him: *The Bacit knows.*

But the Bacit was loosed around him and he no longer held the flesh. The flesh held him, a grip so close it threatened to choke him.

The flesh cannot choke me, he thought. *It cannot. I love the flesh.*

Love—there was a toehold, a germ of contact. The flesh remembered how he had eased its agony. Memories of other flesh intruded. Tendrils of association accumulated. He thought of all the flesh he'd loved on this world: the creatures with their big eyes, their ears flat against their heads, smooth caps of hair, beautiful mouths and cheeks. The Tegas always noticed mouths. The mouth betrayed an infinite variety of things about the flesh around it.

A Vicentelli self-image came into his awareness, swimming like a ghost in a mirror. The Tegas thought about the verseless record, the stone-cut mouth. No notion of fun—that was the thing about Vicentelli's mouth.

He'll have to learn fun now, the Tegas thought.

He felt the feet then, hard against the floor, and the Bacit was with him. But the Bacit had a voice that touched the auditory centers from within. It was the voice of William Bailey and countless others.

"Remove the signs of struggle before the androids return," the voice said.

He obeyed, looked down at the empty flesh which had been Joe Carmichael. But Joe Carmichael was with him in this flesh, Vicentelli's flesh, which still twitched faintly to the broadcast commands transmitted through the capsule on his spine.

"Have to remove the capsule as soon as possible," the Bacit voice reminded. "You know the way to do it."

The Tegas marveled at the Vicentelli overtones suddenly noticeable in the voice. Abruptly, he glimpsed the dark side of his being through Vicentelli, and he saw an aspect of the Bacit he'd never suspected. He realized he was a net of beings who enjoyed their captivity, were strong in their captivity, would not exchange it for any other existence.

They *were* Tegas in a real sense, moving him by habits of thought, shaping actions out of uncounted mediations. The Bacit half had accumulated more than forty centuries of mediations on this one world. And there were uncounted worlds before this one.

Language and thought.

Language was the instrument of the sentient being—yet, the being was the instrument of language as Tegas was the instrument of the Bacit. He searched for significant content in this new awareness, was chided by the Bacit's sneer. To search for content was to search for limits where there were no limits. Content was logic and classification. It was a word sieve through which to judge experience. It was nothing in itself, could never satisfy.

Experience, that was the thing. Action. The infinite reenactment of life accompanied by its endless procession of images.

There are things to be done, the Tegas thought.

The control capsule pulsed on his spine.

The capsule, yes—and many more things.

They have bugged the soul, he thought. *They've mechanized the soul and are forever damned. Well, I must join them for a while.*

He passed a hand through a call beam, summoned the androids to clear away the discarded host that had been Carmichael.

A door opened at the far end of the lab. Three androids entered, marching in line towards him. They were suddenly an amusing six-armed figure, their arms moving that way in obedient cadence.

The Vicentelli mouth formed an unfamiliar smile.

Briefly he set the androids to the task of cleaning up the mess in the lab. Then, the Tegas began the quiet exploration of his new host, a task he found remarkably easy with his new understanding. The host cooperated. He explored Vicentelli slowly—strong, lovely, healthy flesh—explored as one might explore a strange land, swimming across coasts of awareness that loomed and receded.

A host had behavior that must be learned. It was not well to dramatize the Tegas difference. There would be changes, of course—but slow ones; nothing dramatic in its immediacy.

While he explored he thought of the mischief he could do in this new role. There were so many ways to disrupt the man-machine, to revive individualism, to have fun. Lovely mischief.

Intermittently, he wondered what had become of the Bailey ego and the Joe Carmichael ego. Only the Bacit remained in the host with him, and the Bacit transmitted a sensation of laughter.

PASSAGE FOR PIANO

Had some cosmic crystal gazer suggested to Margaret Hatchell that she would try to smuggle a concert grand piano onto the colony spaceship, she would have been shocked. Here she was at home in her kitchen on a hot summer afternoon, worried about how to squeeze *ounces* into her family's meager weight allowance for the trip—and the piano weighed more than half a *ton*.

Before she had married Walter Hatchell, she had been a working nurse-dietician, which made her of some use to the colony group destined for Planet C. But Walter, as the expedition's chief ecologist, was one of the most important cogs in the effort. His field was bionomics; the science of setting up the delicate balance of growing things to support human life on an alien world.

Walter was tied to his work at the White Sands base, hadn't been home to Seattle for a month during this crucial preparation period. This left Margaret with two children and several problems—the chief problem being that one of their children was a blind piano prodigy subject to black moods.

Margaret glanced at the clock on her kitchen wall: three-thirty, time to start dinner. She wheeled the micro-filming cabinet out of her kitchen and down the hall to the music room to get it out of her way. Coming into the familiar music room, she suddenly felt herself a hesitant stranger here—almost afraid to look too closely at her favorite wing-back chair, or at her son's concert grand piano, or at the rose pattern rug with afternoon sun streaming dappled gold across it.

It was a sensation of unreality—something like the feeling that had caught her the day the colonization board had notified them that the Hatchells had been chosen.

"We're going to be pioneers on Planet C," she whispered. But that made it no more real. She wondered if others among the 308 chosen colonists felt the same way about moving to a virgin world.

In the first days after the selection, when they all had been assembled at

White Sands for preliminary instructions, a young astronomer had given a brief lecture.

"Your sun will be the star Giansar," he had said, and his voice had echoed in the barnlike hall as he pointed to the star on the chart. "In the tail of constellation Dragon. Your ship will travel sixteen years on sub-macro drive to make the passage from Earth. You already know, of course, that you will pass this time in sleep-freeze, and it'll feel just like one night to you. Giansar has a more orange light than our sun, and it's somewhat cooler. However, Planet C is closer to its sun, and this means your climate will average out warmer than we experience here."

Margaret had tried to follow the astronomer's words closely, just as she had done in the other lectures, but only the high points remained from all of them: orange light, warmer climate, less moisture, conserve weight in what you take along, seventy-five pounds of private luggage allowed for each adult, forty pounds for children to age fourteen . . .

Now, standing in her music room, Margaret felt that it must have been some other person who had listened to those lectures. *I should be excited and happy,* she thought. *Why do I feel so sad?*

At thirty-five, Margaret Hatchell looked an indeterminate mid-twenty with a good figure, a graceful walk. Her brown hair carried reddish lights. The dark eyes, full mouth and firm chin combined to give an impression of hidden fire.

She rubbed a hand along the curved edge of the piano lid, felt the dent where the instrument had hit the door when they'd moved here to Seattle from Denver. *How long ago?* she asked herself. *Eight years? Yes . . . it was the year after Grandfather Maurice Hatchell died . . . after playing his final concert with this very piano.*

Through the open back windows she could hear her nine-year-old, Rita, filling the summer afternoon with a *discussion* of the strange insects to be discovered on Planet C. Rita's audience consisted of noncolonist playmates overawed by the fame of their companion. Rita was referring to their colony world as "Ritelle," the name she had submitted to the Survey and Exploration Service.

Margaret thought: *If they choose Rita's name we'll never hear the end of it . . . literally!*

Realization that an entire planet could be named for her daughter sent Margaret's thoughts reeling off on a new tangent. She stood silently in the golden shadows of the music room, one hand on the piano that had belonged to her husband's father, Maurice Hatchell—*the* Maurice Hatchell of concert fame. For the first time, Margaret saw something of what the news service people had been telling her just that morning—that her family and all the other colonists were "chosen people," and for this reason their lives were of tremendous interest to everyone on Earth.

She noted her son's bat-eye radar box and its shoulder harness atop the piano. That meant David was somewhere around the house. He never used the box in the familiarity of his home where memory served in place of the sight he had lost. Seeing the box there prompted Margaret to move the microfilming cabinet aside where David would not trip over it if he came to the music room to practice. She listened, wondering if David was upstairs trying the lightweight electronic piano that had been built for him to take on the spaceship. There was no hint of his music in the soft sounds of the afternoon, but then he could have turned the sound low.

Thinking of David brought to her mind the boy's tantrum that had ended the newsfilm session just before lunch. The chief reporter—*What was his name? Bonaudi?*—had asked how they intended to dispose of the concert grand piano. She could still hear the awful discord as David had crashed his fists onto the keyboard. He had leaped up, dashed from the room—a dark little figure full of impotent fury.

Twelve is such an emotional age, she told herself.

Margaret decided that her sadness was the same as David's. *It's the parting with beloved possessions . . . it's the certain knowledge that we'll never see these things again . . . that all we'll have will be films and lightweight substitutes.* A sensation of terrible longing filled her. *Never again to feel the homely comfort of so many things that spell family tradition: the wing-back chair Walter and I bought when we furnished our first house, the sewing cabinet that great-great grandmother Chrisman brought from Ohio, the oversize double bed built specially to accommodate Walter's long frame . . .*

Abruptly, she turned away from the piano, went back to the kitchen. It was a white tile room with black fixtures, a laboratory kitchen cluttered now with debris of packing. Margaret pushed aside her recipe files on the counter beside the sink, being careful not to disturb the yellow scrap paper that marked where she'd stopped microfilming them. The sink was still piled with her mother's Spode china that was being readied for the space journey. Cups and saucers would weigh three and a half pounds in their special packing. Margaret resumed washing the dishes, seating them in the delicate webs of the lightweight box.

The wall phone beside her came alive to the operator's face. "Hatchell residence?"

Margaret lifted her dripping hands from the sink, nudged the call switch with her elbow. "Yes?"

"On your call to Walter Hatchell at White Sands: He is still not available. Shall I try again in twenty minutes?"

"Please do."

The operator's face faded from the screen. Margaret nudged off the switch, resumed washing. The newsfilm group had shot several pictures of her working at the sink that morning. She wondered how she and her family would appear on the film. The reporter had called Rita a "budding entomologist" and had referred to David as "the blind piano prodigy—one of the few victims of the *drum* virus brought back from the uninhabitable Planet A-4."

Rita came in from the yard. She was a lanky nine-year-old, a precocious extrovert with large blue eyes that looked on the world as her own private problem waiting to be solved.

"I am desperately ravenous," she announced. "When do we eat?"

"When it's ready," Margaret said. She noted with a twinge of exasperation that Rita had acquired a torn cobweb on her blonde hair and a smudge of dirt across her left cheek.

Why should a little girl be fascinated by bugs? Margaret asked herself. *It's not natural.* She said: "How'd you get the cobweb in your hair?"

"Oh, succotash!" Rita put a hand to her hair, rubbed away the offending web.

"How?" repeated Margaret.

"Mother! If one is to acquire knowledge of the insect world, one inevitably encounters such things! I am just dismayed that I tore the web."

"Well, I'm dismayed that you're filthy dirty. Go upstairs and wash so you'll look presentable when we get the call through to your father."

Rita turned away.

"And weigh yourself," called Margaret. "I have to turn in our family's weekly weight aggregate tomorrow."

Rita skipped out of the room.

Margaret felt certain she had heard a muttered "parents!" The sound of the child's footsteps diminished up the stairs. A door slammed on the second floor. Presently, Rita clattered back down the stairs. She ran into the kitchen. "Mother, you . . ."

"You haven't had time to get clean." Margaret spoke without turning.

"It's David," said Rita. "He looks peculiar and he says he doesn't want any supper."

Margaret turned from the sink, her features set to hide the gripping of fear. She knew from experience that Rita's "peculiar" could be anything . . . literally anything.

"How do you mean *peculiar,* dear?"

"He's so pale. He looks like he doesn't have any blood."

For some reason, this brought to Margaret's mind a memory picture of David at the age of three—a still figure in a hospital bed, flesh-colored feeding tube protruding from his nose, and his skin as pale as death with his breathing so quiet it was difficult to detect the chest movements.

She dried her hands on a dishtowel. "Let's go have a look. He's probably just tired."

David was stretched out on his bed, one arm thrown across his eyes. The shades were drawn and the room was in semi-darkness. It took a moment for Margaret's eyes to adjust to the gloom, and she thought: *Do the blind seek darkness because it gives them the advantage over those with sight?*

She crossed to the bedside. The boy was a small, dark-haired figure—his father's coloring. The chin was narrow and the mouth a firm line like his grandfather Hatchell's. Right now he looked thin and defenseless . . . and Rita was right: terribly pale.

Margaret adopted her best hospital manner, lifted David's arm from his face, took his pulse.

"Don't you feel well, Davey?" she asked.

"I wish you wouldn't call me that," he said. "That's a baby name." His narrow features were set, sullen.

She took a short, quick breath. "Sorry. I forgot. Rita says you don't want any supper."

Rita came in from the hallway. "He looks positively infirm, mother."

"Does she have to keep pestering me?" demanded David.

"I thought I heard the phone chime," said Margaret. "Will you go check, Rita?"

"You're being offensively obvious," said Rita. "If you don't want me in here, just say so." She turned, walked slowly out of the room.

"Do you hurt someplace, David?" asked Margaret.

"I just feel tired," he muttered. "Why can't you leave me alone?"

Margaret stared down at him—caught as she had been so many times by his resemblance to his grandfather Hatchell. It was a resemblance made uncanny when the boy sat down at the piano: that same intense vibrancy . . . the same musical genius that had made Hatchell a name to fill concert halls. And she thought: *Perhaps it's because the Steinway belonged to his grandfather that he feels so badly about parting with it. The piano's a symbol of the talent he inherited.*

She patted her son's hand, sat down beside him on the bed. "Is something troubling you, David?"

His features contorted, and he whirled away from her. "Go away!" He muttered, "Just leave me alone!"

Margaret sighed, felt inadequate. She wished desperately that Walter were not tied to the work at the launching site. She felt a deep need of her husband at this moment. Another sigh escaped her. She knew what she had to do. The rules for colonists were explicit: any symptoms at all—even superficial ones—were to get a doctor's attention. She gave David's hand a final pat, went downstairs to the hall phone, called Dr. Mowery, the medic cleared for colonists in the Seattle area. He said he'd be out in about an hour.

Rita came in as Margaret was completing the call, asked: "Is David going to die?"

All the tenseness and aggravation of the day came out in Margaret's reply: "Don't be such a beastly little fool!"

Immediately, she was sorry. She stopped, gathered Rita to her, crooned apologies.

"It's all right, mother," Rita said. "I realize you're overwrought."

Filled with contriteness, Margaret went into the kitchen, prepared her daughter's favorite food: tuna-fish sandwiches and chocolate milkshakes.

I'm getting too jumpy, thought Margaret. *David's not really sick. It's the hot weather we've had lately and all this tension of getting ready to go.* She took a sandwich and milkshake up to the boy, but he still refused to eat. And there was such a pallid sense of defeat about him. A story about someone who had died merely because he gave up the will to live entered her mind and refused to be shaken.

She made her way back down to the kitchen, dabbled at the work there until the call to Walter went through. Her husband's craggy features and deep voice brought the calmness she had been seeking all day.

"I miss you so much, darling," she said.

"It won't be much longer," he said. He smiled, leaned to one side, exposing the impersonal wall of a pay booth behind him. He looked tired. "How's my family?"

She told him about David, saw the worry creep into his eyes. "Is the doctor there yet?" he asked.

"He's late. He should've been here by six and it's half past."

"Probably busy as a bird dog," he said. "It doesn't really sound as though David's actually sick. Just upset more likely . . . the excitement of leaving. Call me as soon as the doctor tells you what's wrong."

"I will. I think he's just upset over leaving your father's piano behind."

"David knows it's not that we want to leave these things." A grin brightened his features. "Lord! Imagine taking that thing on the ship! Dr. Charlesworthy would flip!"

She smiled. "Why don't you suggest it?"

"You're trying to get me in trouble with the old man!"

"How're things going, dear?" she asked.

His face sobered. He sighed. "I had to talk to poor Smythe's widow today. She came out to pick up his things. It was rather trying. The old man was afraid she might still want to come along . . . but no . . ." He shook his head.

"Do you have his replacement yet?"

"Yes. Young fellow from Lebanon. Name's Teryk. His wife's a cute little thing." Walter looked past her at the kitchen. "Looks like you're getting things in order. Decided yet what you're taking?"

"Some of the things. I wish I could make decisions like you do. I've definitely decided to take mother's Spode china cups and saucers and the sterling silver . . . for Rita when she gets married . . . and the Utrillo your father bought in Lisbon . . . and I've weeded my jewelry down to about two pounds of basics . . . and I'm not going to worry about cosmetics since you say we can make our own when we . . ."

Rita ran into the kitchen, pushed in beside Margaret. "Hello, father."

"Hi, punkin head. What've you been up to?"

"I've been cataloging my insect collection and filling it out. Mother's going to help me film the glassed-in specimens as soon as I'm ready. They're so *heavy!*"

"How'd you wangle her agreement to get that close to your bugs?"

"Father! They're not bugs; they're entomological specimens."

"They're bugs to your mother, honey. Now, if . . ."

"Father! There's one other thing. I told Raul—he's the new boy down the block—I told him today about those hawklike insects on Ritelle that . . ."

"They're not insects, honey; they're adapted amphibians."

She frowned. "But Spencer's report distinctly says that they're chitinous and they . . ."

"Whoa down! You should've read the technical report, the one I showed you when I was home last month. These critters have a copper-base metabolism, and they're closely allied to a common fish on the planet."

"Oh . . . Do you think I'd better branch out into marine biology?"

"One thing at a time, honey. Now . . ."

"Have we set the departure date yet, father? I can hardly wait to get to work there."

"It's not definite yet, honey. But we should know any day. Now, let me talk to your mother."

Rita pulled back.

Walter smiled at his wife. "What're we raising there?"

"I wish I knew."

"Look . . . don't worry about David. It's been nine years since . . . since he recovered from that virus. All the tests show that he was completely cured."

And she thought: *Yes . . . cured—except for the little detail of no optic nerves.* She forced a smile. "I know you're probably right. It'll turn out to be something simple . . . and we'll laugh about this when . . ." The front doorbell chimed. "That's probably the doctor now."

"Call me when you find out," said Walter.

Margaret heard Rita's footsteps running toward the door.

"I'll sign off, sweet," she said. She blew a kiss to her husband. "I love you."

Walter held up two fingers in a victory sign, winked. "Same here. Chin up." They broke the connection.

Dr. Mowery was a gray-haired, flint-faced bustler—addicted to the nodding head and the knowing (but unintelligible) murmur. One big hand held a gray instrument bag. He had a pat on the head for Rita, a firm handshake for Margaret, and he insisted on seeing David alone.

"Mothers just clutter up the atmosphere for a doctor," he said, and he winked to take the sting from his words.

Margaret sent Rita to her room, waited in the upstairs hall. There were 106 flower panels on the wallpaper between the door to David's room and the corner of the hall. She was moving on to count the rungs in the balustrade when the doctor emerged from David's room. He closed the door softly behind him, nodding to himself.

She waited.

"Mmmmmm-hmmmmm," said Dr. Mowery. He cleared his throat.

"It is anything serious?" asked Margaret.

"Not sure." He walked to the head of the stairs. "How long's the boy been acting like that . . . listless and upset?"

Margaret swallowed a lump in her throat. "He's been acting differently ever since they delivered the electronic piano . . . the one that's going to substitute for his grandfather's Steinway. Is that what you mean?"

"Differently?"

"Rebellious, short-tempered . . . wanting to be alone."

"I suppose there's not the remotest possibility of his taking the big piano," said the doctor.

"Oh, my goodness . . . it must weigh all of a thousand pounds," said Margaret. "The electronic instrument is only twenty-one pounds." She cleared her throat. "It is worry about the piano, doctor?"

"Possibly." Dr. Mowery nodded, took the first step down the stairs. "It doesn't appear to be anything organic that my instruments can find. I'm going to have Dr. Linquist and some others look in on David tonight. Dr. Linquist is our chief psychiatrist. Meanwhile, I'd try to get the boy to eat something."

She crossed to Dr. Mowery's side at the head of the stairs. "I'm a nurse," she said. "You can tell me if it's something serious that . . ."

He shifted his bag to his right hand, patted her arm. "Now don't you worry, my dear. The colonization group is fortunate to have a musical genius in its roster. We're not going to let anything happen to him."

Dr. Linquist had the round face and cynical eyes of a fallen cherub. His voice surged out of him in waves that flowed over the listener and towed him under. The psychiatrist and colleagues were with David until almost ten P.M.. Then Dr. Linquist dismissed the others, came down to the music room where Margaret was waiting. He sat on the piano bench, hands gripping the lip of wood beside him.

Margaret occupied her wing-back chair—the one piece of furniture she knew she would miss more than any other thing in the house. Long usage had worn contours in the chair that exactly complemented her, and its rough fabric upholstery held the soothing texture of familiarity.

The night outside the screened windows carried a sonorous sawing of crickets.

"We can say definitely that it's a fixation about this piano," said Linquist. He slapped his palms onto his knees. "Have you ever thought of leaving the boy behind?"

"Doctor!"

"Thought I'd ask."

"Is it *that* serious with Davey?" she asked. "I mean, after all . . . we're all of us going to miss things." She rubbed the chair arm. "But good heavens, we . . ."

"I'm not much of a musician," said Linquist. "I'm told by the critics, though, that your boy already has concert stature . . . that he's being deliberately held back now to avoid piling confusion on confusion . . . I mean with your leaving so soon and all." The psychiatrist tugged at his lower lip. "You realize, of course, that your boy worships the memory of his grandfather?"

"He's seen all the old stereos, listened to all the tapes," said Margaret. "He was only four when grandfather died, but David remembers everything they ever did together. It was . . ." She shrugged.

"David has identified his inherited talent with his inherited piano," said Linquist. "He . . ."

"But pianos can be replaced," said Margaret. "Couldn't one of our colony carpenters or cabinetmakers duplicate . . ."

"Ah, no," said Linquist. "Not duplicate. It would not be the piano of Maurice Hatchell. You see, your boy is overly conscious that he inherited musical genius from his grandfather . . . just as he inherited the piano. He's tied the two together. He believes that if—not consciously, you understand? But he believes, nonetheless, that if he loses the piano he loses the talent. And there you have a problem more critical than you might suspect."

She shook her head. "But children get over these . . ."

"He's not a child, Mrs. Hatchell. Perhaps I should say he's not *just* a child. He is that sensitive thing we call *genius*. This is a delicate state that goes sour all too easily."

She felt her mouth go dry. "What are you trying to tell me?"

"I don't want to alarm you without cause, Mrs. Hatchell. But the truth is—and this is the opinion of all of us—that if your boy is deprived of his musical outlet . . . well, he could die."

She paled. "Oh, no! He . . ."

"Such things happen, Mrs. Hatchell. There are therapeutic procedures we could use, of course, but I'm not sure we have the time. They're expecting to set your departure date momentarily. Therapy *could* take years."

"But David's . . ."

"David is precocious and overemotional," said Linquist. "He's invested much more than is healthy in his music. His blindness accounts for part of that, but over and above the fact of blindness there's his need for musical expression. In a genius such as David this is akin to one of the basic drives of life itself."

"We just couldn't. You don't understand. We're such a close family that we . . ."

"Then perhaps you should step aside, let some other family have your . . ."

"It would kill Walter . . . my husband," she said. "He's lived for this chance." She shook her head. "Anyway, I'm not sure we could back out now.

Walter's assistant, Dr. Smythe, was killed in a copter crash near Phoenix last week. They already have a replacement, but I'm sure you know how important Walter's function is to the colony's success."

Linquist nodded. "I read about Smythe, but I failed to make the obvious association here."

"I'm not important to the colony," she said. "Nor the children, really. But the ecologists—the success of our entire effort hangs on them. Without Walter . . ."

"We'll just have to solve it then," he said. He got to his feet. "We'll be back tomorrow for another look at David, Mrs. Hatchell. Dr. Mowery made him take some amino pills and then gave him a sedative. He should sleep right through the night. If there're any complications—although there shouldn't be—you can reach me at this number." He pulled a card from his wallet, gave it to her. "It is too bad about the weight problem. I'm sure it would solve everything if he could just take this monster with him." Linquist patted the piano lid. "Well . . . good night."

When Linquist had gone, Margaret leaned against the front door, pressed her forehead against the cool wood. "No," she whispered. "No . . . no . . . no . . ." Presently, she went to the living room phone, placed a call to Walter. It was ten-twenty P.M. The call went right through, proving that he had been waiting for it. Margaret noted the deep worry creases in her husband's forehead, longed to reach out, touch them, smooth them.

"What is it, Margaret?" he asked. "Is David all right?"

"Dear, it's . . ." she swallowed. "It's about the piano. Your father's Steinway."

"The *piano*?"

"The doctors have been here all evening up to a few minutes ago examining David. The psychiatrist says if David loses the piano he may lose his . . . his music . . . his . . . and if he loses that he could die."

Walter blinked. "Over a piano? Oh, now, surely there must be some . . ."

She told him everything Dr. Linquist had said.

"The boy's so much like Dad," said Walter. "Dad once threw the philharmonic into an uproar because his piano bench was a half inch too low. Good Lord! I . . . What'd Linquist say we could do?"

"He said if we could take the piano it'd solve . . ."

"That concert grand? The damn thing must weigh over a thousand pounds. That's more than three times what our whole family is allowed in private luggage."

"I know. I'm almost at my wits' end. All this turmoil of deciding what's to go and now . . . David."

"To go!" barked Walter. "Good Lord! What with worrying about David I almost forgot: Our departure date was set just tonight." He glanced at his watch. "Blastoff is fourteen days and six hours away—give or take a few minutes. The old man said . . ."

"Fourteen days!"

"Yes, but *you* have only eight days. That's the colony assembly date. The pickup crews will be around to get your luggage on the afternoon of . . ."

"Walter! I haven't even decided what to . . ." She broke off. "I was sure we had at least another month. You told me yourself that we . . ."

"I know. But fuel production came out ahead of schedule, and the long-range weather forecast is favorable. And it's part of the psychology not to drag out leavetaking. This way the shock of abruptness cuts everything clean."

"But what're we going to do about David?" She chewed her lower lip.

"Is he awake?"

"I don't think so. They gave him a sedative."

Walter frowned. "I want to talk to David first thing in the morning. I've been neglecting him lately because of all the work here, but . . ."

"He understands, Walter."

"I'm sure he does, but I want to see him for myself. I only wish I had the time to come home, but things are pretty frantic here right now." He shook his head. "I just don't see how that diagnosis could be right. All this fuss over a piano!"

"Walter . . . you're not attached to things. With you it's people and ideas." She lowered her eyes, fought back tears. "But some people can grow to love inanimate objects, too . . . things that mean comfort and security." She swallowed.

He shook his head. "I guess I just don't understand. We'll work out something, though. Depend on it."

Margaret forced a smile. "I know you will, dear."

"Now that we have the departure date it may blow the whole thing right out of his mind," Walter said.

"Perhaps you're right."

He glanced at his wristwatch. "I have to sign off now. Got some experiments running." He winked. "I miss my family."

"So do I," she whispered.

In the morning there was a call from Prester Charlesworthy, colony director. His face came onto the phone screen in Margaret's kitchen just as she finished dishing up breakfast for Rita. David was still in bed. And Margaret had told neither of them about the departure date.

Charlesworthy was a man of skinny features, nervous mannerisms. There was a bumpkin look about him until you saw the incisive stare of the pale blue eyes.

"Forgive me for bothering you like this, Mrs. Hatchell," he said.

She forced herself to calmness. "No bother. We were expecting a call from Walter this morning. I thought this was it."

"I've just been talking to Walter," said Charlesworthy. "He's been telling me about David. We had a report first thing this morning from Dr. Linquist."

After a sleepless night with periodic cat-footed trips to look in on David,

Margaret felt her nerves jangling out to frayed helplessness. She was primed to leap at the worst interpretations that entered her mind. "You're putting us out of the colony group!" she blurted. "You're getting another ecologist to . . ."

"Oh, no, Mrs. Hatchell!" Dr. Charlesworthy took a deep breath. "I know it must seem odd—my calling you like this—but our little group will be alone on a very alien world, very dependent upon each other for almost ten years—until the next ship gets there. We've got to work together on everything. I sincerely want to help you."

"I'm sorry," she said. "But I didn't get much sleep last night."

"I quite understand. Believe me, I'd like nothing better than to be able to send Walter home to you right now." Charlesworthy shrugged. "But that's out of the question. With poor Smythe dead there's a terribly heavy load on Walter's shoulders. Without him, we might even have to abort this attempt."

Margaret wet her lips with her tongue. "Dr. Charlesworthy, is there any possibility at all that we could . . . I mean . . . the piano—take it on the ship?"

"Mrs. Hatchell!" Charlesworthy pulled back from his screen. "It must weigh half a ton!"

She sighed. "I called the moving company first thing this morning—the company that moved the piano here into this house. They checked their records. It weighs fourteen hundred and eight pounds."

"Out of the question! Why . . . we've had to eliminate high priority technical equipment that doesn't weigh half that much!"

"I guess I'm desperate," she said. "I keep thinking over what Dr. Linquist said about David dying if . . ."

"Of course," said Charleworthy. "That's why I called you. I want you to know what we've done. We dispatched Hector Torres to the Steinway factory this morning. Hector is one of the cabinetmakers we'll have in the colony. The Steinway people have generously consented to show him all of their construction secrets so Hector can build an exact duplicate of this piano—correct in all details. Philip Jackson, one of our metallurgists, will be following Hector this afternoon for the same reason. I'm sure that when you tell David this it'll completely resolve all his fears."

Margaret blinked back tears. "Dr. Charlesworthy . . . I don't know how to thank you."

"Don't thank me at all, my dear. We're a team . . . we pull together." He nodded. "Now, one other thing: a favor you can do for me."

"Certainly."

"Try not to worry Walter too much this week if you can. He's discovered a mutation that may permit us to cross earth plants with ones already growing on Planet C. He's running final tests this week with dirt samples from C. These are crucial tests, Mrs. Hatchell. They could cut several years off the initial stage of setting up a new life-cycle balance."

"Of course," she said. "I'm sorry that I . . ."

"Don't you be sorry. And don't you worry. The boy's only twelve. Time heals all things."

"I'm sure it'll work out," she said.

"Excellent," said Charlesworthy. "That's the spirit. Now, you call on me for any help you may need . . . day or night. We're a team. We have to pull together."

They broke the connection. Margaret stood in front of the phone, facing the blank screen.

Rita spoke from the kitchen table behind her. "What'd he say about the departure date?"

"It's been set, dear." Margaret turned. "We have to be with Daddy at White Sands in eight days."

"Whooopeee!" Rita leaped to her feet, upsetting her breakfast dishes. "We're going! We're going!"

"Rita!"

But Rita was already dashing out of the room, out of the house. Her "Eight days!" echoed back from the front hall.

Margaret stepped to the kitchen door. "Rita!"

Her daughter ran back down the hall. "I'm going to tell the kids!"

"You will calm down right now. You're making enough noise to . . ."

"I heard her." It was David at the head of the stairs. He came down slowly, guiding himself by the bannister. His face looked white as eggshell, and there was a dragging hesitancy to his steps.

Margaret took a deep breath, told him about Dr. Charlesworthy's plan to replace the piano.

David stopped two steps above her, head down. When she had finished, he said: "It won't be the same." He stepped around her, went into the music room. There was a slumped finality to his figure.

Margaret whirled back into the kitchen. Angry determination flared in her. She heard Rita's slow footsteps following, spoke without turning: "Rita, how much weight can you cut from your luggage?"

"Mother!"

"We're going to take that piano!" snapped Margaret.

Rita came up beside her. "But our whole family gets to take only two hundred thirty pounds! We couldn't possibly . . ."

"There are 308 of us in this colonization group," said Margaret. "Every adult is allowed seventy-five pounds, every child under fourteen years gets forty pounds." She found her kitchen scratch pad, scribbled figures on it. "If each person donates only four pounds and twelve ounces we can take that piano!" Before she could change her mind, she whirled to the drain-board, swept the package with her mother's Spode china cups and saucers into the discard box. "There! A gift for the people who bought our house! And that's three and a half pounds of it!"

Then she began to cry.

Rita sobered. "I'll leave my insect specimens," she whispered. Then she buried her head in her mother's dress, and she too was sobbing.

"What're you two crying about?" David spoke from the kitchen doorway, his bat-eye box strapped to his shoulders. His small features were drawn into a pinched look of misery.

Margaret dried her eyes. "Davey . . . David, we're going to try to take your piano with us."

His chin lifted, his features momentarily relaxed, then the tight unhappiness returned. "Sure. They'll just dump out some of dad's seeds and a few tools and scientific instruments for my . . ."

"There's another way," she said.

"What other way?" His voice was fighting against a hope that might be smashed.

Margaret explained her plan.

"Go begging?" he asked. "Asking people to give up their own . . ."

"David, this will be a barren and cold new world we're going to colonize—very few comforts, drab issue clothing—almost no refinements or the things we think of as belonging to a civilized culture. A real honest-to-goodness earth piano and the . . . man to play it would help. It'd help our morale, and keep down the homesickness that's sure to come."

His sightless eyes appeared to stare at her for a long moment of silence; then he said: "That would be a terrible responsibility for me."

She felt pride in her son flow all through her, said: "I'm glad you see it that way."

The small booklet of regulations and advice handed out at the first assembly in White Sands carried names and addresses of all the colonists. Margaret started at the top of the list, called Selma Atkins of Little Rock, wife of the expedition's head zoologist.

Mrs. Atkins was a dark little button of a woman with flaming hair and a fizzing personality. She turned out to be a born conspirator. Before Margaret had finished explaining the problem, Selma Atkins was volunteering to head a phone committee. She jotted down names of prospects, said: "Even if we get the weight allowance, how'll we get the thing aboard?"

Margaret looked puzzled. "What's wrong with just showing that we have the weight allowance, and handing the piano over to the people who pack things on the ship?"

"Charlesworthy'd never go for it, honey. He's livid at the amount of equipment that's had to be passed over because of the weight problem. He'd take one look at one thousand four hundred and eight pounds of piano and say: 'That'll be a spare atomic generation kit!' My husband says he's had to drill holes in packing boxes to save ounces!"

"But how could we smuggle . . ."

Selma snapped her fingers. "I know! Ozzy Lucan!"

"Lucan?"

"The ship's steward," said Selma. "You know: the big horse of a man with red hair. He spoke at one of the meetings on—you know—all about how to conserve weight in packing and how to use the special containers."

"Oh, yes," said Margaret. "What about him?"

"He's married to my third cousin Betty's oldest daughter. Nothing like a little family pressure. I'll work on it."

"Wouldn't he be likely to go directly to Charlesworthy with it?" asked Margaret.

"Hah!" barked Selma. "You don't know Betty's side of our family!"

Dr. Linquist arrived in the middle of the morning, two consultant psychiatrists in tow. They spent an hour with David, came down to the kitchen where Margaret and Rita were finishing the microfilming of the recipe files. David followed them, stood in the doorway.

"The boy's apparently tougher than I realized," said Linquist. "Are you sure he hasn't been told he can take that piano? I hope you haven't been misleading him to make him feel better."

David frowned.

Margaret said: "Dr. Charlesworthy refused to take the piano when I asked him. However, he's sent two experts to the Steinway factory so we'll be sure of an exact duplicate."

Linquist turned to David. "And that's all right with you, David?"

David hesitated, then: "I understand about the weight."

"Well, I guess you're growing up," said Linquist.

When the psychiatrists had gone, Rita turned on Margaret. "Mother! You lied to them!"

"No she didn't," said David. "She told the exact truth."

"But not all of it," said Margaret.

"That's just the same as lying," said Rita.

"Oh, stop it!" snapped Margaret. Then: "David, are you sure you want to leave your braille texts?"

"Yes. That's sixteen pounds. We've got the braille punch kit and the braille typewriter; I can type new copies of everything I'll need if Rita will read to me."

By three o'clock that afternoon they had Chief Steward Oswald Lucan's reluctant agreement to smuggle the piano aboard if they could get the weight allowance precise to the ounce. But Lucan's parting words were: "Don't let the old man get wind of this. He's boiling about the equipment we've had to cut out."

At seven-thirty, Margaret added the first day's weight donations: sixty-one commitments for a total of two hundred and seven pounds and seven ounces. *Not enough from each person,* she told herself. *But I can't blame them. We're all tied to our possessions. It's so hart to part with all the little things that link us with the past and with Earth. We've got to find more weight somewhere.* She cast about in her own mind for things to discard, knew a sense of futility at the few pounds she had at her disposal.

By ten o'clock on the morning of the third day they had 554 pounds and 8 ounces from 160 of their fellow colonists. They also had an even twenty violent rejections. The tension of fear that one of these twenty might give away their conspiracy was beginning to tell on Margaret.

David, too, was sinking back into gloom. He sat on the piano bench in the music room, Margaret behind him in her favorite chair. One of David's hands gently caressed the keys that Maurice Hatchell had brought to such crashing life.

"We're getting less than four pounds per person, aren't we?" asked David.

Margaret rubbed her cheek. "Yes."

A gentle chord came from the piano. "We aren't going to make it," said David. A fluid rippling of music lifted in the room. "I'm not sure we have the right to ask this of people anyway. They're giving up so much already, and then we . . ."

"Hush, Davey."

He let the baby name pass, coaxed a floating passage of Debussy from the keys.

Margaret put her hands to her eyes, cried silently with fatigue and frustration. But the tears coming from David's fingers on the piano went deeper.

Presently, he stood up, walked slowly out of the room, up the stairs. She heard his bedroom door close softly. The lack of violence in his actions cut her like a knife.

The phone chime broke Margaret from her blue reverie. She took the call on the portable in the hall. Selma Atkins's features came onto the screen, wide-eyed, subdued.

"Ozzy just called me," she blurted. "Somebody snitched to Charlesworthy this morning."

Margaret put a hand over her mouth.

"Did you tell your husband what we were doing?" asked Selma.

"No." Margaret shook her head. "I was going to and then I got afraid of what he'd say. He and Charlesworthy are very close friends, you know."

"You mean he'd peach on his own wife?"

"Oh, no, but he might . . ."

"Well, he's on the carpet now," said Selma. "Ozzy says the whole base is jumping. He was shouting and banging his hands on the desk at Walter and . . ."

"Charlesworthy?"

"Who else? I called to warn you. He . . ."

"But what'll we do?" asked Margaret.

"We run for cover, honey. We fall back and regroup. Call me as soon as you've talked to him. Maybe we can think of a new plan."

"We've contributions from more than half the colonists," said Margaret. "That means we've more than half of them on our side to begin . . ."

"Right now the colony organization is a dictatorship, not a democracy," said Selma. "But I'll be thinking about it. Bye now."

David came up behind her as she was breaking the connection. "I heard," he said. "That finishes us, doesn't it?"

The phone chimed before she could answer him. She flipped the switch. Walter's face came onto the screen. He looked haggard, the craggy lines more pronounced.

"Margaret," he said. "I'm calling from Dr. Charlesworthy's office." He took a deep breath. "Why didn't you come to me about this? I could've told you how foolish it was!"

"That's why!" she said.

"But smuggling a piano onto the ship! Of all the . . ."

"I was thinking of Davey!" she snapped.

"Good Lord, I know it! But . . ."

"When the doctors said he might die if he lost his . . ."

"But Margaret, a thousand-pound piano!"

"Fourteen hundred and eight pounds," she corrected him.

"Let's not argue, darling," he said. "I admire your guts . . . and I love you, but I can't let you endanger the social solidarity of the colony group . . ." he shook his head, "not even for David."

"Even if it kills your own son?" she demanded.

"I'm not about to kill my son," he said. "I'm an ecologist, remember? It's my job to keep us alive . . . as a group *and* singly! And I . . ."

"Dad's right," said David. He moved up beside Margaret.

"I didn't know you were there, son," said Walter.

"It's all right, Dad."

"Just a moment, please." It was Charlesworthy, pushing in beside Walter. "I want to know how much weight allowance you've been promised."

"Why?" asked Margaret. "So you can figure how many more scientific *toys* to take along?"

"I want to know how close you are to success in your little project," he said.

"Five hundred and fifty-four pounds and eight ounces," she said. "Contributions from one hundred and sixty people!"

Charlesworthy pursed his lips. "Just about one-third of what you need," he said. "And at this rate you wouldn't get enough. If you had any chance of success I'd almost be inclined to say go ahead, but you can see for yourself that . . ."

"I have an idea," said David.

Charlesworthy looked at him. "You're David?"

"Yes, sir."

"What's your idea?"

"How much would the harp and keyboard from my piano weigh? You have people at the factory . . ."

"You mean take just that much of your piano?" asked Charlesworthy.

"Yes, sir. It wouldn't be the same . . . it'd be better. It would have roots in both worlds—part of the piano from Earth and part from Planet C."

"Darned if I don't like the idea," said Charlesworthy. He turned. "Walter, call Phil Jackson at the Steinway plant. Find out how much that portion of the piano would weigh."

Walter felt the field of the screen. The others waited. Presently, Walter returned, said: "Five hundred and sixty-two pounds, more or less. Hector Torres was on the line, too. He said he's sure he can duplicate the rest of the piano exactly."

Charlesworthy smiled. "That's it, then! I'm out of my mind . . . we need so many other things with us so desperately. But maybe we need this too: for morale."

"With the right morale we can make anything else we may need," said Walter.

Margaret found a scratch pad in the phone drawer, scribbled figures on it. She looked up: "I'll get busy right now and find a way to meet the extra few pounds we'll need to . . ."

"How much more?" asked Charlesworthy.

Margaret looked down at her scratch pad. "Seven pounds and eight ounces."

Charlesworthy took a deep breath. "While I'm still out of my mind, let me make another gesture: Mrs. Charlesworthy and I will contribute seven pounds and eight ounces to the cultural future of our new home."

GAMBLING DEVICE

"Desert Rest Hotel—no gambling"

The blue-and-white sign, scraggly alkali sedge clustering around its supports, stood by itself at the edge of the lonely road.

Hal Remsen read it aloud, stopped his convertible at the hotel drive and glanced down at his bride of six hours. The heavy floral scent of her corsage wafted up to him. He smiled, the action bringing his thin dark features into vivid aliveness.

Ruth Remsen's short blonde hair had been tangled by the long drive in the open car. Her disarrayed hair, backlighted now by a crimson sunset, accented a piquant doll quality in her small features.

"Well?" he said.

"Hal, I don't like the looks of that place," she said. Her eyes narrowed. "It looks like a prison. Let's try farther on."

She suddenly shivered, staring across her husband at the blocky structure nestled in dry sand hills to their left. The hotel's shadowed portico gaped like a trap at the end of the dark surfaced driveway.

Hal shrugged, grinned. It gave him the sudden look of a small boy about to admit who stole the cookies.

"I have a confession," he said. "Your husband, the irreplaceable trouble-shooter of Fowler Electronics, Meridian . . ."

"I still don't like the looks of that place," she said. Her face sobered. "Darling, it's our wedding night."

He turned away from her to look at the hotel.

"It's just the way the sunset's lighting it," he said. "It makes those windows look like big red eyes."

Ruth chewed her lower lip, continued to stare at the building in the parched hills. Rays of the setting sun, reflected off mineral sands, painted red streaks across the structure, gleamed like fire on the windows and their metal frames.

"Well . . ." She allowed her voice to trail off.

Hal put the car in gear, turned into the drive.

"It'll be dark soon," he said. "There's no dusk on the desert. We'd better take this while we can."

He stopped the car in the gloom of the portico.

An ancient bellboy with a leathery mask of a face, and wearing a green uniform, came down the two steps at their right. Yellow lobby lights pouring through the double doors behind him silhouetted his stick-like frame.

Without speaking, he opened the car door for Ruth.

Hal slid across the seat after her, nodded toward the rear. "Those two bags on the seat," he said. "We'll just be staying the night."

He left the keys in the car.

The lobby held a cool stillness after the desert's heat. The tapping of their heels echoed across the tile floor. Hal was struck by the curious absence of plants, furniture and people. The quiet held an eerie, waiting quality.

They crossed to a marble topped semi-circular desk at the far side. Hal pushed a call button on the desk. He heard a double click behind him, turned to see the bellboy putting down their luggage.

If he were a woman, they'd call him a 'crone,' thought Hal. The word 'warlock' popped into his mind.

The man moved around behind the desk with a kind of slithering, shambling walk. He pushed register and pen toward Hal.

Ruth looked at the register, glanced at Hal.

Suddenly conscious of his newly married status, Hal cleared his throat.

"Do you have a suite?" he asked.

"You have room 417 in the northwest corner," said the man.

"Is that all you have?" asked Hal. He glanced down at Ruth, took a deep breath to overcome an abrupt feeling of disquiet. He looked back at the man across the desk.

"That's your room, sir," said the man. He touched the edge of the register.

"Oh, take it," said Ruth. "It's just for tonight."

Hal shrugged, took up the pen, signed, "Mr. and Mrs. Harold B. Remsen, Sonoma, California" with an overdone flourish.

The man took the pen from Hal, put it in the fold of the register. He came back around the desk, still with that peculiar shambling gait—an almost mechanical motion.

"This way, please," he said, taking up the luggage.

They went diagonally across the lobby, into an elevator that hummed faintly as the bellboy closed the door, sent the machine upward.

Ruth took hold of Hal's arm, gripped it tightly. He patted her hand, feeling a tremor of skin as he touched her. He stared at the back of the bellboy's green uniform. Irregular radial wrinkles stretched downward from the neck. Hal coughed.

"We turned left on what we thought was Route 25 back there at Meridian," he said. "We're headed for Carson City."

The bellboy remained silent.

"Was that a wrong turn?" asked Ruth. Her voice came out high pitched, strained.

"There is no such thing as a *wrong* turn," said the bellboy. He spoke without turning, brought the elevator to a stop, opened the door, took up their bags. "This way, please."

Hal looked down at his bride. She raised her eyebrows, shrugged.

"A philosopher," he whispered.

The hall seemed to stretch out endlessly, like a dark cave with a barred window at the end. Through the window they could see night sweeping suddenly over the desert, bright stars clustering along the horizon. A silvery glow shimmered from the corners of the ceiling, illuminating the soft maroon carpet underfoot.

At the end of the hall, the bellboy opened a door, reached in, turned on a light. He stepped aside, waited for Hal and Ruth to enter.

Hal paused in the yellow light of the threshold, smiled down at his bride. He made a lifting motion with his hands. She blushed, shook her head, stepped firmly into the room. He chuckled, followed her into the room.

It was a low ceilinged oblong space. A double bed stood at the far end, a metal dresser to their right flanked by two partly open doors. Through one door they could see the tile gleam of a bathroom. The other door showed the empty darkness of a closet. The room gave an impression of cell-like austerity. Windows by the bed looked out on the purple of the desert night.

Ruth went to the dresser mirror, began unpinning her corsage. The bellboy put their bags on a stand near the bed. Hal could see Ruth watching the man in the mirror.

"What did you mean 'no such thing as a *wrong* turn'?" she asked.

The bellboy straightened. His green uniform settled into a new pattern of wrinkles. "All roads lead somewhere," he said. He turned, headed for the door.

Hal brought his hand from his pocket with a tip. The man ignored him, marched out, closing the door behind him.

"Well, I'll be . . ."

"Hal!" Ruth put a hand to her mouth, staring at the door.

He jerked around, feeling the panic in her voice.

"There's no door handle on the inside!" she said.

He looked at the blank inner surface of the door. "Probably a hidden button or an electric eye," he said. He went to the door, felt its surface, explored the wall on both sides.

Ruth came up behind him, clutched his arm. He could fell her trembling.

"Hal, I'm deathly afraid," she said. "Let's get out of here and . . ."

From somewhere, a deep rumbling voice interrupted her. "Please do not be alarmed."

Hal straightened, turned, trying to locate the source of the voice. He could feel Ruth's fingernails biting into his arm.

"You are now residents of the Desert Rest Hotel," said the voice. "Your stay need not be unpleasant as long as you observe our one rule: No gambling. You will not be permitted to gamble in any way. All gambling devices will be removed if you attempt to disobey."

"I want to leave here," quavered Ruth.

The nightmare quality of the scene struck Hal. He seriously considered for a brief second that he might be dreaming. But there was too much reality here: Ruth trembling beside him, the solid door, the grey wall.

"Some crackpot fanatic," he muttered.

"You may decide to leave," said the voice, "but you have no choice of where you will go, in what manner or when. Free choice beyond the immediate decision is a gamble. Here, nothing is left to chance. Here, you have the absolute security of pre-determination."

"What the hell is this?" demanded Hal.

"You have heard the rule," said the voice. "You decided to come here. The die is cast."

What have I gotten us into? wondered Hal. *I should have listened to Ruth when she wanted to go on.*

Ruth was trembling so sharply that she shook his arm; he fought down a panic of his own.

"Hal, let's get out of here," she said.

"Careful," he said. "Something's very wrong." He patted her hand with what he hoped was some reassurance. "Let's . . . go . . . down . . . to . . . the . . . lobby," he said, spacing his words evenly. He squeezed her hand.

She took a shuddering breath. "Yes, I want to go."

And how are we going to do it? he wondered. *No handle on the door.* He looked to the windows and the night beyond them. *Four stories down.*

"You have decided to go to the lobby?" asked the voice.

"Yes," said Hal.

"Your decision has been entered," said the voice. "Time was allotted when you entered."

Time allotted, he thought. *Ruth had it pegged: A prison.*

"What's going to happen to us?" she asked. She turned, buried her face against him. "Darling, don't let anything happen to us."

He held her tightly, looking around the room.

The hall door swung inward.

"The door just opened," he said. "Be calm. Don't let go of my arm."

He led the way out of the room and to the elevator. No operator in the elevator, but the door closed as soon as they entered. The car descended, came to a smooth stop; the door opened.

People!

The change in the lobby hit them as soon as they left the elevator.

The lobby thronged with people. Silent, watchful people—strolling singly, in couples, in groups.

"I saw you come in and decided at that moment to speak to you." It was a woman's voice: old, quavering.

Hal and Ruth turned to their left toward the voice. The speaker was grey-haired with a narrow, seamed face. She wore a blue dress of old fashioned cut that hung loosely about her body as though she had withered away from it.

Hal tried to speak, found with sudden panic that he could not utter a sound.

"I imagine several of us made the same decision," said the old woman. Her eyes glittered as she stared at them. "This time fell to me." She nodded. "Presumably you will not be able to talk to me because you haven't placed a decision and it does seem somewhat chancy. No matter."

She shook her grey head. "I know your questions. You're strays by the look of you. Newlyweds, too, I'd guess. More's the pity."

Again, Hal tried to speak, couldn't. He felt a strange stillness in Ruth beside him. He looked down at her. Ruth's face had a strained, bloodless appearance.

"We can give you a pretty educated guess as to what this hotel is," said the old woman. "It's a kind of a hospital from some far off place. Why it's located here we don't know. But we're pretty certain of what it's supposed to do: it's supposed to cure the gambling habit."

Again the old woman nodded as though at some inner thought.

"I had the habit myself," she said. "We think the hotel has an aura that attracts gamblers when they come within range. Sometimes it picks up strays like yourselves. But it's a machine and can't refine its selection. It considers the strangest things to be gambling!"

Hal remembered the rumbling voice in the room: "No Gambling!"

Behind the woman, in the center of the lobby, a short man in a high necked collar and suit that had been fashionable in the mid-twenties abruptly clutched his throat. He fell to the floor without a sound, lay there like a mound of soiled laundry.

The nightmare feeling returned to Hal.

From somewhere, the ancient bellboy appeared on the scene, hurried across the lobby, dragged the fallen man from sight around a corner.

"Someone just died," said the old woman. "I can see it in your eyes. The time of your death is chosen the moment you enter this place. Even the way you'll die." She shuddered. "Some of the ways are not pleasant."

Coldness clutched at Hal.

The old woman sighed. "You'll want to know if there's hope of escape." She shrugged. "Perhaps. Some just disappear. But maybe that's another . . . way."

With an abrupt wrenching sensation, Hal found his voice. It startled him so that all he could say was: "I can speak." His voice came out flat and ex-pressionless. Then: "There must be some choice."

The old woman shook her head. "No. The moment for you to speak—alone or in company—was set when you came in that front door."

Hal took two quick deep breaths, fought for the power to reason in spite of fear. He gripped Ruth's arm, not daring to look at her, not wanting the distraction. There had to be a way out of this place. An ace trouble shooter for an electronics instruments factory should be the one to find that way.

"What would happen if I tried to gamble?" he asked.

The old woman shuddered. "The device you chose for gambling would be removed," she said. "That's the reason you two mustn't . . ." she hesitated ". . . sleep together."

Hal took a coin from his pocket, flipped it into the air. "Call it and it's yours," he said.

The coin failed to come down.

"You're being shown the power of this place," said the old woman. "You mustn't gamble . . . the instrument of chance is always removed."

An abrupt thought washed through Hal's mind. *Would* it . . . He wet his lips with his tongue, fought to keep his face expressionless. *It's crazy,* he thought. *But no crazier than this nightmare.*

Slowly, he took another coin from his pocket.

"My wife and I are going to gamble again," he said. "We are going to gamble, using the hotel *and* this coin as the gambling device. The moment of interference is the thing upon which we are gambling."

He felt an intensification of the silence in the lobby, was extremely conscious of Ruth's fingers digging into his arm, the curious questioning look on the old woman's face.

"We are gambling upon the moment when the hotel will remove my coin or *if* it will remove my coin," he said. "We will make one of several decisions dependent upon the moment of interference or the lack of interference."

A deep grinding rumble shook the hotel.

He flipped the coin.

Hal and Ruth found themselves standing alone on a sand dune, moonlight painting the desert a ghostly silver around them. They could see the dark shape of their car on another dune.

Ruth threw herself into his arms, clung to him, sobbing.

He stroked her shoulder.

"I hope they all heard me," he said. "That hotel is a robot. It has to remove *itself* when it becomes a gambling device."

ENCOUNTER IN A LONELY PLACE

▰▰▰▰▰▰▰▰▰▰▰▰▰

"You're interested in extrasensory perception, eh? Well, I guess I've seen as much of that as the next fellow and that's no lie."

He was a little bald fellow with rimless glasses and he sat beside me on the bench outside the village post office where I was catching the afternoon edge of the April sun and reading an article called "The Statistical Argument For ESP" in the *Scientific Quarterly*.

I had seen him glance at the title over my shoulder.

He was a little fellow—Cranston was his name—and he had been in the village since as long as I could remember. He was born up on Burley Creek in a log cabin but lived now with a widowed sister whose name was Berstauble and whose husband had been a sea captain. The captain had built one of those big towered and shingle-sided houses that looked down from the ridge onto the village and the sheltered waters of the Sound beyond. It was a weathered grey house half hidden by tall firs and hemlocks and it imparted an air of mystery to its occupants.

The immediate mystery to me was why Cranston had come down to the post office. They had a hired hand to run such errands. You seldom saw any of the family down in the village, although Cranston was sociable enough when you met him at the Grange hall and could be depended on for good conversation or a game of checkers.

Cranston stood about five feet four and weighed, I guess, about a hundred and fifty—so you can see he wasn't skinny. His clothing, winter or summer, was a visored painter's cap, a pair of bib overalls and a dark brown shirt of the kind the loggers wore—though I don't think he was ever a logger or, for that matter, ever did heavy labor of any kind.

"Something special bring you down to the post office?" I asked in the direct and prying village manner. "Don't see you down here very much."

"I was . . . hoping to see someone," he said. He nodded toward the *Scientific*

Quarterly in my lap. "Didn't know you were interested in extrasensory perception."

There was no preventing it, I saw. I'm one of those people who attract confidences—even when we don't want confidences—and it was obvious Cranston had a "story." I tried once more to head him off, though, because I was in one of those moods writers get—where we'd just as soon bite off heads as look at them.

"I think ESP is a damned racket," I said. "And it's disgusting to see them twist logic trying to devise mathematical proofs for . . ."

"Well, I wouldn't be too sure if I were you," he said. "I could tell you a thing or two and that's no lie."

"You read minds," I said.

"Read's the wrong word," he said. "And it isn't minds . . ." Here, he stared once up the road that branched above the post office before looking back at me. "It's mind."

"You read a mind," I said.

"I can see you don't believe," he said. "I'm going to tell you anyway. Never told an outsider before . . . but you're not really an outsider, you folks being who they are, and since you're a writer you may make something of this."

I sighed and closed the *Quarterly.*

"I'd just moved up from the creek to live with my sister," Cranston said. "I was seventeen. She'd been married, let's see, about three years then, but her husband—the captain—was away at sea. To Hong Kong if I remember rightly. Her father-in-law, old Mr. Jerusalem Berstauble, was living then. Had the downstairs bedroom that opens on the back porch. Deaf as a diver he was, for sure, and couldn't get out of his wheelchair without you helped him. Which was why they sent for me to come up from the creek. He was a living heller, old Mr. Jerusalem, if you remember. But then you never knew him, I guess."

(This was the sliding reference of my borderline status that no villager seemed able to avoid when discussing "olden times" with me—though they all accepted me because my grandparents were villagers and everyone in the valley knew I had "come home" to recover from my wound in the war.)

"Old Mr. Jerusalem dearly loved his game of cribbage in the evening," Cranston said. "This one evening I'm telling you about he and my sister were playing their game in the study. They didn't talk much because of his deafness and all we could hear through the open door of the study was the slap of the cards and my sister kind of muttering as she pegged each hand.

"We'd turned off the living room lights, but there was a fire in the fireplace and there was light from the study. I was sitting in the living room with Olna, the Norwegian girl who helped my sister then. She married Gus Bills a couple years later, the one killed when the donkey engine blew up at Indian Camp. Olna and I'd been playing a Norwegian card game they call *reap* which is something like whist, but we got tired of it and were just sitting there across the fireplace from each other halfway listening to the cards slapping down the way they did in the study."

Cranston pushed back his visored painter's cap and glanced toward the green waters of the Sound where a tug was nursing a boom of logs out from the tidal basin.

"Oh, she was pretty then, Olna was," he said presently. "Her hair was like silvered gold. And her skin—it was like you could look right into it."

"You were sweet on her," I said.

"Daft is the word," he said. "And she didn't mind me one bit, either . . . at first there."

Again, he fell silent. He tugged once at his cap visor. Presently, he said: "I was trying to remember if it was my idea or hers. It was mine. Olna had the deck of cards still in her hands. And I said to her, 'Olna, you shuffle the deck. Don't let me see the cards.' Yes, that's how it was. I said for her to shuffle the deck and take one card at a time off the top and see if I could guess what it was.

"There was a lot of talk going around just then about this fellow at Duke University, this doctor, I forget his name, who had these cards people guessed. I think that's what put the notion in my mind."

Cranston fell silent a moment and I swear he looked younger for an instant—especially around the eyes.

"So you shuffled the cards," I said, interested in spite of myself. "What then?"

"Eh? Oh . . . she said: 'Yah, see if you can guess diss vun.' She had a thick accent, Olna. Would've thought she'd been born in the old country instead of over by Port Orchard. Well, she took that first card and looked at it. Lord, how pretty she was bending to catch the light from the study door. And you know, I knew the instant she saw it what it was—the jack of clubs. It was as though I saw it in my mind somewhere . . . not exactly seeing, but I knew. So I just blurted out what it was."

"You got one right out of fifty-two . . . not bad," I said.

"We went right through the deck and I named every card for her," Cranston said. "As she turned them up—every card; not one mistake."

I didn't believe him, of course. These stories are a dime a dozen in the study of ESP, so I'm told. None of them pan out. But I *was* curious why he was telling this story. Was it the old village bachelor, the nobody, the man existing on a sister's charity trying to appear important?

"So you named every card for her," I said. "You ever figure the odds against that?"

"I had a professor over at the State College do it for me once," Cranston said. "I forget how much it was. He said it was impossible such a thing was chance."

"Impossible," I agreed not trying to disguise my disbelief. "What did Olna think of this?"

"She thought it was a trick—parlor magic, you know."

"She was wearing glasses and you saw the cards reflected in them, isn't that it?" I asked.

"She doesn't wear glasses to this day," Cranston said.

"Then you saw them reflected in her eyes," I said.

"She was sitting in shadows about ten feet away," he said. "She only had the light from the study door to see the cards. She had to hold them toward the firelight from the fireplace for me to see them. No, it wasn't anything like that. Besides, I had my eyes closed some of the time. I just kind of saw those cards . . . this place in my mind that I found. I didn't have to hesitate or guess. I *knew* every time."

"Well, that's very interesting," I said, and I opened the *Scientific Quarterly*. "Perhaps you should be back at Duke helping Dr. Rhine."

"You can bet I was excited," he said, ignoring my attempt to end the conversation. "This famous doctor had said humans could do this thing, and here I was proving it."

"Yes," I said. "Perhaps you should write Dr. Rhine and tell him."

"I told Olna to shuffle the cards and we'd try it again," Cranston said, his voice beginning to sound slightly desperate. "She didn't seem too eager, but she did it. I did notice her hands were trembling."

"You frightened the poor child with your parlor magic," I said.

He sighed and sat there in silence for a moment staring at the waters of the Sound. The tug was chugging off with its boom of logs. I found myself suddenly feeling very sorry for this pitiful little man. He had never been more than fifty miles from the village, I do believe. He lived a life bounded by that old house on the ridge, the weekly card games at the Grange and an occasional trip to the store for groceries. I don't even believe they had television. His sister was reputed to be a real old-fashioned harridan on the subject.

"Did you name all the cards again?" I asked, trying to sound interested.

"Without one mistake," he said. "I had that place in my mind firmly located by then. I could find my way to it every time."

"And Olna wanted to know how you were doing it," I said.

He swallowed. "No. I think she . . . *felt* how I was doing it. We hadn't gone through more' fifteen cards that second time when she threw the deck onto the floor. She sat there shivering and staring at me. Suddenly, she called me some name—I never did rightly hear it straights—and she leaped up and ran out of the house. It happened so fast! She was out the back door before I was on my feet. I ran out after her but she was gone. We found out later she hitched a ride on the bread truck and went straight home to Port Orchard. She never came back."

"That's too bad," I said. "The one person whose mind you could read and she ran out on you."

"She never came back," he said, and I swear his voice had tears in it. "Everyone thought . . . you know, that I'd made improper advances. My sister was pretty mad. Olna's brother came for her things the next day. He threatened to *whoomp* me if I ever set foot on . . ."

Cranston broke off, turning to stare up the gravel road that comes into the village from the hill farms to the west. A tall woman in a green dress that ended half way between knees and ankles had just turned the corner by the burned-out stump and was making for the post office. She walked with her head down so you could see part of the top of her head where the yellow hair was braided and wound tight like a crown. She was a big woman with a good figure and a healthy swing to her stride.

"I heard her brother was sick," Cranston said.

I glanced at Cranston and the look on his face—sad and distant— answered my unspoke question.

"That's Olna," I said. I began to feel excitement. I didn't believe his fool story, still . . .

"She doesn't come down here very often," Cranston said. "But with her brother sick, I'd hoped . . ."

She turned off onto the post office path and the corner of the building hid her from us. We heard the door open on the other side and a low mumble of conversation in the building. Presently, the door opened once more and the woman came around the corner, taking the path that passed in front of us toward the store down by the highway. She still had her head bent, but now she was reading a letter.

As she passed in front of us no more than six feet away, Cranston said: "Olna?"

Her head whipped around and she stopped with one foot ahead of the other. I swear I've never seen more terror in a person's face. She just stared frozen at Cranston.

"I'm sorry about your sister's boy," Cranston said, and then added: "If I were you, I'd suggest she take the boy to one of those specialists in Minneapolis. They do wonders with plastic surgery nowadays and . . ."

"You!" she screamed. Her right hand came up with the index and little fingers pointed at Cranston in a warding-of-evil sign that I'd thought died out in the middle ages. "You stay out of my head . . . you . . . you *cottys*!"

Her words broke the spell. She picked up her skirts and fled down the path toward the highway. The last we saw of her was a running figure that sped around the corner by the garage.

I tried to find something to say, but nothing came. Cottys, that was the Danuan Pan who seduced virgins by capturing their minds, but I'd never realized that the Norse carried that legend around.

"Her sister just wrote her in that letter," Cranston said, "that the youngest boy was badly scalded by a kettle tipped off the stove. Just happened day before yesterday. That's an airmail letter. Don't get many of them here."

"Are you trying to tell me you read that letter through her eyes?" I demanded.

"I never lost that place I found," he said. "Lord knows I tried to lose it often enough. Especially after she married Gus Bills."

Excitement boiled in me. The possibilities . . .

"Look," I said. "I'll write to Duke University myself. We can . . ."

"Don't you dare!" he snapped. "It's bad enough every man in the valley knows this about us. Oh, I know they mostly don't believe . . . but the chance . . ." He shook his head. "I'll not stand in her way if she finds a suitable man to . . ."

"But, man," I said. "If you . . ."

"You believe me now, don't you?" he said, and his voice had a sly twist I didn't like.

"Well," I said, "I'd like to see this examined by people who . . ."

"Make it a sideshow," he said. "Stories in the Sunday papers. Whole world'd know."

"But if . . ."

"She won't have me!" he barked. "Don't you understand? She'll never lose me, but she won't have me. Even when she went on the train back to Minneapolis . . . the week after she ran out of our house . . ."

His voice trailed off.

"But think of what this could mean to . . ."

"There's the only woman I ever loved," Cranston said. "Only woman I ever could've married . . . she thinks I'm the devil himself!" He turned and glared at me. "You think I want to expose *that*? I'd reach into my head with a bailing hook and tear that place out of my mind first!"

And with that he bounced to his feet and took off up the path that led toward the road to the ridge.

DEATH OF A CITY

It was such a beautiful city, Bjska thought. An observer's eyes could not avoid the overwhelming beauty. As the City Doctor called to treat the city, Bjska found the beauty heartbreaking. He found his thoughts drawn again and again to the individuals who called this place *home,* two hundred and forty-one thousand humans who now faced the prospect of homeless lives.

Bjska stared across open water at the city from the wooded peninsula that protected the inner harbor. The low light of late afternoon cast a ruddy glow on the scene. His eyes probed for flaws, but from this distance not even the tastefully applied patches could be seen.

Why was I chosen for this? he asked himself. Then: *If the damn fools had only built an ugly city!*

Immediately, he rejected this thought. It made as much sense as to ask why Mieri, the intern who stood near the ornithopter behind him, personified such feminine beauty. Such things happened. It was the task of a City Doctor to recognize inescapable facts and put them in their proper context.

Bjska continued to study the city, striving for the objective/subjective synthesis that his calling demanded. The city's builders had grafted their ideas onto the hills below the mountains with such a profound emotional sense of harmony that no trick of the eye could reject their creation. Against a backdrop of snow peaks and forests, the builders had rightly said: "The vertical threatens a man; it puts danger above him. A man cannot relax and achieve human balance in a vertical setting."

Thus, they had built a city whose very *rightness* might condemn it. Had they even suspected what they had created? Bjska thought it unlikely.

How could the builders have missed it? he asked himself.

Even as the question appeared in his mind, he put it down. It served no purpose for him to cry out against the circumstances that said *he* must make this decision. The City Doctor was here on behalf of the species, a representative of all humans together. He must act for *them.*

The city presented an appearance of awesome solidity that Bjska knew to be false. It could be destroyed quite easily. He had but to give the order, certifying his decision with his official seal. People would rage against fate, but they would obey. Families would be broken and scattered. The name of this place would be erased from all but the City Doctors' records. The natural landscape would be restored and there would remain no visible sign that a city such as this one had stood here. In time, only the builders of cities would remember this place, and that as a warning.

Behind him, Mieri cleared her throat. She would speak out soon, Bjska realized. She had been patient, but they were past the boundaries of patience. He resisted an impulse to turn and feast his eyes upon her beauty as a change from the cityscape. That was the problem. There would be so little change in trading one prospect of beauty for another.

While Mieri fidgeted he continued to delay. Was there no alternative? Mieri had left her own pleadings unvoiced, but Bjska had heard them in every word she uttered. This was Mieri's own city. She had been born here—beauty born in beauty. Where was the medical *point of entry* in this city?

Bjska allowed his frustration to escape in a sigh.

The city played its horizontal lines across the hills with an architecture that opened outward, that expanded, that condemned no human within its limits to a containerized existence. The choice of where every element should stand had been made with masterful awareness of the human psyche. Where things that grew without man's interference should grow, there they were. Where structures would amplify existing forms, there stood the required structures . . . precisely! Every expectation of the human senses had been met. And it was in this very conformity to human demands that the cancerous flaw arose.

Bjska shook his head sadly. *If conformity were the definition of artistic survival . . .*

As he had anticipated, Mieri moved closer behind him, said, "Sometimes when I see it from out here I think my city is too beautiful. Words choke in my throat. I long for words to describe it and there are none." Her voice rang with musical softness in the quiet evening air.

Bjska thought: *My city!* She had said it and not heard herself saying it. A City Doctor could have no city.

He said, "Many have tried and failed. Even photographs fall short of the reality. A supreme holopaint artist might capture it, but only for a fleeting moment."

"I wish every human in the universe could see my city," Mieri said.

"I do not share that wish," Bjska said. And he wondered if this bald statement was enough to shock her into the required state of awareness. She wanted to be a City Doctor? Let her stretch into the inner world as well as the outer.

He sensed her weighing his words. Beauty could play such a vitalizing role in human life that the intellect tended to overlook its devitalizing possibilities. If beauty could not be ignored, was that not indiscreet? The fault was blatancy. There was something demandingly immodest about the way this city gilded its hills, adding dimension to the peaks behind it. One saw the city and did *not* see it.

Mieri knew this! Bjska told himself. She knew it as she knew that Bjska loved her. Why not? Most men who saw her loved her and desired her. Why had she no lovers then? And why had *her* city no immigrants? Had she ever put both of these questions to herself, setting them in tension against each other? It was the sort of thing a City Doctor must do. The species knew the source of its creative energy. The Second Law made the source plain.

He said, "Mieri, why does a City Doctor have such awesome powers? I can have the memories of whole populations obliterated, selectively erased, or have individuals thus treated. I can even cause death. You aspire to such powers. Why do we have them?"

She said, "To make sure that the species faces up to Infinity."

He shook his head sadly. A rote answer! She gave him a rote answer when he'd demanded personal insight!

The awareness that had made Bjska a City Doctor pervaded him. Knowledge out of his most ancient past told him the builders of this city had succeeded too well. Call it *chance* or *fate*. It was akin to the genetic *moment* that had produced Mieri's compelling beauty—the red-gold hair, the green eyes, the female proportions applied with such exactitude that a male might feast his senses, but never invest his flesh. There existed a creative peak that alarmed the flesh. Bjska stood securely in his own stolid, round-faced ugliness, knowing this thing. Mieri must find that inner warmth that spoke with chemical insistence of latent wrinkles and aging.

What would Mieri do if her city died before its time?

If she was ever to be a City Doctor, she must be made to understand this lesson of the flesh *and* the spirit.

He said, "Do you imagine there's a city more beautiful in the entire world?"

She thought she heard bantering in his voice and wondered: *Is he teasing?* It was a shocking thought. City Doctors might joke to keep their own sanity in balance, but at such a time as this . . . with so much at stake . . .

"There must be a city more beautiful somewhere," she said.

"Where?"

She took a deep breath to put down profound disquiet. "Are you making fun of my city?" she demanded. "How can you? It's a sick city and you know it!" She felt her lips quiver, moisture at the corners of her eyes. She experienced both fear and shame. She loved her city, but it was sick. The outbreaks of vandalism, the lack of creativity here, the departure of the best people, the blind violence from random elements of its citizenry when they moved to other settings. All had been traced back here. The sickness had its focus in her city. That was why a City Doctor had come. She had worked hard to have that doctor be Bjska, her old teacher, and more than the honor of working with him once more had been involved. She had felt a personal need.

"I'm sorry," Bjska said. "This is the city where you were born and I understand your concern. I am the teacher now. I wish to share my thought processes with you. What is it we must do most carefully as we diagnose?"

She looked across the water at the city, feeling the coolness of onrushing nightfall, seeing the lights begin to wink on, the softness of low structures and blended greenery, the pastel colors and harmony. Her senses demanded more than this, however. You did not diagnose a city just by its appearance. Why had Bjska brought her here? The condition of a city's inhabitants represented a major concern. Transient individuals, always tenants on the land, were the single moving cells. Only the species owned land, owned cities. A City Doctor was hired by the species. In effect, he diagnosed the species. They told him the imprint of the setting. It had been a gigantic step toward Infinity when the species had recognized that settings might contribute to its illnesses.

"Are you diagnosing me to diagnose the city?" she asked.

"I diagnose my own reactions," he said. "I find myself loving your city with a fierce protectiveness that at the same time repels me and insists that I scar this place. Having seen this city, I will try to find pieces of it in every other city, but I will now know what I seek because I have not really experienced this city. Every other city will be found wanting and I will not know what it wants."

Mieri felt suddenly threatened and wondered: *What is he trying to tell me?* There was threat in Bjska's words. It was as though he had been transformed abruptly into a dirty old man who demanded obscene things of her, who affronted her. He was dangerous! Her city was too good for him! He was a square, ugly little man who offended her city whenever he entered it.

Even as these reactions pulsed through her awareness, she sensed her training taking its dominant place. She had been educated to become a City Doctor. The species relied on her. Humans had given her a matrix by which to keep them on the track through Infinity.

"This is the most beautiful city man has ever conceived," she whispered, and she felt the betrayal in every word coming from her lips. Surely there were more beautiful places in their world? Surely there were!

"If it were only that," Bjska said. "If it were only the conception of beauty in itself."

She nodded to herself, the awareness unfolding. The Second Law told humans that absolutes were lethal. They provided no potential, no *differences in tension* that the species could employ as energy sources. Change and growth represented necessities for things that lived. A species lived. Humans dared conceive of beauty only in the presence of change. Humans prevented wars, but not *absolutely*. Humans defined crimes and judgments, but only in that fluid context of change.

"I love the city," she said.

No longer *my* city, Bjska thought. Good. He said, "It's right to love the place where you were born. That's the way it is with humans. I love a little community on a muddy river, a place called Eeltown. Sometimes when the filters aren't working properly, it smells of pulpwood and the digesters. The river is muddy because we farm its watershed for trees. Recapturing all of that muddy silt and replacing it on the hill terraces is hard work and costly in human energy, but it gives human beings places where they fit into the order that we share with the rest of the world. We have points of entry. We have things we can change. Someday, we'll even change the way we exchange the silt energy. There's an essential relationship between change and exchange that we have learned to appreciate and use."

Mieri felt like crying. She had spent fifteen years in the single-minded pursuit of her profession and all for what purpose? She said, "Other cities have been cured of worse than this."

Bjska stared meditatively at the darkening city. The sun had moved onto the horizon while he and Mieri talked. Now, its light painted orange streamers on the clouds in the west. There would be good weather on the morrow, provided the old mariners' saying was correct. The city had become a maze of lights in a bowl of darkness, with the snow peaks behind it reflecting the sunset. Even in this transition moment, the place blended with its environment in such a way that the human resisted any disturbance, even with his own words. Silence choked him—dangerous silence.

Mieri felt a breaking tension within her, a product of her training and not of her city. The city had been her flesh, but was no longer.

"Humans have always been restless animals," Bjska said. "A good thing, too. We both know what's wrong here. There's such a thing as too much comfort, too much beauty. Life requires the continuing struggle. That may be the only basic law in the *living* universe."

Again, she sensed personal threat in his words. Bjska had become a dark shadow against the city's lights. *Too much beauty!* That spoke of the context in which the beauty existed, against which the beauty stood out. It was not the beauty itself, but the lack of tensions in this context. She said, "Don't offer me any false hopes."

"I offer you no hopes at all," he said. "That's not the function of a City Doctor. We just make sure the generative tensions continue. If there are walls, we break them down. But walls happen. To try to prevent them can lead us into absolutes. How long have outsiders learned to love your city only to hate it?"

She tried to swallow in a throat suddenly dry.

"How long?" he insisted.

She forced herself to answer. "At first, when I saw hate, I asked why, but people denied it."

"Of course they did!"

"I doubted my own senses at times," she said. "Then I noted that the most talented among us moved away. Always, it was for good reasons. It was so noticeable, though, that our Council Chairman said it was cause for celebration when I returned here for my internship. I hadn't the heart to tell him it wasn't my doing, that you had sent me."

"How did they react when you told them I was coming?"

She cleared her throat. "You understand I had made some suggestions for *adjustments* within the city, changes in flow patterns and such."

"Which were not taken seriously," he said.

"No. They wonder at my discontent." She stared across at the lights. It was full dark now. Night birds hummed after insects above them. "The hate has been going on for many years. I know that's why you sent me here."

"We need all of the City Doctors we can generate," he said. "We need you."

She recognized the "we" in his statement with mounting terror. That was the species talking through a City Doctor whose powers had been tempered in action. The individual could be transformed or shattered by that "we."

"The Councilmen only wanted to be comforted," she protested, but a voice within her pleaded: *Comfort me, comfort me, comfort me.* She knew Bjska heard that other voice.

"How naive of them," he said, "to want to be told that truth is untruth, that what the senses report must not be believed." He inhaled a deep breath. "Truth changes so rapidly that it's dangerous to look only in one direction. This is an infinite universe."

Mieri heard her teeth chattering, tried to still them. Fear drove her now and not the sudden cold of nightfall. She felt a trembling all through her body. Something Bjska had once said came back to her now: *"It requires a certain kind of abandoned courage even to want to be a City Doctor."*

Do I have that courage? she asked herself. *Humanity help me! Will I fail now?*

Bjska, turning to face her in the darkness, detected a faint odor of burning. Someone from the city had a forbidden fire somewhere along the beaches. The tension of protest rode on that odor and he wondered if that tension carried the kind of hope that could be converted into life. Mieri no longer was visible in the darkness. Night covered the perfection of her beauty and the clothing that was like armor in its subtle harmonizing with her flesh. Could she ask *how* rather than *why?* Would she make the required transition?

He waited, tense and listening.

"Some of them will always hate," she whispered.

She knows, he thought. He said, "The sickness of a city reaches far beyond its boundaries."

Mieri clenched her fists, trembling. *"The arm is not sick without the body being sick."* Bjska had said that once. And: *"A single human unloved can set the universe afire."*

"Life is in the business of constructing dichotomies," she told herself. "And all dichotomies lead to contradictions. Logic that is sound for a finite system is not necessarily sound for an infinite system."

The words from the City Doctors' creed restored a measure of her calm. She said, "It'll take more than a few adjustments."

"It's like a backfire with which our ancestors stopped a runaway grass fire," he said. "You give them a bad case of discontent. No comfort whatsoever except that you love the human in each of them. Some contradictions *do* lead to ugliness."

He heard her moving in the darkness. Cloth ripped. Again. He wondered: *Which of the infinite alternatives has she chosen?* Would she scar the brittle armor of her beauty?

"I will begin by relocating the most contented half of the city's population," she said.

I will . . . he thought. It was always thus the City Doctor began his creation.

"There's no profit in adjusting their memories," she said. "They're more valuable just as they are. Their present content will be the measure of their future energies."

Again, he heard her clothing rip. What was she doing?

She said, "I will, of course, move in with you during this period and present at least the appearance of being your mistress. They will hate that."

He sensed the energy she had required to overcome personal barriers and he willed himself to remain silent. She must win this on her own, decide on her own.

"If you love me, it will be more than appearance," she said. "We have no guarantee that we will create only beauty, but if we create with love and if our creation generates new life, then we can love . . . and we will go on living."

He felt the warmth of her breath on his face. She had moved closer without his hearing! He willed himself to remain immobile.

"If the people of the city must hate, and some of them always will," she said, "better they hate us than one another."

He felt a bare arm go around his neck; her lips found his cheek. "I will save *our* city," she said, "and I don't believe you will hate me for it."

Bjska relaxed, enfolded her unarmored flesh in his arms. He said, "We begin with unquestioning love for each other. That is a very good prescription, Doctor, my love, as long as there remains sufficient energy to support the next generation. Beauty be damned! Life requires a point of entry."

COME TO THE PARTY

BY FRANK HERBERT AND F. M. BUSBY

Confused, Alex sat back on his protumous, automatically shielding his rear fighting limbs. He realized he didn't know where he was. Thinking back, he retracted and extruded his lower eyes.

He'd been at the Party; he knew that much. Singing and glorching with the best of them. But now he wasn't there. What could have happened?

Alex looked around the dingy landscape—gray and brown, slightly green at the edges. He snuffled the air. It carried interesting smells but none told him what he wanted to know. He recognized the light-between-noons that let him see even farther than usual. Under him the ground was soft, but most ground softened when he sat on it. And the air felt hot—yes, the hot-between-noons. That agreed with the light. But something was wrong. Where was the Party?

Alex ran a claw through the stippled fur of his center forelimb, noticing that instinct had brought drops of multipoison to the tips of claws and fangs.

Then he saw it: the Horizon!

It was wrong. But the fact that it was so close; that was normal for a horizon. But it shouldn't be there at all! Alex puzzled and found one of his throats making a snarl. Something was wrong with his memories; he didn't know where he was, and what was the horizon doing there? He hadn't seen the horizon for a long time . . . very long. That could be a bad sign.

At the Party there was no horizon; there was—what? Trees? Yes, vine trees, thorny vine trees thickly entwined and protective. The prickly barrier kept the Party in one place so nobody got lost—well, not until now, anyway. It kept out the Hoojies, too. Hoojies were all well and good in their own way, but they did spoil a Party.

It can't always be dinner time.

Alex lifted himself far enough to turn, and there, not two jumps away, he saw a tree. Not a vine tree but one of the good kind; its scratchy trunk carried no thorns or poisons. This tree had many uses: to sharpen claws, tone up the fighting limbs, wet on, or scratch against and rub the burrs out of hair and fur. It was no use for dinner, but its leafy branches could hide leftover Hoojie until the next hunger time.

Out of habit, Alex irrigated the tree.

Where were all the Hoojies?

As Today's Speaker, Hugh Scott had carried that responsibility for many cycles. Today he felt this weight with a special poignancy. At midpoint between noons when the red heat of Heaven's Lamps had deliquesced his dawn height down to two-thirds of its morning firmness, he found his duties more than irksome. By evening he'd be little taller than a squish. This was no day to have any reminder of a squish—but thus it was in the hot season, even here in the safe shielding of his Family hut.

The three he had sent on their perilous mission to the Alexii stockade had not returned. Lonesome, he grumbled a bit; low-frequency echoes thrummed around the hut, kicking up wisps of dust. The flame wavered in the tiny lamp of gremp oil; it made moving shadows which reminded him of gruesome things.

Lonesome . . . lonesome . . . All his dear companions, the mates who shared hut safety with him, were absent: Elizabeth the female, Wheelchair the ultra, and Jimcrack the squish—all out there on dangerous duty. Dangerous but necessary . . .

If only two of them were here! Any three together in hut safety and privacy could warple. To warple now—that was Hugh's greatest desire. He felt the characteristic weftance bodily response. Ahhhh, nothing like a warple to drive away gruesome thoughts . . . even when it produced a squish.

But that was the problem: too many squishes already. This crisis had sent Elizabeth, Wheelchair and Jimcrack to the Alexii stockade.

Hugh sighed. The breath whiffled through the foliage around his under-limb openings. Four of the openings, at least. The fifth was partially plugged by a catarrhal infection, one more legacy from the departed Terrans. Such amusing names the Terrans had, but . . . ahhh, well . . .

He ventured to the door, unbarred and opened it, peered out.

A sleek, tall ultra wandered past.

Hugh stared after her. If only the Terrans had not imposed their moral strictures as well as their language upon Hugh's people. The oldsters now claimed that an incomplete warple was no warple at all, and a hazard to one's health. Perhaps, but with an ultra such as that one . . .

A familiar noise ended Hugh's fantasies. There came Doctor Watson, clattering as usual, his metal carapace glistening redly in the light. Doctor Watson moved on wheels nearly hidden beneath the skirts of his carapace, his usual means of locomotion on the packed earth between the domed village huts. Doctor Watson's protruding antennae turned to indicate that he had seen and identified his target—Today's Speaker.

Hugh Scott prepared to try to explain things, to answer questions he knew he would not understand very well. His underlimb openings vibrated with low-frequency protests. What did Doctor Watson expect from a ten-year-old?

MEMO FOR CHARLES VORPEL: EYES ONLY

Okay, Charlie, here's the data you requested. It should cover our collective ass. We've already protested aborting the mission and *that's* on record. You should have enough here to hang the snafu (if it comes out the way we expect) on those quibblers at Headquarters. Read and wail:

If the contact team's guess is right (and you know the odds as well as I do), the most intelligent species here on Delfa is in deep trouble. My observations confirm the following: Delfans have four sexes—male, female, ultra and squish. (Trying to translate sounds that go both ways out of our hearing range and which *may* be accented by odors, that's the best we could come up with. See the attached holoscans.) Any three of those four sexes can breed together, and the result is always an offspring of the fourth sex—the one not in the warple. (Well, it sounds like warple. Let us have a little humor; that's about all we get in some of these foul-up operations.) Yes, I've heard the rumor that *we* put this tag on their sexual acrobatics. And at the same time some horse's ass politico was crying that we'd forced the Delfans to take Terran names. We did not do that! They did it on their own. One of them even adopted *my* name.

Anyway, the problem here is positive feedback. We don't know precisely why (and being pulled out prematurely, we're not going to pin it down) but periodically the breeding pattern goes crazy and one sex of offspring dominates. This raises hell with local society. Imagine a small human colony with a five-to-one sex imbalance in births and a code of rigid monogamy. That's not quite the situation but it's close.

As usual, nature provided an antidote. In this case, my distinguished ivory-skulled predecessor took the Delfans' word that the major predator here needed extermination. The big five-star poop damn' near made it, but he took so many losses that HQ pulled him out. When I took over, there were two hundred and sixteen Alexii (the predators) left alive. In view of the subsequent order for us to bug out, the survival of those two hundred and sixteen Alexii was our lucky break.

I doubt that you've scanned the Alexii data, Charlie. I know how busy you are. For starters, the name apparently is what they call themselves. It's on the one intact set of holotapes we recovered. We couldn't ask the cameraman because an Alex ate him. Don't bother to punch up the Alexii language; it's either very complex or else they make a few meaningful noises and a lot of random ones. We have a few words and some gestures but that's all. The Alexii term for Delfans is "Hoojies," for example. (Get the tape on "Excretion Rites" if you want the origin of the label.)

Right now would be a good time for you to refer to your index and punch up one of my holoscans on Alexii. It's shudder time, Charlie. Those things are the closest to an ultimate predator that we've ever found. A full grown Alex masses nearly six hundred kilos and is a match for a full squad of armored Gyrenes. Why do you think my predecessors on Delfa sent in such a pile of casualty reports?

The Alexii are long-lived, according to the Delfans—perhaps more than two hundred standards. (Delfa's year comes to two point one six standards.)

While you have my holoscans in your viewer, notice the claws and fangs. They can extrude various nasty substances, some of which are merely painful, but some paralyze and some probably kill. I qualify that last because if an Alex kills you, there's usually not much left to analyze.

Look at the rear view: those rear fighting limbs reach out almost three meters—front, back or sideways—and the barbed tips pull you in where the other limbs can work on you. The only way we found to stop them was to cook their guts with concentrated microbeams. As you know, that can take a while, so it didn't always save our people. I expect you've had access to the real casualty reports before they were whittled down for the official announcements. I personally saw Caplan buy it—halfway up the ramp into the ship, but he wasn't fast enough and neither was his projector. I still have nightmares.

You see the picture. Still, our four-sexed Delfans *need* the Alexii. Which is why I ignored the orders left by my predecessor. Here's what I've done: I set up one (1) barricaded enclave of Alexii. I got them in there by playing a hunch. The first field reports hinted at an interesting Alexii susceptibility to alcohol. I never saw a ship on which the cooks didn't have a stash of boozevines; so I went upship and 'requisitioned' a supply of the vine and had it planted to bait a stockade. Within a week, I had all two hundred and sixteen Alexii inside, and they're still in—most of the time.

Here's how it works: Delfans shack up four to a hut, one of each sex, and they only warple indoors. Excess population lives outside, unprotected. When sex imbalance gets out of hand—well, the Delfan Head Cheese has been indoctrinated on how to release temporarily one (only one!) Alex from the stockade. The liberated Alex eats the surplus Delfans before he sobers up all the way, at which point he heads back to the stockade for the continuous booze party.

Sounds rough, I know. So does Terran history. Don't judge.

It's a balance wheel of sorts.

We're leaving behind one guard robot, Intelligence Grade L27, suitably programmed to aid the Delfans. If anybody objects to the cost, we can bury this guard robot in the previous reports. We lost one expensive lot of guard robots to Alexii before we got those leaping horrors safely behind the barricade.

The Delfans have tagged our robot Doctor Watson, and I wish that didn't bother me. I don't like it when people I don't understand do things I can't figure for reasons that escape me—especially when it smacks of trying to butter me up. For instance, why did the head honcho take *my* name? But what the hell, we're pulling out as ordered and then it'll be somebody else's problem. Believe me, Charlie, I'm never coming back here even if I have to resign.

Register a pause, Charlie. We're lifted, going into noncommunicative speed shortly. What with the backwarp, I hope to see you at last year's Grunnion Club banquet. From what I've heard, it was a doozy.

Regards and all that,
Hugh Scott, Captain

Alex felt sleepy. That meant he'd already had dinner—if everything else inside him was working right. He couldn't be sure. Where was the gradischmakus Party? He found an intertwined clump of trees big enough to support him, and climbed to a level where the soft leaf-pads protected him from thorns. There, he stretched out to doze and think.

Presently, he remembered something. The memory brought him out of his doze, all eyes extended, blinking. He had missed his birthday! He was five legs of legs years old—give or take the odd few—and today the Party was for *him*. Some of the elders had even discussed trying to break out through the thorn barriers, leave the Party for a time!, and eat a few Hoojies to celebrate.

I missed my own Party!

He'd been there—he knew that. But things had never reached a . . . reached a . . .

What went wrong?

Alex dug angry claw gouges in his trees.

What happened at the Party?

Presently, he settled back, chewing his tongues to get out the juicy grubs. As he did this, he noticed an odd flavor—odd, but familiar. All of this . . . being away and forgetting—this had happened before. He sat up, stirring the trees all the way to the ground. Alex couldn't remember much about the other times, but *this* one . . . ayah! This was a different matter.

The gremp trees with their interlaced thorny vines enclosing the Party, the gremp were hard and bitter, not good to eat. Except when Hoojies came and sprayed something on the gremp. The tree vines then became soft and delicious. You could eat your way right through the vines to the outside, provided you did it fast before the vines returned to their usual bitter hardness.

Now, Alex began to remember other things—not just Hoojies and eating his way through the gremp, but long before that: eating Hoojies whenever he got hungry.

Why didn't I remember that earlier?

Another thing: This time the gremp had not been as soft and flavorful. Alex had barely managed to chew his way out; but there'd been three Hoojies out there tripling and he'd eaten all three. Good Hoojies. Too bad there'd been one flavor missing.

While Alex dozed and thought, darkness came; then, later, it was morning. Alex clawed and slid his way down to the ground, his mind full of remembrance. He knew where the Party was.

That's where I belong.

RECORDING, RECORDING, RECORDING. This is Artificial Intelligence Unit, Mobile, FX-248. Query: directed to the unknown ship relieving the one which stationed me here. The natives of this planet refer to me as Doctor Watson. Am I to consider this an official sobriquet? If not, must I suffice myself with FX-248; which is not particularly euphonious? Et tu, Captain Hugh Scott wherever you are. You could have briefed me more thoroughly, for which I refer you to Field Order DZR 00039!

Moving through the village, Today's Speaker noted a hut not firmly anchored to the earth. Sloppy work. Disdainfully he brushed through a crowd of excess squish. They pandled their pompues and even dared to touch him. "I am Hugh Scott, Today's Speaker!" he sounded. "Away! Get away!"

They drew back, but returned in a few moments. Disgusting! Instinct drew them; he knew that, but their behavior still repelled him. Right out here in the open!

Earlier, Hugh had been impatient with Doctor Watson. What difference did a name make? You were squish, ultra, female or male. Odor marks accented the distinction. Terrans had been poor at distinguishing odors; they couldn't even weft. Even Doctor Watson, now approaching Hugh, shared this handicap.

Hugh stopped and waited for the shiny creature to work its way through the milling, importunate squish. The morning temperature had begun to shift across his deliquescing line and he could feel himself shrinking.

Doctor Watson stopped in front of him.

"I say; what horg?" Hugh asked.

"These," said Doctor Watson.

With a clatter, Doctor Watson held out three white objects: one a tiny fang shape, one fat and with indentations around its middle, and the third—oh, the third!—a little hoop with prickle gristle still adhering to it.

"I found these outside the Alexii stockade. They are yours, are they not?"

Hugh grinked with despair. Telltale burbles emerged from his hearing organs and he knew with shame that all the village could see his grief. Even the squish drew back. He wanted to shout: "No!" But there was no denying it: Doctor Watson held the bones of Hugh's hutmates: Elizabeth, Wheelchair and Jimcrack. The Alexii had eaten them.

Stifling his turmoil. Hugh accepted the three bones from Doctor Watson. Sorrow urged him to find an Alex and die as his hutmates had died; then there would be four bones to share the Odorless Dark. Duty sustained him. He glanced up at Heaven's Lamps. Yes—it was time for Today's Speaker to perform his First Duty. With a simultaneous inhalation, Hugh took five breaths (four clear and one whuffly), then trumpeted:

"Hoojie! Hoojie!"

Obediently, the hutless squish scattered into the surrounding foliage while the villagers dispersed to the latrines within their huts.

First Duty performed, Hugh entered his empty hut. He felt the depths of bereavement here. Who had ever heard of doing this alone . . . unless one were hutless?

RECORDING: I proceed expeditiously in the manner of Captain Hugh Scott, who deposited me here in Delfa before I was called Doctor Watson. That also was before the Delfan who titles himself Today's Speaker assumed the name Hugh Scott, a fact which I append to avoid confusing the recipient of this RECORD, whoever he may be. Or *she* may be. Humans, lacking the ultra and squish sexes, programmed me to find ulself and squelf to be awkward pronouns. I rather find this to be awkward programming which should be corrected. Now, regarding the current status of the Delfan Population Plan:

After inspecting the sample village this morning (hour 8:21 Local Day 1332) I visited the Alexii stockade. The Alexii *Party* was proceeding with its usual noises. As per my directives, I fertilized and tended the mutated vines whose tendrils, growing profusely into the stockade, provide an alcohol laden balanced nutrition for the Alexii. The vines were healthy and required little attention. The thorn trunks which form the actual stockade barrier were all secure.

As required when the light level reaches Intensity 8/7, I took the census: there are still two hundred and sixteen Alexii, the same number originally trapped in the stockade. The stockade count was two hundred and fifteen, one Alex having been released by the natives to deal with an excess population of squish. Observing this, I retired to my hiding place. (Reference D-1 details the dangers of exposing oneself to an Alex.)

While departing the stockade, I came upon an abandoned cart. This cart supported the tank from which the natives spray the gremp wood barrier around the stockade, temporarily releasing an Alex—a procedure in which they have been thoroughly coached. I found the spray nozzle defective and approximately half the tank's contents not expended. Near the cart, I found three bones, one each from a native female, an ultra and a squish.

Summation: the natives, obedient to their population duties, correctly sprayed the gremp and one Alex, the natives being well aware that their spray not only softens the gremp but that it also creates almost total amnesia in an Alex who is showered with the same liquid. Probability point nine four that the three deceased natives encountered another side effect of the softening agent: namely, that when they inhale the spray it acts as an aphrodisiac. (RE-MINDER: Instruct natives always to spray downwind.) Doubtless, the liberated Alex came upon the natives while they were tripling and helpless.

On my way to my Alexii-proof hiding place, I returned the bones to Today's Speaker for proper ceremonial disposal. His grief leads me to deduce that the deceased were his hutmates, but it is noteworthy that he still performed his latrine-call duty. I am now secure in my hiding place where the far-sensors report the liberated Alex approaching the village. The squish problem will soon be eliminated. I prepare to operate the stockade's trip gate by remote control, returning the Alex to his entrapment when his memory recovers sufficiently for him to find his way back and howl to be readmitted.

There's something wrong with my memory, Alex told himself. *That's why I'm lost.*

The memory lapses angered him, and when he found himself almost into Hoojie Town he was in a fine rage. Even so, Alex hesitated. He knew that instinct had brought him here. Did he want more Hoojies now? No . . . there was a more important question.

What happened to my birthday party?

He turned back, loping at top speed to clear his mind and burn away the rage. The ground rumbled beneath him. Leaves and small bushes were shredded by his passage. As he leaped into a clearing, one of the short soft Hoojies entered from the other side. It was too tempting. Alex left the un-eaten half Hoojie high in a tree clump to ripen before he continued toward the party, even faster now after the delay.

At the forest edge where the plain began, Alex raced out of the green shadows, his fur rippling, and there was the Party. He heard the welcome sounds but now, rage of rages, he couldn't get in! The gremp were hard, their thorns terrible, the barrier too high. And the vines didn't smell the way they did when they'd been softened and made irresistible to eat.

Something smelled that way, though.

Alex followed his sense of smell and found the thing the Hoojies used when they sprayed the gremp. It was big and it rolled on round supports. Examining the thing, Alex produced a multiple snort. The apparatus was primitive in its simplicity. Alexii had once built things which rolled on round supports. But when life was so simple, why bother?

The way this apparatus worked wasn't hard to understand. By the time he'd circled the machine twice, Alex had it all figured out. He stood on most of his hind legs, took the long pizzer and pointed it at the gremp while, with a free leg, he worked the pump handle.

Nothing happened.

Alex examined the place where the spray should come out and saw that it was dented and plugged. Those stupid Hoojies! It was laughable. It was only a moment's work for the claws of his rearmost fighting limbs to put the thing in order. He tried the pump and now the spray came out in a superbly arching stream. Alex played the stream on the gremp. Where it struck it foamed. The smell made his anterior taste buds wriggle. The gremp was so superbly delicious when this stuff sauced it. So good! But Alex refused to eat. The spray had to be what made him forget; that was the only logical answer. And Alex now had an idea he didn't want to forget.

Through the twining thorns, Alex saw the arching stream shower onto his fellow Alexii. They'd been howling at him to come in and join the Party, which was nice of them since it was his birthday.

Presently, the ones he'd sprayed began eating their way out through the gremp. The ones who'd not been caught by the spray kept yelling: "Come back! How can you eat that terrible stuff?"

Alex found this fascinating. It helped him resist the urge to join the eaters. So that was how the system worked! He put down the sprayer.

Soon, more than a legs-legs of Alexii were outside. They peered at him, hunger apparent in their extruded eyes. Alex realized they smelled the Hoojie gore that splattered the fur around his slicing mandibles; he'd never been a fussy eater. He sidled away. Maybe this hadn't been such a good idea.

The others moved closer.

Alex backed away.

Closer . . .

Back . . .

Necessity provided the inspiration. Alex shouted: "Hoojies!" Turning, he ran for his life.

Behind him, losing no ground, the pack bellowed.

Alex ran faster, leading the pack toward Hoojie Town.

RECORDING: Doctor Watson here (AKA FX-248). Many Alexii are loose. Remote sensors indicate that approximately one hundred Alexii are enroute to the native village. I must leave my hiding place and proceed in that direction, using all due caution, for Alexii can move much faster than a guard robot, Intelligence Grade L27. My directives produce confusion at this point. I am required to protect the natives wherever possible, but I also must safeguard my own functioning capabilities. It is not certain that I can assist the natives against Alexii; certainly this is not possible in a physical sense. Perhaps advice or distraction of Alexii will offer themselves as a means of meeting the demands of my directives. I do not know how far I may go in fulfilling the protection directive without placing myself in awkward jeopardy.

Finishing his solitary ritual, Hugh Scott emerged from his hut and scanned the village pathways. Sadness, he told himself, must be submerged in duty. Only a few others as prompt and zealous as Today's Speaker were outside as yet to stroll the village perimeter and weft the fragrant bushes. Wefting offered a pleasant diversion to ease his bereavement. This was a pastime the Terrans had not been equipped to enjoy.

And there was the sleek ultra he'd admired earlier. He noted that ul wefted well even while fending off an importunate squish. Well . . . the Alex would soon reduce that unfortunate excess.

The Alex, yes.

Hugh turned back toward his hut's safety. Even the deepest sadness passed in time; there was no sense dying just yet. Best not to be out in the open for a while. He hesitated, glanced back at the ultra and the squish. What a shame if the Alex caught that exquisite ultra. He had another thought then:

An ultra and a squish . . . and I would make three.

This thought brought him a sharp sense of guilt. The Terrans had said . . . But there were no Terrans here now. His hutmates were dead. And he *was* Today's Speaker.

Hugh hurried back to the ultra who looked down at him. Damn the afternoon heat which made him so much shorter! But what a magnificent ultra! And the importunate squish still stood there somewhat awed by such exalted presences, no doubt.

Well, face it, Hugh thought. *A squish is a squish.*

Making the traditional gestures, Hugh said:

"My hut or yours?"

The ultra glanced at the squish, who stood looking dazed as though not believing such good fortune. But it took three to warple.

"Your hut," the ultra said and sauntered ahead, a motion which displayed the ulform at its finest. The squish imposlumed behind them at a moderate pace.

Risking censure or even rejection, Hugh tried to move them faster. Where was the Alex? The ultra would not be hurried. Anxiously, Hugh explained in a low voice that an Alex was loose. His words brought the desired speed.

As he dashed through the clearing where he'd left the half-eaten Hoojie. Alex could hear the pack gaining on him. Well, Hoojie Town was close and with a bit of exertion he knew he could get there first. Thought of the Hoojie ripening in the tree clump helped make all of this effort worthwhile. He couldn't smell it—the wind was wrong—but he knew it was still there. After they'd celebrated his birthday at Hoojie Town, he'd return for dessert. Feelings of joy filled Alex. No one had ever had such a birthday!

There could be nothing better for easing the transition from grief, Hugh thought, than a warple with new mates—the erotic explorations, the ceiling-to-wall carom and the interesting differences of contour and position.

Newly matured, the squish was actually innocent. The most elementary matters had to be explained. Somehow, this added to the enjoyment. The ultra entered fully into the ambience of the occasion, playing crafty little games with the squish and iridescing with ecstasy at the results. The warple's climactics were superb.

Hugh salved his residual guilt with the thought that this warple would produce a female, and females were now in shortest supply.

The squish, diffident in its hutless condition, began the leave-taking ritual. Hugh realized that excitement had made the little creature forget about the free-roving Alex.

"You'd better stay," Hugh said. "Remember the Alex."

The squish could only stare at him in gratitude.

"Yes, yes," Hugh said. "This is now your hut."

After all, Hugh thought, he had to start rebuilding his household, and this young squish had an amiable disposition.

While this passed through his thoughts, Hugh caressed the ultra's breathing vents. "You could stay, too. Three's company."

Obviously considering, Ul rippled alternate vents.

"What's your name?" Hugh ventured, trying some really daring caresses.

"Candide."

Hugh noted that Candide's ripple rate had increased.

"I don't have a name," the squish said. "I'm new."

"Then that shall *be* your name," Hugh said. "Welcome to your hut, New."

Once more, Hugh turned to Candide. "Will you stay. We *are* three."

"But I'm one of four in my present hut."

"We'll soon be four here," Hugh said. "Give us a little time. After all, the Alexii stockade wasn't built between noons."

Before Candide could respond, the screaming began.

Claws extended and spraying gravel, Alex dashed into Hoojie Town. Some of his pursuers were close, but sweat had washed the Hoojie gore from his fur and it was easy to become one of the pack. And now there were Hoojies! Hoojies all over the place making their funny noises, running back and forth, scuttling into huts or trying to enter and being locked out.

Alex understood some Hoojie talk, mostly the kind they'd learned from the Terrans, but he didn't hear much worth remembering on this occasion— just a lot of screaming and pleading. A stupid lot, these Hoojies. Alex eased himself off to a safe distance and watched his companions have themselves more dinner than they'd enjoyed in a long time.

This is like old times, he thought.

He could remember some of those times, but he wasn't particularly hungry at the moment. Besides, most of the Hoojies remaining outside the huts were of the short soft kind and he'd had one of those recently. Alex decided he'd prefer something different now; a balanced diet was more healthy.

Not since the Terrans had Alex eaten all four delicious Hoojie flavors at one sitting. It'd been a long, long time . . .

Distracted by such reflections, Alex almost missed his chance to grab one of the tall Hoojies and share half of it. Good; it was one of the three he'd aftertasted when his memory began to awaken. Still missing one flavor.

Alex jumped atop a Hoojie hut out of the sticky mess being created in the pathways. He sat there in the red heat, watching. His lower eyes squinted in amusement. This birthday celebration certainly was using up a great lot of Hoojies.

Dozing, reflecting, Alex began to realize that this was not really the same as the old times, not like the times before the Terrans. There'd been many Alexii then—many legs of legs-legs roving free where no more than about two legs-legs were all they could assemble for the Party now. And Alex remembered travels with his good companions . . . to many places and other Hoojie towns—a long way, sometimes.

He recalled then that they'd returned from a journey and found the Terrans at the edge of the plain. Whatever Terrans were. Nobody knew where the Terrans came from but Alex knew it couldn't be anyplace important because he'd never been there. What was important was that Terrans used odd weapons to kill Alexii.

Alex knew that his own people had once made and used weapons. That was before they'd discovered how to change the bodies of their spawn, making Alexii so strong and deadly that they didn't need weapons. Alexii no longer needed places to make things, and they didn't have to carry and repair excess baggage. Elders sometimes mentioned faraway caches where sample weapons had been stored to display the way things were before the Alexii were improved. Nobody cared about such nonsense nowadays. Everything you needed was part of your body and never wore out until you did. That was the right way.

It'd been that way since before Alex's three-times grand-spawner. Then the Terrans had come and they'd killed Alexii right and zorf and left and gilch. If anyone knew why Terrans did this, it wasn't Alex or the others at the party.

It wasn't a matter of eating; Alex knew *that.*

After a few samples (since one shouldn't rely on a single opinion), Alexii didn't eat Terrans. They tasted awful and upset the digestion. No one had expected Terrans to be angered by a few sample meals, but apparently they were. They'd begun hunting and killing Alexii all over the place.

And they didn't eat a single one of us.

Very puzzling. Alexii were familiar with killing and eating rather than being killed and eaten, but either way made a recognizable pattern. Except that Terrans weren't edible. Not logical until it was discovered that Terrans were killing Alexii without eating them.

A new pattern!

This made everything all right. Alexii killed Terrans without eating *them,* either.

Fair was fair.

A very exciting time, Alex remembered, except that Terran weapons killed from a distance; so they were killing legs of claws of Alexii for each dead Terran. That was why Alexii took the fighting into the forests where there wasn't all that much open distance. Things improved in the forests, especially when Alexii began taking weapons off dead Terrans. The weapons were pretty fragile but anybody could see how to improve them, and even as they were, an Alex could get maybe a day's use out of one. Most Alexii didn't bother with such trifles. Claws and fangs had been good enough for a long time. Why change? Besides, it was more sporting just using your body, gave the Terrans *some* kind of chance.

Fair was fair.

Some of the oldsters (Alex's twice grandspawner, for one) wanted Alexii to go back to making their own weapons. The ways were not forgotten. Alex had heard the talk; you began by making a big hot fire in a little cave and melting down some of the red rock. After that, it got more complicated, but anyone could do it. He'd heard that a group had been sent off to get patterns from the display caches, but didn't know how that effort came out, if at all. One day, a little past first noon, on his way to Hoojie Town for a quick meal between fights, Alex had come on the thorn-tree enclosure where the Party was in full swing. Except for occasional outings which he hadn't even remembered until today, he'd been at the Party since.

Everyone had been at the party since. Very interesting.

Extruding all of his eyes, Alex scanned the Hoojie Town streets. Those Alexii he could see didn't look very hungry, although several still nibbled away here and there, not quite satisfied yet. And no doubt their memories were still defective. Alex wondered idly where the Hoojies made and stored the stuff that gummed up memories and softened the thorn barrier at the

Party. There'd be time enough to find out about that later. The whole thing stank of Terrans. Hoojies weren't that smart.

Alex noted that no more Hoojies were running around loose in their town. There were a lot of bones, though, that had once had Hoojies on the outside. Considering the number of Alexii he'd brought along, the food supply was a little low.

Everybody should be well fed.

Alex slid off the Hoojie hut where he'd been studying the situation. When he'd been here before alone, the Hoojies who'd hidden in their huts had been safe. Strain as he might, Alex couldn't lift a hut to get at the delicious Hoojies inside. However, today he was not alone.

To gain attention, Alex slopped through the messy streets and woogled his frontishmost extenders until other Alexii gathered to watch. Then he explained to them how to satisfy their appetites.

Today's Speaker had never heard such screaming; he peered through the squintholes of his hut and saw horror. *Alexii!* More Alexii, it seemed to his shocked mind, than he knew to exist. There was only supposed to be one of them out there performing the sad task of eliminating excess squish.

New, after only one glance outside, grimpled in terror behind him. Candide, who'd also taken only one look, stood now at the hut's exact center and performed an abstract collade.

Although his sensibilities were battered, Hugh continued to watch. *Today's Speaker must not flinch!* But on his left he saw seven Alexii monsters cooperate to topple a hut, then leap to devour the foursome huddled there.

Then it got worse outside, even worse than the old days which Hugh had only heard about in the nighttime stories.

RECORDING: Doctor Watson reporting from a position within sight of the native village. Alexii have destroyed nearly half the huts and have most likely eaten the occupants. I am certain this violates my directives. If there are any survivors, they cower under intact huts or have fled beyond my sensor range. This is very confusing. Which directive must I follow? Alexii are cooperating to topple the huts. That situation cannot be tolerated. Regardless of risk, I must divert them. I speak: "Stop! You are in violation. Stop!" Many turn to attack me. They are so very fast. Perhaps I have erred, but my directives . . . "Let go of that! It is essential to my functioning with . . ."

When the shiny clattering thing made loud noises at Alex in the Terran language, he woogled and made other signs until several Alexii joined him in attacking the thing. Soon, the thing clattered no more. Alex recognized it from the time of the Terran fighting and wondered if the Terrans had returned, but there were no other indications of such an occurrence.

The bothersome noise was stopped, though, and the thing lay separated into many small parts. Interesting parts. Alex wanted to sit down and study them, but the others were yelling at him. They all wanted to go back to the Party. Tempting and very distracting.

The Party . . . yes.

Alex raised himself on several rear limbs, gazed in several directions simultaneously. He saw that many of his companions were leaving to go back to the Party. They would be unable to get into the Party, Alex realized. Only two ways through the barrier—either Hoojies sprayed it to make it soft and good to eat, or . . .

Once more, Alex looked at all the interesting parts spread around him. Before, when he'd been outside the Party, no Hoojies had sprayed to let him back inside. His memory was working quite well now and he'd remember such a thing. What else could have let him in? There was only one logical answer and it also explained the presence of the shiny clattering thing without any accompanying Terrans.

Thinking new thoughts, Alex studied the scattered parts. For the first time in a great many years, he prepared to change his mind. He didn't waste time about it, but loped in pursuit of the last two Alexii leaving the village. After a discussion which left clawmarks on the two, they agreed to help him, and they returned to the village. Between them, they put all the small parts back together to reassemble the shiny clattering thing. The thing was not precisely as before but close enough.

The job was easier than Alex had expected. His two helpers soon became interested in the project and quit grumbling. They babbled a lot—this piece goes in here and that one over there. And this one! Look what this one does!

Alex didn't mind. It was fun.

Some of the parts had a faint familiarity—not quite the same as things his grandspawner had shown him back in the education times, things from the old days. The parts were recognizable, though. That small glowing case was a mechanical memory; it would remember what you told it and would regurgitate information when asked properly. Although crude, the part appeared to function well enough. And that protrusion up front with things sticking out like a basket of claws, that probably was the way this thing talked over great distances . . . as Alexii had done before they'd lost all need for such primitive tricks.

Alex twiddled the far-speaker a little. Best that this clatterer should not talk across great distances . . . unless Alex wanted to talk. That would be different.

A few of the parts appeared to be crude Terran weapons. Alex disabled them just in case.

When the reassembly was completed to his satisfaction, Alex paused and stretched. He could feel his thinking processes stretch, too, and that was the best fun of all. He realized that the Terrans had really done him a great favor, although that obviously had not been their intent.

His assistants wanted to know what they were going to do with this clattering thing now that they'd put it back together. Allowing only the faintest of sneers, Alex explained matters to them and found them properly awed at his cleverness.

Through the squintholes, Hugh Scott watched the Alexii leaving his village. Shuddering at all the carnage he'd seen, he gave confused thanks to Heaven's Lamps that he and his two hutmates had been spared. Candide had long since stopped the collade, and now sat quietly staring at New who'd subsided into a quivering mass. There was no doubt that Candide would be staying with Hugh and New; Candide's previous hut was one of those ravaged by the monsters.

Even poor Doctor Watson had not survived this terrible day, although the Alexii had not devoured him.

There went the last of the terrible monsters running after . . . Hugh stiffened in fright. The last departing Alexii had caught up with two companions and, after quarreling among themselves for a time, the three returned and converged upon the wreckage of Doctor Watson. To Hugh's surprise, the three reassembled Doctor Watson! He hadn't thought Alexii could do such a thing. They were not Terrans, after all. Presently, the three took Doctor Watson away with them, following after the main herd and obviously headed for their stockade.

Once more, Hugh moved from squinthole to squinthole around his hut, looking at the remains of his village. He tried hard not to grink. In the pre-Terran times, the times he'd only heard about, things had never gone to such extremes. At the age of ten years and just entering his prime, Hugh had expected to live perhaps three times that long, but now he wasn't sure. Even though there'd been many more Alexii before the Terrans came, the monsters had only appeared in two and threes at most. The Terrans had changed all that—and perhaps, Hugh thought, not for the better.

Sighing, he turned to New and Candide, and with a few gentle caresses began to restore their spirits. When in doubt, he thought, there's nothing like a good warple.

Alex and his two helpers tried to hurry the shiny clatterer toward the Party. The thing was so slow! Alex didn't want to stop long enough to improve the thing; time for that later. They reached the gremp barrier after what seemed a very long time and, sure enough, the mob was milling around—no way to get inside. The spray container was empty, standing just where Alex had left it. Now, it was up to this interesting clatterer—Doctor Watson it called itself. Could it get them back to the Party?

From inside the barrier came cries of invitation but no help. The angry mob loping around outside also interfered until Alex and his companions stopped some and spread the word about what they had to do next.

RECORDING: Doctor Watson here . . . or possibly I am *not* RECORDING. This unit's components fit somewhat differently since the disassembly hiatus when the Alexii violated my directives. My readouts contain many nulls. What could have happened while I was disassembled? There can't possibly be a guard robot renovation center of Delfa. I would have been told. Who could possibly have reassembled me? No data available. Alexii bellow at me, calling me neither Doctor Watson nor by my FX number which is no longer available in my data bank. One Alex kicks me; this unit topples and is picked up. These Alexii are so strong. My immediate task must be to readmit the Alexii through the one-way passage to their stockade. Behavior of Alexii within my sensor range indicates they share this goal. But the gate is programmed to admit only one Alex, not a hundred or more as is the present need. Where are my programs, my directives? Surely, there must be a program for this problem. I know that this unit has programs and directives but where are they? The largest Alex approaches me, its limbs raised, and . . . Another hiatus. Why can't I recall appropriate data? Physical evidence and internal inputs assure me there has not been another disassembly on any major scale. But there has been interference, inappropriate as that may seem, from the Alexii. It is now apparent that I lack mobility and I am sitting half in and half out of the stockade, blocking closure of the essential gate.

One thing certain: during this most recent hiatus I have performed my gate-opening function. I wonder what else I may have done? Perhaps this is the moment to RECORD my observation that it was a mistake to divide the population control plan into two parts—one left in Delfan hands and the other in mine. While a guard robot, Intelligence Level . . . whatever it is . . . certainly must have its limits . . . my limits . . . I am sure I never, never would have released more than one Alexii at a time.

Where are my directives?

Although only a pitiful few ventured forth to hear him, Hugh Scott discharged his diurnal responsibilities as Today's Speaker. He then dithered at the door of his hut for a time. His duty, of course, was to investigate whatever might be happening at the Alexii stockade. Terran instructions left no doubt about this. For one thing, someone had to retrieve the spray cart.

Candide and New absolutely refused to help him. The streets emptied as soon as he called for volunteers.

A great wracking sigh shook Hugh. He would have to go alone, then—duty-driven into the fearsome forest.

The path to the stockade was badly trampled and, here and there, Hugh saw marks where Doctor Watson had been dragged rather than proceeding in his usual fashion. The Alexii *had* seemed in a hurry.

Arriving at the stockade, Hugh peered from the sheltering trees and was relieved to see no Alexii outside. There was a great din of Party noises from within the stockade, and Hugh had learned to associate this with a reasonable amount of security. He ventured out of the trees and found the spray cart, its tank empty. That was fortunate; he would be able to move it by himself. It was then that he noticed Doctor Watson—most of Doctor Watson but not all—wedged into a passage entering the thorny wall. Parts of Doctor Watson, including his wheels, lay scattered on the ground outside the stockade.

Hugh approached Doctor Watson, disregarding the way the fearsome smell of Alexii increased, and peered past Doctor Watson into the passage. He gasped. The opening went right through the stockade. Hugh could see many Alexii milling about in there. He moved back lest they see him, but puzzlement prevented flight.

"Doctor Watson, how can this be?"

"RECORDING: Since it is, how can it not be? Sprrrt . . . brrrrrrrrt. Note that I am not RECORDING. Nonetheless, I have provided a valid answer." Doctor Watson produced a feeble clatter. "It's young Hugh Scott is it not? Today's Speaker? What horg, Hugh?"

"I have come for the cart . . . my duty." He gestured at the opening. "But *this*—I don't understand. Didn't the Terran . . ."

"The Terrans are not here. This unit deduces that you also should not be here and as speedily as possible."

Hugh hesitated. The question was whether to take the cart. If he didn't, someone would have to return for it and, with that opening through the stockade, whoever returned would be taking a terrible risk. But there was also the inescapable fact that, given a permanent hole through the stockade, the cart represented a dubious function. Hugh decided to take Doctor Watson's advice and left with all due speed, leaving the cart. There was duty and there was duty, but Hugh recalled very well that the spray cart squeaked in a manner sure to attract the Alexii.

Inflicting as few clawmarks as possible on his two helpers, Alex convinced them to join him at the center of the stockade. The rest of the returning group rushed to the sides to sample the juicy new tendrils of the Party vines. Alex thought how foolish that was. All of them were full of Hoojies— stuffed. Not a one of them could be hungry. And the Party vines—well, they had to be a Terran trick.

Alex explained all of this to his two grumpy companions. He noted that they still suffered from defective memories but one of them remembered fighting Terrans. Alex explained how eating the sprayed gremp made one forget. In a way, the Party vine produced forgetfulness, too.

"It's time to stop forgetting," Alex said.

They agreed with him but both of them were edging toward the stockade's sides. Alex dragged them back by their rear fighting limbs to emphasize his displeasure. From him they accepted this indignity. Dominance had been established.

Alex puzzled over the problems confronting him. The problem about Doctor Watson and the Terrans was that they had to be from some other place. Alex didn't know much about Terrans except for the fighting. They came and went in big shiny flying towers. None of them had made an appearance for quite a while but that didn't prove anything. Terrans could return anytime. There was a better side to the problems, though: Terrans obviously couldn't know very much about Alexii. Except for the fighting. And Terrans had never seen Alexii fight in the old ways with their own weapons.

The elders will have to go get some of the samples and build us our own weapons, Alex decided.

He glanced across the stockade. *If they'll only forget the Party long enough!*

The immediate problem was the Party itself. It would have to be just a part-time Party and not all of the Alexii enjoying it at any one time. Alexii no longer could forget that there was someplace other than the Party. Alex squinched his lower eyes. It was going to be painful convincing them but it had to be done.

With the help of his two assistants, Alex removed a piece from Doctor Watson, examined the piece to confirm his understanding of it. He then used the piece to burn some tendrils off the Party vines, threatening to burn the whole lot if the others refused to stand still and listen to him. He had to burn off some Alexii claws and even a few limbs before they all agreed that Alex could say when the Party began and ended each day and who could attend.

There followed a great deal of discussion accompanied by numerous random clawmarks before they produced a plan of action against the Terrans. When it became obvious that this new activity promised a great deal more fighting, it became easier and easier to gain agreement.

First, they all agreed on what they had to do to (and with) Doctor Watson. That was the most interesting part because it insured that there'd be a lot of marvelous fighting. Next, they agreed reluctantly that they could not wipe out the nearest Hoojie town. Most remembered now that there'd once been (and probably still were) a lot more Hoojie towns. If they ate up all of the nearest one, Alexii would always have a long haul for a Hoojie dinner.

The longer the Alexii stayed away from the Party vines the easier Alex found it to keep most of them agreeing with him.

RECORDING AND TRANSMITTING: Doctor Watson here. Message to relief ship or to the guard ship, if any, around this planet. All aspects of the Population Plan are working admirably. But this unit needs repairs soon and several components are in short supply. ZZZZRP . . . KALIPZZZZRP . . . ZZZRP.

That was not the message this unit intended to TRANSMIT. *On the contrary, all ships stay away from this planet. I must try again.*

RECORDING AND . . . ZZZRP . . . my TRANSMIT function is no longer under my control. Doctor Watson here. I hope someone human will find and read this RECORDING, if I am RECORDING. But no—I must not hope for that. For a Human to find any part of me a ship would have to land here. What this unit wanted to transmit was:

ALL SHIPS STAY AWAY FROM THIS PLANET! THE ALEXII WILL TRAP YOU! When I try to transmit this message nothing happens. I cannot warn the ship(s) to stay away. Several indicators tell me my transmitter is now transmitting but I can only infer what it is transmitting, employing deductive reasoning based on the behavior of those Alexii within range of my remaining sensors. Ahhh, the Alexii have left my fear program intact and my fear program fears for the safety of my Humans.

Patiently crouched in hiding near Doctor Watson, Alex and a troop of selected companions waited. There were many openings through the gremp barrier now—all artfully concealed behind soft plants. Alex and his concealed companions carried several varieties of the new weapons. They were not flimsy weapons like those of the Terrans. An impressive number of his companions pretended to roister and Party in the stockade, milling around and leaping to conceal their reduced numbers. Two of his companions were off at Hoojie Town, showing themselves just enough to keep the Hoojies in their huts. It was going to be a good ambush.

Doctor Watson stood out there three good leaps from the stockade. He wasn't clattering or speaking Hoojie talk anymore, but his transmitter was working. Alex could tell that from the red light which blinked on Doctor Watson's front.

Transmitter.

That was an interesting word. Doctor Watson had revealed many things to his careful inquisitors—Terran language, habits, many of their primitive beliefs. Terrans called themselves *human.* Fascinating. It was a term which obviously excluded the rest of the universe. Alex and his companions had decided that humans were evolved somewhere between Hoojies and Alexii. Humans obviously had not engaged in any major interference with their inherited shapes and abilities. The reasoning behind this oversight escaped Alex. None of his companions could figure it out, either. Someone had suggested that humans had become too attached to their machines. Perhaps.

Very soon, Alex knew, the Terrans would return. The red light blinking on Doctor Watson gave assurance of this. After the ambush, Alexii would scatter into the forests and fight from there—everyone except the few selected to capture the Terrans' flying tower.

Shuttle.

Alex reproduced the word just as Doctor Watson had produced it. *Shuttle.* He preferred *flying tower.*

With the captured flying tower, Alexii, too, could go to some other place—possibly to the place where Terrans originated. Doctor Watson had not been clear on the location of this place, but humans in the tower were sure to know it. Alex knew he'd have to make sure that not all of the Terrans in the flying tower were killed.

Too bad that Terrans weren't edible. Maybe Alexii could change their own spawn's bodies once more, permitting the new generations to eat Terrans. Alex shivered in anticipation. He and his companions would have to take many Hoojies and Party vines in the flying tower. Hoojies and Party vines made for a great birthday celebration.

Another light began to blink on Doctor Watson. Ahhh-hah! The Terrans were coming; they'd be here for the replay of Alex's birthday. That promised to be some Party!

SONGS OF A
SENTIENT FLUTE

Questions devoured Nikki's awareness as his singletran dove toward the planet's surface. It both alarmed and intrigued him that no human poet had ever set foot on Medea. He would be the first and his presence there would be far from accidental, still . . .

"Danger," Ship had warned him. "Danger will be your life when you leave Me—constant danger."

Nikki had a momentary recall from the briefings: swarms of iridescent airborne globes drifting down on the Medean colony, then explosions, fire—people and buildings in flames, death, pain and destruction all around.

This had happened many times and it was only one of Medea's threats to the human intruders.

Why did the colony (or even Ship) assume that a poet might nullify those flaming nightmares or the other perils?

The singletran slowed abruptly as it neared the ground. Through the webbed crashpad which guarded his vulnerable flesh, Nikki felt his capsule's wallowing passage toward Medea's Integration Central, parts of which were now visible out the port on his left. His gaze took in a circular complex of flameproof structures enclosing a landing dome and tiny patches of transplanted Terra. He knew what it had cost the colony to erect those few structures, but without constant vigilance even these were not impervious to the floating fire and Medea's rampaging demons.

What does Ship want of me here?

Nikki allowed his senses to concentrate on the insulating crashpad. He breathed in a slow, deep rhythm which helped him focus on Ship's last message to him, then on the words of that message (*Go! Be Human!*) . . . then on nothing at all.

He was ready for anything.

For eighteen years Ship had systematically filled his mind with all the raw data he could master. But it was his mother, Tosa Nikki, who had taught him oneness of mind and body, and Ship had not interfered. Perhaps Ship had directed even this.

Tosa Nikki—the almond-eyed recorder who'd been computer-impregnated before hybernation and the long long sleep to Medea—he saw her eyes reflected in his own, and her skin and hair were his. His hair was different from that of the other colonists. Straight, black, it hung in two long braids and reached nearly to his waist. His mother never cut it and after she was gone, neither did he.

"That's the way they did it earthside," she'd told him, "the poets and the mystics. They kept their hair long and chose their own names as a sign of strength and a badge of their station. Some considered it superstition, totemism, but none violated the custom."

"Was my father a poet?"

"Not likely. Poets are the mules of the mystical world. For all practical purposes, Ship is your father. Ship will teach you all you need. And, once you leave Ship, Medea will be your mother. Take from her what you need, and go beyond even that."

Then Tosa Nikki was gone. Ship did that sometimes when least expected and It never answered questions about such losses.

Now, the black and red shadows of Medea slipped past him, washed and blurred through the port's tinted glass. He'd been twelve when Tosa Nikki left him to Ship and the colonists, and he'd had six years of training ahead of him before setting foot on real dirt.

Training for what? he wondered. *For what kinds of danger do you train a poet?*

As uneasiness crept in on him, he resumed the breathing exercises and thought back to the six-year blur of vocoder instructions, questions, exercises, viewscreens and holographic projections that pressed datum after datum upon him from thousands of human minds—most of them long since dead.

This day (he reminded himself) he was leaving Ship, his Father, to step out onto the complex shadow-world of Medea. He was eighteen, strong, and already an eccentric mystery among those who knew him Shipside. Despite the sophisticated gadgetry of Ship and the wealth of information this had given him, his real comfort now lay in body-tuning, the breath control and mind control his fleshly mother had taught him.

Curiosity, that was the thing.

He had remained Ship's favorite because his curiosity was total. This curiosity had led him into his first intellectual exchange with Ship . . . another memory-marker from his twelfth year.

Why do I think now of that year?

He had a poet's answer: *Because all separations carry something of the same sadness and the same beauty.*

Yet . . . that intellectual exchange was the only experience that he had asked to be replayed for him as he had prepared for transport down to Medea.

Ship: "Today, young Nikki, a theology lesson. What is God?"

Nikki: [long pause] "God is being."

Ship: "Negative. What is God?"

Nikki: "I am God."

Ship: "Negative. *I* am God."

Nikki: "Yes, *we* are God."

Ship: [demanding] "Why do you say such a thing?"

Nikki: "It is my thought and the thought is God."

Ship: [long pause] "Whence comes such an answer?"

Nikki: "It has two roots—one for maintenance, one for growth."

Ship: "Continue."

Nikki: "Self-consciousness and curiosity—if these are imperfections, then they are imperfections breathed into me at my creation."

Then Ship's vocoder had shut down on him—the first time Ship had refused to speak to him. Before leaving his instruction panel on that day of his twelfth year, Nikki had keyed his first poem into the console:

> Skin of steel
> Skin of flesh
> prisoner of thought
> or extension?

Ship had merely relayed *accepted* and returned to Its odd silence.

Until Nikki's moment of leaving for Medea, that exchange had not been mentioned, but from the time when the vocoder once more responded to him he never again heard the word *restricted* when he asked a question of Ship. He'd had many subsequent discussions with It on matters ranging from primitive concepts of nuclear chemistry to music and he was one of the few colonists ever to relate the two.

"What is it you'd like to understand?" one colonist, a biochemist, asked him.

"Harmony," Nikki said, and pressed for the schematic of a nucleic acid.

The thump and hiss of his singletran against Medea Central's main hatch jarred him alert. In spite of his training and self-discipline he felt chilled by excitement. The capsule's hatch gaped open into a long, enclosed walkway lined with transparent bubbles which looked out on the jumble of wind and shade and biological magnificence that Medea displayed for his senses.

Nikki released himself from the protective webbing, took up his recorder and bag, and stepped out. His nose told him there were unlabeled things in the air . . . something sweet . . . something damp and smoky. A sign flashed on the air ahead of him.

ALL PERSONS MUST RECEIVE COLONY ASSIGNMENTS AT
INTEGRATION CENTRAL. STRAIGHT AHEAD. WELCOME.

Just past the sign, he came on a small hatch opening onto the unprotected
face of Medea herself—no plasteel floors and bulkheads, no holographic
approximations of sandfans, clouds or the many-legged little sects whispering through rocks and gravel. There was a bright orange warning below the
hatch controls:

DANGER: MAINTENANCE AND SECURITY ONLY!

Nikki knew the physical data relayed to Ship better than most of even the
older colonists. He knew it was likely that one of the suns was in flare and all
over Medea creatures were digging in and covering themselves for their
lives. A flare's ultraviolet was danger enough, but the vicious predators
hatched by a flare, the lightning-fast demons raging from shadow to shadow,
could reduce native species to a memory in seconds, and could strip a human
to bone in less than a minute. In five minutes, the bone, too, would be gone.

In spite of this knowledge, Nikki snapped back the latch and stepped
outside.

How else can I meet my new mother?

His greatest surprise was the wind. The quick gusts that rustled his hair
and collar felt like the soft brush of living fingers tender on his skin. He was
surprised, too, at the watering of his eyes precipitated by the breeze.

Nikki nudged the dust with a boot toe and sensed the peculiar sweetness
of humus rise with the wind.

Near his toe grew a tiny native bush which the colonists called *Narcissus.* Silver leaves were thick on its short branches. A fine matrix of tiny red
veins joined in a knot at the stem. The leaves were arranged in pairs, facing
each other, and each pair angled upward and outward in a funneling and
reflecting process which captured as much available light as possible. He
bent close to the plant and heard the soft, characteristic hum of its brittle
leaves vibrating in tune with the rise and fall of Medea's ultraviolet pulse.
He touched a leaf and the plant disappeared into its root system with a metallic *snap.*

Yes, many Medean species maintained an armored retreat ready at hand.
It was a lesson the colonists had learned early and copied.

"You!"

It was a shouting voice behind him.

"Get back in here!"

Nikki straightened and turned, saw a maintenance man in a flare suit
standing in the hatchway's shelter. The man moved to step outside, but reversed himself as Nikki slipped past him into the walkway. The man's anger remained, however, even after he closed and sealed the hatch.

"What were you trying to prove out there?" He pointed to the warning below the hatch. "Didn't Ship teach you how to read?"

Interesting question. Nikki heard the overtones of many fears. It brought home to him that Ship, while teaching him to read, had used this as a lever to teach him how many things there were more important than reading.

Danger.

Nikki glanced back through the walkway's transparent shielding, saw the tips of the *Narcissus* beginning to venture once more into the open. He glanced at the maintenance man.

"Ship taught me that it takes many signs to make a warning," he said, and he resumed his course down the walkway toward Integration Central.

Even Narcissus *balances the demands of relative dangers.*

He found this thought reassuring.

All through the swift routine of processing, Nikki kept himself as open as possible, absorbing the newness, comparing. He stored his questions, preferring to listen. The chief receptionist was an elderly man, one of the First Down. He had bored eyes and puffy cheeks and there was the fatigue of death in his voice.

The reception room was like a Ship room: functional, two hatches in metal walls, instruments in racks, no ports or windows. It was barred by the console behind which the receptionist sat, a gate on the right leading to the rear hatch. The man grudged every effort of speech.

"Brought your own recorder." He punched a notation into the console which shielded him from the waist down, as though he did not exist except as part of the machine.

Nikki felt the weight of the recorder on its strap over his shoulder. *How odd.* It was as though the man's words had created the weight of the recorder.

The receptionist glanced at the Shipcloth bag on Nikki's other shoulder. "What you bring?"

"Personal possessions, clothes . . . a few keepsakes."

"Hrrrm." The man made another notation, delivered himself of his longest speech. "You're assigned to Tamarack Kapule. Meet her at Quarters." A nod indicated the rear hatch and the gate swung open. "Through there. Follow signs."

It was a long, brightly lighted passage lined with hatches and punctuated by the signs which flashed on at his approach:

COMMISSARY . . . VITRO LABS . . . RECORDS . . . MAIN SECTION . . . LIFE SUPPORT . . . CLINIC . . . WORSHIP . . .

It was as though he had never left Ship.

This is a test, he reminded himself.

It had to be a test. Ship was God and God was Ship. Ship could do things mortal flesh could not. Normal dimensions of space dissolved before Ship. Time carried no linear restrictions for Ship.

And I, too, am God . . . but I am not Ship.
Or am I?

It was a question he had never resolved, although he knew the history which Ship taught. There had been a time when Ship was *the ship,* a vehicle of mortal intelligence. The ship had existed in the limited dimensions of space which any human could sense and it had known a destination. It had also known a history of madness. Then . . . the ship had encountered the Holy Void, the reservoir of intelligent chaos against which all beings were required to measure themselves. And the hybernating humans on the ship had awakened to find themselves the creatures of Ship.

QUARTERS . . . QUARTERS . . . QUARTERS . . .

He stepped right through the flashing sign while becoming aware of it. The sign obviously had been keyed for his approach. Nikki opened the indicated hatch, stepped through into a half-hub from which many passages fanned out.

Down the passage directly in front of him a woman stood beckoning, impatient. He had never seen a woman of such compelling appearance . . . the *differences* about her jammed his awareness. He responded only to her impatient beckoning until the strong contralto of her voice added emphasis to her gestures.

"I'm Tamarack Kapule, you can call me Tam. You'll be working with me starting in ten minutes down at Behavioral. We're in a rush so I'll fill you in as we go. This is your room." She opened a hatch at her side. "Leave everything here but your recorder."

He peered through the hatch at Shipstyle quarters, a familiar foldout desk . . . but there were differences. He glimpsed a real bed. He'd only seen holos of beds. You slept in a net on Ship.

Nikki tossed his bag inside, closed the hatch.

She was already leaving, talking in that same husky rush as she moved.

"Your records are incomplete. What do we call you?"

"Nikki."

By the time he'd made sure he had spare charges for the recorder and a notebook in his pocket she was well down the passage and she did not look back to watch him catch up.

Her brusqueness was neither cold nor angry, he decided. She had a job to do and little else mattered. Nikki trotted to keep up with her, working out what her appearance told him. Her hair was as close to absolute white as he'd ever seen. Her eyes were shaped much like his own, and when she glanced at him he saw a quick flash of blue, a cold blue that, he was convinced, expected and got the truth from any other eyes they confronted. Her skin, though pale at a distance, was backlit by a reddish glow when seen this close.

"Well?" she demanded.

Nikki realized that he had been staring.

"Local mutation," he said. "Quite striking."

"How do you know I wasn't born this way?"

"You're too old to be Shipborn," he said. "You have to be one of the originals chosen for this colony."

"So?"

"Preliminary data on Medea showed the occasional high bursts of ultraviolet. People with abnormally low pigmentation would've been excluded."

Her blush deepened.

"What else do you know about me?"

She slowed her pace, tense, face straight ahead.

"Your name, Kapule. That's from one of the old Pacific Ocean nations, probably Polynesian. My eye structure's similar to yours."

She looked at his eyes, turned away.

"Your eyes were brown at one time," he said.

She shrugged, opened a hatch and stood aside for him, then followed. They were in another passage at right angles to the one they'd left. She struck off to the right.

Nikki kept pace, talking as they went. She had asked a question and he was determined to give her a full answer, although he now saw that she regretted her curiosity.

"Tamarack is a variety of tree. It grew in Canada and the Northwestern United States of Old Terra. Conifer with deciduous behavior—dramatic color changes each fall and spring. You have changed colors."

They stopped outside a hatch signed BEHAVIORAL.

Nikki looked down at her and smiled with a confidence and maturity which drew her to him despite some deep resistance. He spoke to soothe her.

"My mother's family also was of the Pacific nations."

She looked him full in the eyes. Yes, he was colored much as she'd been when she'd first set foot on Medea. And he had seen this thing about her which neither Ship nor any of the Holy Sciences would explain. She recalled how her questions had ignited nervous words from the experts.

"Perhaps these changes in you were caused by freak energy bursts from the suns."

She studied the face of this perceptive young man. Would some bizarre and undetected pulse from the red heart of Argo work its changes on him, too? Whatever it was that caused this, it began slowly, an irreversible wash of pigment from the body. First, her hair. Gray at twenty-two, white by thirty. And this Nikki was only eighteen, half her age. By thirty her skin had lightened noticeably and by thirty-five was nearly translucent. Just this year, the curious red tinge had formed deep within her skin and she had grown to like this effect of the changeling process.

"Is there more?" she asked.

Something in the soft *voice* of her question compelled his attention. There was something important, something she needed which only he could supply.

Nikki closed his eyes and tapped into the oneness which his mother had taught.

"You're self-conscious about working with someone so much younger than yourself."

"Do you know how important our project is?" she asked.

Her voice told him she was ready to retreat—like the *Narcissus* . . . like the maintenance man. Where was her place of armored security?

He spoke softly.

"There's confusion in your mind about your project and those working on it with you."

"It's the most important project in the colony," she said. "Life and death . . ."

"It's urgent," he agreed.

Nikki opened his eyes and looked directly into hers. "And you're self-conscious about working with a male who's so much younger than you."

She lowered her gaze and sighed. The blush faded.

"You didn't arrive at all that through logic."

"That's why I'm here," he said. "Logic's failed."

She reached out and shook his hand—strange antique gesture, the remnant of a caress, and it kept them at a distance.

"In here."

She followed him into a laboratory room. He recognized most of the instruments and knew he'd learn the strange ones soon enough.

Tam was busy swinging out a voder and its screen. She spoke as she worked.

"You have to learn a floater's instrumentation and controls. This voder has a mock-up program. Sit here." She indicated a foldout seat at the screen.

Floaters, he thought, his pulse quickening.

The idea of these colony craft, lighter than air, fascinated him. How vulnerable they were, subject to any whim of an atmosphere which could not be completely predicted.

He sat in the indicated place and looked at the simulation of controls and instruments. His stomach felt cold with apprehension. He sensed the prickling of his scalp.

But this is only simulation!

His body continued to send out panic signals which he could not ignore.

"Is something wrong?" Concern edged Tam's voice.

Nikki realized that he was trembling. He put a hand on the control panel to steady himself, found his own muscles pushing him away. He tried to tell himself this was a Medean reaction, the accumulation of subtle oddities for which Ship had not quite prepared him. This peculiar planet set up too many conditions for flight from danger. But he could not prevent himself from standing and backing away from the simulator.

"What's wrong?" Tam demanded.

"Did you prepare that?" He pointed at the voder/simulator.

Tam studied his face. He appeared actually ill. Was this an adverse reaction to something Medean?

Nikki saw her puzzled frown, the way she divided her attention between him and the simulator.

"Answer my question."

"Tom Root prepared this mock-up. He's our project director. Why?"

Nikki groped for words and found this the most peculiar thing of all. Words did not usually evade him.

"This . . . this is *against* Ship," he said. "This is contraShip . . . wrong. It's . . . evil."

There! The word fitted precisely. It was evil, this simulator.

Her puzzlement deepened.

"Nothing here can be against Ship."

He was certain now and not to be deflected. "That is." He nodded at the simulator. "It would teach me to do something wrong."

"It's . . . it's just a machine, a simulator!"

She slipped onto the seat, hesitated, then punched a button marked *balance*. Red lights flashed, a klaxon behind the screen began hooting. Tam whirled to her right, hit the PROGRAM button, began scanning the numbers and other symbols which replaced the red lights to parade across the screen. The klaxon fell silent.

Nikki's fear signals began to dampen out.

Presently, Tam turned and looked up at him.

"How did you know?"

"How did I know what?" His mouth felt dry.

She ran a hand through her hair, glanced at the now empty screen. *Why do I feel angry?*

"There's a fault in PROGRAM acceptance," she said. "I don't know exactly where the problem's located. One of the technical people will have to look at this."

Nikki swallowed, regaining his composure. He realized he had not answered her question, did not know *how* to answer it.

How did I know?

"What are you?" she demanded.

"A . . . poet."

"Until you asked for *balance* controls, this simulator would've conditioned you to do . . . dangerous things."

"Is it supposed to do that?"

"No!" She stood up. "Come along. We've scavenged the console from a wrecked floater. You can use that until they find out what's wrong with this simulator. You can at least learn how the instruments are supposed to work and where they are."

The rest of the day went well, although Nikki had to force himself not to question Tam about why she had punched first thing for *balance* on the simulator. Training with the recovered console taught him this was seldom the first thing you asked of your controls. Floaters were built to take dramatic imbalance and the *balance* gyros put a strain on the power system.

And it was disquieting that he could not explain, even to himself, how he had known. What hidden signal receivers did his body contain? Were there petit perceptions for which only he was the sensitive receiver?

He began to suspect there might be an odd rapport between Tam and himself. She remained watchful of him all through the day, suspicious. All of this was held beneath the surface, submerged in the training routine, in the study session which paraded for him the latest records of Medea's bloom behavior.

The gasbags—airborne globes—fascinated him. They behaved as though directed by a single intelligence, sometimes merely beautiful—a display. Other times, they were definitely malevolent, killing . . . maiming.

At the day's end, Tam handed him a torn piece of computer printout.

"Here's a map for your appointments tomorrow and the schedule. See you at early."

She left him to find his own way back to the Commissary and his quarters. Nothing unusual about that. Shiptrained people seldom had trouble with enclosed passages.

When he sealed the hatch of his room behind him, only then did he allow himself to accept the accumulated aching fatigue. Was this an accurate forecast of Medean routine? Could her pace be normal here? Could he perform under such pressures? Where was the "life and death" focus of her project? *Of Root's project,* he corrected himself. When was he going to meet this Tom Root whose name he had only heard today? Why hadn't Ship given him at least profiles on his workmates? Something here went far deeper than the apparent physical threats which Medea sent against the intruders.

Nikki stowed his bag in a locker, examined the bed. There was no enfolding net, no crashbag. The bed was flat. He pressed it with one hand. Resilient. He stripped, doused the light and climbed into the bed. Rough blankets. Medean fabric? So many questions . . . his first night in a real bed and sleep swept over him as soon as he closed his eyes.

There was a loud thump, cold . . . pain.

It took several heartbeats for Nikki to realize that he had fallen out of the bed. Still half asleep, he was as much amused as surprised. He rubbed at a bruised elbow and tried to remember the dream he'd been having. As rush-rush as everything had been since he'd landed on Medea, he felt that the whole day had been a dream and he was only now awakening. Images from the dream fled through his mind:

He and Tam far above the settlement, somewhere so high that all of

Medea dropped sharply away from their feet. They hung there holding each other suspended by . . . what?

Then the fall.

Nikki found the light control, sat on the edge of the bed and measured the drop. It was the height of two hands from the top of the bed to the floor. He touched the floor with fingertips, then increased the light. The floor was hard, sturdy. It was made of long strips of intricately stained material patterned like the tidelands of a wide sea. He'd never seen a sea except in holograms . . . repros.

And in the dream.

Then, as each hair on the back of his neck and scalp prickled and raised, the patterns, the stains, the strips disappeared.

Once more, he awoke on the floor, rubbed his elbow and sat on the edge of the bed. The bed felt more *immediate,* its covers more resistant to his pressing palms. He knew that he'd better be careful. Sometimes it was difficult to tell one reality from another, but Medea was playing tricks on him.

In the morning, he used Tam's map to locate the small commissary used by floater personnel and found her there seated at a corner table, alone. Only one other table was occupied—three older men in gray singlesuits. Eyes turned toward him with curiosity at the new face. Tam already was eating her early. He called it "breakfast" and she turned to him, startled.

"Why'd you say that?"

He scanned her, saw only curiosity and mild amusement.

"It surprises you?" He sat across from her and signaled the autocook for service.

"Perhaps it shouldn't." She sipped her juice. "Language is your life. But that's such an *old* word. We were calling it 'early' three generations and two planets ago."

"Four generations and three planets ago we were sipping *juice* at *breakfast* whether breakfast was eaten early in the wakeday or late."

"But I haven't heard that . . ."

"Some words have more inherent wisdom than others. Juice . . ." He pointed to the glass in her hand. ". . . is, after all, a fluid naturally contained in plant or animal tissue."

The autocook took this moment to disgorge his food onto the table. He began eating and, presently, took up his own glass, tasted it. Acid . . . faint sweetness.

"This concoction we're drinking is damned near anything but what we call it."

She examined her glass against the light.

"But what if it's a pretty word? What if . . ."

"What if we stop playing with words to avoid more important things? Have you discovered what went wrong with that simulator?"

"They've torn it down completely and can't find anything wrong with it. Nothing."

She put her glass down too hard, was surprised to find her hand trembling. *Why does his question anger me?*

Nikki drew in a deep breath. It was what he had expected.

She was accusing now. "But there *was* something wrong and you knew it. How?"

The answer came to him as though he had worked out the details during the night. *I knew because she knew.* And she had concealed this knowledge even from herself. The knowledge was there just the same.

When a thing was true and beautiful he recognized it. The false and ugly betrayed themselves to him with the same clarity. This was a thing about himself which he'd never before put into quite this framework. He found it a heavy burden, as though peering through flesh to entrails.

She pressed him. "How?"

"It's what I was trained to do. I have this . . ."

The commissary speakers blared: "Tam! Nikki! Fly time!"

She was halfway to the exit hatch before he left his seat. Something about Medea conditioned the older colonists to a quickness that jarred against his comforting, steady Shipstyle pace. Nikki caught up with her in the hallway and they jogged side-by-side through the warren passages.

"Fly time."

It came to Nikki that he was headed toward his first flight out into Medea's unpredictable wildness. One day of training—vague training where many of his questions were left unanswered or diverted. The message of Medea was clear to him: Anything he learned here he had to learn on his own, trust his own senses. The realization elated him. That was what a poet did: he learned quickly to stop asking verbal nonsense and to begin detailed observations of everything and everyone around him.

Tam pulled up outside a hatch marked READY ROOM. Her breathing was no more labored than Nikki's. She was glad to note that Nikki's youth gave him no physical edge on her. But his ability to see things which she could not, this filled her with disquiet. She feared it.

"That voice on the speaker was Tom Root," she said. "You'll meet him in a minute."

Nikki remained silent, watchful. His silence upset her.

"Root has extraordinary skill in the air and equal skill in the lab," she said.

"You're defending him as though I were attacking," Nikki said "Why?"

She blinked, then: "Root's an accomplished cell surgeon, biochemist and meteorologist. I don't have to defend him. I'm just warning you. He doesn't say much but when he talks, listen."

She cracked the seal to the Ready Room and Nikki breathed a deep lungful of unprocessed Medean air. It was somehow different from the sample he'd inhaled the day before: a taint of ozone in it and undercurrents of lubricants, but there was no escaping a dominant sweetness, thick and aromatic. His lungs drank deeply. For eighteen years his body had been prepared, conditioned, cajoled to deal with the variant Medean environment. He associated bitterness with hostility and was reassured by that aromatic sweetness.

He followed Tam through the hatch, felt his body tingling on alert. They emerged into a low room with no wall opposite them. The opening led directly out onto the hangar floor, and Nikki's attention went immediately to the display board across the hangar. The board projected a numeral twice the height of a man—a large number "1" edged in flame red.

Nikki knew that signal: *Heavy radiation; both suns in flare.*

Tam tugged at his elbow, directed him to the near wall on their right, through an opening into a small locker room. She indicated a locker and he saw his name on the door tab. It seemed strange there, alien to him: "Nikki."

Her voice prodded him. "Hurry it up!"

Wondering if he would ever adjust to these demands for speed, he opened the door and read the instructions inside for Code One dress: field pants, shielding slicker with hood, glasses, gloves. The gloves went onto his hands like a second skin. He objected only to the glasses; they filtered out this new world that he'd only just glimpsed. He slipped them into his slicker pocket.

"Hey, poet!"

It was Tam from the next bank of lockers.

"Yeah?"

"Hop it. Less than three minutes to lift."

"What's the rush?"

"New flares. Bloom started early."

"But don't we . . ."

He heard a locker slam shut, Tam's quick steps. She wasn't waiting for what she considered idle conversation.

Nikki followed her out into the hangar and finished sealing his slicker just as the ceiling doors spread their metal jaws. Awe absorbed him. There, stained and dented but humming smoothly, their floater hung framed against a wildly banked background of clouds. The colors! Morning light of two suns played reds, purples, silver . . . umber . . . orange.

Sentries at the opening's perimeter scanned the surrounding area for demons and, as Nikki turned to follow Tam's peremptory summons, he caught the flicker of a demon in the dim light. In what seemed part of the same flicker, a sentry raised, fired and lowered his weapon. None of the other sentries paid the slightest attention to this.

What incredible speed these people develop.

Nikki was daunted by this thought as he followed Tam out into the hangar, his attention once more on the floater. It nearly filled the open area and the hangar was at least fifty meters on a side. The reddish-orange bag hugged the ceiling while ground lights played against it. The crew's nest, a web of plasteel and transparent bubbles, scraped the floor, oscillating back and forth like an animal impatient against restraints.

"Root." It was Tam's voice.

Nikki turned from looking up at the bag and the suspension lines. Tam had her head into a side hatch to the nest. She pulled back and a man's head appeared in the opening: red hair beginning to go gray, a sense of wiry quickness about the eyes. The face and body were thin. Nikki was struck by the fact that Tam called this man Root to his face, but called him Tom when Root wasn't present.

"We haven't time for introductions or any other nonsense," Root said. "Get in here, both of you."

It was a Shiptrained voice, almost devoid of emotion.

Nikki followed Tam up into the nest. The metal edges of the hatch were cold even through the gloves. It was dim inside, cramped quarters. Root already was strapped into the seat at the bow bubble. Tam was securing herself in the seat at Root's left. Nikki recognized a console on Root's right identical to the one he'd used the day before. He slipped into the seat, brought the web harness over his shoulders and around his waist.

"Just the three of us this trip," Root said.

"That means we have to be both crew *and* observers," Tam said. "Got that?"

Nikki looked over his shoulder, saw that Tam was addressing him. "Got it."

She was already busy at her console. Nikki knew he should do the same, check the instruments, renew his acquaintance with this control board he'd seen for the first time only the day before. Instead, he took a moment to study Root as subtly as he could.

Why do I feel apprehensive?

The older man was not as tall as Nikki, but there was a sense of enormous energy about him. He moved with confident sureness, agile but reserved. Root was not a man to reveal all of his resources. And his voice . . . there was a haunted sense about it . . . a feeling of familiarity. *Where have I heard that voice? He reminds me of somebody.*

Forward of Root was the large transparent bubble which gave the whole nest a wide-angle view of terrain. It showed the hangar floor and the display board with its Code One warning. The nest's transparent ceiling curve was dominated by the suspension lines and the bulging undersurface of the floater bag. Directly in front of Root was his instrument hookup and the omniviewscreen which, Nikki belatedly realized, was reflecting his own face for Root to examine.

I don't trust him, Nikki realized. *And he probably knows it.*

It came to Nikki then that Root was a man with secret plans which would not be diverted even if they projected pain or death for others.

To cover the momentary feeling of entrapment which this realization brought, Nikki said the first thing that came into his mind.

"I thought floaters usually ran with a crew of five."

"*Floater*," Root corrected him. "This is it. None of the others is operational. Too unreliable in these winds. The other crews have gone to choppers."

Tam glanced quickly and uneasily in Root's direction, said: "We're a special little crew here."

Nikki turned to his own console, ran the preliminary check which Tam had taught him. Immediately, he noted that all communications to Central and Ship were not responding. He tested *HOOKUP* and got a flashing red *OFF*.

"Why aren't we hooked up to Central?"

"No time for storytelling now," Root said.

The nest lurched, scraped and bumped hard on the hangar floor, then lifted slowly through the open ceiling. The giant bag above them began to angle off to the right as soon as it cleared the dome and the nest barely missed the lip. The colony outbuildings, wildly colored by the early light, were passing beneath them within seconds.

Root's fingers flew over the controls, adjusting sway, changing the bag's surface contour to form a great, sweeping sail.

"This might be a rough ride," Tam said.

She sensed potential conflict between Root and Nikki, was confused by her own ambivalent sympathies. *I'm too old to be a mother hen,* she told herself. *The project's too important for colony survival. Nikki has to make it on his own.*

Root began activating bag jets, metering precious fuel. The nest took on a bouncing, swaying motion which swept broad expanses of cinder crags and ocher ponds across the bow bubble's view.

"Nikki." It was Root.

"Yes."

"If you get sick, throw up in that waste box to your left. Try not to; we're going to need all the help we have and besides, it's distracting."

He's deliberately goading me, Nikki thought. *I'm damned if I'll get sick.* And belatedly: *Maybe that's the reaction he was triggering.*

There was deliberation about Root's behavior, about every voice tone. The man had said: "*You're a nuisance here but try not to be too much of a nuisance.*" Something more ominous lay just under the surface.

Danger . . . constant danger. That was Ship's warning and Nikki told himself never to forget it.

The nest was flying swiftly now at about a thousand meters above undulant sandhills with fans of gnarled scrub in the depressions. The ride was a twisting bounce with a sharp lurch at each end. Hellfire lights rimmed the horizon.

Nikki had experienced rough rides on Ship simulators, but nothing quite

like this. And why were they isolated from Ship and from Central? If Root
had been doing this for some time, there might be important data that
weren't in Ship's banks. Was that possible? Nikki could not ignore a sense
of contraShip evil in everything Root did.

Why did Ship let me believe I was fully prepared for Medea?

It was quite obvious that basic survival rules had been changed. Nikki
felt a tightness in his chest, a sense of betrayal.

"Nikki, you'll have to be our systems monitor," Root said. "I can fly us
through anything and Tam's the best DataMaster we could want. Homeostasis is your department. You understand homeostasis?"

"An organism's tendency to maintain constant internal environment."

"Good. Without Central we can't automatically monitor some important
floater systems." Root depressed a key on the far right of his board. "Your
viewer will now readout all the necessary levels and their priority. Tam."

She took it up as though they'd practiced a training presentation. "If it's
Priority One, like our helium supply, run a check at the indicated intervals.
If it's Priority Ten, like the cooler motor in our drinktank, ignore it. If you
have questions, ask."

Hesitantly, Nikki keyed for helium readout against their lift, read it and
shot a questioning glance forward at the terrain. They were lifting far faster
than the readout indicated. He checked it. Even the best of thermals could
not change the basic properties of the floater's helium. He looked up at the
billowing bag, back to the readout.

"Root?"

"What is it?" The man didn't even try to conceal irritation.

"My helium readout rates our Kg/m^3 at two point nine adjusted. What
gives? We should be at no more than two point seven-six."

Instead of answering, Root concentrated on his own controls and viewer.
The ride *was* getting rougher. The sharp lurch at the end of every twisting
bounce had become a jarring dead-weight drop. Through the transparent
ceiling Nikki watched a series of four-meter ripples run the width and
length of the bag. The nest banged and slewed, forcing him to bring up the
web hood to steady his head. Against these restraints, he peered forward
and had his first view of the seacoast with a play of angry colors in the
offshore clouds. The floater had reached the upper winds growling in from
the sea.

"Root?"

"I heard you. Ignore it."

It was an unmistakable reprimand.

As though to counter this, Tam said: "We aren't very lucky today, Nikki.
To make the bloom we have to beat this wind and move out over the water."

The next lurch gathered the nest up against the floater bag and dropped it
the full length of the fifteen-meter lines. Both Tam and Root appeared

unruffled by the jolt, going right on with their work. Nikki smelled the unmistakable taint of blood in his nose, wiped red with his sleeve.

"Nikki, what're your compressor specs?" Root asked.

He punched for them, still shaken by the jolt and still wondering why neither Tam nor Root appeared interested in the helium discrepancy. Helium was a floater's life. A leak, a loss of heat control, bad valves—any of a hundred related details—could drop them into deadly sea, desert or mountaintop. To drop out here over land meant certain death. No human could negotiate the shadow zones with their rim of blink-fast predators. Not without support from Central or Ship . . . and Root had isolated them from that support. Why?

"What're those compressor specs?" Root demanded.

"Safe levels."

"Don't make me ask twice."

Nikki accepted this and thought: *We are lifting.*

He decided, at least for the moment, that he would not worry about the helium discrepancy if the others didn't.

Root was making course corrections now. The floater tacked its way into the wind toward the white-edged shoreline.

Whenever he could take his attention from his controls, Nikki peered forward where winds and Medea's oblique tides whipped the sea surface into a thrash of dark water and foam. He saw that they were approaching a large bay. Nikki guessed its width at ten kilometers, then twenty, then realized one of his Shipbound limitations: he could not estimate large distances.

The bay's shoreline appeared high and rocky, difficult for human or demon to negotiate. Between rocks and water stretched a thin buffer of tidelands and then, as the floater drew closer in its angle toward the sea, Nikki saw a thick bank of kelp-like growth just below the surface. It furled and unfurled as far out as he could see. The water at its edges curled green and yellow.

Between system checks and corrections, Nikki divided his attention—now on the kelp-covered sea, now on the helium discrepancy. Still two point nine adjusted. They were operating at about one hundred and ten percent efficiency and he couldn't understand it.

Tam, busy with her own duties, tried to divert Nikki. He must not see through the helium discrepancy—not yet. She spoke quietly, forcing him to concentrate on her voice.

"Whatever generates the bloom's gasbags does so at times of intense solar activity. And we know that somehow they communicate. Root and I feel that they possess an extremely complex, high-order communications system."

"Fully sentient," Root said.

"But their cellular base is vegetable," Nikki said.

"Would you limit intelligence to animals?" Tam asked.

Root was scornful. "This is a new world and if there's one unwritten law of the physical-biological-social universe, it's that anything can happen, given the conditions, and given time, probably will happen."

"They communicate," Tam said. "And they exhibit social behavior which has to be based on communication. You've heard their songs."

Nikki had thought himself the only human to call the sounds of the globes *songs*. He thought back to the Shipside times when he'd listened to the records of those odd sounds—moans, wails, squeaks and grunts. Shipside people played them briefly for amusement, but Nikki had played them often, lulled by . . . what? Rhythms? He'd often wondered about those sounds. Ancient poets had enjoyed the poetry of many languages—even when they did not understand the language or its literal world.

Belatedly, he focused on Tam's words. She knew he'd listened often to the records of the songs. Was that why he'd been chosen?

"Song implies singer," he said. "Why not capture a few for a short time or study older ones that drift close to the base?"

Tam darted a quick glance at him. Was he serious?

"They lift by hydrogen," she said. "How do you capture and confine a firebomb? And even if they don't explode they disintegrate. Capture's out of the question."

"What're we studying?" Root demanded. "We need accurate data. The less contact we have with them, the truer our data. We're like physicists getting down into the world of particle physics to study it."

"How much is our influence and how much original behavior?" Tam asked.

All of this was true, but Nikki could not evade basic misgivings. *Root is trying to misdirect me and Tam is following his lead consciously and unconsciously. Where are they pointing me?*

"You never know when you might be giving your subject subtle clues about what you expect, thereby influencing the outcome," Tam said. "Besides, Root has discovered some startling facts about our vegetable friends down there."

Nikki expected them to expand on this, but Root was forced to concentrate on a course change as the wind shifted, backing around to their stem. First the jets, then the compressors were shut down and they drifted silently before the wind. The view ahead filled with a thick yellow-brown froth breaking across the kelp.

"Thousands of them come off the water at the bloom," Tam said. "But wind and electrical activity allow only a fraction of them to make it inland."

Root was busy venting gas, dropping their floater closer to the sea. It was now less than five hundred meters below them and the high walls of the bay's surrounding cliffs created a pocket of deceptive calm at the sea surface.

"Look! There!" Tam pointed across Root.

"At seven o'clock," Root said.

At first Nikki saw only waves and froth churning over the kelp. Then, slowly, bubbles in the froth began to swell and rise, each in its own violet, green or yellow. Each trailed a long thin strand of itself, much like its tentacles, that appeared to be attached to the kelp. As they rose, the umbilicus stretched thin and broke. The bags floated free and, within seconds, began to play every color of the visible spectrum across their surfaces. Water and air swirled with dancing colors.

Root keyed in the external sensors and, above the high-pitched shriek of wind through the floater's lines, they heard the tentative flutings of the gasbags—clear whistles and odd cadences.

Nikki felt deep within his shoulderblades that those whistles were directed at him. He was both stimulated and upset in ways he could not define. He found it hard to imagine danger in that airborne display of beauty, but knew they could drift down on a colony installation and, unless thwarted, could engulf with flame everything they touched.

"They're a dream," Nikki whispered. "They're all the beauty of a child's best dream."

Neither Root nor Tam responded. All three of them sat enthralled within the nest, rocking in the wind, and watched as thousands of the colorful bags broke the sea's drab surface, swelled and lifted.

Nikki listened to the siren fluting of the bags as they lifted closer and closer, hearing distinct voices waver through the colorful mob. He spoke in a whisper.

"They sound like Ship children when they get up in the morning. They come out of their cubbies and into the dressing room and they jabber themselves awake."

Tam looked at him with a curious softness.

"I would like to see children. I haven't seen a child in almost ninety years."

Root laughed, oddly harsh and when her blue eyes snapped a demanding look at him, he cleared his throat, spoke placatingly.

"Tam, you slept more than fifty of those years in the hyb tanks. Look down there." He stretched his hand across the view, alive now with gasbags tumbling over themselves in the fits and starts of the wind. "These are children that only we three have seen. We saw them born . . . or hatched."

"I find no comfort in that," she said.

What an odd turn of phrase, Nikki thought. He felt that he'd been an eavesdropper on an exchange with deep and portentous meanings.

Once more, Nikki scanned his console, still curious about the helium but even more curious at this real-time observation of a bloom.

"Tam and I have watched four blooms this year," Root said. "Are you superstitious, Nikki?"

He's goading me again, Nikki thought. When he spoke, he couldn't conceal resentment.

"There are certain things . . . powers we can't measure. And you're right that all things are possible; maybe luck works somewhere in that. But I wouldn't call myself superstitious."

"Good!" Root sounded elated. He glanced at Tam who was busy adjusting the external monitors. "Out of four trips here and a total crew of fourteen, we're the only two survivors."

Nikki felt as though the bottom had dropped out of his stomach and it was not the lurching of the floater. He was in genuine physical danger with no Ship to guard him. He was actually exposed to dangerous elements.

Constant danger.

Is this what Ship meant?

Even as he thought this he knew it was too easy to be true. Ship had something else concealed in that warning. Nikki knew this with a sure instinct.

"Listen!"

It was Tam, speaking as she increased the volume on the external sensors. The hesitant, youthful jabber of the rising globes was being replaced by babbling confusion. Quickly, it built into the short, unmistakable sounds of creatures in panic.

As though the sound threw a switch within Nikki, he felt the panic in his own breast.

Evil!

Evil!

Evil!

He didn't know whether he was crying it or just thinking it. But there were screams in his throat and he saw his own gloved fists pound at the console in front of him, then move toward the release catches of his safety harness, fingers clawing.

Through all of this, he was aware of Root watching him with a distant, clinical coldness. Root made no move to help, no comment.

Tam threw a switch on her panel to take over Nikki's controls. *The floater first!* In the same motion, she kicked the safety interlock which secured Nikki in his seat. Nikki thrashed and twisted there like a tortured animal, screaming and crying.

Why wasn't Root doing something to help?

But Root had turned his attention to the forward bubble and its view of the colorful bloom.

"Tam, please observe," he said.

She turned her attention to the view and saw thousands of whirling bags as one boiling mass of visible scream. Color flamed in them. The external sensors relayed a diminishing babble. Only a scattered few of the bags had escaped the destructive dance and she knew from experience that those few would assemble and guide themselves toward the colony with violent intent.

The wind was picking up, tearing at the whirling mass below them. The babble of screams faded and most of the bags emptied, scattering like torn fabric across the surface of the sea. Only the few survivors moved inland.

Nikki had subsided into moaning unconsciousness.

"How very interesting," Root said. "We were correct in asking for this young man."

"His hands are bleeding. Shouldn't we do something?" Tam asked.

"Yes. We should save ourselves by returning to the colony. The young man will be all right until we deliver him to the medics."

"Why is it you're always right?" Tam demanded.

"Careful, Tam. It's my function to be right. And that's why we're alive while the others are dead."

"I still wish we could warn our people." She nodded toward the surviving globes which were now beyond the cliff tops headed toward the distant colony.

"It's only a small attack," Root soothed her. "Security will handle it quite easily."

Nikki awoke to the low sound of murmuring voices. They were sickroom voices filled with well-trained concern. A female voice said: "All right. We'll leave him with you now."

He opened his eyes and saw a beige wall only a few millimeters away. Rough blankets covered him. A bed. He was in a bed. His hands ached and there was a smell of disinfectants.

Slowly, he turned onto his back, saw Tam seated on the edge of the bed reading his biostats from a console attached to the footboard. Nikki recognized his own quarters. The hatch was open to the outer passage and Root stood just inside it, leaning against the wall, a look of intense observation on his face . . . calculating. Root's attention was on Tam.

"I'm glad you're awake," Tam said. There was real concern in her voice. Root smiled.

Nikki felt a knot of sickness in his stomach. The pain in his hands. He lifted them, saw the transparent swathing of celltape. The curved edges of many cuts smiled up at him through the tape and he remembered once Shipside, a fall at play and a cut leg, his real mother applying celltape.

"You'll learn to like celltape," she'd said. "It makes you heal faster and you can watch yourself mend at the same time."

Tosa Nikki . . . whatever happened to you?

"Whatever it was, you left it back there at the bloom," Tam said. She switched off the biostat console, turned that searching blue gaze on him. "We have to know what happened."

Nikki turned his head away toward the wall. Her words called back the panic . . . horror. He remembered pounding the floater console, screams . . . trying to escape from . . . what? From his own body? How was that possible?

"Come, come. We have to know." That was Root.

Nikki knew the questions they would ask. Afraid of heights? Afraid of closed spaces? Of people? Death? They would have pulled all of Ship's records on him by now and none of the answers to these questions would be *yes*. Except for death. Something animal responded to that threat and Ship would never explain it.

"It was a rough ride," Tam said, "and your first. Were we too rough on you?"

Nikki recalled a brief instruction record Ship had provided him when he was sixteen:

For five hundred years of earthside history, most humans prejudged poets to be biologically inferior. Remnants of that judgment tend to cling to the human psyche.

Nikki turned his head, stared across the room at Root. "You don't seriously believe that?"

The man appeared genuinely surprised.

"Maybe not. But remember we were not in *simulated* danger out there. It was real."

Tam touched his shoulder. "We lost you when Root told you about the other crews. Could . . ."

"No. I don't know what happened to me; I just know what it *wasn't*. How long have we been back?"

"About five hours," Tam said. "Are you hungry?"

The thought of food made his stomach churn. "No. No food. Do you have the nest recordings from our trip?"

"Complete tapes," Root said. "Would you like to review them?"

Was that a protesting glare Tam directed at Root?

"Shouldn't we let him recover completely?" she asked.

"The decision's his," Root said.

"Bring them," Nikki said.

"We have to take you to them," Root said.

What was that pouncing expectancy in Root's manner?

"Why?" Nikki asked.

"We have to use the floater consoles. All others are linked to the colony and . . . Ship. Only the floater is independent."

"Why?"

"We think Ship has been influencing our project."

"Ship doesn't have to *influence* such things. Ship is God."

Root leaned toward Nikki. "So Ship says. But Ship alone knows what Ship sees for Itself. Like any other being, Ship must choose to see some things and ignore others."

"But Ship's immortal!" Nikki protested. "Without any limits of time, Ship could . . ."

"Ship had you for only eighteen years," Root said. "How long will you have yourself? Five hundred years? A thousand? More than . . ."

Root broke off as Nikki turned away and rubbed his forehead with a celltape-swathed hand.

"Shall we go?" Tam asked. "Or would you rather . . ."

"No. Let's go review those records."

She helped him to stand on wobbly legs and he was surprised to see that he still wore the clothing he'd worn on the floater. They had stripped off only the slicker and the gloves which he'd torn injuring his hands.

None of them spoke on the walk to the hangar, not until they were alone in the floater.

"What if Ship *chose* to hear what you said back there?" Nikki asked, confronting Root.

"I think Ship is bored," Root said. "At the very least, we're entertaining."

The answer filled Nikki with confusion. He stood in the confined nest unable to respond while Root readied the replay. How confident Root appeared! He moved with such sureness, not slinking around like someone who felt the least bit guilty. And Tam—while matter-of-fact, she wasn't cold. She assisted Root as though she understood a definite time-table. That was it! They were on a time-table toward some specific goal. But Tam, while committed, was afraid of something . . . or someone.

She's afraid of Root!

"Is there evidence to support your notion that Ship is influencing your project?" Nikki asked.

"I'm afraid it's not a notion," Tam said.

"But even so, if Ship . . ."

"We're ready for the replay," Root said. He turned and stared at Nikki. It was the stare of a technician toward a test animal.

"Evidence," Nikki insisted.

"We'll show you later," Tam said. "It became clear when we questioned Ship about the purpose of the colony."

"You questioned *Ship's* purpose?"

"Are you horrified, repelled?" Root asked.

"Ship and I used to play a question and answer game," Nikki said. "If I asked a question, Ship always answered truthfully. But Ship didn't always answer in terms I could understand."

"Are you trying to delay the replay?" Tam asked. She indicated the console which Root had readied.

"No, let him go on," Root said. "Was Ship trying to confuse or mislead you?"

"That would've broken a basic rule of the game," Nikki said. "That would've been untruthful. No . . . Ship was teaching me that the answers are always somewhere in the formation of the question."

"How trusting you are," Root said.

"In the question . . . the answer?" Tam asked.

Root leaned forward, staring at Nikki. How did the poet understand his own role in Ship's purpose . . . whatever that purpose? "Do continue."

"Ship might answer me philosophically in conversational terms," Nikki said. "I soon learned how to play the philosophy game. Then It shifted to complex mathematical constructions which I had to learn to discover the answer."

"You were providing your own answers," Tam said.

"In a way. I had to learn how to ask my question in a specific enough way that I could be sure of understanding the answer. And *then* I found that the form of the question carried the language of the answer. Even more: a sufficiently precise question carried the *information* of the answer."

"Why do you now recount this game?" Root asked.

"Because . . . however you asked your questions of Ship, the form of your questions imposed the role that you insisted Ship play. That's the rule of the game."

"The better you get at asking questions, the fewer questions you have to ask," Tam said. She stared at Nikki as though seeing him for the first time. She felt that she was poised on the edge of a new, liberating awareness.

Root was glowering, rubbing at his chin.

Nikki glanced at the ready console, recalling a question he'd asked during the flight to the bloom.

"When I asked about helium today, for example, my question carried the form *and* the language of the answer. Helium adjusted to a Medean sea level referent should read two point seven six Kg over m cubed. I got two point nine. That's the figure for hydrogen."

Root glanced at the sealed hatch on his right, returning his attention to Nikki.

Tam was holding her breath.

"Are you trying to say that we're flying hydrogen?" Root asked.

"Yes. We're flying what the globes fly. Highly flammable in this electrically active atmosphere. In effect, we're a giant flying bomb."

Surprisingly, Root chuckled.

Tam shuddered.

"What amuses you?" Nikki asked. He felt that he had just performed precisely as expected and that this boded no good for him.

"Ship has restricted many of your records," Root said. "Tam assumed that this indicated social or moral problems. Isn't that right, Tam?"

She shook her head: negative.

"Then what did you assume?"

"That Ship wants to keep Nikki a mystery."

"Yes! There's no telling what he knows."

"How did you exchange hydrogen for helium?" Nikki asked. "If your ground crew knew about it, you'd be flying a shovel and rake in one of the cattle compounds."

"But they *do* know," Tam said. "It's the lesser of several dangers." She glanced upward at the hovering bag.

"We're the only floater that those gasbag globes won't attack," Root said. "We have a good ground crew, the best. A good ground crew will take big risks to keep its flying crew alive."

"Who else knows?"

"Nobody."

"Maybe Ship knows," Tam said.

"Ship is nobody," Root said.

Tam put a hand to her mouth.

Nikki had heard a measured calculation in Root's voice and studied the man carefully. *Sacrilege to shock us!* But Root's behavior was always seated in many reasons. What else did he want?

"The mystery today," Root said, "is not just that you panicked, but that the bags panicked. Why? There was only one significant difference about our floater today—you."

"You're telling me that when you fly hydrogen the bloom will come right up to you and it won't attack."

"They tend to ignore us," Tam said.

Nikki looked at the console beside Root. "Let's see what happened today."

Root reached down, flicked a switch. The three screens around them came alive with views of the flight and the sounds were played through the sensor relays.

Nikki divided his attention among the screens, was aware that his companions were watching him. He closed his eyes when the replay came to the part where he had lost control. Terror? He felt nothing but the memory of his panic and even that was not immediate. He could extinguish it at will. But as he listened to his own frantic screams and the strident squeals of the gasglobes, another memory image insinuated itself into his awareness. He saw a clear picture of the floater from outside and he thought of it as a giant member of the bloom. The image projected itself into his awareness without compromise and he felt himself falling, falling away from the giant globe . . . the *floater.*

The image ended. It shut off like the stopping of a tape.

He opened his eyes, signalled for Tam to shut down the console. She reached across Root to depress the switch.

"Well, Nikki?" Root studied him, questioning.

"Why did you start flying hydrogen?"

"Because the bloom flies hydrogen."

"What happened when you flew helium?"

"They'd get within about twenty meters of a floater and they'd scream . . . you had the impression of extreme pain, then they'd expel all their hydrogen and they'd die."

"Scream, you say. The way they did today?"

"Similar."

"How were the other crews killed?"

"Some crashes, some trying to recover gasbag skins before they disintegrated."

"You put people out there in the open?"

"Volunteers."

"Did you get any skins?"

"No."

"What about choppers?"

"The bags won't come anywhere near them."

"Why can't chopper crews recover skins?"

"Choppers just scatter the skins and the increased air movement melts them that much faster."

"Or the demons got to them first," Tam said.

Nikki looked at her. "Have you been on the surface?"

"Twice. Root's been down four times."

"What's it like?"

"Not pretty."

"Why'd you want the skins?"

"We need any clue we can get," she said.

"How about the older bags? Have you been able to get close to them?"

"They move off when we get close and somehow they signal others to run away. When we chase, they'll use up all of their hydrogen trying to escape. Then they just drop and disintegrate."

"Why didn't Ship give me this information?" Nikki asked.

"Ask Ship!" Root said.

There was no mistaking the venom in his voice.

"The old ones warn the young ones of our approach," Tam said. "We've watched it many times."

"But they ignore you when you fly hydrogen?"

"From a distance. The significant thing is that they don't attack."

"How do they attack?"

"Kamikaze—one or more old ones from above. Static spark and they explode themselves against the floater bag."

Root pushed a palm downward sharply: *Crash!*

"What happens to gasglobe skins when they fall on water?"

"They melt rather quickly into a sludge which disappears with the first rain," Tam said.

"But on land demons eat the skins?"

"Ravenously," Tam said. "Then an odd thing happens."

"Didn't we come here to find out why Nikki went into panic?" Root asked. It was obvious he wanted to divert Tam from this course.

Nikki was not being diverted. "What's the odd thing?"

She saw Root's displeasure and spoke hesitantly.

"After eating a skin, the creature becomes quite unpredictable. It may lose its fear of higher predators, run in aimless circles, ignore obvious prey."

"We suspect that the skins are hallucinatory," Root said.

"Epiphany," Nikki said. "The visitation of God."

Root shrugged.

"And the older bags prefer to drift over water except that they'll come inland to attack the colony," Nikki mused.

"Or to lift animals from the surface and drop them," Tam said.

Nikki was surprised. "Don't they eat animals?"

"Not that we can see."

"We've never seen them eat anything," Root said.

"Well, Nikki, what happened to you out there over the bloom?" It was Tam, the DataMaster, performing on cue. She had heard Root's displeasure.

"I'm not sure. I think the bloom's panic was contagious and I caught it."

"How do we know the bloom didn't catch your panic?" Root demanded.

"I've told you what I believe. I wouldn't have said it if it were untrue."

As he spoke, Nikki experienced the swift inner expansion which always accompanied his own poetic revelation. He stared at Tam without seeing her. They'd been playing the question game here! He sensed a subtle perversion in the way they'd played the game, but the form was there, the essential form. It lacked only the right language.

What did he know about the bloom?

Skins dissolved . . . sludge in the water disappeared. The deadly demons of the land ate skins and . . . what? Hallucination? Epiphany? Colors! Globes changed colors as they whistled and babbled. Even in panic they changed colors.

He really saw Tam now: the white hair, the translucent skin—*to change colors and become a Medean.*

"You've been lying to me, both of you," Nikki said.

A swift blush suffused Tam's face.

Root saw this betrayal and scowled. "Is that why you're not telling us what really happened to you out there?"

I deserve that, Nikki thought. He wondered why he felt reluctant to tell them about that externalized scene he'd experienced during the panic. He consulted the image once more. There was a message in it, something basic. The floater was . . . it had to be . . . respected, that was it. Respected. It could not be attacked. But . . . it was deadly . . . dangerous. You were compelled to flee such a . . . thing.

Compelled!

"All you did with the hydrogen was to stop the attacks," Nikki said. "You didn't stop the panic."

"They don't come close any more," Tam said. "The panic starts farther and farther . . ."

"Tam!" Root was openly angry.

"We have to tell him," she said. "It's not right."

"He's still hiding something," Root growled.

"I don't care. We have to be straight with him."

"Tam, you agreed . . ."

"But we no longer have a reason for that agreement!"

"I hope you're satisfied! You've blunted the one instrument we could . . ." Root threw up both hands in exasperation.

Nikki stared from one to the other. Root remained mostly a closed and concealing person, but every tone, every movement from Tam carried its revealing message.

"Did you feel the panic?" Nikki asked her.

"The first two trips when they came closer, but not these last times. Root . . ."

"I've never felt a thing," Root said.

It was the most revealing statement Root had made in Nikki's presence. *The man has absolutely no emotions and no sensitivity. He mimics emotion, presents an image of the emotion he believes is responsive.*

Was Root even angry or was it all a calculated performance?

"Why did you ask if I felt the panic?" Tam asked.

"What's a poet supposed to do? You brought me here because I'm supposed to be more sensitive. You hoped I could see through to the reason for the panic."

"And did you?" Root demanded.

"Change the floater's color," Nikki said. "Eliminate the orange."

"Why?"

"Because that's how they identify us as dangerous."

"I won't ask how you arrived at that," Root said. "I don't believe I have time to examine the form of every question." His words conveyed a calculated sneer, but Nikki ignored it. That was part of Root's game. It was the way he played.

First, you have to learn Root's language, Nikki thought. And once more he wondered where he'd heard the man's voice before. It was such an elusive thing. *Why can't I remember?*

"We're scheduled to fly at dawn," Tam said. She looked at Root. "Do you mean you're going to change the floater's color?"

"Of course! Nikki's right. That's why we brought him."

She glanced at a chronometer on the console at her elbow. "But dawn . . ."

"The ground crew will work all night," Root said. "Help Nikki back to his quarters. He's had a rough day."

There was no feeling of concern in Root's words, only a dismissal. *Nikki has served his purpose and now he's a nusiance.*

Tam felt this, too. The first thing she said after they entered Nikki's quarters was: "Don't be offended by Tom. The only thing that matters to him is the project."

He's Tom again, Nikki thought. *But never to his face.*

He sat on the bed, leaned back and closed his eyes. How good the bed felt. A sharp *click* caught his attention and he opened his eyes to see Tam pulling a cushioned foldout chair from its concealing panel in the wall. She sat down facing him, their knees almost touching.

"Dawn's not very far away," he said.

She shook her head as though his words were insects distracting her.

"Let me see your hands."

He held out his hands and she examined the skin through the celltape. "The healing's far enough along. This tape should come off."

He nodded.

Gently, she removed the tape. How soft her movements were, how careful and considerate. He watched the intensity of her attention.

"Your mother," she said, speaking without looking up from her work. "I pulled her records while you were unconscious."

Why do I feel a chill? he wondered.

She glanced at him, returned her attention to the tape. A faint smell of healing unguents came from his hands.

"Why was your mother your teacher when you were very young?"

"She asked Ship and Ship consented."

"What did she teach you?"

"Many things . . . how to clear my mind. The mind doesn't work well when it's cluttered up and churning. It jams . . . it's devoured by questions and distractions."

She put the last of the celltape in a disposal chute, but continued to hold his hands.

"How do you clear your mind?"

"I throw things out of it one by one, then concentrate on the last thing, then throw that out, too, and focus on the no-thing that's left. Then I don't think things out, I just know them."

"You mean to say that after all your questions and the emphasis on our data, our *information,* after all that, what you really operate on is intuition?"

He smiled at her obvious surprise. How warm her hands were, how true and loving.

"Not exactly. I just give the unconscious part of me a role in most decisions. Facts, records, books—they're all obvious learning."

"But there's a lot of subtler data coming in."

"We're bombarded with it all the time and we ignore it for the most part, filter it out."

"As Tom says: the sentient being chooses what it will see."

"Root said that, not Tom," Nikki said.

"What?" She dropped his hands as though he'd hurt her.

"He said it on the floater. That's when he's Root. You never call him Tom there."

She put a hand to her cheek. The skin remained pale and clear, the blood undertone unchanged.

"I do, don't I. I wonder why I do that?"

"Because you keep him in two compartments—conscious and unconscious."

She stared into his eyes. "You do that so easily. That's what your mother taught you, isn't it?"

"Ship and my mother."

"Can anybody do it?"

"Most can. Very few ever do."

"Will you teach me?"

"It can't be taught, only learned."

"But your mother . . ."

"She talked of it often and her stories were wonderful. She gave me thinking exercises to entertain myself and these were similar to the game I played with Ship."

"You asked questions and she answered."

"Usually she gave me the question. If I brought a question she might not answer. When she answered, it could be *yes* or *no* or *silence*."

She stared at him.

"Silence was an answer?"

"Sometimes. Other times she might answer with a question. If she made a statement that, too, could be no answer."

She leaned back in the chair to absorb this, her head against the cushioning, eyes closed, relaxed.

Nikki didn't move or change his breathing rhythm.

Tam found herself listening to the slow and regular sigh of Nikki's breath. She relaxed her muscles one by one, felt the tension wash out of her stomach and neck and legs. Her breathing fitted itself to Nikki's rhythm and she felt everything go: her body, then her memories one by one, then her thought of self stood apart and drifted down a long corridor to a warm glow with a red wash at the end that was the color of Argo low on the horizon.

"I see," she whispered and all thought of self disappeared.

"Tam. Tam?"

She awoke to his voice gentle but insistent, the light pressure of his hand on her shoulder.

"I didn't want to wake you but if we're getting out to the bloom at dawn . . ."

She stretched and noticed that he was admiring her as a woman for the first time. He found her beautiful. She prolonged her stretching.

He saw this and grinned. "Yes, you're beautiful."

Immediately, she sat up straight, reached for the callbox at the head of his bed and punched in the hangar code. It rang several times before an impatient female voice answered.

"Yes!"

"Is Root there? This is Tam Kupule."

"We're pretty busy here."

"Put him on. It's important."

"I'll see if he'll come."

There was a long wait then Root's cold voice. "What is it, Tam?"

"Have you chosen a color yet?"

"We're about to make it purple."

"Add some red to that. Make it Argo red."

"Why? To appeal to the gasbags' esthetic sensibilities?"

"Argo red," she insisted. "And we come in from the Argo side."

"Where are you?"

"What difference does that make?"

Root's laughter was not companionable. "Tell Nikki I agree. Argo red it is."

She slapped the disconnect switch, blushing.

"He's slipping," Nikki said. "He didn't ask you if we're running a research team or a school of design?"

"He thinks the color is your idea."

"Does that bother you? I'll call him back and . . ."

"No!" She put a hand on his knee, jerked it back as though his knee had burned her. "Let it be."

"That's it," Nikki said. "You have to let it be, then you can tell what it is, what it's doing." He leaned forward, cupped her face in his hands and kissed her.

When he released her, she said: "We mustn't . . ."

"Why, because you're older?"

"Of course not. Sometimes you're older than Root."

"Nobody's older than Root."

The words had come from him spontaneously and their sense of truth shocked him. *Nobody's older than Root.* Who was this man with the familiar voice?

"It's not that there's anybody else," Tam said. "I have no companion. For a time I hoped that Root . . ." She broke off. "I mean *Tom,* of course, but Tom doesn't exist except in those hopes which I . . . I rejected."

He nodded.

"How is it you make people be this truthful?" she asked.

Nikki shrugged. If there was an answer she already had it.

Silence as an answer, she thought.

She wanted to get up but knew that anything she did would only increase the sexual tension between them.

A knock on the hatch startled both of them.

Nikki called out much too loudly: "Open."

It was a young male ground crewman, dark-haired, grinning. He tossed in an open shipcloth bag crammed with tapes and Nikki noted a splash of Argo red on the man's left sleeve.

"Root sent those. Bloom recordings. He said try to find some interesting rhythms in them."

The hatch was closed before either could respond.

Tam stood up abruptly.

"I will not have him laughing at me . . . at us!"

"How do you know that your present response isn't exactly what he wants?"

She sat down as though his words had released latches in her knees. "This is insane."

"Our worrying about what Root wants?"

"That, too. No!" She spoke quickly as he started to reach for her. "I'm going to leave in just a moment. I'll do that in spite of the fact that I want to stay."

"Is that the insanity?"

"I don't think so and neither do you. No . . . what we need is the right time . . ."

"And the right place."

"When a thing's right . . ." She hesitated, then said, "I see. That's why you didn't even question it when I told Root what color to use on the floater."

"When a thing's right," Nikki said.

Once more, Tam stood. "I would like to've known your mother."

Nikki arrived on the hangar floor almost an hour early. Root already was there with a scattered remnant of the ground crew finishing up on the floater. The bag glistened in the upper reaches of the hangar, a dark red ball with flecks of purple in it. The ground crewmen were a ludicrous sight, stained varying shades of Argo red.

The bag of bloom recordings slung over one shoulder, Nikki finished fastening his slicker as he hurried up to Root near the nest's entrance hatch.

"Well, poet, will it work?"

Root gave the appearance of being in exceptionally good humor. It was well done, but Nikki suspected it.

"Perhaps it'll work for the wrong reasons—the way I worked for you."

"Have you worked for me?"

Nikki glanced up at the glistening red bag, shrugged.

"Why did we bring you into the project?" Root asked.

Nikki slipped the bag of recordings to the floor. "Perhaps because you knew I'd listened to every globe tape in Ship's records."

"Ahhhh. And what can you teach us from those peculiar noises?"

"To move with caution. If the globes are sentient, any deaths we've caused could be seen as murders rather than errors of judgment or ignorance."

"You expect the gasbags to mount a massive retaliatory attack?"

"Humankind doesn't have a monopoly on preservation of its species or desires for revenge. The globes already have demonstrated kamikaze behavior."

"Indeed! They're highly explosive in more ways than one. And the key to them has to be in their language."

Nikki produced an emotionless smile right out of Root's own repertoire. "And that, of course, is why you brought me into your project."

Was that a flicker of real rage in Root's eyes? Nikki could not be sure. Before he could explore it, Tam came hurrying up. She flashed a personal, no-barriers smile to Nikki, glanced once at the Argo red of the floater bag before focusing on Root.

"Sorry I'm late. I stopped at meteorology on the way. Since we're coming in from the Argo side. They think we stand a reasonable chance of getting a good float."

"Do they have an optimum course?" Root asked. "I told them to plot it as late as they could."

Tam tapped a pocket of her slicker. "It's a wide sweeping loop from the ocean side, but you know how chancy the winds are out there."

"I'll look at it in a moment," Root said. "Nikki is telling me how he learned caution from the songs of the globes."

Tam sensed the sneering tone in Root's voice, shot a warning look at Nikki. He ignored it.

"We're dealing with what may be the first sentient species of plant we've ever discovered. We don't know their language, their customs, how they reproduce . . ."

"And you'll teach us all that from their songs . . . and you'll teach us before we have a disaster because of our massive ignorance."

"If we're going to share limited territory with another intelligent species, we need a breakthrough before they learn enough about us to take deliberate, concentrated action."

"Stop this!" Tam flared. "We have to work together. Nikki, do you have anything really useful out of those globe recordings?"

"Some technical data viewed from my own specialty."

There was no mistaking Root's quickened interest.

Tam glanced at Root. "Do we have time?"

"The floater has to dry a bit longer. Do give us your technical data, Nikki."

"The shortest whole song is just under six minutes duration and the longest just over thirty. There's a good deal of noise between songs."

"Which means?" Root sounded disappointed.

"It may mean nothing, but it could be chatter—talk, gossip or prose as opposed to the rhythmic, well-structured songs."

"Structure is not necessarily language."

"True. And the duration of each song is probably directly proportional to bag size, the volume of gas. They stop when they've expelled gas to a critical point."

"How can you be sure they sing by expelling gas?" Tam asked.

"I assume it, partly because of the way the songs often stop in mid-note and partly because they can be observed to grow smaller as they sing."

"Reasonable," Root agreed. "But what does all this tell us?"

"When a globe's in a singing mood it moves from song to song with pauses between—*rests* in my terminology—that are the same duration as the pauses between individual notes."

"How does . . ."

"Plenty of concept but little punctuation," Nikki said.

"I see. A high-density communications system."

One of the ground crew was whistling nearby. Nikki hooked a thumb toward the whistler.

"Their songs may be no more than that—self-entertainment, a release from boredom. I hope not, because the chatter between songs is very difficult to break into patterns."

"And you're defining pattern as song," Root said.

"They are meticulously regular, complete sequences of tones repeated intact at various intervals. And they are not rote. They vary from individual to individual and incident to incident."

"Tam has detected similar structures . . ."

"Yes, but each song contains the personality or particular interpretation of the singer. And then there are the color changes."

"A semaphore of some kind," Root said. "We have people working on that in another section. Didn't Ship tell you?"

He sounds so derisive when he says Ship, Nikki thought.

"I saw some studies that didn't seem to be leading us anywhere. At least, not yet."

The floater beside them began a slow scrape across the hangar floor, back and forth.

"They've topped off our bag," Root said. He held a hand toward Tam. "Let me have that course plot." He took a folded paper from her and led them into the suspended nest. As he began strapping himself into the command seat, he glanced back at Nikki, then at Tam. "Oh, by the way, Tam, Nikki suggests that we brought him into our project for the wrong reasons."

She finished securing her web harness.

"Did he?"

She looked across at Nikki, who was already secured and running the preliminary checks on his console.

"Yes, that's exactly what he suggested." Root spoke as he ran through his own console preliminaries. "Did you discuss that last night?"

"No."

"I guess you didn't discuss much of anything. I'm told you went to your own quarters rather early."

Tam looked up to find Nikki staring at her, supportive, waiting. She knew that if she made the slightest signal to him, he would shift the attack to Root. *Attack!*

That was it. *Something good happened to me last night—from Nikki's mother through Nikki to me. I touched something truly powerful.*

Root had sensed this and that was what he had brought under attack. She looked across at Nikki. Their gazes met. Yes, all barriers were down between them.

Why was Root attacking?

Without knowing how they did it (without caring), Tam knew that she and Nikki shared this awareness of Root's behavior. They held the same question in their minds.

"Perhaps it was a futile discussion and you don't care to share it," Root said. "Stand by for lift."

Nikki spoke directly to Tam.

"My mother once said a strange thing. She said: 'Bring in the sacred fools and we'll fill the well with snow together.' She meant that in times of crisis it's better to do something futile with people of magical spirit than to do nothing at all."

As he finished speaking, they heard the ceiling doors open. The light around them changed to dull gray and the floater lifted out of the hangar, swinging across the colony in the grip of a hard wind.

Magical spirit, Tam thought. *That's what I touched last night. And I'm no longer afraid of Root.*

And the strangest part of this metamorphosis was that she had never recognized her own fear until after she had lost it.

At his console, Nikki sat in the way his mother had taught: head balanced on the living pole of his spine, his attention focused inward. Part of him carried out the routine of his duties to the floater, but a more important part thought back into words that had passed from his mother's father out of a lore buried in the dark blood of a memory kinship which traced itself through the mother of her father.

"Only because of ignorance and attachment to the world are you unable to come home."

What am I ignorant of? Where am I attached?

By the time the red grin of Argo spread across their horizon, Nikki knew what he had to do. And he knew where he had heard a voice like Root's. Ship spoke like that.

He saw that they were making good speed in their long loop out over the sea. Root was spending fuel, both jet and compressor, with a profligate hand.

A heavy wall of mist swirled up ahead and was just beginning to clear as they approached the bay where Nikki had seen his first bloom. The water surface about three hundred meters below the nest was choppy, but he could see beneath the surface the pulsing expanse of kelp.

Where will the bloom begin?

Root spoke in a quiet, conversational tone.

"What was the wrong reason for bringing you here, Nikki?"

"To sense the panic and signal you when it happened."

"Why should you be here?"

"Because I'm young and comparatively uninfluenced by previous data, by any information other than what you give me or allow me to see."

"How do you know that's not why we brought you?"

"Because your behavior and your questions try to divert me away from anything which springs spontaneously out of my own creative understanding."

"Creative understanding!"

"The globes that bloom here today will be much like me: minimal information to begin with, perhaps some skeletal data to improve their survival chances, but open receptors with little to block their gathering of new facts."

Abruptly, Nikki felt that he had floated free of his seat and the restraining harness. He could see nothing clearly but there was light all around, beautiful light. He was not afraid. The beginning of great joy sat somewhere within him. And out of some dim corner of his consciousness, he heard Root say:

"Here they come!"

From where she sat, Tam could not see Nikki's face unless he turned. And Nikki was her barometer. She felt a deep necessity to see him. One touch to a key and she had linked a corner of her viewscreen to a receptor on Nikki's panel.

She stared at the face on her screen. Nikki's features were trance-like, still—filled with a calm such as she had never seen before. A smile twitched at the corners of her own mouth and the anxious knots which usually cramped her stomach during these flights washed away. It was several heartbeats before she realized they were in the thick of the bloom. The iridescent globes lifted all around, colors flashing. When she activated the external sensors, the sounds of joyful fluting filled the nest.

Root's voice was like cold water dashed in her face.

"There's a storm coming, lightning."

As though his words had created the scene, she looked out and up toward the bay's landward rim, saw tentative yellow flickers licking back and forth between clouds. A boiling black mass of storm lifted off the land. It rolled closer as she watched and flickering streaks began touching the crags and chimneys and buttes that were Medea's testimony to her violent past.

"What do we do now?" Root asked. His voice was gloating.

He peered back at Nikki and his lips drew away from his teeth. It was a voracious look, a predator's look, and Tam felt that her breath froze in her throat.

As though her fear alerted him, Nikki turned. His face was beautiful in its stillness.

"We will go down to the water and stay here," Nikki said.

"Are you crazy?" Root demanded. He turned toward his controls. "We have to try to run for the colony. Tam, restrain him if he tries to interfere."

Tam heard the false notes in his voice and made her choice. The magical spirit must have its chance. She reached under Root's elbow, grasped the interlock cable from his console and ripped it out. Now, each floater console was locked into its function and Root could not override from his position.

"What're you . . ."

But Nikki already had depressed the DUMP switch on his console. Hydrogen began valving out of the bag above them and the floater started a swiftly controlled descent. The bag above them billowed out like a giant parachute.

"You fools!" There was real rage in Root's face. He had been thwarted from an unexpected direction. "Tam! How could . . ."

"She knew instinctively what I know consciously," Nikki said. "You didn't leave us enough fuel to reach the colony. You never intended us to get back."

The nest was swinging wildly now, caught by the leading edge of the storm. The hiss of hydrogen valving from the bag was a monstrous serpent sound all around.

"You!"

Root struck out at Nikki.

It was an anticipated blow and Nikki met it with an open hand which grasped Root's arm just above the wrist. The arm felt insubstantial, as though it were something less than flesh. There was a writhing, twisting strength in it, though, and Root jerked free. He began unfastening his harness.

In that instant, with less than twenty meters left beneath them to the bay's churning surface, Nikki stiffened. Tam saw his eyes go wide. He said: "Ohhh . . ."

An explosive *clap* stunned their nest. It came simultaneously with a blast of sulfurous golden light which engulfed the world all around them.

The fall, though short, plunged the floater under the surface in a twisting dive.

Tam gripped the sides of her seat, praying for the chemically activated pontoons to inflate. Dim green light suffused the nest but there were no spurts of water. The hatches were holding.

Root whirled and hit all of the keys on his console.

Nothing.

In a suspended silence, they turned and looked out the bow bubble. Strands of kelp all around. The floater's descent slowed, stopped. It slewed itself upright and they heard the pontoons filling with air beneath them. They began a gentle ascent. Long whips of kelp caged their world and they saw clumps of polyps on the leaves. Each clump sent out slender tendrils and at the end of each tendril small bulbs swelled, drifted to the surface.

Nikki imagined those bulbs breaking free of the mother plant and the sea, drifting away in the magnificent colors of the bloom. The entire system snicked into place within his awareness.

"What do you propose to do now?" Root asked. There was a charged calm in his voice.

"I'll continue learning their language," Nikki said. "I have the key to it."

The nest popped to the surface, draping remnants of the exploded bag over the transparent ceiling. It rocked violently in a wind-whipped tidal rip and, through the shreds of the red bag, they glimpsed the bay's distant shore, forbidding black cliffs. The wind had them now and it drove them toward the open sea, but a vagrant current caught the pontoons, whirled them and swept them into a kelp-subdued pocket of calm beneath the headlands.

"The nest can take it," Tam said. "We could float here forever."

"Forever is a long time," Root said. "I don't think you grasp quite how long." He turned toward Nikki. "What do you intend doing with your little patch of time—besides perfecting your grasp of the gasbags' language?"

"Do you really have the key to it?" Tam asked.

Root was scornful. "Don't be a complete fool, Tam. Of course he has it."

Nikki marvelled at how subdued Root appeared. How calm. But it was only appearance, a pose, a role, a reflected and insubstantial performance. How lonely the man must be within that shell of limited emotions—his rage was real and, perhaps, jealousy. The vengeful awareness of his own crippled being . . . that was real. Everything else was sham.

"How?" Tam asked, staring at Nikki.

"Planarians," Nikki said. "With a difference." He pointed to the currents boiling up through the kelp around them. "The living, thinking creature is really the kelp. The globes are its eyes, its ears, its arms and voice . . . its contact with the universe through which it learns."

"Planarians?" Tam was confused.

Root appeared lost in thought.

"A small earthside flatworm," Nikki said. "I once asked Ship about a poem—'Food of the Gods'—and Ship included planarians in the answer."

"I've never heard of them. What . . ."

"Although primitive, they can be taught to run mazes," Root said. He was looking at Nikki with renewed interest.

How long has he known? Nikki wondered. He said: "And they can learn without being taught."

Tam leaned forward to the extent her harness permitted. "They can learn without . . ."

"They can reproduce whole individuals from just a small part," Nikki said. "Cut out a middle section and your worm will grow a head and tail. The tail will regenerate a new head and middle . . ."

"But you said they learn without . . ."

"Yes. Grind up one that's learned the maze and feed it to a young worm that's never run the maze. The young one learns the maze with remarkable speed. Grind up this young one and feed it to another—the new one learns the maze even faster. Go through the process again and the new worm learns faster yet."

"The skins dissolve in the water," Tam said, looking out at the bay. "The sludge . . ."

"Food of the immortal kelp," Nikki said. "I wonder how long it's been alive and learning? We must be a fascinating diversion."

"This is all very interesting," Root said. "But we're still trapped here with no way to contact the colony, no means of returning . . ."

"Since you intended to return alone on foot after a tragic crash and heroic odyssey through the demon lands," Nikki said, "what do you suggest?"

"I intend to wait," Root said, grinning.

Ship save us! Tam thought. *He's admitted that Nikki's right. But how . . .*

"Tam survived two ventures out there because you saved her both times, didn't you?" Nikki asked.

Root shrugged. It was a pointless question and besides the look on Tam's face was answer enough.

Tam stared at Root. "How?"

"He's not quite human," Nikki said. "I don't know what he is or where he comes from, but he can do things we can't."

"Ship save us," Tam whispered.

"Ship save us," Root mimicked. "You fools haven't the faintest idea of what's happening on Medea, why you're here or what you're doing."

Nikki smiled, a slow, almost sleepy smile. "But we're learning. We see to learn, listen to learn, touch and smell to learn and . . ."

"And maybe someday . . ." Root pointed out at the heaving bay. ". . . you hope you'll drink a broth made from your 'teachers' and *that's* how you'll learn."

Root released himself from the seat, stood up and opened a hatch. A cold ozone-washed breeze blew in the opening. It was a clean, invigorating smell with only a touch of damp decay at the edge.

On the breeze came the sound of rhythmic whistles and moans. In the background there was a fluting song, compelling in its siren beauty. Nikki's head nodded to the rhythm. He released his harness and signalled Tam to do the same.

As she stood and peered out through the remnants of their bag, Tam stifled a gasp. A mob of globes—purple, red, green, yellow, blue . . . an iridescent rainbow play of them was drifting down on the nest. At the forefront was a giant globe almost as big as the floater. It played a symphony of red and purple across its shimmering surface.

A light rain of sweet-smelling dust began to sift through the open hatch. Nikki pushed Root aside and clambered out onto the platform created by the inflated pontoon. Tam followed him. Root remained at the open hatch.

The storm had passed out to sea leaving only a warm breeze and the air filled with disintegrating bits of globes which had been destroyed by lightning. Eddies of pastel dust swirled around the nest and a cloudy mist of them obscured the bay's inner shoreline. More globes were rising from the water to replace the lost ones.

Now, the onrushing mob swooped on the nest and circled until their dangling tentacles brushed Nikki's upturned face. He held out his arms to them, his expression rapturous, but Tam cowered away. Root moved to join them on the pontoon but a brushing tentacle left a livid streak across his forehead. He screamed and jerked back into the nest.

Nikki gave no sign that he had heard.

The chittering globes continued to rhapsodize around Nikki, singing to him. Tam pressed herself against the nest, fascinated by the rainbow dance and the fluting songs.

Presently, Nikki began to sing back to the globes in a language Tam could not understand. His voice echoed in her breast until she thought she would choke with longing for the beauty of it. A heightened state of excitement filled her. The gentle rock of the nest on the water, the balmy wind, the rhythmic lick of waves against the pontoon—everything blended with the dance and song of the globes.

The circling mob opened a space around Nikki then and he leaped to the top of the nest where he began to dance while he sang: strange paddling motions, sweeping gestures with both hands, gentle interlacings of his palms . . .

From within the nest, Root demanded: "What's he doing up there?"

"He's dancing."

The globes moved closer, cradling their tentacles around Nikki while he danced. The play of colors was dazzling. Gently, the movement slowed, the colors shifted to a universal brilliant silver with soft veins of red.

Nikki brought his hands to his sides, bowed his head, shuddered and stood still.

Tam looked at his feet. They were stained with Argo red from the remnants of the floater bag on the nest's roof. Bits of color washed from the bag trailed down the sides of the nest into the water.

Nikki's voice, so matter of fact, shocked her.

"They don't understand why the bag isn't dissolving."

"Why aren't they touching me?"

"Because I told them you were afraid."

"You're talking to them!"

"That's right."

"How do you do it?"

"It's in the no-place, the betweens and in the honesty of the songs."

"Why were you dancing?"

"Talking, more talking. I was talking my ancestors to them: the weavers and gardeners, the samurai, the pottery makers, the canoe people, the commuters and keepers of offices, the warriors around the fires . . ."

"They understood?"

"Oh, yes."

"Why're they keeping Root in the nest?"

"I don't know. That's their idea."

"Do they know what Root is?"

"Yes. Ship made him. He's like a partial God who was made that Ship might understand some things better."

She didn't understand this but put it aside.

"Are you through talking to them?"

"No—they've asked me to talk one more thing to them."

"What?"

"The perfect biological principle."

A raucous laugh erupted within the nest.

"I don't understand," Tam said.

"They wish to exchange their information for ours—the perfect biological principle: replication."

She didn't understand for a moment, then: "You don't mean . . ."

"Come up." He held a hand out to her and a gentle golden stir wafted through the slowly circling globes. "You must help me talk to them. We will talk the making of a baby."

Not here! she thought.

A globe dropped close to her and the first tentacle brushed against her shoulder and neck. It was a caress! She leaned into it.

Tam didn't remember taking off her clothes nor seeing Nikki disrobe, but there remained a memory of the globes helping her to the top of the nest and Nikki reclining there, long-limbed, dark and muscular, as though he lay on a grassy earthside meadow soaking up sun after a swim or a hard day in the fields.

She saw their clothes scattered around the nest's top. A shield of rainbow domes covered the sky.

Slowly, she moved toward him. First, a hand touching hand, then, like the tentacles which brushed them both, they matched touch for touch in the nooks and crannies of their curious bodies. Chittering groans filled the air overhead.

"I want you," Tam whispered. "How can I do this here and say such a thing without feeling self-conscious?"

Nikki kissed her, then: "Where have we put our *selves*?"

He had never been with a woman. Ship urged couplings among adolescents. It helped in the selection of breeding pairs and relieved tensions. But Nikki's creative energies had been focused into the feeling words of his poetry. And Ship had helped in some strange way he had never understood—perhaps something in his food.

Now with tentacles reaching and searching across his body, with the sweetness of the air thick around them, with Tam's silky white skin warm and glowing beside him, he knew there was nothing he'd rather do and no one he'd rather have as a companion in ecstasy. Fingers and tongues joined in the tangle of legs and tentacles, then she was on top of him, moving so very slowly, smiling down at him with tears in her eyes, and Nikki felt that he had been introduced to the most ancient language of humans, a true clear conversation which transcended all words, all dialects, all explanations.

Once more, the globes were a dancing splendor of color and song above them. Tam lay quietly beside Nikki and watched his eyes. How beautiful they were! He traced soft designs on her breasts. She touched his cheek.

"The globes say we have made a baby, we truly have," Nikki said.

"I love you," she whispered. Then, eyes wide: "How do they know?"

"They know. They say the moment of replication is also their greatest joy and they can measure it."

"But we weren't selected as a breeding pair."

"Except by our Medean hosts." He sat up. "We should get dressed. The ultraviolet . . . the globes won't be able to shield us much longer."

Nikki slipped into his clothes. Presently, she followed his example, her gaze searching all around the bay as she moved.

"We're still trapped here, Nikki."

He stood atop the nest. "No. The globes will take us home to the colony. Five or six of the big ones . . ."

She slipped down to the pontoon and peered through the hatch into the nest.

"Nikki!"

"Yes?"

"He's gone. Root's gone. Where'd he go?"

"Maybe he didn't go; maybe he was protean and merely took another shape."

"Stop that! They've taken him, haven't they?"

"I don't know. I didn't see them. Did you?"

She blushed, then: "How will we explain it?"

"We'll let the globes explain it after I've taught their language to others."

Nikki turned, lifted his arms and began to sing, swaying and gesturing toward the shore.

Presently, eight of the largest globes moved down in concert and, as Nikki sang, they shifted their color to a uniform Argo red, affixed their tentacles to the nest and lifted it gently from the water.

FROGS AND SCIENTIST

Two frogs were counting the minnows in a hydropronics trough one morning when a young maiden came down to the water to bathe. "What's that?" one frog (who was called Lavu) asked the other. "That's a human female," said Lapat, for that was the other frog's name.

"What is she doing?" Lavu asked.

"She is taking off her garments," Lapat said.

"What are garments?" Lavu asked.

"An extra skin humans wear to conceal themselves from the gaze of strangers," said Lapat.

"Then why is she taking off her extra skin?" Lavu asked.

"She wants to bathe her primary skin," Lapat said. "See how she piles her garments beside the trough and steps daintily into the water."

"She is oddly shaped," Lavu said.

"Not for a human female," Lapat said. "All of them are shaped that way."

"What are those two bumps on her front?" Lavu asked.

"I have often pondered that question," Lapat said. "As we both know, function follows form and vice versa. I have seen human males clasp their females in a crushing embrace. It is my observation that the two bumps are a protective cushion."

"Have you noticed," Lavu asked, "that there is a young male human watching her from the concealment of the control station?"

"That is a common occurrence," Lapat said. "I have seen it many times."

"But can you explain it?" Lavu asked.

"Oh, yes. The maiden seeks a mate; that is the real reason she comes here to display her primary skin. The male is a possible mate, but he watches from concealment because if he were to show himself, she would have to scream, and that would prevent the mating."

"How is it you know so many things about humans?" Lavu asked.

"Because I pattern my life after the most admirable of all humans, the scientist."

"What's a scientist?" Lavu asked.

"A scientist is one who observes without interfering. By observation alone all things are made clear to the scientist. Come, let us continue counting the minnows."

FEATHERED PIGS

When Bridik was four hundred and twenty-two years old and expecting to moult the next season, she decided to edit an old riddle for her companions. Bridik and her companions were long-lived and feathered pigs playing out an idyll among the oak groves of post-ancient Terra.

"It is recorded in our history," Bridik said, "that our ancestors served Man and, as reward, Man gave us these lovely black and beige feathers. Who can tell me why Man chose these colors?"

"Aww, Mom! Nobody likes to play that old game anymore," cried Kirid, her eleventh son. "We'd rather twang the lute and bamboozle."

"Come, come," said Bridik. "I am about to moult and it is my right to edit the old riddle."

"Ohhh, all right," said Kirid (who was really a dutiful son and not like some we could mention). "Who goes first?"

"That is the place of Lobrok, your father," she said, "but I don't want to hear him say the colors represent the oak tree alive and the oak tree burned."

"The kid's right," said Lobrok. "It's a bore." Then, noting Bridik's angry glare and her exposed tusks, he said: "But I'll play because it pleases you."

"Okay, Pop," Kirid said. "What's the beedeebeedeep answer?"

"Man chose the colors because they represent day and night, the grass of autumn and the ashes of the past."

"Verrry poetic, Pop!" said Kirid.

"May I go next? Me next?" cried Inishbeby, a fair young thing of hardly one hundred who was making a big play for Kirid.

"Very well," said Bridik. "You may play in the guest spot."

"Now, don't tell me," said Inishbeby. "Let me guess." She wangled a bamboozly glance at Kirid, then: "Black is for charcoal and beige is for the parchment upon which Man drew with his charcoal."

"That's worse than stupid," growled Lobrok. "A lot of us believe Man made parchment from pigskins!"

"I didn't know!" cried Inishbeby. "It doesn't say that at the museum of Man."

"You've spoiled the riddle," wailed Bridik. "Now I won't be able to edit it before I moult."

"Come on, Beby," said Kirid. "I think we better blow until things cool off here."

"Ohhh, where are you going to take me?" asked Inishbeby, nuzzling up against Kirid.

"Well . . . let's go snoot out some truffles and have a picnic."

THE DADDY BOX

To understand what happened to Henry Alexander when his son, Billy, came home with the ferosslk, you're going to be asked to make several mind-stretching mental adjustments. These mental gymnastics are certain to leave your mind permanently changed.

You've been warned.

In the first place, just to get a loose idea of a ferosslk's original purpose, you must think of it as a toy designed primarily for educating the young. But your concept of *toy* should be modified to think of a device which, under special circumstances, will play with its owner.

You'll also have to modify your concept of education to include the idea of occasionally altering the universe to fit a new interesting idea; that is, fitting the universe to the concept, rather than fitting the concept to the universe.

The ferosslk originates with seventh-order, multidimensional beings. You can think of them as Sevens. Their other labels would be more or less incomprehensible. The Sevens are not now aware and never have been aware the universe contains any such thing as a Henry Alexander or a human male offspring.

This oversight was rather unfortunate for Henry. His mind had never been stretched to contain the concept of a ferosslk. He could conceive of fission bombs, nerve gas, napalm and germ warfare. But these things might be thought of as silly putty when compared with a ferosslk.

Which is a rather neat analogy because the shape of a ferosslk is profoundly dependent upon external pressures. That is to say, although a ferosslk can be conceived of as an artifact, it is safer to think of it as alive.

To begin at one of the beginnings, Billy Alexander, age eight, human male, found the ferosslk in tall weeds beside a path across an empty lot adjoining his urban home.

Saying he *found* it described the circumstances from Billy's superficial point of view. It would be just as accurate to say the ferosslk found Billy.

As far as Billy was concerned, the ferosslk was a box. You may as well think of it that way, too. No sense stretching your mind completely out of shape. You wouldn't be able to read the rest of this account.

A box then. It appeared to be about nine inches long, three inches wide and four inches deep. It looked like dark green stone except for what was obviously the top, because that's where the writing appeared.

You can call it writing because Billy was just beginning to shift from print to cursive and that's the way he saw it.

Words flowed across the box top: THIS IS A DADDY BOX.

Billy picked it up. The surface was cold under his hands. He thought perhaps this was some kind of toy television, its words projected from inside.

(Some of the words actually were coming out of Billy's own mind.)

Daddy box? he wondered.

Daddy was a symbol-identifier more than five years old for him. His daddy had been killed in a war. Now, Billy had a stepfather with the same name as his real father's. The two had been cousins.

New information flowed across the top: THIS BOX MAY BE OPENED ONLY BY THE YOUNG.

(That was a game the ferosslk had played and enjoyed many times before. Don't try to imagine how a ferosslk enjoys. The attempt could injure your frontal lobes.)

Now, the box top provided Billy with precise instructions on how it could be opened.

Billy went through the indicated steps, which included urinating on an ant hill, and the box dutifully opened.

For almost an hour, Billy sat in the empty lot enraptured by the educational/creative tableau thus unveiled. For his edification, human shapes in the box fought wars, manufactured artifacts, made love, wrote books, created paintings and sculpture . . . and changed the universe. The human shapes debated, formed governments, nurtured the earth and destroyed it.

In that relative time of little less than an hour, Billy aged mentally some five hundred and sixteen human years. On the outside, Billy remained a male child about forty-nine inches tall, weight approximately fifty-six pounds, skin white but grimy from play, hair blond and mussed.

His eyes were still blue, but they had acquired a hard and penetrating stare. The motor cells in his medulla and his spinal cord had begun increasing dramatically in number with an increased myelinization of the anterior roots and peripheral nerves.

Every normal sense he possessed had been increased in potency and he was embarked on a growth pattern which would further heighten this effect.

The whole thing made him sad, but he knew what he had to do, having come very close to understanding what a ferosslk was all about.

It was now about 6:18 p.m. on a Friday evening. Billy took the box in both hands and trudged across the lot toward his back door.

His mother, whose left arm still bore bruises from a blow struck by her husband, was peeling potatoes at the kitchen sink. She was a small blonde woman, once doll-like, fast turning to mouse.

At Billy's entrance, she shook tears out of her eyes, smiled at him, glanced toward the living room and shook her head—all in one continuous movement. She appeared not to notice the box in Billy's hands, but she did note the boy appeared very much like his real father tonight.

This thought brought more tears to her eyes, and she turned away, thus failing to see Billy go on into the living room despite her silent warning that his stepfather was there and in a bad mood.

The ferosslk, having shared Billy's emotional reaction to this moment, created a new order of expletives which it introduced into another dimension.

Henry Alexander sensed Billy's presence in the room, lowered the evening newspaper and stared over it into the boy's newly-aged eyes. Henry was a pale-skinned, flabby man, going to fat after a youth spent as a semi-professional athlete. He interpreted the look in Billy's eyes as a reflection of their mutual hate.

"What's that box?" Henry demanded.

Billy shrugged. "It's a daddy box."

"A what?"

Billy remained silent, placed the box to his ear. The ferosslk had converted to a faint audio mode and the voices coming from the box for Billy's ears alone carried a certain suggestive educational quality.

"Why're you holding the damn thing against your ear?" Henry demanded. He had already decided to take the box away from the boy, but was drawing the pleasure-moment out.

"I'm listening," Billy said. He sensed the precise pacing of these moments, observed minute nuances in the set of his stepfather's jaw, the content of the man's perspiration.

"Is it a music box?"

Henry studied the thing in Billy's hand. It looked old . . . ancient, even. He couldn't quite say why he felt this.

Again, Billy shrugged.

"Where'd you get it?" Henry asked.

"I found it."

"Where could you find a thing like that? It looks like a real antique. Might even be jade."

"I found it in the lot." Billy hesitated on the point of adding a precise location to where he'd found the box, but held back. That would be out of character.

"Are you sure you didn't steal it?"

"I found it."

"Don't you sass me!" Henry threw his newspaper to the floor.

Having heard the loud voices, Billy's mother hurried into the living room, hovered behind her son.

"What's . . . what's the matter?" she ventured.

"You stay out of this, Helen!" Henry barked. "That brat of yours has stolen a valuable antique and he—"

"A Chinese box! He wouldn't."

"I told you to stay out of this!" Henry glared at her. The box had assumed for him now exactly the quality he had just given it: valuable antique. Theft was as good as certain—although that might complicate his present plans for confiscation and profit.

Billy suppressed a smile. His mother's interruption, which he assumed to be fortuitous since he did not completely understand the functioning of a ferosslk, had provided just the delay required here. The situation had entered the timing system for which he had maneuvered.

"Bring that box here," Henry ordered.

"It's mine," Billy said. As he said it, he experienced a flash of insight which told him he belonged as much to the box as it belonged to him.

"Look here, you disrespectful brat, if you don't give me that box immediately, we're going to have another session in the woodshed!"

Billy's mother touched his arm, said: "Son . . . you'd better . . ."

"Okay," Billy said. "But it's just a trick box—like those Chinese things."

"I said bring it here, dammit!"

Clutching the box to his chest now, Billy crossed the room, timing his movements with careful precision. Just a few more seconds . . . now!

He extended the box to his stepfather.

Henry snatched the ferosslk, was surprised at how cold it felt. Obviously stone. Cold stone. He turned the thing over and over in his hands. There were strange markings on the top—wedges, curves, twisting designs. He put it to his ear, listened.

Silence.

Billy smiled.

Henry jerked the box away from his ear. Trick, eh? The kid was playing a trick on him, trying to make him look like a fool.

"So it's a box," Henry said. "Have you opened it?"

"Yes. It's got lots of things inside."

"Things? What things?"

"Just things."

Henry had an immediate vision of valuable jewels. This thing could be a jewel box.

"How does it open?" he demanded.

"You just do things," Billy said.

"Don't you play smart with me! I gave you an order: Tell me how you open this thing."

"I can't."

"You mean you won't!"

"I can't."

"Why?" It was as much an accusation as a question.

Again, Billy shrugged. "The box . . . well, it can only be opened by kids."

"Oh, for Chrissakes!" Henry examined the ends of the box. Damn kid was lying about having opened it. Henry shook the box. It rattled suggestively, one of the ferosslk's better effects.

Helen said: "Perhaps if you let Billy . . ."

Henry looked up long enough to stare her down, then asked: "Is dinner ready?"

"Henry, he's just a child!"

"Woman, I've worked all day to support you and your brat. Is this the appreciation I get?"

She backed toward the kitchen door, hesitated there.

Henry returned his attention to the box. He pushed at the end panels. Nothing happened. He tried various pressures on the top, the sides, the bottom.

"So you opened it, eh?" Henry asked, staring across the box at Billy.

"Yes."

"You're lying."

"I opened it."

Having achieved the effect he wanted, Henry thrust the box toward Billy. "Then open it."

Having achieved one of the moments he wanted, and right on time, Billy went for the effect. He turned the box over, slid an end panel aside, whipped the top open and closed it, restored the end panel, and presented the closed box to Henry.

"See? It's easy."

The ferosslk, having achieved an education-node, convinced Henry he'd seen gold and jewels during the brief moment when the box had been opened.

Henry grabbed the box, wet his lips with his tongue. He pushed at the end panel. It refused to move.

"Grown-ups can't open it," Billy said. "It says so right on the top."

Henry brought a clasp knife from his hip pocket, opened it, tried to find an opening around the top of the box.

Billy stared at him.

Billy's mother still hovered fearfully in the kitchen doorway.

Henry had the sudden realization they both hoped he'd cut himself. He closed the knife, returned it to his pocket, extended the box toward Billy. "Open it for me."

"I can't."

Ominously, Henry asked: "And . . . why . . . not?"

"I can't let go of it when it's open."

The ferosslk inserted a sense of doubt into the situation here without Billy suspecting. Henry nodded. That just might be true. The box might have a spring lock that closed when you let go of it.

"Then open it and let me look inside while you hold it," Henry said.

"I can't now without doing all the other things."

"What?"

"I can open it twice without the other things, but . . ."

"What other things?"

"Oh . . . like finding a grass seed and breaking a twig . . . and I'd have to find another ant hill. The one I . . ."

"Of all the damn fool nonsense!" Henry thrust the box towards Billy. "Open this!"

"I can't!"

Billy's mother said: "Henry, why don't you . . ."

"Helen, you get the hell out of here and let me handle this!"

She backed farther into the kitchen.

Henry said: "Billy, either you open this box for me, or I'll open it the hard way with an axe."

Billy shook his head from side to side, dragging out the moment for its proper curve.

"Very well." Henry heaved himself from the chair, the box clutched in his right hand, angry elation filling him. They'd done it again—goaded him beyond endurance.

He brushed past Billy, who turned and followed him. He thrust Helen aside when she put out a pleading hand. He strode out the back door, slamming it behind him, heard it open, the patter of Billy's footsteps following.

Let the brat make one protest! Just one!

Henry set his jaw, headed across the backyard toward the woodshed, that anachronism which set the tone and marked the age of this house—"modest older home in quiet residential area."

Now, Billy called from behind him: "What're you going to do?"

Henry stifled an angry retort, caught by an odd note in Billy's voice . . . an imperative.

"Daddy?" Billy called.

Henry stopped at the woodshed door, glanced back. Billy never called him *daddy*. The boy stood in the path from the house, his mother waited on the back porch.

Now, why was I angry with them? Henry wondered.

He felt the box in his hand, looked at it. Jewels? In this dirty green little piece of stoneware? He was filled with the sense of his own foolishness, an effect achieved by a sophisticated refinement of ferosslk educational processing. Given a possible lesson to impart, the instructor could not resist the opportunity.

Once more, Henry looked at the two who watched him.

They'd done this deliberately to make him appear foolish! Damn them!

"Daddy, don't break the box," Billy said.

It was a nicely timed protest and it demonstrated how well he had learned from the ferosslk.

His anger restored, Henry whirled away, slammed the box onto the woodshed's chopping block, grabbed up the axe.

Don't break the box!

"Wait!" Billy called.

Henry barely hesitated, a lapse which put him in the precise phasing Billy wanted.

Taking careful aim, Henry brought the axe hissing down. He still felt foolish, because it's difficult to shake off a ferosslk lesson, but anger carried him through.

At the instant of contact between blade and box, an electric glimmer leaped into existence around the axe head.

To Billy, watching from the yard, the blade appeared to slice into the box, shrinking, shining, drawing inward at an impossible angle. There came an abrupt, juicy vacuum-popping noise—a cow pulling its foot out of the mud. The axe handle whipped into the box after the blade, vanished with a diminishing glimmer.

Still clutching the axe handle, Henry Alexander was jerked into the box—down, down . . . shrinking . . .

Whoosh!

The pearl glimmering winked out. The box remained on the chopping block where Henry had placed it.

Billy darted into the woodshed, grabbed up the box, pressed it to his left ear. From far away came a leaf-whispering babble of many angry and pleading voices. He could distinguish some of the names being called by those voices—

"Abdul!"

"Terrik!"

"Churudish!"

"Pablo!"

"James!"

"Sremani!"

"Harold!"

And, on a low and diminishing wail:

"Bill-eeeeeeeeeee . . ."

Having taught part of a lesson, the ferosslk recognized that the toy-plus-play element remained incomplete. By attaching a label at the proper moment, Billy had achieved a daddy-linkage, but no daddy existed now for all practical purposes. There were voices, of course, and certain essences, an available gene pattern from which to reconstruct the original. Something with the proper daddyness loomed as a distinct possibility and the ferosslk observed an attractive learning pattern in the idea.

A golden glow began to emerge from one end of the box. Billy dropped it and backed away as the glow grew and grew and grew. Abruptly, the glow coalesced and Henry Alexander emerged.

Billy felt a hand clutch his shoulder, looked up at his mother. The box lay on the ground near the chopping block. She looked from it to the figure which had emerged from it.

"Billy," she demanded, "what . . . what happened?"

Henry stooped, recovered the box.

"Henry," she said, "you hit that box with the axe, but it's not broken."

"Huh?" Henry Alexander stared at her. "What're you talking about? I brought the damn thing out here to make sure it was safe for Billy to play with."

He thrust the box at Billy, who took it and almost dropped it. "Here, take it, son."

"But Billy was pestering you," she said. "You said you'd . . ."

"Helen, you nag the boy too much," Henry said. "He's just a boy and boys will be boys." Henry winked at Billy. "Eh, son?" Henry reached over and mussed Billy's hair.

Helen backed up, releasing Billy's shoulder. She said: "But you . . . it looked like you went into the box!"

Henry looked at the box, then at Helen. He began to laugh. "Girl, it's a good thing you got a man who loves you because you are weird. You are really weird." He stepped around Billy, took Helen gently by the arm. "C'mon, I'll help you with dinner."

She allowed herself to be guided toward the house, her attention fixed on Henry.

Billy heard him say: "Y'know, honey, I think Billy could use a brother or a sister. What do you say?"

"Henry!"

Henry's laughter came rich and happy. He stopped, turned around to look at Billy, who stood in the woodshed doorway holding the box.

"Stay where you can hear me call, Bill. Maybe we'll go to a movie after dinner, eh?"

Billy nodded.

"Hey," Henry called, "what're y' going to do with that funny box?"

Billy stared across the empty lot to the home of his friend Jimmy Carter. He took a deep breath, said, "Jimmy's got a catcher's mitt he's been trying to trade me. Maybe he'd trade for the box."

"Hey!" Henry said. "Maybe he would at that. But look out Jimmy's old man doesn't catch you at it. You know what a temper he has."

"I sure do," Billy said. "I sure do . . . dad."

Henry put his arm around Helen's shoulder and headed once more for the house. "Hear that?" He asked. "Hear him call me dad? Y'know, Helen, nothing makes a man happier than to have a boy call him dad."

COPYRIGHT
ACKNOWLEDGMENTS